BAG OF BONES

By Stephen King and published by
Hodder & Stoughton

Carrie
'Salem's Lot
The Shining
Night Shift
The Stand
Christine
Pet Sematary
It
Misery
The Tommyknockers
The Dark Half
The Stand: the Complete and Uncut Edition
Four Past Midnight
Needful Things
Gerald's Game
Dolores Claiborne
Nightmares and Dreamscapes
Insomnia
Rose Madder
Desperation
The Dark Tower I: The Gunslinger
The Dark Tower II: The Drawing of the Three
The Dark Tower III: The Waste Lands
The Dark Tower IV: Wizard and Glass

By Stephen King as Richard Bachman

Thinner
The Bachman Books
The Regulators

stephen
KING

BAG OF BONES

BCA

LONDON NEW YORK SYDNEY TORONTO

Grateful acknowledgement is made for permission to reprint excerpts from the following copyrighted material:

'All She Wants To Do Is Dance' by Danny Kortchmar. Copyright © 1984 WB Music Corp. All rights reserved. Used by permission. WARNER BROS. PUBLICATIONS U.S. INC., Miami, FL. 33014

'As Time Goes By' by Herman Hupfeld. Copyright © 1931 (Renewed) Warner Bros. Inc. All rights reserved. Used by permission. WARNER BROS. PUBLICATIONS U.S. INC., Miami, FL. 33014

'Don't Worry Baby' by Brian Wilson, Roger Christian, Jay Siegel, Philip Margo, Henry Medress, Mitchell Margo. Copyright © 1964 Irving Music, Inc. " Renewed, Assigned to Irving Music, Inc. and Careers-BMG Music Publishing, Inc. All rights reserved. Used by permission. WARNER BROS. PUBLICATIONS U.S. INC., Miami, FL. 33014

Seferis, George; Collected Poems, Copyright © 1967 by Princeton University Press, 1980 by Edmund Keetey and Philip Sherrard Greek © M. Seferiades 1972, 1976. Reprinted by permission of Princeton University Press.

'Welcome to the Jungle' words and music By W. Axl Rose, Slash, Izzy Stradlin', Duff McKagen & Steven Adler. Copyright © 1987 Guns N' Roses Music (ASCAP) International Copyright Secured. All rights reserved. Reprinted by permission of Cherry Lane Music Company.

This edition published 1998
by BCA
By arrangement with Hodder and Stoughton
A division of Hodder Headline PLC

The right of Stephen King to be identified as the Author of
the Work has been asserted by him in accordance with the
Copyright, Designs and Patents Act 1988.

CN 2545

First reprint 1998

Designed by Peter Ward
Typeset by Palimpsest Book Produktion Limited,
Polmont, Stirlingshire
Printed and bound in Germany by
Graphischer Grossbetrieb Pössneck GmbH

This is for Naomi. Still.

AUTHOR'S NOTE

To some extent, this novel deals with the legal aspects of child custody in the State of Maine. I asked for help in understanding this subject from my friend Warren Silver, who is a fine attorney. Warren guided me carefully, and along the way he also told me about a quaint old device called the Stenomask, which I immediately appropriated for my own fell purposes. If I've made procedural mistakes in the story which follows, blame me, not my legal resource. Warren also asked me – rather plaintively – if I could maybe put a 'good' lawyer in my book. All I can say is that I did my best in that regard.

Thanks to my son Owen for technical support in Woodstock, New York, and to my friend (and fellow Rock Bottom Remainder) Ridley Pearson for technical support in Ketchum, Idaho. Thanks to Pam Dorman for her sympathetic and perceptive reading of the first draft. Thanks to Chuck Verrill for a monumental editing job – your personal best, Chuck. Thanks to Susan Moldow, Nan Graham, Jack Romanos, and Carolyn Reidy at Scribner's for care and feeding. And thanks to Tabby, who was there for me again when things got hard. I love you, hon.

S.K.

Yes, Bartleby, stay there behind your screen, thought I;
I shall persecute you no more; you are harmless and
noiseless as any of these old chairs; in short, I never feel
so private as when I know you are here.

'Bartleby'
Herman Melville

Last night I dreamt I went to Manderley again . . .
As I stood there, hushed and still, I could swear that
the house was not an empty shell but lived and breathed
as it had lived before.

Rebecca
Daphne du Maurier

Mars is heaven.
Ray Bradbury

BAG OF BONES

CHAPTER ONE

On a very hot day in August of 1994, my wife told me she was going down to the Derry Rite Aid to pick up a refill on her sinus medicine prescription – this is stuff you can buy over the counter these days, I believe. I'd finished my writing for the day and offered to pick it up for her. She said thanks, but she wanted to get a piece of fish at the supermarket next door, anyway; two birds with one stone and all of that. She blew a kiss at me off the palm of her hand and went out. The next time I saw her, she was on TV. That's how you identify the dead here in Derry – no walking down a subterranean corridor with green tiles on the walls and long fluorescent bars overhead, no naked body rolling out of a chilly drawer on casters; you just go into an office marked PRIVATE and look at a TV screen and say yep or nope.

The Rite Aid and the Shopwell are less than a mile from our house, in a little neighborhood strip mall which also supports a video store, a used book-store named Spread It Around (they do a very brisk business in my old paperbacks), a Radio Shack, and a Fast Foto. It's on Up-Mile Hill, at the intersection of Witcham and Jackson.

She parked in front of Blockbuster Video, went into the drugstore, and did business with Mr Joe Wyzer, who was the druggist in those days; he has since moved on to the Rite Aid in Bangor. At the checkout she picked up one of those little chocolates with marshmallow inside, this one in the shape of a mouse. I found it later, in her purse. I unwrapped it and ate it myself, sitting at the kitchen table with the contents of her red handbag spread out in front of me, and it was like taking Communion. When it was gone

1

except for the taste of chocolate on my tongue and in my throat, I burst into tears. I sat there in the litter of her Kleenex and makeup and keys and half-finished rolls of Certs and cried with my hands over my eyes, the way a kid cries.

The sinus inhaler was in a Rite Aid bag. It had cost twelve dollars and eighteen cents. There was something else in the bag, too – an item which had cost twenty-two-fifty. I looked at this other item for a long time, seeing it but not understanding it. I was surprised, maybe even stunned, but the idea that Johanna Arlen Noonan might have been leading another life, one I knew nothing about, never crossed my mind. Not then.

Jo left the register, walked out into the bright, hammering sun again, swapping her regular glasses for her prescription sunglasses as she did, and just as she stepped from beneath the drugstore's slight overhang (I am imagining a little here, I suppose, crossing over into the country of the novelist a little, but not by much; only by inches, and you can trust me on that), there was that shrewish howl of locked tires on pavement that means there's going to be either an accident or a very close call.

This time it happened – the sort of accident which happened at that stupid X-shaped intersection at least once a week, it seemed. A 1989 Toyota was pulling out of the shopping-center parking lot and turning left on to Jackson Street. Behind the wheel was Mrs Esther Easterling of Barrett's Orchards. She was accompanied by her friend Mrs Irene Deorsey, also of Barrett's Orchards, who had shopped the video store without finding anything she wanted to rent. Too much violence, Irene said. Both women were cigarette widows.

Esther could hardly have missed the orange Public Works dump truck coming down the hill; although she denied this to the police, to the newspaper, and to me when I talked to her some two months later, I think it likely that she just forgot to look. As my own mother (another cigarette widow) used to say, 'The two most common ailments of the elderly are arthritis and forgetfulness. They can be held responsible for neither.'

Driving the Public Works truck was William Fraker, of Old Cape. Mr Fraker was thirty-eight years old on the day of my wife's death, driving with his shirt off and thinking how badly he wanted a cool shower and a cold beer, not necessarily in that order. He and three other men had spent eight hours putting down asphalt patch out on the Harris Avenue Extension near the airport, a hot job on a hot day, and Bill Fraker said yeah, he might have been going a little too fast – maybe forty in a thirty-mile-an-hour zone. He was eager to get back to the garage, sign off on the truck, and get behind the wheel of his own F-150, which had air conditioning. Also, the dump truck's brakes, while good enough to pass inspection, were a long way from tip-top condition. Fraker hit them as soon as he saw the Toyota pull out in front of him (he hit his horn, as well), but it was too late. He heard screaming tires – his own, and Esther's as she belatedly realized her danger – and saw her face for just a moment.

'That was the worst part, somehow,' he told me as we sat on his porch, drinking beers – it was October by then, and although the sun was warm on our faces, we were both wearing sweaters. 'You know how high up you sit in one of those dump trucks?'

I nodded.

'Well, she was looking up to see me – *craning* up, you'd say – and the sun was full in her face. I could see how old she was. I remember thinking, "Holy shit, she's gonna break like glass if I can't stop." But old people are tough, more often than not. They can surprise you. I mean, look at how it turned out, both those old biddies still alive, and your wife . . .'

He stopped then, bright red color dashing into his cheeks, making him look like a boy who has been laughed at in the schoolyard by girls who have noticed his fly is unzipped. It was comical, but if I'd smiled, it only would have confused him.

'Mr Noonan, I'm sorry. My mouth just sort of ran away with me.'

'It's all right,' I told him. 'I'm over the worst of it, anyway.' That was a lie, but it put us back on track.

'Anyway,' he said, 'we hit. There was a loud bang, and a crumping sound when the driver's side of the car caved in. Breaking glass, too. I was thrown against the wheel hard enough so I couldn't draw a breath without it hurting for a week or more, and I had a big bruise right here.' He drew an arc on his chest just below the collarbones. 'I banged my head on the windshield hard enough to crack the glass, but all I got up there was a little purple knob . . . no bleeding, not

3

even a headache. My wife says I've just got a naturally thick skull. I saw the woman driving the Toyota, Mrs Easterling, thrown across the console between the front bucket seats. Then we were finally stopped, all tangled together in the middle of the street, and I got out to see how bad they were. I tell you, I expected to find them both dead.'

Neither of them was dead, neither of them was even unconscious, although Mrs Easterling had three broken ribs and a dislocated hip. Mrs Deorsey, who had been a seat away from the impact, suffered a concussion when she rapped her head on her window. That was all; she was 'treated and released at Home Hospital,' as the *Derry News* always puts it in such cases.

My wife, the former Johanna Arlen of Malden, Massachusetts, saw it all from where she stood outside the drugstore, with her purse slung over her shoulder and her prescription bag in one hand. Like Bill Fraker, she must have thought the occupants of the Toyota were either dead or seriously hurt. The sound of the collision had been a hollow, authoritative bang which rolled through the hot afternoon air like a bowling ball down an alley. The sound of breaking glass edged it like jagged lace. The two vehicles were tangled violently together in the middle of Jackson Street, the dirty orange truck looming over the pale-blue import like a bullying parent over a cowering child.

Johanna began to sprint across the parking lot toward the street. Others were doing the same all around her. One of them, Miss Jill Dunbarry, had been window-shopping at Radio Shack when the accident occurred. She said she thought she remembered running past Johanna – at least she was pretty sure she remembered someone in yellow slacks – but she couldn't be sure. By then, Mrs Easterling was screaming that she was hurt, they were both hurt, wouldn't somebody help her and her friend Irene.

Halfway across the parking lot, near a little cluster of newspaper dispensers, my wife fell down. Her purse-strap stayed over her shoulder, but her prescription bag slipped from her hand, and the sinus inhaler slid halfway out. The other item stayed put.

No one noticed her lying there by the newspaper dispensers; everyone was focused on the tangled vehicles, the screaming women, the spreading puddle of water and antifreeze from the Public Works truck's ruptured radiator. ('That's gas!' the clerk from Fast Foto

4

shouted to anyone who would listen. 'That's gas, watch out she don't blow, fellas!') I suppose one or two of the would-be rescuers might have jumped right over her, perhaps thinking she had fainted. To assume such a thing on a day when the temperature was pushing ninety-five degrees would not have been unreasonable.

Roughly two dozen people from the shopping center clustered around the accident; another four dozen or so came running over from Strawford Park, where a baseball game had been going on. I imagine that all the things you would expect to hear in such situations were said, many of them more than once. Milling around. Someone reaching through the misshapen hole which had been the driver's-side window to pat Esther's trembling old hand. People immediately giving way for Joe Wyzer; at such moments anyone in a white coat automatically becomes the belle of the ball. In the distance, the warble of an ambulance siren rising like shaky air over an incinerator.

All during this, lying unnoticed in the parking lot, was my wife with her purse still over her shoulder (inside, still wrapped in foil, her uneaten chocolate-marshmallow mouse) and her white prescription bag near one outstretched hand. It was Joe Wyzer, hurrying back to the pharmacy to get a compress for Irene Deorsey's head, who spotted her. He recognized her even though she was lying face-down. He recognized her by her red hair, white blouse, and yellow slacks. He recognized her because he had waited on her not fifteen minutes before.

'Mrs Noonan?' he asked, forgetting all about the compress for the dazed but apparently not too badly hurt Irene Deorsey. 'Mrs Noonan, are you all right?' Knowing already (or so I suspect; perhaps I am wrong) that she was not.

He turned her over. It took both hands to do it, and even then he had to work hard, kneeling and pushing and lifting there in the parking lot with the heat baking down from above and then bouncing back up from the asphalt. Dead people put on weight, it seems to me; both in their flesh and in our minds, they put on weight.

There were red marks on her face. When I identified her I could see them clearly even on the video monitor. I started to ask the assistant medical examiner what they were, but then I knew. Late

5

July hot pavement; elementary, my dear Watson. My wife died getting a sunburn.

Wyzer got up, saw that the ambulance had arrived, and ran toward it. He pushed his way though the crowd and grabbed one of the attendants as he got out from behind the wheel. 'There's a woman over there,' Wyzer said, pointing toward the parking lot.

'Guy, we've got two women right here, and a man as well,' the attendant said. He tried to pull away, but Wyzer held on.

'Never mind them right now,' he said. 'They're basically okay. The woman over there isn't.'

The woman over there was dead, and I'm pretty sure Joe Wyzer knew it . . . but he had his priorities straight. Give him that. And he was convincing enough to get both paramedics moving away from the tangle of truck and Toyota, in spite of Esther Easterling's cries of pain and the rumbles of protest from the Greek chorus.

When they got to my wife, one of the paramedics was quick to confirm what Joe Wyzer had already suspected. 'Holy shit,' the other one said. 'What happened to her?'

'Heart, most likely,' the first one said. 'She got excited and it just blew out on her.'

But it wasn't her heart. The autopsy revealed a brain aneurysm which she might have been living with, all unknown, for as long as five years. As she sprinted across the parking lot toward the accident, that weak vessel in her cerebral cortex had blown like a tire, drowning her control-centers in blood and killing her. Death had probably not been instantaneous, the assistant medical examiner told me, but it had still come swiftly enough . . . and she wouldn't have suffered. Just one big black nova, all sensation and thought gone even before she hit the pavement.

'Can I help you in any way, Mr Noonan?' the assistant ME asked, turning me gently away from the still face and closed eyes on the video monitor. 'Do you have questions? I'll answer them if I can.'

'Just one,' I said. I told him what she'd purchased in the drugstore just before she died. Then I asked my question.

The days leading up to the funeral and the funeral itself are dreamlike in my memory — the clearest memory I have is of eating Jo's chocolate mouse and crying . . . crying mostly, I think, because

6

I knew how soon the taste of it would be gone. I had one other crying fit a few days after we buried her, and I will tell you about that one shortly.

I was glad for the arrival of Jo's family, and particularly for the arrival of her oldest brother, Frank. It was Frank Arlen – fifty, red-cheeked, portly, and with a head of lush dark hair – who organized the arrangements . . . who wound up actually *dickering* with the funeral director.

'I can't believe you did that,' I said later, as we sat in a booth at Jack's Pub, drinking beers.

'He was trying to stick it to you, Mikey,' he said. 'I hate guys like that.' He reached into his back pocket, brought out a handkerchief, and wiped absently at his cheeks with it. He hadn't broken down – none of the Arlens broke down, at least not when I was with them – but Frank had leaked steadily all day; he looked like a man suffering from severe conjunctivitis.

There had been six Arlen sibs in all, Jo the youngest and the only girl. She had been the pet of her big brothers. I suspect that if I'd had anything to do with her death, the five of them would have torn me apart with their bare hands. As it was, they formed a protective shield around me instead, and that was good. I suppose I might have muddled through without them, but I don't know how. I was thirty-six, remember. You don't expect to have to bury your wife when you're thirty-six and she herself is two years younger. Death was the last thing on our minds.

'If a guy gets caught taking your stereo out of your car, they call it theft and put him in jail,' Frank said. The Arlens had come from Massachusetts, and I could still hear Malden in Frank's voice – *caught* was *coowat*, *car* was *cah, call* was *caul*. 'If the same guy is trying to sell a grieving husband a three-thousand-dollar casket for forty-five hundred dollars, they call it business and ask him to speak at the Rotary Club luncheon. Greedy asshole, I fed him his lunch, didn't I?'

'Yes. You did.'

'You okay, Mikey?'

'I'm okay.'

'Sincerely okay?'

'How the fuck should I know?' I asked him, loud enough to turn some heads in a nearby booth. And then: 'She was pregnant.'

His face grew very still. *'What?'*

I struggled to keep my voice down. 'Pregnant. Six or seven weeks, according to the . . . you know, the autopsy. Did you know? Did she tell you?'

'No! Christ, no!' But there was a funny look on his face, as if she had told him *something*. 'I knew you were trying, of course . . . she said you had a low sperm count and it might take a little while, but the doctor thought you guys'd probably . . . sooner or later you'd probably . . .' He trailed off, looking down at his hands. 'They can tell that, huh? They check for that?'

'They can tell. As for checking, I don't know if they do it automatically or not. I asked.'

'Why?'

'She didn't just buy sinus medicine before she died. She also bought one of those home pregnancy-testing kits.'

'You had no idea? No clue?'

I shook my head.

He reached across the table and squeezed my shoulder. 'She wanted to be sure, that's all. You know that, don't you?'

A refill on my sinus medicine and a piece of fish, she'd said. Looking like always. A woman off to run a couple of errands. We had been trying to have a kid for eight years, but she had looked just like always.

'Sure,' I said, patting Frank's hand. 'Sure, big guy. I know.'

It was the Arlens – led by Frank – who handled Johanna's sendoff. As the writer of the family, I was assigned the obituary. My brother came up from Virginia with my mom and my aunt and was allowed to tend the guest-book at the viewings. My mother – almost completely ga-ga at the age of sixty-six, although the doctors refused to call it Alzheimer's – lived in Memphis with her sister, two years younger and only slightly less wonky. They were in charge of cutting the cake and the pies at the funeral reception.

Everything else was arranged by the Arlens, from the viewing hours to the components of the funeral ceremony. Frank and Victor, the second-youngest brother, spoke brief tributes. Jo's dad offered a prayer for his daughter's soul. And at the end, Pete Breedlove, the boy who cut our grass in the summer and raked our yard in the fall, brought everyone to tears by singing 'Blessed Assurance, Jesus Is Mine,' which Frank said had been Jo's favorite hymn as a girl. How Frank found Pete and persuaded him to sing at the funeral is something I never found out.

We got through it – the afternoon and evening viewings on Tuesday, the funeral service on Wednesday morning, then the little pray-over at Fairlawn Cemetery. What I remember most was thinking how hot it was, how lost I felt without having Jo to talk to, and that I wished I had bought a new pair of shoes. Jo would have pestered me to death about the ones I was wearing, if she had been there.

Later on I talked to my brother, Sid, told him we *had* to do something about our mother and Aunt Francine before the two of them disappeared completely into the Twilight Zone. They were too young for a nursing home; what did Sid advise?

He advised something, but I'll be damned if I know what it was. I agreed to it, I remember that, but not what it was. Later that day, Siddy, our Mom, and our aunt climbed back into Siddy's rental car for the drive to Boston, where they would spend the night and then grab the *Southern Crescent* the following day. My brother is happy enough to chaperone the old folks, but he doesn't fly, even if the tickets are on me. He claims there are no breakdown lanes in the sky if the engine quits.

Most of the Arlens left the next day. Once more it was dog-hot, the sun glaring out of a white-haze sky and lying on everything like melted brass. They stood in front of our house – which had become solely my house by then – with three taxis lined up at the curb behind them, big galoots hugging one another amid the litter of tote-bags and saying their goodbyes in those foggy Massachusetts accents.

Frank stayed another day. We picked a big bunch of flowers behind the house – not those ghastly-smelling hothouse things whose aroma I always associate with death and organ-music but real flowers, the kind Jo liked best – and stuck them in a couple of coffee cans I found in the back pantry. We went out to Fairlawn and put them on the new grave. Then we just sat there for awhile under the beating sun.

'She was always just the sweetest thing in my life,' Frank said at last in a strange, muffled voice. 'We took care of Jo when we were kids. Us guys. No one messed with Jo, I'll tell you. Anyone tried, we'd feed em their lunch.'

'She told me a lot of stories.'

'Good ones?'

'Yeah, real good.'

'I'm going to miss her so much.'

'Me, too,' I said. 'Frank . . . listen . . . I know you were her favorite brother. She never called you, maybe just to say that she missed a period or was feeling whoopsy in the morning? You can tell me. I won't be pissed.'

'But she didn't. Honest to God. *Was* she whoopsy in the morning?'

'Not that I saw.' And that was just it. I hadn't seen *anything*. Of course I'd been writing, and when I write I pretty much trance out. But she knew where I went in those trances. She could have found me and shaken me fully awake. Why hadn't she? Why would she hide good news? Not wanting to tell me until she was sure was plausible . . . but it somehow wasn't Jo.

'Was it a boy or a girl?' he asked.

'A girl.'

We'd had names picked out and waiting for most of our marriage. A boy would have been Andrew. Our daughter would have been Kia. Kia Jane Noonan.

Frank, divorced six years and on his own, had been staying with me. On our way back to the house he said, 'I worry about you, Mikey. You haven't got much family to fall back on at a time like this, and what you do have is far away.'

'I'll be all right,' I said.

He nodded. 'That's what we say, anyway, isn't it?'

'We?'

'Guys. "I'll be all right." And if we're not, we try to make sure no one knows it.' He looked at me, eyes still leaking, handkerchief in one big sunburned hand. 'If you're not all right, Mikey, and you don't want to call your brother – I saw the way you looked at him – let me be your brother. For Jo's sake if not your own.'

'Okay,' I said, respecting and appreciating the offer, also knowing I would do no such thing. I don't call people for help. It's not because of the way I was raised, at least I don't think so; it's the way I was made. Johanna once said that if I was drowning at Dark Score Lake, where we have a summer home, I would die silently fifty feet out from the public beach rather than yell for help. It's not a question of love or affection. I can give those and I can take them. I feel pain like anyone else. I need to touch and be touched. But if someone asks me, 'Are you all right?' I can't answer no. I can't say help me.

A couple of hours later Frank left for the southern end of the state. When he opened the car door, I was touched to see that the taped book he was listening to was one of mine. He hugged me, then surprised me with a kiss on the mouth, a good hard smack. 'If you need to talk, call,' he said. 'And if you need to be with someone, just come.'

I nodded.

'And be careful.'

That startled me. The combination of heat and grief had made me feel as if I had been living in a dream for the last few days, but that got through.

'Careful of what?'

'I don't know,' he said. 'I don't know, Mikey.' Then he got into his car – he was so big and it was so little that he looked as if he were wearing it – and drove away. The sun was going down by then. Do you know how the sun looks at the end of a hot day in August, all orange and somehow *squashed*, as if an invisible hand were pushing down on the top of it and at any moment it might just pop like an overfilled mosquito and splatter all over the horizon? It was like that. In the east, where it was already dark, thunder was rumbling. But there was no rain that night, only a dark that came down as thick and stifling as a blanket. All the same, I slipped in front of the word processor and wrote for an hour or so. It went pretty well, as I remember. And you know, even when it doesn't, it passes the time.

My second crying fit came three or four days after the funeral. That sense of being in a dream persisted – I walked, I talked, I answered the phone, I worked on my book, which had been about eighty per cent complete when Jo died – but all the time there was this clear sense of disconnection, a feeling that everything was going on at a distance from the real me, that I was more or less phoning it in.

Denise Breedlove, Pete's mother, called and asked if I wouldn't like her to bring a couple of her friends over one day the following week and give the big old Edwardian pile I now lived in alone – rolling around in it like the last pea in a restaurant-sized can – a good stem-to-stern cleaning. They would do it, she said, for a hundred dollars split even among the three of them, and mostly because it wasn't good for me to go on without it. There had to be a scrubbing after a death, she said, even if the death didn't happen in the house itself.

I told her it was a fine idea, but I would pay her and the women she brought a hundred dollars each for six hours' work. At the end of the six hours, I wanted the job done. And if it wasn't, I told her, it would be done, anyway.

'Mr Noonan, that's far too much,' she said.

'Maybe and maybe not, but it's what I'm paying,' I said. 'Will you do it?'

She said she would, of course she would.

Perhaps predictably, I found myself going through the house on the evening before they came, doing a pre-cleaning inspection. I guess I didn't want the women (two of whom would be complete strangers to me) finding anything that would embarrass them or me: a pair of Johanna's silk panties stuffed down behind the sofa cushions, perhaps ('We are often overcome on the sofa, Michael,' she said to me once, 'have you noticed?'), or beer cans under the loveseat on the sunporch, maybe even an unflushed toilet. In truth, I can't tell you any one thing I was looking for; that sense of operating in a dream still held firm control over my mind. The clearest thoughts I had during those days were either about the end of the novel I was writing (the psychotic killer had lured my heroine to a high-rise building and meant to push her off the roof) or about the Norco Home Pregnancy Test Jo had bought on the day she died. Sinus prescription, she had said. Piece of fish for supper, she had said. And her eyes had shown me nothing else I needed to look at twice.

Near the end of my 'pre-cleaning,' I looked under our bed and saw an open paperback on Jo's side. She hadn't been dead long, but few

12

household lands are so dusty as the Kingdom of Underbed, and the light-gray coating I saw on the book when I brought it out made me think of Johanna's face and hands in her coffin – Jo in the Kingdom of Underground. Did it get dusty inside a coffin? Surely not, but—

I pushed the thought away. It pretended to go, but all day long it kept creeping back, like Tolstoy's white bear.

Johanna and I had both been English majors at the University of Maine, and like many others, I reckon, we fell in love to the sound of Shakespeare and the Tilbury Town cynicism of Edwin Arlington Robinson. Yet the writer who had bound us closest together was no college-friendly poet or essayist but W. Somerset Maugham, that elderly globetrotting novelist-playwright with the reptile's face (always obscured by cigarette smoke in his photographs, it seems) and the romantic's heart. So it did not surprise me much to find that the book under the bed was *The Moon and Sixpence*. I had read it myself as a late teenager, not once but twice, identifying passionately with the character of Charles Strickland. (It was writing I wanted to do in the South Seas, of course, not painting.)

She had been using a playing card from some defunct deck as her place-marker, and as I opened the book, I thought of something she had said when I was first getting to know her. In Twentieth-Century British Lit, this had been, probably in 1980. Johanna Arlen had been a fiery little sophomore. I was a senior, picking up the Twentieth-Century Brits simply because I had time on my hands that last semester. 'A hundred years from now,' she had said, 'the shame of the mid-twentieth-century literary critics will be that they embraced Lawrence and ignored Maugham.' This was greeted with contemptuously good-natured laughter (they all knew *Women in Love* was one of the greatest damn books ever written), but I didn't laugh. I fell in love.

The playing card marked pages 102 and 103 – Dirk Stroeve has just discovered that his wife has left him for Strickland, Maugham's version of Paul Gauguin. The narrator tries to buck Stroeve up. *My dear fellow, don't be unhappy. She'll come back . . .*

'Easy for you to say,' I murmured to the room which now belonged just to me.

I turned the page and read this: *Strickland's injurious calm robbed Stroeve of his self-control. Blind rage seized him, and without knowing*

13

what he was doing he flung himself on Strickland. Strickland was taken by surprise and he staggered, but he was very strong, even after his illness, and in a moment, he did not exactly know how, Stroeve found himself on the floor.

'You funny little man,' said Strickland.

It occurred to me that Jo was never going to turn the page and hear Strickland call the pathetic Stroeve a funny little man. In a moment of brilliant epiphany I have never forgotten – how could I? it was one of the worst moments of my life – I understood it wasn't a mistake that would be rectified, or a dream from which I would awaken. Johanna was dead.

My strength was robbed by grief. If the bed hadn't been there, I would have fallen to the floor. We weep from our eyes, it's all we can do, but on that evening I felt as if every pore of my body were weeping, every crack and cranny. I sat there on her side of the bed, with her dusty paperback copy of *The Moon and Sixpence* in my hand, and I wailed. I think it was surprise as much as pain; in spite of the corpse I had seen and identified on a high-resolution video monitor, in spite of the funeral and Pete Breedlove singing 'Blessed Assurance' in his high, sweet tenor voice, in spite of the graveside service with its ashes to ashes and dust to dust, I hadn't really believed it. The Penguin paperback did for me what the big gray coffin had not: it insisted she was dead.

You funny little man, said Strickland.

I lay back on our bed, crossed my forearms over my face, and cried myself to sleep that way as children do when they're unhappy. I had an awful dream. In it I woke up, saw the paperback of *The Moon and Sixpence* still lying on the coverlet beside me, and decided to put it back under the bed where I had found it. You know how confused dreams are – logic like Dalí clocks gone so soft they lie over the branches of trees like throw-rugs.

I put the playing-card bookmark back between pages 102 and 103 – a turn of the index finger away from *You funny little man, said Strickland* now and forever – and rolled on to my side, hanging my head over the edge of the bed, meaning to put the book back exactly where I had found it.

Jo was lying there amid the dust-kitties. A strand of cobweb hung down from the bottom of the box spring and caressed her cheek like a

14

feather. Her red hair looked dull, but her eyes were dark and alert and baleful in her white face. And when she spoke, I knew that death had driven her insane.

'Give me that,' she hissed. 'It's my dust-catcher.' She snatched it out of my hand before I could offer it to her. For a moment our fingers touched, and hers were as cold as twigs after a frost. She opened the book to her place, the playing card fluttering out, and placed Somerset Maugham over her face – a shroud of words. As she crossed her hands on her bosom and lay still, I realized she was wearing the blue dress I had buried her in. She had come out of her grave to hide under our bed.

I awoke with a muffled cry and a painful jerk that almost tumbled me off the side of the bed. I hadn't been asleep long – the tears were still damp on my cheeks, and my eyelids had that funny stretched feel they get after a bout of weeping. The dream had been so vivid that I had to roll on my side, hang my head down, and peer under the bed, sure she would be there with the book over her face, that she would reach out with her cold fingers to touch me.

There was nothing there, of course – dreams are just dreams. Nevertheless, I spent the rest of the night on the couch in my study. It was the right choice, I guess, because there were no more dreams that night. Only the nothingness of good sleep.

CHAPTER TWO

I never suffered from writer's block during the ten years of my marriage, and did not suffer it immediately after Johanna's death. I was in fact so unfamiliar with the condition that it had pretty well set in before I knew anything out of the ordinary was going on. I think this was because in my heart I believed that such conditions only affected 'literary' types of the sort who are discussed, deconstructed, and sometimes dismissed in *The New York Review of Books*.

My writing career and my marriage covered almost exactly the same span. I finished the first draft of my first novel, *Being Two*, not long after Jo and I became officially engaged (I popped an opal ring on the third finger of her left hand, a hundred and ten bucks at Day's Jewellers, and quite a bit more than I could afford at the time . . . but Johanna seemed utterly thrilled with it), and I finished my last novel, *All the Way from the Top*, about a month after she was declared dead. This was the one about the psychotic killer with the love of high places. It was published in the fall of 1995. I have published other novels since then – a paradox I can explain – but I don't think there'll be a Michael Noonan novel on any list in the foreseeable future. I know what writer's block is now, all right. I know more about it than I ever wanted to.

When I hesitantly showed Jo the first draft of *Being Two*, she read it in one evening, curled up in her favorite chair, wearing nothing but panties and a tee-shirt with the Maine black bear on the front, drinking glass after glass of iced tea. I went out to the garage (we were renting a house in Bangor with another couple on as shaky financial

16

ground as we were . . . and no, Jo and I weren't quite married at that point, although as far as I know, that opal ring never left her finger) and puttered aimlessly, feeling like a guy in a *New Yorker* cartoon – one of those about funny fellows in the delivery waiting room. As I remember, I fucked up a so-simple-a-child-can-do-it birdhouse kit and almost cut off the index finger of my left hand. Every twenty minutes or so I'd go back inside and peek at Jo. If she noticed, she gave no sign. I took that as hopeful.

I was sitting on the back stoop, looking up at the stars and smoking, when she came out, sat down beside me, and put her hand on the back of my neck.

'Well?' I said.

'It's good,' she said. 'Now why don't you come inside and do me?' And before I could answer, the panties she had been wearing dropped in my lap in a little whisper of nylon.

Afterward, lying in bed and eating oranges (a vice we later outgrew), I asked her: 'Good as in publishable?'

'Well,' she said, 'I don't know anything about the glamorous world of publishing, but I've been reading for pleasure all my life – *Curious George* was my first love, if you want to know—'

'I don't.'

She leaned over and popped an orange segment into my mouth, her breast warm and provocative against my arm. '—and I read this with great pleasure. My prediction is that your career as a reporter for the *Derry News* is never going to survive its rookie stage. I think I'm going to be a novelist's wife.'

Her words thrilled me – actually brought goosebumps out on my arms. No, she didn't know anything about the glamorous world of publishing, but if she believed, I believed . . . and belief turned out to be the right course. I got an agent through my old creative-writing teacher (who read my novel and damned it with faint praise, seeing its commercial qualities as a kind of heresy, I think), and the agent sold *Being Two* to Random House, the first publisher to see it.

Jo was right about my career as a reporter, as well. I spent four months covering flower shows, drag races, and bean suppers at about a hundred a week before my first check from Random House came in – $27,000, after the agent's commission had been deducted. I wasn't

17

in the newsroom long enough to get even that first minor bump in salary, but they had a going-away party for me just the same. At Jack's Pub, this was, now that I think of it. There was a banner hung over the tables in the back room which said GOOD LUCK MIKE – WRITE ON! Later, when we got home, Johanna said that if envy was acid, there would have been nothing left of me but my belt-buckle and three teeth.

Later, in bed with the lights out – the last orange eaten and the last cigarette shared – I said, 'No one's ever going to confuse it with *Look Homeward, Angel*, are they?' My book, I meant. She knew it, just as she knew I had been fairly depressed by my old creative-writing teacher's response to *Two*.

'You aren't going to pull a lot of frustrated-artist crap on me, are you?' she asked, getting up on one elbow. 'If you are, I wish you'd tell me now, so I can pick up one of those do-it-yourself divorce kits first thing in the morning.'

I was amused, but also a little hurt. 'Did you see that first press release from Random House?' I knew she had. 'They're just about calling me V. C. Andrews with a prick, for God's sake.'

'Well,' she said, lightly grabbing the object in question, 'you *do* have a prick. As far as what they're calling you ... Mike, when I was in third grade, Patty Banning used to call me a booger-hooker. But I wasn't.'

'Perception is everything.'

'Bullshit.' She was still holding my dick and now gave it a formidable squeeze that hurt a little and felt absolutely wonderful at the same time. That crazy old trouser mouse never really cared what it got in those days, as long as there was a lot of it. '*Happiness* is everything. Are you happy when you write, Mike?'

'Sure.' It was what she knew, anyway.

'And does your conscience bother you when you write?'

'When I write, there's nothing I'd rather do except this,' I said, and rolled on top of her.

'Oh dear,' she said in that prissy little voice that always cracked me up. 'There's a penis between us.'

And as we made love, I realized a wonderful thing or two: that she had meant it when she said she really liked my book (hell, I'd known she liked it just from the way she sat in the wing chair reading

18

it, with a lock of hair falling over her brow and her bare legs tucked beneath her), and that I didn't need to be ashamed of what I had written . . . not in her eyes, at least. And one other wonderful thing: her perception, joined with my own to make the true binocular vision nothing but marriage allows, was the only perception that mattered.

Thank God she was a Maugham fan.

I was V. C. Andrews with a prick for ten years . . . fourteen, if you add in the post-Johanna years. The first five were with Random; then my agent got a huge offer from Putnam and I jumped.

You've seen my name on a lot of bestseller lists . . . if, that is, your Sunday paper carries a list that goes up to fifteen instead of just listing the top ten. I was never a Clancy, Ludlum, or Grisham, but I moved a fair number of hardcovers (V. C. Andrews never did, Harold Oblowski, my agent, told me once; the lady was pretty much a paperback phenomenon) and once got as high as number five on the *Times* list . . . that was with my second book, *The Red-Shirt Man*. Ironically, one of the books that kept me from going higher was *Steel Machine*, by Thad Beaumont (writing as George Stark). The Beaumonts had a summer place in Castle Rock back in those days, not even fifty miles south of our place on Dark Score Lake. Thad's dead now. Suicide. I don't know if it had anything to do with writer's block or not.

I stood just outside the magic circle of the mega-bestsellers, but I never minded that. We owned two homes by the time I was thirty-one: the lovely old Edwardian in Derry and, in western Maine, a lakeside log home almost big enough to be called a lodge – that was Sara Laughs, so called by the locals for nearly a century. And we owned both places free and clear at a time of life when many couples consider themselves lucky just to have fought their way to mortgage approval on a starter home. We were healthy, faithful, and with our fun-bones still fully attached. I wasn't Thomas Wolfe (not even Tom Wolfe or Tobias Wolff), but I was being paid to do what I loved, and there's no gig on earth better than that; it's like a license to steal.

I was what midlist fiction used to be in the forties: critically ignored, genre-oriented (in my case the genre was Lovely Young

Woman on Her Own Meets Fascinating Stranger), but well compensated and with the kind of shabby acceptance accorded to state-sanctioned whorehouses in Nevada, the feeling seeming to be that some outlet for the baser instincts should be provided and someone had to do That Sort of Thing. I did That Sort of Thing enthusiastically (and sometimes with Jo's enthusiastic connivance, if I came to a particularly problematic plot crossroads), and at some point around the time of George Bush's election, our accountant told us we were millionaires.

We weren't rich enough to own a jet (Grisham) or a pro football team (Clancy), but by the standards of Derry, Maine, we were quite rolling in it. We made love thousands of times, saw thousands of movies, read thousands of books (Jo storing hers under her side of the bed at the end of the day, more often than not). And perhaps the greatest blessing was that we never knew how short the time was.

More than once I wondered if breaking the ritual was what led to the writer's block. In the daytime I could dismiss this as supernatural twaddle, but at night that was harder to do. At night your thoughts have an unpleasant way of slipping their collars and running free. And if you've spent most of your adult life making fictions, I'm sure those collars are even looser and the dogs less eager to wear them. Was it Shaw or Oscar Wilde who said a writer was a man who had taught his mind to misbehave?

And is it really so far-fetched to think that breaking the ritual might have played a part in my sudden and unexpected (unexpected by me, at least) silence? When you make your daily bread in the land of make-believe, the line between what is and what seems to be is much finer. Painters sometimes refuse to paint without wearing a certain hat, and baseball players who are hitting well won't change their socks.

The ritual started with the second book, which was the only one I remember being nervous about – I suppose I'd absorbed a fair amount of that sophomore-jinx stuff; the idea that one hit might only be a fluke. I remember an American Lit lecturer's once saying that of modern American writers, only Harper Lee had found a foolproof way of avoiding the second-book blues.

20

When I reached the end of *The Red-Shirt Man*, I stopped just short of finishing. The Edwardian on Benton Street in Derry was still two years in the future at that point, but we had purchased Sara Laughs, the place on Dark Score (not anywhere near as furnished as it later became, and Jo's studio not yet built, but nice), and that's where we were.

I pushed back from my typewriter – I was still clinging to my old IBM Selectric in those days – and went into the kitchen. It was mid-September, most of the summer people were gone, and the crying of the loons on the lake sounded inexpressibly lovely. The sun was going down, and the lake itself had become a still and heatless plate of fire. This is one of the most vivid memories I have, so clear I sometimes feel I could step right into it and live it all again. What things, if any, would I do differently? I sometimes wonder about that.

Early that evening I had put a bottle of Taittinger and two flutes in the fridge. Now I took them out, put them on a tin tray that was usually employed to transport pitchers of iced tea or Kool-Aid from the kitchen to the deck, and carried it before me into the living room.

Johanna was deep in her ratty old easy chair, reading a book (not Maugham that night but William Denbrough, one of her contemporary favorites). 'Ooo,' she said, looking up and marking her place. 'Champagne. What's the occasion?' As if, you understand, she didn't know.

'I'm done,' I said. '*Mon livre est tout fini.*'

'Well,' she said, smiling and taking one of the flutes as I bent down to her with the tray, 'then *that's* all right, isn't it?'

I realize now that the essence of the ritual – the part that was alive and powerful, like the one true magic word in a mouthful of gibberish – was that phrase. We almost always had champagne, and she almost always came into the office with me afterward for the other thing, but not always.

Once, five years or so before she died, she was in Ireland, vacationing with a girlfriend, when I finished a book. I drank the champagne by myself that time, and entered the last line by myself as well (by then I was using a Macintosh which did a billion different things and which I used for only one) and never lost a minute's sleep over it. But I called her at the inn where she and her friend Bryn were staying; I told her I had finished, and listened as she said the words I'd called to hear – words that slipped into an Irish telephone line, travelled to a microwave transmitter, rose like a prayer to some satellite, and then came back down to my ear: 'Well, then *that's* all right, isn't it?'

This custom began, as I say, after the second book. When we'd each had a glass of champagne and a refill, I took her into the office, where a single sheet of paper still stuck out of my forest-green Selectric. On the lake, one last loon cried down dark, that call that always sounds to me like something rusty turning slowly in the wind.

'I thought you said you were done,' she said.

'Everything but the last line,' I said. 'The book, such as it is, is dedicated to you, and I want you to put down the last bit.'

She didn't laugh or protest or get gushy, just looked at me to see if I really meant it. I nodded that I did, and she sat in my chair. She had been swimming earlier, and her hair was pulled back and threaded through a white elastic thing. It was wet, and two shades darker red than usual. I touched it. It was like touching damp silk.

'Paragraph indent?' she asked, as seriously as a girl from the steno pool about to take dictation from the big boss.

'No,' I said, 'this continues.' And then I spoke the line I'd been holding in my head ever since I got up to pour the champagne. '"He slipped the chain over her head, and then the two of them walked down the steps to where the car was parked."'

She typed it, then looked around and up at me expectantly. 'That's it,' I said. 'You can write The End, I guess.'

Jo hit the RETURN button twice, centered the carriage, and typed The End under the last line of prose, the IBM's Courier type ball (my favorite) spinning out the letters in their obedient dance.

'What's the chain he slips over her head?' she asked me.

'You'll have to read the book to find out.'

With her sitting in my desk chair and me standing beside her, she was in perfect position to put her face where she did. When she spoke, her lips moved against the most sensitive part of me. There were a pair of cotton shorts between us and that was all.

'Ve haff vays off making you talk,' she said.

22

'I'll just bet you do,' I said.

I at least made a stab at the ritual on the day I finished *All the Way from the Top*. It felt hollow, form from which the magical substance had departed, but I'd expected that. I didn't do it out of superstition but out of respect and love. A kind of memorial, if you will. Or, if you will, Johanna's real funeral service, finally taking place a month after she was in the ground.

It was the last third of September, and still hot – the hottest late summer I can remember. All during that final sad push on the book, I kept thinking how much I missed her . . . but that never slowed me down. And here's something else: hot as it was in Derry, so hot I usually worked in nothing but a pair of boxer shorts, I never once thought of going to our place at the lake. It was as if my memory of Sara Laughs had been entirely wiped from my mind. Perhaps that was because by the time I finished *Top*, that truth was finally sinking in. She wasn't just in Ireland this time.

My office at the lake is tiny, but has a view. The office in Derry is long, book-lined, and windowless. On this particular evening, the overhead fans – there are three of them – were on and paddling at the soupy air. I came in dressed in shorts, a tee-shirt, and rubber thong sandals, carrying a tin Coke tray with the bottle of champagne and the two chilled glasses on it. At the far end of that railroad-car room, under an eave so steep I'd had to almost crouch so as not to bang my head when I got up (over the years I'd also had to withstand Jo's protests that I'd picked the absolute worst place in the room for a workstation), the screen of my Macintosh glowed with words.

I thought I was probably inviting another storm of grief – maybe the worst storm – but I went ahead anyway . . . and our emotions always surprise us, don't they? There was no weeping and wailing that night; I guess all that was out of my system. Instead there was a deep and wretched sense of loss – the empty chair where she used to like to sit and read, the empty table where she would always set her glass too close to the edge.

I poured a glass of champagne, let the foam settle, then picked it up. 'I'm done, Jo,' I said as I sat there beneath the paddling fans. 'So *that's* all right, isn't it?'

There was no response. In light of all that came later, I think that's worth repeating – there was no response. I didn't sense, as I later did, that I was not alone in a room which appeared empty.

I drank the champagne, put the glass back on the Coke tray, then filled the other one. I took it over to the Mac and sat down where Johanna would have been sitting, if not for everyone's favorite loving God. No weeping and wailing, but my eyes prickled with tears. The words on the screen were these:

```
today wasn't so bad, she supposed. She crossed the grass
to her car, and laughed when she saw the white square of
paper under the windshield. Cam Delancey, who refused to
be discouraged, or to take no for an answer, had invited her
to another of his Thursday-night wine-tasting parties.
She took the paper, started to tear it up, then changed her
mind and stuck it in the hip pocket of her jeans, instead.
```

'No paragraph indent,' I said, 'this continues.' Then I keyboarded the line I'd been holding in my head ever since I got up to get the champagne.

```
There was a whole world out there; Cam Delancey's wine-
tasting was as good a place to start as any.
```

I stopped, looking at the little flashing cursor. The tears were still prickling at the corners of my eyes, but I repeat that there were no cold drafts around my ankles, no spectral fingers at the nape of my neck. I hit RETURN twice. I clicked on CENTER. I typed The End below the last line of prose, and then I toasted the screen with what should have been Jo's glass of champagne.

'Here's to you, babe,' I said. 'I wish you were here. I miss you like hell.' My voice wavered a little on that last word, but didn't break. I drank the Taittinger, saved my final line of copy, transferred the whole works to floppy disks, then backed them up. And except for notes, grocery lists, and checks, that was the last writing I did for four years.

24

CHAPTER THREE

My publisher didn't know, my editor Debra Weinstock didn't know, my agent Harold Oblowski didn't know. Frank Arlen didn't know, either, although on more than one occasion I had been tempted to tell him. *Let me be your brother, for Jo's sake if not your own,* he told me on the day he went back to his printing business and mostly solitary life in the southern Maine town of Sanford. I had never expected to take him up on that, and didn't – not in the elemental cry-for-help way he might have been thinking about – but I phoned him every couple of weeks or so. Guy-talk, you know – *How's it going, Not too bad, cold as a witch's tit, Yeah, here, too, You want to go down to Boston if I can get Bruins tickets, Maybe next year, pretty busy right now, Yeah, I know how that is, seeya, Mikey, Okay, Frank, keep your wee-wee in the teepee.* Guy-talk.

I'm pretty sure that once or twice he asked me if I was working on a new book, and I think I said—

Oh, fuck it – that's a lie, okay? One so ingrown that now I'm even telling it to myself. He asked, all right, and I always said yeah, I was working on a new book, it was going good, real good. I was tempted more than once to tell him *I can't write two paragraphs without going into total mental and physical doglock – my heartbeat doubles, then triples, I get short of breath and then start to pant, my eyes feel like they're going to pop out of my head and hang there on my cheeks. I'm like a claustrophobe in a sinking submarine. That's how it's going, thanks for asking,* but I never did. I don't call for help. I *can't* call for help. I think I told you that.

*　　*　　*

From my admittedly prejudiced standpoint, successful novelists – even modestly successful novelists – have got the best gig in the creative arts. It's true that people buy more CDs than books, go to more movies, and watch a *lot* more TV. But the arc of productivity is longer for novelists, perhaps because readers are a little brighter than fans of the non-written arts, and thus have marginally longer memories. David Soul of *Starsky and Hutch* is God knows where, same with that peculiar white rapper Vanilla Ice, but in 1994, Herman Wouk, James Michener, and Norman Mailer were all still around; talk about when dinosaurs walked the earth.

Arthur Hailey was writing a new book (that was the rumor, anyway, and it turned out to be true), Thomas Harris could take seven years between Lecters and still produce bestsellers, and although not heard from in almost forty years, J. D. Salinger was still a hot topic in English classes and informal coffee-house literary groups. Readers have a loyalty that cannot be matched anywhere else in the creative arts, which explains why so many writers who have run out of gas can keep coasting anyway, propelled on to the bestseller lists by the magic words AUTHOR OF on the covers of their books.

What the publisher wants in return, especially from an author who can be counted on to sell 500,000 or so copies of each novel in hardcover and a million more in paperback, is perfectly simple: a book a year. That, the wallahs in New York have determined, is the optimum. Three hundred and eighty pages bound by string or glue every twelve months, a beginning, a middle, and an end, continuing main character like Kinsey Millhone or Kay Scarpetta optional but very much preferred. Readers love continuing characters; it's like coming back to family.

Less than a book a year and you're screwing up the publisher's investment in you, hampering your business manager's ability to continue floating all of your credit cards, and jeopardizing your agent's ability to pay his shrink on time. Also, there's always *some* fan attrition when you take too long. Can't be helped. Just as, if you publish too much, there are readers who'll say, 'Phew, I've had enough of this guy for awhile, it's all starting to taste like beans.'

I tell you all this so you'll understand how I could spend four years using my computer as the world's most expensive Scrabble board, and no one ever suspected. Writer's block? What writer's block?

26

We don't got no steenkin writer's block. How could anyone think such a thing when there was a new Michael Noonan suspense novel appearing each fall just like clockwork, perfect for your late-summer pleasure reading, folks, and by the way, don't forget that the holidays are coming and that all your relatives would also probably enjoy the new Noonan, which can be had at Borders at a thirty per cent discount, oy vay, such a deal.

The secret is simple, and I am not the only popular novelist in America who knows it – if the rumors are correct, Danielle Steel (to name just one) has been using the Noonan Formula for decades. You see, although I have published a book a year starting with *Being Two* in 1984, I wrote *two* books in four of those ten years, publishing one and ratholing the other.

I don't remember ever talking about this with Jo, and since she never asked, I always assumed she understood what I was doing: saving up nuts. It wasn't writer's block I was thinking of, though. Shit, I was just having fun.

By February of 1995, after crashing and burning with at least two good ideas (that particular creative function – the *Eureka!* thing – has never stopped, which creates its own special version of hell), I could no longer deny the obvious: I was in the worst sort of trouble a writer can get into, barring Alzheimer's or a cataclysmic stroke. Still, I had four cardboard manuscript boxes in the big safe-deposit box I keep up at Fidelity Union. They were marked *Promise, Threat, Darcy*, and *Top*. Around Valentine's Day, my agent called, moderately nervous – I usually delivered my latest masterpiece to him by January, and here it was already half-past February. They would have to crash production to get this year's Mike Noonan out in time for the annual Christmas buying orgasm. Was everything all right?

This was my first chance to say things were a country mile from all right, but Mr Harold Oblowski of 225 Park Avenue wasn't the sort of man you said such things to. He was a fine agent, both liked and loathed in publishing circles (sometimes by the same people at the same time), but he didn't adapt well to bad news from the dark and oil-streaked levels where the goods were actually produced. He would have freaked and been on the next plane to Derry, ready to give me creative mouth-to-mouth, adamant in his resolve not to leave until he had yanked me out of my fugue. No, I liked Harold right where he was, in his thirty-eighth-floor office with its kickass view of the East Side.

I told him what a coincidence, Harold, you calling on the very day I finished the new one, gosharooty, how 'bout that, I'll send it out FedEx, you'll have it tomorrow. Harold assured me solemnly that there was no coincidence about it, that where his writers were concerned, he was telepathic. Then he congratulated me and hung up. Two hours later I received his bouquet – every bit as fulsome and silky as one of his Jimmy Hollywood ascots.

After putting the flowers in the dining room, where I rarely went since Jo died, I went down to Fidelity Union. I used my key, the bank manager used his, and soon enough I was on my way to FedEx with the manuscript of *All the Way from the Top*. I took the most recent book because it was the one closest to the front of the box, that's all. In November it was published just in time for the Christmas rush. I dedicated it to the memory of my late, beloved wife, Johanna. It went to number eleven on the *Times* bestseller list, and everyone went home happy. Even me. Because things would get better, wouldn't they? No one had *terminal* writer's block, did they (well, with the possible exception of Harper Lee)? All I had to do was relax, as the chorus girl said to the archbishop. And thank God I'd been a good squirrel and saved up my nuts.

I was still optimistic the following year when I drove down to the Federal Express office with *Threatening Behavior*. That one was written in the fall of 1991, and had been one of Jo's favorites. Optimism had faded quite a little bit by March of 1997, when I drove through a wet snowstorm with *Darcy's Admirer*, although when people asked me how it was going ('Writing any good books lately?' is the existential way most seem to phrase the question), I still answered good, fine, yeah, writing lots of good books lately, they're pouring out of me like shit out of a cow's ass.

After Harold had read *Darcy* and pronounced it my best ever, a bestseller which was also *serious*, I hesitantly broached the idea of taking a year off. He responded immediately with the question I detest above all others: was I all right? Sure, I told him, fine as freckles, just thinking about easing off a little.

There followed one of those patented Harold Oblowski silences, which were meant to convey that you were being a terrific asshole, but because Harold liked you so much, he was trying to think of the gentlest possible way of telling you so. This is a wonderful trick, but one I saw through about six years ago. Actually, it was Jo who saw through it. 'He's only pretending compassion,' she said. 'Actually, he's like a cop in one of those old *film noir* movies, keeping his mouth shut so you'll blunder ahead and end up confessing to everything.'

This time I kept my mouth shut – just switched the phone from my right ear to my left, and rocked back a little further in my office chair. When I did, my eye fell on the framed photograph over my computer – Sara Laughs, our place on Dark Score Lake. I hadn't been there in eons, and for a moment I consciously wondered why.

Then Harold's voice – cautious, comforting, the voice of a sane man trying to talk a lunatic out of what he hopes will be no more than a passing delusion – was back in my ear. 'That might not be a good idea, Mike – not at this stage of your career.'

'This isn't a stage,' I said. 'I peaked in 1991 – since then, my sales haven't really gone up or down. This is a *plateau*, Harold.'

'Yes,' he said, 'and writers who've reached that steady state really only have two choices in terms of sales – they can continue as they are, or they can go down.'

So I go down, I thought of saying . . . but didn't. I didn't want Harold to know exactly how deep this went, or how shaky the ground under me was. I didn't want him to know that I was now having heart palpitations – yes, I mean this literally – almost every time I opened the Word Six program on my computer and looked at the blank screen and flashing cursor.

'Yeah,' I said. 'Okay. Message received.'

'You're sure you're all right?'

'Does the book read like I'm wrong, Harold?'

'Hell, no – it's a helluva yarn. Your personal best, I told you. A great read but also fucking *serious shit*. If Saul Bellow wrote romantic suspense fiction, this is what he'd write. But . . . you're not having any trouble with the next one, are you? I know you're still missing Jo, hell, we all are—'

'No,' I said. 'No trouble at all.'

Another of those long silences ensued. I endured it. At last Harold said, 'Grisham could afford to take a year off. Clancy could. Thomas Harris, the long silences are a part of his mystique. But where you are, life is even tougher than at the very top, Mike. There are five writers for every one of those spots down on the list, and you know who they are – hell, they're your neighbors three months a year. Some are going up, the way Patricia Cornwell went up with her last two books, some are going down, and some are staying steady, like you. If Tom Clancy were to go on hiatus for five years and then bring Jack Ryan back, he'd come back strong, no argument. If *you* go on hiatus for five years, maybe you don't come back at all. My advice is—'

'Make hay while the sun shines.'

'Took the words right out of my mouth.'

We talked a little more, then said our goodbyes. I leaned back further in my office chair – not all the way to the tipover point but close – and looked at the photo of our western Maine retreat. Sara Laughs, sort of like the title of that hoary old Hall and Oates ballad. Jo had loved it more, true enough, but only by a little, so why had I been staying away? Bill Dean, the caretaker, took down the storm shutters every spring and put them back up every fall, drained the pipes in the fall and made sure the pump was running in the spring, checked the generator and took care to see that all the maintenance tags were current, anchored the swimming float fifty yards or so off our little lick of beach after each Memorial Day.

Bill had the chimney cleaned in the early summer of '96, although there hadn't been a fire in the fireplace for two years or more. I paid him quarterly, as is the custom with caretakers in that part of the world; Bill Dean, an old Yankee from a long line of them, cashed my checks and didn't ask why I never used my place anymore. I'd only been down two or three times since Jo died, and not a single overnight. Good thing Bill didn't ask, because I don't know what answer I would have given him. I hadn't even really thought about Sara Laughs until my conversation with Harold.

Thinking of Harold, I looked away from the photo and back at the phone. Imagined saying to him, *So I go down, so what? The world comes to an end? Please. It isn't as if I had a wife and family to support – the wife died in a drugstore parking lot, if you please (or even if you don't please), and the kid we wanted so badly and tried for so long went with her. I don't crave the fame, either – if writers who fill the lower slots on the* Times *bestseller list can be said to be famous – and I don't fall asleep dreaming of book club sales. So why? Why does it even bother me?*

30

But that last one I *could* answer. Because it felt like giving up. Because without my wife *and* my work, I was a superfluous man living alone in a big house that was all paid for, doing nothing but the newspaper crossword over lunch.

I pushed on with what passed for my life. I forgot about Sara Laughs (or some part of me that didn't want to go there buried the idea) and spent another sweltering, miserable summer in Derry. I put a cruciverbalist program on my PowerBook and began making my own crossword puzzles. I took an interim appointment on the local YMCA's board of directors and judged the Summer Arts Competition in Waterville. I did a series of TV ads for the local homeless shelter, which was staggering toward bankruptcy, then served on *that* board for awhile. (At one public meeting of this latter board a woman called me a friend of degenerates, to which I replied, 'Thanks! I needed that.' This resulted in a loud outburst of applause which I still don't understand.) I tried some one-on-one counselling and gave it up after five appointments, deciding that the counsellor's problems were far worse than mine. I sponsored an Asian child and bowled with a league.

Sometimes I tried to write, and every time I did, I locked up. Once, when I tried to force a sentence or two (any sentence or two, just as long as they came fresh-baked out of my own head), I had to grab the wastebasket and vomit into it. I vomited until I thought it was going to kill me . . . and I did have to literally crawl away from the desk and the computer, pulling myself across the deep-pile rug on my hands and knees. By the time I got to the other side of the room, it was better. I could even look back over my shoulder at the VDT screen. I just couldn't get near it. Later that day, I approached it with my eyes shut and turned it off.

More and more often during those late-summer days I thought of Dennison Carville, the creative-writing teacher who'd helped me connect with Harold and who had damned *Being Two* with such faint praise. Carville once said something I never forgot, attributing it to Thomas Hardy, the Victorian novelist and poet. Perhaps Hardy *did* say it, but I've never found it repeated, not in *Bartlett's*, not in the Hardy biography I read between the publications of *All the Way from the Top* and *Threatening Behavior*. I have an idea Carville may have

31

made it up himself and then attributed it to Hardy in order to give it more weight. It's a ploy I have used myself from time to time, I'm ashamed to say.

In any case, I thought about this quote more and more as I struggled with the panic in my body and the frozen feeling in my head, that awful *locked-up* feeling. It seemed to sum up my despair and my growing certainty that I would never be able to write again (what a tragedy, V. C. Andrews with a prick felled by writer's block). It was this quote that suggested any effort I made to better my situation might be meaningless even if it succeeded.

According to gloomy old Dennison Carville, the aspiring novelist should understand from the outset that fiction's goals were forever beyond his reach, that the job was an exercise in futility. 'Compared to the dullest human being actually walking about on the face of the earth and casting his shadow there,' Hardy supposedly said, 'the most brilliantly drawn character in a novel is but a bag of bones.' I understood because that was what I felt like in those interminable, dissembling days: a bag of bones.

Last night I dreamt I went to Manderley again.

If there is any more beautiful and haunting first line in English fiction, I've never read it. And it was a line I had cause to think of a lot during the fall of 1997 and the winter of 1998. I didn't dream of Manderley, of course; but of Sara Laughs, which Jo sometimes called 'the hideout.' A fair enough description, I guess, for a place so far up in the western Maine woods that it's not really even in a town at all, but in an unincorporated area designated on state maps as TR-90.

The last of these dreams was a nightmare, but until that one they had a kind of surreal simplicity. They were dreams I'd awake from wanting to turn on the bedroom light so I could reconfirm my place in reality before going back to sleep. You know how the air feels before a thunderstorm, how everything gets still and colors seem to stand out with the brilliance of things seen during a high fever? My winter dreams of Sara Laughs were like that, each leaving me with a feeling that was not quite sickness. *I've dreamt again of Manderley*, I would think sometimes, and sometimes I would lie in bed with the light on, listening to the wind outside, looking into the bedroom's shadowy corners, and thinking that Rebecca de Winter hadn't drowned in a bay but in Dark Score Lake. That she had gone down, gurgling and flailing, her strange black eyes full of water, while the loons cried out indifferently in the twilight. Sometimes I would get up and drink a glass of water. Sometimes I just turned off the light after I was once more sure of where I was, rolled over on my side again, and went back to sleep.

In the daytime I rarely thought of Sara Laughs at all, and it was only much later that I realized something is badly out of whack when there is such a dichotomy between a person's waking and sleeping lives.

I think that Harold Oblowski's call in October of 1997 was what kicked off the dreams. Harold's ostensible reason for calling was to congratulate me on the impending release of *Darcy's Admirer*, which was entertaining as hell and which also contained some *extremely thought-provoking shit*. I suspected he had at least one other item on his agenda – Harold usually does – and I was right. He'd had lunch with Debra Weinstock, my editor, the day before, and they had gotten talking about the fall of 1998.

'Looks crowded,' he said, meaning the fall lists, meaning specifically the *fiction* half of the fall lists. 'And there are some surprise additions. Dean Koontz—'

'I thought he usually published in January,' I said.

'He does, but Debra hears this one may be delayed. He wants to add a section, or something. Also there's a Harold Robbins, *The Predators*—'

'Big deal.'

'Robbins still has his fans, Mike, still has his fans. As you yourself have pointed out on more than one occasion, fiction writers have a long arc.'

'Uh-huh.' I switched the telephone to the other ear and leaned back in my chair. I caught a glimpse of the framed Sara Laughs photo over my desk when I did. I would be visiting it at greater length and proximity that night in my dreams, although I didn't know that then; all I knew then was that I wished like almighty fuck that Harold Oblowski would hurry up and get to the point.

'I sense impatience, Michael my boy,' Harold said. 'Did I catch you at your desk? Are you writing?'

'Just finished for the day,' I said. 'I am thinking about lunch, however.'

'I'll be quick,' he promised, 'but hang with me, this is important. There may be as many as five other writers that we didn't expect publishing next fall: Ken Follett . . . it's supposed to be his best since *Eye of the Needle* . . . Belva Plain . . . John Jakes . . .'

'None of those guys plays tennis on my court,' I said, although I knew that was not exactly Harold's point; Harold's point was that there are only fifteen slots on the *Times* list.

'How about Jean Auel, finally publishing the next of her sex-among-the-cave-people epics?'

I sat up. 'Jean Auel? Really?'

'Well . . . not a hundred per cent, but it looks good. Last but not least is a new Mary Higgins Clark. I know what tennis court she plays on, and so do you.'

If I'd gotten that sort of news six or seven years earlier, when I'd felt I had a great deal more to protect, I would have been frothing; Mary Higgins Clark *did* play on the same court, shared exactly the same audience, and so far our publishing schedules had been arranged to keep us out of each other's way . . . which was to my benefit rather than hers, let me assure you. Going nose to nose, she would cream me. As the late Jim Croce so wisely observed, you don't tug on Superman's cape, you don't spit into the wind, you don't pull the mask off that old Lone Ranger, and you don't mess around with Mary Higgins Clark. Not if you're Michael Noonan, anyway.

'How did this happen?' I asked.

I don't think my tone was particularly ominous, but Harold replied in the nervous, stumbling-all-over-his-own-words fashion of a man who suspects he may be fired or even beheaded for bearing evil tidings.

'I don't know. She just happened to get an extra idea this year, I guess. That does happen, I've been told.'

As a fellow who had taken his share of double-dips I knew it did, so I simply asked Harold what he wanted. It seemed the quickest and easiest way to get him to relinquish the phone. The answer was no surprise; what he and Debra *both* wanted – not to mention all the rest of my Putnam pals – was a book they could publish in late summer of '98, thus getting in front of Ms Clark and the rest of the competition by a couple of months. Then, in November, the Putnam sales reps would give the novel a healthy second push, with the Christmas season in mind.

'So they *say*,' I replied. Like most novelists (and in this regard the successful are no different from the unsuccessful, indicating there might be some merit to the idea as well as the usual free-floating paranoia), I never trusted publishers' promises.

'I think you can believe them on this, Mike – *Darcy's Admirer* was the last book of your old contract, remember.' Harold sounded almost sprightly at the thought of forthcoming contract negotiations with Debra Weinstock and Phyllis Grann at Putnam. 'The big thing is they still like you. They'd like you even more, I think, if they saw pages with your name on them before Thanksgiving.'

'They want me to give them the next book in November? Next *month*?' I injected what I hoped was the right note of incredulity into my voice, just as if I hadn't had *Helen's Promise* in a safe-deposit box for almost eleven years. It had been the first nut I had stored; it was now the only nut I had left.

'No, no, you could have until January fifteenth, at least,' he said, trying to sound magnanimous. I found myself wondering where he and Debra had gotten their lunch. Some fly place, I would have bet my life on that. Maybe Four Seasons. Johanna always used to call that place Frankie Valli and the Four Seasons. 'It means they'd have to crash production, *seriously* crash it, but they're willing to do that. The real question is whether or not *you* could crash production.'

'I think I could, but it'll cost em,' I said. 'Tell them to think of it as being like same-day service on your dry-cleaning.'

'Oh what a rotten shame for them!' Harold sounded as if he were maybe jacking off and had reached the point where Old Faithful splurts and everybody snaps their Instamatics.

'How much do you think—'

'A surcharge tacked on to the advance is probably the way to go,' he said. 'They'll get pouty of course, claim that the move is in your interest, too. *Primarily* in your interest, even. But based on the extra-work argument . . . the midnight oil you'll have to burn . . .'

'The mental agony of creation . . . the pangs of premature birth . . .'

'Right . . . right . . . I think a ten per cent surcharge sounds about right.' He spoke judiciously, like a man trying to be just as damned fair as he possibly could. Myself, I was wondering how many women would induce birth a month or so early if they got paid two or three hundred grand extra for doing so. Probably some questions are best left unanswered.

And in my case, what difference did it make? The goddam thing was written, wasn't it?

'Well, see if you can make the deal,' I said.

'Yes, but I don't think we want to be talking about just a single book here, okay? I think—'

'Harold, what I want right now is to eat some lunch.'

'You sound a little tense, Michael. Is everything—'

'Everything is fine. Talk to them about just one book, with a sweetener for speeding up production at my end. Okay?'

'Okay,' he said after one of his most significant pauses. 'But I hope this doesn't mean that you won't entertain a three- or four-book contract later on. Make hay while the sun shines, remember. It's the motto of champions.'

'Cross each bridge when you come to it is the motto of champions,' I said, and that night I dreamt I went to Sara Laughs again.

In that dream — in all the dreams I had that fall and winter — I am walking up the lane to the lodge. The lane is a two-mile loop through the woods with ends opening on to Route 68. It has a number at either end (Lane Forty-two, if it matters) in case you have to call in a fire, but no name. Nor did Jo and I ever give it one, not even between ourselves. It is narrow, really just a double rut with timothy and witchgrass growing on the crown. When you drive in, you can hear that grass whispering like low voices against the undercarriage of your car or truck.

I don't drive in the dream, though. I never drive. In these dreams I walk.

The trees huddle in close on either side of the lane. The darkening sky overhead is little more than a slot. Soon I will be able to see the first peeping stars. Sunset is past. Crickets chirr. Loons cry on the lake. Small things — chipmunks, probably, or the occasional squirrel — rustle in the woods.

Now I come to a dirt driveway sloping down the hill on my right. It is our driveway, marked with a little wooden sign which reads SARA LAUGHS. I stand at the head of it, but I don't go down. Below is the lodge. It's all logs and added-on wings, with a deck jutting out behind. Fourteen rooms in all, a ridiculous number of rooms. It should look ugly and awkward, but somehow it does not. There is a brave-dowager quality to Sara, the look of a lady pressing resolutely on toward her hundredth year, still taking pretty good strides in spite of her arthritic hips and gimpy old knees.

The central section is the oldest, dating back to 1900 or so. Other sections were added in the thirties, forties, and sixties. Once it was a hunting lodge; for a brief period in the early seventies it was home to a small commune of transcendental hippies. These were lease or rental deals; the owners from the late forties until 1984 were the Hingermans, Darren and Marie . . . then Marie alone when Darren died in 1971. The only visible addition from our period of ownership is the tiny DSS dish mounted on the central roofpeak. That was Johanna's idea, and she never really got a chance to enjoy it.

Beyond the house, the lake glimmers in the afterglow of sunset. The driveway, I see, is carpeted with brown pine needles and littered with fallen branches. The bushes which grow on either side of it have run wild, reaching out to one another like lovers across the narrowed gap which separates them. If you brought a car down here, the branches would scrape and squeal unpleasantly against its sides. Below, I see, there's moss growing on the logs of the main house, and three large sunflowers with faces like searchlights have grown up through the boards of the little driveway-side stoop. The overall feeling is not neglect, exactly, but *forgottenness*.

There is a breath of breeze, and its coldness on my skin makes me realize that I have been sweating. I can smell pine – a smell which is both sour and clean at the same time – and the faint but somehow tremendous smell of the lake. Dark Score is one of the cleanest, deepest lakes in Maine. It was bigger until the late thirties, Marie Hingerman told us; that was when Western Maine Electric, working hand in hand with the mills and paper operations around Rumford, had gotten state approval to dam the Gessa River. Marie also showed us some charming photographs of white-frocked ladies and vested gentlemen in canoes – these snaps were from the time

37

of the First World War, she said, and pointed to one of the young women, frozen forever on the rim of the Jazz Age with a dripping paddle upraised. 'That's my mother,' she said, 'and the man she's threatening with the paddle is my father.'

Loons crying, their voices like loss. Now I can see Venus in the darkening sky. Star light, star bright, wish I may, wish I might . . . in these dreams I always wish for Johanna.

With my wish made, I try to walk down the driveway. Of course I do. It's my house, isn't it? Where else would I go but my house, now that it's getting dark and now that the stealthy rustling in the woods seems both closer and somehow more purposeful? Where else *can* I go? It's dark, and it will be frightening to go into that dark place alone (suppose Sara resents having been left so long alone? suppose she's angry?), but I must. If the electricity's off, I'll light one of the hurricane lamps we keep in a kitchen cabinet.

Except I can't go down. My legs won't move. It's as if my body knows something about the house down there that my brain does not. The breeze rises again, chilling gooseflesh out on to my skin, and I wonder what I have done to get myself all sweaty like this. Have I been running? And if so, what have I been running toward? Or from?

My hair is sweaty, too; it lies on my brow in an unpleasantly heavy clump. I raise my hand to brush it away and see there is a shallow cut, fairly recent, running across the back, just beyond the knuckles. Sometimes this cut is on my right hand, sometimes it's on the left. I think, *If this is a dream, the details are good.* Always that same thought: *If this is a dream, the details are good.* It's the absolute truth. They are a novelist's details . . . but in dreams, perhaps everyone is a novelist. How is one to know?

Now Sara Laughs is only a dark hulk down below, and I realize I don't want to go down there, anyway. I am a man who has trained his mind to misbehave, and I can imagine too many things waiting for me inside. A rabid raccoon crouched in a corner of the kitchen. Bats in the bathroom – if disturbed they'll crowd the air around my cringing face, squeaking and fluttering against my cheeks with their dusty wings. Even one of William Denbrough's famous Creatures from Beyond the Universe, now hiding under the porch and watching me approach with glittering, pus-rimmed eyes.

38

'Well, I can't stay up here,' I say, but my legs won't move, and it seems I *will* be staying up here, where the driveway meets the lane; that I will be staying up here, like it or not.

Now the rustling in the woods behind me sounds not like small animals (most of them would by then be nested or burrowed for the night, anyway) but approaching footsteps. I try to turn and see, but I can't even do that . . .

. . . and that was where I usually woke up. The first thing I always did was to turn over, establishing my return to reality by demonstrating to myself that my body would once more obey my mind. Sometimes – most times, actually – I would find myself thinking *Manderley, I have dreamt again of Manderley.* There was something creepy about this (there's something creepy about any repeating dream, I think, about knowing your subconscious is digging obsessively at some object that won't be dislodged), but I would be lying if I didn't add that some part of me enjoyed the breathless summer calm in which the dream always wrapped me, and that part also enjoyed the sadness and foreboding I felt when I awoke. There was an exotic strangeness to the dream that was missing from my waking life, now that the road leading out of my imagination was so effectively blocked.

The only time I remember being really frightened (and I must tell you I don't completely trust any of these memories, because for so long they didn't seem to exist at all) was when I awoke one night speaking quite clearly into the dark of my bedroom: 'Something's behind me, don't let it get me, something in the woods, please don't let it get me.' It wasn't the words themselves that frightened me so much as the tone in which they were spoken. It was the voice of a man on the raw edge of panic, and hardly seemed like my own voice at all.

Two days before Christmas of 1997, I once more drove down to Fidelity Union, where once more the bank manager escorted me to my safe-deposit box in the fluorescent-lit catacombs. As we walked down the stairs, he assured me (for the dozenth time, at least) that his wife was a *huge* fan of my work, she'd read all my books, couldn't get enough. For the dozenth time (at least) I replied that now I must get *him* in my clutches. He responded with his usual chuckle. I thought of this oft-repeated exchange as Banker's Communion.

Mr Quinlan inserted his key in Slot A and turned it. Then, as discreetly as a pimp who has conveyed a customer to a whore's crib, he left. I inserted my own key in Slot B, turned it, and opened the drawer. It looked very vast now. The one remaining manuscript box seemed almost to quail in the far corner, like an abandoned puppy who somehow knows his sibs have been taken off and gassed. *Promise* was scrawled across the top in fat black letters. I could barely remember what the goddam story was about.

I snatched that time-traveller from the eighties and slammed the safe-deposit box shut. Nothing left in there now but dust. *Give me that*, Jo had hissed in my dream — it was the first time I'd thought of that one in years. *Give me that, it's my dust-catcher.*

'Mr Quinlan, I'm finished,' I called. My voice sounded rough and unsteady to my own ears, but Quinlan seemed to sense nothing wrong . . . or perhaps he was just being discreet. I can't have been the only customer, after all, who found his or her visits to this financial version of Forest Lawn emotionally distressful.

'I'm really going to read one of your books,' he said, dropping an involuntary little glance at the box I was holding (I suppose I could have brought a briefcase to put it in, but on those expeditions I never did). 'In fact, I think I'll put it on my list of New Year's resolutions.'

'You do that,' I said. 'You just do that, Mr Quinlan.'

'Mark,' he said. 'Please.' He'd said this before, too.

I had composed two letters, which I slipped into the manuscript box before setting out for Federal Express. Both had been written on my computer, which my body would let me use as long as I chose the Note Pad function. It was only opening Word Six that caused the storms to start. I never tried to compose a novel using the Note Pad function, understanding that if I did, I'd likely lose that option, too . . . not to mention my ability to play Scrabble and do crosswords on the machine. I had tried a couple of times to compose longhand, with spectacular lack of success. The problem wasn't what I had once heard described as 'screen shyness'; I had proved that to myself.

One of the notes was to Harold, the other to Debra Weinstock, and both said pretty much the same thing: here's the new book,

Helen's Promise, hope you like it as much as I do, if it seems a little rough it's because I had to work a lot of extra hours to finish it this soon, Merry Christmas, Happy Hanukkah, Erin Go Bragh, trick or treat, hope someone gives you a fucking pony.

I stood for almost an hour in a line of shuffling, bitter-eyed late mailers (Christmas is such a carefree, low-pressure time – that's one of the things I love about it), with *Helen's Promise* under my left arm and a paperback copy of Nelson DeMille's *The Charm School* in my right hand. I read almost fifty pages before entrusting my final unpublished novel to a harried-looking clerk. When I wished her a Merry Christmas she shuddered and said nothing.

41

CHAPTER FOUR

The phone was ringing when I walked in my front door. It was Frank Arlen, asking me if I'd like to join him for Christmas. Join *them*, as a matter of fact; all of his brothers and their families were coming.

I opened my mouth to say no – the last thing on earth I needed was a crazed Irish Christmas with everybody drinking whiskey and waxing sentimental about Jo while perhaps two dozen snotcaked rugrats crawled around the floor – and heard myself saying I'd come.

Frank sounded as surprised as I felt, but honestly delighted. 'Fantastic!' he cried. 'When can you get here?'

I was in the hall, my galoshes dripping on the tile, and from where I was standing I could look through the arch and into the living room. There was no Christmas tree; I hadn't bothered with one since Jo died. The room looked both ghastly and much too big to me . . . a roller rink furnished in Early American.

'I've been out running errands,' I said. 'How about I throw some underwear in a bag, get back into the car, and come south while the heater's still blowing warm air?'

'Tremendous,' Frank said without a moment's hesitation. 'We can have us a sane bachelor evening before the Sons and Daughters of East Malden start arriving. I'm pouring you a drink as soon as I get off the telephone.'

'Then I guess I better get rolling,' I said.

That was hands down the best holiday since Johanna died. The only good holiday, I guess. For four days I was an honorary Arlen. I drank too much, toasted Johanna's memory too many times . . . and knew, somehow, that she'd be pleased to know I was doing it. Two babies spit up on me, one dog got into bed with me in the middle of the night, and Nicky Arlen's sister-in-law made a bleary pass at me on the night after Christmas, when she caught me alone in the kitchen making a turkey sandwich. I kissed her because she clearly wanted to be kissed, and an adventurous (or perhaps 'mischievous' is the word I want) hand groped me for a moment in a place where no one other than myself had groped in almost three and a half years. It was a shock, but not an entirely unpleasant one.

It went no further – in a houseful of Arlens and with Susy Donahue not quite officially divorced yet (like me, she was an honorary Arlen that Christmas), it hardly could have done – but I decided it was time to leave . . . unless, that was, I wanted to go driving at high speed down a narrow street that most likely ended in a brick wall. I left on the twenty-seventh, very glad that I had come, and I gave Frank a fierce goodbye hug as we stood by my car. For four days I hadn't thought at all about how there was now only dust in my safe-deposit box at Fidelity Union, and for four nights I had slept straight through until eight in the morning, sometimes waking up with a sour stomach and a hangover headache, but never once in the middle of the night with the thought *Manderley, I have dreamt again of Manderley* going through my mind. I got back to Derry feeling refreshed and renewed.

The first day of 1998 dawned clear and cold and still and beautiful. I got up, showered, then stood at the bedroom window, drinking coffee. It suddenly occurred to me – with all the simple, powerful reality of ideas like up is over your head and down is under your feet – that I could write now. It was a new year, something had changed, and I could write now if I wanted to. The rock had rolled away.

I went into the study, sat down at the computer, and turned it on. My heart was beating normally, there was no sweat on my forehead or the back of my neck, and my hands were warm. I pulled down the main menu, the one you get when you click on the apple, and there was my old pal Word Six. I clicked on it. The pen-and-parchment logo came up, and when it did I suddenly couldn't breathe. It was as if iron bands had been clamped around my chest.

I pushed back from the desk, gagging and clawing at the round

43

neck of the sweatshirt I was wearing. The wheels of my office chair caught on a little throw rug – one of Jo's finds in the last year of her life – and I tipped right over backward. My head banged the floor and I saw a fountain of bright sparks go whizzing across my field of vision. I suppose I was lucky not to black out, but I think my real luck on New Year's Morning of 1998 was that I tipped over the way I did. If I'd only pushed back from the desk so that I was still looking at the logo – and at the hideous blank screen which followed it – I think I might have choked to death.

When I staggered to my feet, I was at least able to breathe. My throat felt the size of a straw, and each inhale made a weird screaming sound, but I was breathing. I lurched into the bathroom and threw up in the basin with such force that vomit splashed the mirror. I grayed out and my knees buckled. This time it was my brow I struck, thunking it against the lip of the basin, and although the back of my head didn't bleed (there was a very respectable lump there by noon, though), my forehead did, a little. This latter bump also left a purple mark, which I of course lied about, telling folks who asked that I'd run into the bathroom door in the middle of the night, silly me, that'll teach a fella to get up at two A.M. without turning on a lamp.

When I regained complete consciousness (if there is such a state), I was curled on the floor. I got up, disinfected the cut on my forehead, and sat on the lip of the tub with my head lowered to my knees until I felt confident enough to stand up. I sat there for fifteen minutes, I guess, and in that space of time I decided that barring some miracle, my career was over. Harold would scream in pain and Debra would moan in disbelief, but what could they do? Send out the Publication Police? Threaten me with the Book-of-the-Month Club Gestapo? Even if they could, what difference would it make? You couldn't get sap out of a brick or blood out of a stone. Barring some miraculous recovery, my life as a writer was over.

And if it is? I asked myself. *What's on for the back forty, Mike? You can play a lot of Scrabble in forty years, go on a lot of Crossword Cruises, drink a lot of whiskey. But is that enough? What else are you going to put on your back forty?*

I didn't want to think about that, not then. The next forty years

44

could take care of themselves; I would be happy just to get through New Year's Day of 1998.

When I felt I had myself under control, I went back into my study, shuffled to the computer with my eyes resolutely on my feet, felt around for the right button, and turned off the machine. You can damage the program shutting down like that without putting it away, but under the circumstances, I hardly thought it mattered.

That night I once again dreamed I was walking at twilight on Lane Forty-two, which leads to Sara Laughs; once more I wished on the evening star as the loons cried on the lake, and once more I sensed something in the woods behind me, edging ever closer. It seemed my Christmas holiday was over.

That was a hard, cold winter, lots of snow and in February a flu epidemic that did for an awful lot of Derry's old folks. It took them the way a hard wind will take old trees after an ice storm. It missed me completely. I hadn't so much as a case of the sniffles that winter.

In March, I flew to Providence and took part in Will Weng's New England Crossword Challenge. I placed fourth and won fifty bucks. I framed the uncashed check and hung it in the living room. Once upon a time, most of my framed Certificates of Triumph (Jo's phrase; all the good phrases are Jo's phrases, it seems to me) went up on my office walls, but by March of 1998, I wasn't going in there very much. When I wanted to play Scrabble against the computer or do a tourney-level crossword puzzle, I used the PowerBook and sat at the kitchen table.

I remember sitting there one day, opening the PowerBook's main menu, going down to the crossword puzzles . . . then dropping the cursor two or three items further, until it had highlighted my old pal, Word Six.

What swept over me then wasn't frustration or impotent, balked fury (I'd experienced a lot of both since finishing *All the Way from the Top*), but sadness and simple longing. Looking at the Word Six icon was suddenly like looking at the pictures of Jo I kept in my wallet. Studying those, I'd sometimes think that I would sell my immortal soul in order to have her back again . . . and on that day in March, I thought I would sell my soul to be able to write a story again.

45

Go on and try it, then, a voice whispered. *Maybe things have changed*.

Except that nothing had changed, and I knew it. So instead of opening Word Six, I moved it across to the trash barrel in the lower righthand corner of the screen, and dropped it in. Goodbye, old pal.

Debra Weinstock called a lot that winter, mostly with good news. Early in March she reported that *Helen's Promise* had been picked as one half of the Literary Guild's main selection for August, the other half being a legal thriller by Steve Martini, another veteran of the eight-to-fifteen segment of the *Times* bestseller list. And my British publisher, Debra said, loved *Helen*, was sure it would be my 'breakthrough book.' (My British sales had always lagged.)

'*Promise* is sort of a new direction for you,' Debra said. 'Wouldn't you say?'

'I kind of thought it was,' I confessed, and wondered how Debbie would respond if I told her my new-direction book had been written almost a dozen years ago.

'It's got . . . I don't know . . . a kind of *maturity*.'

'Thanks.'

'Mike? I think the connection's going. You sound muffled.'

Sure I did. I was biting down on the side of my hand to keep from howling with laughter. Now, cautiously, I took it out of my mouth and examined the bite-marks. 'Better?'

'Yes, lots. So what's the new one about? Give me a hint.'

'You know the answer to that one, kiddo.'

Debra laughed. '"You'll have to read the book to find out, Josephine,"' she said. 'Right?'

'Yessum.'

'Well, keep it coming. Your pals at Putnam's are crazy about the way you're taking it to the next level.'

I said goodbye, I hung up the telephone, and then I laughed wildly for about ten minutes. Laughed until I was crying. That's me, though. Always taking it to the next level.

During this period I also agreed to do a phone interview with a *Newsweek* writer who was putting together a piece on The New American Gothic (whatever that was, other than a phrase which might sell a few magazines), and to sit for a *Publishers Weekly* interview which would appear just before publication of *Helen's Promise*. I agreed to these because they both sounded softball, the sort of interviews you could do over the phone while you read your mail. And Debra was delighted because I ordinarily say no to all the publicity. I hate that part of the job and always have, especially the hell of the live TV chat-show, where nobody's ever read your goddam book and the first question is always 'Where in the world do you get those wacky ideas?' The publicity process is like going to a sushi bar where you're the sushi, and it was great to get past it this time with the feeling that I'd been able to give Debra some good news she could take to her bosses. 'Yes,' she could say, 'he's still being a booger about publicity, but I got him to do a couple of things.'

All through this my dreams of Sara Laughs were going on – not every night but every second or third night, with me never thinking of them in the daytime. I did my crosswords, I bought myself an acoustic steel guitar and started learning how to play it (I was never going to be invited to tour with Patty Loveless or Alan Jackson, however), I scanned each day's bloated obituaries in the *Derry News* for names that I knew. I was pretty much dozing on my feet, in other words.

What brought all this to an end was a call from Harold Oblowski not more than three days after Debra's book club call. It was storming outside – a vicious snow-changing-over-to-sleet event that proved to be the last and biggest blast of the winter. By mid-evening the power would be off all over Derry, but when Harold called at five P.M., things were just getting cranked up.

'I just had a very good conversation with your editor,' Harold said. 'A very enlightening, very *energizing* conversation. Just got off the phone, in fact.'

'Oh?'

'Oh indeed. There's a feeling at Putnam, Michael, that this latest book of yours may have a positive effect on your sales position in the market. It's very strong.'

'Yes,' I said, 'I'm taking it to the next level.'

'Huh?'

'I'm just blabbing, Harold. Go on.'

'Well . . . Helen Nearing's a great lead character, and Skate is your best villain ever.'

I said nothing.

'Debra raised the possibility of making *Helen's Promise* the opener of a three-book contract. A very *lucrative* three-book contract. All without any prompting from me. Three is one more than any publisher has wanted to commit to 'til now. I mentioned nine million dollars, three million per book, in other words, expecting her to laugh . . . but an agent has to start *somewhere*, and I always choose the highest ground I can find. I think I must have Roman military officers somewhere back in my family tree.'

Ethiopian rug-merchants, more like it, I thought, but didn't say. I felt the way you do when the dentist has gone a little heavy on the Novocain and flooded your lips and tongue as well as your bad tooth and the patch of gum surrounding it. If I tried to talk, I'd probably only flap and spread spit. Harold was almost purring. A three-book contract for the new, mature Michael Noonan. Tall tickets, baby.

This time I didn't feel like laughing. This time I felt like screaming. Harold went on, happy and oblivious. Harold didn't know the bookberry tree had died. Harold didn't know the new Mike Noonan had cataclysmic shortness of breath and projectile-vomiting fits every time he tried to write.

'You want to hear how she came back to me, Michael?'

'Lay it on me.'

'She said, "Well, nine's obviously high, but it's as good a place to start as any. We feel this new book is a big step forward for him." This is extraordinary. *Extraordinary*. Now, I haven't given anything away, wanted to talk to you first, of course, but I think we're looking at seven-point-five, minimum. In fact—'

'No.'

He paused a moment. Long enough for me to realize I was gripping the phone so hard it hurt my hand. I had to make a conscious effort to relax my grip. 'Mike, if you'll just hear me out—'

'I don't need to hear you out. I don't want to talk about a new contract.'

'Pardon me for disagreeing, but there'll never be a better time. Think about it, for Christ's sake. We're talking top dollar here. If

48

you wait until after *Helen's Promise* is published, I can't guarantee that the same offer—'

'I know you can't,' I said. 'I don't want guarantees, I don't want offers, *I don't want to talk contract.*'

'You don't need to shout, Mike, I can hear you.'

Had I been shouting? Yes, I suppose I had been.

'Are you dissatisfied with Putnam's? I think Debra would be very distressed to hear that. I also think Phyllis Grann would do damned near anything to address any concerns you might have.'

Are you sleeping with Debra, Harold? I thought, and all at once it seemed like the most logical idea in the world – that dumpy, fiftyish, balding little Harold Oblowski was making it with my blonde, aristocratic, Smith-educated editor. *Are you sleeping with her, do you talk about my future while you're lying in bed together in a room at the Plaza? Are the pair of you trying to figure how many golden eggs you can get out of this tired old goose before you finally wring its neck and turn it into pâté? Is that what you're up to?*

'Harold, I can't talk about this now, and I *won't* talk about this now.'

'What's wrong? Why are you so upset? I thought you'd be pleased. Hell, I thought you'd be over the fucking moon.'

'There's nothing wrong. It's just a bad time for me to talk long-term contract. You'll have to pardon me, Harold. I have something coming out of the oven.'

'Can we at least discuss this next w—'

'*No,*' I said, and hung up. I think it was the first time in my adult life that I'd hung up on someone who wasn't a telephone salesman.

I had nothing coming out of the oven, of course, and I was too upset to even think about putting something in. I went into the living room instead, poured myself a short whiskey, and sat down in front of the TV. I sat there for almost four hours, looking at everything and seeing nothing. Outside, the storm continued cranking up. Tomorrow there would be trees down all over Derry and the world would look like an ice sculpture.

At quarter past nine the power went out, came back on for thirty seconds or so, then went out and stayed out. I took this as a suggestion to stop thinking about Harold's useless contract and how Jo would have chortled at the idea of nine million dollars. I got up, unplugged the blacked-out TV so it wouldn't come blaring on at two in the morning (I needn't have worried; the power was off in Derry for nearly two days), and went upstairs. I dropped my clothes at the foot of the bed, crawled in without even bothering to brush my teeth, and was asleep in less than five minutes. I don't know how long after that it was that the nightmare came.

It was the last dream I had in what I now think of as my 'Manderley series,' the culminating dream. It was made even worse, I suppose, by the unrelievable blackness to which I awoke.

It started like the others. I'm walking up the lane, listening to the crickets and the loons, looking mostly at the darkening slot of sky overhead. I reach the driveway, and here something *has* changed; someone has put a little sticker on the SARA LAUGHS sign. I lean closer and see it's a radio station sticker. WBLM, it says. 102.9, PORTLAND'S ROCK AND ROLL BLIMP.

From the sticker I look back up into the sky, and there is Venus. I wish on her as I always do, I wish for Johanna with the dank and vaguely tremendous smell of the lake in my nose.

Something lumbers in the woods, rattling old leaves and breaking a branch. It sounds big.

Better get down there, a voice in my head tells me. *Something has taken out a contract on you, Michael. A three-book contract, and that's the worst kind.*

I can't move, I can never move, I can only stand here. I've got walker's block.

But that's just talk. I *can* walk. This time I *can* walk. I am delighted. I have had a major breakthrough. In the dream I think *This changes everything! This changes everything!*

Down the driveway I walk, deeper and deeper into the clean but sour smell of pine, stepping over some of the fallen branches, kicking others out of the way. I raise my hand to brush the damp hair off my forehead and see the little scratch running across the back of it. I stop to look at it, curious.

No time for that, the dream-voice says. *Get down there. You've got a book to write.*

I can't write, I reply. *That part's over. I'm on the back forty now.*

No, the voice says. There is something relentless about it that scares me. *You had writer's walk, not writer's block, and as you can see, it's gone. Now hurry up and get down there.*

I'm afraid, I tell the voice.

Afraid of what?

Well . . . what if Mrs Danvers is down there?

The voice doesn't answer. It knows I'm not afraid of Rebecca de Winter's housekeeper, she's just a character in an old book, nothing but a bag of bones. So I begin walking again. I have no choice, it seems, but at every step my terror increases, and by the time I'm halfway down to the shadowy sprawling bulk of the log house, fear has sunk into my bones like fever. Something is wrong here, something is all twisted up.

I'll run away, I think. *I'll run back the way I came, like the gingerbread man I'll run, run all the way back to Derry, if that's what it takes, and I'll never come here anymore.*

Except I can hear slobbering breath behind me in the growing gloom, and padding footsteps. The thing in the woods is now the thing in the driveway. It's right behind me. If I turn around the sight of it will knock the sanity out of my head in a single roundhouse slap. Something with red eyes, something slumped and hungry.

The house is my only hope of safety.

I walk on. The crowding bushes clutch like hands. In the light of a rising moon (the moon has never risen before in this dream, but I have never stayed in it this long before), the rustling leaves look like sardonic faces. I see winking eyes and smiling mouths. Below me are the black windows of the house and I know that there will be no power when I get inside, the storm has knocked the power out, I will flick the lightswitch up and down, up and down, until something reaches out and takes my wrist and pulls me like a lover deeper into the dark.

I am three quarters of the way down the driveway now. I can see the railroad-tie steps leading down to the lake, and I can see the float out there on the water, a black square in a track of moonlight. Bill Dean has put it out. I can also see an oblong something lying at the place where the driveway ends at the stoop. There has never been such an object before. What can it be?

Another two or three steps, and I know. It's a coffin, the one

51

Frank Arlen dickered for . . . because, he said, the mortician was trying to stick it to me. It's Jo's coffin, and lying on its side with the top partway open, enough for me to see it's empty.

I think I want to scream. I think I mean to turn around and run back up the driveway – I will take my chances with the thing behind me. But before I can, the back door of Sara Laughs opens, and a terrible figure comes darting out into the growing darkness. It is human, this figure, and yet it's not. It is a crumpled white thing with baggy arms upraised. There is no face where its face should be, and yet it is shrieking in a glottal, loonlike voice. It must be Johanna. She was able to escape her coffin, but not her winding shroud. She is all tangled up in it.

How hideously *speedy* this creature is! It doesn't drift as one imagines ghosts drifting, but *races* across the stoop toward the driveway. It has been waiting down here during all the dreams when I had been frozen, and now that I have finally been able to walk down, it means to have me. I'll scream when it wraps me in its silk arms, and I will scream when I smell its rotting, bug-raddled flesh and see its dark staring eyes through the fine weave of the cloth. I will scream as the sanity leaves my mind forever. I will scream . . . but there is no one out here to hear me. Only the loons will hear me. I have come again to Manderley, and this time I will never leave.

The shrieking white thing reached for me and I woke up on the floor of my bedroom, crying out in a cracked, horrified voice and slamming my head repeatedly against something. How long before I finally realized I was no longer asleep, that I wasn't at Sara Laughs? How long before I realized that I had fallen out of bed at some point and had crawled across the room in my sleep, that I was on my hands and knees in a corner, butting my head against the place where the walls came together, doing it over and over again like a lunatic in an asylum?

I didn't know, couldn't with the power out and the bedside clock dead. I know that at first I couldn't move out of the corner because it felt safer than the wider room would have done, and I know that for a long time the dream's force held me even after I woke up (mostly, I imagine, because I couldn't turn on a light and dispel its power). I was afraid that if I crawled out of my corner, the white thing would burst out of my bathroom, shrieking its dead shriek, eager to finish what it had started. I know I was shivering all over, and that I was cold and wet from the waist down, because my bladder had let go.

I stayed there in the corner, gasping and wet, staring into the darkness, wondering if you could have a nightmare powerful enough in its imagery to drive you insane. I thought then (and think now) that I almost found out on that night in March.

Finally I felt able to leave the corner. Halfway across the floor I pulled off my wet pajama pants, and when I did that, I got disoriented. What followed was a miserable and surreal five minutes in which I crawled aimlessly back and forth in my familiar bedroom, bumping into stuff and moaning each time I hit something with a blind, flailing hand. Each thing I touched at first seemed like that awful white thing. Nothing I touched felt like anything I knew. With the reassuring green numerals of the bedside clock gone and my sense of direction temporarily lost, I could have been crawling around a mosque in Addis Ababa.

At last I ran shoulder-first into the bed. I stood up, yanked the pillowcase off the extra pillow, and wiped my groin and upper legs with it. Then I crawled back into bed, pulled the blankets up, and lay there shivering, listening to the steady tick of sleet on the windows.

There was no sleep for me for the rest of that night, and the dream didn't fade as dreams usually do upon waking. I lay on my side, the shivers slowly subsiding, thinking of her coffin lying there in the driveway, thinking that it made a kind of mad sense – Jo had loved Sara, and if she were to haunt anyplace, it would be there. But why would she want to hurt me? Why would my Jo ever want to hurt me? I could think of no reason.

Somehow the time passed, and there came a moment when I realized that the air had turned a dark shade of gray; the shapes of the furniture loomed in it like sentinels in fog. That was a little better. That was more like it. I would light the kitchen woodstove, I decided, and make strong coffee. Begin the work of getting this behind me.

I swung my legs out of bed and raised my hand to brush my sweat-damp hair off my forehead. I froze with the hand in

53

front of my eyes. I must have scraped it while I was crawling, disoriented, in the dark and trying to find my way back to bed. There was a shallow, clotted cut across the back, just below the knuckles.

CHAPTER FIVE

Once, when I was sixteen, a plane went supersonic directly over my head. I was walking in the woods when it happened, thinking of some story I was going to write, perhaps, or how great it would be if Doreen Fournier weakened some Friday night and let me take off her panties while we were parked at the end of Cushman Road.

In any case I was travelling far roads in my own mind, and when that boom went off, I was caught totally by surprise. I went flat on the leafy ground with my hands over my head and my heart drumming crazily, sure I'd reached the end of my life (and while I was still a virgin). In my forty years, that was the only thing which equalled the final dream of the 'Manderley series' for utter terror.

I lay on the ground, waiting for the hammer to fall, and when thirty seconds or so passed and no hammer *did* fall, I began to realize it had just been some jet-jockey from the Brunswick Naval Air Station, too eager to wait until he was out over the Atlantic before going to Mach 1. But, holy shit, who ever could have guessed that it would be so *loud*?

I got slowly to my feet, and as I stood there with my heart finally slowing down, I realized I wasn't the only thing that had been scared witless by that sudden clear-sky boom. For the first time in my memory, the little patch of woods behind our house in Prout's Neck was entirely silent. I stood there in a dusty bar of sunlight, crumbled leaves all over my tee-shirt and jeans, holding my breath, listening. I had never heard a silence like it. Even on a cold day in January, the woods would have been full of conversation.

At last a finch sang. There were two or three seconds of silence, and then a jay replied. Another two or three seconds went by, and then a crow added his two cents' worth. A woodpecker began to hammer for grubs. A chipmunk bumbled through some underbrush on my left. A minute after I had stood up, the woods were fully alive with little noises again; it was back to business as usual, and I continued with my own. I never forgot that unexpected boom, though, or the deathly silence which followed it.

I thought of that June day often in the wake of the nightmare, and there was nothing so remarkable in that. Things had changed, somehow, or *could* change . . . but first comes silence while we assure ourselves that we are still unhurt and that the danger – if there *was* danger – is gone.

Derry was shut down for most of the following week, anyway. Ice and high winds caused a great deal of damage during the storm, and a sudden twenty-degree plunge in the temperature afterward made the digging out hard and the cleanup slow. Added to that, the atmosphere after a March storm is always dour and pessimistic; we get them up this way every year (and two or three in April for good measure, if we're not lucky), but we never seem to expect them. Every time we get clouted, we take it personally.

On a day toward the end of that week, the weather finally started to break. I took advantage, going out for a cup of coffee and a mid-morning pastry at the little restaurant three doors down from the Rite Aid where Johanna did her last errand. I was sipping and chewing and working the newspaper crossword when someone asked, 'Could I share your booth, Mr Noonan? It's pretty crowded in here today.'

I looked up and saw an old man that I knew but couldn't quite place.

'Ralph Roberts,' he said. 'I volunteer down at the Red Cross. Me and my wife, Lois.'

'Oh, okay, sure,' I said. I give blood at the Red Cross every six weeks or so. Ralph Roberts was one of the old parties who passed out juice and cookies afterward, telling you not to get up or make any sudden movements if you felt woozy. 'Please, sit down.'

He looked at my paper, folded open to the crossword and lying in a patch of sun, as he slid into the booth. 'Don't you find that doing the crossword in the *Derry News* is sort of like striking out the pitcher in a baseball game?' he asked.

I laughed and nodded. 'I do it for the same reason folks climb Mount Everest, Mr Roberts . . . because it's there. Only with the *News* crossword, no one ever falls off.'

'Call me Ralph. Please.'

'Okay. And I'm Mike.'

'Good.' He grinned, revealing teeth that were crooked and a little yellow, but all his own. 'I like getting to the first names. It's like being able to take off your tie. Was quite a little cap of wind we had, wasn't it?'

'Yes,' I said, 'but it's warming up nicely now.' The thermometer had made one of its nimble March leaps, climbing from twenty-five degrees the night before to fifty that morning. Better than the rise in air-temperature, the sun was warm again on your face. It was that warmth that had coaxed me out of the house.

'Spring'll get here, I guess. Some years it gets a little lost, but it always seems to find its way back home.' He sipped his coffee, then set the cup down. 'Haven't seen you at the Red Cross lately.'

'I'm recycling,' I said, but that was a fib; I'd come eligible to give another pint two weeks ago. The reminder card was up on the refrigerator. It had just slipped my mind. 'Next week, for sure.'

'I only mention it because I know you're an A, and we can always use that.'

'Save me a couch.'

'Count on it. Everything going all right? I only ask because you look tired. If it's insomnia, I can sympathize, believe me.'

He *did* have the look of an insomniac, I thought – too wide around the eyes, somehow. But he was also a man in his mid- to late seventies, and I don't think anyone gets that far without showing it. Stick around a little while, and life maybe only jabs at your cheeks and eyes. Stick around a long while and you end up looking like Jake La Motta after a hard fifteen.

I opened my mouth to say what I always do when someone asks me if I'm all right, then wondered why I always felt I had to pull that tiresome Marlboro Man shit, just who I was trying to fool. What did I think would happen if I told the guy who gave me a chocolate-chip cookie down at the Red Cross after the nurse took the needle out of my arm that I wasn't feeling a hundred per cent? Earthquakes? Fire and flood? Shit.

'No,' I said, 'I really haven't been feeling so great, Ralph.'

'Flu? It's been going around.'

'Nah. The flu missed me this time, actually. And I've been sleeping all right.' Which was true – there had been no recurrence of the Sara Laughs dream in either the normal or the high-octane version. 'I think I've just got the blues.'

'Well, you ought to take a vacation,' he said, then sipped his coffee. When he looked up at me again, he frowned and set his cup down. 'What? Is something wrong?'

No, I thought of saying. *You were just the first bird to sing into the silence, Ralph, that's all.*

'No, nothing wrong,' I said, and then, because I sort of wanted to see how the words tasted coming out of my own mouth, I repeated them. 'A vacation.'

'Ayuh,' he said, smiling. 'People do it all the time.'

People do it all the time. He was right about that; even people who couldn't strictly afford to went on vacation. When they got tired. When they got all balled up in their own shit. When the world was too much with them, getting and spending.

I could certainly afford a vacation, and I could certainly take the time off from work – *what* work, ha-ha? – and yet I'd needed the Red Cross cookie-man to point out what should have been self-evident to a college-educated guy like me: that I hadn't been on an actual vacation since Jo and I had gone to Bermuda, the winter before she died. My particular grindstone was no longer turning, but I had kept my nose to it all the same.

It wasn't until that summer, when I read Ralph Robert's obituary in the *News* (he was struck by a car), that I fully realized how much I owed him. That advice was better than any glass of orange juice I ever got after giving blood, let me tell you.

When I left the restaurant, I didn't go home but tramped over half of the damned town, the section of newspaper with the partly completed crossword puzzle in it clamped under one arm. I walked until I was chilled in spite of the warming temperatures. I didn't think

58

about anything, and yet I thought about everything. It was a special kind of thinking, the sort I'd always done when I was getting close to writing a book, and although I hadn't thought that way in years, I fell into it easily and naturally, as if I had never been away.

It's like some guys with a big truck have pulled up in your driveway and are moving things into your basement. I can't explain it any better than that. You can't see what these things are because they're all wrapped up in padded quilts, but you don't need to see them. It's furniture, everything you need to make your house a home, make it just right, just the way you wanted it.

When the guys have hopped back into their truck and driven away, you go down to the basement and walk around (the way I went walking around Derry that late morning, slopping up hill and down dale in my old galoshes), touching a padded curve here, a padded angle there. Is this one a sofa? Is that one a dresser? It doesn't matter. Everything is here, the movers didn't forget a thing, and although you'll have to get it all upstairs yourself (straining your poor old back in the process, more often than not), that's okay. The important thing is that the delivery was complete.

This time I thought – hoped – the delivery truck had brought the stuff I needed for the back forty: the years I might have to spend in a No Writing Zone. To the cellar door they had come, and they had knocked politely, and when after several months there was still no answer, they had finally fetched a battering ram. HEY BUDDY, HOPE THE NOISE DIDN'T SCARE YOU TOO BAD, SORRY ABOUT THE DOOR!

I didn't care about the door; I cared about the furniture. Any pieces broken or missing? I didn't think so. I thought all I had to do was get it upstairs, pull off the furniture pads, and put it where it belonged.

On my way back home, I passed The Shade, Derry's charming little revival movie house, which has prospered in spite of (or perhaps because of) the video revolution. This month they were showing classic SF from the fifties, but April was dedicated to Humphrey Bogart, Jo's all-time favorite. I stood under the marquee for several moments, studying one of the Coming Attractions posters. Then I went home, picked a travel agent pretty much at random from the phone book, and told the guy I wanted to go to Key Largo. Key

West, you mean, the guy said. No, I told him, I mean Key Largo, just like in the movie with Bogie and Bacall. Three weeks. Then I rethought that. I was wealthy, I was on my own, and I was retired. What was this 'three weeks' shit? Make it six, I said. Find me a cottage or something. Going to be expensive, he said. I told him I didn't care. When I came back to Derry, it would be spring.

In the meantime, I had some furniture to unwrap.

I was enchanted with Key Largo for the first month and bored out of my mind for the last two weeks. I stayed, though, because boredom is good. People with a high tolerance for boredom can get a lot of thinking done. I ate about a billion shrimp, drank about a thousand margaritas, and read twenty-three John D. MacDonald novels by actual count. I burned, peeled, and finally tanned. I bought a long-billed cap with PARROTHEAD printed on it in bright green thread. I walked the same stretch of beach until I knew everybody by first name. And I unwrapped furniture. A lot of it I didn't like, but there was no doubt that it all fit the house.

I thought about Jo and our life together. I thought about saying to her that no one was ever going to confuse *Being Two* with *Look Homeward, Angel*. '*You aren't going to pull a lot of frustrated-artist crap on me, are you, Noonan?*' she had replied . . . and during my time on Key Largo, those words kept coming back, always in Jo's voice: crap, frustrated-artist crap, all that fucking schoolboy frustrated-artist crap.

I thought about Jo in her long red woods apron, coming to me with a hatful of black trumpet mushrooms, laughing and triumphant: '*Nobody on the TR eats better than the Noonans tonight!*' she'd cried. I thought of her painting her toenails, bent over between her own thighs in the way only women doing that particular piece of business can manage. I thought of her throwing a book at me because I laughed at some new haircut. I thought of her trying to learn how to play a breakdown on her banjo and of how she looked braless in a thin sweater. I thought of her crying and laughing and angry. I thought of her telling me it was crap, all that frustrated-artist crap.

And I thought about the dreams, especially the culminating dream. I could do that easily, because it never faded as the more ordinary ones do. The final Sara Laughs dream and my very first wet

60

dream (coming upon a girl lying naked in a hammock and eating a plum) are the only two that remain perfectly clear to me, year after year; the rest are either hazy fragments or completely forgotten.

There were a great many clear details to the Sara dreams – the loons, the crickets, the evening star and my wish upon it, just to name a few – but I thought most of those things were just verisimilitude. Scene-setting, if you will. As such, they could be dismissed from my considerations. That left three major elements, three large pieces of furniture to be unwrapped.

As I sat on the beach, watching the sun go down between my sandy toes, I didn't think you had to be a shrink to see how those three things went together.

In the Sara dreams, the major elements were the woods behind me, the house below me, and Michael Noonan himself, frozen in the middle. It's getting dark and there's danger in the woods. It will be frightening to go to the house below, perhaps because it's been empty so long, but I never doubt I must go there; scary or not, it's the only shelter I have. Except I can't do it. I can't move. I've got writer's walk.

In the nightmare I am finally able to go toward shelter, only the shelter proves false. Proves more dangerous than I had ever expected in my . . . well, yes, in my wildest dreams. My dead wife rushes out, screaming and still tangled in her shroud, to attack me. Even five weeks later and almost three thousand miles from Derry, remembering that speedy white thing with its baggy arms would make me shiver and look back over my shoulder.

But *was* it Johanna? I didn't really know, did I? The thing was all wrapped up. The coffin looked like the one in which she had been buried, true, but that might just be misdirection.

Writer's *walk*, writer's *block*.

I can't write, I told the voice in the dream. The voice says I can. The voice says the writer's block is gone, and I believe it because the writer's *walk* is gone, I'm finally headed down the driveway, going to shelter. I'm afraid, though. Even before the shapeless white thing makes its appearance, I'm terrified. I say it's Mrs Danvers I'm afraid of, but that's just my dreaming mind getting Sara Laughs and Manderley all mixed up. I'm afraid of—

61

'I'm afraid of writing,' I heard myself saying out loud. 'I'm afraid to even try.'

This was the night before I finally flew back to Maine, and I was half-past sober, going on drunk. By the end of my vacation, I was drinking a lot of evenings. 'It's not the block that scares me, it's *undoing* the block. I'm really fucked, boys and girls. I'm fucked big-time.'

Fucked or not, I had an idea I'd finally reached the heart of the matter. I was afraid of undoing the block, maybe afraid of picking up the strands of my life and going on without Jo. Yet some deep part of my mind believed I must do it; that's what the menacing noises behind me in the woods were about. And belief counts for a lot. Too much, maybe, especially if you're imaginative. When an imaginative person gets into mental trouble, the line between seeming and being has a way of disappearing.

Things in the woods, yes, sir. I had one of them right there in my hand as I was thinking these things. I lifted my drink, holding it toward the western sky so that the setting sun seemed to be burning in the glass. I was drinking a lot, and maybe that was okay on Key Largo – hell, people were supposed to drink a lot on vacation, it was almost the law – but I'd been drinking too much even before I left. The kind of drinking that could get out of hand in no time at all. The kind that could get a man in trouble.

Things in the woods, and the potentially safe place guarded by a scary bugbear that was not my wife, but perhaps my wife's memory. It made sense, because Sara Laughs had always been Jo's favorite place on earth. That thought led to another, one that made me swing my legs over the side of the chaise I'd been reclining on and sit up in excitement. Sara Laughs had also been the place where the ritual had begun . . . champagne, last line, and the all-important benediction: *Well, then*, that's *all right, isn't it?*

Did I want things to be all right again? Did I truly want that? A month or a year before, I mightn't have been sure, but now I was. The answer was yes. I wanted to move on – let go of my dead wife, rehab my heart, move on. But to do that, I'd have to go back.

Back to the log house. Back to Sara Laughs.

'Yeah,' I said, and my body broke out in gooseflesh. 'Yeah, you got it.'

So why not?

The question made me feel as stupid as Ralph Roberts's observation that I needed a vacation. If I needed to go back to Sara Laughs now that my vacation was over, indeed why not? It might be a little scary the first night or two, a hangover from my final dream, but just being there might dissolve the dream faster.

And (this last thought I allowed in only one humble corner of my conscious mind) something *might* happen with my writing. It wasn't likely . . . but it wasn't impossible, either. *Barring a miracle*, hadn't that been my thought on New Year's Day as I sat on the rim of the tub, holding a damp washcloth to the cut on my forehead? Yes. *Barring a miracle*. Sometimes blind people fall down, knock their heads, and regain their sight. Sometimes maybe cripples *are* able to throw their crutches away when they get to the top of the church steps.

I had eight or nine months before Harold and Debra started really bugging me for the next novel. I decided to spend the time at Sara Laughs. It would take me a little while to tie things up in Derry, and awhile for Bill Dean to get the house on the lake ready for a year-round resident, but I could be down there by the Fourth of July, easily. I decided that was a good date to shoot for, not just the birthday of our country, but pretty much the end of bug season in western Maine.

By the day I packed up my vacation gear (the John D. MacDonald paperbacks I left for the cabin's next inhabitant), shaved a week's worth of stubble off a face so tanned it no longer looked like my own to me, and flew back to Maine, I was decided: I'd go back to the place my subconscious mind had identified as shelter against the deepening dark; I'd go back even though my mind had also suggested that doing so would not be without risks. I would not go back expecting Sara to be Lourdes . . . but I would allow myself to hope, and when I saw the evening star peeping out over the lake for the first time, I would allow myself to wish on it.

Only one thing didn't fit into my neat deconstruction of the Sara dreams, and because I couldn't explain it, I tried to ignore it. I didn't have much luck, though; part of me was still a writer, I guess, and a writer is a man who has taught his mind to misbehave.

It was the cut on the back of my hand. That cut had been in

all the dreams, I would swear it had . . . and then it had actually appeared. You didn't get that sort of shit in the works of Dr Freud; stuff like that was strictly for the Psychic Friends hotline.

It was a coincidence, that's all, I thought as my plane started its descent. I was in seat A-2 (the nice thing about flying up front is that if the plane goes down, you're first to the crash site) and looking at pine forests as we slipped along the glidepath toward Bangor International Airport. The snow was gone for another year; I had vacationed it to death. *Only coincidence. How many times have you cut your hands in your life? I mean, they're always out front, aren't they, waving themselves around? Practically begging for it.*

All that should have rung true, and yet somehow it didn't, quite. It should have, but . . . well . . .

It was the boys in the basement. They were the ones who didn't buy it. The boys in the basement didn't buy it at all.

At that point there was a thump as the 737 touched down, and I put the whole line of thought out of my mind.

One afternoon shortly after arriving back home, I rummaged the closets until I found the shoeboxes containing Jo's old photographs. I sorted them, then studied my way through the ones of Dark Score Lake. There were a staggering number of these, but because Johanna was the shutterbug, there weren't many with her in them. I found one, though, that I remembered taking in 1990 or '91.

Sometimes even an untalented photographer can take a good picture – if seven hundred monkeys spent seven hundred years bashing away at seven hundred typewriters, and all that – and this was good. In it Jo was standing on the float with the sun going down red-gold behind her. She was just out of the water, dripping wet, wearing a two-piece swimming suit, gray with red piping. I had caught her laughing and brushing her soaked hair back from her forehead and temples. Her nipples were very prominent against the cups of her halter. She looked like an actress on a movie poster for one of those guilty-pleasure B-pictures about monsters at Party Beach or a serial killer stalking the campus.

I was sucker-punched by a sudden powerful lust for her. I wanted her upstairs just as she was in that photograph, with strands of her hair pasted to her cheeks and that wet bathing suit clinging to her.

I wanted to suck her nipples through the halter top, taste the cloth and feel their hardness through it. I wanted to suck water out of the cotton like milk, then yank the bottom of her suit off and fuck her until we both exploded.

Hands shaking a little, I put the photograph aside, with some others I liked (although there were no others I liked in quite that same way). I had a huge hard-on, one of those ones that feel like stone covered with skin. Get one of those and until it goes away you are good for nothing.

The quickest way to solve a problem like that when there's no woman around willing to help you solve it is to masturbate, but that time the idea never even crossed my mind. Instead I walked restlessly through the upstairs rooms of my house with my fists opening and closing and what looked like a hood ornament stuffed down the front of my jeans.

Anger may be a normal stage of the grieving process – I've read that it is – but I was never angry at Johanna in the wake of her death until the day I found that picture. Then, wow. There I was, walking around with a boner that just wouldn't quit, *furious* with her. Stupid bitch, why had she been running on one of the hottest days of the year? Stupid, inconsiderate bitch to leave me alone like this, not even able to work.

I sat down on the stairs and wondered what I should do. A drink was what I should do, I decided, and then maybe another drink to scratch the first one's back. I actually got up before deciding that wasn't a very good idea at all.

I went into my office instead, turned on the computer, and did a crossword puzzle. That night when I went to bed, I thought of looking at the picture of Jo in her bathing suit again. I decided that was almost as bad an idea as a few drinks when I was feeling angry and depressed. *But I'll have the dream tonight*, I thought as I turned off the light. *I'll have the dream for sure*.

I didn't, though. My dreams of Sara Laughs seemed to be finished.

A week's thought made the idea of at least summering at the lake seem better than ever. So, on a Saturday afternoon in early May when I calculated that any self-respecting Maine caretaker would be home watching the Red Sox, I called Bill Dean and told him I'd be at my lake place from the Fourth of July or so . . . and that if things went as I hoped, I'd be spending the fall and winter there as well.

'Well, that's good,' he said. 'That's real good news. A lot of folks down here've missed you, Mike. Quite a few that want to condole with you about your wife, don't you know.'

Was there the faintest note of reproach in his voice, or was that just my imagination? Certainly Jo and I had cast a shadow in the area; we had made significant contributions to the little library which served the Motton–Kashwakamak–Castle View area, and Jo had headed the successful fund drive to get an area bookmobile up and running. In addition to that, she had been part of a ladies' sewing circle (afghans were her specialty), and a member in good standing of the Castle County Crafts Co-op. Visits to the sick . . . helping out with the annual volunteer fire department blood drive . . . womaning a booth during Summerfest in Castle Rock . . . and stuff like that was only where she had started. She didn't do it in any ostentatious Lady Bountiful way, either, but unobtrusively and humbly, with her head lowered (often to hide a rather sharp smile, I should add – my Jo had a Biercean sense of humor). Christ, I thought, maybe old Bill had a right to sound reproachful.

'People miss her,' I said.

'Ayuh, they do.'

'I still miss her a lot myself. I think that's why I've stayed away from the lake. That's where a lot of our good times were.'

'I s'pose so. But it'll be damned good to see you down this way. I'll get busy. The place is all right – you could move into it this afternoon, if you was a mind – but when a house has stood empty the way Sara has, it gets stale.'

'I know.'

'I'll get Brenda Meserve to clean the whole shebang from top to bottom. Same gal you always had, don't you know.'

'Brenda's a little old for comprehensive spring cleaning, isn't she?' The lady in question was about sixty-five, stout, kind, and gleefully vulgar. She was especially fond of jokes about the travelling salesman who spent the night like a rabbit, jumping from hole to hole. No Mrs Danvers she.

'Ladies like Brenda Meserve never get too old to oversee the festivities,' Bill said. 'She'll get two or three girls to do the vacuuming and heavy lifting. Set you back maybe three hundred dollars. Sound all right?'

'Like a bargain.'

'The well needs to be tested, and the gennie, too, although I'm sure both of em's okay. I seen a hornet's nest by Jo's old studio that I want to smoke before the woods get dry. Oh, and the roof of the old house – you know, the middle piece – needs to be reshingled. I shoulda talked to you about that last year, but with you not using the place, I let her slide. You stand good for that, too?'

'Yes, up to ten grand. Beyond that, call me.'

'If we have to go over ten, I'll smile and kiss a pig.'

'Try to have it all done before I get down there, okay?'

'Coss. You'll want your privacy, I know that . . . just so long's you know you won't get any right away. We was shocked when she went so young; all of us were. Shocked and sad. She was a dear.' From a Yankee mouth, that word rhymes with *Leah*.

'Thank you, Bill.' I felt tears prickle my eyes. Grief is like a drunken houseguest, always coming back for one more goodbye hug. 'Thanks for saying.'

'You'll get your share of carrot-cakes, chummy.' He laughed, but a little doubtfully, as if afraid he was committing an impropriety.

'I can eat a lot of carrot-cake,' I said, 'and if folks overdo it, well, hasn't Kenny Auster still got that big Irish wolfhound?'

'Yuh, that thing'd eat cake 'til he busted!' Bill cried in high good humor. He cackled until he was coughing. I waited, smiling a little myself. 'Blueberry, he calls that dog, damned if I know why. Ain't he the gormiest thing!' I assumed he meant the dog and not the dog's master. Kenny Auster, not much more than five feet tall and neatly made, was the opposite of gormy, that peculiar Maine adjective that means clumsy, awkward, and clay-footed.

I suddenly realized that I missed these people – Bill and Brenda and Buddy Jellison and Kenny Auster and all the others who lived year-round at the lake. I even missed Blueberry, the Irish wolfhound, who trotted everywhere with his head up just as if he had half a brain in it and long strands of saliva depending from his jaws.

'I've also got to get down there and clean up the winter blowdown,' Bill said. He sounded embarrassed. 'It ain't bad this

67

year – that last big storm was all snow over our way, thank God – but there's still a fair amount of happy crappy I ain't got to yet. I shoulda put it behind me long before now. You not using the place ain't an excuse. I been cashing your checks.' There was something amusing about listening to the grizzled old fart beating his breast; Jo would have kicked her feet and giggled, I'm quite sure.

'If everything's right and running by July fourth, Bill, I'll be happy.'

'You'll be happy as a clam in a mudflat, then. That's a promise.' Bill sounded as happy as a clam in a mudflat himself, and I was glad. 'Gointer come down and write a book by the water? Like in the old days? Not that the last couple ain't been fine, my wife couldn't put that last one down, but—'

'I don't know,' I said, which was the truth. And then an idea struck me. 'Bill, would you do me a favour before you clean up the driveway and turn Brenda Meserve loose?'

'Happy to if I can,' he said, so I told him what I wanted.

Four days later, I got a little package with this laconic return address: DEAN/GEN DELIV/TR-90 (DARK SCORE). I opened it and shook out twenty photographs which had been taken with one of those little cameras you use once and then throw away.

Bill had filled out the roll with various views of the house, most conveying that subtle air of neglect a place gets when it's not used enough . . . even a place that's caretook (to use Bill's word) gets that neglected feel after awhile.

I barely glanced at these. The first four were the ones I wanted, and I lined them up on the kitchen table, where the strong sunlight would fall directly on them. Bill had taken these from the top of the driveway, pointing the disposable camera down at the sprawl of Sara Laughs. I could see the moss which had grown not only on the logs of the main house, but on the logs of the north and south wings, as well. I could see the litter of fallen branches and the drifts of pine needles on the driveway. Bill must have been tempted to clear all that away before taking his snaps, but he hadn't. I'd told him exactly what I wanted – 'warts and all' was the phrase I had used – and Bill had given it to me.

The bushes on either side of the driveway had thickened a lot

68

since Jo and I had spent any significant amount of time at the lake; they hadn't exactly run wild, but yes, some of the longer branches did seem to yearn toward each other across the asphalt like separated lovers.

Yet what my eye came back to again and again was the stoop at the foot of the driveway. The other resemblances between the photographs and my dreams of Sara Laughs might only be coincidental (or the writer's often surprisingly practical imagination at work), but I could explain the sunflowers growing out through the boards of the stoop no more than I had been able to explain the cut on the back of my hand.

I turned one of the photos over. On the back, in a spidery script, Bill had written: *These fellows are way early . . . and trespassing!*

I flipped back to the picture side. Three sunflowers, growing up through the boards of the stoop. Not two, not four, but three large sunflowers with faces like searchlights.

Just like the ones in my dream.

CHAPTER SIX

On July 3rd of 1998, I threw two suitcases and my PowerBook in the trunk of my mid-sized Chevrolet, started to back down the driveway, then stopped and went into the house again. It felt empty and somehow forlorn, like a faithful lover who has been dropped and cannot understand why. The furniture wasn't covered and the power was still on (I understood that The Great Lake Experiment might turn out to be a swift and total failure), but 14 Benton Street felt deserted, all the same. Rooms too full of furniture to echo still did when I walked through them, and everywhere there seemed to be too much dusty light.

In my study, the VDT was hooded like an executioner against the dust. I knelt before it and opened one of the desk drawers. Inside were four reams of paper. I took one, started away with it under my arm, then had a second thought and turned back. I had put that provocative photo of Jo in her swimsuit in the wide center drawer. Now I took it, tore the paper wrapping from the end of the ream of paper, and slid the photo halfway in, like a bookmark. If I *did* perchance begin to write again, and if the writing marched, I would meet Johanna right around page two hundred and fifty.

I left the house, locked the back door, got into my car, and drove away. I have never been back.

I'd been tempted to go down to the lake and check out the work – which turned out to be quite a bit more extensive than Bill Dean had originally expected – on several occasions. What kept me away was a feeling, never quite articulated by my conscious mind but still

70

very powerful, that I wasn't supposed to do it that way; that when I next came to Sara, it should be to unpack and stay.

Bill hired out Kenny Auster to shingle the roof, and got Kenny's cousin, Timmy Larribee, to 'scrape the old girl down,' a cleansing process akin to pot-scrubbing that is sometimes employed with log homes. Bill also had a plumber in to check out the pipes, and got my okay to replace some of the older plumbing and the well-pump.

Bill fussed about all these expenses over the telephone; I let him. When it comes to fifth- or sixth-generation Yankees and the expenditure of money, you might as well just stand back and let them get it out of their systems. Laying out the green just seems wrong to a Yankee, somehow, like petting in public. As for myself, I didn't mind the outgo a bit. I live frugally, for the most part, not out of any moral code but because my imagination, very lively in most other respects, doesn't work very well on the subject of money. My idea of a spree is three days in Boston, a Red Sox game, a trip to Tower Records and Video, plus a visit to the Wordsworth bookstore in Cambridge. Living like that doesn't make much of a dent in the interest, let alone the principal; I had a good money manager down in Waterville, and on the day I locked the door of the Derry house and headed west to TR-90, I was worth slightly over five million dollars. Not much compared to Bill Gates, but big numbers for this area, and I could afford to be cheerful about the high cost of house repairs.

That was a strange late spring and early summer for me. What I did mostly was wait, close up my town affairs, talk to Bill Dean when he called with the latest round of problems, and try not to think. I did the *Publishers Weekly* interview, and when the interviewer asked me if I'd had any trouble getting back to work 'in the wake of my bereavement,' I said no with an absolutely straight face. Why not? It was true. My troubles hadn't started until I'd finished *All the Way from the Top*; until then, I had been going on like gangbusters.

In mid-June, I met Frank Arlen for lunch at the Starlite Cafe. The Starlite is in Lewiston, which is the geographical midpoint between his town and mine. Over dessert (the Starlite's famous strawberry shortcake), Frank asked if I was seeing anyone. I looked at him with surprise.

'What are you gaping at?' he asked, his face registering one of the nine hundred unnamed emotions – this one of those somewhere between amusement and irritation. 'I certainly wouldn't think of it as two-timing Jo. She'll have been dead four years come August.'

'No,' I said. 'I'm not seeing anybody.'

He looked at me silently. I looked back for a few seconds, then started fiddling my spoon through the whipped cream on top of my shortcake. The biscuits were still warm from the oven, and the cream was melting. It made me think of that silly old song about how someone left the cake out in the rain.

'*Have* you seen anybody, Mike?'

'I'm not sure that's any business of yours.'

'Oh for Christ's sake. On your vacation? Did you—'

I made myself look up from the melting whipped cream. 'No,' I said. 'I did not.'

He was silent for another moment or two. I thought he was getting ready to move on to another topic. That would have been fine with me. Instead, he came right out and asked me if I had been laid at all since Johanna died. He would have accepted a lie on that subject even if he didn't entirely believe it – men lie about sex all the time. But I told the truth . . . and with a certain perverse pleasure.

'No.'

'Not a single time?'

'Not a single time.'

'What about a massage parlor? You know, to at least get a—'

'No.'

He sat there tapping his spoon against the rim of the bowl with his dessert in it. He hadn't taken a single bite. He was looking at me as though I were some new and oogy specimen of bug. I didn't like it much, but I suppose I understood it.

I had been close to what is these days called 'a relationship' on two occasions, neither of them on Key Largo, where I had observed roughly two thousand pretty women walking around dressed in only a stitch and a promise. Once it had been a red-haired waitress, Kelli, at a restaurant out on the Extension where I often had lunch. After awhile we got talking, joking around, and then there started to be some of that eye-contact, you know the kind I'm talking about, looks that go on just a little too long. I started to notice her legs, and the way her uniform pulled against her hip when she turned, and she noticed me noticing.

And there was a woman at Nu You, the place where I used to work out. A tall woman who favored pink jog-bras and black bike shorts. Quite yummy. Also, I liked the stuff she brought to read while she pedaled one of the stationary bikes on those endless aerobic trips to nowhere – not *Mademoiselle* or *Cosmo*, but novels by people like John Irving and Ellen Gilchrist. I like people who read actual books, and not just because I once wrote them myself. Book-readers are just as willing as anyone else to start out with the weather, but as a general rule they can actually go on from there.

The name of the blonde in the pink tops and black shorts was Adria Bundy. We started talking about books as we pedaled side by side ever deeper into nowhere, and there came a point where I was spotting her one or two mornings a week in the weight room. There's something oddly intimate about spotting. The prone position of the lifter is part of it, I suppose (especially when the lifter is a woman), but not all or even most of it. Mostly it's the dependence factor. Although it hardly ever comes to that point, the lifter is trusting the spotter with his or her life. And, at some point in the winter of 1996, those looks started as she lay on the bench and I stood over her, looking down into her upside-down face. The ones that go on just a little too long.

Kelli was around thirty, Adria perhaps a little younger. Kelli was divorced, Adria never married. In neither case would I have been robbing the cradle, and I think either would have been happy to go to bed with me on a provisional basis. Kind of a honey-bump test-drive. Yet what I did in Kelli's case was to find a different restaurant to eat my lunch at, and when the YMCA sent me a free exercise tryout offer, I took them up on it and just never went back to Nu You. I remember walking past Adria Bundy one day on the street six months or so after I made the change, and although I said hi, I made sure not to see her puzzled, slightly hurt gaze.

In a purely physical way I wanted them both (in fact, I seem to remember a dream in which I *had* them both, in the same bed and at the same time), and yet I wanted neither. Part of it was my inability to write – my life was quite fucked up enough, thank you, without adding any additional complications. Part of it was the work involved in making sure that the woman who is returning your glances is interested in you and not your rather extravagant bank account.

Most of it, I think, was that there was just too much Jo still in my head and heart. There was no room for anyone else, even after four years. It was sorrow like cholesterol, and if you think that's funny or weird, be grateful.

'What about friends?' Frank asked, at last beginning to eat his strawberry shortcake. 'You've got friends you see, don't you?'

'Yes,' I said. 'Plenty of friends.' Which was a lie, but I *did* have lots of crosswords to do, lots of books to read, and lots of movies to watch on my VCR at night; I could practically recite the FBI warning about unlawful copying by heart. When it came to real live people, the only ones I called when I got ready to leave Derry were my doctor and my dentist, and most of the mail I sent out that June consisted of change-of-address cards to magazines like *Harper's* and *National Geographic*.

'Frank,' I said, 'you sound like a Jewish mother.'

'Sometimes when I'm with you I *feel* like a Jewish mother,' he said. 'One who believes in the curative powers of baked potatoes instead of matzo balls. You look better than you have in a long time, finally put on some weight, I think—'

'Too much.'

'Bullshit, you looked like Ichabod Crane when you came for Christmas. Also, you've got some sun on your face and arms.'

'I've been walking a lot.'

'So you look better . . . except for your eyes. Sometimes you get this look in your eyes, and I worry about you every time I see it. I think Jo would be glad *someone's* worrying.'

'What look is this?' I asked.

'Your basic thousand-yard stare. Want the truth? You look like someone who's caught on something and can't get loose.'

I left Derry at three-thirty, stopped in Rumford for supper, then drove slowly on through the rising hills of western Maine as the sun lowered. I had planned my times of departure and arrival carefully, if not quite consciously, and as I passed out of Motton and into the unincorporated township of TR-90, I became aware of the heavy way my heart was beating. There was sweat on my face and arms in spite of the car's air conditioning. Nothing on the radio sounded right, all the music like screaming, and I turned it off.

I was scared, and had good reason to be. Even setting aside the

74

peculiar cross-pollination between the dreams and things in the real world (as I was able to do quite easily, dismissing the cut on my hand and the sunflowers growing through the boards of the back stoop as either coincidence or so much psychic fluff), I had reason to be scared. Because they hadn't been ordinary dreams, and my decision to go back to the lake after all this time hadn't been an ordinary decision. I didn't feel like a modern *fin-de-millénaire* man on a spiritual quest to face his fears (I'm okay, you're okay, let's all have an emotional circle-jerk while William Ackerman plays softly in the background); I felt more like some crazy Old Testament prophet going out into the desert to live on locusts and alkali water because God had summoned him in a dream.

I was in trouble, my life was a moderate-going-on-severe mess, and not being able to write was only part of it. I wasn't raping kids or running around Times Square preaching conspiracy theories through a bullhorn, but I was in trouble just the same. I had lost my place in things and couldn't find it again. No surprise there; after all, life's not a book. What I was engaging in on that hot July evening was self-induced shock therapy, and give me at least this much credit – I knew it.

You come to Dark Score this way: I-95 from Derry to Newport; Route 2 from Newport to Bethel (with a stop in Rumford, which used to stink like hell's front porch until the paper-driven economy pretty much ground to a halt during Reagan's second term); Route 5 from Bethel to Waterford. Then you take Route 68, the old County Road, across Castle View, through Motton (where downtown consists of a converted barn which sells videos, beer, and second-hand rifles), and then past the sign which reads TR-90 and the one reading GAME WARDEN IS BEST ASSISTANCE IN EMERGENCY, DIAL 1–800–555–GAME OR * 72 ON CELLULAR PHONE. To this, in spray paint, someone has added FUCK THE EAGLES.

Five miles past that sign, you come to a narrow lane on the right, marked only by a square of tin with the faded number 42 on it. Above this, like umlauts, are a couple of .22 holes.

I turned into this lane just about when I had expected to – it was 7:16 P.M., EDT, by the clock on the Chevrolet's dashboard.

And the feeling was coming home.

*   *   *

I drove in two tenths of a mile by the odometer, listening to the grass which crowned the lane whickering against the undercarriage of my car, listening to the occasional branch which scraped across the roof or knocked on the passenger side like a fist.

At last I parked and turned the engine off. I got out, walked to the rear of the car, lay down on my belly, and began pulling all of the grass which touched the Chevy's hot exhaust system. It had been a dry summer, and it was best to take precautions. I had come at this exact hour in order to replicate my dreams, hoping for some further insight into them or for an idea of what to do next. What I had not come to do was start a forest fire.

Once this was done I stood up and looked around. The crickets sang, as they had in my dreams, and the trees huddled close on either side of the lane, as they always did in my dreams. Overhead, the sky was a fading strip of blue.

I set off, walking up the righthand wheelrut. Jo and I had had one neighbor at this end of the road, old Lars Washburn, but now Lars's driveway was overgrown with juniper bushes and blocked by a rusty length of chain. Nailed to a tree on the left of the chain was NO TRESPASSING. Nailed to one on the right was NEXT CENTURY REAL ESTATE, and a local number. The words were faded and hard to read in the growing gloom.

I walked on, once more conscious of my heavily beating heart and of the way the mosquitoes were buzzing around my face and arms. Their peak season was past, but I was sweating a lot, and that's a smell they like. It must remind them of blood.

Just how scared was I as I approached Sara Laughs? I don't remember. I suspect that fright, like pain, is one of those things that slip our minds once they have passed. What I *do* remember is a feeling I'd had before when I was down here, especially when I was walking this road by myself. It was a sense that reality was thin. I think it *is* thin, you know, thin as lake ice after a thaw, and we fill our lives with noise and light and motion to hide that thinness from ourselves. But in places like Lane Forty-two, you find that all the smoke and mirrors have been removed. What's left is the sound of crickets and the sight of green leaves darkening toward black; branches that make shapes like faces; the sound of your heart in your chest, the beat of the blood against the backs of

76

your eyes, and the look of the sky as the day's blue blood runs out of its cheek.

What comes in when daylight leaves is a kind of certainty: that beneath the skin there is a secret, some mystery both black and bright. You feel this mystery in every breath, you see it in every shadow, you expect to plunge into it at every turn of a step. It is here; you slip across it on a kind of breathless curve like a skater turning for home.

I stopped for a moment about half a mile south of where I'd left the car, and still half a mile north of the driveway. Here the road curves sharply, and on the right is an open field which slants steeply down toward the lake. Tidwell's Meadow is what the locals call it, or sometimes the Old Camp. It was here that Sara Tidwell and her curious tribe built their cabins, at least according to Marie Hingerman (and once, when I asked Bill Dean, he agreed this was the place . . . although he didn't seem interested in continuing the conversation, which struck me at the time as a bit odd).

I stood there for a moment, looking down at the north end of Dark Score. The water was glassy and calm, still candy-colored in the afterglow of sunset, without a single ripple or a single small craft to be seen. The boat-people would all be down at the marina or at Warrington's Sunset Bar by now, I guessed, eating lobster rolls and drinking big mixed drinks. Later a few of them, buzzed on speed and martinis, would go bolting up and down the lake by moonlight. I wondered if I would be around to hear them. I thought there was a fair chance that by then I'd be on my way back to Derry, either terrified by what I'd found or disillusioned because I had found nothing at all.

'You funny little man, said Strickland.'

I didn't know I was going to speak until the words were out of my mouth, and why those words in particular I had no idea. I remembered my dream of Jo under the bed and shuddered. A mosquito whined in my ear. I slapped it and walked on.

In the end, my arrival at the head of the driveway was almost too perfectly timed, the sense of having re-entered my dream almost too complete. Even the balloons tied to the SARA LAUGHS sign (one white and one blue, both with WELCOME BACK MIKE! carefully printed on them in black ink) and floating against the ever-darkening backdrop of the trees seemed to intensify the *déjà vu* I had quite deliberately induced, for no two dreams are exactly the same, are they? Things made by hands and minds can never be quite the same, even when they try their best to be identical, because we're never the same from day to day or even moment to moment.

I walked to the sign, feeling the mystery of this place at twilight. I squeezed down on the board, feeling its rough reality, and then I ran the ball of my thumb over the letters, daring the splinters and reading with my skin like a blind man reading Braille: *S* and *A* and *R* and *A*; *L* and *A* and *U* and *G* and *H* and *S*.

The driveway had been cleared of fallen needles and blown-down branches, but Dark Score glimmered a fading rose just as it had in my dreams, and the sprawled hulk of the house was the same. Bill had thoughtfully left the light over the back stoop burning, and the sunflowers growing through the boards had long since been cut down, but everything else was the same.

I looked overhead, at the slot of sky over the lane. Nothing . . . I waited . . . and nothing . . . waiting still . . . and then there it was, right where the center of my gaze had been trained. At one moment there was only the fading sky (with indigo just starting to rise up from the edges like an infusion of ink), and at the next Venus was glowing there, bright and steady. People talk about watching the stars come out, and I suppose some people do, but I think that was the only time in my life that I actually saw one appear. I wished on it, too, but this time it was real time, and I did not wish for Jo.

'Help me,' I said, looking at the star. I would have said more, but I didn't know what to say. I didn't know what kind of help I needed.

That's enough, a voice in my mind said uneasily. *That's enough, now. Go on back and get your car.*

Except that wasn't the plan. The plan was to go down the driveway, just as I had in the final dream, the nightmare. The plan was to prove to myself that there was no shroud-wrapped monster lurking in the shadows of the big old log house down there. The plan was pretty much based on that bit of New Age wisdom which says the word 'fear' stands for Face Everything And Recover. But, standing there and looking down at that spark of porch light (it looked very small in the growing darkness), it occurred to me that there's

78

another bit of wisdom, one not quite so good-morning-starshine, which suggests fear is actually an acronym for Fuck Everything And Run. Standing there by myself in the woods as the light left the sky, that seemed like the smarter interpretation, no two ways about it.

I looked down and was a little amused to see that I had taken one of the balloons – untied it without even noticing as I thought things over. It floated serenely up from my hand at the end of its string, the words printed on it now impossible to read in the growing dark.

Maybe it's all moot, anyway; maybe I won't be able to move. Maybe that old devil writer's walk has got hold of me again, and I'll just stand here like a statue until someone comes along and hauls me away.

But this was real time in the real world, and in the real world there was no such thing as writer's walk. I opened my hand. As the string I'd been holding floated free, I walked under the rising balloon and started down the driveway. Foot followed foot, pretty much as they had ever since I'd first learned this trick back in 1959. I went deeper and deeper into the clean but sour smell of pine, and once I caught myself taking an extra-big step, avoiding a fallen branch that had been in the dream but wasn't here in reality.

My heart was still thudding hard, and sweat was still pouring out of me, oiling my skin and drawing mosquitoes. I raised a hand to brush the hair off my brow, then stopped, holding it splay-fingered out in front of my eyes. I put the other one next to it. Neither was marked; there wasn't even a shadow of scar from the cut I'd given myself while crawling around my bedroom during the ice-storm.

'I'm all right,' I said. 'I'm all right.'

You funny little man, said Strickland, a voice answered. It wasn't mine, wasn't Jo's; it was the UFO voice that had narrated my nightmare, the one which had driven me on even when I wanted to stop. The voice of some outsider.

I started walking again. I was better than halfway down the driveway now. I had reached the point where, in the dream, I told the voice that I was afraid of Mrs Danvers.

'I'm afraid of Mrs D,' I said, trying the words aloud in the growing dark. 'What if the bad old housekeeper's down there?'

A loon cried on the lake, but the voice didn't answer. I suppose it didn't have to. There *was* no Mrs Danvers, she was only a bag of bones in an old book, and the voice knew it.

I began walking again. I passed the big pine that Jo had once banged into in our Jeep, trying to back up the driveway. How she had sworn! Like a sailor! I had managed to keep a straight face until she got to 'Fuck a duck,' and then I'd lost it, leaning against the side of the Jeep with the heels of my hands pressed against my temples, howling until tears rolled down my cheeks, and Jo glaring hot blue sparks at me the whole time.

I could see the mark about three feet up on the trunk of the tree, the white seeming to float above the dark bark in the gloom. It was just here that the unease which pervaded the other dreams had skewed into something far worse. Even before the shrouded thing had come bursting out of the house, I had felt something was all wrong, all twisted up; I had felt that somehow the house itself had gone insane. It was at this point, passing the old scarred pine, that I had wanted to run like the gingerbread man.

I didn't feel that now. I was afraid, yes, but not in terror. There was nothing behind me, for one thing, no sound of slobbering breath. The worst thing a man was likely to come upon in these woods was an irritated moose. Or, I supposed, if he was really unlucky, a pissed-off bear.

In the dream there had been a moon at least three quarters full, but there was no moon in the sky above me that night. Nor would there be; in glancing over the weather page in that morning's *Derry News*, I had noticed that the moon was new.

Even the most powerful *déjà vu* is fragile, and at the thought of that moonless sky, mine broke. The sensation of reliving my nightmare departed so abruptly that I even wondered why I had done this, what I had hoped to prove or accomplish. Now I'd have to go all the way back down the dark lane to retrieve my car.

All right, but I'd do it with a flashlight from the house. One of them would surely still be just inside the—

A series of jagged explosions ran themselves off on the far side of the lake, the last loud enough to echo against the hills. I stopped, drawing in a quick breath. Moments before, those unexpected bangs probably would have sent me running back up the driveway in a panic, but now I had only that brief, startled moment. It was firecrackers, of course, the last one – the loudest one – maybe an

80

M-80. Tomorrow was the Fourth of July, and across the lake kids were celebrating early, as kids are wont to do.

I walked on. The bushes still reached like hands, but they had been pruned back and their reach wasn't very threatening. I didn't have to worry about the power being out, either; I was now close enough to the back stoop to see moths fluttering around the light Bill Dean had left on for me. Even if the power *had* been out (in the western part of the state a lot of the lines are still above ground, and it goes out a lot), the gennie would have kicked in automatically.

Yet I was awed by how much of my dream was actually here, even with the powerful sense of repetition – of *reliving* – departed. Jo's planters were where they'd always been, flanking the path which leads down to Sara's little lick of beach; I suppose Brenda Meserve had found them stacked in the cellar and had had one of her crew set them out again. Nothing was growing in them yet, but I suspected that stuff would be soon. And even without the moon of my dream, I could see the black square on the water, standing about fifty yards offshore. The swimming float.

No oblong shape lying overturned in front of the stoop, though; no coffin. Still, my heart was beating hard again, and I think if more firecrackers had gone off on the Kashwakamak side of the lake just then, I might have screamed.

You funny little man, said Strickland.

Give me that, it's my dust-catcher.

What if death drives us insane? What if we survive, but it drives us insane? What then?

I had reached the point where, in my nightmare, the door banged open and that white shape came hurtling out with its wrapped arms upraised. I took one more step and then stopped, hearing the harsh sound of my respiration as I drew each breath down my throat and then pushed it back out over the dry floor of my tongue. There was no return of the *déjà vu*, but for a moment I thought the shape would appear anyway – here in the real world, in real time. I stood waiting for it with my sweaty hands clenched. I drew in another dry breath, and this time I held it.

The soft lap of water against the shore.

A breeze that patted my face and rattled the bushes.

A loon cried out on the lake; moths battered the stoop light.

81

No shroud-monster threw open the door, and through the big windows to the left and right of the door, I could see nothing moving, white or otherwise. There was a note above the knob, probably from Bill, and that was it. I let out my breath in a rush and walked the rest of the way down the driveway to Sara Laughs.

The note was indeed from Bill Dean. It said that Brenda had done some shopping for me; the supermarket receipt was on the kitchen table, and I would find the pantry well stocked with canned goods. She'd gone easy with the perishables, but there was milk, butter, half-and-half, and hamburger, that staple of single-guy cuisine.

I will see you next Mon., Bill had written. *If I had my druthers I'd be here to say hello in person but the good wife says it's our turn to do the holiday trotting and so we are going down to Virginia (hot!!) to spend the 4th with her sister. If you need anything or run into problems . . .*

He had jotted his sister-in-law's phone number in Virginia as well as Butch Wiggins's number in town, which locals just call 'the TR,' as in 'Me and mother got tired of Bethel and moved our trailer over to the TR.' There were other numbers, as well – the plumber, the electrician, Brenda Meserve, even the TV guy over in Harrison who had repositioned the DSS dish for maximum reception. Bill was taking no chances. I turned the note over, imagining a final P.S.: *Say, Mike, if nuclear war should break out before me and Yvette get back from Virginia—*

Something moved behind me.

I whirled on my heels, the note dropping from my hand. It fluttered to the boards of the back stoop like a larger, whiter version of the moths banging the bulb overhead. In that instant I was sure it would be the shroud-thing, an insane revenant in my wife's decaying body, *Give me my dust-catcher, give it to me, how dare you come down here and disturb my rest, how dare you come to Manderley again, and now that you're here, how will you ever get away? Into the mystery with you, you silly little man. Into the mystery with you.*

Nothing there. It had just been the breeze again, stirring the bushes around a little . . . except I had felt no breeze against my sweaty skin, not that time.

'Well it must have been, there's nothing there,' I said.

The sound of your voice when you're alone can be either scary or reassuring. That time it was the latter. I bent over, picked up Bill's note, and stuffed it into my back pocket. Then I rummaged out my keyring. I stood under the stoop light in the big, swooping shadows of the lightstruck moths, picking through my keys until I found the one I wanted. It had a funny disused look, and as I rubbed my thumb along its serrated edge, I wondered again why I hadn't come down here – except for a couple of quick broad daylight errands – in all the months and years since Jo had died. Surely if she had been alive, she would have insisted—

But then a peculiar realization came to me: it wasn't just a matter of *since Jo died*. It was easy to think of it that way; never once during my six weeks on Key Largo had I thought of it any other way . . . but now, actually standing here in the shadows of the dancing moths (it was like standing under some weird organic disco ball) and listening to the loons out on the lake, I remembered that although Johanna had died in August of 1994, she had died in Derry. It had been miserably hot in the city . . . so why had we been there? Why hadn't we been sitting out on our shady deck on the lake side of the house, drinking iced tea in our bathing suits, watching the boats go back and forth and commenting on the form of the various water-skiers? What had she been doing in that damned Rite Aid parking lot to begin with, when during any other August we would have been miles from there?

Nor was that all. We usually stayed at Sara until the end of September – it was a peaceful, pretty time, as warm as summer. But in '93 we'd left with August only a week gone. I knew, because I could remember Johanna going to New York with me later that month, some kind of publishing deal and the usual attendant publicity crap. It had been dog-hot in Manhattan, the hydrants spraying in the East Village and the uptown streets sizzling. On one night of that trip we'd seen *The Phantom of the Opera*. Near the end Jo had leaned over to me and whispered, 'Oh fuck! The Phantom is snivelling again!' I had spent the rest of the show trying to keep from bursting into wild peals of laughter. Jo could be evil that way.

Why had she come with me that August? Jo didn't like New York even in April or October, when it's sort of pretty. I didn't know. I couldn't remember. All I was sure of was that she had never been back to Sara Laughs after early August of 1993 . . . and before long I wasn't even sure of that.

I slipped the key into the lock and turned it. I'd go inside, flip on the kitchen overheads, grab a flashlight, and go back for the car. If I didn't, some drunk guy with a cottage at the far south end of the lane would come in too fast, rear-end my Chevy, and sue me for a billion dollars.

The house had been aired out and didn't smell a bit musty; instead of still, stale air, there was a faint and pleasing aroma of pine. I reached for the light inside the door, and then, somewhere in the blackness of the house, a child began to sob. My hand froze where it was and my flesh went cold. I didn't panic, exactly, but all rational thought left my mind. It was weeping, a child's weeping, but I hadn't a clue as to where it was coming from.

Then it began to fade. Not to grow softer but to *fade*, as if someone had picked that kid up and was carrying it away down some long corridor . . . not that any such corridor existed in Sara Laughs. Even the one running through the middle of the house, connecting the central section to the two wings, isn't really long.

Fading . . . faded . . . almost gone.

I stood in the dark with my cold skin crawling and my hand on the lightswitch. Part of me wanted to boogie, to just go flying out of there as fast as my little legs could carry me, running like the gingerbread man. Another part, however – the rational part – was already reasserting itself.

I flicked the switch, the part that wanted to run saying forget it, it won't work, it's the dream, stupid, it's your dream coming true. But it *did* work. The foyer light came on in a shadow-dispelling rush, revealing Jo's lumpy little pottery collection to the left and the bookcase to the right, stuff I hadn't looked at in four years or more, but still here and still the same. On a middle shelf of the bookcase I could see the three early Elmore Leonard novels – *Swag*, *The Big Bounce*, and *Mr Majestyk* – that I had put aside against a spell of rainy weather; you have to be ready for rain when you're at camp. Without a good book, even two days of rain in the woods can be enough to drive you bonkers.

There was a final whisper of weeping, then silence. In it, I could hear ticking from the kitchen. The clock by the stove, one of Jo's rare lapses into bad taste, is Felix the Cat with big eyes that shift from side to side as his pendulum tail flicks back and forth. I think it's been in every cheap horror movie ever made.

'Who's here?' I called. I took a step toward the kitchen, just a dim space floating beyond the foyer, then stopped. In the dark the house was a cavern. The sound of the weeping could have come from anywhere. Including my own imagination. 'Is someone here?'

No answer . . . but I didn't think the sound had been in my head. If it had been, writer's block was the least of my worries.

Standing on the bookcase to the left of the Elmore Leonards was a long-barrelled flashlight, the kind that holds eight D-cells and will temporarily blind you if someone shines it directly into your eyes. I grasped it, and until it nearly slipped through my hand I hadn't really realized how heavily I was sweating, or how scared I was. I juggled it, heart beating hard, half-expecting that creepy sobbing to begin again, half-expecting the shroud-thing to come floating out of the black living room with its shapeless arms raised; some old hack of a politician back from the grave and ready to give it another shot. Vote the straight Resurrection ticket, brethren, and you will be saved.

I got control of the light and turned it on. It shot a bright straight beam into the living room, picking out the moosehead over the fieldstone fireplace; it shone in the head's glass eyes like two lights burning under water. I saw the old cane-and-bamboo chairs; the old couch; the scarred dining-room table you had to balance by shimming one leg with a folded playing card or a couple of beer coasters; I saw no ghosts; I decided this was a seriously fucked-up carnival just the same. In the words of the immortal Cole Porter, let's call the whole thing off. If I headed east as soon as I got back to my car, I could be in Derry by midnight. Sleeping in my own bed.

I turned out the foyer light and stood with the flash drawing its line across the dark. I listened to the tick of that stupid cat-clock, which Bill must have set going, and to the familiar chugging cycle of the refrigerator. As I listened to them, I realized that I had never expected to hear either sound again. As for the crying . . .

Had there *been* crying? Had there really?

Yes. Crying or *something*. Just what now seemed moot. What seemed germane was that coming here had been a dangerous idea and a stupid course of action for a man who has taught his mind to misbehave. As I stood in the foyer with no light but the flash and the glow falling in the windows from the bulb over the back stoop, I realized that the line between what I knew was real and what I knew was only my imagination had pretty much disappeared.

I left the house, checked to make sure the door was locked, and walked back up the driveway, swinging the flashlight beam from side to side like a pendulum – like the tail of old Felix the Krazy Kat in the kitchen. It occurred to me, as I struck north along the lane, that I would have to make up some sort of story for Bill Dean. It wouldn't do to say, 'Well, Bill, I got down there and heard a kid bawling in my locked house, and it scared me so bad I turned into the gingerbread man and ran back to Derry. I'll send you the flashlight I took; put it back on the shelf next to the paperbacks, would you?' That wasn't any good because the story would get around and people would say, 'Not surprised. Wrote too many books, probably. Work like that has got to soften a man's head. Now he's scared of his own shadow. Occupational hazard.'

Even if I never came down here again in my life, I didn't want to leave people on the TR with that opinion of me, that half-contemptuous, see-what-you-get-for-thinking-too-much attitude. It's one a lot of folks seem to have about people who live by their imaginations.

I'd tell Bill I got sick. In a way it was true. Or no . . . better to tell him someone *else* got sick . . . a friend . . . someone in Derry I'd been seeing . . . a lady-friend, perhaps. 'Bill, this friend of mine, this *lady*-friend of mine got sick, you see, and so . . .'

I stopped suddenly, the light shining on the front of my car. I had walked the mile in the dark without noticing many of the sounds in the woods, and dismissing even the bigger of them as deer settling down for the night. I hadn't turned around to see if the shroud-thing (or maybe some spectral crying child) was following me. I had gotten involved in making up a story and then embellishing it, doing it in my head instead of on paper this time but going down all the same well-known paths. I had gotten so involved that I had neglected to be afraid. My heartbeat was back to normal, the sweat was drying on my skin, and the mosquitoes had stopped whining in my ears. And as I stood there, a thought occurred to me. It was as if my mind had been waiting patiently for me to calm down enough so it could remind me of some essential fact.

The pipes. Bill had gotten my go-ahead to replace most of the old stuff, and the plumber had done so. Very recently he'd done so.

'Air in the pipes,' I said, running the beam of the eight-cell flashlight over the grille of my Chevrolet. 'That's what I heard.'

I waited to see if the deeper part of my mind would call this a stupid, rationalizing lie. It didn't . . . because, I suppose, it realized it could be true. Airy pipes can sound like people talking, dogs barking, or children crying. Perhaps the plumber had bled them and the sound had been something else . . . but perhaps he hadn't. The question was whether or not I was going to jump in my car, back two tenths of a mile to the highway, and then return to Derry, all on the basis of a sound I had heard for ten seconds (maybe only five), and while in an excited, stressful state of mind.

I decided the answer was no. It might take only one more peculiar thing to turn me around – probably gibbering like a character on *Tales from the Crypt* – but the sound I'd heard in the foyer wasn't enough. Not when making a go of it at Sara Laughs might mean so much.

I hear voices in my head, and have for as long as I can remember. I don't know if that's part of the necessary equipment for being a writer or not; I've never asked another one. I never felt the need to, because I know all the voices I hear are versions of me. Still, they often seem like very real versions of other people, and none is more real to me – or more familiar – than Jo's voice. Now that voice came, sounding interested, amused in an ironic but gentle way . . . and approving.

Going to fight, Mike?

'Yeah,' I said, standing there in the dark and picking out gleams of chrome with my flashlight. 'Think so, babe.'

Well, then – that's all right, isn't it?

Yes. It was. I got into my car, started it up, and drove slowly down the lane. And when I got to the driveway, I turned in.

There was no crying the second time I entered the house. I walked slowly through the downstairs, keeping the flashlight in my hand until I had turned on every light I could find; if there were people still boating on the north end of the lake, old Sara probably looked like some weird Spielbergian flying saucer hovering above them.

87

I think houses live their own lives along a time-stream that's different from the ones upon which their owners float, one that's slower. In a house, especially an old one, the past is closer. In my life Johanna had been dead nearly four years, but to Sara, she was much nearer than that. It wasn't until I was actually inside, with all the lights on and the flash returned to its spot on the bookshelf, that I realized how much I had been dreading my arrival. Of having my grief reawakened by signs of Johanna's interrupted life. A book with a corner turned down on the table at one end of the sofa, where Jo had liked to recline in her nightgown, reading and eating plums; the cardboard cannister of Quaker Oats, which was all she ever wanted for breakfast, on a shelf in the pantry; her old green robe hung on the back of the bathroom door in the south wing, which Bill Dean still called 'the new wing,' although it had been built before we ever saw Sara Laughs.

Brenda Meserve had done a good job – a humane job – of removing these signs and signals, but she couldn't get them all. Jo's hardcover set of Sayers's Peter Wimsey novels still held pride of place at the center of the living-room bookcase. Jo had always called the moosehead over the fireplace Bunter, and once, for no reason I could remember (certainly it seemed a very un-Bunterlike accessory), she had hung a bell around the moose's hairy neck. It hung there still, on a red velvet ribbon. Mrs Meserve might have puzzled over that bell, wondering whether to leave it up or take it down, not knowing that when Jo and I made love on the living-room couch (and yes, we were often overcome there), we referred to the act as 'ringing Bunter's bell.' Brenda Meserve had done her best, but any good marriage is secret territory, a necessary white space on society's map. What others don't know about it is what makes it yours.

I walked around, touching things, looking at things, seeing them new. Jo seemed everywhere to me, and after a little while I dropped into one of the old cane chairs in front of the TV. The cushion wheezed under me, and I could hear Jo saying, 'Well *excuse* yourself, Michael!'

I put my face in my hands and cried. I suppose it was the last of my mourning, but that made it no easier to bear. I cried until I thought something inside me would break if I didn't stop. When it finally let me go, my face was drenched, I had the hiccups, and I thought I had never felt so tired in my life. I felt strained all over my body – partly from the walking I'd done, I suppose, but mostly just from the tension of getting here . . . and deciding to stay here. To fight. That weird phantom crying I'd heard when I first stepped into the place, although it seemed very distant now, hadn't helped.

I washed my face at the kitchen sink, rubbing away the tears with the heels of my hands and clearing my clogged nose. Then I carried my suitcases down to the guest bedroom in the north wing. I had no intention of sleeping in the south wing, in the master bedroom where I had last slept with Jo.

That was a choice Brenda Meserve had foreseen. There was a bouquet of fresh wildflowers on the bureau, and a card: WELCOME BACK, MR NOONAN. If I hadn't been emotionally exhausted, I suppose looking at that message, in Mrs Meserve's spiky copperplate handwriting, would have brought on another fit of the weeps. I put my face in the flowers and breathed deeply. They smelled good, like sunshine. Then I took off my clothes, leaving them where they dropped, and turned back the coverlet on the bed. Fresh sheets, fresh pillowcases; same old Noonan sliding between the former and dropping his head on to the latter.

I lay there with the bedside lamp on, looking up at the shadows on the ceiling, almost unable to believe I was in this place and this bed. There had been no shroud-thing to greet me, of course . . . but I had an idea it might well find me in my dreams.

Sometimes – for me, at least – there's a transitional bump between waking and sleeping. Not that night. I slipped away without knowing it, and woke the next morning with sunlight shining in through the window and the bedside lamp still on. There had been no dreams that I could remember, only a vague sensation that I had awakened sometime briefly in the night and heard a bell ringing, very thin and far away.

CHAPTER SEVEN

The little girl – actually she wasn't much more than a baby – came walking up the middle of Route 68, dressed in a red bathing suit, yellow plastic flip-flops, and a Boston Red Sox baseball cap turned around backwards. I had just driven past the Lakeview General Store and Dickie Brooks's All-Purpose Garage, and the speed limit there drops from fifty-five to thirty-five. Thank God I was obeying it that day, otherwise I might have killed her.

It was my first day back. I'd gotten up late and spent most of the morning walking in the woods which run along the lakeshore, seeing what was the same and what had changed. The water looked a little lower and there were fewer boats than I would have expected, especially on summer's biggest holiday, but otherwise I might never have been away. I even seemed to be slapping at the same bugs.

Around eleven my stomach alerted me to the fact that I'd skipped breakfast. I decided a trip to the Village Cafe was in order. The restaurant at Warrington's was trendier by far, but I'd be stared at there. The Village Cafe would be better – if it was still doing business. Buddy Jellison was an ill-tempered fuck, but he had always been the best fry-cook in western Maine and what my stomach wanted was a big greasy Villageburger.

Now this little girl, walking straight up the white line and looking like a majorette leading an invisible parade.

At thirty-five miles per I saw her in plenty of time, but this road was busy in the summer, and very few people bothered creeping through the reduced speed zone. There were only a dozen Castle County police cruisers, after all, and not many of them bothered with the TR unless they were specifically called there.

I pulled over to the shoulder, put the Chevy in PARK, and was out before the dust had even begun to settle. The day was muggy and close and still, the clouds seeming low enough to touch. The kid – a little blondie with a snub nose and scabbed knees – stood on the white line as if it were a tightrope and watched me approach with no more fear than a fawn.

'Hi,' she said. 'I go beach. Mummy 'on't take me and I'm mad as hell.' She stamped her foot to show she knew as well as anybody what mad as hell was all about. Three or four was my guess. Well-spoken in her fashion and cute as hell, but still no more than three or four.

'Well, the beach is a good place to go on the Fourth, all right,' I said, 'but—'

'Fourth of July and fireworks *too*,' she agreed, making 'too' sound exotic and sweet, like a word in Vietnamese.

'—but if you try to walk there on the highway, you're more apt to wind up in Castle Rock Hospital.'

I decided I wasn't going to stand there playing Misterogers with her in the middle of Route 68, not with a curve only fifty yards to the south and a car apt to come wheeling around it at sixty miles an hour at any time. I could hear a motor, actually, and it was revving hard.

I picked the kid up and carried her over to where my car was idling, and although she seemed perfectly content to be carried and not frightened a bit, I felt like Chester the Molester the second I had my arm locked under her bottom. I was very aware that anyone sitting around in the combined office and waiting room of Brooksie's Garage could look out and see me. This is one of the strange midlife realities of my generation: we can't touch a child who isn't our own without fearing others will see something lecherous in our touching . . . or without thinking, way down deep in the sewers of our psyches, that there probably *is* something lecherous in it. I got her out of the road, though. I did that much. Let the Marching Mothers of Western Maine come after me and do their worst.

'You take me beach?' the little girl asked. She was bright-eyed, smiling. I figured that she'd probably be pregnant by the time she was twelve, especially given the cool way she was wearing her baseball cap. 'Got your suitie?'

'Actually I think I left my suitie at home. Don't you hate that? Honey, where's your mom?'

As if in direct answer to my question, the car I'd heard came busting out of a road on the near side of the curve. It was a Jeep Scout with mud splashed high up on both sides. The motor was growling like something up a tree and pissed off about it. A woman's head was poked out the side window. Little cutie's mom must have been too scared to sit down; she was driving in a mad crouch, and if a car *had* been coming around that particular curve in Route 68 when she pulled out, my friend in the red bathing suit would likely have become an orphan on the spot.

The Scout fishtailed, the head dropped back down inside the cab, and there was a grinding as the driver upshifted, trying to take her old heap from zero to sixty in maybe nine seconds. If pure terror could have done the job, I'm sure she would have succeeded.

'That's Mattie,' the girl in the bathing suit said. 'I'm mad at her. I'm running away to have a Fourth at the beach. If she's mad I go to my white nana.'

I had no idea what she was talking about, but it *did* cross my mind that Miss Bosox of 1998 could have her Fourth at the beach; I would settle for a fifth of something whole-grain at home. Meanwhile, I was waving the arm not under the kid's butt back and forth over my head, and hard enough to blow around wisps of the girl's fine blonde hair.

'Hey!' I shouted. 'Hey, lady! I got her!'

The Scout sped by, still accelerating and still sounding pissed off about it. The exhaust was blowing clouds of blue smoke. There was a further hideous grinding from the Scout's old transmission. It was like some crazy version of *Let's Make a Deal*: 'Mattie, you've succeeded in getting into second gear – would you like to quit and take the Maytag washer, or do you want to try for third?'

I did the only thing I could think of, which was to step out on to the road, turn toward the Jeep, which was now speeding away from me (the smell of the oil was thick and acrid), and hold the kid up high over my head, hoping Mattie would see us in her rearview mirror. I no longer felt like Chester the Molester; now I felt like a cruel auctioneer in a Disney cartoon, offering the cutest li'l piglet in the litter to the highest bidder. It worked, though. The Scout's mudcaked taillights came on and there was a demonic howling as the badly used brakes locked. Right in front of Brooksie's, this was. If there *were* any old-timers in for a good Fourth of July gossip, they would now have plenty to gossip about. I thought they would especially enjoy the part where Mom screamed at me to unhand her baby. When you return to your summer home after a long absence, it's always nice to get off on the right foot.

The backup lights flared and the Jeep began reversing down the road at a good twenty miles an hour. Now the transmission sounded not pissed off but panicky – please, it was saying, please stop, you're killing me. The Scout's rear end wagged from side to side like the tail of a happy dog. I watched it coming at me, hypnotized – now in the northbound lane, now across the white line and into the southbound lane, now overcorrecting so that the lefthand tires spumed dust off the shoulder.

'Mattie go fast,' my new girlfriend said in a conversational, isn't-this-interesting voice. She had one arm slung around my neck; we were chums, by God.

But what the kid said woke me up. Mattie go fast, all right, *too* fast. Mattie would, more likely than not, clean out the rear end of my Chevrolet. And if I just stood here, Baby Snooks and I were apt to end up as toothpaste between the two vehicles.

I backed the length of my car, keeping my eyes fixed on the Jeep and yelling, 'Slow down, Mattie! Slow down!'

Cutie-pie liked that. 'S'yo down!' she yelled, starting to laugh. 'S'yo down, you old Mattie, s'yo down!'

The brakes screamed in fresh agony. The Jeep took one last walloping, unhappy jerk backward as Mattie stopped without benefit of the clutch. That final lunge took the Scout's rear bumper so close to the rear bumper of my Chevy that you could have bridged the gap with a cigarette. The smell of oil in the air was huge and furry. The kid was waving a hand in front of her face and coughing theatrically.

The driver's door flew open; Mattie Devore flew out like a circus acrobat shot from a cannon, if you can imagine a circus acrobat dressed in old paisley shorts and a cotton smock top. My first thought was that the little girl's big sister had been babysitting her, that Mattie and Mommy were two different people. I knew that little kids often spend a period of their development calling their parents by their first names, but this pale-cheeked blonde girl looked all of twelve, fourteen at the outside. I decided her mad handling of the Scout hadn't been terror for her child (or not *just* terror) but total automotive inexperience.

There was something else, too, okay? Another assumption that I made. The muddy four-wheel-drive, the baggy paisley shorts, the smock that all but screamed Kmart, the long yellow hair held back with those little red elastics, and most of all the inattention that allows the three-year-old in your care to go wandering off in the first place . . . all those things said trailer-trash to me. I know how that sounds, but I had some basis for it. Also, I'm Irish, goddammit. My ancestors were trailer-trash when the trailers were still horse-drawn caravans.

'*Stinky-phew!*' the little girl said, still waving a pudgy hand at the air in front of her face. 'Scoutie *stink!*'

Where Scoutie's bathing suitie? I thought, and then my new girlfriend was snatched out of my arms. Now that she was closer, my idea that Mattie was the bathing beauty's sister took a hit. Mattie wouldn't be middle-aged until well into the next century, but she wasn't twelve or fourteen, either. I now guessed twenty, maybe a year younger. When she snatched the baby away, I saw the wedding ring on her left hand. I also saw the dark circles under her eyes, gray skin dusting to purple. She was young, but I thought it was a mother's terror and exhaustion I was looking at.

I expected her to swat the tot, because that's how trailer-trash moms react to being tired and scared. When she did, I would stop her, one way or another – distract her into turning her anger on me, if that was what it took. There was nothing very noble in this, I should add; all I really wanted to do was to postpone the fanny-whacking, shoulder-shaking, and in-your-face shouting to a time and place where I wouldn't have to watch it. It was my first day back in town; I didn't want to spend any of it watching an inattentive slut abuse her child.

Instead of shaking her and shouting 'Where did you think you were going, you little bitch?' Mattie first hugged the child (who hugged back enthusiastically, showing absolutely no sign of fear) and then covered her face with kisses.

'Why did you do that?' she cried. 'What was in your head? When I couldn't find you, I died.'

Mattie burst into tears. The child in the bathing suit looked at her with an expression of surprise so big and complete it would have been comical under other circumstances. Then her own face crumpled up. I stood back, watched them crying and hugging, and felt ashamed of my preconceptions.

A car went by and slowed down. An elderly couple – Ma and Pa Kettle on their way to the store for that holiday box of Grape Nuts – gawked out. I gave them an impatient wave with both hands, the kind that says what are *you* staring at, go on, put an egg in your shoe and beat it. They sped up, but I didn't see an out-of-state license plate, as I'd hoped I might. This version of Ma and Pa were locals, and the story would be fleeting its rounds soon enough: Mattie the teenage bride and her little bundle of joy (said bundle undoubtedly conceived in the back seat of a car or the bed of a pickup truck some months before the legitimizing ceremony), bawling their eyes out at the side of the road. With a stranger. No, not exactly a stranger. Mike Noonan, the writer fella from upstate.

'I wanted to go to the beach and *suh-suh-swim!*' the little girl wept, and now it was 'swim' that sounded exotic – the Vietnamese word for 'ecstasy,' perhaps.

'I said I'd take you this afternoon.' Mattie was still sniffing, but getting herself under control. 'Don't do that again, little guy, please don't you ever do that again, Mommy was so scared.'

'I won't,' the kid said. 'I really won't.' Still crying, she hugged the older girl tight, laying her head against the side of Mattie's neck. Her baseball cap fell off. I picked it up, beginning to feel very much like an outsider here. I poked the blue-and-red cap at Mattie's hand until her fingers closed on it.

I decided I also felt pretty good about the way things had turned out, and maybe I had a right to. I've presented the incident as if it was amusing, and it was, but it was the sort of amusing you never see until later. When it was happening, it was terrifying. Suppose there had been a truck coming from the other direction? Coming around that curve, and coming too fast?

A vehicle *did* come around it, a pickup of the type no tourist ever drives. Two more locals gawked their way by.

'Ma'am?' I said. 'Mattie? I think I'd better get going. Glad your little girl is all right.' The minute it was out, I felt an almost irresistible urge to laugh. I could picture me drawling this speech to Mattie (a name that belonged in a movie like. *Unforgiven* or *True Grit* if any name ever did) with my thumbs hooked into the belt of my chaps and my Stetson pushed back to reveal my noble brow. I felt an insane urge to add, 'You're right purty, ma'am, ain't you the new schoolteacher?'

She turned to me and I saw that she *was* right purty. Even with circles under her eyes and her blonde hair sticking off in gobs to either side of her head. And I thought she was doing okay for a girl probably not yet old enough to buy a drink in a bar. At least she hadn't belted the baby.

'Thank you so much,' she said. 'Was she right *in* the road?' Say she wasn't, her eyes begged. At least say she was walking along the shoulder.

'Well—'

'I walked on the line,' the girl said, pointing. 'It's like the crossmock.' Her voice took on a faintly righteous tone. 'Crossmock is safe.'

Mattie's cheeks, already white, turned whiter. I didn't like seeing her that way, and didn't like to think of her driving home that way, especially with a kid.

'Where do you live, Mrs—?'

'Devore,' she said. 'I'm Mattie Devore.' She shifted the child and put out her hand. I shook it. The morning was warm, and it was going to be hot by mid-afternoon – beach weather for sure – but the fingers I touched were icy. 'We live just there.'

She pointed to the intersection the Scout had shot out of, and I could see – surprise, surprise – a doublewide trailer set off in a grove of pines about two hundred feet up the little feeder road. Wasp Hill Road, I recalled. It ran about half a mile from Route 68 to the water – what was known as the Middle Bay. Ah yes, doc, it's all coming back to me now. I'm once more riding the Dark Score range. Saving little kids is my specialty.

Still, I was relieved to see that she lived close by – less than a quarter of a mile from the place where our respective vehicles were parked with their tails almost touching – and when I thought about

❖

it, it stood to reason. A child as young as the bathing beauty couldn't have walked far . . . although this one had already demonstrated a fair degree of determination. I thought Mother's haggard look was even more suggestive of the daughter's will. I was glad I was too old to be one of her future boyfriends; she would have them jumping through hoops all through high school and college. Hoops of fire, likely.

Well, the high-school part, anyway. Girls from the doublewide side of town did not, as a general rule, go to college unless there was a juco or a voke-tech handy. And she would only have them jumping until the right boy (or more likely the wrong one) came sweeping around the Great Curve of Life and ran her down in the highway, her all the while unaware that the white line and the crossmock were two different things. Then the whole cycle would repeat itself.

Christ almighty, Noonan, quit it, I told myself. *She's three years old and you've already got her with three kids of her own, two with ringworm and one retarded.*

'Thank you *so* much,' Mattie repeated.

'That's okay,' I said, and snubbed the little girl's nose. Although her cheeks were still wet with tears, she grinned at me sunnily enough in response. 'This is a very verbal little girl.'

'Very verbal, and very wilful.' Now Mattie did give her child a little shake, but the kid showed no fear, no sign that shaking or hitting was the order of most days. On the contrary, her smile widened. Her mother smiled back. And yes – once you got past the slopped-together look of her, she was most extraordinarily pretty. Put her in a tennis dress at the Castle Rock Country Club (where she'd likely never go in her life, except maybe as a maid or a waitress), and she would maybe be more than pretty. A young Grace Kelly, perhaps.

Then she looked back at me, her eyes very wide and grave.

'Mr Noonan, I'm not a bad mother,' she said.

I felt a start at my name coming from her mouth, but it was only momentary. She was the right age, after all, and my books were probably better for her than spending her afternoons in front of *General Hospital* and *One Life to Live*. A little, anyway.

'We had an argument about when we were going to the beach. I wanted to hang out the clothes, have lunch, and go this afternoon. Kyra wanted—' She broke off. 'What? What did I say?'

97

'Her name is Kia? Did—' Before I could say anything else, the most extraordinary thing happened: my mouth was full of water. So full I felt a moment's panic, like someone who is swimming in the ocean and swallows a wave-wash. Only this wasn't a salt taste; it was cold and fresh, with a faint metal tang like blood.

I turned my head aside and spat. I expected a gush of liquid to pour out of my mouth – the sort of gush you sometimes get when commencing artificial respiration on a near-drowning victim. What came out instead was what usually comes out when you spit on a hot day: a little white pellet. And that sensation was gone even before the little white pellet struck the dirt of the shoulder. In an instant, as if it had never been there.

'That man spitted,' the girl said matter-of-factly.

'Sorry,' I said. I was also bewildered. What in God's name had *that* been about? 'I guess I had a little delayed reaction.'

Mattie looked concerned, as though I were eighty instead of forty. I thought that maybe to a girl her age, forty *is* eighty. 'Do you want to come up to the house? I'll give you a glass of water.'

'No, I'm fine now.'

'All right. Mr Noonan . . . all I mean is that nothing like this has ever happened to me before. I was hanging sheets . . . she was inside watching a *Mighty Mouse* cartoon on the VCR . . . then, when I went in to get more pins . . .' She looked at the girl, who was no longer smiling. It was starting to get through to her now. Her eyes were big, and ready to fill with tears. 'She was gone. I thought for a minute I'd die of fear.'

Now the kid's mouth began to tremble, and her eyes filled up right on schedule. She began to weep. Mattie stroked her hair, soothing the small head until it lay against the Kmart smock top.

'That's all right, Ki,' she said. 'It turned out okay this time, but you can't go out in the road. It's dangerous. Little things get run over in the road, and you're a little thing. The most precious little thing in the world.'

She cried harder. It was the exhausted sound of a child who needed a nap before any more adventures, to the beach or anywhere else.

'Kia bad, Kia bad,' she sobbed against her mother's neck.

'No, honey, only three,' Mattie said, and if I had harbored any further thoughts about her being a bad mother, they melted away then. Or perhaps they'd already gone – after all, the kid was round, comely, well-kept, and unbruised.

On one level, those things registered. On another I was trying to cope with the strange thing that had just happened, and the equally strange thing I thought I was hearing – that the little girl I had carried off the white line had the name we had planned to give our child, if our child turned out to be a girl.

'Kia,' I said. Marvelled, really. As if my touch might break her, I tentatively stroked the back of her head. Her hair was sun-warm and fine.

'No,' Mattie said. 'That's the best she can say it now. *Kyra,* not Kia. It's from the Greek. It means ladylike.' She shifted, a little self-conscious. 'I picked it out of a baby-name book. While I was pregnant, I kind of went Oprah. Better than going postal, I guess.'

'It's a lovely name,' I said. 'And I don't think you're a bad mom.'

What went through my mind right then was a story Frank Arlen had told over a meal at Christmas – it had been about Petie, the youngest brother, and Frank had had the whole table in stitches. Even Petie, who claimed not to remember a bit of the incident, laughed until tears streamed down his cheeks.

One Easter, Frank said, when Petie was about five, their folks had gotten them up for an Easter-egg hunt. The two parents had hidden over a hundred colored hardboiled eggs around the house the evening before, after getting the kids over to their grandparents'. A high old Easter morning was had by all, at least until Johanna looked up from the patio, where she was counting her share of the spoils, and shrieked. There was Petie, crawling gaily around on the second-floor overhang at the back of the house, not six feet from the drop to the concrete patio.

Mr Arlen had rescued Petie while the rest of the family stood below, holding hands, frozen with horror and fascination. Mrs Arlen had repeated the Hail Mary over and over ('so fast she sounded like one of the chipmunks on that old "Witch Doctor" record,' Frank had said, laughing harder than ever) until her husband had disappeared back into the open bedroom window with Petie in his arms. Then she had swooned to the pavement, breaking her nose.

99

When asked for an explanation, Petie had told them he'd wanted to check the rain-gutter for eggs.

I suppose every family has at least one story like that; the survival of the world's Peties and Kyras is a convincing argument – in the minds of parents, anyway – for the existence of God.

'I was so scared,' Mattie said, now looking fourteen again. Fifteen at most.

'But it's over,' I said. 'And Kyra's not going to go walking in the road anymore. Are you, Kyra?'

She shook her head against her mother's shoulder without raising it. I had an idea she'd probably be asleep before Mattie got her back to the good old doublewide.

'You don't know how bizarre this is for me,' Mattie said. 'One of my favorite writers comes out of nowhere and saves my kid. I knew you had a place on the TR, that big old log house everyone calls Sara Laughs, but folks say you don't come here anymore since your wife died.'

'For a long time I didn't,' I said. 'If Sara was a marriage instead of a house, you'd call this a trial reconciliation.'

She smiled fleetingly, then looked grave again. 'I want to ask you for something. A favor.'

'Ask away.'

'Don't talk about this. It's not a good time for Ki and me.'

'Why not?'

She bit her lip and seemed to consider answering the question – one I might not have asked, given an extra moment to consider – and then shook her head. 'It's just not. And I'd be so grateful if you didn't talk about what just happened in town. More grateful than you'll ever know.'

'No problem.'

'You mean it?'

'Sure. I'm basically a summer person who hasn't been around for awhile . . . which means I don't have many folks to talk to anyway.' There was Bill Dean, of course, but I could keep quiet around him. Not that he wouldn't know. If this little lady thought the locals weren't going to find out about her daughter's attempt to get to the beach by shank's mare, she was fooling herself. 'I think we've

100

been noticed already, though. Take a look up at Brooksie's Garage. Peek, don't stare.'

She did, and sighed. Two old men were standing on the tarmac where there had been gas pumps once upon a time. One was very likely Brooksie himself; I thought I could see the remnants of the flyaway red hair which had always made him look like a downeast version of Bozo the Clown. The other, old enough to make Brooksie look like a wee slip of a lad, was leaning on a gold-headed cane in a way that was queerly vulpine.

'I can't do anything about them,' she said, sounding depressed. '*Nobody* can do anything about them. I guess I should count myself lucky it's a holiday and there's only two of them.'

'Besides,' I added, 'they probably didn't see much.' Which ignored two things: first, that half a dozen cars and pick-em-ups had gone by while we had been standing here, and second, that whatever Brooksie and his elderly friend hadn't seen, they would be more than happy to make up.

On Mattie's shoulder, Kyra gave a ladylike snore. Mattie glanced at her and gave her a smile full of rue and love. 'I'm sorry we had to meet under circumstances that make me look like such a dope, because I really am a big fan. They say at the bookstore in Castle Rock that you've got a new one coming out this summer.'

I nodded. 'It's called *Helen's Promise*.'

She grinned. 'Good title.'

'Thanks. You better get your buddy back home before she breaks your arm.'

'Yeah.'

There are people in this world who have a knack for asking embarrassing, awkward questions without meaning to – it's like a talent for walking into doors. I am one of that tribe, and as I walked with her toward the passenger side of the Scout, I found a good one. And yet it was hard to blame myself too enthusiastically. I had seen the wedding ring on her hand, after all.

'Will you tell your husband?'

Her smile stayed on, but it paled somehow. And tightened. If it were possible to delete a spoken question the way you can delete a line of type when you're writing a story, I would have done it.

'He died last August.'

'Mattie, I'm sorry. Open mouth, insert foot.'

'You couldn't know. A girl my age isn't even supposed to be married, is she? And if she is, her husband's supposed to be in the army, or something.'

There was a pink baby-seat – also Kmart, I guessed – on the passenger side of the Scout. Mattie tried to boost Kyra in, but I could see she was struggling. I stepped forward to help her, and for just a moment, as I reached past her to grab a plump leg, the back of my hand brushed her breast. She couldn't step back unless she wanted to risk Kyra's slithering out of the seat and on to the floor, but I could feel her recording the touch. My husband's dead, not a threat, so the big-deal writer thinks it's okay to cop a little feel on a hot summer morning. And what can I say? Mr Big Deal came along and hauled my kid out of the road, maybe saved her life.

No, Mattie, I may be forty going on a hundred, but I was not copping a feel. Except I couldn't say that; it would only make things worse. I felt my cheeks flush a little.

'How old *are* you?' I asked, when we had the baby squared away and were back at a safe distance.

She gave me a look. Tired or not, she had it together again. 'Old enough to know the situation I'm in.' She held out her hand. 'Thanks again, Mr Noonan. God sent you along at the right time.'

'Nah, God just told me I needed a hamburger at the Village Cafe,' I said. 'Or maybe it was His opposite number. Please say Buddy's still doing business at the same old stand.'

She smiled. It warmed her face back up again, and I was happy to see it. 'He'll still be there when Ki's kids are old enough to try buying beer with fake IDs. Unless someone wanders in off the road and asks for something like shrimp tetrazzini. If that happened he'd probably drop dead of a heart attack.'

'Yeah. When I get copies of the new book, I'll drop one off.'

The smile continued to hang in there, but now it shaded toward caution. 'You don't need to do that, Mr Noonan.'

'No, but I will. My agent gets me fifty comps. I find that as I get older, they go further.'

Perhaps she heard more in my voice than I had meant to put there – people do sometimes, I guess.

'All right. I'll look forward to it.'

I took another look at the baby, sleeping in that queerly casual way they have – her head tilted over on her shoulder, her lovely little lips pursed and blowing a bubble. Their skin is what kills me – so fine and perfect there seem to be no pores at all. Her Sox hat was askew. Mattie watched me reach in and readjust it so the visor's shade fell across her closed eyes.

'Kyra,' I said.

Mattie nodded. 'Ladylike.'

'Kia is an African name,' I said. 'It means "season's beginning."' I left her then, giving her a little wave as I headed back to the driver's side of the Chevy. I could feel her curious eyes on me, and I had the oddest feeling that I was going to cry.

That feeling stayed with me long after the two of them were out of sight; was still with me when I got to the Village Cafe. I pulled into the dirt parking lot to the left of the off-brand gas pumps and just sat there for a little while, thinking about Jo and about a home pregnancy-testing kit which had cost twenty-two-fifty. A little secret she'd wanted to keep until she was absolutely sure. That must have been it; what else could it have been?

'Kia,' I said. 'Season's beginning.' But that made me feel like crying again, so I got out of the car and slammed the door hard behind me, as if I could keep the sadness inside that way.

CHAPTER EIGHT

Buddy Jellison was just the same, all right – same dirty cooks' whites and splotchy white apron, same flyaway gray hair under a paper cap stained with either beef-blood or strawberry juice. Even, from the look, the same oatmeal-cookie crumbs caught in his ragged mustache. He was maybe fifty-five and maybe seventy, which in some genetically favored men seems to be still within the farthest borders of middle age. He was huge and shambly – probably six-four, three hundred pounds – and just as full of grace, wit, and *joie de vivre* as he had been four years before.

'You want a menu or do you remember?' he grunted, as if I'd last been in yesterday.

'You still make the Villageburger Deluxe?'

'Does a crow still shit in the pine tops?' Pale eyes regarding me. No condolences, which was fine by me.

'Most likely. I'll have one with everything – a Villageburger, not a crow – plus a chocolate frappe. Good to see you again.'

I offered my hand. He looked surprised but touched it with his own. Unlike the whites, the apron, and the hat, the hand was clean. Even the nails were clean. 'Yuh,' he said, then turned to the sallow woman chopping onions beside the grill. 'Villageburger, Audrey,' he said. 'Drag it through the garden.'

I'm ordinarily a sit-at-the-counter kind of guy, but that day I took a booth near the cooler and waited for Buddy to yell that it was ready – Audrey short-orders, but she doesn't waitress. I wanted to think, and Buddy's was a good place to do it. There were a couple of locals eating sandwiches and drinking sodas straight from the can,

104

but that was about it; people with summer cottages would have to be starving to eat at the Village Cafe, and even then you'd likely have to haul them through the door kicking and screaming. The floor was faded green linoleum with a rolling topography of hills and valleys. Like Buddy's uniform, it was none too clean (the summer people who came in probably failed to notice his hands). The woodwork was greasy and dark. Above it, where the plaster started, there were a number of bumper-stickers – Buddy's idea of decoration.

HORN BROKEN – WATCH FOR FINGER.
WIFE AND DOG MISSING. REWARD FOR DOG.
THERE'S NO TOWN DRUNK HERE, WE ALL TAKE TURNS.

Humor is almost always anger with its makeup on, I think, but in little towns the makeup tends to be thin. Three overhead fans paddled apathetically at the hot air, and to the left of the soft-drink cooler were two dangling strips of flypaper, both liberally stippled with wildlife, some of it still struggling feebly. If you could look at those and still eat, your digestion was probably doing okay.

I thought about a similarity of names which was surely, *had* to be, a coincidence. I thought about a young, pretty girl who had become a mother at sixteen or seventeen and a widow at nineteen or twenty. I thought about inadvertently touching her breast, and how the world judged men in their forties who suddenly discovered the fascinating world of young women and their accessories. Most of all I thought of the queer thing that had happened to me when Mattie had told me the kid's name – that sense that my mouth and throat were suddenly flooded with cold, mineral-tangy water. That *rush*.

When my burger was ready, Buddy had to call twice. When I went over to get it, he said: 'You back to stay or to clear out?'

'Why?' I asked. 'Did you miss me, Buddy?'

'Nup,' he said, 'but at least you're from in-state. Did you know that "Massachusetts" is Piscataqua for "asshole"?'

'You're as funny as ever,' I said.

'Yuh. I'm goin on fuckin Letterman. Explain to him why God gave seagulls wings.'

'Why was that, Buddy?'

'So they could beat the fuckin Frenchmen to the dump.'

105

I got a newspaper from the rack and a straw for my frappe. Then I detoured to the pay phone and, tucking my paper under my arm, opened the phone book. You could actually walk around with it if you wanted; it wasn't tethered to the phone. Who, after all, would want to steal a Castle County telephone directory?

There were over twenty Devores, which didn't surprise me very much – it's one of those names, like Pelkey or Bowie or Toothaker, that you kept coming across if you lived down here. I imagine it's the same everywhere – some families breed more and travel less, that's all.

There was a Devore listing for 'RD Wsp Hll Rd,' but it wasn't for a Mattie, Mathilda, Martha, or M. It was for Lance. I looked at the front of the phone book and saw it was a 1997 model, printed and mailed while Mattie's husband was still in the land of the living. Okay . . . but there was something else about that name. Devore, Devore, let us now praise famous Devores; wherefore art thou Devore? But it wouldn't come, whatever it was.

I ate my burger, drank my liquefied ice cream, and tried not to look at what was caught on the flypaper.

While I was waiting for the sallow, silent Audrey to give me my change (you could still eat all week in the Village Cafe for fifty dollars . . . if your blood-vessels could stand it, that was), I read the sticker pasted to the cash register. It was another Buddy Jellison special: CYBERSPACE SCARED ME SO BAD I DOWNLOADED IN MY PANTS. This didn't exactly convulse me with mirth, but it *did* provide the key for solving one of the day's mysteries: why the name Devore had seemed not just familiar but evocative.

I was financially well-off, rich by the standards of many. There was at least one person with ties to the TR, however, who was rich by the standards of everybody, and filthy rich by the standards of most year-round residents of the lakes region. If, that was, he was still eating, breathing, and walking around.

'Audrey, is Max Devore still alive?'

She gave me a little smile. 'Oh, ayuh. But we don't see him in here too often.'

That got the laugh out of me that all of Buddy's joke stickers hadn't been able to elicit. Audrey, who had always been yellowish and who now looked like a candidate for a liver transplant, snickered herself. Buddy gave us a librarian's prim glare from the far end of the counter, where he was reading a flyer about the holiday NASCAR race at Oxford Plains.

I drove back the way I had come. A big hamburger is a bad meal to eat in the middle of a hot day; it leaves you feeling sleepy and heavy-witted. All I wanted was to go home (I'd been there less than twenty-four hours and was already thinking of it as home), flop on the bed in the north bedroom under the revolving fan, and sleep for a couple of hours.

When I passed Wasp Hill Road, I slowed down. The laundry was hanging listlessly on the lines, and there was a scatter of toys in the front yard, but the Scout was gone. Mattie and Kyra had donned their suities, I imagined, and headed on down to the public beachie. I'd liked them both, and quite a lot. Mattie's short-lived marriage had probably hooked her somehow to Max Devore . . . but looking at the rusty doublewide trailer with its dirt driveway and balding front yard, remembering Mattie's baggy shorts and Kmart smock top, I had to doubt that the hook was a strong one.

Before retiring to Palm Springs in the late eighties, Maxwell William Devore had been a driving force in the computer revolution. It's primarily a young people's revolution, but Devore did okay for a golden oldie – knew the playing-field and understood the rules. He started when memory was stored on magnetic tape instead of in computer chips and a warehouse-sized cruncher called UNIVAC was state-of-the-art. He was fluent in COBOL and spoke FORTRAN like a native. As the field expanded beyond his ability to keep up, expanded to the point where it began to define the world, he bought the talent he needed to keep growing.

His company, Visions, had created scanning programs which could upload hard copy on to floppy disks almost instantaneously; it created graphic-imaging programs which had become the industry standard; it created Pixel Easel, which allowed laptop users to mouse-paint . . . to actually fingerpaint, if their gadget came equipped with what Jo had called 'the clitoral cursor.' Devore had invented none of this later stuff, but he'd understood that it *could* be invented and had hired people to do it. He held dozens of patents and co-held hundreds more. He was supposedly worth something like six hundred million dollars, depending on how technology stocks were doing on any given day.

On the TR he was reputed to be crusty and unpleasant. No surprise there; to a Nazarene, can any good thing come out of Nazareth? And folks said he was eccentric, of course. Listen to the old-timers who remember the rich and successful in their salad days (and all the old-timers claim they do), and you'll hear that they ate the wallpaper, fucked the dog, and showed up at church suppers wearing nothing but their pee-stained BVDs. Even if all that was true in Devore's case, and even if he was Scrooge McDuck in the bargain, I doubted that he'd allow two of his closer relatives to live in a doublewide trailer.

I drove up the lane above the lake, then paused at the head of my driveway, looking at the sign there: SARA LAUGHS burned into a length of varnished board nailed to a handy tree. It's the way they do things down here. Looking at it brought back the last dream of the Manderley series. In that dream someone had slapped a radio-station sticker on the sign, the way you're always seeing stickers slapped on turnpike toll-collection baskets in the exact-change lanes.

I got out of my car, went to the sign, and studied it. No sticker. The sunflowers had been down there, growing out of the stoop – I had a photo in my suitcase that proved it – but there was no radio-station sticker on the house sign. Proving exactly what? Come on, Noonan, get a grip.

I started back to the car – the door was open, the Beach Boys spilling out of the speakers – then changed my mind and went back to the sign again. In the dream, the sticker had been pasted just above the RA of SARA and the LAU of LAUGHS. I touched my fingers to that spot and thought they came away feeling slightly sticky. Of course that could have been the feel of varnish on a hot day. Or my imagination.

I drove down to the house, parked, set the emergency brake (on the slopes around Dark Score and the dozen or so other lakes in western Maine, you always set your brake), and listened to the rest of 'Don't Worry, Baby,' which I've always thought was the best of the Beach Boys' songs, great not in spite of the sappy lyrics but because of them. If you knew how much I love you, baby, Brian Wilson sings, nothing could go wrong with you. And oh folks, wouldn't that be a world.

I sat there listening and looked at the cabinet set against the right side of the stoop. We kept our garbage in there to foil the neighborhood raccoons. Even cans with snap-down lids won't always do that; if the coons are hungry enough, they somehow manage the lids with their clever little hands.

You're not going to do what you're thinking of doing, I told myself. *I mean . . . are you?*

It seemed I was – or that I was at least going to have a go. When the Beach Boys gave way to Rare Earth, I got out of the car, opened the storage cabinet, and pulled out two plastic garbage cans. There was a guy named Stan Proulx who came down to yank the trash twice a week (or there was four years ago, I reminded myself), one of Bill Dean's farflung network of part-timers working for cash off the books, but I didn't think Stan would have been down to collect the current accumulation of swill because of the holiday, and I was right. There were two plastic garbage bags in each can. I hauled them out (cursing myself for a fool even while I was doing it) and untwisted the yellow ties.

I really don't think I was so obsessed that I would have dumped a bunch of wet garbage out on my stoop if it had come to that (of course I'll never know for sure, and maybe that's for the best), but it didn't. No one had lived in the house for four years, remember, and it's occupancy that produces garbage – everything from coffee-grounds to used sanitary napkins. The stuff in these bags was dry trash swept together and carted out by Brenda Meserve's cleaning crew.

There were nine vacuum cleaner disposal bags containing forty-eight months of dust, dirt, and dead flies. There were wads of paper towels, some smelling of aromatic furniture polish and others of the sharper but still pleasant aroma of Windex. There was a moldy mattress pad and a silk jacket which had that unmistakable dined-upon-by-moths look. The jacket certainly caused me no regrets; a mistake of my young manhood, it looked like something from the Beatles' 'I Am the Walrus' era. Goo-goo-joob, baby.

There was a box filled with broken glass . . . another filled with unrecognizable (and presumably out-of-date) plumbing fixtures . . . a torn and filthy square of carpet . . . done-to-death dishtowels, faded and ragged . . . the old oven-gloves I'd used when cooking burgers and chicken on the barbecue . . .

The sticker was in a twist at the bottom of the second bag. I'd known I would find it – from the moment I'd felt that faintly tacky patch on the sign, I'd known – but I'd needed to see it for myself. The same way old Doubting Thomas had needed to get the blood under his fingernails, I suppose.

I placed my find on a board of the sunwarmed stoop and smoothed it out with my hand. It was shredded around the edges. I guessed Bill had probably used a putty-knife to scrape it off. He hadn't wanted Mr Noonan to come back to the lake after four years and discover some beered-up kid had slapped a radio-station sticker on his driveway sign. Gorry, no, 't'wouldn't be proper, deah. So off it had come and into the trash it had gone and here it was again, another piece of my nightmare unearthed and not much the worse for wear. I ran my fingers over it. WBLM, 102.9, PORTLAND'S ROCK AND ROLL BLIMP.

I told myself I didn't have to be afraid. That it meant nothing, just as all the rest of it meant nothing. Then I got the broom out of the cabinet, swept all the trash together, and dumped it back in the plastic bags. The sticker went in with the rest.

I went inside meaning to shower the dust and grime away, then spied my own bathing suitie, still lying in one of my open suitcases, and decided to go swimming instead. The suit was a jolly number, covered with spouting whales, that I had purchased in Key Largo. I thought my pal in the Bosox cap would have approved. I checked my watch and saw that I had finished my Villageburger forty-five minutes ago. Close enough for government work, *Kemo Sabe*, especially after engaging in an energetic game of Trash-Bag Treasure Hunt.

I pulled on my suit and walked down the railroad-tie steps which lead from Sara to the water. My flip-flops snapped and flapped. A few late mosquitoes hummed. The lake gleamed in front of me, still and inviting under that low humid sky. Running north and south along its edge, bordering the entire east side of the lake, was a right-of-way path (it's called 'common property' in the deeds) which folks on the TR simply call The Street. If one were to turn left on to The Street at the foot of my steps, one could walk all the way down to the Dark Score Marina, passing Warrington's and Buddy Jellison's scuzzy little eatery on the way . . . not to mention four dozen summer cottages, discreetly tucked into sloping groves of spruce and pine. Turn right and you could walk to Halo Bay, although it would take you a day to do it with The Street overgrown the way it is now.

I stood there for a moment on the path, then ran forward and leaped into the water. Even as I flew through the air with the greatest of ease, it occurred to me that the last time I had jumped in like this, I had been holding my wife's hand.

Touching down was almost a catastrophe. The water was cold enough to remind me that I was forty, not fourteen, and for a moment my heart stopped dead in my chest. As Dark Score Lake closed over my head, I felt quite sure that I wasn't going to come up alive. I'd be found drifting face-down between the swimming float and my little stretch of The Street, a victim of cold water and a greasy Villageburger. They'd carve 'Your Mother Always Said To Wait At Least An Hour' on my tombstone.

Then my feet landed in the stones and slimy weedstuff growing along the bottom, my heart kick-started, and I shoved upward like a guy planning to slam-dunk home the last score of a close basketball game. As I returned to the air, I gasped. Water went in my mouth and I coughed it back out, patting one hand against my chest in an effort to encourage my heart – come on, baby, keep going, you can do it.

I came back down standing waist-deep in the lake and with my mouth full of that cold taste – lakewater with an undertinge of minerals, the kind you'd have to correct for when you washed your clothes. It was exactly what I had tasted while standing on the shoulder of Route 68. It was what I had tasted when Mattie Devore told me her daughter's name.

I made a psychological connection, that's all. From the similarity of the names to my dead wife to this lake. Which—

'Which I have tasted a time or two before,' I said out loud. As if to underline the fact, I scooped up a palmful of water – some of the cleanest and clearest in the state, according to the analysis reports I and all the other members of the so-called Western Lakes Association get each year – and drank it down. There was no revelation, no sudden weird flashes in my head. It was just Dark Score, first in my mouth and then in my stomach.

I swam out to the float, climbed the three-rung ladder on the side, and flopped on the hot boards, feeling suddenly very glad I

111

had come. In spite of everything. Tomorrow I would start putting together some sort of life down here . . . trying to, anyway. For now it was enough to be lying with my head in the crook of one arm, on the verge of a doze, confident that the day's adventures were over.

As it happened, that was not quite true.

During our first summer on the TR, Jo and I discovered it was possible to see the Castle Rock fireworks show from the deck overlooking the lake. I remembered this just as it was drawing down toward dark, and thought that this year I would spend that time in the living room, watching a movie on the video player. Reliving all the Fourth of July twilights we had spent out there, drinking beer and laughing as the big ones went off, would be a bad idea. I was lonely enough without that, lonely in a way of which I had not been conscious in Derry. Then I wondered what I had come down here for, if not to finally face Johanna's memory — all of it — and put it to loving rest. Certainly the possibility of writing again had never seemed more distant than it did that night.

There was no beer — I'd forgotten to get a sixpack either at the General Store or at the Village Cafe — but there was soda, courtesy of Brenda Meserve. I got a can of Pepsi and settled in to watch the lightshow, hoping it wouldn't hurt too much. Hoping, I supposed, that I wouldn't cry. Not that I was kidding myself; there were more tears here, all right. I'd just have to get through them.

The first explosion of the night had just gone off — a spangly burst of blue with the bang travelling far behind — when the phone rang. It made me jump as the faint explosion from Castle Rock had not. I decided it was probably Bill Dean, calling long-distance to see if I was settling in all right.

In the summer before Jo died, we'd gotten a wireless phone so we could prowl the downstairs while we talked, a thing we both liked to do. I went through the sliding glass door into the living room, punched the pickup button, and said, 'Hello, this is Mike,' as I went back to my deck-chair and sat down. Far across the lake, exploding below the low clouds hanging over Castle View, were green and yellow starbursts, followed by soundless flashes that would eventually reach me as noise.

For a moment there was nothing from the phone, and then a

112

man's raspy voice – an elderly voice but not Bill Dean's – said, 'Noonan? Mr Noonan?'

'Yes?' A huge spangle of gold lit up the west, shivering the low clouds with brief filigree. It made me think of the award shows you see on television, all those beautiful women in shining dresses.

'Devore.'

'Yes?' I said again, cautiously.

'Max Devore.'

We don't see him in here too often, Audrey had said. I had taken that for Yankee wit, but apparently she'd been serious. Wonders never ceased.

Okay, what next? I was at a total loss for conversational gambits. I thought of asking him how he'd gotten my number, which was unlisted, but what would be the point? When you were worth over half a billion dollars – if this really was *the* Max Devore I was talking to – you could get any old unlisted number you wanted.

I settled for saying yes again, this time without the little uptilt at the end.

Another silence followed. When I broke it and began asking questions, he would be in charge of the conversation . . . if we could be said to be having a conversation at that point. A good gambit, but I had the advantage of my long association with Harold Oblowski to fall back on – Harold, master of the pregnant pause. I sat tight, cunning little cordless phone to my ear, and watched the show in the west. Red bursting into blue, green into gold; unseen women walked the clouds in glowing award-show evening dresses.

'I understand you met my daughter-in-law today,' he said at last. He sounded annoyed.

'I may have done,' I said, trying not to sound surprised. 'May I ask why you're calling, Mr Devore?'

'I understand there was an incident.'

White lights danced in the sky – they could have been exploding spacecraft. Then, trailing after, the bangs. *I've discovered the secret of time travel*, I thought. *It's an auditory phenomenon.*

My hand was holding the phone far too tightly, and I made it relax. Maxwell Devore. Half a billion dollars. Not in Palm Springs as I had supposed, but close – right here on the TR, if the characteristic underhum on the line could be trusted.

113

'I'm concerned for my granddaughter.' His voice was raspier than ever. He was angry, and it showed – this was a man who hadn't had to conceal his emotions in a lot of years. 'I understand my daughter-in-law's attention wandered again. It wanders often.'

Now half a dozen colored starbursts lit the night, blooming like flowers in an old Disney nature film. I could imagine the crowds gathered on Castle View sitting cross-legged on their blankets, eating ice cream cones and drinking beer and all going *Oooooh* at the same time. That's what makes any successful work of art, I think – everybody goes *Oooooh* at the same time.

You're scared of this guy, aren't you? Jo asked. *Okay, maybe you're right to be scared. A man who feels he can be angry whenever he wants to at whoever he wants to . . . that's a man who can be dangerous.*

Then Mattie's voice: *Mr Noonan, I'm not a bad mother. Nothing like this has ever happened to me before.*

Of course that's what most bad mothers say in such circumstances, I imagined . . . but I had believed her.

Also, goddammit, my number was unlisted. I had been sitting here with a soda, watching the fireworks, bothering nobody, and this guy had—

'Mr Devore, I don't have any idea what—'

'Don't give me that, with all due respect don't give me that, Mr Noonan, you were seen talking to them.' He sounded as I imagine Joe McCarthy sounded to those poor shmucks who ended up being branded dirty commies when they came before his committee.

Be careful, Mike, Jo said. *Beware of Maxwell's silver hammer.*

'I did see and speak to a woman and a little girl this morning,' I said. 'I presume they're the ones you're talking about.'

'No, you saw a *toddler* walking on the road *alone*,' he said. 'And then you saw a woman chasing after her. My daughter-in-law, in that old thing she drives. The child could have been run down. Why are you protecting that young woman, Mr Noonan? Did she promise you something? You're certainly doing the child no favors, I can tell you that much.'

She promised to take me back to her trailer and then take me around the world, I thought of saying. *She promised to keep her mouth open the whole time if I'd keep mine shut – is that what you want to hear?*

Yes, Jo said. *Very likely that is what he wants to hear. Very likely*

114

what he wants to believe. Don't let him provoke you into a burst of your sophomore sarcasm, Mike – you could regret it.

Why was I bothering to protect Mattie Devore, anyway? I didn't know. Didn't have the slightest idea of what I might be getting into here, for that matter. I only knew that she had looked tired, and the child hadn't been bruised or frightened or sullen.

'There *was* a car. An old Jeep.'

'That's more like it.' Satisfaction. And sharp interest. Greed, almost. 'What did—'

'I guess I assumed they came in the car together,' I said. There was a certain giddy pleasure in discovering my capacity for invention had not deserted me – I felt like a pitcher who can no longer do it in front of a crowd, but who can still throw a pretty good slider in the old back yard. 'The little girl might have had some daisies.' All the careful qualifications, as if I were testifying in court instead of sitting on my deck. Harold would have been proud. Well, no. Harold would have been horrified that I was having such a conversation at all.

'I think I assumed they were picking wildflowers. My memory of the incident isn't all that clear, unfortunately. I'm a writer, Mr Devore, and when I'm driving I often drift off into my own private—'

'You're lying.' The anger was right out in the open now, bright and pulsing like a boil. As I had suspected, it hadn't taken much effort to escort this guy past the social niceties.

'Mr Devore. The computer Devore, I assume?'

'You assume correctly.'

Jo always grew cooler in tone and expression as her not inconsiderable temper grew hotter. Now I heard myself emulating her in a way that was frankly eerie. 'Mr Devore, I'm not accustomed to being called in the evening by men I don't know, nor do I intend to prolong the conversation when a man who does so calls me a liar. Good evening, sir.'

'If everything was fine, then why did you stop?'

'I've been away from the TR for some time, and I wanted to know if the Village Cafe was still open. Oh, by the way – I don't know where you got my telephone number, but I know where you can put it. Good night.'

I broke the connection with my thumb and then just looked at the phone, as if I had never seen such a gadget in my life. The hand holding it was trembling. My heart was beating hard; I could feel it in my neck and wrists as well as my chest. I wondered if I could have told Devore to stick my phone number up his ass if I hadn't had a few million rattling around in the bank myself.

The Battle of the Titans, dear, Jo said in her cool voice. *And all over a teenage girl in a trailer. She didn't even have any breasts to speak of.*

I laughed out loud. Battle of the Titans? Hardly. Some old robber baron from the turn of the century had said, 'These days a man with a million dollars thinks he's rich.' Devore would likely have the same opinion of me, and in the wider scheme of things he would be right.

Now the western sky was alight with unnatural, pulsing color. It was the finale.

'What was that all about?' I asked.

No answer; only a loon calling across the lake. Protesting all the unaccustomed noise in the sky, as likely as not.

I got up, went inside, and put the phone back in its charging cradle, realizing as I did that I was expecting it to ring again, expecting Devore to start spouting movie clichés: *If you get in my way I'll* and *I'm warning you, friend, not to* and *Let me give you a piece of good advice before you.*

The phone didn't ring. I poured the rest of my soda down my gullet, which was understandably dry, and decided to go to bed. At least there hadn't been any weeping and wailing out there on the deck; Devore had pulled me out of myself. In a weird way, I was grateful to him.

I went into the north bedroom, undressed, and lay down. I thought about the little girl, Kyra, and the mother that could have been her older sister. Devore was pissed at Mattie, that much was clear, and if I was a financial nonentity to the guy, what must she be to him? And what kind of resources would she have if he had taken against her? That was a pretty nasty thought, actually, and it was the one I fell asleep on.

I got up three hours later to eliminate the can of soda I had unwisely downed before retiring, and as I stood before the bowl, pissing with one eye open, I heard the sobbing again. A child somewhere in the dark, lost and frightened . . . or perhaps just *pretending* to be lost and frightened.

116

'Don't,' I said. I was standing naked before the toilet bowl, my back alive with gooseflesh. 'Please don't start up with this shit, it's scary.'

The crying dwindled as it had before, seeming to diminish like something carried down a tunnel. I went back to bed, turned on my side, and closed my eyes.

'It was a dream,' I said. 'Just another Manderley dream.'

I knew better, but I also knew I was going back to sleep, and right then that seemed like the important thing. As I drifted off, I thought in a voice that was purely my own: *She is alive. Sara is alive.*

And I understood something, too: she belonged to me. I had reclaimed her. For good or ill, I had come home.

CHAPTER NINE

At nine o'clock the following morning I filled a squeeze-bottle with grapefruit juice and set out for a good long walk south along The Street. The day was bright and already hot. It was also silent – the kind of silence you experience only after a Saturday holiday, I think, one composed of equal parts holiness and hangover. I could see two or three fishermen parked far out on the lake, but not a single power-boat burred, not a single gaggle of kids shouted and splashed. I passed half a dozen cottages on the slope above me, and although all of them were likely inhabited at this time of year, the only signs of life I saw were bathing suits hung over the deck rail at the Passendales' and a half-deflated fluorescent-green seahorse on the Rimers' stub of a dock.

But did the Passendales' little gray cottage still belong to the Passendales? Did the Batchelders' amusing circular summer-camp with its Cinerama picture-window pointing at the lake and the mountains beyond still belong to the Batchelders? No way of telling, of course. Four years can bring a lot of changes.

I walked and made no effort to think – an old trick from my writing days. Work your body, rest your mind, let the boys in the basement do their jobs. I made my way past camps where Jo and I had once had drinks and barbecues and attended the occasional card-party, I soaked up the silence like a sponge, I drank my juice, I armed sweat off my forehead, and I waited to see what thoughts might come.

The first was an odd realization: that the crying child in the night seemed somehow more real than the call from Max Devore.

Had I actually been phoned by a rich and obviously bad-tempered techno-mogul on my first full evening back on the TR? Had said mogul actually called me a liar at one point? (I was, considering the tale I had told, but that was beside the point.) I knew it had happened, but it was actually easier to believe in The Ghost of Dark Score Lake, known around some campfires as The Mysterious Crying Kiddie.

My next thought – this was just before I finished my juice – was that I should call Mattie Devore and tell her what had happened. I decided it was a natural impulse but probably a bad idea. I was too old to believe in such simplicities as The Damsel in Distress versus The Wicked Stepfather . . . or, in this case, Father-in-Law. I had my own fish to fry this summer, and I didn't want to complicate my job by getting into a potentially ugly dispute between Mr Computer and Ms Doublewide. Devore had rubbed my fur the wrong way – and vigorously – but that probably wasn't personal, only something he did as a matter of course. Hey, some guys snap bra-straps. Did I want to get in his face on this? No. I did not. I had saved Little Miss Red Sox, I had gotten myself an inadvertent feel of Mom's small but pleasantly firm breast, I had learned that Kyra was Greek for ladylike. Any more than that would be gluttony, by God.

I stopped at that point, feet as well as brain, realizing I'd walked all the way to Warrington's, a vast barnboard structure which locals sometimes called the country club. It was, sort of – there was a six-hole golf course, a stable and riding trails, a restaurant, a bar, and lodging for perhaps three dozen in the main building and the eight or nine satellite cabins. There was even a two-lane bowling alley, although you and your competition had to take turns setting up the pins. Warrington's had been built around the beginning of World War I. That made it younger than Sara Laughs, but not by much.

A long dock led out to a smaller building called The Sunset Bar. It was there that Warrington's summer guests would gather for drinks at the end of the day (and some for Bloody Marys at the beginning). And when I glanced out that way, I realized I was no longer alone. There was a woman on the porch standing to the left of the floating bar's door, watching me.

She gave me a pretty good jump. My nerves weren't in their best condition right then, and that probably had something to do with it . . . but I think she would have given me a jump in any case. Part of it was her stillness. Part was her extraordinary thinness. Most of it was her face. Have you ever seen that Edvard Munch drawing, *The Cry*? Well, if you imagine that screaming face at rest, mouth closed and eyes watchful, you'll have a pretty good image of the woman standing at the end of the dock with one long-fingered hand resting on the rail. Although I must tell you that my first thought was not *Edvard Munch* but *Mrs Danvers*.

She looked about seventy and was wearing black shorts over a black tank bathing suit. The combination looked strangely formal, a variation on the ever-popular little black cocktail dress. Her skin was cream-white, except above her nearly flat bosom and along her bony shoulders. There it swam with large brown age-spots. Her face was a wedge featuring prominent, skull-like cheekbones and an unlined lamp of brow. Beneath that bulge, her eyes were lost in sockets of shadow. White hair hung scant and lank around her ears and down to the prominent shelf of her jaw.

God, she's thin, I thought. *She's nothing but a bag of—*

A shudder twisted through me at that. It was a strong one, as if someone were spinning a wire in my flesh. I didn't want her to notice it – what a way to start a summer day, by revolting a guy so badly that he stood there shaking and grimacing in front of you – so I raised my hand and waved. I tried to smile, as well. Hello there, lady standing out by the floating bar. Hello there, you old bag of bones, you scared the living shit out of me but it doesn't take much these days and I forgive you. How the fuck ya doin? I wondered if my smile looked as much like a grimace to her as it felt to me.

She didn't wave back.

Feeling quite a bit like a fool – THERE'S NO VILLAGE IDIOT HERE, WE ALL TAKE TURNS – I ended my wave in a kind of half-assed salute and headed back the way I'd come. Five steps and I had to look over my shoulder; the sensation of her watching me was so strong it was like a hand pressing between my shoulderblades.

The dock where she'd been was completely deserted. I squinted my eyes, at first sure she must have just retreated deeper into the shadow thrown by the little *boozehaus*, but she was gone. As if she had been a ghost herself.

She stepped into the bar, hon, Jo said. *You know that, don't you? I mean . . . you* do *know it, right?*

120

'Right, right,' I murmured, setting off north along The Street toward home. 'Of course I do. Where else?' Except it didn't seem to me that there had been time; it didn't seem to me that she could have stepped in, even in her bare feet, without me hearing her. Not on such a quiet morning.

Jo again: *Perhaps she's stealthy.*

'Yes,' I murmured. I did a lot of talking out loud before that summer was over. 'Yes, perhaps she is. Perhaps she's stealthy.' Sure. Like Mrs Danvers.

I stopped again and looked back, but the right-of-way path had followed the lake around a little bit of curve, and I could no longer see either Warrington's or The Sunset Bar. And really, I thought, that was just as well.

On my way back, I tried to list the oddities which had preceded and then surrounded my return to Sara Laughs: the repeating dreams; the sunflowers; the radio-station sticker; the weeping in the night. I supposed that my encounter with Mattie and Kyra, plus the follow-up phone-call from Mr Pixel Easel, also qualified as passing strange . . . but not in the same way as a child you heard sobbing in the night.

And what about the fact that we had been in Derry instead of on Dark Score when Johanna died? Did that qualify for the list? I didn't know. I couldn't even remember why that was. In the fall and winter of 1993 I'd been fiddling with a screenplay for *The Red-Shirt Man*. In February of '94 I got going on *All the Way from the Top*, and that absorbed most of my attention. Besides, deciding to go west to the TR, west to Sara . . .

'That was Jo's job,' I told the day, and as soon as I heard the words I understood how true they were. We'd both loved the old girl, but saying 'Hey Irish, let's get our asses over to the TR for a few days' had been Jo's job. She might say it any time . . . except, in the year before her death she hadn't said it once. And I had never thought to say it for her. Had somehow forgotten all about Sara Laughs, it seemed, even when summer came around. Was it possible to be that absorbed in a writing project? It didn't seem likely . . . but what other explanation was there?

Something was very wrong with this picture, but I didn't know what it was. Not from nothin.

That made me think of Sara Tidwell, and the lyrics to one of her songs. She had never been recorded, but I owned the Blind Lemon Jefferson version of this particular tune. One verse went:

It ain't nuthin but a barn-dance sugar
It ain't nuthin but a round-and-round
Let me kiss you on your sweet lips sugar
You the good thing that I found.

I loved that song, and had always wondered how it would have sounded coming out of a woman's mouth instead of from that whiskey-voiced old troubadour. Out of Sara Tidwell's mouth. I bet she sang sweet. And boy, I bet she could swing it.

I had gotten back to my own place again. I looked around, saw no one in the immediate vicinity (although I could now hear the day's first ski-boat burring away downwater), stripped to my underpants, and swam out to the float. I didn't climb it, only lay beside it holding on to the ladder with one hand and lazily kicking my feet. It was nice enough, but what was I going to do with the rest of the day?

I decided to spend it cleaning my work area on the second floor. When that was done, maybe I'd go out and look around in Jo's studio. If I didn't lose my courage, that was.

I swam back, kicking easily along, raising my head in and out of water which flowed along my body like cool silk. I felt like an otter. I was most of the way to the shore when I raised my dripping face and saw a woman standing on The Street, watching me. She was as thin as the one I'd seen down at Warrington's . . . but this one was green. Green and pointing north along the path like a dryad in some old legend.

I gasped, swallowed water, coughed it back out. I stood up in chest-deep water and wiped my streaming eyes. Then I laughed (albeit a little doubtfully). The woman was green because she was a birch growing a little to the north of where my set of railroad-tie steps ended at The Street. And even with my eyes clear of water, there was something creepy about how the leaves around the ivory-streaked-with-black trunk almost made a peering face. The air was perfectly still and so the face was perfectly still (as still as the face of the woman in the black shorts and bathing suit

122

had been), but on a breezy day it would seem to smile or frown . . . or perhaps to laugh. Behind it there grew a sickly pine. One bare branch jutted off to the north. It was this I had mistaken for a skinny arm and a bony, pointing hand.

It wasn't the first time I'd spooked myself like that. I see things, that's all. Write enough stories and every shadow on the floor looks like a footprint, every line in the dirt like a secret message. Which did not, of course, ease the task of deciding what was really peculiar at Sara Laughs and what was peculiar only because my *mind* was peculiar.

I glanced around, saw I still had this part of the lake to myself (although not for much longer; the bee-buzz of the first power boat had been joined by a second and third), and stripped off my soggy underpants. I wrung them out, put them on top of my shorts and shirt, and walked naked up the railroad-tie steps with my clothes held against my chest. I pretended I was Bunter, bringing breakfast and the morning paper to Lord Peter Wimsey. By the time I got back inside the house I was grinning like a fool.

The second floor was stifling in spite of the open windows, and I saw why as soon as I got to the top of the stairs. Jo and I had shared space up here, she on the left (only a little room, really just a cubby, which was all she needed with the studio north of the house), me on the right. At the far end of the hall was the grilled snout of the monster air-conditioning unit we'd bought the year after we bought the lodge. Looking at it, I realized I had missed its characteristic hum without even being aware of it. There was a sign taped to it which said, *Mr Noonan: Broken. Blows hot air when you turn it on & sounds full of broken glass. Dean says the part it needs is promised from Western Auto in Castle Rock. I'll believe it when I see it. B. Meserve.*

I grinned at that last – it was Mrs M. right down to the ground – and then tried the switch. Machinery often responds favorably when it senses a penis-equipped human in the vicinity, Jo used to claim, but not this time. I listened to the air conditioner grind for five seconds or so, then snapped it off. 'Damn thing shit the bed,' as TR folks like to say. And until it was fixed, I wouldn't even be doing crossword puzzles up here.

I looked in my office just the same, as curious about what I might feel as about what I might find. The answer was next to nothing. There was the desk where I had finished *The Red-Shirt Man*, thus proving to myself that the first time wasn't a fluke; there was the photo of Richard Nixon, arms raised, flashing the double V-for-Victory sign, with the caption WOULD YOU BUY A USED CAR FROM THIS MAN? running beneath; there was the rag rug Jo had hooked for me a winter or two before she had discovered the wonderful world of afghans and pretty much gave up hooking.

It wasn't quite the office of a stranger, but every item (most of all, the weirdly empty surface of the desk) said that it *was* the work-space of an earlier-generation Mike Noonan. Men's lives, I had read once, are usually defined by two primary forces: work and marriage. In my life the marriage was over and the career on what appeared to be permanent hiatus. Given that, it didn't seem strange to me that now the space where I'd spent so many days, usually in a state of real happiness as I made up various imaginary lives, seemed to mean nothing. It was like looking at the office of an employee who had been fired . . . or who had died suddenly.

I started to leave, then had an idea. The filing cabinet in the corner was crammed with papers – bank statements (most eight or ten years out of date), correspondence (mostly never answered), a few story fragments – but I didn't find what I was looking for. I moved on to the closet, where the temperature had to be at least a hundred and ten degrees, and in a cardboard box which Mrs M. had marked GADGETS, I unearthed it – a Sanyo Memo-Scriber Debra Weinstock gave me at the conclusion of our work on the first of the Putnam's books. It could be set to turn itself on when you started to talk; it dropped into its PAUSE mode when you stopped to think.

I never asked Debra if the thing just caught her eye and she thought, 'Why, I'll bet any self-respecting popular novelist would enjoy owning one of these babies,' or if it was something a little more specific . . . some sort of hint, perhaps? Verbalize those little faxes from your subconscious while they're still fresh, Noonan? I hadn't known then and didn't now. But I had it, a genuine pro-quality dictating machine and there were at least a dozen cassette tapes in my car, home dubs I'd made to listen to while driving. I would insert one in the Memo-Scriber tonight, slide the volume control as high as it would go, and put the machine in its DICTATE mode. Then, if the noise I'd heard at least twice now repeated itself, I would have it on tape. I could play it for Bill Dean and ask him what *he* thought it was.

What if I hear the sobbing child tonight and the machine never kicks on?

'Well then, I'll know something else,' I told the empty, sunlit office. I was standing there in the doorway with the Memo-Scriber under my arm, looking at the empty desk and sweating like a pig. 'Or at least suspect it.'

Jo's nook across the hall made my office seem crowded and homey by comparison. Never overfull, it was now nothing but a square room-shaped space. The rug was gone, her photos were gone, even the desk was gone. This looked like a do-it-yourself project which had been abandoned after ninety per cent of the work had been done. Jo had been scrubbed out of it – *scraped* out of it – and I felt a moment's unreasonable anger at Brenda Meserve. I thought of what my mother usually said when I'd done something on my own initiative of which she disapproved: 'You took a little too much on y'self, didn't you?' That was my feeling about Jo's little bit of office: that in emptying it to the walls this way, Mrs Meserve had taken a little too much on herself.

Maybe it wasn't Mrs M. who cleaned it out, the UFO voice said. *Maybe Jo did it herself. Ever think of that, sport?*

'That's stupid,' I said. 'Why would she? I hardly think she had a premonition of her own death. Considering she'd just bought—'

But I didn't want to say it. Not out loud. It seemed like a bad idea somehow.

I turned to leave the room, and a sudden sigh of cool air, amazing in that heat, rushed past the sides of my face. Not my body; just my face. It was the most extraordinary sensation, like hands patting briefly but gently at my cheeks and forehead. At the same time there was a sighing in my ears . . . except that's not quite right. It was a susurrus that went *past* my ears, like a whispered message spoken in a hurry.

I turned, expecting to see the curtains over the room's window in motion . . . but they hung perfectly straight.

'Jo?' I said, and hearing her name made me shiver so violently that I almost dropped the Memo-Scriber. 'Jo, was that you?'

Nothing. No phantom hands patting my skin, no motion from

125

the curtains . . . which there certainly would have been if there had been an actual draft. All was quiet. There was only a tall man with a sweaty face and a tape-recorder under his arm standing in the doorway of a bare room . . . but that was when I first began to really believe that I wasn't alone in Sara Laughs.

So what? I asked myself. *Even if it should be true, so what? Ghosts can't hurt anyone.*

That's what I thought then.

When I visited Jo's studio (her *air-conditioned* studio) after lunch, I felt quite a lot better about Brenda Meserve – she hadn't taken too much on herself after all. The few items I especially remembered from Jo's little office – the framed square of her first afghan, the green rag rug, her framed poster depicting the wildflowers of Maine – had been put out here, along with almost everything else I remembered. It was as if Mrs M. had sent a message – *I can't ease your pain or shorten your sadness, and I can't prevent the wounds that coming back here may reopen, but I can put all the stuff that may hurt you in one place, so you won't be stumbling over it unexpected or unprepared. I can do that much.*

Out here were no bare walls; out here the walls jostled with my wife's spirit and creativity. There were knitted things (some serious, many whimsical), batik squares, rag dolls popping out of what she called 'my baby collages,' an abstract desert painting made from strips of yellow, black, and orange silk, her flower photographs, even, on top of her bookshelf, what appeared to be a sculpture-in-progress of Sara Laughs herself. It was made out of toothpicks and lollipop sticks.

In one corner was her little loom and a wooden cabinet with a sign reading JO'S KNITTING STUFF! NO TRESPASSING! hung over the pull-knob. In another was the banjo she had tried to learn and then given up on, saying it hurt her fingers too much. In a third was a kayak paddle and a pair of Rollerblades with scuffed toes and little purple pompoms on the tips of the laces.

The thing which caught and held my eye was sitting on the old rolltop desk in the center of the room. During the many good summers, falls, and winter weekends we had spent here, that desktop would have been littered with spools of thread, skeins of yarn, pincushions, sketches, maybe a book about the Spanish Revolution or famous American dogs. Johanna could be aggravating, at least to me, because she imposed no real system or order on what she did. She could also be daunting, even overwhelming at times. She was a brilliant scatterbrain, and her desk had always reflected that.

But not now. It was possible to think that Mrs M. had cleared the litter from the top of it and plunked down what was now there, but impossible to believe. Why would she? It made no sense.

The object was covered with a gray plastic hood. I reached out to touch it, and my hand faltered an inch or two short as a memory of an old dream

(*give me that it's my dust-catcher*)

slipped across my mind much as that queer draft had slipped across my face. Then it was gone, and I pulled the plastic cover off. Underneath it was my old green IBM Selectric, which I hadn't seen or thought of in years. I leaned closer, knowing that the typewriter ball would be Courier – my old favorite – even before I saw it.

What in God's name was my old typewriter doing out here?

Johanna painted (although not very well), she took photographs (very good ones indeed) and sometimes sold them, she knitted, she crocheted, she wove and dyed cloth, she could play eight or ten basic chords on the guitar. She *could* write, of course; most English majors can, which is why they become English majors. Did she demonstrate any blazing degree of literary creativity? No. After a few experiments with poetry as an undergrad, she gave up that particular branch of the arts as a bad job. *You write for both of us, Mike*, she had said once. *That's all yours; I'll just take a little taste of everything else.* Given the quality of her poems as opposed to the quality of her silks, photographs, and knitted art, I thought that was probably wise.

But here was my old IBM. Why?

'Letters,' I said. 'She found it down in the cellar or something, and rescued it to write letters on.'

Except that wasn't Jo. She showed me most of her letters, often urging me to write little postscripts of my own, guilt-tripping me with that old saying about how the shoemaker's kids always go barefoot ('and the writer's friends would never hear from him if it weren't for Alexander Graham Bell,' she was apt to add). I hadn't seen a typed personal letter from my wife in all the time we'd been married – if nothing else, she would have considered it shitty etiquette. She *could* type, producing mistake-free business letters slowly yet methodically, but she always used my desktop computer or her own PowerBook for those chores.

'What were you up to, hon?' I asked, then began to investigate her desk drawers.

Brenda Meserve had made an effort with these, but Jo's fundamental nature had defeated her. Surface order (spools of thread segregated by color, for instance) quickly gave way to Jo's old dear jumble. I found enough of her in those drawers to hurt my heart with a hundred unexpected memories, but I found no paperwork which had been typed on my old IBM, with or without the Courier ball. Not so much as a single page.

When I was finished with my hunt, I leaned back in my chair (*her* chair) and looked at the little framed photo on her desk, one I couldn't remember ever seeing before. Jo had most likely printed it herself (the original might have come out of some local's attic) and then hand-tinted the result. The final product looked like a wanted poster colorized by Ted Turner.

I picked it up and ran the ball of my thumb over the glass facing, bemused. Sara Tidwell, the turn-of-the-century blues shouter whose last known port of call had been right here in TR-90. When she and her folks — some of them friends, most of them relatives — had left the TR, they had gone on to Castle Rock for a little while . . . then had simply disappeared, like a cloud over the horizon or mist on a summer morning.

She was smiling just a little in the picture, but the smile was hard to read. Her eyes were half-closed. The string of her guitar — not a strap but a string — was visible over one shoulder. In the background I could see a black man wearing a derby at a killer angle (one thing about musicians: they really know how to wear hats) and standing beside what appeared to be a washtub bass.

Jo had tinted Sara's skin to a *café au lait* shade, maybe based on other pictures she'd seen (there are quite a few knocking around, most showing Sara with her head thrown back and her hair hanging almost to her waist as she bellows out her famous carefree yell of a laugh), although none would have been in color. Not at the turn of the century. Sara Tidwell hadn't just left her mark in old photographs, either. I recalled Dickie Brooks, owner of the All-Purpose Garage, once telling me that his father claimed to have won a teddy bear at the Castle County Fair's shooting-pitch, and to have given it to Sara Tidwell. She had rewarded him, Dickie said, with a kiss. According to Dickie the old man never forgot it, said it was the best kiss of his life . . . although I doubt if he said it in his wife's hearing.

In this photo she was only smiling. Sara Tidwell, known as Sara Laughs. Never recorded, but her songs had lived just the same. One of them, 'Walk Me Baby,' bears a remarkable resemblance to 'Walk This Way,' by Aerosmith. Today the lady would be known as an African-American. In 1984, when Johanna and I bought the lodge and consequently got interested in her, she would have been known as a Black. In her own time she would have been called a Negress or a darkie or possibly an octoroon. And a nigger, of course. There would have been plenty of folks free with that one. And did I believe that she had kissed Dickie Brooks's father – a white man – in front of half of Castle County? No, I did not. Still, who could say for sure? No one. That was the entrancing thing about the past.

'It ain't nuthin but a barn-dance, sugar,' I sang, putting the picture back on the desk. 'It ain't nuthin but a round-and-round.'

I picked up the typewriter cover, then decided to leave it off. As I stood, my eyes went back to Sara, standing there with her eyes closed and the string which served her as a guitar strap visible over one shoulder. Something in her face and smile had always struck me as familiar, and suddenly it came to me. She looked oddly like Robert Johnson, whose primitive licks hid behind the chords of almost every Led Zeppelin and Yardbirds song ever recorded. Who, according to the legend, had gone down to the crossroads and sold his soul to Satan for seven years of fast living, high-tension liquor, and streetlife babies. And for a jukejoint brand of immortality, of course. Which he had gotten. Robert Johnson, supposedly poisoned over a woman.

In the late afternoon I went down to the store and saw a good-looking piece of flounder in the cold-case. It looked like supper to me. I bought a bottle of white wine to go with it, and while I was waiting my turn at the cash register, a trembling old man's voice spoke up behind me. 'See you made a new friend yes'ty.' The Yankee accent was so thick that it sounded almost like a joke . . . except the accent itself is only part of it; mostly, I've come

129

to believe, it's that singsong tone – real Mainers all sound like auctioneers.

I turned and saw the geezer who had been standing out on the garage tarmac the day before, watching along with Dickie Brooks as I got to know Kyra, Mattie, and Scoutie. He still had the gold-headed cane, and I now recognized it. Sometime in the 1950s, the *Boston Post* had donated one of those canes to every county in the New England states. They were given to the oldest residents and passed along from old fart to old fart. And the joke of it was that the *Post* had gone toes-up years ago.

'Actually two new friends,' I replied, trying to dredge up his name. I couldn't, but I remembered him from when Jo had been alive, holding down one of the overstuffed chairs in Dickie's waiting room, discussing weather and politics, politics and weather, as the hammers whanged and the air-compressor chugged. A regular. And if something happened out there on Highway 68, eye-God, he was there to see it.

'I hear Mattie Devore can be quite a dear,' he said – *heah, Devoah, deeah* – and one of his crusty eyelids drooped. I have seen a fair number of salacious winks in my time, but none that was a patch on the one tipped me by that old man with the gold-headed cane. I felt a strong urge to knock his waxy beak of a nose off. The sound of it parting company from his face would be like the crack of a dead branch broken over a bent knee.

'Do you hear a lot, old-timer?' I asked.

'Oh, ayuh!' he said. His lips – dark as strips of liver – parted in a grin. His gums swarmed with white patches. He had a couple of yellow teeth still planted in the top one, and a couple more on the bottom. 'And she gut that little one – cunnin, she is! Ayuh!'

'Cunnin as a cat a-runnin,' I agreed.

He blinked at me, a little surprised to hear such an old one out of my presumably newfangled mouth, and then that reprehensible grin widened. 'Her don't mind her, though,' he said. 'Baby gut the run of the place, don'tcha know.'

I became aware – better belated than never – that half a dozen people were watching and listening to us. 'That wasn't my impression,' I said, raising my voice a bit. 'No, that wasn't my impression at all.'

He only grinned . . . that old man's grin that says *Oh, ayuh, deah; I know one worth two of that.*

I left the store feeling worried for Mattie Devore. Too many people were minding her business, it seemed to me.

When I got home, I took my bottle of wine into the kitchen – it could chill while I got the barbecue going out on the deck. I reached for the fridge door, then paused. Perhaps as many as four dozen little magnets had been scattered randomly across the front – vegetables, fruits, plastic letters and numbers, even a good selection of the California Raisins – but they weren't random anymore. Now they formed a circle on the front of the refrigerator. Someone had been in here. Someone had come in and . . .

Rearranged the magnets on the fridge? If so, that was a burglar who needed to do some heavy remedial work. I touched one of them – gingerly, with just the tip of my finger. Then, suddenly angry with myself, I reached out and spread them again, doing it with enough force to knock a couple to the floor. I didn't pick them up.

That night, before going to bed, I placed the Memo-Scriber on the table beneath Bunter the Great Stuffed Moose, turning it on and putting it in the DICTATE mode. Then I slipped in one of my old home-dubbed cassettes, zeroed the counter, and went to bed, where I slept without dreams or other interruption for eight hours.

The next morning, Monday, was the sort of day the tourists come to Maine for – the air so sunny-clean that the hills across the lake seemed to be under subtle magnification. Mount Washington, New England's highest, floated in the farthest distance.

I put on the coffee, then went into the living room, whistling. All my imaginings of the last few days seemed silly this morning. Then the whistle died away. The Memo-Scriber's counter, set to 000 when I went to bed, was now at 012.

I rewound it, hesitated with my finger over the PLAY button, told myself (in Jo's voice) not to be a fool, and pushed it.

'*Oh Mike,*' a voice whispered – mourned, almost – on the tape, and I found myself having to press the heel of one hand to my mouth to hold back a scream. It was what I had heard in Jo's office when the draft rushed past the sides of my face . . . only now the words were slowed down just enough for me to understand them. '*Oh Mike,*' it said again. There was a faint click. The machine had shut down for some length of time. And then, once more, spoken in the living room as I had slept in the north wing: '*Oh Mike.*'

Then it was gone.

CHAPTER TEN

Around nine o'clock, a pickup came down the driveway and parked behind my Chevrolet. The truck was new – a Dodge Ram so clean and chrome-shiny it looked as if the ten-day plates had just come off that morning – but it was the same shade of off-white as the last one and the sign on the driver's door was the one I remembered: WILLIAM 'BILL' DEAN CAMP CHECKING CARETAKING LIGHT CARPENTRY, plus his telephone number. I went out on the back stoop to meet him, coffee cup in my hand.

'Mike!' Bill cried, climbing down from behind the wheel. Yankee men don't hug – that's a truism you can put right up there with tough guys don't dance and real men don't eat quiche – but Bill pumped my hand almost hard enough to slop coffee from a cup that was three-quarters empty, and gave me a hearty clap on the back. His grin revealed a splendidly blatant set of false teeth – the kind which used to be called Roebuckers, because you got them from the catalogue. It occurred to me in passing that my ancient interlocutor from the Lakeview General Store could have used a pair. It certainly would have improved mealtimes for the nosy old fuck. 'Mike, you're a sight for sore eyes!'

'Good to see you, too,' I said, grinning. Nor was it a false grin; I felt all right. Things with the power to scare the living shit out of you on a thundery midnight in most cases seem only interesting in the bright light of a summer morning. 'You're looking well, my friend.'

It was true. Bill was four years older and a little grayer around the edges, but otherwise the same. Sixty-five? Seventy? It didn't

133

matter. There was no waxy look of ill health about him, and none of the falling-away in the face, principally around the eyes and in the cheeks, that I associate with encroaching infirmity.

'So're you,' he said, letting go of my hand. 'We was all so sorry about Jo, Mike. Folks in town thought the world of her. It was a shock, with her so young. My wife asked if I'd give you her condolences special. Jo made her an afghan the year she had the pneumonia, and Yvette ain't never forgot it.'

'Thanks,' I said, and my voice wasn't quite my own for a moment or two. It seemed that in the TR my wife was hardly dead at all. 'And thank Yvette, too.'

'Yuh. Everythin okay with the house? Other'n the air conditioner, I mean. Buggardly thing! Them at the Western Auto promised me that part last week, and now they're saying maybe not until August first.'

'It's okay. I've got my PowerBook. If I want to use it, the kitchen table will do fine for a desk.' And I *would* want to use it – so many crosswords, so little time.

'Got your hot water okay?'

'All that's fine, but there is one problem.'

I stopped. How did you tell your caretaker you thought your house was haunted? Probably there was no good way; probably the best thing to do was to go at it head-on. I had questions, but I didn't want just to nibble around the edges of the subject and be coy. For one thing, Bill would sense it. He might have bought his false teeth out of a catalogue, but he wasn't stupid.

'What's on your mind, Mike? Shoot.'

'I don't know how you're going to take this, but—'

He smiled in the way of a man who suddenly understands and held up his hand. 'Guess maybe I know already.'

'You do?' I felt an enormous sense of relief, and I could hardly wait to find out what he had experienced in Sara, perhaps while checking for dead lightbulbs or making sure the roof was holding the snow all right. 'What did *you* hear?'

'Mostly what Royce Merrill and Dickie Brooks have been telling,' he said. 'Beyond that, I don't know much. Me and Mother's been in Virginia, remember. Only got back last night around eight o'clock. Still, it's the big topic down to the store.'

For a moment I remained so fixed on Sara Laughs that I had no idea what he was talking about. All I could think was that folks were gossiping about the strange noises in my house. Then the name Royce Merrill clicked and everything else clicked with it. Merrill was the elderly possum with the gold-headed cane and the salacious wink. Old Four-Teeth. My caretaker wasn't talking about ghostly noises; he was talking about Mattie Devore.

'Let's get you a cup of coffee,' I said. 'I need you to tell me what I'm stepping in here.'

When we were seated on the deck, me with fresh coffee and Bill with a cup of tea ('Coffee burns me at both ends these days,' he said), I asked him first to tell me the Royce Merrill–Dickie Brooks version of my encounter with Mattie and Kyra.

It turned out to be better than I had expected. Both old men had seen me standing at the side of the road with the little girl in my arms, and they had observed my Chevy parked halfway into the ditch with the driver's side door open, but apparently neither of them had seen Kyra using the white line of Route 68 as a tightrope. As if to compensate for this, however, Royce claimed that Mattie had given me a big *my hero* hug and a kiss on the mouth.

'Did he get the part about how I grabbed her by the ass and slipped her some tongue?' I asked.

Bill grinned. 'Royce's imagination ain't stretched that far since he was fifty or so, and that was forty or more year ago.'

'I never touched her.' Well . . . there had been that moment when the back of my hand went sliding along the curve of her breast, but that had been inadvertent, whatever the young lady herself might think about it.

'Shite, you don't need to tell me that,' he said. '*But . . .*'

He said that *but* the way my mother always had, letting it trail off on its own, like the tail of some ill-omened kite.

'But what?'

'You'd do well to keep your distance from her,' he said. 'She's nice enough – almost a town girl, don't you know – but she's trouble.' He paused. 'No, that ain't quite fair to her. She's *in* trouble.'

'The old man wants custody of the baby, doesn't he?'

Bill set his teacup down on the deck rail and looked at me with

135

his eyebrows raised. Reflections from the lake ran up his cheek in ripples, giving him an exotic look. 'How'd you know?'

'Guesswork, but of the educated variety. Her father-in-law called me Saturday night during the fireworks. And while he never came right out and stated his purpose, I doubt if Max Devore came all the way back to TR-90 in western Maine to repo his daughter-in-law's Jeep and trailer. So what's the story, Bill?'

For several moments he only looked at me. It was almost the look of a man who knows you have contracted a serious disease and isn't sure how much he ought to tell you. Being looked at that way made me profoundly uneasy. It also made me feel that I might be putting Bill Dean on the spot. Devore had roots here, after all. And, as much as Bill might like me, I didn't. Jo and I were from away. It could have been worse – it could have been Massachusetts or New York – but Derry, although in Maine, was still away.

'Bill? I could use a little navigational help if you—'

'You want to stay out of his way,' he said. His easy smile was gone. 'The man's mad.'

For a moment I thought Bill only meant Devore was pissed off at me, and then I took another look at his face. No, I decided, he didn't mean pissed off; he had used the word 'mad' in the most literal way.

'Mad how?' I asked. 'Mad like Charles Manson? Like Hannibal Lecter? How?'

'Say like Howard Hughes,' he said. 'Ever read any of the stories about him? The lengths he'd go to to get the things he wanted? It didn't matter if it was a special kind of hot dog they only sold in L.A. or an airplane designer he wanted to steal from Lockheed or McDonnell-Douglas, he had to have what he wanted, and he wouldn't rest until it was under his hand. Devore is the same way. He always was – even as a boy he was willful, according to the stories you hear in town.

'My own dad had one he used to tell. He said little Max Devore broke into Scant Larribee's tack-shed one winter because he wanted the Flexible Flyer Scant give his boy Scooter for Christmas. Back around 1923, this would have been. Devore cut both his hands on broken glass, Dad said, but he got the sled. They found him near midnight, sliding down Sugar Maple Hill, holding his hands up to his chest when he went down. He'd bled all over his mittens and his snowsuit. There's other stories you'll hear about Maxie Devore as a kid – if you ask you'll hear fifty different ones – and some may even be true. That one about the sled *is* true, though. I'd bet the farm on it. Because my father didn't lie. It was against his religion.'

'Baptist?'

'Nosir, Yankee.'

'1923 was many moons ago, Bill. Sometimes people change.'

'Ayuh, but mostly they don't. I haven't seen Devore since he come back and moved into Warrington's, so I can't say for sure, but I've heard things that make me think that if he *has* changed, it's for the worse. He didn't come all the way across the country 'cause he wanted a vacation. He wants the *kid*. To him she's just another version of Scooter Larribee's Flexible Flyer. And my strong advice to you is that you don't want to be the window-glass between him and her.'

I sipped my coffee and looked out at the lake. Bill gave me time to think, scraping one of his workboots across a splatter of birdshit on the boards while I did it. Crowshit, I reckoned; only crows crap in such long and exuberant splatters.

One thing seemed absolutely sure: Mattie Devore was roughly nine miles up Shit Creek with no paddle. I'm not the cynic I was at twenty – is anyone? – but I wasn't naïve enough or idealistic enough to believe the law would protect Ms Doublewide against Mr Computer . . . not if Mr Computer decided to play dirty. As a boy he'd taken the sled he wanted and gone sliding by himself at midnight, bleeding hands not a concern. And as a man? An old man who had been getting every sled he wanted for the last forty years or so?

'What's the story with Mattie, Bill? Tell me.'

It didn't take him long. Country stories are, by and large, simple stories. Which isn't to say they're not often interesting.

Mattie Devore had started life as Mattie Stanchfield, not quite from the TR but from just over the line in Motton. Her father had been a logger, her mother a home beautician (which made it, in a ghastly way, the perfect country marriage). There were three kids. When Dave Stanchfield missed a curve over in Lovell and drove a fully loaded pulptruck into Kewadin Pond, his widow 'kinda lost heart,' as they say. She died soon after. There had been no insurance, other than what Stanchfield had been obliged to carry on his Jimmy and his skidder.

Talk about your Brothers Grimm, huh? Subtract the Fisher-Price toys behind the house, the two pole hairdryers in the basement beauty salon, the old rustbucket Toyota in the driveway, and you were right there: *Once upon a time there lived a poor widow and her three children.*

Mattie is the princess of the piece – poor but beautiful (that she *was* beautiful I could personally testify). Now enter the prince. In this case he's a gangly stuttering redhead named Lance Devore. The child of Max Devore's sunset years. When Lance met Mattie, he was twenty-one. She had just turned seventeen. The meeting took place at Warrington's, where Mattie had landed a summer job as a waitress.

Lance Devore was staying across the lake on the Upper Bay, but on Tuesday nights there were pickup softball games at Warrington's, the townies against the summer folks, and he usually canoed across to play. Softball is a great thing for the Lance Devores of the world; when you're standing at the plate with a bat in your hands, it doesn't matter if you're gangly. And it sure doesn't matter if you stutter.

'He confused em quite considerable over to Warrington's,' Bill said. 'They didn't know which team he belonged on – the Locals or the Aways. Lance didn't care; either side was fine with him. Some weeks he'd play for one, some weeks t'other. Either one was more than happy to have him, too, as he could hit a ton and field like an angel. They'd put him at first base a lot because he was tall, but he was really wasted there. At second or shortstop . . . my! He'd jump and twirl around like that guy Noriega.'

'You might mean Nureyev,' I said.

He shrugged. 'Point is, he was somethin to see. And folks liked him. He fit in. It's mostly young folks that play, you know, and to them it's how you do, not who you are. Besides, a lot of em don't know Max Devore from a hole in the ground.'

'Unless they read *The Wall Street Journal* and the computer magazines,' I said. 'In those, you run across the name Devore about as often as you run across the name of God in the Bible.'

'No foolin?'

'Well, I guess that in the computer magazines God is more often spelled Gates, but you know what I mean.'

'I s'pose. But even so, it's been sixty-five years since Max Devore spent any real time in the TR. You know what happened when he left, don't you?'

'No, why would I?'

He looked at me, surprised. Then a kind of veil seemed to fall over his eyes. He blinked and it cleared. 'Tell you another time – it ain't no secret – but I need to be over to the Harrimans' by eleven to check their sump-pump. Don't want to get sidetracked. Point I was tryin to make is just this: Lance Devore was accepted as a nice young fella who could hit a softball three hundred and fifty feet into the trees if he struck it just right. There was no one old enough to hold his old man against him – not at Warrington's on Tuesday nights, there wasn't – and no one held it against him that his family had dough, either. Hell, there are lots of wealthy people here in the summer. You know that. None worth as much as Max Devore, but bein rich is only a matter of degree.'

That wasn't true, and I had just enough money to know it. Wealth is like the Richter scale – once you pass a certain point, the jumps from one level to the next aren't double or triple but some amazing and ruinous multiple you don't even want to think about. Fitzgerald had it straight, although I guess he didn't believe his own insight: the very rich *are* different from you and me. I thought of telling Bill that, and decided to keep my mouth shut. He had a sump-pump to fix.

Kyra's parents met over a keg of beer stuck in a mudhole. Mattie was running the usual Tuesday-night keg out to the softball field from the main building on a handcart. She'd gotten it most of the way from the restaurant wing with no trouble, but there had been heavy rain earlier in the week, and the cart finally bogged down in a soft spot. Lance's team was up, and Lance was sitting at the end of the bench, waiting his turn to hit. He saw the girl in the white shorts and blue Warrington's polo shirt struggling with the bogged handcart, and got up to help her. Three weeks later they were inseparable and Mattie was pregnant; ten weeks later they were married; thirty-seven months later, Lance Devore was in a coffin, done with softball and cold beer on a summer evening, done with what he called 'woodsing,' done with fatherhood, done with love for the beautiful princess. Just another early finish, hold the happily ever after.

Bill Dean didn't describe their meeting in any detail; he only said, 'They met at the field – she was runnin out the beer and he helped her out of a boghole when she got her handcart stuck.'

Mattie never said much about that part of it, so I don't know much. Except I do ... and although some of the details might be wrong, I'd bet you a dollar to a hundred I got most of them right. That was my summer for knowing things I had no business knowing.

It's hot, for one thing – '94 is the hottest summer of the decade and July is the hottest month of the summer. President Clinton is being upstaged by Newt and the Republicans. Folks are saying old Slick Willie may not even run for a second term. Boris Yeltsin is reputed to be either dying of heart disease or in a dry-out clinic. The Red Sox are looking better than they have any right to. In Derry, Johanna Arlen Noonan is maybe starting to feel a little whoopsy in the morning. If so, she does not speak of it to her husband.

I see Mattie in her blue polo shirt with her name sewn in white script above her left breast. Her white shorts make a pleasing contrast to her tanned legs. I also see her wearing a blue gimme cap with the red *W* for Warrington's above the long bill. Her pretty dark-blonde hair is pulled through the hole at the back of the cap and falls to the collar of her shirt. I see her trying to yank the handcart out of the mud without upsetting the keg of beer. Her head is down; the shadow thrown by the bill of the cap obscures all of her face but her mouth and small set chin.

'Luh–let m–me h–h–help,' Lance says, and she looks up. The shadow cast by the cap's bill falls away, he sees her big blue eyes – the ones she'll pass on to their daughter. One look into those eyes and the war is over without a single shot fired; he belongs to her as surely as any young man ever belonged to any young woman.

The rest, as they say around here, was just courtin.

The old man had three children, but Lance was the only one he seemed to care about. ('Daughter's crazier'n a shithouse mouse,' Bill said matter-of-factly. 'In some laughin academy in Washington State. Think I heard she caught her a cancer, too.') The fact that Lance had no interest in computers and software actually seemed to please his

140

father. He had another son who was capable of running the business. In another way, however, Lance Devore's older half-brother wasn't capable at all: there would be no grandchildren from that one.

'Rump-wrangler,' Bill said. 'Understand there's a lot of that goin around out there in California.'

There was a fair amount of it going around on the TR, too, I imagined, but thought it not my place to offer sexual instruction to my caretaker.

Lance Devore had been attending Reed College in Oregon, majoring in forestry – the kind of guy who falls in love with green flannel pants, red suspenders, and the sight of condors at dawn. A Brothers Grimm woodcutter, in fact, once you got past the academic jargon. In the summer between his junior and senior years, his father had summoned him to the family compound in Palm Springs, and had presented him with a boxy lawyer's suitcase crammed with maps, aerial photos, and legal papers. These had little order that Lance could see, but I doubt that he cared. Imagine a comic-book collector given a crate crammed with rare old copies of *Donald Duck*. Imagine a movie collector given the rough cut of a never-released film starring Humphrey Bogart and Marilyn Monroe. Then imagine this avid young forester realizing that his father owned not just acres or square miles in the vast unincorporated forests of western Maine, but entire *realms*.

Although Max Devore had left the TR in 1933, he'd kept a lively interest in the area where he'd grown up, subscribing to area newspapers and getting magazines such as *Down East* and *The Maine Times*. In the early eighties, he had begun to buy long columns of land just east of the Maine–New Hampshire border. God knew there had been plenty for sale; the paper companies which owned most of it had fallen into a recessionary pit, and many had become convinced that their New England holdings and operations would be the best place to begin retrenching. So this land, stolen from the Indians and clear-cut ruthlessly in the twenties and fifties, came into Max Devore's hands. He might have bought it just because it was there, a good bargain he could afford to take advantage of. He might have bought it as a way of demonstrating to himself that he had really survived his childhood; had, in point of fact, triumphed over it.

Or he might have bought it as a toy for his beloved younger son.

141

In the years when Devore was making his major land purchases in western Maine, Lance would have been just a kid . . . but old enough for a perceptive father to see where his interests were tending.

Devore asked Lance to spend the summer of 1994 surveying purchases which were, for the most part, already ten years old. He wanted the boy to put the paperwork in order, but he wanted more than that – he wanted Lance to make sense of it. It wasn't a land-use recommendation he was looking for, exactly, although I guess he would have listened if Lance had wanted to make one; he simply wanted a sense of what he had purchased. Would Lance take a summer in western Maine trying to find out what *his* sense of it was? At a salary of two or three thousand dollars a month?

I imagine Lance's reply was a more polite version of Buddy Jellison's 'Does a crow shit in the pine tops?'

The kid arrived in June of 1994 and set up shop in a tent on the far side of Dark Score Lake. He was due back at Reed in late August. Instead, though, he decided to take a year's leave of absence. His father wasn't pleased. His father smelled what he called 'girl trouble.'

'Yeah, but it's a damned long sniff from California to Maine,' Bill Dean said, leaning against the driver's door of his truck with his sunburned arms folded. 'He had someone a lot closer than Palm Springs doin his sniffin for him.'

'What are you talking about?' I asked.

''Bout *talk*. People do it for free, and most are willing to do even more if they're paid.'

'People like Royce Merrill?'

'Royce might be one,' he agreed, 'but he wouldn't be the only one. Times around here don't go between bad and good; if you're a local, they mostly go between bad and worse. So when a guy like Max Devore sends a guy out with a supply of fifty- and hundred-dollar bills . . .'

'Was it someone local? A lawyer?'

Not a lawyer; a real estate broker named Richard Osgood ('a greasy kind of fella' was Bill Dean's judgment of him) who denned and did business in Motton. Eventually Osgood *had* hired a lawyer from Castle Rock. The greasy fella's initial job, when the summer of '94 ended and Lance Devore remained in the

142

TR, was to find out what the hell was going on and put a stop to it.

'And then?' I asked.

Bill glanced at his watch, glanced at the sky, then centered his gaze on me. He gave a funny little shrug, as if to say, 'We're both men of the world, in a quiet and settled sort of way – you don't need to ask a silly question like that.'

'Then Lance Devore and Mattie Stanchfield got married in the Grace Baptist Church right up there on Highway 68. There were tales made the rounds about what Osgood might've done to keep it from comin off – I heard he even tried to bribe Reverend Gooch into refusin to hitch em, but I think that's stupid, they just would have gone someplace else. 'Sides, I don't see much sense in repeating what I don't know for sure.'

Bill unfolded an arm, and began to tick items off on the leathery fingers of his right hand.

'They got married in the middle of September, 1995, I know that.' Out popped the thumb. 'People looked around with some curiosity to see if the groom's father would put in an appearance, but he never did.' Out popped the forefinger. Added to the thumb, it made a pistol. 'Mattie had a baby in April of '95, making the kiddie a dight premature . . . but not enough to matter. I seen it in the store with my own eyes when it wasn't a week old, and it was just the right size.' Out with the second finger. 'I don't know that Lance Devore's old man absolutely refused to help em financially, but I *do* know they were living in that trailer down below Dickie's Garage, and that makes me think they were havin a pretty hard skate.'

'Devore put on the choke-chain,' I said. 'It's what a guy used to getting his own way would do . . . but if he loved the boy the way you seem to think, he might have come around.'

'Maybe, maybe not.' He glanced at his watch again. 'Let me finish up quick and get out of your sunshine . . . but you ought to hear one more little story, because it really shows how the land lies.

'In July of last year, less'n a month before he died, Lance Devore shows up at the post office counter in the Lakeview General. He's got a manila envelope he wants to send, but first he needs to show Carla DeCinces what's inside. She said he was all fluffed out, like daddies sometimes get over their kids when they're small.'

143

I nodded, amused at the idea of skinny, stuttery Lance Devore all fluffed out. But I could see it in my mind's eye, and the image was also sort of sweet.

'It was a studio pitcher they'd gotten taken over in the Rock. Showed the kid . . . what's her name? Kayla?'

'Kyra.'

'Ayuh, they call em anything these days, don't they? It showed Kyra sittin in a big leather chair, with a pair of joke spectacles on her little snub of a nose, lookin at one of the aerial photos of the woods over across the lake in TR-100 or TR-110 – part of what the old man had picked up, anyway. Carla said the baby had a surprised look on her face, as if she hadn't suspected there could be so much woods in the whole world. Said it was *awful* cunnin, she did.'

'Cunnin as a cat a-runnin,' I murmured.

'And the envelope – Registered, Express Mail – was addressed to Maxwell Devore, in Palm Springs, California.'

'Leading you to deduce that the old man either thawed enough to ask for a picture of his only grandchild, or that Lance Devore thought a picture *might* thaw him.'

Bill nodded, looking as pleased as a parent whose child has managed a difficult sum. 'Don't know if it did,' he said. 'Wasn't enough time to tell, one way or the other. Lance had bought one of those little satellite dishes, like what you've got here. There was a bad storm the day he put it up – hail, high wind, blowdowns along the lakeshore, lots of lightnin. That was along toward evening. Lance put his dish up in the afternoon, all done and safe, except around the time the storm commenced he remembered he'd left his socket wrench on the trailer roof. He went up to get it so it wouldn't get all wet n rusty—'

'He was struck by lightning? Jesus, Bill!'

'Lightnin struck, all right, but it hit across the way. You go past the place where Wasp Hill Road runs into 68 and you'll see the stump of the tree that stroke knocked over. Lance was comin down the ladder with his socket wrench when it hit. If you've never had a lightnin bolt tear right over your head, you don't know how scary it is – it's like havin a drunk driver veer across into your lane, headed right for you, and then swing back on to his own side just in time. Close lightnin makes your hair stand up – makes your damned *prick*

144

stand up. It's apt to play the radio on your steel fillins, it makes your ears hum, and it makes the air taste roasted. Lance fell off the ladder. If he had time to think anything before he hit the ground, I bet he thought he *was* electrocuted. Poor boy. He loved the TR, but it wasn't lucky for him.'

'Broke his neck?'

'Ayuh. With all the thunder, Mattie never heard him fall or yell or anything. She looked out a minute or two later when it started to hail and he still wasn't in. And there he was, layin on the ground and lookin up into the friggin hail with his eyes open.'

Bill looked at his watch one final time, then swung open the door to his truck. 'The old man wouldn't come for their weddin, but he came for his son's funeral and he's been here ever since. He didn't want nawthin to do with the young woman—'

'But he wants the kid,' I said. It was no more than what I already knew, but I felt a sinking in the pit of my stomach just the same. *Don't talk about this*, Mattie had asked me on the morning of the Fourth. *It's not a good time for Ki and me.* 'How far along in the process has he gotten?'

'On the third turn and headin into the home stretch, I sh'd say. There'll be a hearin in Castle County Superior Court, maybe later this month, maybe next. The judge could rule then to hand the girl over, or put it off until fall. I don't think it matters which, because the one thing that's never going to happen on God's green earth is a rulin in favor of the mother. One way or another, that little girl is goin to grow up in California.'

Put that way, it gave me a very nasty little chill.

Bill slid behind the wheel of his truck. 'Stay out of it, Mike,' he said. 'Stay away from Mattie Devore and her daughter. And if you get called to court on account of seein the two of em on Saturday, smile a lot and say as little as you can.'

'Max Devore's charging that she's unfit to raise the child.'

'Ayuh.'

'Bill, I *saw* the child, and she's fine.'

He grinned again, but this time there was no amusement in it. ''Magine she is. But that's not the point. Stay clear of their business, old boy. It's my job to tell you that; with Jo gone, I guess I'm the only caretaker you got.' He slammed the door of his Ram, started the engine, reached for the gearshift, then dropped his hand again as something else occurred to him. 'If you get a chance, you ought to look for the owls.'

'What owls?'

'There's a couple of plastic owls around here someplace. They might be in y'basement or out in Jo's studio. They come in by mail-order the fall before she passed on.'

'The fall of 1993?'

'Ayuh.'

'That can't be right.' We hadn't used Sara in the fall of 1993.

''Tis, though. I was down here puttin on the storm doors when Jo showed up. We had us a natter, and then the UPS truck come. I lugged the box into the entry and had a coffee – I was still drinkin it then – while she took the owls out of the carton and showed em off to me. Gorry, but they looked real! She left not ten minutes after. It was like she'd come down to do that errand special, although why anyone'd drive all the way from Derry to take delivery of a couple of plastic owls I don't know.'

'When in the fall was it, Bill? Do you remember?'

'Second week of November,' he said promptly. 'Me n the wife went up to Lewiston later that afternoon, to 'Vette's sister's. It was her birthday. On our way back we stopped at the Castle Rock Agway so 'Vette could get her Thanksgiving turkey.' He looked at me curiously. 'You really didn't know about them owls?'

'No.'

'That's a touch peculiar, wouldn't you say?'

'Maybe she told me and I forgot,' I said. 'I guess it doesn't matter much now in any case.' Yet it seemed to matter. It was a small thing, but it seemed to matter. 'Why would Jo want a couple of plastic owls to begin with?'

'To keep the crows from shittin up the woodwork, like they're doing out on your deck. Crows see those plastic owls, they veer off.'

I burst out laughing in spite of my puzzlement . . . or perhaps because of it. 'Yeah? That really works?'

'Ayuh, long's you move em every now and then so the crows don't get suspicious. Crows are just about the smartest birds going, you know. You look for those owls, save yourself a lot of mess.'

'I will,' I said. Plastic owls to scare the crows away – it was exactly the sort of knowledge Jo would come by (she was like a crow herself in that way, picking up glittery pieces of information that happened to catch her interest) and act upon without bothering to tell me. All at once I was lonely for her again – missing her like hell.

'Good. Some day when I've got more time, we'll walk the place all the way around. Woods too, if you want. I think you'll be satisfied.'

'I'm sure I will. Where's Devore staying?'

The bushy eyebrows went up. 'Warrington's. Him and you's practically neighbors. I thought you must know.'

I remembered the woman I'd seen – black bathing suit and black shorts somehow combining to give her an exotic cocktail-party look – and nodded. 'I met his wife.'

Bill laughed heartily enough at that to feel in need of his handkerchief. He fished it off the dashboard (a blue paisley thing the size of a football pennant) and wiped his eyes.

'What's so funny?' I asked.

'Skinny woman? White hair? Face sort of like a kid's Halloween mask?'

It was my turn to laugh. 'That's her.'

'She ain't his wife, she's his whatdoyoucallit, personal assistant. Rogette Whitmore is her name.' He pronounced it ro-GET, with a hard G. 'Devore's wives're all dead. The last one twenty years.'

'What kind of name is Rogette? French?'

'California,' he said, and shrugged as if that one word explained everything. 'There's people in town scared of her.'

'Is that so?'

'Ayuh.' Bill hesitated, then added with one of those smiles we put on when we want others to know that *we* know we're saying something silly: 'Brenda Meserve says she's a witch.'

'And the two of them have been staying at Warrington's almost a year?'

"Ayuh. The Whitmore woman comes n goes, but mostly she's been here. Thinkin in town is that they'll stay until the custody case is finished off, then all go back to California on Devore's private jet. Leave Osgood to sell Warrington's, and—'

'Sell it? What do you mean, *sell* it?'

147

'I thought you must know,' Bill said, dropping his gearshift into drive. 'When old Hugh Emerson told Devore they closed the lodge after Thanksgiving, Devore told him he had no intention of moving. Said he was comfortable where he was and meant to stay put.'

'He bought the place.' I had been by turns surprised, amused, and angered over the last twenty minutes, but never exactly dumb-founded. Now I was. 'He bought Warrington's Lodge so he wouldn't have to move to Lookout Rock Hotel over in Castle View, or rent a house.'

'Ayuh, so he did. Nine buildins, includin the main lodge and The Sunset Bar; twelve acres of woods, a six-hole golf course, and five hundred feet of shorefront on The Street. Plus a two-lane bowlin alley and a softball field. Four and a quarter million. His friend Osgood did the deal and Devore paid with a personal check. I wonder how he found room for all those zeros. See you, Mike.'

With that he backed up the driveway, leaving me to stand on the stoop, looking after him with my mouth open.

Plastic owls.

Bill had told me roughly two dozen interesting things in between peeks at his watch, but the one which stayed on top of the pile was the fact (and I did accept it as a fact; he had been too positive for me not to) that Jo had come down here to take delivery on a couple of plastic goddam owls.

Had she told me?

She might have. I didn't remember her doing so, and it seemed to me that I would have, but Jo used to claim that when I got in the zone it was no good to tell me anything; stuff went in one ear and out the other. Sometimes she'd pin little notes – errands to run, calls to make – to my shirt, as if I were a first-grader. But wouldn't I recall if she'd said 'I'm going down to Sara, hon, UPS is delivering something I want to receive personally, interested in keeping a lady company?' Hell, wouldn't I have *gone*? I always liked an excuse to go to the TR. Except I'd been writing and maybe pushing it a little . . . notes pinned to the sleeve of my shirt . . . *If you go out when you're finished, we need milk and orange juice . . .*

I inspected what little was left of Jo's vegetable garden with July sun beating down on my neck and thought about the owls, the plastic goddam owls. Suppose Jo *had* told me she was coming down here to Sara Laughs? Suppose I had declined almost without hearing the offer because I was in the writing zone? Even if you granted those things, there was another question: why had she felt the need to come down here personally when she could have just called someone and asked them to meet the delivery truck? Kenny Auster would have been happy to do it, ditto Mrs M. And Bill Dean, our caretaker, had actually been here. This led to other questions – one was why she hadn't just had UPS deliver the damned things to Derry – and finally I decided I couldn't live without actually seeing a bona fide plastic owl for myself. Maybe, I thought, going back to the house, I'd put one on the roof of my Chevy when it was parked in the driveway. Forestall future bombing runs.

I paused in the entry, struck by a sudden idea, and called Ward Hankins, the guy in Waterville who handles my taxes and my few non-writing-related business affairs.

'Mike!' he said heartily. 'How's the lake?'

'The lake's cool and the weather's hot, just the way we like it,' I said. 'Ward, you keep all the records we send you for five years, don't you? Just in case IRS decides to give us some grief?'

'Five is accepted practice,' he said, 'but I hold your stuff for seven – in the eyes of the tax boys, you're a mighty fat pigeon.'

Better a fat pigeon than a plastic owl, I thought but didn't say. What I said was, 'That includes desk calendars, right? Mine and Jo's, up until she died?'

'You bet. Since neither of you kept diaries, it was the best way to cross-reference receipts and claimed expenses with—'

'Could you find Jo's desk calendar for 1993 and see what she had going in the second week of November?'

'I'd be happy to. What in particular are you looking for?'

For a moment I saw myself sitting at my kitchen table in Derry on my first night as a widower, holding up a box with the words Norco Home Pregnancy Test printed on the side. Exactly what *was* I looking for at this late date? Considering that I had loved the lady and she was almost four years in her grave, what *was* I looking for? Besides trouble, that was?

'I'm looking for two plastic owls,' I said. Ward probably thought

I was talking to him, but I'm not sure I was. 'I know that sounds weird, but it's what I'm doing. Can you call me back?'

'Within the hour.'

'Good man,' I said, and hung up.

Now for the actual owls themselves. Where was the most likely spot to store two such interesting artifacts?

My eyes went to the cellar door. Elementary, my dear Watson.

The cellar stairs were dark and mildly dank. As I stood on the landing groping for the lightswitch, the door banged shut behind me with such force that I cried out in surprise. There was no breeze, no draft, the day was perfectly still, but the door banged shut just the same. Or was sucked shut.

I stood in the dark at the top of the stairs, feeling for the lightswitch, smelling that oozy smell that even good concrete foundations get after awhile if there is no proper airing-out. It was cold, much colder than it had been on the other side of the door. I wasn't alone and I knew it. I was afraid, I'd be a liar to say I wasn't . . . but I was also fascinated. Something was with me. *Something was in here with me.*

I dropped my hand away from the wall where the switch was and just stood with my arms at my sides. Some time passed. I don't know how much. My heart was beating furiously in my chest; I could feel it in my temples. It was cold. 'Hello?' I asked.

Nothing in response. I could hear the faint, irregular drip of water as condensation fell from one of the pipes down below, I could hear my own breathing, and faintly – far away, in another world where the sun was out – I could hear the triumphant caw of a crow. Perhaps it had just dropped a load on the hood of my car. *I really need an owl,* I thought. *In fact, I don't know how I ever got along without one.*

'Hello?' I asked again. 'Can you talk?'

Nothing.

I wet my lips. I should have felt silly, perhaps, standing there in the dark and calling to the ghosts. But I didn't. Not a bit. The damp had been replaced by a coldness I could feel, and I had company. Oh, yes. 'Can you tap, then? If you can shut the door, you must be able to tap.'

I stood there and listened to the isolated drips from the pipes.

There was nothing else. I was reaching out for the lightswitch again when there was a soft thud from not far below me. The cellar of Sara Laughs is high, and the upper three feet of the concrete – the part which lies against the ground's frost-belt – had been insulated with big silver-backed panels of Insu-Gard. The sound that I heard was, I am quite sure, a fist striking against one of these.

Just a fist hitting a square of insulation, but every gut and muscle of my body seemed to come unwound. My hair stood up. My eyesockets seemed to be expanding and my eyeballs contracting, as if my head were trying to turn into a skull. Every inch of my skin broke out in gooseflesh. Something was in here with me. Very likely something dead. I could no longer have turned on the light if I'd wanted to. I no longer had the strength to raise my arm.

I tried to talk, and at last, in a husky whisper I hardly recognized, I said: 'Are you really there?'

Thud.

'Who are you?' I could still do no better than that husky whisper, the voice of a man giving last instructions to his family as he lies on his deathbed. This time there was nothing from below.

I tried to think, and what came to my struggling mind was Tony Curtis as Harry Houdini in some old movie. According to the film, Houdini had been the Diogenes of the Ouija board circuit, a guy who spent his spare time just looking for an honest medium. He'd attended one séance where the dead communicated by—

'Tap once for yes, twice for no,' I said. 'Can you do that?'

Thud.

It was on the stairs below me . . . but not *too* far below. Five steps down, six or seven at most. Not quite close enough to touch if I should reach out and wave my hand in the black basement air . . . a thing I could imagine, but not actually imagine doing.

'Are you . . .' My voice trailed off. There was simply no strength in my diaphragm. Chilly air lay on my chest like a flatiron. I gathered all my will and tried again. 'Are you Jo?'

Thud. That soft fist on the insulation. A pause, and then: *Thud-thud*.

Yes and no.

Then, with no idea why I was asking such an inane question: 'Are the owls down here?'

151

Thud-thud.

'Do you know where they are?'

Thud.

'Should I look for them?'

Thud! Very hard.

Why did she want them? I could ask, but the thing on the stairs had no way to an—

Hot fingers touched my eyes and I almost screamed before realizing it was sweat. I raised my hands in the dark and wiped the heels of them up my face to the hairline. They skidded as if on oil. Cold or not, I was all but bathing in my own sweat.

'Are you Lance Devore?'

Thud-thud, at once.

'Is it safe for me at Sara? Am I safe?'

Thud. A pause. And I *knew* it was a pause, that the thing on the stairs wasn't finished. Then: *Thud-thud.* Yes, I was safe. No, I wasn't safe.

I had regained marginal control of my arm. I reached out, felt along the wall, and found the lightswitch. I settled my fingers on it. Now the sweat on my face felt as if it were turning to ice.

'Are you the person who cries in the night?' I asked.

Thud-thud from below me, and between the two thuds, I flicked the switch. The cellar globes came on. So did a brilliant hanging bulb – at least a hundred and twenty-five watts – over the landing. There was no time for anyone to hide, let alone get away, and no one there to try, either. Also, Mrs Meserve – admirable in so many ways – had neglected to sweep the cellar stairs. When I went down to where I estimated the thudding sounds had been coming from, I left tracks in the light dust. But mine were the only ones.

I blew out breath in front of me and could see it. So it *had* been cold, still *was* cold . . . but it was warming up fast. I blew out another breath and could see just a hint of fog. A third exhale and there was nothing.

I ran my palm over one of the insulated squares. Smooth. I pushed a finger at it, and although I didn't push with any real force, my finger left a dimple in the silvery surface. Easy as pie. If someone had been thumping a fist down here, this stuff should be pitted, the thin silver

152

skin perhaps even broken to reveal the pink fill underneath. But all the squares were smooth.

'Are you still there?' I asked.

No response, and yet I had a sense that my visitor *was* still there. Somewhere.

'I hope I didn't offend you by turning on the light,' I said, and now I did feel slightly odd, standing on my cellar stairs and talking out loud, sermonizing to the spiders. 'I wanted to see you if I could.' I had no idea if that was true or not.

Suddenly – so suddenly I almost lost my balance and tumbled down the stairs – I whirled around, convinced the shroud-creature was behind me, that it had been the thing knocking, *it*, no polite M. R. James ghost but a horror from around the rim of the universe.

There was nothing.

I turned around again, took two or three deep, steadying breaths, and then went the rest of the way down the cellar stairs. Beneath them was a perfectly serviceable canoe, complete with paddle. In the corner was the gas stove we'd replaced after buying the place; also the claw-foot tub Jo had wanted (over my objections) to turn into a planter. I found a trunk filled with vaguely recalled table-linen, a box of mildewy cassette tapes (groups like the Delfonics, Funkadelic, and .38 Special), several cartons of old dishes. There was a life down here, but ultimately not a very interesting one. Unlike the life I'd sensed in Jo's studio, this one hadn't been cut short but evolved out of, shed like old skin, and that was all right. Was, in fact, the natural order of things.

There was a photo album on a shelf of knickknacks and I took it down, both curious and wary. No bombshells this time, however; nearly all the pix were landscape shots of Sara Laughs as it had been when we bought it. I found a picture of Jo in bellbottoms, though (her hair parted in the middle and white lipstick on her mouth), and one of Michael Noonan wearing a flowered shirt and muttonchop sideburns that made me cringe (the bachelor Mike in the photo was a Barry White kind of guy I didn't want to recognize and yet did).

I found Jo's old broken treadmill, a rake I'd want if I was still around here come fall, a snowblower I'd want even more if I was around come winter, and several cans of paint. What I didn't find was any plastic owls. My insulation-thumping pal had been right.

Upstairs the telephone started ringing.

I hurried to answer it, going out through the cellar door and *then* reaching back in to flick off the lightswitch. This amused me and at the same time seemed like perfectly normal behavior . . . just as being careful not to step on sidewalk cracks had seemed like perfectly normal behavior to me when I was a kid. And even if it wasn't normal, what did it matter? I'd only been back at Sara for three days, but already I'd postulated Noonan's First Law of Eccentricity: when you're on your own, strange behavior really doesn't seem strange at all.

I snagged the cordless. 'Hello?'

'Hi, Mike. It's Ward.'

'That was quick.'

'The file-room's just a short walk down the hall,' he said. 'Easy as pie. There's only one thing on Jo's calendar for the second week of November in 1993. It says "S-Ks of Maine, Freep, 11 A.M." That's on Tuesday the sixteenth. Does it help?'

'Yes,' I said. 'Thank you, Ward. It helps a lot.'

I broke the connection and put the phone back in its cradle. Yes, it helped. S-Ks of Maine was Soup Kitchens of Maine. Jo had been on their board of directors from 1992 until her death. Freep was Freeport. It must have been a board meeting. They had probably discussed plans for feeding the homeless on Thanksgiving . . . and then Jo had driven the seventy or so miles to the TR in order to take delivery of two plastic owls. It didn't answer all the questions, but aren't there always questions in the wake of a loved one's death? And no statute of limitations on when they come up.

The UFO voice spoke up then. *While you're right here by the phone*, it said, *why not call Bonnie Amudson? Say hi, see how she's doing?*

Jo had been on four different boards during the nineties, all of them doing charitable work. Her friend Bonnie had persuaded her on to the Soup Kitchens board when a seat fell vacant. They had gone to a lot of the meetings together. Not the one in November of 1993, presumably, and Bonnie could hardly be expected to remember that one particular meeting almost five years later . . . but if she saved her old minutes-of-the-meeting sheets . . .

Exactly what the fuck was I thinking of? Calling Bonnie, making nice, then asking her to check her December minutes? Was I going to ask her if the attendance report had my wife absent from the November meeting? Was I going to ask if maybe Jo had seemed different that last year of her life? And when Bonnie asked me why I wanted to know, what would I say?

Give me that, Jo had snarled in my dream of her. In that dream she hadn't looked like Jo at all, she'd looked like some other woman, maybe like the one in the Book of Proverbs, the strange woman whose lips were as honey but whose heart was full of gall and wormwood. A strange woman with fingers as cold as twigs after a frost. *Give me that, it's my dust-catcher.*

I went to the cellar door and touched the knob. I turned it . . . then let it go. I didn't want to look down there into the dark, didn't want to risk the chance that something might start thumping again. It was better to leave that door shut. What I wanted was something cold to drink. I went into the kitchen, reached for the fridge door, then stopped. The magnets were back in a circle again, but this time four letters and one number had been pulled into the center and lined up there. They spelled a single lower-case word:

hel1o

There was something here. Even back in broad daylight I had no doubt of that. I'd asked if it was safe for me to be here and had received a mixed message . . . but that didn't matter. If I left Sara now, there was nowhere to go. I had a key to the house in Derry, but matters had to be resolved here. I knew that, too.

'Hello,' I said, and opened the fridge to get a soda. 'Whoever or whatever you are, hello.'

155

CHAPTER ELEVEN

I woke in the early hours of the following morning convinced that there was someone in the north bedroom with me. I sat up against the pillows, rubbed my eyes, and saw a dark, shouldery shape standing between me and the window.

'Who are you?' I asked, thinking that it wouldn't reply in words; it would, instead, thump on the wall. Once for yes, twice for no – what's on your mind, Houdini? But the figure standing by the window made no reply at all. I groped up, found the string hanging from the light over the bed, and yanked it. My mouth was turned down in a grimace, my midsection tensed so tight it felt as if bullets would have bounced off.

'Oh shit,' I said. 'Fuck me 'til I cry.'

Dangling from a hanger I'd hooked over the curtain rod was my old suede jacket. I'd parked it there while unpacking and had then forgotten to store it away in the closet. I tried to laugh and couldn't. At three in the morning it just didn't seem that funny.

I turned off the light and lay back down with my eyes open, waiting for Bunter's bell to ring or the childish sobbing to start. I was still listening when I fell asleep.

Seven hours or so later, as I was getting ready to go out to Jo's studio and see if the plastic owls were in the storage area, where I hadn't checked the day before, a late-model Ford rolled down my driveway and stopped nose to nose with my Chevy. I had gotten as far as the short path between the house and the studio, but now I came back. The day was hot and breathless, and I was wearing nothing but a pair of cut-off jeans and plastic flip-flops on my feet.

Jo always claimed that the Cleveland style of dressing divided itself naturally into two subgenres: Full Cleveland and Cleveland Casual. My visitor that Tuesday morning was wearing Cleveland Casual – you had your Hawaiian shirt with pineapples and monkeys, your tan slacks from Banana Republic, your white loafers. Socks are optional, but white footgear is a necessary part of the Cleveland look, as is at least one piece of gaudy gold jewelry. This fellow was totally okay in the latter department: he had a Rolex on one wrist and a gold-link chain around his neck. The tail of his shirt was out, and there was a suspicious lump at the back. It was either a gun or a beeper and looked too big to be a beeper. I glanced at the car again. Blackwall tires. And on the dashboard, oh look at this, a covered blue bubble. The better to creep up on you unsuspected, Gramma.

'Michael Noonan?' He was handsome in a way that would be attractive to certain women – the kind who cringe when anybody in their immediate vicinity raises his voice, the kind who rarely call the police when things go wrong at home because, on some miserable secret level, they believe they deserve things to go wrong at home. Wrong things that result in black eyes, dislocated elbows, the occasional cigarette burn on the booby. These are women who more often than not call their husbands or lovers Daddy, as in 'Can I bring you a beer, daddy?' or 'Did you have a hard day at work, daddy?'

'Yes, I'm Michael Noonan. How can I help you?'

This version of daddy turned, bent, and grabbed something from the litter of paperwork on the passenger side of the front seat. Beneath the dash, a two-way radio squawked once, briefly, and fell silent. He turned back to me with a long, buff-colored folder in one hand. Held it out. 'This is yours.'

When I didn't take it, he stepped forward and tried to poke it into one of my palms, which would presumably cause me to close my fingers in a kind of reflex. Instead I raised both hands to shoulder-level, as if he had just told me to put em up, Muggsy.

He looked at me patiently, his face as Irish as the Arlen brothers' but without the Arlen look of kindness, openness, and curiosity. What was there in place of those things was a species of sour amusement, as if he'd seen all of the world's pissier behavior, most of it twice. One

157

of his eyebrows had been split open a long time ago, and his cheeks had that reddish windburned look that indicates either ruddy good health or a deep interest in grain-alcohol products. He looked like he could knock you into the gutter and then sit on you to keep you there. I been good, daddy, get off me, don't be mean.

'Don't make this tough. You're gonna take service of this and we both know it, so don't make this tough.'

'Show me some ID first.'

He sighed, rolled his eyes, then reached into one of his shirt pockets. He brought out a leather folder and flipped it open. There was a badge and a photo ID. My new friend was George Footman, Deputy Sheriff, Castle County. The photo was flat and shadowless, like something an assault victim would see in a mugbook.

'Okay?' he asked.

I took the buff-backed document when he held it out again. He stood there, broadcasting that sense of curdled amusement as I scanned it. I had been subpoenaed to appear in the Castle Rock office of Elmer Durgin, Attorney-at-Law, at ten o'clock on the morning of 10 July 1998 – Friday, in other words. Said Elmer Durgin had been appointed guardian *ad litem* of Kyra Elizabeth Devore, a minor child. He would take a deposition from me concerning any knowledge I might have of Kyra Elizabeth Devore in regard to her well-being. This deposition would be taken on behalf of Castle County Superior Court and Judge Noble Rancourt. A stenographer would be present. I was assured that this was the court's depo, and nothing to do with either 𝔓laintiff or 𝔇efendant.

Footman said, 'It's my job to remind you of the penalties should you fail—'

'Thanks, but let's just assume you told me all about those, okay? I'll be there.' I made shooing gestures at his car. I felt deeply disgusted . . . and I felt *interfered with*. I had never been served with a process before, and I didn't care for it.

He went back to his car, started to swing in, then stopped with one hairy arm hung over the top of the open door. His Rolex gleamed in the hazy sunlight.

'Let me give you a piece of advice,' he said, and that was enough to tell me anything else I needed to know about the guy. 'Don't fuck with Mr Devore.'

'Or he'll squash me like a bug,' I said.

'Huh?'

'Your actual lines are "Let me give you a piece of advice – don't fuck with Mr Devore or he'll squash you like a bug."'

I could see by his expression – half past perplexed, going on angry – that he had meant to say something very much like that. Obviously we'd seen the same movies, including all those in which Robert De Niro plays a psycho. Then his face cleared.

'Oh sure, you're the writer,' he said.

'That's what they tell me.'

'You can say stuff like that 'cause you're a writer.'

'Well, it's a free country, isn't it?'

'Ain't you a smartass, now.'

'How long have you been working for Max Devore, Deputy? And does the County Sheriff's office know you're moonlighting?'

'They know. It's not a problem. *You're* the one that might have the problem, Mr Smartass Writer.'

I decided it was time to quit this before we descended to the kaka-poopie stage of name-calling.

'Get out of my driveway, please, Deputy.'

He looked at me a moment longer, obviously searching for that perfect capper line and not finding it. He needed a Mr Smartass Writer to help him, that was all. 'I'll be looking for you on Friday,' he said.

'Does that mean you're going to buy me lunch? Don't worry, I'm a fairly cheap date.'

His reddish cheeks darkened a degree further, and I could see what they were going to look like when he was sixty, if he didn't lay off the firewater in the meantime. He got back into his Ford and reversed up my driveway hard enough to make his tires holler. I stood where I was, watching him go. Once he was headed back out Lane Forty-two to the highway, I went into the house. It occurred to me that Deputy Footman's extra-curricular job must pay well, if he could afford a Rolex. On the other hand, maybe it was a knockoff.

Settle down, Michael, Jo's voice advised. *The red rag is gone now, no one's waving anything in front of you, so just settle—*

I shut her voice out. I didn't want to settle down; I wanted to settle *up*. I had been *interfered with*.

159

I walked over to the hall desk where Jo and I had always kept our pending documents (and our desk calendars, now that I thought about it), and tacked the summons to the bulletin board by one corner of its buff-colored jacket. With that much accomplished, I raised my fist in front of my eyes, looked at the wedding ring on it for a moment, then slammed it against the wall beside the bookcase. I did it hard enough to make an entire row of paperbacks jump. I thought about Mattie Devore's baggy shorts and Kmart smock, then about her father-in-law paying four and a quarter million dollars for Warrington's. Writing a personal goddamned check. I thought about Bill Dean saying that one way or another, that little girl was going to grow up in California.

I walked back and forth through the house, still simmering, and finally ended up in front of the fridge. The circle of magnets was the same, but the letters inside had changed. Instead of

hel1o

they now read

help   r

'Helper?' I said, and as soon as I heard the word out loud, I understood. The letters on the fridge consisted of only a single alphabet (no, not even that, I saw; *g* and *x* had been lost someplace), and I'd have to get more. If the front of my Kenmore was going to become a Ouija board, I'd need a good supply of letters. Especially vowels. In the meantime, I moved the *h* and the *e* in front of the *r*. Now the message read

lp her

I scattered the circle of fruit and vegetable magnets with my palm, spread the letters, and resumed pacing. I had made a decision not to get between Devore and his daughter-in-law, but I'd wound up between them anyway. A deputy in Cleveland clothing had shown up in my driveway, complicating a life that already had its problems . . . and scaring me a little in the bargain. But at least it was a fear of something I could see and understand. All at once I decided I wanted to do more with the summer than worry about ghosts, crying kids, and what my wife had been up to four or five years ago . . . if, in fact, she had been up to anything. I couldn't write books, but that didn't mean I had to pick scabs.

Help her.

I decided I would at least try.

'Harold Oblowski Literary Agency.'

'Come to Belize with me, Nola,' I said. 'I need you. We'll make beautiful love at midnight, when the full moon turns the beach to a bone.'

'Hello, Mr Noonan,' she said. No sense of humor had Nola. No sense of romance, either. In some ways that made her perfect for the Oblowski Agency. 'Would you like to speak to Harold?'

'If he's in.'

'He is. Please hold.'

One nice thing about being a bestselling author – even one whose books only appear, as a general rule, on lists that go to fifteen – is that your agent almost always happens to be in. Another is if he's vacationing on Nantucket, he'll be in to you there. A third is that the time you spend on hold is usually quite short.

'Mike!' he cried. 'How's the lake? I thought about you all weekend!'

Yeah, I thought, *and pigs will whistle.*

'Things are fine in general but shitty in one particular, Harold. I need to talk to a lawyer. I thought first about calling Ward Hankins for a recommendation, but then I decided I wanted somebody a little more high-powered than Ward was likely to know. Someone with filed teeth and a taste for human flesh would be nice.'

This time Harold didn't bother with the long pause routine. 'What's up, Mike? Are you in trouble?'

Thump once for yes, twice for no, I thought, and for one wild moment thought of actually doing just that. I remembered finishing Christy Brown's memoir, *Down All the Days*, and wondering what it would be like to write an entire book with the pen grasped between the toes of your left foot. Now I wondered what it would be like to go through eternity with no way to communicate but rapping on the cellar wall. And even then only certain people would be able to hear and understand you . . . and only those certain people at certain times.

Jo, was it you? And if it was, why did you answer both ways?

'Mike? Are you there?'

'Yes. This isn't really my trouble, Harold, so cool your jets. I *do* have a problem, though. Your main guy is Goldacre, right?'

'Right. I'll call him right aw—'

'But he deals primarily with contracts law.' I was thinking out loud now, and when I paused, Harold didn't fill it. Sometimes he's an all right guy. Most times, really. 'Call him for me anyway, would you? Tell him I need to talk to an attorney with a good working knowledge of child custody law. Have him put me in touch with the best one who's free to take a case immediately. One who can be in court with me Friday, if that's necessary.'

'Is it paternity?' he asked, sounding both respectful and afraid.

'No, *custody*.' I thought about telling him to get the whole story from the Lawyer To Be Named Later, but Harold deserved better . . . and would demand to hear my version sooner or later anyway, no matter what the lawyer told him. I gave him an account of my Fourth of July morning and its aftermath. I stuck with the Devores, mentioning nothing about voices, crying children, or thumps in the dark. Harold only interrupted once, and that was when he realized who the villain of the piece was.

'You're asking for trouble,' he said. 'You know that, don't you?'

'I'm in for a certain measure of it in any case,' I said. 'I've decided I want to dish out a little as well, that's all.'

'You will not have the peace and quiet that a writer needs to do his best work,' Harold said in an amusingly prim voice. I wondered what the reaction would be if I said that was okay, I hadn't written anything more riveting than a grocery list since Jo died, and maybe this would stir me up a little. But I didn't. Never let em see you sweat, the Noonan clan's motto. Someone should carve DON'T WORRY I'M FINE on the door of the family crypt.

Then I thought: *help   r.*

'That young woman needs a friend,' I said, 'and Jo would have wanted me to be one to her. Jo didn't like it when the little folks got stepped on.'

'You think?'

'Yeah.'

'Okay, I'll see who I can find. And Mike . . . do you want me to come up on Friday for this depo?'

'No.' It came out sounding needlessly abrupt and was followed by a silence that seemed not calculated but hurt. 'Listen, Harold, my caretaker said the actual custody hearing is scheduled soon. If it happens and you still want to come up, I'll give you a call. I can always use your moral support – you know that.'

'In my case it's *im*moral support,' he replied, but he sounded cheery again.

We said goodbye. I walked back to the fridge and looked at the magnets. They were still scattered hell to breakfast, and that was sort of a relief. Even the spirits must have to rest sometimes.

I took the cordless phone, went out on to the deck, and plonked down in the chair where I'd been on the night of the Fourth, when Devore called. Even after my visit from 'daddy,' I could still hardly believe that conversation. Devore had called me a liar; I had told him to stick my telephone number up his ass. We were off to a great start as neighbors.

I pulled the chair a little closer to the edge of the deck, which dropped a giddy forty feet or so to the slope between Sara's backside and the lake. I looked for the green woman I'd seen while swimming, telling myself not to be a dope – things like that you can see only from one angle, stand even ten feet off to one side or the other and there's nothing to look at. But this was apparently a case of the exception proving the rule. I was both amused and a little uneasy to realize that the birch down there by The Street looked like a woman from the land side as well as from the lake. Some of it was due to the pine just behind it – that bare branch jutting off to the north like a bony pointing arm – but not all of it. From back here the birch's white limbs and narrow leaves still made a woman's shape, and when the wind shook the lower levels of the tree, the green and silver swirled like long skirts.

I had said no to Harold's well-meant offer to come up almost before it was fully articulated, and as I looked at the tree-woman, rather ghostly in her own right, I knew why: Harold was loud, Harold was insensitive to nuance, Harold might frighten off whatever was

163

here. I didn't want that. I was scared, yes – standing on those dark cellar stairs and listening to the thumps from just below me, I had been fucking terrified – but I had also felt fully alive for the first time in years. I was touching something in Sara that was entirely beyond my experience, and it fascinated me.

The cordless phone rang in my lap, making me jump. I grabbed it, expecting Max Devore or perhaps Footman, his overgolded minion. It turned out to be a lawyer named John Storrow, who sounded as if he might have graduated from law school fairly recently – like last week. Still, he worked for the firm of Avery, McLain, and Bernstein on Park Avenue, and Park Avenue is a pretty good address for a lawyer, even one who still has a few of his milk-teeth. If Henry Goldacre said Storrow was good, he probably was. And his specialty was custody law.

'Now tell me what's happening up there,' he said when the introductions were over and the background had been sketched in.

I did my best, feeling my spirits rise a little as the tale wound on. There's something oddly comforting about talking to a legal guy once the billable-hours clock has started running; you have passed the magical point at which *a* lawyer becomes *your* lawyer. Your lawyer is warm, your lawyer is sympathetic, your lawyer makes notes on a yellow pad and nods in all the right places. Most of the questions your lawyer asks are questions you can answer. And if you can't, your lawyer will help you find a way to do so, by God. Your lawyer is always on your side. Your enemies are his enemies. To him you are never shit but always Shinola.

When I had finished, John Storrow said: 'Wow. I'm surprised the papers haven't gotten hold of this.'

'That never occurred to me.' But I could see his point. The Devore family saga wasn't for the *New York Times* or *Boston Globe*, probably not even for the *Derry News*, but in weekly supermarket tabs like *The National Enquirer* or *Inside View*, it would fit like a glove – instead of the girl, King Kong decides to snatch the girl's innocent child and carry it with him to the top of the Empire State Building. Oh, eek, unhand that baby, you brute. It wasn't front-page stuff, no blood or celebrity morgue shots, but as a page nine shouter it would do nicely. In my mind I composed a headline blaring over side-by-side pix of Warrington's Lodge and

164

Mattie's rusty doublewide: **COMPU-KING LIVES IN SPLENDOR AS HE TRIES TO TAKE YOUNG BEAUTY'S ONLY CHILD**. Probably too long, I decided. I wasn't writing anymore and still I needed an editor. That was pretty sad when you stopped to think about it.

'Perhaps at some point we'll see that they do get the story,' Storrow said in a musing tone. I realized that this was a man I could grow attached to, at least in my present angry mood. He grew brisker. 'Who'm I representing here, Mr Noonan? You or the young lady? I vote for the young lady.'

'The young lady doesn't even know I've called you. She may think I've taken a bit too much on myself. She may, in fact, give me the rough side of her tongue.'

'Why would she do that?'

'Because she's a Yankee – a *Maine* Yankee, the worst kind. On a given day, they can make the Irish look logical.'

'Perhaps, but she's the one with the target pinned to her shirt. I suggest that you call and tell her that.'

I promised I would. It wasn't a hard promise to make, either. I'd known I'd have to be in touch with her ever since I had accepted the summons from Deputy Footman. 'And who stands for Michael Noonan come Friday morning?'

Storrow laughed dryly. 'I'll find someone local to do that. He'll go into this Durgin's office with you, sit quietly with his briefcase on his lap, and listen. I may be in town by that point – I won't know until I talk to Ms Devore – but I won't be in Durgin's office. When the custody hearing comes around, though, you'll see my face in the place.'

'All right, good. Call me with the name of my new lawyer. My other new lawyer.'

'Uh-huh. In the meantime, talk to the young lady. Get me a job.'

'I'll try.'

'Also try to stay visible if you're with her,' he said. 'If we give the bad guys room to get nasty, they'll get nasty. There's nothing like that between you, is there? Nothing nasty? Sorry to have to ask, but I *do* have to ask.'

'No,' I said. 'It's been quite some time since I've been up to anything nasty with anyone.'

165

'I'm tempted to commiserate, Mr Noonan, but under the circumstances—'

'Mike. Make it Mike.'

'Good. I like that. And I'm John. People are going to talk about your involvement anyway. You know that, don't you?'

'Sure. People know I can afford you. They'll speculate about how *she* can afford *me*. Pretty young widow, middle-aged widower. Sex would seem the most likely.'

'You're a realist.'

'I don't really think I am, but I know a hawk from a handsaw.'

'I hope you do, because the ride could get rough. This is an extremely rich man we're going up against.' Yet he didn't sound scared. He sounded almost . . . *greedy*. He sounded the way part of me had felt when I saw that the magnets on the fridge were back in a circle.

'I know he is.'

'In court that won't matter a whole helluva lot, because there's a certain amount of money on the other side. Also, the judge is going to be very aware that this one is a powderkeg. That can be useful.'

'What's the best thing we've got going for us?' I asked this thinking of Kyra's rosy, unmarked face and her complete lack of fear in the presence of her mother. I asked it thinking John would reply that the charges were clearly unfounded. I thought wrong.

'The best thing? Devore's age. He's got to be older than God.'

'Based on what I've heard over the weekend, I think he must be eighty-five. That would make God older.'

'Yeah, but as a potential dad he makes Tony Randall look like a teenager,' John said, and now he sounded positively gloating. 'Think of it, Michael – the kid graduates from high school the year Gramps turns one hundred. Also there's a chance the old man's overreached himself. Do you know what a guardian *ad litem* is?'

'No.'

'Essentially it's a lawyer the court appoints to protect the interests of the child. A fee for the service comes out of court costs, but it's a pittance. Most people who agree to serve as guardian *ad litem* have strictly altruistic motives . . . but not all of them. In any case, the *ad litem* puts his own spin on the case. Judges don't have to take the guy's advice, but they almost always do. It makes a judge look stupid to reject the advice of his own appointee, and the thing a judge hates above all others is looking stupid.'

'Devore will have his own lawyer?'

John laughed. 'How about half a dozen at the actual custody hearing?'

'Are you serious?'

'The guy is eighty-five. That's too old for Ferraris, too old for bungee jumping in Tibet, and too old for whores unless he's a mighty man. What does that leave for him to spend his money on?'

'Lawyers,' I said bleakly.

'Yep.'

'And Mattie Devore? What does she get?'

'Thanks to you, she gets me,' John Storrow said. 'It's like a John Grisham novel, isn't it? Pure gold. Meantime, I'm interested in Durgin, the *ad litem*. If Devore hasn't been expecting any real trouble, he may have been unwise enough to put temptation in Durgin's way. And Durgin may have been stupid enough to succumb. Hey, who knows what we might find?'

But I was a turn back. 'She gets you,' I said. 'Thanks to me. And if I wasn't here to stick in my oar? What would she get then?'

'*Bubkes*. That's Yiddish. It means—'

'I know what it means,' I said. 'That's incredible.'

'Nope, just American justice. You know the lady with the scales? The one who stands outside most city courthouses?'

'Uh-huh.'

'Slap some handcuffs on that broad's wrists and some tape over her mouth to go along with the blindfold, rape her and roll her in the mud. You like that image? I don't, but it's a fair representation of how the law works in custody cases where the plaintiff is rich and the defendant is poor. And sexual equality has actually made it worse, because while mothers still tend to be poor, they are no longer seen as the automatic choice for custody.'

'Mattie Devore's got to have you, doesn't she?'

'Yes,' John said simply. 'Call me tomorrow and tell me that she will.'

'I hope I can do that.'

'So do I. And listen – there's one more thing.'

'What?'

167

'You lied to Devore on the telephone.'

'Bullshit!'

'Nope, nope, I hate to contradict my sister's favorite author, but you did and you know it. You told Devore that mother and child were out together, the kid was picking flowers, everything was fine. You put everything in there except Bambi and Thumper.'

I was sitting up straight in my deck-chair now. I felt sandbagged. I also felt that my own cleverness had been overlooked. 'Hey, no, think again. I never came out and *said* anything. I told him I assumed. I used the word more than once. I remember that very clearly.'

'Uh-huh, and if he was taping your conversation, you'll get a chance to actually count how many times you used it.'

At first I didn't answer. I was thinking back to the conversation I'd had with him, remembering the underhum on the phone line, the characteristic underhum I remembered from all my previous summers at Sara Laughs. Had that steady low *mmmmm* been even more noticeable on Saturday night?

'I guess maybe there could be a tape,' I said reluctantly.

'Uh-huh. And if Devore's lawyer gets it to the *ad litem*, how do you think you'll sound?'

'Careful,' I said. 'Maybe like a man with something to hide.'

'Or a man spinning yarns. And you're good at that, aren't you? After all, it's what you do for a living. At the custody hearing, Devore's lawyer is apt to mention that. If he then produces one of the people who passed you shortly after Mattie arrived on the scene . . . a person who testifies that the young lady seemed upset and flustered . . . how do you think you'll sound then?'

'Like a liar,' I said, and then: 'Ah, fuck.'

'Fear not, Mike. Be of good cheer.'

'What should I do?'

'Spike their guns before they can fire them. Tell Durgin exactly what happened. Get it in the depo. Emphasize the fact that the little girl thought she was walking safely. Make sure you get in that "crossmock" thing. I love that.'

'Then if they have a tape they'll play it and I'll look like a story-changing schmuck.'

'I don't think so. You weren't a sworn witness when you talked to Devore, were you? There you were, sitting out on your deck

168

and minding your own business, watching the fireworks show. Out of the blue this grouchy old asshole calls you. Starts ranting. Didn't even give him your number, did you?'

'No.'

'Your *unlisted* number.'

'No.'

'And while he *said* he was Maxwell Devore, he could have been anyone, right?'

'Right.'

'He could have been the Shah of Iran.'

'No, the Shah's dead.'

'The Shah's out, then. But he could have been a nosy neighbor . . . or a prankster.'

'Yes.'

'And you said what you said with all those possibilities in mind. But now that you're part of an official court proceeding, you're telling the whole truth and nothing but.'

'You bet.' That good *my-lawyer* feeling had deserted me for a bit, but it was back full-force now.

'You can't do better than the truth, Mike,' he said solemnly. 'Except maybe in a few cases, and this isn't one. Are we clear on that?'

'Yes.'

'All right, we're done. I want to hear from either you or Mattie Devore around elevenish tomorrow. It ought to be her.'

'I'll try.'

'If she really balks, you know what to do, don't you?'

'I think so. Thanks, John.'

'One way or another, we'll talk very soon,' he said, and hung up.

I sat where I was for awhile. Once I pushed the button which opened the line on the cordless phone, then pushed it again to close it. I had to talk to Mattie, but I wasn't quite ready yet. I decided to take a walk instead.

If she really balks, you know what to do, don't you?

Of course. Remind her that she couldn't afford to be proud. That she couldn't afford to go all Yankee, refusing charity from Michael Noonan, author of *Being Two*, *The Red-Shirt Man*, and the soon-to-be-published *Helen's Promise*. Remind her that she could have her pride or her daughter, but likely not both.

Hey, Mattie, pick one.

I walked almost to the end of the lane, stopping at Tidwell's Meadow with its pretty view down to the cup of the lake and across to the White Mountains. The water dreamed under a hazy sky, looking gray when you tipped your head one way, blue when you tipped it the other. That sense of mystery was very much with me. That sense of Manderley.

Over forty black people had settled here at the turn of the century – lit here for awhile, anyway – according to Marie Hingerman (also according to *A History of Castle County and Castle Rock*, a weighty tome published in 1977, the county's bicentennial year). Pretty special black people, too: most of them related, most of them talented, most of them part of a musical group which had first been called The Red-Top Boys and then Sara Tidwell and the Red-Top Boys. They had bought the meadow and a good-sized tract of lakeside land from a man named Douglas Day. The money had been saved up over a period of ten years, according to Sonny Tidwell, who did the dickering (as a Red-Top, Son Tidwell had played what was then known as 'chickenscratch guitar').

There had been a vast uproar about it in town, and even a meeting to protest 'the advent of these darkies, which come in a Horde.' Things had settled down and turned out okay, as things have a way of doing, more often than not. The shanty town most locals had expected on Day's Hill (for so Tidwell's Meadow was called in 1900, when Son Tidwell bought the land on behalf of his extensive clan) had never appeared. Instead, a number of neat white cabins sprang up, surrounding a larger building that might have been intended as a group meeting place, a rehearsal area, or perhaps, at some point, a performance hall.

Sara and the Red-Top Boys (sometimes there was a Red-Top Girl in there, as well; membership in the band was fluid, changing with every performance) played around western Maine for over a year, maybe closer to two years. In towns all up and down the Western Line – Farmington, Skowhegan, Bridgton, Gates Falls, Castle Rock, Motton, Fryeburg – you'll still come across their old show-posters at barn bazaars and junkatoriums. Sara and the Red-Tops were great favorites on the circuit, and they got along all right at home on the TR, too, which never surprised me. At the end of the day Robert Frost – that utilitarian and often unpleasant poet – was right: in the northeastern three we really do believe that good fences make good neighbors. We squawk and then keep a miserly peace, the kind with gimlet eyes and a tucked-down mouth. 'They pay their bills,' we say. 'I ain't never had to shoot one a their dogs,' we say. 'They keep themselves to themselves,' we say, as if isolation were a virtue. And, of course, the defining virtue: 'They don't take charity.'

And at some point, Sara Tidwell became Sara Laughs.

In the end, though, TR-90 mustn't have been what they wanted, because after playing a county fair or two in the late summer of 1901, the clan moved on. Their neat little cabins provided summer-rental income for the Day family until 1933, when they burned in the summer fires which charred the east and north sides of the lake. End of story.

Except for her music, that was. Her music had lived.

I got up from the rock I had been sitting on, stretched my arms and my back, and walked back down the lane, singing one of her songs as I went.

CHAPTER TWELVE

During my hike back down the lane to the house, I tried to think about nothing at all. My first editor used to say that eighty-five per cent of what goes on in a novelist's head is none of his business, a sentiment I've never believed should be restricted to just writers. So-called higher thought is, by and large, highly overrated. When trouble comes and steps have to be taken, I find it's generally better to just stand aside and let the boys in the basement do their work. That's blue-collar labor down there, non-union guys with lots of muscles and tattoos. Instinct is their specialty, and they refer problems upstairs for actual cogitation only as a last resort.

When I tried to call Mattie Devore, an extremely peculiar thing happened – one that had nothing at all to do with spooks, as far as I could tell. Instead of an open-hum line when I pushed the cordless's ON button, I got silence. Then, just as I was thinking I must have left the phone in the north bedroom off the hook, I realized it wasn't *complete* silence. Distant as a radio transmission from deep space, cheerful and quacky as an animated duck, some guy with a fair amount of Brooklyn in his voice was singing: 'He followed her to school one day, school one day, school one day. He followed her to school one day, which was against the rule.'

I opened my mouth to ask who was there, but before I could, a woman's voice said 'Hello?' She sounded perplexed and doubtful.

'Mattie?' In my confusion it never occurred to me to call her something more formal, like Ms or Mrs Devore. Nor did it seem odd that I should know who it was, based on a single word, even though

172

our only previous conversation had been relatively brief. Maybe the guys in the basement recognized the background music and made the connection to Kyra.

'Mr Noonan?' She sounded more bewildered than ever. 'The phone never even rang!'

'I must have picked mine up just as your call was going through,' I said. 'That happens from time to time.' But how many times, I wondered, did it happen when the person calling you was the one you yourself had been planning to call? Maybe quite often, actually. Telepathy or coincidence? Live or Memorex? Either way, it seemed almost magical. I looked across the long, low living room, into the glassy eyes of Bunter the moose, and thought: *Yes, but maybe this is a magic place now.*

'I suppose,' she said doubtfully. 'I apologize about calling in the first place – it's a presumption. Your number's unlisted, I know.'

Oh, don't worry about that, I thought. *Everyone's got this old number by now. In fact, I'm thinking about putting it in the Yellow Pages.*

'I got it from your file at the library,' she went on, sounding embarrassed. 'That's where I work.' In the background, 'The Hokey Cokey' had given way to 'The Farmer in the Dell.'

'It's quite all right,' I said. 'Especially since you're the person I was picking up the phone to call.'

'Me? Why?'

'Ladies first.'

She gave a brief, nervous laugh. 'I wanted to invite you to dinner. That is, Ki and I want to invite you to dinner. I should have done it before now. You were awfully good to us the other day. Will you come?'

'Yes,' I said with no hesitation at all. 'With thanks. We've got some things to talk about, anyway.'

There was a pause. In the background, the mouse was taking the cheese. As a kid I used to think all these things happened in a vast gray factory called The Hi-Ho Dairy-O.

'Mattie? Still there?'

'He's dragged you into it, hasn't he? That awful old man.' Now her voice sounded not nervous but somehow dead.

'Well, yes and no. You could argue that fate dragged me into

173

it, or coincidence, or God. I wasn't there that morning because of Max Devore; I was chasing the elusive Villageburger.'

She didn't laugh, but her voice brightened a little, and I was glad. People who talk in that dead, affectless way are, by and large, frightened people. Sometimes people who have been outright terrorized. 'I'm still sorry for dragging you into my trouble.' I had an idea she might start to wonder who was dragging whom after I pitched her on John Storrow, and was glad it was a discussion I wouldn't have to have with her on the phone.

'In any case, I'd love to come to dinner. When?'

'Would this evening be too soon?'

'Absolutely not.'

'That's wonderful. We have to eat early, though, so my little guy doesn't fall asleep in her dessert. Is six okay?'

'Yes.'

'Ki will be excited. We don't have much company.'

'She hasn't been wandering again, has she?'

I thought she might be offended. Instead, this time she *did* laugh. 'God, no. All the fuss on Saturday scared her. Now she comes in to tell me if she's switching from the swing in the side yard to the sandbox in back. She's talked about you a lot, though. She calls you "that tall guy who carrot me." I think she's worried you might be mad at her.'

'Tell her I'm not,' I said. 'No, check that. I'll tell her myself. Can I bring anything?'

'Bottle of wine?' she asked, a little doubtfully. 'Or maybe that's pretentious – I was only going to cook hamburgers on the grill and make potato salad.'

'I'll bring an unpretentious bottle.'

'Thank you,' she said. 'This is sort of exciting. We never have company.'

I was horrified to find myself on the verge of saying that I thought it was sort of exciting, too, my first date in four years and all. 'Thanks so much for thinking of me.'

As I hung up I remembered John Storrow advising me to try and stay visible with her, not to hand over any extra grist for the town gossip mill. If she was barbecuing, we'd probably be out where people could see we had our clothes on . . . for most of the evening, anyway. She would, however, likely do the polite thing at some point and invite me inside. I would then do the polite thing and go. Admire her velvet Elvis painting on the wall, or her commemorative plates from the Franklin Mint, or whatever she had going in the way of trailer decoration; I'd let Kyra show me her bedroom and exclaim with wonder over her excellent assortment of stuffed animals and her favorite dolly, if that was required. There are all sorts of priorities in life. Some your lawyer can understand, but I suspect there are quite a few he can't.

'Am I handling this right, Bunter?' I asked the stuffed moose. 'Bellow once for yes, twice for no.'

I was halfway down the hall leading to the north wing, thinking of nothing but a cool shower, when from behind me, very soft, came a brief ring of the bell around Bunter's neck. I stopped, head cocked, my shirt held in one hand, waiting for the bell to ring again. It didn't. After a minute, I went the rest of the way to the bathroom and flipped on the shower.

The Lakeview General had a pretty good selection of wines tucked away in one corner — not much local demand for it, maybe, but the tourists probably bought a fair quantity — and I selected a bottle of Mondavi red. It was probably a bit more expensive than Mattie had had in mind, but I could peel the price-sticker off and hope she wouldn't know the difference. There was a line at the checkout, mostly folks with damp tee-shirts pulled on over their bathing suits and sand from the public beach sticking to their legs. While I was waiting my turn, my eye happened on the impulse items which are always stocked near the counter. Among them were several plastic bags labeled MAGNABET, each bag showing a cartoon refrigerator with the message BACK SOON stuck to it. According to the written info, there were two sets of consonants in each Magnabet, PLUS EXTRA VOWELS. I grabbed two sets . . . then added a third, thinking that Mattie Devore's kid was probably just the right age for such an item.

Kyra saw me pulling into the weedy dooryard, jumped off the slumpy little swingset beside the trailer, bolted to her mother, and hid behind her. When I approached the hibachi which had been set up beside the cinderblock front steps, the child who'd spoken to me so fearlessly on

Saturday was just a peeking blue eye and a chubby hand grasping a fold of her mother's sundress below the hip.

Two hours brought considerable changes, however. As twilight deepened, Kyra sat on my lap in the trailer's living room, listening carefully – if with growing wooziness – as I read her the ever-enthralling story of Cinderella. The couch we were on was a shade of brown which can by law be sold only in discount stores, and extremely lumpy into the bargain, but I still felt ashamed of my casual preconceptions about what I would find inside this trailer. On the wall above and behind us there was an Edward Hopper print – that one of a lonely lunch counter late at night – and across the room, over the small Formica-topped table in the kitchen nook, was one of Vincent van Gogh's '*Sunflowers*.' Even more than the Hopper, it looked at home in Mattie Devore's doublewide. I have no idea why that should have been true, but it was.

'Glass slipper will cut her footie,' Ki said in a muzzy, considering way.

'No way,' I said. 'Slipper-glass was specially made in the Kingdom of Grimoire. Smooth and unbreakable, as long as you didn't sing high C while wearing them.'

'I get a pair?'

'Sorry, Ki,' I said, 'no one knows how to make slipper-glass anymore. It's a lost art, like Toledo steel.' It was hot in the trailer and she was hot against my shirt, where her upper body lay, but I wouldn't have changed it. Having a kid on my lap was pretty great. Outside, her mother was singing and gathering up dishes from the card table we'd used for our picnic. Hearing her sing was also pretty great.

'Go on, go on,' Kyra said, pointing to the picture of Cinderella scrubbing the floor. The little girl peeking nervously around her mother's leg was gone; the angry I'm-going-to-the-damn-beach girl of Saturday morning was gone; here was only a sleepy kid who was pretty and bright and trusting. 'Before I can't hold it anymore.'

'Do you need to go pee-pee?'

'No,' she said, looking at me with some disdain. 'Besides, that's you-rinating. Peas are what you eat with meatloaf, that's what Mattie says. And I already went. But if you don't go fast on the story, I'll fall to sleep.'

'You can't hurry stories with magic in them, Ki.'

'Well go as fast as you can.'

'Okay.' I turned the page. Here was Cinderella, trying to be a good sport, waving goodbye to her asshole sisters as they went off to the ball dressed like starlets at a disco. '"No sooner had Cinderella said goodbye to Tammy Faye and Vanna—"'

'Those are the sisters' names?'

'The ones I made up for them, yes. Is that okay?'

'Sure.' She settled more comfortably on my lap and dropped her head against my chest again.

'"No sooner had Cinderella said goodbye to Tammy Faye and Vanna than a bright light suddenly appeared in the corner of the kitchen. Stepping out of it was a beautiful lady in a silver gown. The jewels in her hair glowed like stars."'

'Fairy godmother,' Kyra said matter-of-factly.

'Yes.'

Mattie came in carrying the remaining half-bottle of Mondavi and the blackened barbecue implements. Her sundress was bright red. On her feet she wore low-topped sneakers so white that they seemed to flash in the gloom. Her hair was tied back and although she still wasn't the gorgeous country-club babe I had briefly envisioned, she was very pretty. Now she looked at Kyra, looked at me, raised her eyebrows, made a lifting gesture with her arms. I shook my head, sending back a message that neither of us was ready quite yet.

I resumed reading while Mattie went to work scrubbing her few cooking tools. She was still humming. By the time she had finished with the spatula, Ki's body had taken on an additional relaxation which I recognized at once – she'd conked out, and hard. I closed the *Little Golden Treasury of Fairy Tales* and put it on the coffee-table beside a couple of other stacked books – whatever Mattie was reading, I presumed. I looked up, saw her looking back at me from the kitchen, and flicked her the V-for-Victory sign. 'Noonan, the winner by a technical knockout in the eighth round,' I said.

Mattie dried her hands on a dishtowel and came over. 'Give her to me.'

I stood up with Kyra in my arms instead. 'I'll carry. Where?'

She pointed. 'On the left.'

I carried the baby down the hallway, which was narrow enough

177

so I had to be careful not to bump her feet on one side or the top of her head on the other. At the end of the hall was the bathroom, stringently clean. On the right was a closed door which led, I assumed, into the bedroom Mattie had once shared with Lance Devore and where she now slept alone. If there was a boyfriend who overnighted even some of the time, Mattie had done a good job of erasing his presence from the trailer.

I slid carefully through the door on the left and looked at the little bed with its ruffled coverlet of cabbage roses, the table with the dollhouse on it, the picture of the Emerald City on one wall, the sign (done in shiny stick-on letters) on another one that read CASA KYRA. Devore wanted to take her away from here, a place where nothing was wrong – where, to the contrary, everything was perfectly right. Casa Kyra was the room of a little girl who was growing up okay.

'Put her on the bed and then go pour yourself another glass of wine,' Mattie said. 'I'll zip her into her pj's and join you. I know we've got stuff to talk about.'

'Okay.' I put her down, then bent a little farther, meaning to plant a kiss on her nose. I almost thought better of it, then did it anyway. When I left, Mattie was smiling, so I guess it was okay.

I poured myself a little more wine, walked back into the scrap of living room with it, and looked at the two books beside Ki's fairy-tale collection. I'm always curious about what people are reading; the only better insight into them is the contents of their medicine cabinets, and rummaging through your host's drugs and nostrums is frowned upon by the better class.

The books were different enough to qualify as schizoid. One, with a playing-card bookmark about three-quarters of the way through, was the paperback edition of Richard North Patterson's *Silent Witness*. I applauded her taste; Patterson and DeMille are probably the best of the current popular novelists. The other, a hardcover tome of some weight, was *The Collected Short Works of Herman Melville*. About as far from Richard North Patterson as you could get. According to the faded purple ink stamped on the thickness of the pages, this volume belonged to Four Lakes Community Library. That was a lovely little stone building about five miles south of Dark Score Lake, where Route 68 passes off the

TR and into Motton. Where Mattie worked, presumably. I opened to her bookmark, another playing card, and saw she was reading 'Bartleby.'

'I don't understand that,' she said from behind me, startling me so badly that I almost dropped the books. 'I like it – it's a good enough story – but I haven't the slightest idea what it means. The other one, now, I've even figured out who did it.'

'It's a strange pair to read in tandem,' I said, putting them back down.

'The Patterson I'm reading for pleasure,' Mattie said. She went into the kitchen, looked briefly (and with some longing, I thought) at the bottle of wine, then opened the fridge and took out a pitcher of Kool-Aid. On the fridge door were words her daughter had already assembled from her Magnabet bag: KI and MATTIE and HOHO (Santa Claus, I presumed). 'Well, I'm reading them both for pleasure, I guess, but we're due to discuss "Bartleby" in this little group I'm a part of. We meet Thursday nights at the library. I've still got about ten pages to go.'

'A readers' circle.'

'Uh-huh. Mrs Briggs leads. She formed it long before I was born. She's the head librarian at Four Lakes, you know.'

'I do. Lindy Briggs is my caretaker's sister-in-law.'

Mattie smiled. 'Small world, isn't it?'

'No, it's a big world but a small town.'

She started to lean back against the counter with her glass of Kool-Aid, then thought better of it. 'Why don't we go outside and sit? That way anyone passing can see that we're still dressed and that we don't have anything on inside-out.'

I looked at her, startled. She looked back with a kind of cynical good humor. It wasn't an expression that looked particularly at home on her face.

'I may only be twenty-one, but I'm not stupid,' she said. 'He's watching me. I know it, and you probably do, too. On another night I might be tempted to say fuck him if he can't take a joke, but it's cooler out there and the smoke from the hibachi will keep the worst of the bugs away. Have I shocked you? If so, I'm sorry.'

'You haven't.' She had, a little. 'No need to apologize.'

We carried our drinks down the not-quite-steady cinderblock

steps and sat side-by-side in a couple of lawn-chairs. To the left of us the coals in the hibachi glowed soft rose in the growing gloom. Mattie leaned back, placed the cold curve of her glass briefly against her forehead, then drank most of what was left, the ice cubes sliding against her teeth with a click and a rattle. Crickets hummed in the woods behind the trailer and across the road. Farther up Highway 68, I could see the bright white fluorescents over the gas island at the Lakeview General. The seat of my chair was a little baggy, the interwoven straps a little frayed, and the old girl canted pretty severely to the left, but there was still no place I'd rather have been sitting just then. This evening had turned out to be a quiet little miracle . . . at least, so far. We still had John Storrow to get to.

'I'm glad you came on a Tuesday,' she said. 'Tuesday nights are hard for me. I'm always thinking of the ballgame down at Warrington's. The guys'll be picking up the gear by now – the bats and bases and catcher's mask – and putting it back in the storage cabinet behind home plate. Drinking their last beers and smoking their last cigarettes. That's where I met my husband, you know. I'm sure you've been told all that by now.'

I couldn't see her face clearly, but I could hear the faint tinge of bitterness which had crept into her voice, and guessed she was still wearing the cynical expression. It was too old for her, but I thought she'd come by it honestly enough. Although if she didn't watch out, it would take root and grow.

'I heard a version from Bill, yes – Lindy's brother-in-law.'

'Oh ayuh – our story's on retail. You can get it at the store, or the Village Cafe, or at that old blabbermouth's garage . . . which my father-in-law rescued from Western Savings, by the way. He stepped in just before the bank could foreclose. Now Dickie Brooks and his cronies think Max Devore is walking talking Jesus. I hope you got a fairer version from Mr Dean than you'd get at the All-Purpose. You must've, or you wouldn't have risked eating hamburgers with Jezebel.'

I wanted to get away from that, if I could – her anger was understandable but useless. Of course it was easier for me to see that; it wasn't my kid who had been turned into the handkerchief tied at the center of a tug-of-war rope. 'They still play softball at Warrington's? Even though Devore bought the place?'

'Yes indeed. He goes down to the field in his motorized wheelchair every Tuesday evening and watches. There are other things he's done since he came back here that are just attempts to buy the town's good opinion, but I think he genuinely loves the softball games. The Whitmore woman goes, too. Brings an extra oxygen tank along in a little red wheelbarrow with a whitewall tire on the front. She keeps a fielder's mitt in there, too, in case any foul pops come up over the backstop to where he sits. He caught one near the start of the season, I heard, and got a standing O from the players and the folks who come to watch.'

'Going to the games puts him in touch with his son, you think?'

Mattie smiled grimly. 'I don't think Lance so much as crosses his mind, not when he's at the ballfield. They play hard at Warrington's – slide into home with their feet up, jump into the puckerbrush for the flyballs, curse each other when they do something wrong – and that's what old Max Devore enjoys, that's why he never misses a Tuesday-evening game. He likes to watch them slide and get up bleeding.'

'Is that how Lance played?'

She thought about it carefully. 'He played hard, but he wasn't crazed. He was there just for the fun of it. We all were. We women – shit, really just us girls, Barney Therriault's wife Cindy was only sixteen – we'd stand behind the backstop on the first-base side, smoking cigarettes or waving punks to keep the bugs away, cheering our guys when they did something good, laughing when they did something stupid. We'd swap sodas or share a can of beer. I'd admire Helen Geary's twins and she'd kiss Ki under the chin until Ki giggled. Sometimes we'd go down to the Village Cafe afterward and Buddy'd make us pizzas, losers pay. All friends again, you know, after the game. We'd sit there laughing and yelling and blowing straw-wrappers around, some of the guys half-loaded but nobody mean. In those days they got all the mean out on the ballfield. And you know what? None of them come to see me. Not Helen Geary, who was my best friend. Not Richie Lattimore, who was Lance's best friend – the two of them would talk about rocks and birds and the kinds of trees there were across the lake for hours on end. They came to the funeral, and for a little while after, and then . . . you

181

know what it was like? When I was a kid, our well dried up. For a while you'd get a trickle when you turned on the tap, but then there was just air. Just air.' The cynicism was gone and there was only hurt in her voice. 'I saw Helen at Christmas, and we promised to get together for the twins' birthday, but we never did. I think she's scared to come near me.'

'Because of the old man?'

'Who else? But that's okay, life goes on.' She sat up, drank the rest of her Kool-Aid, and set the glass aside. 'What about you, Mike? Did you come back to write a book? Are you going to name the TR?' This was a local *bon mot* that I remembered with an almost painful twinge of nostalgia. Locals with great plans were said to be bent on naming the TR.

'No,' I said, and then astonished myself by saying: 'I don't do that anymore.'

I think I expected her to leap to her feet, overturning her chair and uttering a sharp cry of horrified denial. All of which says a good deal about me, I suppose, and none of it flattering.

'You've retired?' she asked, sounding calm and remarkably unhorrified. 'Or is it writer's block?'

'Well, it's certainly not *chosen* retirement.' I realized the conversation had taken a rather amusing turn. I'd come primarily to sell her on John Storrow – to shove John Storrow down her throat, if that was what it took – and instead I was for the first time discussing my inability to work. For the first time with anyone.

'So it's a block.'

'I used to think so, but now I'm not so sure. I think novelists may come equipped with a certain number of stories to tell – they're built into the software. And when they're gone, they're gone.'

'I doubt that,' she said. 'Maybe you'll write now that you're down here. Maybe that's part of the reason you came back.'

'Maybe you're right.'

'Are you scared?'

'Sometimes. Mostly about what I'll do for the rest of my life. I'm no good at boats in bottles, and my wife was the one with the green thumb.'

'I'm scared, too,' she said. 'Scared a lot. All the time now, it seems like.'

'That he'll win his custody case? Mattie, that's what I—'

'The custody case is only part of it,' she said. 'I'm scared just to be here, on the TR. It started early this summer, long after I knew Devore meant to get Ki away from me if he could. And it's getting worse. In a way it's like watching thunderheads gather over New Hampshire and then come piling across the lake. I can't put it any better than that, except . . .' She shifted, crossing her legs and then bending forward to pull the skirt of her dress against the line of her shin, as if she were cold. 'Except that I've woken up several times lately, sure that I wasn't in the bedroom alone. Once when I was sure I wasn't in the *bed* alone. Sometimes it's just a feeling – like a headache, only in your nerves – and sometimes I think I can hear whispering, or crying. I made a cake one night – about two weeks ago, this was – and forgot to put the flour away. The next morning the cannister was overturned, and the flour was spilled on the counter. Someone had written "hello" in it. I thought at first it was Ki, but she said she didn't do it. Besides, it wasn't her printing, hers is all straggly. I don't know if she could even write hello. Hi, maybe, but . . . Mike, you don't think he could be sending someone around to try and freak me out, do you? I mean that's just stupid, right?'

'I don't know,' I said. I thought of something thumping the insulation in the dark as I stood on the stairs. I thought of hello printed with magnets on my refrigerator door, and a child sobbing in the dark. My skin felt more than cold; it felt numb. A headache in the nerves, that was good, that was exactly how you felt when something reached around the wall of the real world and touched you on the nape of the neck.

'Maybe it's ghosts,' she said, and smiled in an uncertain way that was more frightened than amused.

I opened my mouth to tell her about what had been happening at Sara Laughs, then closed it again. There was a clear choice to be made here: either we could be sidetracked into a discussion of the paranormal, or we could come back to the visible world. The one where Max Devore was trying to steal himself a kid.

'Yeah,' I said. 'The spirits are about to speak.'

'I wish I could see your face better. There was something on it just then. What?'

183

'I don't know,' I said. 'But right now I think we'd better talk about Kyra. Okay?'

'Okay.' In the faint glow of the hibachi I could see her settling herself in her chair, as if to take a blow.

'I've been subpoenaed to give a deposition in Castle Rock on Friday. Before Elmer Durgin, who is Kyra's guardian *ad litem*—'

'That pompous little toad isn't Ki's anything!' she burst out. 'He's in my father-in-law's hip pocket, just like Dickie Osgood, old Max's pet real estate guy! Dickie and Elmer Durgin drink together down at The Mellow Tiger, or at least they did until this business really got going. Then someone probably told them it would look bad, and they stopped.'

'The papers were served by a deputy named George Footman.'

'Just one more of the usual suspects,' Mattie said in a thin voice. 'Dickie Osgood's a snake, but George Footman's a junkyard dog. He's been suspended off the cops twice. Once more and he can work for Max Devore full-time.'

'Well, he scared me. I tried not to show it, but he did. And people who scare me make me angry. I called my agent in New York and then hired a lawyer. One who makes a specialty of child-custody cases.'

I tried to see how she was taking this and couldn't, although we were sitting fairly close together. But she still had that set look, like a woman who expects to take some hard blows. Or perhaps for Mattie the blows had already started to fall.

Slowly, not allowing myself to rush, I went through my conversation with John Storrow. I emphasized what Storrow had said about sexual equality – that it was apt to be a negative force in her case, making it easier for Judge Rancourt to take Kyra away. I also came down hard on the fact that Devore could have all the lawyers he wanted – not to mention sympathetic witnesses, with Richard Osgood running around the TR and spreading Devore's dough – but that the court wasn't obligated to treat her to so much as an ice cream cone. I finished by telling her that John wanted to talk to one of us tomorrow at eleven, and that it should be her. Then I waited. The silence spun out, broken only by crickets and the faint revving of some kid's unmuffled truck. Up Route 68, the white fluorescents went out as the Lakeview Market finished another day of summer

184

trade. I didn't like Mattie's quiet; it seemed like the prelude to an explosion. A *Yankee* explosion. I held my peace and waited for her to ask me what gave me the right to meddle in her business.

When she finally spoke, her voice was low and defeated. It hurt to hear her sounding that way, but like the cynical look on her face earlier, it wasn't surprising. And I hardened myself against it as best I could. Hey, Mattie, tough old world. Pick one.

'Why would you do this?' she asked. 'Why would you hire an expensive New York lawyer to take my case? That *is* what you're offering, isn't it? It's got to be, because *I* sure can't hire him. I got thirty thousand dollars' insurance money when Lance died, and was lucky to get that. It was a policy he bought from one of his Warrington's friends, almost as a joke, but without it I would have lost the trailer last winter. They may love Dickie Brooks at Western Savings, but they don't give a rat's ass for Mattie Stanchfield Devore. After taxes I make about a hundred a week at the library. So you're offering to pay. Right?'

'Right.'

'Why? You don't even know us.'

'Because . . .' I trailed off. I seem to remember wanting Jo to step in at that point, asking my mind to supply her voice, which I could then pass on to Mattie in my own. But Jo didn't come. I was flying solo.

'Because now I do nothing that makes a difference,' I said at last, and once again the words astonished me. 'And I *do* know you. I've eaten your food, I've read Ki a story and had her fall asleep in my lap . . . and maybe I saved her life the other day when I grabbed her out of the road. We'll never know for sure, but maybe I did. You know what the Chinese say about something like that?'

I didn't expect an answer, the question was more rhetorical than real, but she surprised me. Not for the last time, either. 'That if you save someone's life, you're responsible for them.'

'Yes. It's also about what's fair and what's right, but I think mostly it's about wanting to be part of something where I make a difference. I look back on the four years since my wife died, and there's nothing there. Not even a book where Marjorie the shy typist meets a handsome stranger.'

She sat thinking this over, watching as a fully loaded pulptruck

185

snored past on the highway, its headlights glaring and its load of logs swaying from side to side like the hips of an overweight woman. 'Don't you *root* for us,' she said at last. She spoke in a low, unexpectedly fierce voice. 'Don't you root for us like he roots for his team-of-the-week down at the softball field. I need help and I know it, but I won't have that. I *can't* have it. We're not a game, Ki and me. You understand?'

'Perfectly.'

'You know what people in town will say, don't you?'

'Yes.'

'I'm a lucky girl, don't you think? First I marry the son of an extremely rich man, and after *he* dies, I fall under the protective wing of another rich guy. Next I'll probably move in with Donald Trump.'

'Cut it out.'

'I'd probably believe it myself, if I were on the other side. But I wonder if anyone notices that lucky Mattie is still living in a Modair trailer and can't afford health insurance. Or that her kid got most of her vaccinations from the County Nurse. My parents died when I was fifteen. I have a brother and a sister, but they're both a lot older and both out of state. My parents were drunks – not physically abusive, but there was plenty of the other kinds. It was like growing up in a . . . a roach motel. My dad was a pulper, my mom was a bourbon beautician whose one ambition was to own a Mary Kay pink Cadillac. He drowned in Kewadin Pond. She drowned in her own vomit about six months later. How do you like it so far?'

'Not very much. I'm sorry.'

'After Mom's funeral my brother, Hugh, offered to take me back to Rhode Island, but I could tell his wife wasn't exactly nuts about having a fifteen-year-old join the family, and I can't say that I blamed her. Also, I'd just made the jv cheering squad. That seems like supreme diddlyshit now, but it was a very big deal then.'

Of course it had been a big deal, especially to the child of alcoholics. The only one still living at home. Being that last child, watching as the disease really digs its claws in, can be one of the world's loneliest jobs. Last one out of the sacred ginmill please turn off the lights.

'I ended up going to live with my aunt Florence, just two miles

186

down the road. It took us about three weeks to discover we didn't like each other very much, but we made it work for two years. Then, between my junior and senior years, I got a summer job at Warrington's and met Lance. When he asked me to marry him, Aunt Flo refused to give permission. When I told her I was pregnant, she emancipated me so I didn't need it.'

'You dropped out of school?'

She grimaced, nodded. 'I didn't want to spend six months having people watch me swell up like a balloon. Lance supported me. He said I could take the equivalency test. I did last year. It was easy. And now Ki and I are on our own. Even if my aunt agreed to help me, what could she do? She works in the Castle Rock Gore-Tex factory and makes about sixteen thousand dollars a year.'

I nodded again, thinking that my last check for French royalties had been about that. My last *quarterly* check. Then I remembered something Ki had told me on the day I met her.

'When I was carrying Kyra out of the road, she said that if you were mad, she'd go to her white nana. If your folks are dead, who did she—' Except I didn't really have to ask; I only had to make one or two simple connections. 'Rogette Whitmore's the white nana? Devore's assistant? But that means . . .'

'That Ki's been with them. Yes, you bet. Until late last month, I allowed her to visit her grandpa – and Rogette by association, of course – quite often. Once or twice a week, and sometimes for an overnight. She likes her "whita poppa" – at least she did at first – and she absolutely adores that creepy woman.' I thought Mattie shivered in the gloom, although the night was still very warm.

'Devore called to say he was coming east for Lance's funeral and to ask if he could see his granddaughter while he was here. Nice as pie, he was, just as if he'd never tried to buy me off when Lance told him we were going to get married.'

'Did he?'

'Uh-huh. The first offer was a hundred thousand. That was in August of 1994, after Lance called him to say we were getting married in mid-September. I kept quiet about it. A week later, the offer went up to two hundred thousand.'

'For what, precisely?'

'To remove my bitch-hooks and relocate with no forwarding

187

address. This time I did tell Lance, and he hit the roof. Called his old man and said we were going to be married whether he liked it or not. Told him that if he ever wanted to see his grandchild, he had better cut the shit and behave.'

With another parent, I thought, that was probably the most reasonable response Lance Devore could have made. I respected him for it. The only problem was that he wasn't dealing with a reasonable man; he was dealing with the fellow who, as a child, had stolen Scooter Larribee's new sled.

'These offers were made by Devore himself, over the telephone. Both when Lance wasn't around. Then, about ten days before the wedding, I had a visit from Dickie Osgood. I was to make a call to a number in Delaware, and when I did . . .' Mattie shook her head. 'You wouldn't believe it. It's like something out of one of your books.'

'May I guess?'

'If you want.'

'He tried to buy the child. He tried to buy Kyra.'

Her eyes widened. A scantling moon had come up and I could see that look of surprise well enough.

'How much?' I asked. 'I'm curious. How much for you to give birth, leave Devore's grandchild with Lance, then scat?'

'Two million dollars,' she whispered. 'Deposited in the bank of my choice, as long as it was west of the Mississippi and I signed an agreement to stay away from her – and from Lance – until at least April twentieth, 2016.'

'The year Ki turns twenty-one.'

'Yes.'

'And Osgood doesn't know any of the details, so Devore's skirts remain clean here in town.'

'Uh-huh. And the two million was only the start. There was to be an additional million on Ki's fifth, tenth, fifteenth, and twentieth birthdays.' She shook her head in a disbelieving way. 'The linoleum keeps bubbling up in the kitchen, the showerhead keeps falling into the tub, and the whole damn rig cants to the east these days, but I could have been the six-million-dollar wom-an.'

Did you ever consider taking the offer, Mattie? I wondered . . . but

188

that was a question I'd never ask, curiosity so unseemly it deserved no satisfaction.

'Did you tell Lance?'

'I tried not to. He was already furious with his father, and I didn't want to make it worse. I didn't want that much hate at the start of our marriage, no matter how good the reasons for hating might be . . . and I didn't want Lance to . . . later on with me, you know . . .' She raised her hands, then dropped them back on her thighs. The gesture was both weary and oddly endearing.

'You didn't want Lance turning on you ten years later and saying "You came between me and my father, you bitch."'

'Something like that. But in the end, I couldn't keep it to myself. I was just this kid from the sticks, didn't own a pair of pantyhose until I was eleven, wore my hair in nothing but braids or a ponytail until I was thirteen, thought the whole state of New York was New York City . . . and this guy . . . this *phantom father* . . . had offered me *six million bucks*. It terrified me. I had dreams about him coming in the night like a troll and stealing my baby out of her crib. He'd come wriggling through the window like a snake . . .'

'Dragging his oxygen tank behind him, no doubt.'

She smiled. 'I didn't know about the oxygen then. Or Rogette Whitmore, either. All I'm trying to say is that I was seventeen and not good at keeping secrets.' I had to restrain my own smile at the way she said this – as if decades of experience now lay between that naïve, frightened child and this mature woman with the mail-order diploma.

'Lance was angry.'

'So angry he replied to his father by e-mail instead of calling. He stuttered, you see, and the more upset he was, the worse his stutter became. A phone conversation would have been impossible.'

Now, at last, I thought I had a clear picture. Lance Devore had written his father an unthinkable letter – unthinkable, that was, if you happened to be Max Devore. The letter said that Lance didn't want to hear from his father again, and Mattie didn't, either. He wouldn't be welcome in their home (the Modair trailer wasn't quite the humble woodcutter's cottage of a Brothers Grimm tale, but it was close enough for kissing). He wouldn't be welcome to visit following the birth of their baby, and if he had the gall to send the child a present then or later, it would be returned. Stay out of my life, Dad. This time you've gone too far to forgive.

There are undoubtedly diplomatic ways of handling an offended child, some wise and some crafty . . . but ask yourself this: would a diplomatic father have gotten himself into such a situation to begin with? Would a man with even minimal insight into human nature have offered his son's fiancée a bounty (one so enormous it probably had little real sense or meaning to her) to give up her firstborn child? And he'd offered this devil's bargain to a girl-woman of seventeen, an age when the romantic view of life is at absolute high tide. If nothing else, Devore should have waited awhile before making his final offer. You could argue that he didn't know if he *had* awhile, but it wouldn't be a persuasive argument. I thought Mattie was right – deep in that wrinkled old prune which served him as a heart, Max Devore thought he was going to live forever.

In the end, he hadn't been able to restrain himself. There was the sled he wanted, the sled he just had to have, on the other side of the window. All he had to do was break the glass and take it. He'd been doing it all his life, and so he had reacted to his son's e-mail not craftily, as a man of his years and abilities should have done, but furiously, as the child would have done if the glass in the shed window had proved immune to his hammering fists. Lance didn't want him meddling? Fine! Lance could live with his backwoods Daisy Mae in a tent or a trailer or a goddamned cowbarn. He could give up the cushy surveying job, as well, and find real employment. See how the other half lived!

In other words, you can't quit on me, son. You're fired.

'We didn't fall into each other's arms at the funeral,' Mattie said, 'don't get that idea. But he was decent to me – which I didn't expect – and I tried to be decent to him. He offered me a stipend, which I refused. I was afraid there might be legal ramifications.'

'I doubt it, but I like your caution. What happened when he saw Kyra for the first time, Mattie? Do you remember?'

'I'll never forget it.' She reached into the pocket of her dress, found a battered pack of cigarettes, and shook one out. She looked at it with a mixture of greed and disgust. 'I quit these because Lance said we couldn't really afford them, and I knew he was right. But the habit creeps back. I only smoke a pack a week, and I know damned

190

well even that's too much, but sometimes I need the comfort. Do you want one?'

I shook my head. She lit up, and in the momentary flare of the match, her face was way past pretty. What had the old man made of *her*? I wondered.

'He met his granddaughter for the first time beside a hearse,' Mattie said. 'We were at Dakin's Funeral Home in Motton. It was the "viewing." Do you know about that?'

'Oh yes,' I said, thinking of Jo.

'The casket was closed but they still call it a viewing. Weird. I came out to have a cigarette. I told Ki to sit on the funeral parlor steps so she wouldn't get the smoke, and I went a little way down the walk. This big gray limo pulled up. I'd never seen anything like it before, except on TV. I knew who it was right away. I put my cigarettes back in my purse and told Ki to come. She toddled down the walk and took hold of my hand. The limo door opened, and Rogette Whitmore got out. She had an oxygen mask in one hand, but he didn't need it, at least not then. He got out after her. A tall man – not as tall as you, Mike, but tall – wearing a gray suit and black shoes as shiny as mirrors.'

She paused, thinking. Her cigarette rose briefly to her mouth, then went back down to the arm of her chair, a red firefly in the weak moonlight.

'At first he didn't say anything. The woman tried to take his arm and help him climb the three or four steps from the road to the walk, but he shook her off. He got to where we were standing under his own power, although I could hear him wheezing way down deep in his chest. It was the sound a machine makes when it needs oil. I don't know how much he can walk now, but it's probably not much. Those few steps pretty well did him in, and that was almost a year ago. He looked at me for a second or two, then bent forward with his big, bony old hands on his knees. He looked at Kyra and she looked up at him.'

Yes. I could see it . . . except not in color, not in an image like a photograph. I saw it as a woodcut, just one more harsh illustration from *Grimm's Fairy Tales*. The little girl looks up wide-eyed at the rich old man – once a boy who went triumphantly sliding on a stolen sled, now at the other end of his life and just one more bag

191

of bones. In my imagining, Ki was wearing a hooded jacket and Devore's grandpa mask was slightly askew, allowing me to see the tufted wolf-pelt beneath. What big eyes you have, Grandpa, what a big nose you have, Grandpa, what big teeth you have, too.

'He picked her up. I don't know how much effort it cost him, but he did. And – the oddest thing – Ki *let* herself be picked up. He was a complete stranger to her, and old people always seem to scare little children, but she let him pick her up. "Do you know who I am?" he asked her. She shook her head, but the way she was looking at him . . . it was as if she *almost* knew. Do you think that's possible?'

'Yes.'

'He said, "I'm your grandpa." And I almost grabbed her back, Mike, because I had this crazy idea . . . I don't know . . .'

'That he was going to eat her up?'

Her cigarette paused in front of her mouth. Her eyes were round. 'How do you know that? How *can* you know that?'

'Because in my mind's eye it looks like a fairy-tale. Little Red Riding Hood and the Old Gray Wolf. What did he do then?'

'Ate her up with his eyes. Since then he's taught her to play checkers and Candyland and box-dots. She's only three, but he's taught her to add and subtract. She has her own room at Warrington's and her own little computer in it, and God knows what he's taught her to do with that . . . but that first time he only looked at her. It was the hungriest look I've ever seen in my life.

'And she looked back. It couldn't have been more than ten or twenty seconds, but it seemed like forever. Then he tried to hand her back to me. He'd used up all his strength, though, and if I hadn't been right there to take her, I think he would have dropped her on the cement walk.

'He staggered a little, and Rogette Whitmore put an arm around him. That was when he took the oxygen mask from her – there was a little air-bottle attached to it on an elastic – and put it over his mouth and nose. A couple of deep breaths and he seemed more or less all right again. He gave it back to Rogette and really seemed to see me for the first time. He said, "I've been a fool, haven't I?" I said, "Yes, sir, I think you have." He gave me a look, very black, when I said that. I think if he'd been even five years younger, he might have hit me for it.'

'But he wasn't and he didn't.'

'No. He said, "I want to go inside. Will you help me do that?"
I said I would. We went up the mortuary steps with Rogette on one
side of him, me on the other, and Kyra walking along behind. I felt
sort of like a harem girl. It wasn't a very nice feeling. When we got
into the vestibule, he sat down to catch his breath and take a little
more oxygen. Rogette turned to Kyra. I think that woman's got a
scary face, it reminds me of some painting or other—'

'*The Cry?* The one by Munch?'

'I'm pretty sure that's the one.' She dropped her cigarette – she'd
smoked it all the way down to the filter – and stepped on it, grinding
it into the bony, rock-riddled ground with one white sneaker. 'But
Ki wasn't scared of her a bit. Not then, not later. She bent down
to Kyra and said, "What rhymes with lady?" and Kyra said "Shady!"
right off. Even at two she loved rhymes. Rogette reached into her
purse and brought out a Hershey's Kiss. Ki looked at me to see if
she had permission and I said, "All right, but just one, and I don't
want to see any of it on your dress." Ki popped it into her mouth
and smiled at Rogette as if they'd been friends since forever.

'By then Devore had his breath back, but he looked tired – the
most tired man I've ever seen. He reminded me of something in
the Bible, about how in the days of our old age we say we have
no pleasure in them. My heart kind of broke for him. Maybe he
saw it, because he reached for my hand. He said, "Don't shut me
out." And at that moment I could see Lance in his face. I started to
cry. I said, 'I won't unless you make me."'

I could see them there in the funeral home's foyer, him sitting,
her standing, the little girl looking on in wide-eyed puzzlement as
she sucked the sweet Hershey's Kiss. Canned organ music in the
background. Poor old Max Devore had been crafty enough on the
day of his son's viewing, I thought. Don't shut me out, indeed.

*I tried to buy you off and when that didn't work I upped the stakes
and tried to buy the baby. When that also failed, I told my son that you
and he and my grandchild could choke on the dirt of your own decision.
In a way, I'm the reason he was where he was when he fell and broke
his neck, but don't shut me out, Mattie, I'm just a poor old geezer, so
don't shut me out.*

'I was stupid, wasn't I?'

193

'You expected him to be better than he was. If that makes you stupid, Mattie, the world could use more of it.'

'I *did* have my doubts,' she said. 'It's why I wouldn't take any of his money, and by last October he'd quit asking. But I let him see her. I suppose, yeah, part of it was the idea there might be something in it for Ki later on, but I honestly didn't think about that so much. Mostly it was him being her only blood link to her father. I wanted her to enjoy that the way any kid enjoys having a grandparent. What I didn't want was for her to be infected by all the crap that went on before Lance died.

'At first it seemed to be working. Then, little by little, things changed. I realized that Ki didn't like her "white poppa" so much, for one thing. Her feelings about Rogette are the same, but Max Devore's started to make her nervous in some way I don't understand and she can't explain. I asked her once if he'd ever touched her anywhere that made her feel funny. I showed her the places I meant, and she said no. I believe her, but . . . he said something or did something. I'm almost sure of it.'

'Could be no more than the sound of his breathing getting worse,' I said. 'That alone might be enough to scare a child. Or maybe he had some kind of spell while she was there. What about you, Mattie?'

'Well . . . one day in February Lindy Briggs told me that George Footman had been in to check the fire extinguishers and the smoke detectors in the library. He also asked if Lindy had found any beer cans or liquor bottles in the trash lately. Or cigarette butts that were obviously homemade.'

'Roaches, in other words.'

'Uh-huh. And Dickie Osgood has been visiting my old friends, I hear. Chatting. Panning for gold. Digging the dirt.'

'Is there any to dig?'

'Not much, thank God.'

I hoped she was right, and I hoped that if there was stuff she wasn't telling me, John Storrow would get it out of her.

'But through all this you let Ki go on seeing him.'

'What would pulling the plug on the visits have accomplished? And I thought that allowing them to go on would at least keep him from speeding up any plans he might have.'

That, I thought, made a lonely kind of sense.

'Then, in the spring, I started to get some extremely creepy, scary feelings.'

'Creepy how? Scary how?'

'I don't know.' She took out her cigarettes, looked at them, then stuffed the pack back in her pocket. 'It wasn't just that my father-in-law was looking for dirty laundry in my closets, either. It was Ki. I started to worry about Ki all the time she was with him . . . with *them*. Rogette would come in the BMW they'd bought or leased, and Ki would be sitting out on the steps waiting for her. With her bag of toys if it was a day-visit, with her little pink Minnie Mouse suitcase if it was an overnight. And she'd always come back with one more thing than she left with. My father-in-law's a great believer in presents. Before popping her into the car, Rogette would give me that cold little smile of hers and say, "Seven o'clock then, we'll give her supper" or "Eight o'clock then, and a nice hot breakfast before she leaves." I'd say okay, and then Rogette would reach into her bag and hold out a Hershey's Kiss to Ki just the way you'd hold a biscuit out to a dog to make it shake hands. She'd say a word and Kyra would rhyme it. Rogette would toss her her treat – woof-woof, good dog, I always used to think – and off they'd go. Come seven in the evening or eight in the morning, the BMW would pull in right where your car's parked now. You could set your clock by the woman. But I got worried.'

'That they might get tired of the legal process and just snatch her?' This seemed to me a reasonable concern – so reasonable I could hardly believe Mattie had ever let her little girl go to the old man in the first place. In custody cases, as in the rest of life, possession tends to be nine-tenths of the law, and if Mattie was telling the truth about her past and present, a custody hearing was apt to turn into a tiresome production even for the rich Mr Devore. Snatching might, in the end, look like a more efficient solution.

'Not exactly,' she said. 'I guess it's the logical thing, but that wasn't really it. I just got afraid. There was nothing I could put my finger on. It would get to be quarter past six in the evening and I'd think, "This time that white-haired bitch isn't going to bring her back. This time she's going to . . ."'

I waited. When nothing came I said, 'Going to what?'

'I told you, I don't know,' she said. 'But I've been afraid for

195

Ki since spring. By the time June came around, I couldn't stand it anymore, and I put a stop to the visits. Kyra's been off-and-on pissed at me ever since. I'm pretty sure that's most of what that Fourth of July escapade was about. She doesn't talk about her grandfather very much, but she's always popping out with "What do you think the white nana's doing now, Mattie?" or "Do you think the white nana would like my new dress?" Or she'll run up to me and say "Sing, ring, king, thing," and ask for a treat.'

'What was the reaction from Devore?'

'Complete fury. He called again and again, first asking what was wrong, then making threats.'

'Physical threats?'

'Custody threats. He was going to take her away, when he was finished with me I'd stand before the whole world as an unfit mother, I didn't have a chance, my only hope was to relent and *let me see my granddaughter, goddammit*.'

I nodded. '"Please don't shut me out" doesn't sound like the guy who called while I was watching the fireworks, but that does.'

'I've also gotten calls from Dickie Osgood, and a number of other locals,' she said. 'Including Lance's old friend Richie Lattimore. Richie said I wasn't being true to Lance's memory.'

'What about George Footman?'

'He cruises by once in awhile. Lets me know he's watching. He hasn't called or stopped in. You asked about physical threats – just seeing Footman's cruiser on my road feels like a physical threat to me. He scares me. But these days it seems as if everything does.'

'Even though Kyra's visits have stopped.'

'Even though. It feels . . . thundery. Like something's going to happen. And every day that feeling seems to get stronger.'

'John Storrow's number,' I said. 'Do you want it?'

She sat quietly, looking into her lap. Then she raised her head and nodded. 'Give it to me. And thank you. From the bottom of my heart.'

I had the number on a pink memo-slip in my front pocket. She grasped it but did not immediately take it. Our fingers were touching, and she was looking at me with disconcerting steadiness. It was as if she knew more about my motives than I did myself.

'What can I do to repay you?' she asked, and there it was.

196

'Tell Storrow everything you've told me.' I let go of the pink slip and stood up. 'That'll do just fine. And now I have to get along. Will you call and tell me how you made out with him?'

'Of course.'

We walked to my car. I turned to her when we got there. For a moment I thought she was going to put her arms around me and hug me, a thank-you gesture that might have led anywhere in our current mood – one so heightened it was almost melodramatic. But it was a melodramatic situation, a fairy-tale where there's good and bad and a lot of repressed sex running under both.

Then headlights appeared over the brow of the hill where the market stood and swept past the All-Purpose Garage. They moved toward us, brightening. Mattie stood back and actually put her hands behind her, like a child who has been scolded. The car passed, leaving us in the dark again . . . but the moment had passed, too. If there had been a moment.

'Thanks for dinner,' I said. 'It was wonderful.'

'Thanks for the lawyer, I'm sure he'll be wonderful, too,' she said, and we both laughed. The electricity went out of the air. 'He spoke of you once, you know. Devore.'

I looked at her in surprise. 'I'm amazed he even knew who I was. Before this, I mean.'

'He knows, all right. He spoke of you with what I think was genuine affection.'

'You're kidding. You must be.'

'I'm not. He said that your great-grandfather and his great-grandfather worked the same camps and were neighbors when they weren't in the woods – I think he said not far from where Boyd's Marina is now. "They shit in the same pit," is the way he put it. Charming, huh? He said he guessed that if a couple of loggers from the TR could produce millionaires, the system was working the way it was supposed to. "Even if it took three generations to do it," he said. At the time I took it as a veiled criticism of Lance.'

'It's ridiculous, however he meant it,' I said. 'My family is from the coast. Prout's Neck. Other side of the state. My dad was a fisherman and so was his father before him. My great-grandfather, too. They trapped lobsters and threw nets, they didn't cut trees.' All that was true, and yet my mind tried to fix on something. Some

197

memory connected to what she was saying. Perhaps if I slept on it, it would come back to me.

'Could he have been talking about someone in your wife's family?'

'Nope. There are Arlens in Maine – they're a big family – but most are still in Massachusetts. They do all sorts of things now, but if you go back to the eighteen-eighties, the majority would have been quarrymen and stonecutters in the Malden–Lynn area. Devore was pulling your leg, Mattie.' But even then I suppose I knew he wasn't. He might have gotten some part of the story wrong – even the sharpest guys begin to lose the edge of their recollection by the time they turn eighty-five – but Max Devore wasn't much of a leg-puller. I had an image of unseen cables stretching beneath the surface of the earth here on the TR – stretching in all directions, unseen but very powerful.

My hand was resting on top of my car door, and now she touched it briefly. 'Can I ask you one other question before you go? It's stupid, I warn you.'

'Go ahead. Stupid questions are a specialty of mine.'

'Do you have any idea at *all* what that "Bartleby" story is about?'

I wanted to laugh, but there was enough moonlight for me to see she was serious, and that I'd hurt her feelings if I did. She was a member of Lindy Briggs's readers' circle (where I had once spoken in the late eighties), probably the youngest by at least twenty years, and she was afraid of appearing stupid.

'I have to speak first next time,' she said, 'and I'd like to give more than just a summary of the story so they know I've read it. I've thought about it until my head aches, and I just don't see. I doubt if it's one of those stories where everything comes magically clear in the last few pages, either. And I feel like I *should* see – that it's right there in front of me.'

That made me think of the cables again – cables running in every direction, a subcutaneous webwork connecting people and places. You couldn't see them, but you could feel them. Especially if you tried to get away. Meanwhile Mattie was waiting, looking at me with hope and anxiety.

'Okay, listen up, school's in session,' I said.

'I am. Believe me.'

'Most critics think *Huckleberry Finn* is the first modern American novel, and that's fair enough, but if "Bartleby" were a hundred pages longer, I think I'd put my money there. Do you know what a scrivener was?'

'A secretary?'

'That's too grand. A copyist. Sort of like Bob Cratchit in *A Christmas Carol*. Only Dickens gives Bob a past and a family life. Melville gives Bartleby neither. He's the first existential character in American fiction, a guy with no ties . . . no ties to, you know . . .'

A couple of loggers who could produce millionaires. They shit in the same pit.

'Mike?'

'What?'

'Are you okay?'

'Sure.' I focused my mind as best I could. 'Bartleby is tied to life only by work. In that way he's a twentieth-century American type, not much different from Sloan Wilson's Man in the Gray Flannel Suit, or – in the dark version – Michael Corleone in *The Godfather*. But then Bartleby begins to question even work, the god of middle-class American males.'

She looked excited now, and I thought it was a shame she'd missed her last year of high school. For her and also for her teachers. 'That's why he starts saying "I prefer not to"?'

'Yes. Think of Bartleby as a . . . a hot-air balloon. Only one rope still tethers him to the earth, and that rope is his scrivening. We can measure the rot in that last rope by the steadily increasing number of things Bartleby prefers not to do. Finally the rope breaks and Bartleby floats away. It's a goddam disturbing story, isn't it?'

'One night I dreamed about him,' she said. 'I opened the trailer door and there he was, sitting on the steps in his old black suit. Thin. Not much hair. I said, "Will you move, please? I have to go out and hang the clothes now." And he said, "I prefer not to." Yes, I guess you could call it disturbing.'

'Then it still works,' I said, and got into my car. 'Call me. Tell me how it goes with John Storrow.'

'I will. And anything I can do to repay, just ask.'

199

Just ask. How young did you have to be, how beautifully ignorant, to issue that kind of blank check?

My window was open. I reached through it and squeezed her hand. She squeezed back, and hard.

'You miss your wife a lot, don't you?' she said.

'It shows?'

'Sometimes.' She was no longer squeezing, but she was still holding my hand. 'When you were reading to Ki, you looked both happy and sad at the same time. I only saw her once, your wife, but I thought she was very beautiful.'

I had been thinking about the touch of our hands, concentrating on that. Now I forgot about it entirely. 'When did you see her? And where? Do you remember?'

She smiled as if those were very silly questions. 'I remember. It was at the ballfield, on the night I met my husband.'

Very slowly I withdrew my hand from hers. So far as I knew, neither Jo nor I had been near TR-90 all that summer of '94 . . . but what I knew was apparently wrong. Jo had been down on a Tuesday in early July. She had even gone to the softball game.

'Are you sure it was Jo?' I asked.

Mattie was looking off toward the road. It wasn't my wife she was thinking about; I would have bet the house and lot on it – either house, either lot. It was Lance. Maybe that was good. If she was thinking about him, she probably wouldn't look too closely at me, and I didn't think I had much control of my expression just then. She might have seen more on my face than I wanted to show.

'Yes,' she said. 'I was standing with Jenna McCoy and Helen Geary – this was after Lance helped me with a keg of beer I got stuck in the mud – and then asked if I was going for pizza with the rest of them after the game – and Jenna said, "Look, it's Mrs Noonan," and Helen said, "She's the writer's wife, Mattie, isn't that a cool blouse?" The blouse was all covered with blue roses.'

I remembered it very well. Jo liked it because it was a joke – there *are* no blue roses, not in nature and not in cultivation. Once when she was wearing it she had thrown her arms extravagantly around my neck, swooned her hips forward against mine, and cried that she was my blue rose and I must stroke her until she turned pink. Remembering that hurt, and badly.

'She was over on the third-base side, behind the chickenwire screen,' Mattie said, 'with some guy who was wearing an old brown jacket with patches on the elbows. They were laughing together over something, and then she turned her head a little and looked right at me.' She was quiet for a moment, standing there beside my car in her red dress. She raised her hair off the back of her neck, held it, then let it drop again. 'Right *at* me. Really seeing me. And she had a look about her . . . she'd just been laughing but this look was sad, somehow. It was as if she knew me. Then the guy put his arm around her waist and they walked away.'

Silence except for the crickets and the far-off drone of a truck. Mattie only stood there for a moment, as if dreaming with her eyes open, and then she felt something and looked back at me.

'Is something wrong?'

'No. Except who was this guy with his arm around my wife?'

She laughed a little uncertainly. 'Well I doubt if he was her boyfriend, you know. He was quite a bit older. Fifty, at least.' *So what?* I thought. I myself was forty, but that didn't mean I had missed the way Mattie moved inside her dress, or lifted her hair from the nape of her neck. 'I mean . . . you're kidding, right?'

'I don't really know. There's a lot of things I don't know these days, it seems. But the lady's dead in any case, so how can it matter?'

Mattie was looking distressed. 'If I put my foot in something, Mike, I'm sorry.'

'Who *was* the man? Do you know?'

She shook her head. 'I thought he was a summer person – there was that feeling about him, maybe just because he was wearing a jacket on a hot summer evening – but if he was, he wasn't staying at Warrington's. I knew most of them.'

'And they walked off together?'

'Yes.' Sounding reluctant.

'Toward the parking lot?'

'Yes.' More reluctant still. And this time she was lying. I knew it with a queer certainty that went far beyond intuition; it was almost like mind-reading.

I reached through the window and took her hand again. 'You said if I could think of anything you could do to repay me, to just ask. I'm asking. Tell me the truth, Mattie.'

201

She bit her lip, looking down at my hand lying over hers. Then she looked up at my face. 'He was a burly guy. The old sportcoat made him look a little like a college professor, but he could have been a carpenter for all I know. His hair was black. He had a tan. They had a laugh together, a good one, and then she looked at me and the laugh went out of her face. After that he put an arm around her and they walked away.' She paused. 'Not toward the parking lot, though. Toward The Street.'

The Street. From there they could have walked north along the edge of the lake until they came to Sara Laughs. And then? Who knew?

'She never told me she came down here that summer,' I said.

Mattie seemed to try several responses and find none of them to her liking. I gave her her hand back. It was time for me to go. In fact I had started to wish I'd left five minutes sooner.

'Mike, I'm sure—'

'No,' I said. 'You're not. Neither am I. But I loved her a lot and I'm going to try and let this go. It probably signifies nothing, and besides – what else can I do? Thanks for dinner.'

'You're welcome.' Mattie looked so much like crying that I picked her hand up again and kissed the back of it. 'I feel like a dope.'

'You're not a dope,' I said.

I gave her hand another kiss, then drove away. And that was my date, the first one in four years.

Driving home I thought of an old saying about how one person can never truly know another. It's easy to give that idea lip service, but it's a jolt – as horrible and unexpected as severe air turbulence on a previously calm airline flight – to discover it's a literal fact in one's own life. I kept remembering our visit to a fertility doc after we'd been trying to make a baby for almost two years with no success. The doctor had told us I had a low sperm count – not disastrously low, but down enough to account for Jo's failure to conceive.

'If you want a kid, you'll likely have one without any special help,' the doc had said. 'Both the odds and time are still on your side. It could happen tomorrow or it could happen four years from now. Will you ever fill the house with babies? Probably not. But you

202

might have two, and you'll almost certainly have one if you keep doing the thing that makes them.' She had grinned. 'Remember, the pleasure is in the journey.'

There had been a lot of pleasure, all right, many ringings of Bunter's bell, but there had been no baby. Then Johanna had died running across a shopping-center parking lot on a hot day, and one of the items in her bag had been a Norco Home Pregnancy Test which she had not told me she had intended to buy. No more than she'd told me she had bought a couple of plastic owls to keep the crows from shitting on the lakeside deck.

What else hadn't she told me?

'Stop,' I muttered. 'For Christ's sake stop thinking about it.'

But I couldn't.

When I got back to Sara, the fruit and vegetable magnets on the refrigerator were in a circle again. Three letters had been clustered in the middle:

g d

o

I moved the *o* up to where I thought it belonged, making 'god' or maybe an abridged version of 'good.' Which meant exactly what? 'I could speculate about that, but I prefer not to,' I told the empty house. I looked at Bunter the moose, willing the bell around his moth-eaten neck to ring. When it didn't, I opened my two new Magnabet packages and stuck the letters on the fridge door, spreading them out. Then I went down to the north wing, undressed, and brushed my teeth.

As I bared my fangs for the mirror in a sudsy cartoon scowl, I considered calling Ward Hankins again tomorrow morning. I could tell him that my search for the elusive plastic owls had progressed from November of 1993 to July of 1994. What meetings had Jo put on her calendar for that month? What excuses to be out of Derry? And once I had finished with Ward, I could tackle Jo's friend Bonnie Amudson, ask her if anything had been going on with Jo in the last summer of her life.

Let her rest in peace, why don't you? It was the UFO voice. *What*

203

good will it do you to do otherwise? Assume she popped over to the TR after one of her board meetings, maybe just on a whim, met an old friend, took him back to the house for a bite of dinner. Just *dinner.*

And never told me? I asked the UFO voice, spitting out a mouthful of toothpaste and then rinsing. *Never said a single word?*

How do you know she didn't? the voice returned, and that froze me in the act of putting my toothbrush back in the medicine cabinet. The UFO voice had a point. I had been deep into *All the Way from the Top* by July of '94. Jo could have come in and told me she'd seen Lon Chaney Junior dancing with the queen, doing the Werewolves of London, and I probably would have said 'Uh-huh, honey, that's nice' as I went on proofing copy.

'Bullshit,' I said to my reflection. 'That's just bullshit.'

Except it wasn't. When I was really driving on a book I more or less fell out of the world; other than a quick scan of the sports pages, I didn't even read the newspaper. So yes – it *was* possible that Jo had told me she'd run over to the TR after a board meeting in Lewiston or Freeport, it *was* possible that she'd told me she'd run into an old friend – perhaps another student from the photography seminar she'd attended at Bates in 1991 – and it *was* possible she'd told me they'd had dinner together on our deck, eating black trumpet mushrooms she'd picked herself as the sun went down. It was possible she'd told me these things and I hadn't registered a word of what she was saying.

And did I really think I'd get anything I could trust out of Bonnie Amudson? She'd been Jo's friend, not mine, and Bonnie might feel the statute of limitations hadn't run out on any secrets my wife had told her.

The bottom line was as simple as it was brutal: Jo was four years dead. Best to love her and let all troubling questions lapse. I took a final mouthful of water directly from the tap, swished it around in my mouth, and spat it out.

When I returned to the kitchen to set the coffee-maker for seven A.M. I saw a new message in a new circle of magnets. It read

blue rose liar ha ha

I looked at it for a second or two, wondering what had put it there, and why.

Wondering if it was true.

I stretched out a hand and scattered all the letters far and wide. Then I went to bed.

CHAPTER THIRTEEN

I caught the measles when I was eight, and I was very ill. 'I thought you were going to die,' my father told me once, and he was not a man given to exaggeration. He told me about how he and my mother had dunked me in a tub of cold water one night, both of them at least half-convinced the shock of it would stop my heart, but both of them completely convinced that I'd burn up before their eyes if they didn't do *something*. I had begun to speak in a loud, monotonously discursive voice about the bright figures I saw in the room – angels come to bear me away, my terrified mother was sure – and the last time my father took my temperature before the cold plunge, he said that the mercury on the old Johnson & Johnson rectal thermometer had stood at a hundred and six degrees. After that, he said, he didn't dare take it anymore.

I don't remember any bright figures, but I remember a strange period of time that was like being in a funhouse corridor where several different movies were showing at once. The world grew elastic, bulging in places where it had never bulged before, wavering in places where it had always been solid. People – most of them seeming impossibly tall – darted in and out of my room on scissoring, cartoonish legs. Their words all came out booming, with instant echoes. Someone shook a pair of baby-shoes in my face. I seem to remember my brother, Siddy, sticking his hand into his shirt and making repeated arm-fart noises. Continuity broke down. Everything came in segments, weird wieners on a poison string.

In the years between then and the summer I returned to Sara Laughs, I had the usual sicknesses, infections, and insults to the body, but never anything like that feverish interlude when I was eight. I never expected to – believing, I suppose, that such experiences are unique to children, people with malaria, or maybe those suffering catastrophic mental breakdowns. But on the night of July seventh and the morning of July eighth, I lived through a period of time remarkably like that childhood delirium. Dreaming, waking, moving – they were all one. I'll tell you as best I can, but nothing I say can convey the strangeness of that experience. It was as if I had found a secret passage hidden just beyond the wall of the world and went crawling along it.

First there was music. Not Dixieland, because there were no horns, but *like* Dixieland. A primitive, reeling kind of bebop. Three or four acoustic guitars, a harmonica, a stand-up bass (or maybe a pair). Behind all of this was a hard, happy drumming that didn't sound as if it was coming from a real drum; it sounded as if someone with a lot of percussive talent was whopping on a bunch of boxes. Then a woman's voice joined in – a contralto voice, not quite mannish, roughing over the high notes. It was laughing and urgent and ominous all at the same time, and I knew at once that I was hearing Sara Tidwell, who had never cut a record in her life. I was hearing Sara Laughs, and man, she was *rocking*.

> *'You know we're goin back to MANderley,*
> *We're gonna dance on the SANderley,*
> *I'm gonna sing with the BANderley,*
> *We gonna ball all we CANderley—*
> *Ball me, baby, yeah!'*

The basses – yes, there were two – broke out in a barn-yard shuffle like the break in Elvis's version of 'Baby Let's Play House,' and then there was a guitar solo: Son Tidwell playing that chickenscratch thing.

Lights gleamed in the dark, and I thought of a song from the fifties – Claudine Clark singing 'Party Lights'. And here they were, Japanese lanterns hung from the trees above the path of railroad-tie steps leading from the house to the water. Party lights casting mystic circles of radiance in the dark: red blue and green.

Behind me, Sara was singing the bridge to her Manderley song – mama likes it nasty, mama likes it strong, mama likes to party all night long – but it was fading. Sara and the Red-Top Boys had set up their bandstand in the driveway by the sound, about where George Footman had parked when he came to serve me with Max Devore's subpoena. I was descending toward the lake through circles of radiance, past party lights surrounded by soft-winged moths. One had found its way inside a lamp and it cast a monstrous, batlike shadow against the ribbed paper. The flower-boxes Jo had put beside the steps were full of night-blooming roses. In the light of the Japanese lanterns they looked blue.

Now the band was only a faint murmur; I could hear Sara shouting out the lyric, laughing her way through it as though it were the funniest thing she'd ever heard, all that Manderley-sanderley-canderley stuff, but I could no longer make out the individual words. Much clearer was the lap of the lake against the rocks at the foot of the steps, the hollow clunk of the cannisters under the swimming float, and the cry of a loon drifting out of the darkness. Someone was standing on The Street to my right, at the edge of the lake. I couldn't see his face, but I could see the brown sportcoat and the tee-shirt he was wearing beneath it. The lapels cut off some of the letters of the message, so it looked like this:

ORMA

ER

OUN

I knew what it said anyway – in dreams you almost always know, don't you? NORMAL SPERM COUNT, a Village Cafe yuck-it-up special if ever there was one.

I was in the north bedroom dreaming all this, and here I woke up enough to *know* I was dreaming . . . except it was like waking into another dream, because Bunter's bell was ringing madly and there was someone standing in the hall. Mr Normal Sperm Count? No, not him. The shadow-shape falling on the door wasn't quite human. It was slumped, the arms indistinct. I sat up into the silver shaking of the bell, clutching a loose puddle of sheet against my naked waist, sure it was the shroud-thing out there – the shroud-thing had come out of its grave to get me.

'Please don't,' I said in a dry and trembling voice. 'Please don't, please.'

The shadow on the door raised its arms. '*It ain't nuthin but a barn-dance sugar!*' Sara Tidwell's laughing, furious voice sang. '*It ain't nuthin but a round-and-round!*'

I lay back down and pulled the sheet over my face in a childish act of denial . . . and there I stood on our little lick of beach, wearing just my undershorts. My feet were ankle-deep in the water. It was warm the way the lake gets by midsummer. My dim shadow was cast two ways, in one direction by the scantling moon which rode low above the water, in another by the Japanese lantern with the moth caught inside it. The man who'd been standing on the path was gone but he had left a plastic owl to mark his place. It stared at me with frozen, gold-ringed eyes.

'Hey, Irish!'

I looked out at the swimming float. Jo stood there. She must have just climbed out of the water, because she was still dripping and her hair was plastered against her cheeks. She was wearing the two-piece swimsuit from the photo I'd found, gray with red piping.

'It's been a long time, Irish – what do you say?'

'Say about what?' I called back, although I knew.

'About this!' She put her hands over her breasts and squeezed. Water ran out between her fingers and trickled across her knuckles.

'Come on, Irish,' she said from beside and above me, 'come on, you bastard, let's go.' I felt her strip down the sheet, pulling it easily out of my sleep-numbed fingers. I shut my eyes, but she took my hand and placed it between her legs. As I found that velvety seam and began to stroke it open, she began to rub the back of my neck with her fingers.

'You're not Jo,' I said. 'Who are you?'

But no one was there to answer. I was in the woods. It was dark, and on the lake the loons were crying. I was walking the path to Jo's studio. It wasn't a dream; I could feel the cool air against my skin and the occasional bite of a rock into my bare sole or heel. A mosquito buzzed around my ear and I waved it away. I was wearing Jockey

209

shorts, and at every step they pulled against a huge and throbbing erection.

'What the hell is this?' I asked as Jo's little barnboard studio loomed in the dark. I looked behind me and saw Sara on her hill, not the woman but the house, a long lodge jutting toward the nightbound lake. 'What's happening to me?'

'Everything's all right, Mike,' Jo said. She was standing on the float, watching as I swam toward her. She put her hands behind her neck like a calendar model, lifting her breasts more fully into the damp halter. As in the photo, I could see her nipples poking out the cloth. I was swimming in my underpants, and with the same huge erection.

'Everything's all right, Mike,' Mattie said in the north bedroom, and I opened my eyes. She was sitting beside me on the bed, smooth and naked in the weak glow of the nightlight. Her hair was down, hanging to her shoulders. Her breasts were tiny, the size of teacups, but the nipples were large and distended. Between her legs, where my hand still lingered, was a powderpuff of blonde hair, smooth as down. Her body was wrapped in shadows like moth-wings, like rose-petals. There was something desperately attractive about her as she sat there – she was like the prize you know you'll never win at the carny shooting gallery or the county fair ringtoss. The one they keep on the top shelf. She reached under the sheet and folded her fingers over the stretched material of my undershorts.

Everything's all right, this ain't nuthin but a round-and-round, said the UFO voice as I climbed the steps to my wife's studio. I stooped, fished for the key from beneath the mat, and took it out.

I climbed the ladder to the float, wet and dripping, preceded by my engorged sex – is there anything, I wonder, so unintentionally comic as a sexually aroused man? Jo stood on the boards in her wet bathing suit. I pulled Mattie into bed with me. I opened the door to Jo's studio. All of these things happened at the same time, weaving in and out of each other like strands of some exotic rope or belt. The thing with Jo felt the most like a dream, the thing in the studio, me crossing the floor and looking down at my old green IBM, the least. Mattie in the north bedroom was somewhere in between.

On the float Jo said, 'Do what you want.' In the north bedroom

210

Mattie said, 'Do what you want.' In the studio, no one had to tell me anything. In there I knew *exactly* what I wanted.

On the float I bent my head and put my mouth on one of Jo's breasts and sucked the cloth-covered nipple into my mouth. I tasted damp fabric and dank lake. She reached for me where I stuck out and I slapped her hand away. If she touched me I would come at once. I sucked, drinking back trickles of cotton-water, groping with my own hands, first caressing her ass and then yanking down the bottom half of her suit. I got it off her and she dropped to her knees. I did too, finally getting rid of my wet, clinging underpants and tossing them on top of her bikini panty. We faced each other that way, me naked, her almost.

'Who was the guy at the game?' I panted. 'Who was he, Jo?'

'No one in particular, Irish. Just another bag of bones.'

She laughed, then leaned back on her haunches and stared at me. Her navel was a tiny black cup. There was something queerly, attractively snakelike in her posture. 'Everything down there is death,' she said, and pressed her cold palms and white, pruney fingers to my cheeks. She turned my head and then bent it so I was looking into the lake. Under the water I saw decomposing bodies slipping by, pulled by some deep current. Their wet eyes stared. Their fish-nibbled noses gaped. Their tongues lolled between white lips like tendrils of waterweed. Some of the dead trailed pallid balloons of jellyfish guts; some were little more than bone. Yet not even the sight of this floating charnel parade could divert me from what I wanted. I shrugged my head free of her hands, pushed her down on the boards, and finally cooled what was so hard and contentious, sinking it deep. Her moon-silvered eyes stared up at me, through me, and I saw that one pupil was larger than the other. That was how her eyes had looked on the TV monitor when I had identified her in the Derry County Morgue. She was dead. My wife was dead and I was fucking her corpse. Nor could even that realization stop me. 'Who was he?' I cried at her, covering her cold flesh as it lay on the wet boards. 'Who was he, Jo, for Christ's sake tell me who he was!'

In the north bedroom I pulled Mattie on top of me, relishing the feel of those small breasts against my chest and the length of her entwining legs. Then I rolled her over on the far side of the bed. I felt her hand reaching for me, and slapped it away – if she touched me

211

where she meant to touch me, I would come in an instant. 'Spread your legs, hurry,' I said, and she did. I closed my eyes, shutting out all other sensory input in favor of this. I pressed forward, then stopped. I made one little adjustment, pushing at my engorged penis with the side of my hand, then rolled my hips and slipped into her like a finger in a silk-lined glove. She looked up at me, wide-eyed, then put a hand on my cheek and turned my head. 'Everything out there is death,' she said, as if only explaining the obvious. In the window I saw Fifth Avenue between Fiftieth and Sixtieth – all those trendy shops, Bijan and Bally, Tiffany and Bergdorf's and Steuben Glass. And here came Harold Oblowski, northbound and swinging his pigskin briefcase (the one Jo and I had given him for Christmas the year before she died). Beside him, carrying a Barnes and Noble bag by the handles, was the bountiful, beauteous Nola, his secretary. Except her bounty was gone. This was a grinning, yellow-jawed skeleton in a Donna Karan suit and alligator pumps; scrawny, beringed bones instead of fingers gripped the bag-handles. Harold's teeth jutted in his usual agent's grin, now extended to the point of obscenity. His favorite suit, the doublebreasted charcoal-gray from Paul Stuart, flapped on him like a sail in a fresh breeze. All around them, on both sides of the street, walked the living dead – mommy mummies leading baby corpses by the hands or wheeling them in expensive prams, zombie doormen, reanimated skateboarders. Here a tall black man with a last few strips of flesh hanging from his face like cured deer-hide walked his skeletal Alsatian. The cab-drivers were rotting to raga music. The faces looking down from the passing buses were skulls, each wearing its own version of Harold's grin – *Hey, how are ya, how's the wife, how's the kids, writing any good books lately?* The peanut vendors were putrefying. Yet none of it could quench me. I was on fire. I slipped my hands under her buttocks, lifting her, biting at the sheet (the pattern, I saw with no surprise, was blue roses) until I pulled it free of the mattress to keep from biting her on the neck, the shoulder, the breasts, anywhere my teeth could reach. 'Tell me who he was!' I shouted at her. 'You know, I know you do!' My voice was so muffled by my mouthful of bed-linen that I doubted if anyone but me could have understood it. 'Tell me, you bitch!'

On the path between Jo's studio and the house I stood in the dark with the typewriter in my arms and that dream-spanning erection quivering below its metal bulk – all that ready and nothing willing. Except maybe for the night breeze. Then I became aware I was no longer alone. The shroud-thing was behind me, called like the moths to the party lights. It laughed – a brazen, smoke-broken laugh that could belong to only one woman. I didn't see the hand that reached around my hip to grip me – the typewriter was in the way – but I didn't need to see it to know its color was brown. It squeezed, slowly tightening, the fingers wriggling.

'What do you want to know, sugar?' she asked from behind me. Still laughing. Still teasing. 'Do you really want to know at all? Do you want to know or do you want to feel?'

'Oh, you're killing me!' I cried. The typewriter – thirty or so pounds of IBM Selectric – was shaking back and forth in my arms. I could feel my muscles twanging like guitar strings.

'Do you want to know who he was, sugar? That nasty man?'

'*Just do me, you bitch!*' I screamed. She laughed again – that harsh laughter that was almost like a cough – and squeezed me where the squeezing was best.

'You hold still, now,' she said. 'You hold still, pretty boy, 'less you want me to take fright and yank this thing of yours right out by the . . .' I lost the rest as the whole world exploded in an orgasm so deep and strong that I thought it would simply tear me apart. I snapped my head back like a man being hung and ejaculated looking up at the stars. I screamed – I had to – and on the lake, two loons screamed back.

At the same time I was on the float. Jo was gone, but I could faintly hear the sound of the band – Sara and Sonny and the Red-Top Boys tearing through 'Black Mountain Rag.' I sat up, dazed and spent, fucked hollow. I couldn't see the path leading up to the house, but I could discern its switchback course by the Japanese lanterns. My underpants lay beside me in a little wet heap. I picked them up and started to put them on, only because I didn't want to swim back to shore with them in my hand. I stopped with them stretched between my knees, looking at my fingers. They were slimed with decaying flesh. Puffing out from beneath several of the nails were clumps of torn-out hair. Corpsehair.

'Oh Jesus,' I moaned. The strength went out of me. I flopped into wetness. I was in the north-wing bedroom. What I had landed in was hot, and at first I thought it was come. The dim glow of the nightlight showed darker stuff, however. Mattie was gone and the bed was full of blood. Lying in the middle of that soaking pool was something I at first glance took to be a clump of flesh or a piece of organ. I looked more closely and saw it was a stuffed animal, a black-furred object matted red with blood. I lay on my side looking at it, wanting to bolt out of the bed and flee from the room but unable to do it. My muscles were in a dead swoon. Who had I really been having sex with in this bed? And what had I done to her? In God's name, what?

'I don't believe these lies,' I heard myself say, and as though it were an incantation, I was slapped back together. That isn't exactly what happened, but it's the only way of saying it that seems to come close to whatever did. There were three of me – one on the float, one in the north bedroom, one on the path – and each one felt that hard slap, as if the wind had grown a fist. There was rushing blackness, and in it the steady silver shaking of Bunter's bell. Then it faded, and I faded with it. For a little while I was nowhere at all.

I came back to the casual chatter of birds on summer vacation and to that peculiar red darkness that means the sun is shining through your closed eyelids. My neck was stiff, my head was canted at a weird angle, my legs were folded awkwardly beneath me, and I was hot.

I lifted my head with a wince, knowing even as I opened my eyes that I was no longer in bed, no longer on the swimming float, no longer on the path between the house and the studio. It was floorboards under me, hard and uncompromising.

The light was dazzling. I squinched my eyes closed again and groaned like a man with a hangover. I eased them back open behind my cupped hands, gave them time to adjust, then cautiously uncovered them, sat all the way up, and looked around. I was in the upstairs hall, lying under the broken air conditioner. Mrs Meserve's note still hung from it. Sitting outside my office door was the green IBM with a piece of paper rolled into it. I looked down at my feet and saw that they were dirty. Pine needles were stuck to my soles, and one toe was scratched. I got up, staggered a little (my right leg had gone to sleep), then braced a hand against the wall and stood steady. I looked down at myself. I was wearing the Jockeys I'd gone to bed in, and I didn't look as if I'd had an accident in them. I pulled out the waistband and peeked inside. My cock looked as it usually did; small and soft, curled up and asleep in its thatch of hair. If Noonan's Folly had been adventuring in the night, there was no sign of it now.

'It sure felt like an adventure,' I croaked. I armed sweat off my forehead. It was stifling up here. 'Not the kind I ever read about in *The Hardy Boys*, though.'

Then I remembered the blood-soaked sheet in the north bedroom, and the stuffed animal lying on its side in the middle of it. There was no sense of relief attached to the memory, that thank-God-it-was-only-a-dream feeling you get after a particularly nasty nightmare. It felt as real as any of the things I'd experienced in my measles fever-delirium . . . and all those things *had* been real, just distorted by my overheated brain.

I staggered to the stairs and limped down them, holding tight to the bannister in case my tingling leg should buckle. At the foot I looked dazedly around the living room, as if seeing it for the first time, and then limped down the north-wing corridor.

The bedroom door was ajar and for a moment I couldn't bring myself to push it all the way open and go in. I was very badly scared, and my mind kept trying to replay an old episode of *Alfred Hitchcock Presents*, the one about the man who strangles his wife during an alcoholic blackout. He spends the whole half hour looking for her, and finally finds her in the pantry, bloated and open-eyed. Kyra Devore was the only kid of stuffed-animal age I'd met recently, but she had been sleeping peacefully under her cabbage-rose coverlet when I left her mother and headed home. It was stupid to think I had driven all the way back to Wasp Hill Road, probably wearing nothing but my Jockeys, that I had—

What? Raped the woman? Brought the child here? In my sleep?

I got the typewriter, in my sleep, didn't I? It's sitting right upstairs in the goddam hallway.

Big difference between going thirty yards through the woods and five miles down the road to—

I wasn't going to stand out here listening to those quarrelling voices in my head. If I wasn't crazy – and I didn't think I was – listening to those contentious assholes would probably send me

215

there, and by the express. I reached out and pushed the bedroom door open.

For a moment I actually *saw* a spreading octopus-pattern of blood soaking into the sheet, that's how real and focused my terror was. Then I closed my eyes tight, opened them, and looked again. The sheets were rumpled, the bottom one mostly pulled free. I could see the quilted satin hide of the mattress. One pillow lay on the far edge of the bed. The other was scrunched down at the foot. The throw rug – a piece of Jo's work – was askew, and my water-glass lay overturned on the nighttable. The bedroom looked as if it might have been the site of a brawl or an orgy, but not a murder. There was no blood and no little stuffed animal with black fur.

I dropped to my knees and looked under the bed. Nothing there – not even dust-kitties, thanks to Brenda Meserve. I looked at the ground-sheet again, first passing a hand over its rumpled topography, then pulling it back down and re-securing the elasticized corners. Great invention, those sheets; if women gave out the Medal of Freedom instead of a bunch of white politicians who never made a bed or washed a load of clothes in their lives, the guy who thought up fitted sheets would undoubtedly have gotten a piece of that tin by now. In a Rose Garden ceremony.

With the sheet pulled taut, I looked again. No blood, not a single drop. There was no stiffening patch of semen, either. The former I hadn't really expected (or so I was already telling myself), but what about the latter? At the very least, I'd had the world's most creative wet-dream – a triptych in which I had screwed two women and gotten a handjob from a third, all at the same time. I thought I had that morning-after feeling, too, the one you get when the previous night's sex has been of the headbusting variety. But if there had been fireworks, where was the burnt gunpowder?

'In Jo's studio, most likely,' I told the empty, sunny room. 'Or on the path between here and there. Just be glad you didn't leave it in Mattie Devore, bucko. An affair with a post-adolescent widow you don't need.'

A part of me disagreed; a part of me thought Mattie Devore was exactly what I *did* need. But I hadn't had sex with her last night, any more than I had had sex with my dead wife out on the swimming float or gotten a handjob from Sara Tidwell. Now that I saw I hadn't killed

216

a nice little kid either, my thoughts turned back to the typewriter. Why had I gotten it? Why bother?

Oh man. What a silly question. My wife might have been keeping secrets from me, maybe even having an affair; there might be ghosts in the house; there might be a rich old man half a mile south who wanted to put a sharp stick into me and then break it off; there might be a few toys in my own humble attic, for that matter. But as I stood there in a bright shaft of sunlight, looking at my shadow on the far wall, only one thought seemed to matter: I had gone out to my wife's studio and gotten my old typewriter, and there was only one reason to do something like that.

I went into the bathroom, wanting to get rid of the sweat on my body and the dirt on my feet before doing anything else. I reached for the shower-handle, then stopped. The tub was full of water. Either I had for some reason filled it during my sleepwalk . . . or something else had. I reached for the drain-lever, then stopped again, remembering that moment on the shoulder of Route 68 when my mouth had filled up with the taste of cold water. I realized I was waiting for it to happen again. When it didn't, I opened the bathtub drain to let out the standing water and started the shower.

I could have brought the Selectric downstairs, perhaps even lugged it out on to the deck where there was a little breeze coming over the surface of the lake, but I didn't. I had brought it all the way to the door of my office, and my office was where I'd work . . . if I *could* work. I'd work in there even if the temperature beneath the roofpeak built to a hundred and twenty degrees . . . which, by three in the afternoon, it just might.

The paper rolled into the machine was an old pink-carbon receipt from Click!, the photo shop in Castle Rock where Jo had bought her supplies when we were down here. I'd put it in so that the blank side faced the Courier type-ball. On it I had typed the names of my little harem, as if I had tried in some struggling way to report on my three-faceted dream even while it was going on:

Jo Sara Mattie Jo Sara Mattie Mattie Mattie Sara Sara Jo Johanna Sara Jo MattieSaraJo.

Below this, in lower case:

`normal sperm count sperm norm all's rosy`

I opened the office door, carried the typewriter in, and put it in its old place beneath the poster of Richard Nixon. I pulled the pink slip out of the roller, balled it up, and tossed it into the wastebasket. Then I picked up the Selectric's plug and stuck it in the baseboard socket. My heart was beating hard and fast, the way it had when I was thirteen and climbing the ladder to the high board at the Y-pool. I had climbed that ladder three times when I was twelve and then slunk back down it again; once I turned thirteen, there could be no chickening out – I really had to do it.

I thought I'd seen a fan hiding in the far corner of the closet, behind the box marked GADGETS. I started in that direction, then turned around again with a ragged little laugh. I'd had moments of confidence before, hadn't I? Yes. And then the iron bands had clamped around my chest. It would be stupid to get out the fan and then discover I had no business in this room after all.

'Take it easy,' I said, 'take it easy.' But I couldn't, no more than that narrow-chested boy in the ridiculous purple bathing suit had been able to take it easy when he walked to the end of the diving board, the pool so green below him, the upraised faces of the boys and girls in it so small, so *small*.

I bent to one of the drawers on the right side of the desk and pulled so hard it came all the way out. I got my bare foot out of its landing zone just in time and barked a gust of loud, humorless laughter. There was half a ream of paper in the drawer. The edges had that faintly crispy look paper gets when it's been sitting for a long time. I no more than saw it before remembering I had brought my own supply – stuff a good deal fresher than this. I left it where it was and put the drawer back in its hole. It took several tries to get it on its tracks; my hands were shaking.

At last I sat down in my desk chair, hearing the same old creaks as it took my weight and the same old rumble of the casters as I rolled it forward, snugging my legs into the kneehole. Then I sat facing the keyboard, sweating hard, still remembering the high board at the Y, how springy it had been under my bare feet as I walked its

218

length, remembering the echoing quality of the voices below me, remembering the smell of chlorine and the steady low throb of the air-exchangers: *fwung-fwung-fwung-fwung*, as if the water had its own secret heartbeat. I had stood at the end of the board wondering (and not for the first time!) if you could be paralyzed if you hit the water wrong. Probably not, but you could die of fear. There were documented cases of that in *Ripley's Believe It or Not*, which served me as science between the ages of eight and fourteen.

Go on! Jo's voice cried. My version of her voice was usually calm and collected; this time it was shrill. *Stop dithering and go on!*

I reached for the IBM's rocker-switch, now remembering the day I had dropped my Word Six program into the PowerBook's trash. *Goodbye, old pal*, I had thought.

'Please let this work,' I said. 'Please.'

I lowered my hand and flicked the switch. The machine came on. The Courier ball did a preliminary twirl, like a ballet dancer standing in the wings, waiting to go on. I picked up a piece of paper, saw my sweaty fingers were leaving marks, and didn't care. I rolled it into the machine, centered it, then wrote

Chapter One

and waited for the storm to break.

CHAPTER FOURTEEN

The ringing of the phone – or, more accurately, the way I *received* the ringing of the phone – was as familiar as the creaks of my chair or the hum of the old IBM Selectric. It seemed to come from far away at first, then to approach like a whistling train coming down on a crossing.

There was no extension in my office or Jo's; the upstairs phone, an old-fashioned rotary-dial, was on a table in the hall between them – in what Jo used to call 'no-man's-land.' The temperature out there must have been at least ninety degrees, but the air still felt cool on my skin after the office. I was so oiled with sweat that I looked like a slightly pot-bellied version of the muscle-boys I sometimes saw when I was working out.

'Hello?'

'Mike? Did I wake you? Were you sleeping?' It was Mattie, but a different one from last night. This one wasn't afraid or even tentative; this one sounded so happy she was almost bubbling over. It was almost certainly the Mattie who had attracted Lance Devore.

'Not sleeping,' I said. 'Writing a little.'

'Get out! I thought you were retired.'

'I thought so, too,' I said, 'but maybe I was a little hasty. What's going on? You sound over the moon.'

'I just got off the phone with John Storrow—'

Really? How long had I been on the second floor, anyway? I looked at my wrist and saw nothing but a pale circle. It was half-past freckles and skin o'clock, as we used to say when we were kids; my watch was downstairs in the north bedroom, probably lying in a puddle of water from my overturned night-glass.

'—his age, and that he can subpoena the other son!'

'Whoa,' I said. 'You lost me. Go back and slow down.'

She did. Telling the hard news didn't take long (it rarely does): Storrow was coming up tomorrow. He would land at County Airport and stay at the Lookout Rock Hotel on Castle View. The two of them would spend most of Friday discussing the case. 'Oh, and he found a lawyer for you,' she said. 'To go with you to your deposition. I think he's from Lewiston.'

It all sounded good, but what mattered a lot more than the bare facts was that Mattie had recovered her will to fight. Until this morning (if it *was* still morning; the light coming in the window above the broken air conditioner suggested that if it was, it wouldn't be much longer) I hadn't realized how gloomy the young woman in the red sundress and tidy white sneakers had been. How far down the road to believing she would lose her child.

'This is great. I'm so glad, Mattie.'

'And you did it. If you were here, I'd give you the biggest kiss you ever had.'

'He told you you could win, didn't he?'

'Yes.'

'And you believe him.'

'Yes!' Then her voice dropped a little. 'He wasn't exactly thrilled when I told him I'd had you over to dinner last night, though.'

'No,' I said. 'I didn't think he would be.'

'I told him we ate in the yard and he said we only had to be inside together for sixty seconds to start the gossip.'

'I'd say he's got an insultingly low opinion of Yankee lovin',' I said, 'but of course he's from New York.'

She laughed harder than my little joke warranted, I thought. Out of semi-hysterical relief that she now had a couple of protectors? Because the whole subject of sex was a tender one for her just now? Best not to speculate.

'He didn't paddle me too hard about it, but he made it clear that he would if we did it again. When this is over, though, I'm having you for a *real* meal. We'll have everything you like, just the way you like it.'

221

Everything you like, just the way you like it. And she was, by God and Sonny Jesus, completely unaware that what she was saying might have another meaning – I would have bet on it. I closed my eyes for a moment, smiling. Why not smile? Everything she was saying sounded absolutely great, especially once you cleared the confines of Michael Noonan's dirty mind. It sounded like we might have the expected fairy-tale ending, if we could keep our courage and hold our course. And if I could restrain myself from making a pass at a girl young enough to be my daughter . . . outside of my dreams, that was. If I couldn't, I probably deserved whatever I got. But Kyra wouldn't. She was the hood ornament in all this, doomed to go wherever the car took her. If I got any of the wrong ideas, I'd do well to remember that.

'If the judge sends Devore home empty-handed, I'll take you out to Renoir Nights in Portland and buy you nine courses of French chow,' I said. 'Storrow, too. I'll even spring for the legal beagle I'm dating on Friday. So who's better than me, huh?'

'No one I know,' she said, sounding serious. 'I'll pay you back for this, Mike. I'm down now, but I won't always be down. If it takes me the rest of my life, I'll pay you back.'

'Mattie, you don't have to—'

'I *do*,' she said with quiet vehemence. 'I *do*. And I have to do something else today, too.'

'What's that?' I loved hearing her sound the way she did this morning – so happy and free, like a prisoner who has just been pardoned and let out of jail – but already I was looking longingly at the door to my office. I couldn't do much more today, I'd end up baked like an apple if I tried, but I wanted another page or two, at least. *Do what you want*, both women had said in my dreams. *Do what you want.*

'I have to buy Kyra the big teddybear they have at the Castle Rock Wal-Mart,' she said. 'I'll tell her it's for being a good girl because I can't tell her it's for walking in the middle of the road when you were coming the other way.'

'Just not a black one,' I said. The words were out of my mouth before I knew they were even in my head.

'Huh?' Sounding startled and doubtful.

'I said bring me back one,' I said, the words once again out and down the wire before I even knew they were there.

'Maybe I will,' she said, sounding amused. Then her tone grew serious again. 'And if I said anything last night that made you unhappy, even for a minute, I'm sorry. I never for the world—'

'Don't worry,' I said. 'I'm not unhappy. A little confused, that's all. In fact I'd pretty much forgotten about Jo's mystery date.' A lie, but in what seemed to me to be a good cause.

'That's probably for the best. I won't keep you – go on back to work. It's what you want to do, isn't it?'

I was startled. 'What makes you say that?'

'I don't know, I just . . .' She stopped. And I suddenly knew two things: What she had been about to say, and that she wouldn't say it. *I dreamed about you last night. I dreamed about us together. We were going to make love and one of us said 'Do what you want.' Or maybe, I don't know, maybe we both said it.*

Perhaps sometimes ghosts were alive – minds and desires divorced from their bodies, unlocked impulses floating unseen. Ghosts from the id, spooks from low places.

'Mattie? Still there?'

'Sure, you bet. Do you want me to stay in touch? Or will you hear all you need from John Storrow?'

'If you don't stay in touch, I'll be pissed at you. Royally.'

She laughed. 'I will, then. But not when you're working. Goodbye, Mike. And thanks again. So much.'

I told her goodbye, then stood there for a moment looking at the old-fashioned Bakelite phone handset after she had hung up. She'd call and keep me updated, but not when I was working. How would she know when that was? She just would. As I'd known last night that she was lying when she said Jo and the man with the elbow patches on the sleeves of his sportcoat had walked off toward the parking lot. Mattie had been wearing a pair of white shorts and a halter top when she called me, no dress or skirt required today because it was Wednesday and the library was closed on Wednesday.

You don't know any of that. You're just making it up.

But I wasn't. If I'd been making it up, I probably would have put her in something a little more suggestive – a Merry Widow from Victoria's Secret, perhaps.

That thought called up another. *Do what you want*, they had said. Both of them. *Do what you want*. And that was a line I knew. While on Key Largo I'd read an *Atlantic Monthly* essay on pornography by some feminist. I wasn't sure which one, only that it hadn't been Naomi Wolf or Camille Paglia. This woman had been of the conservative stripe, and she had used that phrase. Sally Tisdale, maybe? Or was my mind just hearing echo-distortions of Sara Tidwell? Whoever it had been, she'd claimed that 'do what *I* want' was the basis of erotica which appealed to women and 'do what *you* want' was the basis of pornography which appealed to men. Women imagine speaking the former line in sexual situations; men imagine having the latter line spoken *to* them. And, the writer went on, when real-world sex goes bad – sometimes turning violent, sometimes shaming, sometimes just unsuccessful from the female partner's point of view – porn is often the unindicted co-conspirator. The man is apt to round on the woman angrily and cry, 'You wanted me to! Quit lying and admit it! You *wanted* me to!'

The writer claimed it was what every man hoped to hear in the bedroom: Do what you want. Bite me, sodomize me, lick between my toes, drink wine out of my navel, give me a hairbrush and raise your ass for me to paddle, it doesn't matter. Do what you want. The door is closed and we are here, but really only *you* are here, I am just a willing extension of your fantasies and only *you* are here. I have no wants of my own, no needs of my own, no taboos. Do what you want to this shadow, this fantasy, this ghost.

I'd thought the essayist at least fifty per cent full of shit; the assumption that a man can find real sexual pleasure only by turning a woman into a kind of jackoff accessory says more about the observer than the participants. This lady had had a lot of jargon and a fair amount of wit, but underneath she was only saying what Somerset Maugham, Jo's old favorite, had had Sadie Thompson say in 'Rain,' a story written eighty years before: men are pigs, filthy, dirty pigs, all of them. But we are *not* pigs, as a rule, or at least not unless we are pushed to the final extremity. And if we are pushed to it, the issue is rarely sex; it's usually territory. I've heard feminists argue that to men sex and territory are interchangeable, and that is very far from the truth.

I padded back to the office, opened the door, and behind me

224

the telephone rang again. And here was another familiar sensation, back for a return visit after four years: that anger at the telephone, the urge to simply rip it out of the wall and fire it across the room. Why did the whole world have to call while I was writing? Why couldn't they just . . . well . . . let me do what I wanted?

I gave a doubtful laugh and returned to the phone, seeing the wet handprint on it from my last call.

'Hello?'

'I said to stay visible while you were with her.'

'Good morning to you, too, Lawyer Storrow.'

'You must be in another time-zone up there, chum. I've got one-fifteen down here in New York.'

'I had dinner with her,' I said. 'Outside. It's true that I read the little kid a story and helped put her to bed, but—'

'I imagine half the town thinks you're bopping each other's brains out by now, and the other half will think it if I have to show up for her in court.' But he didn't sound really angry; I thought he sounded as though he was having a happy-face day.

'Can they make you tell who's paying for your services?' I asked. 'At the custody hearing, I mean?'

'Nope.'

'At my deposition on Friday?'

'Christ, no. Durgin would lose all credibility as guardian *ad litem* if he went in that direction. Also, they have reasons to steer clear of the sex angle. Their focus is on Mattie as neglectful and perhaps abusive. Proving that Mom isn't a nun quit working around the time *Kramer vs. Kramer* came out in the movie theaters. Nor is that the only problem they have with the issue.' He now sounded positively gleeful.

'Tell me.'

'Max Devore is eighty-five and divorced. Twice divorced, in point of fact. Before awarding custody to a single man of his age, secondary custody has to be taken into consideration. It is, in fact, the single most important issue, other than the allegations of abuse and neglect levelled at the mother.'

'What are those allegations? Do you know?'

'No. Mattie doesn't either, because they're fabrications. She's a sweetie, by the way—'

225

'Yeah, she is.'

'—and I think she's going to make a great witness. I can't wait to meet her in person. Meantime, don't sidetrack me. We're talking about secondary custody, right?'

'Right.'

'Devore has a son and a daughter from his first marriage. The daughter has been declared mentally incompetent and lives in an institution somewhere in California – Modesto, I think. Not a good bet for custody.'

'It wouldn't seem so.'

'The son, Roger, is . . .' I heard a faint fluttering of notebook pages. 'fifty-four. So he's not exactly a spring chicken, either. Still, there are lots of guys who become daddies at that age nowadays; it's a brave new world. But Roger is a homosexual.'

I thought of Bill Dean saying, *Rump-wrangler. Understand there's a lot of that goin around out there in California.*

'I thought you said sex doesn't matter.'

'Maybe I should have said *hetero* sex doesn't matter. In certain states – California is one of them – *homo* sex doesn't matter, either . . . or not as much. But this case isn't going to be adjudicated in California. It's going to be adjudicated in Maine, where folks are less enlightened about how well two married men – married to each other, I mean – can raise a little girl.'

'Roger Devore is *married*?' Okay. I admit it. I now felt a certain horrified glee myself. I was ashamed of it – Roger Devore was just a guy living his life, and he might not have had much or anything to do with his elderly dad's current enterprise – but I felt it just the same.

'He and a software designer named Morris Ridding tied the knot in 1996,' John said. 'I found that on the first computer sweep. And if this does wind up in court, I intend to make as much of it as I possibly can. I don't know how much that will be – at this point it's impossible to predict – but if I get a chance to paint a picture of that bright-eyed, cheerful little girl growing up with two elderly gays who probably spend most of their lives in computer chat-rooms speculating about what Captain Kirk and Mr Spock might have done after the lights were out in officers' country . . . well, if I get that chance, I'll take it.'

226

'It seems a little mean,' I said. I heard myself speaking in the tone of a man who wants to be dissuaded, perhaps even laughed at, but that didn't happen.

'Of course it's mean. It feels like swerving up on to the sidewalk to knock over a couple of innocent bystanders. Roger Devore and Morris Ridding don't deal drugs, traffic in little boys, or rob old ladies. But this is custody, and custody does an even better job than divorce of turning human beings into insects. This one isn't as bad as it could be, but it's bad enough because it's so *naked*. Max Devore came up there to his old hometown for one reason and one reason only: to buy a kid. That makes me mad.'

I grinned, imagining a lawyer who looked like Elmer Fudd standing outside of a rabbit-hole marked DEVORE with a shotgun.

'My message to Devore is going to be very simple: the price of the kid just went up. Probably to a figure higher than even he can afford.'

'*If* it goes to court – you've said that a couple of times now. Do you think there's a chance Devore might just drop it and go away?'

'A pretty good one, yeah. I'd say an excellent one if he wasn't old and used to getting his own way. There's also the question of whether or not he's still sharp enough to know where his best interest lies. I'll try for a meeting with him and his lawyer while I'm up there, but so far I haven't managed to get past his secretary.'

'Rogette Whitmore?'

'No, I think she's a step further up the ladder. I haven't talked to her yet, either. But I will.'

'Try either Richard Osgood or George Footman,' I said. 'Either of them may be able to put you in touch with Devore or Devore's chief counsel.'

'I'll want to talk to the Whitmore woman in any case. Men like Devore tend to grow more and more dependent on their close advisors as they grow older, and she could be a key to getting him to let this go. She could also be a headache for us. She might urge him to fight, possibly because she really thinks he can win and possibly because she wants to watch the fur fly. Also, she might marry him.'

'*Marry* him?'

227

'Why not? He could have her sign a pre-nup – I could no more introduce that in court than his lawyers could go fishing for who hired Mattie's lawyer – and it would strengthen his chances.'

'John, I've seen the woman. She's got to be seventy herself.'

'But she's a potential female player in a custody case involving a little girl, and she's a layer between old man Devore and the married gay couple. We just need to keep it in mind.'

'Okay.' I looked at the office door again, but not so longingly. There comes a point when you're done for the day whether you want to be or not, and I thought I had reached that point. Perhaps in the evening . . .

'The lawyer I got for you is named Romeo Bissonette.' He paused. 'Can that be a real name?'

'Is he from Lewiston?'

'Yes, how did you know?'

'Because in Maine, especially around Lewiston, that can be a real name. Am I supposed to go see him?' I didn't want to go see him. It was fifty miles to Lewiston over two-lane roads which would now be crawling with campers and Winnebagos. What I wanted was to go swimming and then take a long nap. A long *dreamless* nap.

'You don't need to. Call him and talk to him a little. He's only a safety net, really – he'll object if the questioning leaves the incident on the morning of July Fourth. About that incident you tell the truth, the whole truth, and nothing but the truth. Got it?'

'Yes.'

'Talk to him before, then meet him on Friday at . . . wait . . . it's right here . . .' The notebook pages fluttered again. 'Meet him at the Route 120 Diner at nine-fifteen. Coffee. Talk a little, get to know each other, maybe flip for the check. I'll be with Mattie, getting as much as I can. We may want to hire a private dick.'

'I love it when you talk dirty.'

'Uh-huh. I'm going to see that bills go to your guy Goldacre. He'll send them to your agent, and your agent can—'

'No,' I said. 'Instruct Goldacre to send them directly here. Harold's a Jewish mother. How much is this going to cost me?'

'Seventy-five thousand dollars, minimum,' he said with no hesitation at all. With no apology in his voice, either.

'Don't tell Mattie.'

228

'All right. Are you having any fun yet, Mike?'

'You know, I sort of am,' I said thoughtfully.

'For seventy-five grand, you should.' We said our goodbyes and John hung up.

As I put my own phone back into its cradle, it occurred to me that I had lived more in the last five days than I had in the last four years.

This time the phone didn't ring and I made it all the way back into the office, but I knew I was definitely done for the day. I sat down at the IBM, hit the RETURN key a couple of times, and was beginning to write myself a next-note at the bottom of the page I'd been working on when the phone interrupted me. What a sour little doodad the telephone is, and what little good news we get from it! Today had been an exception, though, and I thought I could sign off with a grin. I was working, after all – *working*. Part of me still marvelled that I was sitting here at all, breathing easily, my heart beating steadily in my chest, and not even a glimmer of an anxiety attack on my personal event horizon. I wrote:

```
[NEXT: Drake to Raiford. Stops on the way at vegetable
stand to talk to the guy who runs it, old source, needs a
good & colorful name. Straw hat. DisneyWorld tee-shirt.
They talk about Shackleford.]
```

I turned the roller until the IBM spat this page out, stuck it on top of the manuscript and jotted a final note to myself: 'Call Ted Rosencrief about Raiford.' Rosencrief was a retired Navy man who lived in Derry. I had employed him as a research assistant on several books, using him on one project to find out how paper was made, what the migratory habits of certain common birds were for another, a little bit about the architecture of pyramid burial rooms for a third. And it's always 'a little bit' I want, never 'the whole damn thing.' As a writer, my motto has always been don't confuse me with the facts. The Arthur Hailey type of faction is beyond me – I can't read it, let alone write it. I want to know just enough so I can lie colorfully. Rosie knew that, and we had always worked well together.

This time I needed to know a little bit about Florida's Raiford

Prison, and what the deathhouse down there is really like. I also needed a little bit on the psychology of serial killers. I thought Rosie would probably be glad to hear from me . . . almost as glad as I was to finally have something to call him about.

I picked up the eight double-spaced pages I had written and fanned through them, still amazed at their existence. Had an old IBM typewriter and a Courier type-ball been the secret all along? That was certainly how it seemed.

What had come out was also amazing. I'd had ideas during my four-year sabbatical; there had been no writer's block in that regard. One had been really great, the sort of thing which certainly would have become a novel if I'd still been able to write novels. Half a dozen to a dozen were of the sort I'd classify 'pretty good,' meaning they'd do in a pinch . . . or if they happened to unexpectedly grow tall and mysterious overnight, like Jack's beanstalk. Sometimes they do. Most were glimmers, little 'what-ifs' that came and went like shooting stars while I was driving or walking or just lying in bed at night and waiting to go to sleep.

The Red-Shirt Man was a what-if. One day I saw a man in a bright red shirt washing the show windows of the JC Penney store in Derry – this was not long before Penney's moved out to the mall. A young man and woman walked under his ladder . . . very bad luck, according to the old superstition. These two didn't know *where* they were walking, though – they were holding hands, drinking deeply of each other's eyes, as completely in love as any two twenty-year-olds in the history of the world. The man was tall, and as I watched, the top of his head came within an ace of clipping the window-washer's feet. If that had happened, the whole works might have gone over.

The entire incident was history in five seconds. Writing *The Red-Shirt Man* took five months. Except in truth, the entire book was done in a what-if second. I imagined a collision instead of a near-miss. Everything else followed from there. The writing was just secretarial.

The idea I was currently working on wasn't one of Mike's Really Great Ideas (Jo's voice carefully made the capitals), but it wasn't a what-if, either. Nor was it much like my old gothic suspense yarns; V. C. Andrews with a prick was nowhere in sight this time. But it felt solid, like the real thing, and this morning it had come out as naturally as a breath.

Andy Drake was a private investigator in Key Largo. He was forty years old, divorced, the father of a three-year-old girl. At the open he was in the Key West home of a woman named Regina Whiting. Mrs Whiting also had a little girl, hers five years old. Mrs Whiting was married to an extremely rich developer who did not know what Andy Drake knew: that until 1992, Regina Taylor Whiting had been Tiffany Taylor, a high-priced Miami call-girl.

That much I had written before the phone started ringing. Here is what I knew beyond that point, the secretarial work I'd do over the next several weeks, assuming that my marvellously recovered ability to work held up:

One day when Karen Whiting was three, the phone had rung while she and her mother were sitting in the patio hot tub. Regina thought of asking the yard-guy to answer it, then decided to get it herself – their regular man was out with the flu, and she didn't feel comfortable about asking a stranger for a favor. Cautioning her daughter to sit still, Regina hopped out to answer the phone. When Karen put up a hand to keep from being splashed as her mother left the tub, she dropped the doll she had been bathing. When she bent to pick it up, her hair became caught in one of the hot tub's powerful intakes. (It was reading of a fatal accident like this that had originally kicked the story off in my mind two or three years before.)

The yard-man, some no-name in a khaki shirt sent over by a day-labor outfit, saw what was happening. He raced across the lawn, dove headfirst into the tub, and yanked the child from the bottom, leaving hair and a good chunk of scalp clogging the jet when he did. He'd give her artificial respiration until she began to breathe again. (This would be a wonderful, suspenseful scene, and I couldn't wait to write it.) He would refuse all of the hysterical, relieved mother's offers of recompense, although he'd finally give her an address so that her husband could talk to him. Only both the address and his name, John Sanborn, would turn out to be a fake.

Two years later the ex-hooker with the respectable second life sees the man who saved her child on the front page of the Miami paper. His name is given as John Shackleford and he has been arrested for the rape-murder of a nine-year-old girl. And, the article goes on, he is suspected in over forty other murders, many of the victims children. 'Have you caught Baseball Cap?' one of the reporters would yell at the press conference. 'Is John Shackleford Baseball Cap?'

'Well,' I said, going downstairs, 'they sure *think* he is.'

I could hear too many boats out on the lake this afternoon to make nude bathing an option. I pulled on my suit, slung a towel over my shoulders, and started down the path – the one which had been lined with glowing paper lanterns in my dream – to wash off the sweat of my nightmares and my unexpected morning's labors.

There are twenty-three railroad-tie steps between Sara and the lake. I had gone down only four or five before the enormity of what had just happened hit me. My mouth began to tremble. The colors of the trees and the sky mixed together as my eyes teared up. A sound began to come out of me – a kind of muffled groaning. The strength ran out of my legs and I sat down hard on a railroad tie. For a moment I thought it was over, mostly just a false alarm, and then I began to cry. I stuffed one end of the towel in my mouth during the worst of it, afraid that if the boaters on the lake heard the sounds coming out of me, they'd think someone up here was being murdered.

I cried in grief for the empty years I had spent without Jo, without friends, and without my work. I cried in gratitude because those workless years seemed to be over. It was too early to tell for sure – one swallow doesn't make a summer and eight pages of hard copy don't make a career resuscitation – but I thought it really might be so. And I cried out of fear, as well, as we do when some awful experience is finally over or when some terrible accident has been narrowly averted. I cried because I suddenly realized that I had been walking a white line ever since Jo died, walking straight down the middle of the road. By some miracle, I had been carried out of harm's way. I had no idea who had done the carrying, but that was all right – it was a question that could wait for another day.

I cried it all out of me. Then I went on down to the lake and waded in. The cool water felt more than good on my overheated body; it felt like a resurrection.

232

CHAPTER FIFTEEN

'State your name for the record.'

'Michael Noonan.'

'Your address?'

'Derry is my permanent address, 14 Benton Street, but I also maintain a home in TR-90, on Dark Score Lake. The mailing address is Box 832. The actual house is on Lane Forty-two, off Route 68.'

Elmer Durgin, Kyra Devore's guardian *ad litem*, waved a pudgy hand in front of his face, either to shoo away some troublesome insect or to tell me that was enough. I agreed that it was. I felt rather like the little girl in *Our Town* who gave her address as Grover's Corner, New Hampshire, America, the Northern Hemisphere, the World, the Solar System, the Milky Way Galaxy, the Mind of God. Mostly I was nervous. I'd reached the age of forty still a virgin in the area of court proceedings, and although we were in the conference room of Durgin, Peters, and Jarrette on Bridge Street in Castle Rock, this was still a court proceeding.

There was one mentionably odd detail to these festivities. The stenographer wasn't using one of those keyboards-on-a-post that look like adding machines, but a Stenomask, a gadget which fit over the lower half of his face. I had seen them before, but only in old black-and-white crime movies, the ones where Dan Duryea or John Payne is always driving around in a Buick with portholes on the sides, looking grim and smoking a Camel. Glancing over into the corner and seeing a guy who looked like the world's oldest fighter-pilot was weird enough, but hearing everything you said immediately repeated in a muffled monotone was even weirder.

'Thank you, Mr Noonan. My wife has read all your books and says you are her favorite author. I just wanted to get that on the record.' Durgin chuckled fatly. Why not? He was a fat guy. Most fat people I like – they have expansive natures to go with their expansive waistlines. But there *is* a subgroup which I think of as the Evil Little Fat Folks. You don't want to fuck with the ELFFs if you can help it; they will burn your house and rape your dog if you give them half an excuse and a quarter of an opportunity. Few of them stand over five-foot-two (Durgin's height, I estimated), and many are under five feet. They smile a lot, but their eyes don't smile. The Evil Little Fat Folks hate the whole world. Mostly they hate folks who can look down the length of their bodies and still see their own feet. This included me, although just barely.

'Please thank your wife for me, Mr Durgin. I'm sure she could recommend one for you to start on.'

Durgin chuckled. On his right, Durgin's assistant – a pretty young woman who looked approximately seventeen minutes out of law school – chuckled. On my left, Romeo Bissonette chuckled. In the corner, the world's oldest F-111 pilot only went on muttering into his Stenomask.

'I'll wait for the big-screen version,' he said. His eyes gave an ugly little gleam, as if he knew a feature film had never been made from any of my books – only a made-for-TV movie of *Being Two* that pulled ratings roughly equal to the National Sofa Refinishing Championships. I hoped that we'd completed this chubby little fuck's idea of the pleasantries.

'I am Kyra Devore's guardian *ad litem*,' he said. 'Do you know what that means, Mr Noonan?'

'I believe I do.'

'It means,' Durgin rolled on, 'that I've been appointed by Judge Rancourt to decide – if I can – where Kyra Devore's best interests lie, should a custody judgment become necessary. Judge Rancourt would not, in such an event, be required to base his decision on my conclusions, but in many cases that is what happens.'

He looked at me with his hands folded on a blank legal pad. The pretty assistant, on the other hand, was scribbling madly. Perhaps she didn't trust the fighter-pilot. Durgin looked as if he expected a round of applause.

'Was that a question, Mr Durgin?' I asked, and Romeo Bissonette delivered a light, practiced chip to my ankle. I didn't need to look at him to know it wasn't an accident.

Durgin pursed lips so smooth and damp that he looked as if he were wearing a clear gloss on them. On his shining pate, roughly two dozen strands of hair were combed in smooth little arcs. He gave me a patient, measuring look. Behind it was all the intransigent ugliness of an Evil Little Fat Folk. The pleasantries were over, all right. I was sure of it.

'No, Mr Noonan, that was not a question. I simply thought you might like to know why we've had to ask you to come away from your lovely lake on such a pleasant morning. Perhaps I was wrong. Now, if—'

There was a peremptory knock on the door, followed by your friend and his, George Footman. Today Cleveland Casual had been replaced by a khaki Deputy Sheriff's uniform, complete with Sam Browne belt and sidearm. He helped himself to a good look at the assistant's bustline, displayed in a blue silk blouse, then handed her a folder and a cassette tape recorder. He gave me one brief gander before leaving. *I remember you, buddy,* that glance said. *The smartass writer, the cheap date.*

Romeo Bissonette tipped his head toward me. He used the side of his hand to bridge the gap between his mouth and my ear. 'Devore's tape,' he said.

I nodded to show I understood, then turned to Durgin again.

'Mr Noonan, you've met Kyra Devore and her mother, Mary Devore, haven't you?'

How did you get Mattie out of Mary, I wondered . . . and then knew, just as I had known about the white shorts and halter top. *Mattie* was how Ki had first tried to say *Mary*.

'Mr Noonan, are we keeping you up?'

'There's no need to be sarcastic, is there?' Bissonette asked. His tone was mild, but Elmer Durgin gave him a look which suggested that, should the ELFFs succeed in their goal of world domination, Bissonette would be aboard the first gulag-bound boxcar.

'I'm sorry,' I said before Durgin could reply. 'I just got derailed there for a second or two.'

'New story idea?' Durgin asked, smiling his glossy smile. He looked like a swamp-toad in a sportcoat. He turned to the old jet pilot, told him to strike that last, then repeated his question about Kyra and Mattie.

Yes, I said, I had met them.

'Once or more than once?'

'More than once.'

'How many times have you met them?'

'Twice.'

'Have you also spoken to Mary Devore on the phone?'

Already these questions were moving in a direction that made me uncomfortable.

'Yes.'

'How many times?'

'Three times.' The third had come the day before, when she had asked if I would join her and John Storrow for a picnic lunch on the town common after my deposition. Lunch right there in the middle of town before God and everybody . . . although, with a New York lawyer to play chaperone, what harm in that?

'Have you spoken to Kyra Devore on the telephone?'

What an odd question! Not one anybody had prepared me for, either. I supposed that was at least partly why he had asked it.

'Mr Noonan?'

'Yes, I've spoken to her once.'

'Can you tell us the nature of that conversation?'

'Well . . .' I looked doubtfully at Bissonette, but there was no help there. He obviously didn't know, either. 'Mattie—'

'Pardon me?' Durgin leaned forward as much as he could. His eyes were intent in their pink pockets of flesh. 'Mattie?'

'Mattie Devore. *Mary* Devore.'

'You call her Mattie?'

'Yes,' I said, and had a wild impulse to add: *In bed! In bed I call her that! 'Oh Mattie, don't stop, don't stop,' I cry!* 'It's the name she gave me when she introduced herself. I met her—'

'We may get to that, but right now I'm interested in your telephone conversation with Kyra Devore. When was that?'

'It was yesterday.'

'July ninth, 1998.'

'Yes.'

'Who placed that call?'

'Ma . . . Mary Devore.' *Now he'll ask why she called*, I thought, *and I'll say she wanted to have yet another sex marathon, foreplay to consist of feeding each other chocolate-dipped strawberries while we look at pictures of naked malformed dwarves.*

'How did Kyra Devore happen to speak to you?'

'She asked if she could. I heard her saying to her mother that she had to tell me something.'

'What was it she had to tell you?'

'That she had her first bubble bath.'

'Did she also say she coughed?'

I was quiet, looking at him. In that moment I understood why people hate lawyers, especially when they've been dusted over by one who's good at the job.

'Mr Noonan, would you like me to repeat the question?'

'No,' I said, wondering where he'd gotten his information. Had these bastards tapped Mattie's phone? My phone? Both? Perhaps for the first time I understood on a gut level what it must be like to have half a billion dollars. With that much dough you could tap a lot of telephones. 'She said her mother pushed bubbles in her face and she coughed. But she was—'

'Thank you, Mr Noonan, now let's turn to—'

'Let him finish,' Bissonette said. I had an idea he had already taken a bigger part in the proceedings than he had expected to, but he didn't seem to mind. He was a sleepy-looking man with a bloodhound's face. 'This isn't a courtroom, and you're not cross-examining him.'

'I have the little girl's welfare to think of,' Durgin said. He sounded both pompous and humble at the same time, a combination that went together like chocolate sauce on creamed corn. 'It's a responsibility I take very seriously. If I seemed to be badgering you, Mr Noonan, I apologize.'

I didn't bother accepting his apology – that would have made us both phonies. 'All I was going to say is that Ki was laughing when she said it. She said she and her mother had a bubble-fight. When her mother came back on, she was laughing, too.'

Durgin had opened the folder Footman had brought him and was paging rapidly through it while I spoke, as if he weren't hearing a word. 'Her mother . . . Mattie, as you call her.'

'Yes. Mattie as I call her. How do you know about our private telephone conversation in the first place?'

'That's none of your business, Mr Noonan.' He selected a single sheet of paper, then closed the folder. He held the paper up briefly, like a doctor studying an X-ray, and I could see it was covered with single-spaced typing. 'Let's turn to your initial meeting with Mary and Kyra Devore. That was on the Fourth of July, wasn't it?'

'Yes.'

Durgin was nodding. 'The morning of the Fourth. And you met Kyra Devore first.'

'Yes.'

'You met her first because her mother wasn't with her at that time, was she?'

'That's a badly phrased question, Mr Durgin, but I guess the answer is yes.'

'I'm flattered to have my grammar corrected by a man who's been on the bestseller lists,' Durgin said, smiling. The smile suggested that he'd like to see me sitting next to Romeo Bissonette in that first gulag-bound boxcar. 'Tell us about your meeting, first with Kyra Devore and then with Mary Devore. Or Mattie, if you like that better.'

I told the story. When I was finished, Durgin centered the tape player in front of him. The nails of his pudgy fingers looked as glossy as his lips.

'Mr Noonan, you could have run Kyra over, isn't that true?'

'Absolutely not. I was going thirty-five – that's the speed limit there by the store. I saw her in plenty of time to stop.'

'Suppose you had been coming the other way, though – heading north instead of south. Would you still have seen her in plenty of time?'

That was a fairer question than some of his others, actually. Someone coming the other way would have had a far shorter time to react. Still . . .

'Yes,' I said.

Durgin went up with the eyebrows. 'You're sure of that?'

'Yes, Mr Durgin. I might have had to come down a little harder on the brakes, but—'

'At thirty-five.'

'Yes, at thirty-five. I told you, that's the speed limit—'

'—on that particular stretch of Route 68. Yes, you told me that. You did. Is it your experience that most people obey the speed limit on that part of the road?'

'I haven't spent much time on the TR since 1993, so I can't—'

'Come on, Mr Noonan – this isn't a scene from one of your books. Just answer my questions, or we'll be here all morning.'

'I'm doing my best, Mr Durgin.'

He sighed, put-upon. 'You've owned your place on Dark Score Lake since the eighties, haven't you? And the speed limit around the Lakeview General Store, the post office, and Dick Brooks's All-Purpose Garage – what's called The North Village – hasn't changed since then, has it?'

'No,' I admitted.

'Returning to my original question, then – in your observation, do most people on that stretch of road obey the thirty-five-mile-an-hour limit?'

'I can't say if it's most, because I've never done a traffic survey, but I guess a lot don't.'

'Would you like to hear Castle County Sheriff's Deputy Footman testify on where the greatest number of speeding tickets are given out in TR-90, Mr Noonan?'

'No,' I said, quite honestly.

'Did other vehicles pass you while you were speaking first with Kyra Devore and then with Mary Devore?'

'Yes.'

'How many?'

'I don't know exactly. A couple.'

'Could it have been three?'

'I guess.'

'Five?'

'No, probably not so many.'

'But you don't know, exactly, do you?'

'No.'

'Because Kyra Devore was upset.'

'Actually she had it together pretty well for a—'

'Did she cry in your presence?'

'Well . . . yes.'

239

'Did her mother make her cry?'

'That's unfair.'

'As unfair as allowing a three-year-old to go strolling down the middle of a busy highway on a holiday morning, in your opinion, or perhaps not quite as unfair as that?'

'Jeepers, lay off,' Mr Bissonette said mildly. There was distress on his bloodhound's face.

'I withdraw the question,' Durgin said.

'Which one?' I asked.

He looked at me tiredly, as if to say he had to put up with assholes like me all the time and he was used to how we behaved. 'How many cars went by from the time you picked the child up and carried her to safety to the time when you and the Devores parted company?'

I hated that 'carried her to safety' bit, but even as I formulated my answer, the old guy was muttering the question into his Stenomask. And it was in fact what I had done. There was no getting around it.

'I told you, I don't know for sure.'

'Well, give me a guesstimate.'

Guesstimate. One of my all-time least favorite words. A Paul Harvey word. 'There might have been three.'

'Including Mary Devore herself? Driving a—' He consulted the paper he'd taken from the folder. '—a 1982 Jeep Scout?'

I thought of Ki saying *Mattie go fast* and understood where Durgin was heading now. And there was nothing I could do about it.

'Yes, it was her and it was a Scout. I don't know what year.'

'Was she driving below the posted speed limit, at the posted speed limit, or above the posted speed limit when she passed the place where you were standing with Kyra in your arms?'

She'd been doing at least fifty, but I told Durgin I couldn't say for sure. He urged me to try – *I know you are unfamiliar with the hangman's knot, Mr Noonan, but I'm sure you can make one if you really work at it* – and I declined as politely as I could.

He picked up the paper again. 'Mr Noonan, would it surprise you to know that two witnesses – Richard Brooks, Junior, the owner of Dick's All-Purpose Garage, and Royce Merrill, a retired carpenter – claim that Mrs Devore was doing well over thirty-five when she passed your location?'

240

'I don't know,' I said. 'I was concerned with the little girl.'

'Would it surprise you to know that Royce Merrill estimated her speed at *sixty* miles an hour?'

'That's ridiculous. When she hit the brakes she would have skidded sideways and landed upside down in the ditch.'

'The skid-marks measured by Deputy Footman indicate a speed of at least fifty miles an hour,' Durgin said. It wasn't a question, but he looked at me almost roguishly, as if inviting me to struggle a little more and sink a little deeper into this nasty pit. I said nothing. Durgin folded his pudgy little hands and leaned over them toward me. The roguish look was gone.

'Mr Noonan, if you hadn't carried Kyra Devore to the side of the road – if you hadn't rescued her – mightn't *her own mother* have run her over?'

Here was the really loaded question, and how should I answer it? Bissonette was certainly not flashing any helpful signals; he seemed to be trying to make meaningful eye-contact with the pretty assistant. I thought of the book Mattie was reading in tandem with 'Bartleby' – *Silent Witness*, by Richard North Patterson. Unlike the Grisham brand, Patterson's lawyers almost always seemed to know what they were doing. *Objection, your honor, calls for speculation on the part of the witness*.

I shrugged. 'Sorry, counsellor, can't say – left my crystal ball at home.'

Again I saw the ugly flash in Durgin's eyes. 'Mr Noonan, I can assure you that if you don't answer that question here, you are apt to be called back from Malibu or Fire Island or wherever it is you're going to write your next opus to answer it later on.'

I shrugged. 'I've already told you I was concerned with the child. I can't tell you how fast the mother was going, or how good Royce Merrill's vision is, or if Deputy Footman even measured the right set of skid-marks. There's a whole bunch of rubber on that part of the road, I can tell you. Suppose she *was* going fifty? Even fifty-five, let's say that. She's twenty-one years old, Durgin. At the age of twenty-one, a person's driving skills are at their peak. She probably would have swerved around the child, and easily.'

'I think that's quite enough.'

'Why? Because you're not getting what you wanted?' Bissonette's shoe clipped my ankle again, but I ignored it. 'If you're on Kyra's side, why do you sound as though you're on her grandfather's?'

A baleful little smile touched Durgin's lips. The kind that says *Okay, smart guy, you want to play?* He pulled the tape-recorder a little closer to him. 'Since you have mentioned Kyra's grandfather, Mr Maxwell Devore of Palm Springs, let's talk about him a little, shall we?'

'It's your show.'

'Have you ever spoken with Maxwell Devore?'

'Yes.'

'In person or on the phone?'

'Phone.' I thought about adding that he had somehow gotten hold of my unlisted number, then remembered that Mattie had, too, and decided to keep my mouth shut on that subject.

'When was this?'

'Last Saturday night. The night of the Fourth. He called while I was watching the fireworks.'

'And was the subject of your conversation that morning's little adventure?' As he asked, Durgin reached into his pocket and brought out a cassette tape. There was an ostentatious quality to this gesture; in that moment he looked like a parlor magician showing you both sides of a silk handkerchief. And he was bluffing. I couldn't be sure of that . . . and yet I was. Devore had taped our conversation, all right – that underhum really had been too loud, and on some level I'd been aware of that fact even while I was talking to him – and I thought it really was on the cassette Durgin was now slotting into the cassette player . . . but it was a bluff.

'I don't recall,' I said.

Durgin's hand froze in the act of snapping the cassette's transparent loading panel shut. He looked at me with frank disbelief . . . and something else. I thought the something else was surprised anger.

'You don't recall? Come now, Mr Noonan. Surely writers *train* themselves to recall conversations, and this one was only a week ago. Tell me what you talked about.'

'I really can't say,' I told him in a stolid, colorless voice.

For a moment Durgin looked almost panicky. Then his features smoothed. One polished fingernail slipped back and forth over keys marked REW, FF, PLAY, and REC. 'How did Mr Devore begin the conversation?' he asked.

'He said hello,' I said mildly, and there was a short muffled sound from behind the Stenomask. It could have been the old guy clearing his throat; it could have been a suppressed laugh.

Spots of color were blooming in Durgin's cheeks. 'After hello? What then?'

'I don't recall.'

'Did he ask you about that morning?'

'I don't recall.'

'Didn't you tell him that Mary Devore and her daughter were together, Mr Noonan? That they were together picking flowers? Isn't that what you told this worried grandfather when he inquired about the incident which was the talk of the township that Fourth of July?'

'Oh boy,' Bissonette said. He raised one hand over the table, then touched the palm with the fingers of the other, making a ref's *T*. 'Time out.'

Durgin looked at him. The flush in his cheeks was more pronounced now, and his lips had pulled back enough to show the tips of small, neatly capped teeth. 'What do *you* want?' he almost snarled, as if Bissonette had just dropped by to tell him about the Mormon Way or perhaps the Rosicrucians.

'I want you to stop leading this guy, and I want that whole thing about picking flowers stricken from the record,' Bissonette said.

'Why?' Durgin snapped.

'Because you're trying to get stuff on the record that this witness won't say. If you want to break here for awhile so we can make a conference call to Judge Rancourt, get his opinion—'

'I withdraw the question,' Durgin said. He looked at me with a kind of helpless, surly rage. 'Mr Noonan, do you want to help me do my job?'

'I want to help Kyra Devore if I can,' I said.

'Very well.' He nodded as if no distinction had been made. 'Then please tell me what you and Maxwell Devore talked about.'

'I can't recall.' I caught his eyes and held them. 'Perhaps,' I said, 'you can refresh my recollection.'

There was a moment of silence, like that which sometimes strikes

243

a high-stakes poker game just after the last of the bets have been made and just before the players show their hands. Even the old fighter-pilot was quiet, his eyes unblinking above the mask. Then Durgin pushed the cassette player aside with the heel of his hand (the set of his mouth said he felt about it just then as I often felt about the telephone) and went back to the morning of July Fourth. He never asked about my dinner with Mattie and Ki on Tuesday night, and never returned to my telephone conversation with Devore – the one where I had said all those awkward and easily disprovable things.

I went on answering questions until eleven-thirty, but the interview really ended when Durgin pushed the tape-player away with the heel of his hand. I knew it, and I'm pretty sure he did, too.

'Mike! Mike, over here!'

Mattie was waving from one of the tables in the picnic area behind the town common's bandstand. She looked vibrant and happy. I waved back and made my way in that direction, weaving between little kids playing tag, skirting a couple of teenagers making out on the grass, and ducking a Frisbee which a German Shepherd leaped up and caught smartly.

There was a tall, skinny redhead with her, but I barely got a chance to notice him. Mattie met me while I was still on the gravel path, put her arms around me, hugged me – it was no prudey little ass-poking-out hug, either – and then kissed me on the mouth hard enough to push my lips against my teeth. There was a hearty smack when she disengaged. She pulled back and looked at me with undisguised delight. 'Was it the biggest kiss you've ever had?'

'The biggest in at least four years,' I said. 'Will you settle for that?' And if she didn't step away from me in the next few seconds, she was going to have physical proof of how much I had enjoyed it.

'I guess I'll have to.' She turned to the redheaded guy with a funny kind of defiance. 'Was that all right?'

'Probably not,' he said, 'but at least you're not currently in view of those old boys at the All-Purpose Garage. Mike, I'm John Storrow. Nice to meet you in person.'

I liked him at once, maybe because I'd come upon him dressed in his three-piece New York suit and primly setting out paper plates on a picnic table while his curly red hair blew around his head like kelp. His skin was fair and freckled, the kind which would never tan, only burn and then peel in great eczema-like patches. When we shook, his hand seemed to be all knuckles. He had to be at least thirty, but he looked Mattie's age, and I guessed it would be another five years before he was able to get a drink without showing his driver's license.

'Sit down,' he said. 'We've got a five-course lunch, courtesy of Castle Rock Variety – grinders, which are for some strange reason called "Italian sandwiches" up here . . . mozzarella sticks . . . garlic fries . . . Twinkies.'

'That's only four,' I said.

'I forgot the soft-drink course,' he said, and pulled three long-neck bottles of S'OK birch beer out of a brown bag. 'Let's eat. Mattie runs the library from two to eight on Fridays and Saturdays, and this would be a bad time for her to be missing work.'

'How did the readers' circle go last night?' I asked. 'Lindy Briggs didn't eat you alive, I see.'

She laughed, clasped her hands, and shook them over her head. 'I was a hit! An absolute smashola! I didn't dare tell them I got all my best insights from you—'

'Thank God for small favors,' Storrow said. He was freeing his own sandwich from its string and butcher-paper wrapping, doing it carefully and a little dubiously, using just the tips of his fingers.

'—so I said I looked in a couple of books and found some leads there. It was sort of wonderful. I felt like a college kid.'

'Good.'

'Bissonette?' John Storrow asked. 'Where's he? I never met a guy named Romeo before.'

'Said he had to go right back to Lewiston. Sorry.'

'Actually it's best we stay small, at least to begin with.' He bit into his sandwich – they come tucked into long sub rolls – and looked at me, surprised. 'This isn't bad.'

'Eat more than three and you're hooked for life,' Mattie said, and chomped heartily into her own.

'Tell us about the depo,' John said, and while they ate, I talked. When I finished, I picked up my own sandwich and played a little catch-up. I'd forgotten how good an Italian can be – sweet, sour, and oily all at the same time. Of course nothing that tastes that good

245

can be healthy; that's a given. I suppose one could formulate a similar postulate about full-body hugs from young girls in legal trouble.

'Very interesting,' John said. 'Very interesting indeed.' He took a mozzarella stick from its grease-stained bag, broke it open, and looked with a kind of fascinated horror at the clotted white gunk inside. 'People up here eat this?' he asked.

'People in New York eat fish-bladders,' I said. 'Raw.'

'Touché.' He dipped a piece into the plastic container of spaghetti sauce (in this context it is called 'cheese-dip' in western Maine), then ate it.

'Well?' I asked.

'Not bad. They ought to be a lot hotter, though.'

Yes, he was right about that. Eating cold mozzarella sticks is a little like eating cold snot, an observation I thought I would keep to myself on this beautiful midsummer Friday.

'If Durgin had the tape, why wouldn't he play it?' Mattie asked. 'I don't understand.'

John stretched his arms out, cracked his knuckles, and looked at her benignly. 'We'll probably never know for sure,' he said.

He thought Devore was going to drop the suit – it was in every line of his body-language and every inflection of his voice. That was hopeful, but it would be good if Mattie didn't allow herself to become *too* hopeful. John Storrow wasn't as young as he looked, and probably not as guileless, either (or so I fervently hoped), but he *was* young. And neither he nor Mattie knew the story of Scooter Larribee's sled. Or had seen Bill Dean's face when he told it.

'Want to hear some possibilities?'

'Sure,' I said.

John put down his sandwich, wiped his fingers, and then began to tick off points. 'First, *he* made the call. Taped conversations have a highly dubious value under those circumstances. Second, he didn't exactly come off like Captain Kangaroo, did he?'

'No.'

'Third, your fabrication impugns *you*, Mike, but not really very much, and it doesn't impugn Mattie at all. And by the way, that thing about Mattie pushing bubbles in Kyra's face, I love that. If that's the best they can do, they better give it up right now. Last

246

– and this is where the truth probably lies – I think Devore's got Nixon's Disease.'

'Nixon's Disease?' Mattie asked.

'The tape Durgin had isn't the only tape. Can't be. And your father-in-law is afraid that if he introduces one tape made by whatever system he's got in Warrington's, we might subpoena all of them. And I'd damn well try.'

She looked bewildered. 'What could be on them? And if it's bad, why not just destroy them?'

'Maybe he can't,' I said. 'Maybe he needs them for other reasons.'

'It doesn't really matter,' John said. 'Durgin was bluffing, and *that's* what matters.' He hit the heel of his hand lightly against the picnic table. 'I think he's going to drop it. I really do.'

'It's too early to start thinking like that,' I said at once, but I could tell by Mattie's face – shining more brightly than ever – that the damage was done.

'Fill him in on what else you've been doing,' Mattie told John. 'Then I've got to get to the library.'

'Where do you send Kyra on your workdays?' I asked.

'Mrs Cullum's. She lives two miles up the Wasp Hill Road. Also in July there's VBS from ten until three. That's Vacation Bible School. Ki loves it, especially the singing and the flannel-board stories about Noah and Moses. The bus drops her off at Arlene's, and I pick her up around quarter of nine.' She smiled a little wistfully. 'By then she's usually fast asleep on the couch.'

John held forth for the next ten minutes or so. He hadn't been on the case long, but had already started a lot of balls rolling. A fellow in California was gathering facts about Roger Devore and Morris Ridding ('gathering facts' sounded so much better than 'snooping'). John was particularly interested in learning about the quality of Roger Devore's relations with his father, and if Roger was on record concerning his little niece from Maine. John had also mapped out a campaign to learn as much as possible about Max Devore's movements and activities since he'd come back to TR-90. To that end he had the name of a private investigator, one recommended by Romeo Bissonette, my rent-a-lawyer.

As he spoke, paging rapidly through a little notebook he drew from the inside pocket of his suitcoat, I remembered what he'd said about Lady Justice during our telephone conversation: *Slap some handcuffs on that broad's wrists and some tape over her mouth to go along with the blindfold, rape her and roll her in the mud.* That was maybe a bit too strong for what we were doing, but I thought at the very least we were shoving her around a little. I imagined poor Roger Devore up on the stand, having flown three thousand miles in order to be questioned about his sexual preferences. I had to keep reminding myself that his father had put him in that position, not Mattie or me or John Storrow.

'Have you gotten any closer to a meeting with Devore and his chief legal advisor?' I asked.

'Don't know for sure. The line is in the water, the offer is on the table, the puck's on the ice, pick your favorite metaphor, mix em and match em if you desire.'

'Got your irons in the fire,' Mattie said.

'Your checkers on the board,' I added.

We looked at each other and laughed. John regarded us sadly, then sighed, picked up his sandwich, and began to eat again.

'You really have to meet him with his lawyer more or less dancing attendance?' I asked.

'Would you like to win this thing, then discover Devore can do it all again based on unethical behavior by Mary Devore's legal resource?' John returned.

'Don't even joke about it!' Mattie cried.

'I wasn't joking,' John said. 'It has to be with his lawyer, yes. I don't think it's going to happen, not on this trip. I haven't even got a look at the old *cockuh*, and I have to tell you my curiosity is killing me.'

'If that's all it takes to make you happy, show up behind the backstop at the softball field next Tuesday evening,' Mattie said. 'He'll be there in his fancy wheelchair, laughing and clapping and sucking his damned old oxygen every fifteen minutes or so.'

'Not a bad idea,' John said. 'I have to go back to New York for the weekend – I'm leaving *après* Osgood – but maybe I'll show up on Tuesday. I might even bring my glove.' He began clearing up our litter, and once again I thought he looked both prissy and endearing

248

at the same time, like Stan Laurel wearing an apron. Mattie eased him aside and took over.

'No one ate any Twinkies,' she said, a little sadly.

'Take them home to your daughter,' John said.

'No way. I don't let her eat stuff like this. What kind of mother do you think I am?'

She saw our expressions, replayed what she'd just said, then burst out laughing. We joined her.

Mattie's old Scout was parked in one of the slant spaces behind the war memorial, which in Castle Rock is a World War I soldier with a generous helping of birdshit on his pie-dish helmet. A brand-new Taurus with a Hertz decal above the inspection sticker was parked next to it. John tossed his briefcase — reassuringly thin and not very ostentatious — into the back seat.

'If I can make it back on Tuesday, I'll call you,' he told Mattie. 'If I'm able to get an appointment with your father-in-law through this man Osgood, I will also call you.'

'I'll buy the Italian sandwiches,' Mattie said.

He smiled, then grasped her arm in one hand and mine in the other. He looked like a newly ordained minister getting ready to marry his first couple.

'You two talk on the telephone if you need to,' he said, 'always remembering that one or both lines may be tapped. Meet in the market if you happen to. Mike, you might feel a need to drop by the local library and check out a book.'

'Not until you renew your card, though,' Mattie said, giving me a demure glance.

'But no more visits to Mattie's trailer. Is that understood?'

I said yes; she said yes; John Storrow looked unconvinced. It made me wonder if he was seeing something in our faces or bodies that shouldn't be there.

'They are committed to a line of attack which probably isn't going to work,' he said. 'We can't risk giving them the chance to change course. That means innuendos about the two of you; it also means innuendos about Mike and Kyra.'

Mattie's shocked expression made her look twelve again. 'Mike and Kyra! What are you talking about?'

249

'Allegations of child molestation thrown up by people so desperate they'll try anything.'

'That's ridiculous,' she said. 'And if my father-in-law wanted to sling that kind of mud—'

John nodded. 'Yes, we'd be obligated to sling it right back. Newspaper coverage from coast to coast would follow, maybe even Court TV, God bless and save us. We want none of that if we can avoid it. It's not good for the grownups, and it's not good for the child. Now or later.'

He bent and kissed Mattie's cheek.

'I'm sorry about all this,' he said, and he did sound genuinely sorry. 'Custody's just this way.'

'I think you warned me. It's just that . . . the idea someone might make a thing like that up just because there was no other way for them to win . . .'

'Let me warn you again,' he said. His face came as close to grim as its young and good-natured features would probably allow. 'What we have is a very rich man with a very shaky case. The combination could be like working with old dynamite.'

I turned to Mattie. 'Are you still worried about Ki? Still feel she's in danger?'

I saw her think about hedging her response – out of plain old Yankee reserve, quite likely – and then decide not to. Deciding, perhaps, that hedging was a luxury she couldn't afford.

'Yes. But it's just a feeling, you know.'

John was frowning. I supposed the idea that Devore might resort to extralegal means of obtaining what he wanted had occurred to him, as well. 'Keep your eye on her as much as you can,' he said. 'I respect intuition. Is yours based on anything concrete?'

'No,' Mattie answered, and her quick glance in my direction asked me to keep my mouth shut. 'Not really.' She opened the Scout's door and tossed in the little brown bag with the Twinkies in it – she had decided to keep them after all. Then she turned to John and me with an expression that was close to anger. 'I'm not sure how to follow that advice, anyway. I work five days a week, and in August, when we do the microfiche update, it'll be six. Right now Ki gets her lunch at Vacation Bible School and her dinner from Arlene Cullum. I see her in the mornings. The rest of the time . . .'

250

I knew what she was going to say before she said it; the expression was an old one. '. . .she's on the TR.'

'I could help you find an *au pair*,' I said, thinking it would be a hell of a lot cheaper than John Storrow.

'No,' they said in such perfect unison that they glanced at each other and laughed. But even while she was laughing, Mattie looked tense and unhappy.

'We're not going to leave a paper trail for Durgin or Devore's custody team to exploit,' John said. 'Who pays me is one thing. Who pays Mattie's child-care help is another.'

'Besides, I've taken enough from you,' Mattie said. 'More than I can sleep easy on. I'm not going to get in any deeper just because I've been having megrims.' She climbed into the Scout and closed the door.

I rested my hands on her open window. Now we were on the same level, and the eye-contact was so strong it was disconcerting. 'Mattie, I don't have anything else to spend it on. Really.'

'When it comes to John's fee, I accept that. Because John's fee is about Ki.' She put her hand over mine and squeezed briefly. 'This other is about me. All right?'

'Yeah. But you need to tell your babysitter and the people who run this Bible thing that you've got a custody case on your hands, a potentially bitter one, and Kyra's not to go anywhere with anyone, even someone they know, without your say-so.'

She smiled. 'It's already been done. On John's advice. Stay in touch, Mike.' She lifted my hand, gave it a hearty smack, and drove away.

'What do you think?' I asked John as we watched the Scout blow oil on its way to the new Prouty Bridge, which spans Castle Stream and spills outbound traffic on to Highway 68.

'I think it's grand she has a well-heeled benefactor and a smart lawyer,' John said. He paused, then added: 'But I'll tell you something – she somehow doesn't feel lucky to me at all. There's a feeling I get . . . I don't know . . .'

'That there's a cloud around her you can't quite see.'

'Maybe. Maybe that's it.' He raked his hands through the restless mass of his red hair. 'I just know it's something sad.'

I knew exactly what he meant . . . except for me there was more.

I wanted to be in bed with her, sad or not, right or not. I wanted to feel her hands on me, tugging and pressing, patting and stroking. I wanted to be able to smell her skin and taste her hair. I wanted to have her lips against my ear, her breath tickling the fine hairs within its cup as she told me to do what I wanted, whatever I wanted.

I got back to Sara Laughs shortly before two o'clock and let myself in, thinking about nothing but my study and the IBM with the Courier ball. I was writing again – *writing*. I could still hardly believe it. I'd work (not that it felt much like work after a four-year layoff) until maybe six o'clock, swim, then go down to the Village Cafe for one of Buddy's cholesterol-rich specialties.

The moment I stepped through the door, Bunter's bell began to ring stridently. I stopped in the foyer, my hand frozen on the knob. The house was hot and bright, not a shadow anywhere, but the gooseflesh forming on my arms felt like midnight.

'Who's here?' I called.

The bell stopped ringing. There was a moment of silence, and then a woman shrieked. It came from everywhere, pouring out of the sunny, mote-laden air like sweat out of hot skin. It was a scream of outrage, anger, grief . . . but mostly, I think, of horror. And I screamed in response. I couldn't help it. I had been frightened standing in the dark cellar stairwell, listening to the unseen fist thump on the insulation, but this was far worse.

It never stopped, that scream. It faded, as the child's sobs had faded; faded as if the person screaming was being carried rapidly down a long corridor and away from me.

At last it was gone.

I leaned against the bookcase, my palm pressed against my tee-shirt, my heart galloping beneath it. I was gasping for breath, and my muscles had that queer *exploded* feel they get after you've had a bad scare.

A minute passed. My heartbeat gradually slowed, and my breathing slowed with it. I straightened up, took a tottery step, and when my legs held me, took two more. I stood in the kitchen doorway, looking across to the living room. Above the fireplace, Bunter the moose looked glassily back at me. The bell around his neck hung still and chimeless. A hot sunpoint glowed on its

252

side. The only sound was that stupid Felix the Cat clock in the kitchen.

The thought nagging at me, even then, was that the screaming woman had been Jo, that Sara Laughs was being haunted by my wife, and that she was in pain. Dead or not, she was in pain.

'Jo?' I asked quietly. 'Jo, are you—'

The sobbing began again – the sound of a terrified child. At the same moment my mouth and nose once more filled with the iron taste of the lake. I put one hand to my throat, gagging and frightened, then leaned over the sink and spat. It was as it had been before – instead of voiding a gush of water, nothing came out but a little spit. The waterlogged feeling was gone as if it had never been there.

I stayed where I was, grasping the counter and bent over the sink, probably looking like a drunk who has finished the party by upchucking most of the night's bottled cheer. I felt like that, too – stunned and bleary, too overloaded to really understand what was going on.

At last I straightened up again, took the towel folded over the dishwasher's handle, and wiped my face with it. There was tea in the fridge, and I wanted a tall, ice-choked glass of it in the worst way. I reached for the doorhandle and froze. The fruit and vegetable magnets were drawn into a circle again. In the center was this:

help im drown

That's it, I thought. *I'm getting out of here. Right now. Today.*

Yet an hour later I was up in my stifling study with a glass of tea on the desk beside me (the cubes in it long since melted), dressed only in my bathing trunks and lost in the world I was making – the one where a private detective named Andy Drake was trying to prove that John Shackleford was not the serial killer nicknamed Baseball Cap.

This is how we go on: one day at a time, one meal at a time, one pain at a time, one breath at a time. Dentists go on one root-canal at a time; boat-builders go on one hull at a time. If you write books, you go on one page at a time. We turn from all we know and all we fear. We study catalogues, watch football games, choose Sprint over AT&T. We count the birds in the sky and will not turn from the

253

window when we hear the footsteps behind us as something comes up the hall; we say yes, I agree that clouds often look like other things – fish and unicorns and men on horseback – but they are really only clouds. Even when the lightning flashes inside them we say they are only clouds and turn our attention to the next meal, the next pain, the next breath, the next page. This is how we go on.

CHAPTER SIXTEEN

The book was big, okay? The book was major.

I was afraid to change *rooms*, let alone pack up the typewriter and my slim just-begun manuscript and take it back to Derry. That would be as dangerous as taking an infant out in a windstorm. So I stayed, always reserving the right to move out if things got too weird (the way smokers reserve the right to quit if their coughs get too heavy), and a week passed. Things happened during that week, but until I met Max Devore on The Street the following Friday – the seventeenth of July, it would have been – the most important thing was that I continued to work on a novel which would, if finished, be called *My Childhood Friend*. Perhaps we always think what was lost was the best . . . or would have been the best. I don't know for sure. What I *do* know is that my real life that week had mostly to do with Andy Drake, John Shackleford, and a shadowy figure standing in the deep background. Raymond Garraty, John Shackleford's childhood friend. A man who sometimes wore a baseball cap.

During that week, the manifestations in the house continued, but at a lower level – there was nothing like that bloodcurdling scream. Sometimes Bunter's bell rang, and sometimes the fruit and vegetable magnets would re-form themselves into a circle . . . never with words in the middle, though; not that week. One morning I got up and the sugar cannister was overturned, making me think of Mattie's story about the flour. Nothing was written in the spill, but there was a squiggle—

—as though something had tried to write and failed. If so, I sympathized. I knew what *that* was like.

My depo before the redoubtable Elmer Durgin was on Friday the tenth. On the following Tuesday I took The Street down to Warrington's softball field, hoping for my own peek at Max Devore. It was going on six o'clock when I got within hearing range of the shouts, cheers, and batted balls. A path marked with rustic signs (curlicued *W*'s burned into oak arrows) led past an abandoned boathouse, a couple of sheds, and a gazebo half-buried in blackberry creepers. I eventually came out in deep center field. A litter of potato-chip bags, candy-wrappers, and beer cans suggested that others sometimes watched the games from this vantage-point. I couldn't help thinking about Jo and her mysterious friend, the guy in the old brown sportcoat, the burly guy who had slipped an arm around her waist and led her away from the game, laughing, back toward The Street. Twice over the weekend I'd come close to calling Bonnie Amudson seeing if maybe I could chase that guy down, put a name on him, and both times I had backed off. Sleeping dogs, I told myself each time. Sleeping dogs, Michael.

I had the area beyond deep center to myself that evening, and it felt like the right distance from home plate, considering the man who usually parked his wheelchair behind the backstop had called me a liar and I had invited him to store my telephone number where the sunshine grows dim.

I needn't have worried in any case. Devore wasn't in attendance, nor was the lovely Rogette.

I did spot Mattie behind the casually maintained chickenwire barrier on the first-base line. John Storrow was beside her, wearing jeans and a polo shirt, his red hair mostly corralled by a Mets cap. They stood watching the game and chatting like old friends for two innings before they saw me – more than enough time for me to feel envious of John's position, and a little jealous as well.

Finally someone lofted a long fly to center, where the edge of the woods served as the only fence. The center fielder backed up, but it was going to be far over his head. It was hit to my depth, off to my right. I moved in that direction without thinking, high-footing through the shrubs that formed a zone between the mown outfield and the trees, hoping I wasn't running through poison ivy. I caught the softball in my outstretched left hand, and laughed when some of the spectators cheered. The center fielder applauded me by tapping his bare right hand into the pocket of his glove. The batter, meanwhile, circled the bases serenely, knowing he had hit a ground-rule home run.

I tossed the ball to the fielder, and as I returned to my original post among the candy-wrappers and beer cans, I looked back in and saw Mattie and John looking at me.

If anything confirms the idea that we're just another species of animal, one with a slightly bigger brain and a *much* bigger idea of our own importance in the scheme of things, it's how much we can convey by gesture when we absolutely have to. Mattie clasped her hands to her chest, tilted her head to the left, raised her eyebrows – *My hero*. I held my hands to my shoulders and flipped the palms skyward – *Shucks, ma'am, 't'warn't nothin.* John lowered his head and put his fingers to his brow, as if something there hurt – *You lucky sonofabitch.*

With those comments out of the way, I pointed at the backstop and shrugged a question. Both Mattie and John shrugged back. An inning later a little boy who looked like one giant exploding freckle ran out to where I was, his oversized Michael Jordan jersey churning around his shins like a dress.

'Guy down there gimme fifty cent to say you should call im later on at his hotel over in the Rock,' he said, pointing at John. 'He say you gimme another fifty cent if there was an answer.'

'Tell him I'll call him around nine-thirty,' I said. 'I don't have any change, though. Can you take a buck?'

'Hey, yeah, swank.' He snatched it, turned away, then turned back. He grinned, revealing a set of teeth caught between Act I and Act II. With the softball players in the background, he looked like a Norman Rockwell archetype. 'Guy also say tell you that was a bullshit catch.'

'Tell him people used to say the same thing about Willie Mays all the time.'

'Willie who?'

Ah, youth. Ah, mores. 'Just tell him, son. He'll know.'

I stayed another inning, but by then the game was getting drunk,

Devore still hadn't shown, and I went back home the way I had come. I met one fisherman standing out on a rock and two young people strolling along The Street toward Warrington's, their hands linked. They said hi and I hi'd them back. I felt lonely and content at the same time. I believe that is a rare kind of happiness.

Some people check their phone answering machines when they get home; that summer I always checked the front of the fridge. Eenie-meenie-chili-beanie, as Bullwinkle Moose used to say, the spirits are about to speak. That night they hadn't, although the fruit and vegetable magnets had re-formed into a sinuous shape like a snake or perhaps the letter *S* taking a nap:

A little later I called John and asked him where Devore had been, and he repeated in words what he had already told me, and much more economically, by gesture. 'It's the first game he's missed since he came back,' he said. 'Mattie tried asking a few people if he was okay, and the consensus seemed to be that he was . . . at least as far as anyone knew.'

'What do you mean she *tried* asking a few people?'

'I mean that several wouldn't even talk to her. "Cut her dead," my parents' generation would have said.' *Watch it, buddy*, I thought but didn't say, *that's only half a step from my generation*. 'One of her old girlfriends spoke to her finally, but there's a general attitude about Mattie Devore. That man Osgood may be a shitty salesman, but as Devore's Mr Moneyguy he's doing a wonderful job of separating Mattie from the other folks in the town. *Is* it a town, Mike? I don't quite get that part.'

'It's just the TR,' I said absently. 'There's no real way to explain it. Do you actually believe Devore's bribing *everyone*? That doesn't say much for the old Wordsworthian idea of pastoral innocence and goodness, does it?'

'He's spreading money and using Osgood – maybe Footman, too – to spread stories. And the folks around here seem at least as honest as honest politicians.'

'The ones who stay bought?'

'Yeah. Oh, and I saw one of Devore's potential star witnesses in the Case of the Runaway Child. Royce Merrill. He was over by the equipment shed with some of his cronies. Did you happen to notice him?'

I said I had not.

'Guy must be a hundred and thirty,' John said. 'He's got a cane with a gold head the size of an elephant's asshole.'

'That's a *Boston Post* cane. The oldest person in the area gets to keep it.'

'And I have no doubt he came by it honestly. If Devore's lawyers put him on the stand, I'll debone him.' There was something chilling in John's gleeful confidence.

'I'm sure,' I said. 'How did Mattie take getting cut dead by her old friends?' I was thinking of her saying that she hated Tuesday nights, hated to think of the softball games going on as they always had at the field where she had met her late husband.

'She did okay,' John said. 'I think she's given most of them up as a lost cause, anyway.' I had my doubts about that – I seem to remember that at twenty-one lost causes are sort of a specialty – but I didn't say anything. 'She's hanging in. She's been lonely and scared, I think that in her own mind she might already have begun the process of giving Kyra up, but she's got her confidence back now. Mostly thanks to meeting you. Talk about your fantastically lucky breaks.'

Well, maybe. I flashed on Jo's brother Frank once saying to me that he didn't think there was any such thing as luck, only fate and inspired choices. And then I remembered that image of the TR crisscrossed with invisible cables, connections that were unseen but as strong as steel.

'John, I forgot to ask the most important question of all the other day, after I gave my depo. This custody case we're all so concerned about . . . has it even been scheduled?'

'Good question. I've checked three ways to Sunday, and Bissonette has, too. Unless Devore and his people have pulled something really slippery, like filing in another court district, I don't think it has been.'

'Could they do that? File in another district?'

'Maybe. But probably not without us finding out.'

'So what does it mean?'

'That Devore's on the verge of giving up,' John said promptly. 'As of now I see no other way of explaining it. I'm going back to

259

New York first thing tomorrow, but I'll stay in touch. If anything comes up here, you do the same.'

I said I would and went to bed. No female visitors came to share my dreams. That was sort of a relief.

When I came downstairs to recharge my iced-tea glass late Wednesday morning, Brenda Meserve had erected the laundry whirligig on the back stoop and was hanging out my clothes. This she did as her mother had no doubt taught her, with pants and shirts on the outside and undies on the inside, where any passing nosyparkers couldn't see what you chose to wear closest to your skin.

'You can take these in around four o'clock,' Mrs M. said as she prepared to leave. She looked at me with the bright and cynical eye of a woman who has been 'doing for' well-off men her entire life. 'Don't you forget and leave em out all night – dewy clothes don't ever feel fresh until they're warshed again.'

I told her most humbly that I would remember to take in my clothes. I then asked her – feeling like a spy working an embassy party for information – if the house felt all right to her.

'All right how?' she asked, cocking one wild eyebrow at me.

'Well, I've heard funny noises a couple of times. In the night.'

She sniffed. 'It's a log house, ennit? Built in relays, so to speak. It settles, one wing against t'other. That's what you hear, most likely.'

'No ghosts, huh?' I said, as if disappointed.

'Not that I've ever seen,' she said, matter-of-fact as an accountant, 'but my ma said there's plenty down here. She said this whole lake is haunted. By the Micmacs that lived here until they was driven out by General Wing, by all the men who went away to the Civil War and died there – over six hundred went from this part of the world, Mr Noonan, and less than a hundred and fifty came back . . . at least in their bodies. Ma said this side of Dark Score's also haunted by the ghost of that Negro boy who died here, poor tyke. He belonged to one of the Red-Tops, you know.'

'No – I know about Sara and the Red-Tops, but not this.' I paused. 'Did he drown?'

'Nawp, caught in an animal trap. Struggled there for most of a whole day, screaming for help. Finally they found him. They saved the foot, but they shouldn't have. Blood-poisoning set in, and the

260

boy died. Summer of ought-one, that was. It's why they left, I guess – it was too sad to stay. But my ma used to claim the little fella, *he* stayed. She used to say that he's still on the TR.'

I wondered what Mrs M. would say if I told her that the little fella had very likely been here to greet me when I arrived from Derry, and had been back on several occasions since.

'Then there was Kenny Auster's father, Normal,' she said. 'You know that story, don't you? Oh, that's a terrible story.' She looked rather pleased – either at knowing such a terrible story or at having the chance to tell it.

'No,' I said. 'I know Kenny, though. He's the one with the wolfhound. Blueberry.'

'Ayuh. He carpenters a tad and caretakes a tad, just like his father before him. His dad caretook many of these places, you know, and back just after the Second World War was over, Normal Auster drownded Kenny's little brother in his back yard. This was when they lived on Wasp Hill, down where the road splits, one side goin to the old boat-landin and the other to the marina. He didn't drown the tyke in the lake, though. He put him on the ground under the pump and just held him there until the baby was full of water and dead.'

I stood there looking at her, the clothes behind us snapping on their whirligig. I thought of my mouth and nose and throat full of that cold mineral taste that could have been well-water as well as lakewater; down here all of it comes from the same deep aquifers. I thought of the message on the refrigerator: *help im drown.*

'He left the baby laying right under the pump. He had a new Chevrolet, and he drove it down here to Lane Forty-two. Took his shotgun, too.'

'You aren't going to tell me Kenny Auster's dad committed suicide in my house, are you, Mrs Meserve?'

She shook her head. 'Nawp. He did it on the Brickers' lakeside deck. Sat down on their porch glider and blew his damned baby-murdering head off.'

'The Brickers? I don't—'

'You wouldn't. Hasn't been any Brickers on the lake since the sixties. They were from Delaware. Quality folks. You'd think of it as the Warshburn place, I guess, although they're gone, now, too. Place is empty. Every now and then that stark naturalborn fool Osgood

261

brings someone down and shows it off, but he'll never sell it at the price he's asking. Mark my words.'

The Washburns I had known – had played bridge with them a time or two. Nice enough people, although probably not what Mrs M., with her queer backcountry snobbishness, would have called 'quality.' Their place was maybe an eighth of a mile north of mine along The Street. Past that point, there's nothing much – the drop to the lake gets steep, and the woods are massed tangles of second growth and blackberry bushes. The Street goes on to the tip of Halo Bay at the far north end of Dark Score, but once Lane Forty-two curves back to the highway, the path is for the most part used only by berry-picking expeditions in the summer and hunters in the fall.

Normal, I thought. Hell of a name for a guy who had drowned his infant son under the backyard pump.

'Did he leave a note? Any explanation?'

'Nawp. But you'll hear folks say he haunts the lake, too. Little towns are most likely full of haunts, but I couldn't say aye, no, or maybe, myself; I ain't the sensitive type. All I know about your place, Mr Noonan, is that it smells damp no matter how much I try to get it aired out. I 'magine that's logs. Log buildins don't go well with lakes. The damp gets into the wood.'

She had set her purse down between her Reeboks; now she bent and picked it up. It was a countrywoman's purse, black, styleless (except for the gold grommets holding the handles on), and utilitarian. She could have carried a good selection of kitchen appliances in there if she had wanted to.

'I can't stand here natterin all day long, though, much as I might like to. I got one more place to go before I can call it quits. Summer's ha'vest time in this part of the world, you know. Now remember to take those clothes in before dark, Mr Noonan. Don't let em get all dewy.'

'I won't.' And I didn't. But when I went out to take them in, dressed in my bathing trunks and coated with sweat from the oven I'd been working in (I had to get the air conditioner fixed, just *had* to), I saw that something had altered Mrs M.'s arrangements. My jeans and shirts now hung around the pole. The underwear and socks, which had been decorously hidden when Mrs M. drove up the driveway in her old Ford, were now on the outside. It was as if my unseen guest – *one* of my unseen guests – was saying ha ha ha.

I went to the library the next day, and made renewing my library card my first order of business. Lindy Briggs herself took my four bucks and entered me into the computer, first telling me how sorry she had been to hear about Jo's death. And, as with Bill, I sensed a certain reproach in her tone, as if I were to blame for such improperly delayed condolences. I supposed I was.

'Lindy, do you have a town history?' I asked when we had finished the proprieties concerning my wife.

'We have two,' she said, then leaned toward me over the desk, a little woman in a violently patterned sleeveless dress, her hair a gray puffball around her head, her bright eyes swimming behind her bifocals. In a confidential voice she added, 'Neither is much good.'

'Which one is better?' I asked, matching her tone.

'Probably the one by Edward Osteen. He was a summer resident until the mid-fifties and lived here full-time when he retired. He wrote *Dark Score Days* in 1965 or '66. He had it privately published because he couldn't find a commercial house that would take it. Even the regional publishers passed.' She sighed. 'The locals bought it, but that's not many books, is it?'

'No, I suppose not,' I said.

'He just wasn't much of a writer. Not much of a photographer, either – those little black-and-white snaps of his make my *eyes* hurt. Still, he tells some good stories. The Micmac Drive, General Wing's trick horse, the twister in the eighteen-eighties, the fires in the nineteen-thirties . . .'

'Anything about Sara and the Red-Tops?'

She nodded, smiling. 'Finally got around to looking up the history of your own place, did you? I'm glad to hear it. He found an old photo of them, and it's in there. He thought it was taken at the Fryeburg Fair in 1900. Ed used to say he'd give a lot to hear a record made by that bunch.'

'So would I, but none were ever made.' A haiku by the Greek poet George Seferis suddenly occurred to me: *Are these the voices of our dead friends / or just the gramophone?* 'What happened to Mr Osteen? I don't recall the name.'

'Died not a year or two before you and Jo bought your place on the lake,' she said. 'Cancer.'

'You said there were two histories?'

'The other one you probably know – *A History of Castle County and Castle Rock*. Done for the county centennial, and dry as dust. Eddie Osteen's book isn't very well written, but he wasn't dry. You have to give him that much. You should find them both over there.' She pointed to shelves with a sign over them which read OF MAINE INTEREST. 'They don't circulate.' Then she brightened. 'Although we will happily take any nickels you should feel moved to feed into our photocopy machine.'

Mattie was sitting in the far corner next to a boy in a turned-around baseball cap, showing him how to use the microfilm reader. She looked up at me, smiled, and mouthed the words *Nice catch*. Referring to my lucky grab at Warrington's, presumably. I gave a modest little shrug before turning to the OF MAINE INTEREST shelves. But she was right – lucky or not, it *had* been a nice catch.

'What are you looking for?'

I was so deep into the two histories I'd found that Mattie's voice made me jump. I turned around and smiled, first aware that she was wearing some light and pleasant perfume, second that Lindy Briggs was watching us from the main desk, her welcoming smile put away.

'Background on the area where I live,' I said. 'Old stories. My housekeeper got me interested.' Then, in a lower voice: 'Teacher's watching. Don't look around.'

Mattie looked startled – and, I thought, a little worried. As it turned out, she was right to be worried. In a voice that was low-pitched yet still designed to carry at least as far as the desk, she asked if she could reshelve either book for me. I gave her both. As she picked them up she said in what was almost a con's whisper: 'That lawyer who represented you last Friday got John a private detective. He says they may have found something interesting about the guardian *ad litem*.'

I walked over to the OF MAINE INTEREST shelves with her, hoping I wasn't getting her in trouble, and asked if she knew what the something interesting might be. She shook her head, gave me a professional little librarian's smile, and I went away.

264

On the ride back to the house, I tried to think about what I'd read, but there wasn't much. Osteen was a bad writer who had taken bad pictures, and while his stories were colorful, they were also pretty thin on the ground. He mentioned Sara and the Red-Tops, all right, but he referred to them as a 'Dixie-Land octet,' and even I knew that wasn't right. The Red-Tops might have played some Dixieland, but they had primarily been a blues group (Friday and Saturday nights) and a gospel group (Sunday mornings). Osteen's two-page summary of the Red-Tops stay on the TR made it clear that he had heard no one else's covers of Sara's tunes.

He confirmed that a child had died of blood-poisoning caused by a traphold wound, a story which sounded like Brenda Meserve's . . . but why wouldn't it? Osteen had likely heard it from Mrs M.'s father or grandfather. He also said that the boy was Son Tidwell's only child, and that the guitar-player's real name was Reginald. The Tidwells had supposedly drifted north from the whorehouse district of New Orleans – the fabled crib-and-club streets which had been known around the turn of the century as Storyville.

There was no mention of Sara and the Red-Tops in the more formal history of Castle County, and no mention of Kenny Auster's drownded little brother in either book. Not long before Mattie came over to speak to me, I'd had a wild idea: that Son Tidwell and Sara Tidwell were man and wife, and that the little boy (not named by Osteen) had been their son. I found the picture Lindy had mentioned and studied it closely. It showed at least a dozen black people standing in a stiff group in front of what looked like a cattle exhibition. There was an old-fashioned Ferris wheel in the background. It could well have been taken at the Fryeburg Fair, and as old and faded as it was, it had a simple, elemental power that all Osteen's own photos put together could not match. You have seen photographs of western and Depression-era bandidos that have that same look of eerie truth – stern faces above tight ties and collars, eyes not quite lost in the shadows of antique hatbrims.

Sara stood front and center, wearing a black dress and her guitar. She was not outright smiling in this picture, but there seemed to be a smile in her eyes, and I thought they were like the eyes in some paintings, the ones that seem to follow you wherever you move in the room. I studied the photo and thought of her almost spiteful voice

265

in my dream: *What do you want to know, sugar?* I suppose I wanted to know about her and the others – who they had been, what they were to each other when they weren't singing and playing, why they'd left, where they'd gone.

Both of her hands were clearly visible, one posed on the strings of her guitar, the other on the frets, where she had been making a G-chord on an October Fair-day in the year 1900. Her fingers were long, artistic, bare of rings. That didn't necessarily mean that she and Son Tidwell weren't married, of course, and even if they hadn't been, the little boy who'd been caught in the trap could have been born on the wrong side of the blanket. Except the same ghost of a smile lurked in Son Tidwell's eyes. The resemblance was remarkable. I had an idea that the two of them had been brother and sister, not man and wife.

I thought about these things on my way home, and I thought about cables that were felt rather than seen ... but mostly I found myself thinking about Lindy Briggs – the way she had smiled at me, the way, a little later on, she had not smiled at her bright young librarian with the high-school certification. That worried me.

Then I got back to the house, and all I worried about was my story and the people in it – bags of bones which were putting on flesh daily.

Michael Noonan, Max Devore, and Rogette Whitmore played out their horrible little comedy scene Friday evening. Two other things which bear narrating happened before that.

The first was a call from John Storrow on Thursday night. I was sitting in front of the TV with a baseball game running soundlessly in front of me (the MUTE button with which most remote controls come equipped may be the twentieth century's finest invention). I was thinking about Sara Tidwell and Son Tidwell and Son Tidwell's little boy. I was thinking about Storyville, a name any writer just had to love. And in the back of my mind I was thinking about my wife, who had died pregnant.

'Hello?' I said.

'Mike, I have some wonderful news,' John said. He sounded near to bursting. 'Romeo Bissonette may be a weird name, but there's nothing weird about the detective-guy he found for me. His name is George Kennedy, like the actor. He's good, and he's *fast*. This guy could work in New York.'

'If that's the highest compliment you can think of, you need to get out of the city more.'

He went on as if he hadn't heard. 'Kennedy's real job is with a security firm – the other stuff is strictly in the moonlight. Which is a great loss, believe me. He got most of this on the phone. I can't believe it.'

'What specifically can't you believe?'

'Jackpot, baby.' Again he spoke in that tone of greedy satisfaction which I found both troubling and reassuring. 'Elmer Durgin has done the following things since late May: paid off his car; paid off his camp in Rangely Lakes; caught up on about ninety years of child support—'

'Nobody pays child support for ninety years,' I said, but I was just running my mouth to hear it go . . . to let off some of my own building excitement, in truth. ''T'ain't possible, McGee.'

'It is if you have seven kids,' John said, and began howling with laughter.

I thought of the pudgy self-satisfied face, the cupid-bow mouth, the nails that looked polished and prissy. 'He *don't*,' I said.

'He *do*,' John said, still laughing. He sounded like a complete lunatic – manic, hold the depressive. 'He really do! Ranging in ages from f-fourteen to th-th-*three*! What a b-busy p-p-potent little prick he must have!' More helpless howls. And by now I was howling right along with him – I'd caught it like the mumps. 'Kennedy is going to f-f-fax me p-pictures of the whole . . . fam' . . . damily!' We broke up completely, laughing together long-distance. I could picture John Storrow sitting alone in his Park Avenue office, bellowing like a lunatic and scaring the cleaning ladies.

'That doesn't matter, though,' he said when he could talk coherently again. 'You see what matters, don't you?'

'Yes,' I said. 'How could he be so stupid?' Meaning Durgin, but also meaning Devore. John understood, I think, that we were talking about both *he's* at the same time.

'Elmer Durgin's a little lawyer from a little township tucked away in the big woods of western Maine, that's all. How could he know that some guardian angel would come along with the resources to smoke him out? He also bought a boat, by the way. Two weeks ago. It's a twin outboard. A big 'un. It's over, Mike. The home team scores nine runs in the bottom of the ninth and the fucking pennant is *ours*.'

'If you say so.' But my hand went off on its own expedition, made a loose fist, and knocked on the good solid wood of the coffee-table.

'And hey, the softball game wasn't a total loss.' John was still talking between little giggling outbursts like helium balloons.

'No?'

'I'm taken with her.'

'Her?'

'Mattie,' he said patiently. 'Mattie Devore.' A pause, then: 'Mike? Are you there?'

'Yeah,' I said. 'Phone slipped. Sorry.' The phone hadn't slipped as much as an inch, but it came out sounding natural enough, I thought. And if it hadn't, so what? When it came to Mattie, I would be – in John's mind, at least – below suspicion. Like the country-house staff in an Agatha Christie. He was twenty-eight, maybe thirty. The idea that a man twelve years older might be sexually attracted to Mattie had probably never crossed his mind . . . or maybe just for a second or two there on the common, before he dismissed it as ludicrous. The way Mattie herself had dismissed the idea of Jo and the man in the brown sportcoat.

'I can't do my courtship dance while I'm representing her,' he said, 'wouldn't be ethical. Wouldn't be safe, either. Later, though . . . you can never tell.'

'No,' I said, hearing my voice as you sometimes do in moments when you are caught completely flat-footed, hearing it as though it were coming from someone else. Someone on the radio or the record-player, maybe. Are these the voices of our dead friends, or just the gramophone? I thought of his hands, the fingers long and slender and without a ring on any of them. Like Sara's hands in that old photo. 'No, you can never tell.'

We said goodbye, and I sat watching the muted baseball game. I thought about getting up to get a beer, but it seemed too far to the refrigerator – a safari, in fact. What I felt was a kind of dull hurt, followed by a better emotion: rueful relief, I guess you'd call it. Was he too old for her? No, I didn't think so. Just about right. Prince Charming No. 2, this time in a three-piece suit. Mattie's luck with men might finally be changing, and if so I should be glad. I *would* be glad. And relieved. Because I had a book to write, and never mind the look of white sneakers flashing below a red sundress in the deepening gloom, or the ember of her cigarette dancing in the dark.

Still, I felt really lonely for the first time since I saw Kyra marching up the white line of Route 68 in her bathing suit and flip-flops.

'You funny little man, said Strickland,' I told the empty room. It came out before I knew I was going to say anything, and when it did, the channel on the TV changed. It went from baseball to a rerun of *All in the Family* and then to *Ren & Stimpy*. I glanced down at the remote control. It was still on the coffee-table where I'd left it. The TV channel changed again, and this time I was looking at Humphrey Bogart and Ingrid Bergman. There was an airplane in the background, and I didn't need to pick up the remote and turn on the sound to know that Humphrey was telling Ingrid that she was getting on that plane. My wife's all-time favorite movie. She bawled at the end without fail.

'Jo?' I asked. 'Are you here?'

Bunter's bell rang once. Very faintly. There had been several presences in the house, I was sure of it . . . but tonight, for the first time, I was positive it was Jo who was with me.

'Who was he, hon?' I asked. 'The guy at the softball field, who was he?'

Bunter's bell hung still and quiet. She was in the room, though. I sensed her, something like a held breath.

I remembered the ugly, gibing little message on the refrigerator after my dinner with Mattie and Ki: *blue rose liar ha ha*.

'Who was he?' My voice was unsteady, sounding on the verge of tears. 'What were you doing down here with some guy? Were you . . .' But I couldn't bring myself to ask if she had been lying to me, cheating on me. I couldn't ask even though the presence I felt might be, let's face it, only in my own head.

The TV switched away from *Casablanca* and here was everybody's favorite lawyer, Perry Mason, on Nick at Nite. Perry's nemesis, Hamilton Burger, was questioning a distraught-looking woman, and all at once the sound blared on, making me jump.

'I am *not* a liar!' some long-ago TV actress cried. For a moment she looked right out at me, and I was stunned breathless to see Jo Noonan's eyes in that black-and-white fifties face. 'I *never* lied, Mr Burger, never!'

'I submit that you did!' Burger responded. He moved in on her, leering like a vampire. 'I submit that you—'

The TV suddenly went off. Bunter's bell gave a single brisk shake, and then whatever had been here was gone. But I felt better. *I am not a liar . . . I never lied, never.*

I could believe that if I chose to.

If I chose.

I went to bed, and there were no dreams.

I had taken to starting work early, before the heat could really get a hold on the study. I'd drink some juice, gobble some toast, then sit behind the IBM until almost noon, watching the Courier ball dance and twirl as the pages floated through the machine and came out with writing on them. That old magic, so strange and wonderful. It never really felt like work to me, although I called it that; it felt like some weird kind of mental trampoline I bounced on. Those were springs that took away all the weight of the world for awhile.

At noon I'd break, drive down to Buddy Jellison's greaseatorium for something nasty, then return and work for another hour or so. After that I would swim and take a long, dreamless nap in the north bedroom. I had barely poked my head into the master bedroom at the south end of the house, and if Mrs M. thought this was odd, she kept it to herself.

On Friday the seventeenth, I stopped at the Lakeview General on my way back to the house to gas up my Chevrolet. There are pumps at the All-Purpose Garage, and the go-juice was a penny or two cheaper, but I didn't like the vibe. Today, as I stood in front of the store with the pump on automatic feed, looking off toward the mountains, Bill Dean's Dodge Ram pulled in on the other side of the island. He climbed down and gave me a smile. 'How's it going, Mike?'

'Pretty fair.'

'Brenda says you're writin up a storm.'

'I am,' I said, and it was on the tip of my tongue to ask for an update on the broken second-floor air conditioner. The tip of my tongue was where it stayed. I was still too nervous about my rediscovered ability to want to change anything about the environment in which I was doing it. Stupid, maybe, but sometimes things work just because you think they work. It's as good a definition of faith as any.

'Well, I'm glad to hear it. Very glad.' I thought *he* was sincere enough, but he somehow didn't sound like Bill. Not the one who had greeted me back, anyway.

'I've been looking up some old stuff about my side of the lake,' I said.

'Sara and the Red-Tops? You always were sort of int'rested in them, I remember.'

'Them, yes, but not just them. Lots of history. I was talking to Mrs M., and she told me about Normal Auster. Kenny's father.'

Bill's smile stayed on, and he only paused a moment in the act of unscrewing the cap on his gas tank, but I still had a sense, quite clear, that he had frozen inside. 'You wouldn't write about a thing like that, would you, Mike? Because there's a lot of people around here that'd feel it bad and take it wrong. I told Jo the same thing.'

'Jo?' I felt an urge to step between the two pumps and over the island so I could grab him by the arm. 'What's Jo got to do with this?'

He looked at me cautiously and long. 'She didn't tell you?'

'What are you talking about?'

'She thought she might write something about Sara and the Red-Tops for one of the local papers.' Bill was picking his words very slowly. I have a clear memory of that, and of how hot the sun was, beating down on my neck, and the sharpness of our shadows on the asphalt. He began to pump his gas, and the sound of the pump's motor was also very sharp. 'I think she even mentioned *Yankee* magazine. I c'd be wrong about that, but I don't think I am.'

I was speechless. Why would she have kept quiet about the idea to try her hand at a little local history? Because she might have thought she was poaching on my territory? That was ridiculous. She had known me better than that . . . hadn't she?

'When did you have this conversation, Bill? Do you remember?'

'Coss I do,' he said. 'Same day she come down to take delivery of those plastic owls. Only I raised the subject, because folks had told me she was asking around.'

'Prying?'

'I didn't say that,' he said stiffly, 'you did.'

True, but I thought prying was what he meant. 'Go on.'

'Nothing to go on about. I told her there were sore toes here and there in the TR, same as there are anyplace, and ast her not to tread on any corns if she could help it. She said she understood. Maybe she did, maybe she didn't. All I know is she kep' on asking questions. Listenin to stories from old fools with more time than sense.'

'When was this?'

'Fall of '93, winter and spring of '94. Went all around town, she did – even over to Motton and Harlow – with her notebook and little tape-recorder. Anyway, that's all I know.'

I realized a stunning thing: Bill was lying. If you'd asked me before that day, I'd have laughed and told you Bill Dean didn't have a lie in him. And he must not have had many, because he did it badly.

I thought of calling him on it, but to what end? I needed to think, and I couldn't do it here – my mind was roaring. Given time, that roar might subside and I'd see it was really nothing, no big deal, but I needed that time. When you start finding out unexpected things about a loved one who's been dead awhile, it rocks you. Take it from me, it does.

Bill's eyes had shifted away from mine, but now they shifted back. He looked both earnest and – I could have sworn it – a little scared.

'She ast about little Kerry Auster, and that's a good example of what I mean about steppin on sore toes. That's not the stuff for a newspaper story or a magazine article. Normal just snapped. No one knows why. It was a terrible tragedy, senseless, and there's still people who could be hurt by it. In little towns things are kind of connected under the surface—'

Yes, like cables you couldn't quite see.

'—and the past dies slower. Sara and those others, that's a little different. They were just . . . just wanderers . . . from away. Jo could have stuck to those folks and it would've been all right. And say – for all I know, she did. Because I never saw a single word she ever wrote. If she did write.'

About that he was telling the truth, I felt. But I knew something else, knew it as surely as I'd known Mattie had been wearing white shorts when she called me on her day off. *Sara and those others were just wanderers from away*, Bill had said, but he hesitated in the middle of his thought, substituting *wanderers* for the word which had come naturally to mind. *Niggers* was the word he hadn't said. *Sara and those others were just niggers from away.*

All at once I found myself thinking of an old story by Ray Bradbury, 'Mars Is Heaven.' The first space travellers to Mars discover it's Green Town, Illinois, and all their well-loved friends and relatives are there. Only the friends and relatives are really alien monsters, and in the night, while the space travellers think they are sleeping in the beds of their long-dead kinfolk in a place that must be heaven, they are slaughtered to the last man.

'Bill, you're sure she was up here a few times in the off-season?'

'Ayuh. 'T'wasn't just a few times, either. Might have been a dozen times or more. Day-trips, don't you know.'

'Did you ever see a fellow with her? Burly guy, black hair?'

He thought about it. I tried not to hold my breath. At last he shook his head. 'Few times I saw her, she was alone. But I didn't see her every time she came. Sometimes I only heard she'd been on the TR after she 'us gone again. Saw her in June of '94, headed up toward Halo Bay in that little car a hers. She waved, I waved back. Went down to the house later that evenin to see if she needed anythin, but she'd gone. I didn't see her again. When she died later on that summer, me and 'Vette were so shocked.'

Whatever she was looking for, she must never have written any of it down. I would have found the manuscript.

Was that true, though? She had made many trips down here with no apparent attempts at concealment, on one of them she had even been accompanied by a strange man, and I had only found out about these visits by accident.

'This is hard to talk about,' Bill said, 'but since we've gotten started hard, we might as well go the rest of the way. Livin in the TR is like the way we used to sleep four or even five in a bed when it was January and true cold. If everyone rests easy, you do all right. But if one person gets restless, gets tossing and turning, no one can sleep. Right now you're the restless one. That's how people see it.'

He waited to see what I'd say. When almost twenty seconds passed without a word from me (Harold Oblowski would have been proud), he shuffled his feet and went on.

'There are people in town uneasy about the interest you've taken in Mattie Devore, for instance. Now I'm not sayin there's anythin goin on between the two of you – although there's folks who *do* say it – but if you want to stay on the TR you're makin it tough on yourself.'

'Why?'

'Comes back to what I said a week and a half ago. She's trouble.'

'As I recall, Bill, you said she was *in* trouble. And she is. I'm trying to help her out of it. There's nothing going on between us but that.'

'*I* seem to recall telling you that Max Devore is nuts,' he said. 'If you make him mad, we all pay the price.' The pump clicked off and he racked it up. Then he sighed, raised his hands, dropped them. 'You think this is easy for me to say?'

'You think it's easy for me to listen to?'

'All right, ayuh, we're in the same skiff. But Mattie Devore isn't the only person on the TR livin hand-to-mouth, you know. There's others got their woes, as well. Can't you understand that?'

Maybe he saw that I understood too much and too well, because his shoulders slumped.

'If you're asking me to stand aside and let Devore take Mattie's baby without a fight, you can forget it,' I said. 'And I hope that's not it. Because I think I'd have to be quits with a man who'd ask another man to do something like that.'

'I wouldn't ask it now anywise,' he said, his accent thickening almost to the point of contempt. 'It'd be too late, wouldn't it?' And then, unexpectedly, he softened. 'Christ, man, I'm worried about *you*. Let the rest of it go hang, all right? Hang high where the crows can pick it.' He was lying again, but this time I didn't mind so much, because I thought he was lying to himself. 'But you need to have a care. When I said Devore was crazy, that was no figure of speech. Do you think he'll bother with court if court can't get him what he wants? Folks died in those summer fires back in 1933. Good people. One related to me. They burned over half the goddam county and

274

Max Devore set em. That was his going-away present to the TR. It could never be proved, but he did it. Back then he was young and broke, not yet twenty and no law in his pocket. What do you think he'd do now?'

He looked at me searchingly. I said nothing.

Bill nodded as if I *had* spoken. 'Think about it. And you remember this, Mike: no man who didn't care for you would ever talk to you straight as I have.'

'How straight was that, Bill?' I was faintly aware of some tourist walking from his Volvo to the store and looking at us curiously, and when I replayed the scene in my mind later on, I realized we must have looked like guys on the verge of a fistfight. I remember that I felt like crying out of sadness and bewilderment and an incompletely defined sense of betrayal, but I also remember being furious with this lanky old man – him in his shining-clean cotton undershirt and his mouthful of false teeth. So maybe we *were* close to fighting, and I just didn't know it at the time.

'Straight as I could be,' he said, and turned away to go inside and pay for his gas.

'My house is haunted,' I said.

He stopped, back to me, shoulders hunched as if to absorb a blow. Then, slowly, he turned back. 'Sara Laughs has always been haunted, Mike. You've stirred em up. P'raps you should go back to Derry and let em settle. That might be the best thing.' He paused, as if replaying this last to see if he agreed with it, then nodded. He nodded as slowly as he had turned. 'Ayuh, that might be best all around.'

When I got back to Sara I called Ward Hankins. Then I finally made that call to Bonnie Amudson. Part of me was rooting for her not to be in at the travel agency in Augusta she co-owned, but she was. Halfway through my talk with her, the fax began to print out Xeroxed pages from Jo's appointment calendars. On the first one Ward had scrawled, 'Hope this helps.'

I didn't rehearse what I was going to say to Bonnie; I felt that to do so would be a recipe for disaster. I told her that Jo had been writing something – maybe an article, maybe a series of them – about the township where our summer house was located, and that some of the locals had apparently been cheesed off by her curiosity.

Some still were. Had she talked to Bonnie? Perhaps showed her an early draft?

'No, huh-uh.' Bonnie sounded honestly surprised. 'She used to show me her photos, and more herb samples than I honestly cared to see, but she never showed me anything she was writing. In fact, I remember her once saying that she'd decided to leave the writing to you and just—'

'—take a little taste of everything else, right?'

'Yes.'

I thought this was a good place to end the conversation, but the guys in the basement seemed to have other ideas. 'Was she seeing anyone, Bonnie?'

Silence from the other end. With a hand that seemed at least four miles down my arm, I plucked the fax sheets out of the basket. Ten of them – November of 1993 to August of 1994. Jottings everywhere in Jo's neat hand. Had we even had a fax before she died? I couldn't remember. There was so fucking much I couldn't remember.

'Bonnie? If you know something, please tell me. Jo's dead, but I'm not. I can forgive her if I have to, but I can't forgive what I don't underst—'

'I'm sorry,' she said, and gave a nervous little laugh. 'It's just that I didn't understand at first. "Seeing anyone," that was just so . . . so foreign to Jo . . . the Jo I knew . . . that I couldn't figure out what you were talking about. I thought maybe you meant a shrink, but you didn't, did you? You meant seeing someone like seeing a guy. A boyfriend.'

'That's what I meant.' Thumbing through the faxed calendar sheets now, my hand not quite back to its proper distance from my eyes but getting there, getting there. I felt relief at the honest bewilderment in Bonnie's voice, but not as much as I'd expected. Because I'd known. I hadn't even needed the woman in the old *Perry Mason* episode to put in her two cents, not really. It was Jo we were talking about, after all. *Jo*.

'Mike,' Bonnie was saying, very softly, as if I might be crazy, 'she loved you. She loved *you*.'

'Yes. I suppose she did.' The calendar pages showed how busy my wife had been. How productive. S-Ks of Maine . . . the soup kitchens. WomShel, a county-to-county network of shelters for

276

battered women. TeenShel. Friends of Me. Libes. She had been at two or three meetings a month – two or three a *week* at some points – and I'd barely noticed. I had been too busy with my women in jeopardy. 'I loved her too, Bonnie, but she was up to something in the last ten months of her life. She didn't give you any hint of what it might have been when you were riding to meetings of the Soup Kitchens board or the Friends of Maine Libraries?'

Silence from the other end.

'Bonnie?'

I took the phone away from my ear to see if the red LOW BATTERY light was on, and it squawked my name. I put it back.

'Bonnie, what is it?'

'There *were* no long drives those last nine or ten months. We talked on the phone and I remember once we had lunch in Waterville, but there *were* no long drives. She quit.'

I thumbed through the fax-sheets again. Meetings noted everywhere in Jo's neat hand, Soup Kitchens of Maine among them.

'I don't understand. She quit the Soup Kitchens board?'

Another moment of silence. Then, speaking carefully: 'No, Mike. She quit *all* of them. She finished with Woman Shelters and Teen Shelters at the end of '93 – her term was up then. The other two, Soup Kitchens and Friends of Maine Libraries . . . she resigned in October or November of 1993.'

Meetings noted on all the sheets Ward had sent me. Dozens of them. Meetings in 1993, meetings in 1994. Meetings of boards to which she'd no longer belonged. She had been down here. On all those supposed meeting-days, Jo had been on the TR. I would have bet my life on it.

But why?

CHAPTER SEVENTEEN

Devore was mad, all right, mad as a hatter, and he couldn't have caught me at a worse, weaker, more terrified moment. And I think that everything from that moment on was almost pre-ordained. From there to the terrible storm they still talk about in this part of the world, it all came down like a rockslide.

I felt fine the rest of Friday afternoon – my talk with Bonnie left a lot of questions unanswered, but it had been a tonic just the same. I made a vegetable stir-fry (atonement for my latest plunge into the Fry-O-Lator at the Village Cafe) and ate it while I watched the evening news. On the other side of the lake the sun was sliding down toward the mountains and flooding the living room with gold. When Tom Brokaw closed up shop, I decided to take a walk north along The Street – I'd go as far as I could and still be assured of getting home by dark, and as I went I'd think about the things Bill Dean and Bonnie Amudson had told me. I'd think about them the way I sometimes walked and thought about plot-snags in whatever I was working on.

I walked down the railroad-tie steps, still feeling perfectly fine (confused, but fine), started off along The Street, then paused to look at the Green Lady. Even with the evening sun shining fully upon her, it was hard to see her for what she actually was – just a birch tree with a half-dead pine standing behind it, one branch of the latter making a pointing arm. It was as if the Green Lady were saying go north, young man, go north. Well, I wasn't exactly young, but I could go north, all right. For awhile, at least.

Yet I stood a moment longer, uneasily studying the face I could see in the bushes, not liking the way the little shake of breeze seemed to make what was nearly a mouth sneer and grin. I think perhaps I started to feel a little bad then, was too preoccupied to notice it. I set off north, wondering what, exactly, Jo might have written . . . for by then I was starting to believe she might have written something, after all. Why else had I found my old typewriter in her studio? I would go through the place, I decided. I would go through it carefully and . . .

help im drown

The voice came from the woods, the water, from myself. A wave of lightheadedness passed through my thoughts, lifting and scattering them like leaves in a breeze. I stopped. All at once I had never felt so bad, so *blighted*, in my life. My chest was tight. My stomach folded in on itself like a cold flower. My eyes filled with chilly water that was nothing like tears, and I knew what was coming. *No*, I tried to say, but the word wouldn't come out.

My mouth filled with the cold taste of lakewater instead, all those dark minerals, and suddenly the trees were shimmering before my eyes as if I were looking up at them through clear liquid, and the pressure on my chest had become dreadfully localized and taken the shapes of hands. They were holding me down.

'Won't it stop doing that?' someone asked – almost cried. There was no one on The Street but me, yet I heard that voice clearly. 'Won't it ever stop doing that?'

What came next was no outer voice but alien thoughts in my own head. They beat against the walls of my skull like moths trapped inside a light-fixture . . . or inside a Japanese lantern.

help I'm drown
help I'm drown
blue-cap man say git me
blue-cap man say dassn't let me ramble
help I'm drown
lost my berries they on the path
he holdin me
he face shimmer n look bad
lemme up lemme up O sweet Jesus lemme up
oxen free allee allee oxen free PLEASE
OXEN FREE you go on and stop now ALLEE OXEN FREE
she scream my name
she scream it so LOUD

279

I bent forward in an utter panic, opened my mouth, and from my gaping, straining mouth there poured a cold flood of . . .

Nothing at all.

The horror of it passed and yet it didn't pass. I still felt terribly sick to my stomach, as if I had eaten something to which my body had taken a violent offense, some kind of ant-powder or maybe a killer mushroom, the kind Jo's fungi guides pictured inside red borders. I staggered forward half a dozen steps, gagging dryly from a throat which still believed it was wet. There was another birch where the bank dropped to the lake, arching its white belly gracefully over the water as if to see its reflection by evening's flattering light. I grabbed it like a drunk grabbing a lamppost.

The pressure in my chest began to ease, but it left an ache as real as rain. I hung against the tree, heart fluttering, and suddenly I became aware that something stank – an evil, polluted smell worse than a clogged septic pool which has simmered all summer under the blazing sun. With it was a sense of some hideous presence giving off that odor, something which should have been dead and wasn't.

Oh stop, allee allee oxen free, I'll do anything only stop, I tried to say, and still nothing came out. Then it was gone. I could smell nothing but the lake and the woods . . . but I could see something: a boy in the lake, a little drowned dark boy lying on his back. His cheeks were puffed out. His mouth hung slackly open. His eyes were as white as the eyes of a statue.

My mouth filled with the unmerciful iron of the lake again. Help me, lemme up, help I'm drown. I leaned out, screaming inside my head, screaming down at the dead face, and I realized *I was looking up at myself,* looking up through the rose-shimmer of sunset water at a white man in blue jeans and a yellow polo shirt holding onto a trembling birch and trying to scream, his liquid face in motion, his eyes momentarily blotted out by the passage of a small perch coursing after a tasty bug, I was both the dark boy and the white man, drowned in the water and drowning in the air, is this right, is this what's happening, tap once for yes twice for no.

I retched nothing but a single runner of spit, and, impossibly, a fish jumped at it. They'll jump at almost anything at sunset; something in the dying light must make them crazy. The fish hit the water again about seven feet from the bank, spanking out a circular silver ripple, and it was gone – the taste in my mouth, the horrible smell, the shimmering drowned face of the Negro child – a Negro, that was how he would have thought of himself – whose name had almost surely been Tidwell.

I looked to my right and saw a gray forehead of rock poking out of the mulch. I thought, *There, right there,* and as if in confirmation, that horrible putrescent smell puffed at me again, seemingly from the ground.

I closed my eyes, still hanging onto the birch for dear life, feeling weak and sick and ill, and that was when Max Devore, that madman, spoke from behind me. 'Say there, whoremaster, where's your whore?'

I turned and there he was, with Rogette Whitmore by his side. It was the only time I ever met him, but once was enough. Believe me, once was more than enough.

His wheelchair hardly looked like a wheelchair at all. What it looked like was a motorcycle sidecar crossed with a lunar lander. Half a dozen chrome wheels ran along both sides. Bigger wheels – four of them, I think – ran in a row across the back. None looked to be exactly on the same level, and I realized each was tied into its own suspension-bed. Devore would have a smooth ride over ground a lot rougher than The Street. Above the back wheels was an enclosed engine compartment. Hiding Devore's legs was a fiberglass nacelle, black with red pinstriping, that would not have looked out of place on a racing car. Implanted in the center of it was a gadget that looked like my DSS satellite dish . . . some sort of computerized avoidance system, I guessed. Maybe even an autopilot. The armrests were wide and covered with controls. Holstered on the left side of this machine was a green oxygen tank four feet long. A hose went to a clear plastic accordion tube; the accordion tube led to a mask which rested in Devore's lap. It made me think of the old guy's Stenomask. Coming on the heels of what had just happened, I might have considered this Tom Clancyish vehicle an hallucination, except for the bumper-sticker on the nacelle, below the dish. I BLEED DODGER BLUE, it said.

This evening the woman I had seen outside The Sunset Bar at Warrington's was wearing a white blouse with long sleeves and black pants so tapered they made her legs look like sheathed swords. Her narrow face and hollow cheeks made her resemble Edvard Munch's screamer more than ever. Her white hair hung around her face in a lank cowl. Her lips were painted so brightly red she seemed to be bleeding from the mouth.

She was old and she was ugly, but she was a prize compared to Mattie's father-in-law. Scrawny, blue-lipped, the skin around his eyes and the corners of his mouth a dark exploded purple, he looked like something an archeologist might find in the burial room of a pyramid, surrounded by his stuffed wives and pets, bedizened with his favorite jewels. A few wisps of white hair still clung to his scaly skull; more tufts sprang from enormous ears which seemed to have melted like wax sculptures left out in the sun. He was wearing white cotton pants and a billowy blue shirt. Add a little black beret and he would have looked like a French artist from the nineteenth century at the end of a very long life.

Across his lap was a cane of some black wood. Snugged over the end was a bright red bicycle grip. The fingers grasping it looked powerful, but they were going as black as the cane itself. His circulation was failing, and I couldn't imagine what his feet and his lower legs must look like.

'Whore run off and left you, has she?'

I tried to say something. A croak came out of my mouth, nothing more. I was still holding the birch. I let go of it and tried to straighten up, but my legs were still weak and I had to grab it again.

He nudged a silver toggle switch and the chair came ten feet closer, halving the distance between us. The sound it made was a silky whisper; watching it was like watching an evil magic carpet. Its many wheels rose and fell independent of one another and flashed in the declining sun, which had begun to take on a reddish cast. And as he came closer, I felt the sense of the man. His body was rotting out from under him, but the force around him was undeniable and daunting, like an electrical storm. The woman paced beside him, regarding me with silent amusement. Her eyes were pinkish. I assumed then that they were gray and had picked up a bit of the coming sunset, but I think now she was an albino.

'I always liked a whore,' he said. He drew the word out, making it *horrrrrr*. 'Didn't I, Rogette?'

282

'Yes, sir,' she said. 'In their place.'

'Sometimes their place was on my face!' he cried with a kind of insane perkiness, as if she had contradicted him. 'Where is she, young man? Whose face is she sitting on right now? I wonder. That smart lawyer you found? Oh, I know all about him, right down to the Unsatisfactory Conduct he got in the third grade. I make it my business to know things. It's the secret of my success.'

With an enormous effort, I straightened up. 'What are you doing here?'

'Having a constitutional, same as you. And no law against it, is there? The Street belongs to anyone who wants to use it. You haven't been here long, young whoremaster, but surely you've been here long enough to know that. It's our version of the town common, where good pups and vile dogs may walk side by side.'

Once more using the hand not bunched around the red bicycle grip, he picked up the oxygen mask, sucked deeply, then dropped it back in his lap. He grinned – an unspeakable grin of complicity that revealed gums the color of iodine.

'She good? That little *honrrm* of yours? She must be good to have kept my son prisoner in that nasty little trailer where she lives. And then along comes you even before the worms had finished with my boy's eyes. Does her cunt *suck*?'

'Shut up.'

Rogette Whitmore threw back her head and laughed. The sound was like the scream of a rabbit caught in an owl's talons, and my flesh crawled. I had an idea she was as crazy as he was. Thank God they were old. 'You struck a nerve there, Max,' she said.

'What do you want?' I took a breath . . . and caught a taste of that putrescence again. I gagged. I didn't want to, but I couldn't help it.

Devore straightened in his chair and breathed deeply, as if to mock me. In that moment he looked like Robert Duvall in *Apocalypse Now*, striding along the beach and telling the world how much he loved the smell of napalm in the morning. His grin widened. 'Lovely place, just here, isn't it? A cozy spot to stop and think, wouldn't you say?' He looked around. 'This is where it happened, all right. Ayuh.'

'Where the boy drowned.'

I thought Whitmore's smile looked momentarily uneasy at that. Devore didn't. He clutched for his translucent oxygen mask with an old man's overwide grip, fingers that grope rather than reach. I could see little bubbles of mucus clinging to the inside. He sucked deep again, put it down again.

'Thirty or more folks have drowned in this lake, and that's just the ones they know about,' he said. 'What's one boy, more or less?'

'I don't get it. Were there *two* Tidwell boys who died here? The one that got blood-poisoning and the one—'

'Do you care about your soul, Mr Noonan? Your immortal soul? God's butterfly caught in a cocoon of flesh that will soon stink like mine?'

I said nothing. The strangeness of what had happened before he arrived was passing. What replaced it was his incredible personal magnetism. I have never in my life felt so much raw force. There was nothing supernatural about it, either, and *raw* is exactly the right word. I might have run. Under other circumstances, I'm sure I would have. It certainly wasn't bravery that kept me where I was; my legs still felt rubbery, and I was afraid I might fall down.

'I'm going to give you one chance to save your soul,' Devore said. He raised a bony finger to illustrate the concept of one. 'Go away, my fine whoremaster. Right now, in the clothes you stand up in. Don't bother to pack a bag, don't even stop to make sure you turned off the stove-burners. Go. Leave the whore and leave the whorelet.'

'Leave them to you.'

'Ayuh, to me. I'll do the things that need to be done. Souls are for liberal arts majors, Noonan. I was an engineer.'

'Go fuck yourself.'

Rogette Whitmore made that screaming-rabbit sound again.

The old man sat in his chair, head lowered, grinning sallowly up at me and looking like something raised from the dead. 'Are you sure you want to be the one, Noonan? It doesn't matter to her, you know – you or me, it's all the same to her.'

'I don't know what you're talking about.' I drew another deep breath, and this time the air tasted all right. I took a step away from the birch, and my legs were all right, too. 'And I don't care. You're never getting Kyra. Never in what remains of your scaly life. I'll never see that happen.'

'Pal, you'll see plenty,' Devore said, grinning and showing me his iodine gums. 'Before July's done, you'll likely have seen so much you'll wish you'd ripped the living eyes out of your head in June.'

'I'm going home. Let me pass.'

'Go home then, how could I stop you?' he asked. 'The Street belongs to everyone.' He groped the oxygen mask out of his lap again and took another healthy pull. He dropped it into his lap and settled his left hand on the arm of his Buck Rogers wheelchair.

I stepped toward him, and almost before I knew what was happening, he ran the wheelchair at me. He could have hit me and hurt me quite badly – broken one or both of my legs, I don't doubt – but he stopped just short. I leaped back, but only because he allowed me to. I was aware that Whitmore was laughing again.

'What's the matter, Noonan?'

'Get out of my way. I'm warning you.'

'Whore made you jumpy, has she?'

I started to my left, meaning to go by him on that side, but in a flash he had turned the chair, shot it forward, and cut me off.

'Get out of the TR, Noonan. I'm giving you good ad—'

I broke to the right, this time on the lake side, and would have slipped by him quite neatly except for the fist, very small and hard, that hammered the left side of my face. The white-haired bitch was wearing a ring, and the stone cut me behind the ear. I felt the sting and the warm flow of blood. I pivoted, stuck out both hands, and pushed her. She fell to the needle-carpeted path with a squawk of surprised outrage. At the next instant something clouted me on the back of the head. A momentary orange glow lit up my sight. I staggered backward in what felt like slow motion, waving my arms, and Devore came into view again. He was slued around in his wheelchair, scaly head thrust forward, the cane he'd hit me with still upraised. If he had been ten years younger, I believe he would have fractured my skull instead of just creating that momentary orange light.

I ran into my old friend the birch tree. I raised my hand to my ear and looked unbelievingly at the blood on the tips of my fingers. My head ached from the blow he had fetched me.

Whitmore was struggling to her feet, brushing pine needles from her slacks and looking at me with a furious smile. Her cheeks had filled in with a thin pink flush. Her too-red lips were pulled back

285

to show small teeth. In the light of the setting sun her eyes looked as if they were burning.

'Get out of my way,' I said, but my voice sounded small and weak.

'No,' Devore said, and laid the black barrel of his cane on the nacelle that curved over the front of his chair. Now I could see the little boy who had been determined to have the sled no matter how badly he cut his hands getting it. I could see him very clearly. 'No, you whore-fucking sissy. I *won't*.'

He shoved the silver toggle switch again and the wheelchair rushed silently at me. If I had stayed where I was, he would have run me through with his cane as surely as any evil duke was ever run through in an Alexandre Dumas story. He probably would have crushed the fragile bones in his right hand and torn his right arm clean out of its socket in the collision, but this man had never cared about such things; he left cost-counting to the little people. If I had hesitated out of shock or incredulity, he would have killed me, I'm sure of it. Instead, I rolled to my left. My sneakers slid on the needle-slippery embankment for a moment. Then they lost contact with the earth and I was falling.

I hit the water awkwardly and much too close to the bank. My left foot struck a submerged root and twisted. The pain was huge, something that felt like a thunderclap sounds. I opened my mouth to scream and the lake poured in – that cold metallic dark taste, this time for real. I coughed it out and sneezed it out and floundered away from where I had landed, thinking *The boy, the dead boy's down here, what if he reaches up and grabs me?*

I turned over on my back, still flailing and coughing, very aware of my jeans clinging clammily to my legs and crotch, thinking absurdly about my wallet – I didn't care about the credit cards or driver's license, but I had two good snapshots of Jo in there, and they would be ruined.

Devore had almost run himself over the embankment, I saw, and for a moment I thought he still might go. The front of his chair jutted over the place where I had fallen (I could see the short tracks of my sneakers just to the left of the birch's partially exposed roots), and although the forward wheels were still grounded, the crumbly earth was running out from beneath them in dry little avalanches that rolled down the slope and pit-a-patted into the water, creating interlocking ripple patterns. Whitmore was clinging to the back of the chair, yanking on it, but it was much too heavy for her; if Devore was to be saved, he would have to save himself. Standing waist-deep in the lake with my clothes floating around me, I rooted for him to go over.

The purplish claw of his left hand recaptured the silver toggle switch after several attempts. One finger hooked it backward, and the chair reversed away from the embankment with a final shower of stones and dirt. Whitmore leaped prankishly to one side to keep her feet from being run over.

Devore fiddled some more with his controls, turned the chair to face me where I stood in the water, some seven feet out from the overhanging birch, and then nudged the chair forward until he was on the edge of The Street but safely away from the dropoff. Whitmore had turned away from us entirely; she was bent over with her butt poking in my direction. If I thought about her at all, and I can't remember that I did, I suppose I thought she was getting her breath back.

Devore appeared to be in the best shape of the three of us, not even needing a hit from the oxygen mask sitting in his lap. The late light was full in his face, making him look like a half-rotted jack-o'-lantern which has been soaked with gas and set on fire.

'Enjoying your swim?' he asked, and laughed.

I looked around, hoping to see a strolling couple or perhaps a fisherman looking for a place where he could wet his line one more time before dark . . . and yet at the same time I hoped I'd see no one. I was angry, hurt, and scared. Most of all I was embarrassed. I had been dunked in the lake by a man of eighty-five . . . a man who showed every sign of hanging around and making sport of me.

I began wading to my right – south, back toward my house. The water was about waist-deep, cool and almost refreshing now that I was used to it. My sneakers squelched over rocks and submerged tree-branches. The ankle I'd twisted still hurt, but it was supporting me. Whether it would continue to once I got out of the lake was another question.

Devore twiddled his controls some more. The chair pivoted

and came rolling slowly along The Street, keeping pace with me easily.

'I didn't introduce you properly to Rogette, did I?' he said. 'She was quite an athlete in college, you know. Softball and field hockey were her specialties, and she's held onto at least some of her skills. Rogette, demonstrate your skills for this young man.'

Whitmore passed the slowly moving wheelchair on the left. For a moment she was blocked out by it. When I could see her again, I could also see what she was holding. She hadn't been bent over to get her breath.

Smiling, she strode to the edge of the embankment with her left arm curled against her midriff, cradling the rocks she had picked up from the edge of the path. She selected a chunk roughly the size of a golfball, drew her hand back to her ear, and threw it at me. Hard. It whizzed by my left temple and splashed into the water behind me.

'Hey!' I shouted, more startled than afraid. Even after everything that had preceded it, I couldn't believe this was happening.

'What's wrong with you, Rogette?' Devore asked chidingly. 'You never used to throw like a girl. Get him!'

The second rock passed two inches over my head. The third was a potential tooth-smasher. I batted it away with an angry, fearful shout, not noticing until later that it had bruised my palm. At the moment I was only aware of her hateful, smiling face – the face of a woman who has plunked down two dollars in a carny shooting-pitch and means to win the big stuffed teddybear even if she has to blast away all night.

And she threw *fast*. The rocks hailed down around me, some splashing into the ruddy water to my left or right, creating little geysers. I began to backpedal, afraid to turn and swim for it, afraid that she would throw a really big one the minute I did. Still, I had to get out of her range. Devore, meanwhile, was laughing a wheezy old man's laugh, his wretched face crunched in on itself like the face of a malicious apple-doll.

One of her rocks struck me a hard, painful blow on the collarbone and bounced high into the air. I cried out, and she did, too: '*Hai!*,' like a karate fighter who's gotten in a good kick.

So much for orderly retreat. I turned, swam for deeper water, and the bitch brained me. The first two rocks she threw after I began

288

to swim seemed to be range-finders. There was a pause when I had time to think *I'm doing it, I'm getting beyond her area of* . . . and then something hit the back of my head. I felt it and heard it the same way – it went *CLONK!*, like something you'd read in a Batman comic.

The surface of the lake went from bright orange to bright red to dark scarlet. Faintly I could hear Devore yelling approval and Whitmore squealing her strange laugh. I took in another mouthful of iron-tasting water and was so dazed I had to remind myself to spit it out, not swallow it. My feet now felt too heavy for swimming, and my goddam sneakers weighed a ton. I put them down to stand up and couldn't find the bottom – I had gotten beyond my depth. I looked in toward the shore. It was spectacular, blazing in the sunset like stage-scenery lit with bright orange and red gels. I was probably twenty feet out from the shore now. Devore and Whitmore were at the edge of The Street, watching. They looked like Dad and Mom in a Grant Wood painting. Devore was using the mask again, but I could see him grinning inside it. Whitmore was grinning, too.

More water sloshed in my mouth. I spit most of it out, but some went down, making me cough and half-retch. I started to sink below the surface and fought my way back up, not swimming but only splashing wildly, expending nine times the energy I needed to stay afloat. Panic made its first appearance, nibbling through my dazed bewilderment with sharp little rat teeth. I realized I could hear a high, sweet buzzing. How many blows had my poor old head taken? One from Whitmore's fist . . . one from Devore's cane . . . one rock . . . or had it been two? Christ, I couldn't remember.

Get hold of yourself, for God's sake – you're not going to let him beat you this way, are you? Drown you like that little boy was drowned?

No, not if I could help it.

I trod water and ran my left hand down the back of my head. Not too far above the nape I encountered a goose-egg that was still rising. When I pressed on it the pain made me feel like throwing up and fainting at the same time. Tears rose in my eyes and rolled down my cheeks. There were only traces of blood on the tips of my fingers when I looked at them, but it was hard to tell about cuts when you were in the water.

'You look like a woodchuck caught out in the rain, Noonan!'

Now his voice seemed to roll to where I was, as if across a great distance.

'Fuck you!' I called. 'I'll see you in jail for this!'

He looked at Whitmore. She looked back with an identical expression, and they both laughed. If someone had put an Uzi in my hands at that moment, I would have killed them with no hesitation and then asked for a second clip so I could machine-gun the bodies.

With no Uzi to hand, I began to dogpaddle south, toward my house. They paced me along The Street, he rolling in his whisper-quiet wheelchair, she walking beside him as solemn as a nun and pausing every now and then to pick up a likely-looking rock.

I hadn't swum enough to be tired, but I was. It was mostly shock, I suppose. Finally I tried to draw a breath at the wrong time, swallowed more water, and panicked completely. I began to swim in toward the shore, wanting to get to where I could stand up. Rogette Whitmore began to fire rocks at me immediately, first using the ones she had lined up between her left arm and her midriff, then those she'd stockpiled in Devore's lap. She was warmed up, she wasn't throwing like a girl anymore, and her aim was deadly. Stones splashed all around me. I batted another away – a big one that likely would have cut open my forehead if it had hit – but her follow-up struck my bicep and tore a long scratch there. Enough. I rolled over and swam back out beyond her range, gasping for breath, trying to keep my head up in spite of the growing ache in the back of my neck.

When I was clear, I trod water and looked in at them. Whitmore had come all the way to the edge of the embankment, wanting to get every foot of distance she could. Hell, every damned inch. Devore was parked behind her in his wheelchair. They were both still grinning, and now their faces were as red as the faces of imps in hell. Red sky at night, sailor's delight. Another twenty minutes and it would be getting dark. Could I keep my head above water for another twenty minutes? I thought so, if I didn't panic again, but not much longer. I thought of drowning in the dark, looking up and seeing Venus just before I went under for the last time, and the panic-rat slashed me with its teeth again. The panic-rat was worse than Rogette and her rocks, much worse.

Maybe not worse than Devore.

I looked both ways along the lakefront, checking The Street wherever it wove out of the trees for a dozen feet or a dozen yards. I didn't care about being embarrassed anymore, but I saw no one. Dear God, where was everybody? Gone to the Mountain View in Fryeburg for pizza, or the Village Cafe for milkshakes?

'What do you want?' I called in to Devore. 'Do you want me to tell you I'll butt out of your business? Okay, I'll butt out!'

He laughed.

Well, I hadn't expected it to work. Even if I'd been sincere about it, he wouldn't have believed me.

'We just want to see how long you can swim,' Whitmore said, and threw another rock – a long, lazy toss that fell about five feet short of where I was.

They mean to kill me, I thought. *They really do.*

Yes. And what was more, they might well get away with it. A crazy idea, both plausible and implausible at the same time, rose in my mind. I could see Rogette Whitmore tacking a notice to the COMMUNITY DOIN's board outside the Lakeview General Store.

TO THE MARTIANS OF TR-90, GREETINGS!

Mr MAXWELL DEVORE, everyone's favorite Martian, will give each resident of the TR ONE HUNDRED DOLLARS if no one will use The Street on FRIDAY EVENING, THE 17th OF JULY, between the hours of SEVEN and NINE P.M. Keep our 'SUMMER FRIENDS' away, too! And remember: GOOD MARTIANS are like GOOD MONKEYS: they SEE no evil, HEAR no evil, and SPEAK no evil!

I couldn't really believe it, not even in my current situation . . . and yet I almost could. At the very least I had to grant him the luck of the devil.

Tired. My sneakers heavier than ever. I tried to push one of them off and succeeded only in taking in another mouthful of lakewater. They stood watching me, Devore occasionally picking the mask up from his lap and having a revivifying suck.

I couldn't wait until dark. The sun exits in a hurry here in western Maine – as it does, I guess, in mountain country everywhere – but the twilights are long and lingering. By the time it got dark enough in the west for me to move without being seen, the moon would have risen in the east.

I found myself imagining my obituary in *The New York Times*, the headline reading POPULAR ROMANTIC SUSPENSE NOVELIST DROWNS IN MAINE. Debra Weinstock would provide them with the author photo from the forthcoming *Helen's Promise*. Harold Oblowski would say all the right things, and he'd also remember to put a modest (but not tiny) death notice in *Publishers Weekly*. He would go half-and-half with Putnam's on it, and—

I sank, swallowed more water, and spat it out. I began pummelling the lake again and forced myself to stop. From the shore, I could hear Rogette Whitmore's tinkling laughter. *You bitch*, I thought. *You scrawny bi—*

Mike, Jo said.

Her voice was in my head, but it wasn't the one I make when I'm imagining her side of a mental dialogue or when I just miss her and need to whistle her up for awhile. As if to underline this, something splashed to my right, splashed hard. When I looked in that direction I saw no fish, not even a ripple. What I saw instead was our swimming float, anchored about a hundred yards away in the sunset-colored water.

'I can't swim that far, baby,' I croaked.

'Did you say something, Noonan?' Devore called from the shore. He cupped a mocking hand to one of his huge waxlump ears. 'Couldn't quite make it out! You sound all out of breath!' More tinkling laughter from Whitmore. He was Johnny Carson; she was Ed McMahon.

You can make it. I'll help you.

The float, I realized, might be my only chance – there wasn't another one on this part of the shore, and it was at least ten yards beyond Whitmore's longest rockshot so far. I began to dogpaddle in that direction, my arms now as leaden as my feet. Each time I felt my head on the verge of going under I paused, treading water, telling myself to take it easy, I was in pretty good shape and doing okay, telling myself that if I didn't panic I'd be all right. The old bitch and the even older bastard resumed pacing me, but they saw where I was headed and the laughter stopped. So did the taunts.

For a long time the swimming float seemed to draw no closer. I told myself that was just because the light was fading, the color of the water draining from red to purple to a near-black that was the color of Devore's gums, but I was able to muster less and less conviction for this idea as my breath shortened and my arms grew heavier.

When I was still thirty yards away a cramp struck my left leg. I rolled sideways like a swamped sailboat, trying to reach the bunched muscle. More water poured down my throat. I tried to cough it out, then retched and went under with my stomach still trying to heave and my fingers still looking for the knotted place above the knee.

I'm really drowning, I thought, strangely calm now that it was happening. *This is how it happens, this is it.*

Then I felt a hand seize me by the nape of the neck. The pain of having my hair yanked brought me back to reality in a flash – it was better than an epinephrine injection. I felt another hand clamp around my left leg; there was a brief but terrific sense of heat. The cramp let go and I broke the surface swimming – *really* swimming this time, not just dogpaddling, and in what seemed like seconds I was clinging to the ladder on the side of the float, breathing in great, snatching gasps, waiting to see if I was going to be all right or if my heart was going to detonate in my chest like a grenade. At last my lungs started to overcome my oxygen debt, and everything began to calm down. I gave it another minute, then climbed out of the water and into what was now the ashes of twilight. I stood facing west for a little while, bent over with my hands on my knees, dripping on the boards. Then I turned around, meaning this time to flip them not just a single bird but that fabled double eagle. There was no one to flip it to. The Street was empty. Devore and Rogette Whitmore were gone.

Maybe they were gone. I'd do well to remember there was a lot of Street I couldn't see.

I sat crosslegged on the float until the moon rose, waiting and watching for any movement. Half an hour, I think. Maybe forty-five minutes. I checked my watch, but got no help there; it had shipped some water and stopped at 7:30 P.M. To the other satisfactions Devore owed me I could now add the price of one Timex Indiglo – that's $29.95, asshole, cough it up.

At last I climbed back down the ladder, slipped into the water, and stroked for shore as quietly as I could. I was rested, my head had stopped aching (although the knot above the nape of my neck still throbbed steadily), and I no longer felt off-balance and incredulous. In some ways, that had been the worst of it – trying to cope not just with the apparition of the drowned boy, the flying rocks, and the lake, but with the pervasive sense that none of this could be happening, that rich old software moguls did not try to drown novelists who strayed into their line of sight.

Had tonight's adventure been a case of simply straying into Devore's view, though? A coincidental meeting, no more than that? Wasn't it likely he'd been having me watched ever since the Fourth of July, maybe from the other side of the lake, by people with high-powered optical equipment? Paranoid bullshit, I would have said . . . at least I would have said it before the two of them almost sank me in Dark Score Lake like a kid's paper boat in a mudpuddle.

I decided I didn't care who might be watching from the other side of the lake. I didn't care if the two of them were still lurking on one of the tree-shielded parts of The Street, either. I swam until I could feel strands of waterweed tickling my ankles and see the crescent of my beach. Then I stood up, wincing at the air, which now felt cold on my skin. I limped to shore, one hand raised to fend off a hail of rocks, but no rocks came. I stood for a moment on The Street, my jeans and polo shirt dripping, looking first one way, then the other. It seemed I had this little part of the world to myself. Last, I looked back at the water, where weak moonlight beat a track from the thumbnail of beach out to the swimming float.

'Thanks, Jo,' I said, then started up the railroad ties to the house. I got about halfway, then had to stop and sit down. I had never been so utterly tired in my whole life.

CHAPTER EIGHTEEN

I climbed the stairs to the deck instead of going around to the front door, still moving slowly and marvelling at how my legs felt twice their normal weight. When I stepped into the living room I looked around with the wide eyes of someone who has been away for a decade and returns to find everything just as he left it – Bunter the moose on the wall, the *Boston Globe* on the couch, a compilation of *Tough Stuff* crossword puzzles on the end-table, the plate on the counter with the remains of my stir-fry still on it. Looking at these things brought the realization home full force – I had gone for a walk, leaving all this normal light clutter behind, and had almost died instead. Had almost been murdered.

I began to shake. I went into the north-wing bathroom, took off my wet clothes, and threw them into the tub – *splat*. Then, still shaking, I turned and stared at myself in the mirror over the washbasin. I looked like someone who has been on the losing side in a barroom brawl. One bicep bore a long, clotting gash. A blackish-purple bruise was unfurling what looked like shadowy wings on my left collarbone. There was a bloody furrow on my neck and behind my ear, where the lovely Rogette had caught me with the stone in her ring.

I took my shaving mirror and used it to check the back of my head. 'Can't you get that through your thick skull?' my mother used to shout at me and Sid when we were kids, and now I thanked God that Ma had apparently been right about the thickness factor, at least in my case. The spot where Devore had struck me with his cane looked like the cone of a recently extinct volcano. Whitmore's bullseye had left a red wound that would need stitches if I wanted to avoid a scar. Blood, rusty and thin, stained the nape of my neck all around the hairline. God knew how much had flowed out of that unpleasant-looking red mouth and been washed away by the lake.

I poured hydrogen peroxide into my cupped palm, steeled myself, and slapped it on to the gash back there like aftershave. The bite was monstrous, and I had to tighten my lips to keep from crying out. When the pain started to fade a little, I soaked cotton balls with more peroxide and cleaned my other wounds.

I showered, threw on a tee-shirt and a pair of jeans, then went into the hall to phone the County Sheriff. There was no need for directory assistance; the Castle Rock PD and County Sheriff's numbers were on the IN CASE OF EMERGENCY card thumbtacked to the bulletin board, along with numbers for the fire department, the ambulance service, and the 900-number where you could get three answers to that day's *Times* crossword puzzle for a buck-fifty.

I dialed the first three numbers fast, then began to slow down. I got as far as 955–960 before stopping altogether. I stood there in the hall with the phone pressed against my ear, visualizing another headline, this one not in the decorous *Times* but the rowdy *New York Post*. **NOVELIST TO AGING COMPU-KING: 'YOU BIG BULLY!'** Along with side-by-side pictures of me, looking roughly my age, and Max Devore, looking roughly a hundred and six. The *Post* would have great fun telling its readers how Devore (along with his companion, an elderly lady who might weigh ninety pounds soaking wet) had lumped up a novelist half his age – a guy who looked, in his photograph, at least, reasonably trim and fit.

The phone got tired of holding only six of the required seven numbers in its rudimentary brain, double-clicked, and dumped me back to an open line. I took the handset away from my ear, stared at it for a moment, and then set it gently back down in its cradle.

I'm not a sissy about the sometimes whimsical, sometimes hateful attention of the press, but I'm wary, as I would be around a bad-tempered fur-bearing mammal. America has turned the people who entertain it into weird high-class whores, and the media jeers at any 'celeb' who dares complain about his or her treatment. 'Quitcha bitchin!' cry the newspapers and the TV gossip shows (the tone is one of mingled triumph and indignation). 'Didja really think we paid

296

ya the big bucks just to sing a song or swing a Louisville Slugger? Wrong, asshole! We pay so we can be amazed when you do it well – whatever "it" happens to be in your particular case – and also because it's gratifying when you fuck up. The truth is you're supplies. If you cease to be amusing, we can always kill you and eat you.'

They can't *really* eat you, of course. They can print pictures of you with your shirt off and say you're running to fat, they can talk about how much you drink or how many pills you take or snicker about the night you pulled some starlet on to your lap at Spago and tried to stick your tongue in her ear, but they can't really eat you. So it wasn't the thought of the *Post* calling me a crybaby or being a part of Jay Leno's opening monologue that made me put the phone down; it was the realization that I had no proof. No one had seen us. And, I realized, finding an alibi for himself and his personal assistant would be the easiest thing in the world for Max Devore.

There was one other thing, too, the capper; imagining the County Sheriff sending out George Footman, aka daddy, to take my statement on how the mean man had knocked li'l Mikey into the lake. How the three of them would laugh later about that!

I called John Storrow instead, wanting him to tell me I was doing the right thing, the only thing that made any sense. Wanting him to remind me that only desperate men were driven to such desperate lengths (I would ignore, at least for the time being, how the two of them had laughed, as if they were having the time of their lives), and that nothing had changed in regard to Ki Devore – her grandfather's custody case still sucked bogwater.

I got John's recording machine at home and left a message – just call Mike Noonan, no emergency, but feel free to call late. Then I tried his office, mindful of the scripture according to John Grisham: young lawyers work until they drop. I listened to the firm's recording machine, then followed instructions and punched STO on my phone keypad, the first three letters of John's last name.

There was a click and he came on the line – another recorded version, unfortunately. 'Hi, this is John Storrow. I've gone up to Philly for the weekend to see my mom and dad. I'll be in the office on Monday; for the rest of the week, I'll be out on business. From Tuesday to Friday you'll probably have the most luck trying to reach me at . . .'

The number he gave began 207–955, which meant Castle Rock. I imagined it was the hotel where he'd stayed before, the nice one up on the View. 'Mike Noonan,' I said. 'Call me when you can. I left a message on your apartment machine, too.'

I went in the kitchen to get a beer, then only stood there in front of the refrigerator, playing with the magnets. Whoremaster, he'd called me. *Say there, whoremaster, where's your whore?* A minute later he had offered to save my soul. Quite funny, really. Like an alcoholic offering to take care of your liquor cabinet. *He spoke of you with what I think was genuine affection,* Mattie had said. *Your great-grandfather and his great-grandfather shit in the same pit.*

I left the fridge with all the beer still safe inside, went back to the phone, and called Mattie.

'Hi,' said another obviously recorded voice. I was on a roll. 'It's me, but either I'm out or not able to come to the phone right this minute. Leave a message, okay?' A pause, the mike rustling, a distant whisper, and then Kyra, so loud she almost blew my ear off: '*Leave a HAPPY message!*' What followed was laughter from both of them, cut off by the beep.

'Hi, Mattie, it's Mike Noonan,' I said. 'I just wanted—'

I don't know how I would have finished that thought, and I didn't have to. There was a click and then Mattie herself said, 'Hello, Mike.' There was such a difference between this dreary, defeated-sounding voice and the cheerful one on the tape that for a moment I was silenced. Then I asked her what was wrong.

'Nothing,' she said, then began to cry. 'Everything. I lost my job. Lindy fired me.'

Firing wasn't what Lindy had called it, of course. She'd called it 'belt-tightening,' but it was firing, all right, and I knew that if I looked into the funding of the Four Lakes Consolidated Library, I would discover that one of the chief supporters over the years had been Mr Max Devore. And he'd continue to be one of the chief supporters . . . if, that was, Lindy Briggs played ball.

'We shouldn't have talked where she could see us doing it,' I said, knowing I could have stayed away from the library completely and Mattie would be just as gone. 'And we probably should have seen this coming.'

298

'John Storrow *did* see it.' She was still crying, but making an effort to get it under control. 'He said Max Devore would probably want to make sure I was as deep in the corner as he could push me, come the custody hearing. He said Devore would want to make sure I answered "I'm unemployed, your honor," when the judge asked where I worked. I told John Mrs Briggs would never do anything so low, especially to a girl who'd given such a brilliant talk on Melville's "Bartleby." Do you know what he told me?'

'No.'

'He said, "You're very young." I thought that was a patronizing thing to say, but he was right, wasn't he?'

'Mattie—'

'What am I going to do, Mike? What am I going to do?' The panic-rat had moved on down to Wasp Hill Road, it sounded like.

I thought, quite coldly: *Why not become my mistress? Your title will be 'research assistant,' a perfectly jake occupation as far as the IRS is concerned. I'll throw in clothes, a couple of charge cards, a house — say goodbye to the rustbucket doublewide on Wasp Hill Road — and a two-week vacation: how does February on Maui sound? Plus Ki's education, of course, and a hefty cash bonus at the end of the year. I'll be considerate, too. Considerate and discreet. Once or twice a week, and never until your little girl is fast asleep. All you have to do is say yes and give me a key. All you have to do is slide over when I slide in. All you have to do is let me do what I want — all through the dark, all through the night, let me touch where I want to touch, let me do what I want to do, never say no, never say stop.*

I closed my eyes.

'Mike? Are you there?'

'Sure,' I said. I touched the throbbing gash at the back of my head and winced. 'You're going to do just fine, Mattie. You—'

'The trailer's not paid for!' she nearly wailed. 'I have two overdue phone bills and they're threatening to cut off the service! There's something wrong with the Jeep's transmission, and the rear axle, as well! I can pay for Ki's last week of Vacation Bible School, I guess – Mrs Briggs gave me three weeks' pay in lieu of notice – but how will I buy her *shoes*? She outgrows everything so *fast* . . . there's holes in all her shorts and most of her g-g-goddam underwear . . .'

She was starting to weep again.

299

'I'm going to take care of you until you get back on your feet,' I said.

'No, I can't let—'

'You can. And for Kyra's sake, you will. Later on, if you still want to, you can pay me back. We'll keep tabs on every dollar and dime, if you like. But I'm going to take care of you.' *And you'll never take off your clothes when I'm with you. That's a promise, and I'm going to keep it.*

'Mike, you don't have to do this.'

'Maybe, maybe not. But I *am* going to do it. You just try and stop me.' I'd called meaning to tell her what had happened to me – giving her the humorous version – but that now seemed like the worst idea in the world. 'This custody thing is going to be over before you know it, and if you can't find anyone brave enough to put you to work down here once it is, I'll find someone up in Derry who'll do it. Besides, tell me the truth – aren't you starting to feel that it might be time for a change of scenery?'

She managed a scrap of a laugh. 'I guess you could say that.'

'Heard from John today?'

'Actually, yes. He's visiting his parents in Philadelphia but he gave me the number there. I called him.'

He'd said he was taken with her. Perhaps she was taken with him, as well. I told myself the thorny little tug I felt across my emotions at the idea was only my imagination. Tried to tell myself that, anyway. 'What did he say about you losing your job the way you did?'

'The same things you said. But he didn't make me feel safe. You do. I don't know why.' I did. I was an older man, and that is our chief attraction to young women: we make them feel safe. 'He's coming up again Tuesday morning. I said I'd have lunch with him.'

Smoothly, not a tremor or hesitation in my voice, I said: 'Maybe I could join you.'

Mattie's own voice warmed at the suggestion; her ready acceptance made me feel paradoxically guilty. 'That would be great! Why don't I call him and suggest that you both come over here? I could barbecue again. Maybe I'll keep Ki home from VBS and make it a foursome. She's hoping you'll read her another story. She really enjoyed that.'

'That sounds great,' I said, and meant it. Adding Kyra made it all

300

seem more natural, less of an intrusion on my part. Also less like a date on theirs. John could not be accused of taking an unethical interest in his client. In the end he'd probably thank me. 'I believe Ki might be ready to move on to "Hansel and Gretel." How are you, Mattie? All right?'

'Much better than I was before you called.'

'Good. Things are going to be all right.'

'Promise me.'

'I think I just did.'

There was a slight pause. 'Are *you* all right, Mike? You sound a little . . . I don't know . . . a little strange.'

'I'm okay,' I said, and I was, for someone who had been pretty sure he was drowning less than an hour ago. 'Can I ask you one question before I go? Because this is driving me crazy.'

'Of course.'

'The night we had dinner, you said Devore told you his great-grandfather and mine knew each other. Pretty well, according to him.'

'He said they shit in the same pit. I thought that was elegant.'

'Did he say anything else? Think hard.'

She did, but came up with nothing. I told her to call me if something about that conversation did occur to her, or if she got lonely or scared, or if she started to feel worried about anything. I didn't like to say too much, but I had already decided I'd have to have a frank talk with John about my latest adventure. It might be prudent to have the private detective from Lewiston – George Kennedy, like the actor – put a man or two on the TR to keep an eye on Mattie and Kyra. Max Devore was mad, just as my caretaker had said. I hadn't understood then, but I did now. Any time I started to doubt, all I had to do was touch the back of my head.

I returned to the fridge and once more forgot to open it. My hands went to the magnets instead and again began moving them around, watching as words formed, broke apart, evolved. It was a peculiar kind of writing . . . but it *was* writing. I could tell by the way I was starting to trance out.

That half-hypnotized state is one you cultivate until you can switch it on and off at will . . . at least you can when things are going well. The intuitive part of the mind unlocks itself when you

301

begin work and rises to a height of about six feet (maybe ten on good days). Once there, it simply hovers, sending black-magic messages and bright pictures. For the balance of the day that part is locked to the rest of the machinery and goes pretty much forgotten . . . except on certain occasions when it comes loose on its own and you trance out unexpectedly, your mind making associations which have nothing to do with rational thought and glaring with unexpected images. That is in some ways the strangest part of the creative process. The muses are ghosts, and sometimes they come uninvited.

My house is haunted.

Sara Laughs has always been haunted . . . you've stirred em up.

stirred, I wrote on the refrigerator. But it didn't look right, so I made a circle of fruit and vegetable magnets around it. That was better, much. I stood there for a moment, hands crossed over my chest as I crossed them at my desk when I was stuck for a word or a phrase, then took off *stirr* and put on *haunt,* making *haunted.*

'It's haunted in the circle,' I said, and barely heard the faint chime of Bunter's bell, as if in agreement.

I took the letters off, and as I did found myself thinking how odd it was to have a lawyer named Romeo—

(*romeo* went in the circle)

—and a detective named George Kennedy.

(*george* went up on the fridge)

I wondered if Kennedy could help me with Andy Drake—

(*drake* on the fridge)

—maybe give me some insights. I'd never written about a private detective before and it's the little stuff—

(*rake* off, leave the *d,* add *etails*)

—that makes the difference. I turned a 3 on its back and put an *I* beneath it, making a pitchfork. The devil's in the details.

From there I went somewhere else. I don't know where, exactly, because I was tranced out, that intuitive part of my mind up so high a search-party couldn't have found it. I stood in front of my fridge and played with the letters, spelling out little pieces of thought without even thinking about them. You mightn't believe such a thing is possible, but every writer knows it is.

What brought me back was light splashing across the windows of the foyer. I looked up and saw the shape of a car pulling to a stop behind my Chevrolet. A cramp of terror seized my belly. That was a moment when I would have given everything I owned for a loaded gun. Because it was Footman. Had to be. Devore had called him when he and Whitmore got back to Warrington's, had told him Noonan refuses to be a good Martian so get over there and fix him.

When the driver's door opened and the dome-light in the visitor's car came on, I breathed a conditional sigh of relief. I didn't know who it was, but it sure wasn't 'daddy.' This fellow didn't look as if he could take care of a housefly with a rolled-up newspaper ... although, I supposed, there were plenty of people who had made that same mistake about Jeffrey Dahmer.

Above the fridge was a cluster of aereosol cans, all of them old and probably not ozone-friendly. I didn't know how Mrs M. had missed them, but I was pleased she had. I took the first one my hand touched – Black Flag, excellent choice – thumbed off the cap, and stuck the can in the left front pocket of my jeans. Then I turned to the drawers on the right of the sink. The top one contained silverware. The second one held what Jo called 'kitchenshit' – everything from poultry thermometers to those gadgets you stick in corncobs so you don't burn your fingers off. The third one down held a generous selection of mismatched steak knives. I took one, put it in the right front pocket of my jeans, and went to the door.

The man on my stoop jumped a little when I turned on the outside light, then blinked through the door at me like a nearsighted rabbit. He was about five-four, skinny, pale. He wore his hair cropped in the sort of cut known as a wiffle in my boyhood days. His eyes were brown. Guarding them was a pair of horn-rimmed glasses with greasy-looking lenses. His little hands hung at his sides. One held the handle of a flat leather case, the other a small white oblong. I didn't think it was my destiny to be killed by a man with a business card in one hand, so I opened the door.

The guy smiled, the anxious sort of smile people always seem to wear in Woody Allen movies. He was wearing a Woody Allen outfit too, I saw – faded plaid shirt a little too short at the wrists, chinos a little too baggy in the crotch. *Someone must have told him about the resemblance*, I thought. *That's got to be it.*

'Mr Noonan?'

'Yes?'

He handed me the card. NEXT CENTURY REAL ESTATE, it said in raised gold letters. Below this, in more modest black, was my visitor's name.

'I'm Richard Osgood,' he said as if I couldn't read, and held out his hand. The American male's need to respond to that gesture in kind is deeply ingrained, but that night I resisted it. He held his little pink paw out a moment longer, then lowered it and wiped the palm nervously against his chinos. 'I have a message for you. From Mr Devore.'

I waited.

'May I come in?'

'No,' I said.

He took a step backward, wiped his hand on his pants again, and seemed to gather himself. 'I hardly think there's any need to be rude, Mr Noonan.'

I wasn't being rude. If I'd wanted to be rude, I would have treated him to a faceful of roach-repellent. 'Max Devore and his minder tried to drown me in the lake this evening. If my manners seem a little off to you, that's probably it.'

Osgood's look of shock was real, I think. 'You must be working too hard on your latest project, Mr Noonan. Max Devore is going to be eighty-six on his next birthday – if he makes it, which now seems to be in some doubt. Poor old fella can hardly even walk from his chair to his bed anymore. As for Rogette—'

'I see your point,' I said. 'In fact I saw it twenty minutes ago, without any help from you. I hardly believe it myself, and I was there. Give me whatever it is you have for me.'

'Fine,' he said in a prissy little 'all right, *be* that way' voice. He unzipped a pouch on the front of his leather bag and brought out a white envelope, business-sized and sealed. I took it, hoping Osgood couldn't sense how hard my heart was thumping. Devore moved pretty damned fast for a man who travelled with an oxygen tank. The question was, what kind of move was this?

'Thanks,' I said, beginning to close the door. 'I'd tip you the price of a drink, but I left my wallet on the dresser.'

'Wait! You're supposed to read it and give me an answer.'

304

I raised my eyebrows. 'I don't know where Devore got the notion that he could order me around, but I have no intention of allowing his ideas to influence my behavior. Buzz off.'

His lips turned down, creating deep dimples at the corners of his mouth, and all at once he didn't look like Woody Allen at all. He looked like a fifty-year-old real estate broker who had sold his soul to the devil and now couldn't stand to see anyone yank the boss's forked tail. 'Piece of friendly advice, Mr Noonan – you want to watch it. Max Devore is no man to fool around with.'

'Luckily for me, I'm not fooling around.'

I closed the door and stood in the foyer, holding the envelope and watching Mr Next Century Real Estate. He looked pissed off and confused – no one had given him the bum's rush just lately, I guessed. Maybe it would do him some good. Lend a little perspective to his life. Remind him that, Max Devore or no Max Devore, Richie Osgood would still never stand more than five-feet-seven. Even in cowboy boots.

'Mr Devore wants an answer!' he called through the closed door.

'I'll phone,' I called back, then slowly raised my middle fingers in the double eagle I'd hoped to give Max and Rogette earlier. 'In the meantime, perhaps you could convey this.'

I almost expected him to take off his glasses and rub his eyes. He walked back to his car instead, tossed his case in, then followed it. I watched until he had backed up to the lane and I was sure he was gone. Then I went into the living room and opened the envelope. Inside was a single sheet of paper, faintly scented with the perfume my mother had worn when I was just a kid. White Shoulders, I think it's called. Across the top – neat, ladylike, printed in slightly raised letters – was

ROGETTE D. WHITMORE

Below it was this message, written in a slightly shaky feminine hand:

8:30 P.M.

Dear Mr Noonan,

Max wishes me to convey how glad he was to meet you! I must echo that sentiment. You are a very amusing and entertaining fellow! We enjoyed your antics ever so much.

Now to business. M. offers you a very simple deal: if you promise to cease asking questions about him, and if you promise to cease all legal maneuvering – if you promise to let him rest in peace, so to speak – then Mr Devore promises to cease efforts to gain custody of his granddaughter. If this suits, you need only tell Mr Osgood 'I agree.' He will carry the message! Max hopes to return to California by private jet very soon – he has business which can be put off no longer, although he has enjoyed his time here and has found you particularly interesting. He wants me to remind you that custody has its responsibilities, and urges you not to forget he said so.

Rogette

P.S. He reminds me that you didn't answer his question – does her cunt suck? Max is quite curious on that point.

R.

I read this note over a second time, then a third. I started to put it on the table, then read it a fourth time. It was as if I couldn't get the sense of it. I had to restrain an urge to fly to the telephone and call Mattie at once. It's over, Mattie, I'd say. Taking your job and dunking me in the lake were the last two shots of the war. He's giving up.

No. Not until I was absolutely sure.

I called Warrington's instead, where I got my fourth answering machine of the night. Devore and Whitmore hadn't bothered with anything warm and fuzzy, either; a voice as cold as a motel ice-machine simply told me to leave my message at the sound of the beep.

'It's Noonan,' I said. Before I could go any further there was a click as someone picked up.

'Did you enjoy your swim?' Rogette Whitmore asked in a smoky, mocking voice. If I hadn't seen her in the flesh, I might have imagined a Barbara Stanwyck type at her most coldly attractive, coiled on a red velvet couch in a peach-silk dressing gown, telephone in one hand, ivory cigarette holder in the other.

'If I'd caught up with you, Ms Whitmore, I would have made you understand my feelings perfectly.'

'Oooo,' she said. 'My thighs are a-tingle.'

'Please spare me the image of your thighs.'

'Sticks and stones, Mr Noonan,' she said. 'To what do we owe the pleasure of your call?'

'I sent Mr Osgood away without a reply.'

'Max thought you might. He said, "Our young whoremaster believes in the value of a personal response. You can tell that just looking at him."'

'He gets the uglies when he loses, doesn't he?'

'Mr Devore doesn't *lose.*' Her voice dropped at least forty degrees and all the mocking good humor bailed out on the way down. 'He may change his goals, but he doesn't *lose.* You were the one who looked like a loser tonight, Mr Noonan, paddling around and yelling out there in the lake. You were scared, weren't you?'

'Yes. Badly.'

'You were right to be. I wonder if you know how lucky you are?'

'May I tell you something?'

'Of course, Mike – may I call you Mike?'

'Why don't you just stick with Mr Noonan. Now – are you listening?'

'With bated breath.'

'Your boss is old, he's nutty, and I suspect he's past the point where he could effectively manage a Yahtzee scorecard, let alone a custody suit. He was whipped a week ago.'

'Do you have a point?'

'As a matter of fact I do, so get it right: if either of you ever tries anything remotely like that again, I'll come after that old fuck and jam his snot-smeared oxygen mask so far up his ass he'll be able to aerate his lungs from the bottom. And if I see you on The Street, Ms Whitmore, I'll use you for a shotput. Do you understand me?'

I stopped, breathing hard, amazed and also rather disgusted with myself. If you had told me I'd had such a speech in me, I would have scoffed.

After a long silence I said: 'Ms Whitmore? Still there?'

'I'm here,' she said. I wanted her to be furious, but she actually sounded amused. 'Who has the uglies now, Mr Noonan?'

'I do,' I said, 'and don't you forget it, you rock-throwing bitch.'

'What is your answer to Mr Devore?'

'We have a deal. I shut up, the lawyers shut up, he gets out of Mattie and Kyra's life. If, on the other hand, he continues to—'

'I know, I know, you'll bore him and stroke him. I wonder how you'll feel about all this a week from now, you arrogant, stupid creature?'

Before I could reply – it was on the tip of my tongue to tell her that even at her best she still threw like a girl – she was gone.

I stood there with the telephone in my hand for a few seconds, then hung it up. Was it a trick? It felt like a trick, but at the same time it didn't. John needed to know about this. He hadn't left his parents' number on his answering machine, but Mattie had it. If I called her back, though, I'd be obligated to tell her what had just happened. It might be a good idea to put off any further calls until tomorrow. To sleep on it.

I stuck my hand in my pocket and damned near impaled it on the steak knife hiding there. I'd forgotten all about it. I took it out, carried it back into the kitchen, and returned it to the drawer. Next I fished out the aerosol can, turned to put it back on top of the fridge with its elderly brothers, then stopped. Inside the circle of fruit and vegetable magnets was this:

d
go
w
19n

Had I done that myself? Had I been so far into the zone, so tranced out, that I had put a mini-crossword on the refrigerator without remembering it? And if so, what did it mean?

Maybe someone else put it up, I thought. *One of my invisible roommates.*

'Go down 19n,' I said, reaching out and touching the letters. A compass heading? Or maybe it meant *Go 19 Down*. That suggested crosswords again. Sometimes in a puzzle you get a clue which reads simply *See 19 Across* or *See 19 Down*. If that was the meaning here, what puzzle was I supposed to check?

'I could use a little help here,' I said, but there was no answer – not from the astral plane, not from inside my own head. I finally got the can of beer I'd been promising myself and took it back to the sofa. I picked up my *Tough Stuff* crossword book and looked at the puzzle I was currently working. 'Liquor Is Quicker,' it was called, and it was filled with the stupid puns which only crossword addicts find amusing. Tipsy actor? Marlon Brandy. Tipsy southern novel? Tequila Mockingbird. Drives the DA to drink? Bourbon of proof. And the definition of 19 Down was Oriental nurse, which every cruciverbalist in the universe knows is amah. Nothing in 'Liquor Is Quicker' connected to what was going on in my life, at least that I could see.

I thumbed through some of the other puzzles in the book, looking at 19 Downs. Marble worker's tool (chisel). CNN's favorite howler, 2 wds (wolfblitzer). Ethanol and dimethyl ether, e.g. (isomers). I tossed the book aside in disgust. Who said it had to be this particular crossword collection, anyway? There were probably fifty others in the house, four or five in the drawer of the very end-table on which my beer can stood. I leaned back on the sofa and closed my eyes.

I always liked a whore . . . sometimes their place was on my face.

This is where good pups and vile dogs may walk side by side.

There's no town drunk here, we all take turns.

This is where it happened. Ayuh.

I fell asleep and woke up three hours later with a stiff neck and a terrible throb in the back of my head. Thunder was rumbling thickly far off in the White Mountains, and the house seemed very hot. When I got up from the couch, the backs of my thighs more or less peeled away from the fabric. I shuffled down to the north wing like an old, old man, looked at my wet clothes, thought about taking them into the laundry room, and then decided if I bent over that far, my head might explode.

'You ghosts take care of it,' I muttered. 'If you can change the pants and the underwear around on the whirligig, you can put my clothes in the hamper.'

I urinated, took three Tylenol, and went to bed. At some point I woke a second time and heard the phantom child sobbing.

'Stop,' I told it. 'Stop it, Ki, no one's going to take you anywhere. You're safe.' Then I went back to sleep again.

CHAPTER NINETEEN

The telephone was ringing. I climbed toward it from a drowning dream where I couldn't catch my breath, rising into early sunlight, wincing at the pain in the back of my head as I swung my feet out of bed. The phone would quit before I got to it, they almost always do in such situations, and then I'd lie back down and spend a fruitless ten minutes wondering who it had been before getting up for good.

Ringgg . . . ringgg . . . ringgg . . .

Was that ten? A dozen? I'd lost count. Someone was really dedicated. I hoped it wasn't trouble, but in my experience people don't try that hard when the news is good. I touched my fingers gingerly to the back of my head. It hurt plenty, but that deep, sick ache seemed to be gone. And there was no blood on my fingers when I looked at them.

I padded down the hall and picked up the phone. 'Hello?'

'Well, you won't have to worry about testifyin at the kid's custody hearin anymore, at least.'

'Bill?'

'Ayuh.'

'How did you know . . .' I leaned around the corner and peered at the waggy, annoying cat-clock. Twenty minutes past seven and already sweltering. Hotter'n a bugger, as us TR Martians like to say. 'How do you know he decided—'

'I don't know nothing about his business one way or t'other.' Bill sounded touchy. 'He never called to ask my advice, and I never called to give him any.'

'What's happened? What's going on?'

'You haven't had the TV on yet?'

'I don't even have the coffee on yet.'

No apology from Bill; he was a fellow who believed that people who didn't get up until after six A.M. deserved whatever they got. I was awake now, though. And had a pretty good idea of what was coming.

'Devore killed himself last night, Mike. Got into a tub of warm water and pulled a plastic bag over his head. Mustn't have taken long, with his lungs the way they were.'

No, I thought, probably not long. In spite of the humid summer heat that already lay on the house, I shivered.

'Who found him? The woman?'

'Ayuh, sure.'

'What time?'

'"Shortly before midnight," they said on the Channel 6 news.'

Right around the time I had awakened on the couch and taken myself stiffly off to bed, in other words.

'Is she implicated?'

'Did she play Kevorkian, you mean? The news report I saw didn't say nothin about that. The gossip-mill down to the Lakeview General will be turnin brisk by now, but I ain't been down yet for my share of the grain. If she helped him, I don't think she'll ever see trouble for it, do you? He was eighty-five and not well.'

'Do you know if he'll be buried on the TR?'

'California. She said there'd be services in Palm Springs on Tuesday.'

A sense of surpassing oddness swept over me as I realized the source of Mattie's problems might be lying in a chapel filled with flowers at the same time The Friends of Kyra Devore were digesting their lunches and getting ready to start throwing the Frisbee around. *It's going to be a celebration,* I thought wonderingly. *I don't know how they're going to handle it in The Little Chapel of the Microchips in Palm Springs, but on Wasp Hill Road they're going to be dancing and throwing their arms in the sky and hollering Yes, lawd.*

I'd never been glad to hear of anyone's death before in my life, but I was glad to hear of Devore's. I was sorry to feel that way, but I did. The old bastard had dumped me in the lake . . . but before the night was over, he was the one who had

312

drowned. Inside a plastic bag he had drowned, sitting in a tub of tepid water.

'Any idea how the TV guys got on to it so fast?' It wasn't *superfast*, not with seven hours between the discovery of the body and the seven o'clock news, but TV news people have a tendency to be lazy.

'Whitmore called em. Had a press conference right there in Warrin'ton's parlor at two o'clock this morning. Took questions settin on that big maroon plush sofa, the one Jo always used to say should be in a saloon oil paintin with a naked woman lyin on it. Remember?'

'Yeah.'

'I saw a coupla County deputies walkin around in the background, plus a fella I reckonized from Jaquard's Funeral Home in Motton.'

'That's bizarre,' I said.

'Ayuh, body still upstairs, most likely, while Whitmore was runnin her gums ... but she claimed she was just followin the boss's orders. Said he left a tape sayin he'd done it on Friday night so as not to affect the cump'ny stock price and wanted Rogette to call in the press right off and assure folks that the cump'ny was solid, that between his son and the Board of Directors, everythin was goin to be just acey-deucey. Then she told about the services in Palm Springs.'

'He commits suicide, then holds a two A.M. press conference by proxy to soothe the stockholders.'

'Ayuh. And it sounds just like him.'

A silence fell between us on the line. I tried to think and couldn't. All I knew was that I wanted to go upstairs and work, aching head or no aching head. I wanted to rejoin Andy Drake, John Shackleford, and Shackleford's childhood friend, the awful Ray Garraty. There was madness in my story, but it was a madness I understood.

'Bill,' I said at last, 'are we still friends?'

'Christ, yes,' he said promptly. 'But if there's people around who seem a little stand-offy to you, you'll know why, won't you?'

Sure I'd know. Many would blame the old man's death on me. It was crazy, given his physical condition, and it would by no means be a majority opinion, but the idea would gain a certain amount of credence, at least in the short run – I knew that as well as I knew the truth about John Shackleford's childhood friend.

313

Kiddies, once upon a time there was a goose that flew back to the little unincorporated township where it had lived as a downy gosling. It began laying lovely golden eggs, and the townsfolk all gathered around to marvel and receive their share. Now, however, that goose was cooked and someone had to take the heat. I'd get some, but Mattie's kitchen might get a few degrees toastier than mine; she'd had the temerity to fight for her child instead of silently handing Ki over.

'Keep your head down the next few weeks,' Bill said. 'That'd be my idea. In fact, if you had business that took you right out of the TR until all this settles down, that might be for the best.'

'I appreciate the sense of what you're saying, but I can't. I'm writing a book. If I pick up my shit and move, it's apt to die on me. It's happened before, and I don't want it to happen this time.'

'Pretty good yarn, is it?'

'Not bad, but that's not the important thing. It's . . . well, let's just say this one's important to me for other reasons.'

'Wouldn't it travel as far as Derry?'

'Are you trying to get rid of me, William?'

'I'm tryin to keep an eye out, that's all – caretakin's my job, y'know. And don't say you weren't warned: the hive's gonna buzz. There's two stories goin around about you, Mike. One is that you're shacking with Mattie Devore. The other is that you came back to write a hatchet-job on the TR. Pull out all the old skeletons you can find.'

'Finish what Jo started, in other words. Who's been spreading that story, Bill?'

Silence from Bill. We were back on earthquake ground again, and this time that ground felt shakier than ever.

'The book I'm working on is a novel,' I said. 'Set in Florida.'

'Oh, ayuh?' You wouldn't think three little syllables could have so much relief in them.

'Think you could kind of pass that around?'

'I think I could,' he said. 'If you tell Brenda Meserve, it'd get around even faster and go even farther.'

'Okay, I will. As far as Mattie goes—'

'Mike, you don't have to—'

'I'm not shacking with her. That was never the deal. The deal

314

was like walking down the street, turning the corner, and seeing a big guy beating up a little guy.' I paused. 'She and her lawyer are planning a barbecue at her place Tuesday noon. I'm planning to join them. Are people from town going to think we're dancing on Devore's grave?'

'Some will. Royce Merrill will. Dickie Brooks will. Old ladies in pants, Yvette calls em.'

'Well fuck them,' I said. 'Every last one.'

'I understand how you feel, but tell her not to shove it in folks' faces,' he almost pleaded. 'Do that much, Mike. It wouldn't kill her to drag her grill around back of her trailer, would it? At least with it there, folks lookin out from the store or the garage wouldn't see nothing but the smoke.'

'I'll pass on the message. And if I make the party, I'll put the barbecue around back myself.'

'You'd do well to stay away from that girl and her child,' Bill said. 'You can tell me it's none of my business, but I'm talkin to you like a Dutch uncle, tellin you for your own good.'

I had a flash of my dream then. The slick, exquisite tightness as I slipped inside her. The little breasts with their hard nipples. Her voice in the darkness, telling me to do what I wanted. My body responded almost instantly. 'I know you are,' I said.

'All right.' He sounded relieved that I wasn't going to scold him – take him to school, he would have said. 'I'll let you go n have your breakfast.'

'I appreciate you calling.'

'Almost didn't. Yvette talked me into it. She said, "You always liked Mike and Jo Noonan best of all the ones you did for. Don't you get in bad with him now that he's back home."'

'Tell her I appreciate it,' I said.

I hung up the phone and looked at it thoughtfully. We seemed to be on good terms again . . . but I didn't think we were exactly friends. Certainly not the way we had been. That had changed when I realized Bill was lying to me about some things and holding back about others; it had also changed when I realized what he had almost called Sara and the Red-Tops.

You can't condemn a man for what may only be a figment of your own imagination.

315

True, and I'd try not to do it . . . but I knew what I knew.

I went into the living room, snapped on the TV, then snapped it off again. My satellite dish got fifty or sixty different channels, and not a one of them local. There was a portable TV in the kitchen, however, and if I dipped its rabbit-ears toward the lake I'd be able to get WMTW, the ABC affiliate in western Maine.

I snatched up Rogette's note, went into the kitchen, and turned on the little Sony tucked under the cabinets with the coffee-maker. *Good Morning America* was on, but they would be breaking for the local news soon. In the meantime I scanned the note, this time concentrating on the mode of expression rather than the message, which had taken all of my attention the night before.

Hopes to return to California by private jet very soon, she had written.

Has business which can be put off no longer, she had written.

If you promise to let him rest in peace, she had written.

It was a goddam suicide note.

'You knew,' I said, rubbing my thumb over the raised letters of her name. 'You knew when you wrote this, and probably when you were chucking rocks at me. But why?'

Custody has its responsibilities, she had written. *Don't forget he said so.*

But the custody business was over, right? Not even a judge that was bought and paid for could award custody to a dead man.

GMA finally gave way to the local report, where Max Devore's suicide was the leader. The TV picture was snowy, but I could see the maroon sofa Bill had mentioned, and Rogette Whitmore sitting on it with her hands folded composedly in her lap. I thought one of the deputies in the background was George Footman, although the snow was too heavy for me to be completely sure.

Mr Devore had spoken frequently over the last eight months of ending his life Whitmore said. He had been very unwell. He had asked her to come out with him the previous evening, and she realized now that he had wanted to look at one final sunset. It had been a glorious one, too, she added. I could have corroborated that; I remembered the sunset very well, having almost drowned by its light.

Rogette was reading Devore's statement when my phone rang again. It was Mattie, and she was crying in hard gusts.

'The news,' she said, 'Mike, did you see . . . do you know . . .'

At first that was all she could manage that was coherent. I told her I did know, Bill Dean had called me and then I'd caught some of it on the local news. She tried to reply and couldn't speak. Guilt, relief, horror, even hilarity – I heard all those things in her crying. I asked where Ki was. I could sympathize with how Mattie felt – until turning on the news this morning she'd believed old Max Devore was her bitterest enemy – but I didn't like the idea of a three-year-old girl watching her mom fall apart.

'Out back,' she managed. 'She's had her breakfast. Now she's having a d-doll p-p-p . . . doll pi-p-pic—'

'Doll picnic. Yes. Good. Let it go, then. All of it. Let it out.'

She cried for two minutes at least, maybe longer. I stood with the telephone pressed to my ear, sweating in the July heat, trying to be patient.

I'm going to give you one chance to save your soul, Devore had told me, but this morning he was dead and his soul was wherever it was. He was dead, Mattie was free, I was writing. Life should have felt wonderful, but it didn't.

At last she began to get her control back. 'I'm sorry. I haven't cried like that – really, really cried – since Lance died.'

'It's understandable and you're allowed.'

'Come to lunch,' she said. 'Come to lunch *please*, Mike. Ki's going to spend the afternoon with a friend she met at Vacation Bible School, and we can talk. I need to talk to someone . . . God, my head is spinning. Please say you'll come.'

'I'd love to, but it's a bad idea. Especially with Ki gone.'

I gave her an edited version of my conversation with Bill Dean. She listened carefully. I thought there might be an angry outburst when I finished, but I'd forgotten one simple fact: Mattie Stanchfield Devore had lived around here all her life. She knew how things worked.

'I understand that things will heal quicker if I keep my eyes down, my mouth shut, and my knees together,' she said, 'and I'll do my best to go along, but diplomacy only stretches so far. That old man was trying to take my daughter away, don't they realize that down at the goddam general store?'

'*I* realize it.'

317

'I know. That's why I wanted to talk to you.'

'What if we had an early supper on the Castle Rock common? Same place as Friday? Say five-ish?'

'I'd have to bring Ki—'

'Fine,' I said. 'Bring her. Tell her I know "Hansel and Gretel" by heart and am willing to share. Will you call John in Philly? Give him the details?'

'Yes. I'll wait another hour or so. God, I'm so happy. I know that's wrong, but I'm so happy I could *burst*!'

'That makes two of us.' There was a pause on the other end. I heard a long, watery intake of breath. 'Mattie? All right?'

'Yes, but how do you tell a three-year-old her grandfather died?'

Tell her the old fuck slipped and fell headfirst into a Glad Bag, I thought, then pressed the back of my hand against my mouth to stifle a spate of lunatic cackles.

'I don't know, but you'll have to do it as soon as she comes in.'

'I will? Why?'

'Because she's going to see you. She's going to see your face.'

I lasted exactly two hours in the upstairs study, and then the heat drove me out – the thermometer on the stoop read ninety-five degrees at ten o'clock. I guessed it might be five degrees warmer on the second floor.

Hoping I wasn't making a mistake, I unplugged the IBM and carried it downstairs. I was working without a shirt, and as I crossed the living room, the back of the typewriter slipped in the sweat coating my midriff and I almost dropped the outdated sonofabitch on my toes. That made me think of my ankle, the one I'd hurt when I fell into the lake, and I set the typewriter aside to look at it. It was colorful, black and purple and reddish at the edges, but not terribly inflated. I guessed my immersion in the cool water had helped keep the swelling down.

I put the typewriter on the deck table, rummaged out an extension cord, plugged in beneath Bunter's watchful eye, and sat down facing the hazy blue-gray surface of the lake. I waited for one of my old anxiety attacks to hit – the clenched stomach, the throbbing eyes, and, worst of all, that sensation of invisible steel bands clamped around my chest, making it impossible to breathe. Nothing like that happened. The words flowed as easily down here as they had upstairs, and my naked upper body was loving the little breeze that puffed in off the lake every now and again. I forgot about Max Devore, Mattie Devore, Kyra Devore. I forgot about Jo Noonan and Sara Tidwell. I forgot about myself. For two hours I was back in Florida. John Shackleford's execution was nearing. Andy Drake was racing the clock.

It was the telephone that brought me back, and for once I didn't resent interruption. If undisturbed, I might have gone on writing until I simply melted into a sweaty pile of goo on the deck.

It was my brother. We talked about Mom – in Siddy's opinion she was now short an entire roof instead of just a few shingles – and her sister, Francine, who had broken her hip in June. Sid wanted to know how I was doing, and I told him I was doing all right, I'd had some problems getting going on a new book but now seemed to be back on track (in my family, the only permissible time to discuss trouble is when it's over). And how was the Sidster? Kickin, he said, which I assumed meant just fine – Siddy has a twelve-year-old, and consequently his slang is always up-to-date. The new accounting business was starting to take hold, although he'd been scared for awhile (first I knew of it, of course). He could never thank me enough for the bridge loan I'd made him last November. I replied that it was the least I could do, which was the absolute truth, especially when I considered how much more time – both in person and on the phone – he spent with our mother than I did.

'Well, I'll let you go,' Siddy told me after a few more pleasantries – he never says goodbye or so long when he's on the phone, it's always *well, I'll let you go*, as if he's been holding you hostage. 'You want to keep cool up there, Mike – Weather Channel says it's going to be hotter than hell in New England all weekend.'

'There's always the lake if things get too bad. Hey Sid?'

'Hey what?' Like *I'll let you go, Hey what* went back to childhood. It was sort of comforting; it was also sort of spooky.

'Our folks all came from Prout's Neck, right? I mean on Daddy's side.' Mom came from another world entirely – one where the men wear Lacoste polo shirts, the women always wear full slips under their dresses, and everyone knows the second verse of 'Dixie'

319

by heart. She had met my dad in Portland while competing in a college cheerleading event. Materfamilias came from Memphis quality, darlin, and didn't let you forget it.

'I guess so,' he said. 'Yeah. But don't go asking me a lot of family-tree questions, Mike – I'm still not sure what the difference is between a nephew and a cousin, and I told Jo the same thing.'

'Did you?' Everything inside me had gone very still . . . but I can't say I was surprised. Not by then.

'Uh-huh, you bet.'

'What did she want to know?'

'Everything I knew. Which isn't much. I could have told her all about Ma's great-great-grandfather, the one who got killed by the Indians, but Jo didn't seem to care about any of Ma's folks.'

'When would this have been?'

'Does it matter?'

'It might.'

'Okay, let's see. I think it was around the time Patrick had his appendectomy. Yeah, I'm sure it was. February of '94. It might have been March, but I'm pretty sure it was February.'

Six months from the Rite Aid parking lot. Jo moving into the shadow of her own death like a woman stepping beneath the shade of an awning. Not pregnant, though, not yet. Jo making day-trips to the TR. Jo asking questions, some of the sort that made people feel bad, according to Bill Dean . . . but she'd gone on asking just the same. Yeah. Because once she got on to something, Jo was like a terrier with a rag in its jaws. Had she been asking questions of the man in the brown sportcoat? Who *was* the man in the brown sportcoat?

'Pat was in the hospital, sure. Dr Alpert said he was doing fine, but when the phone rang I jumped for it – I half-expected it to be him, Alpert, saying Pat had had a relapse or something.'

'Where in God's name did you get this sense of impending doom, Sid?'

'I dunno, buddy, but it's there. Anyway, it's not Alpert, it's Johanna. She wants to know if we had any ancestors – three, maybe even four generations back – who lived there where you are, or in one of the surrounding towns. I told her I didn't know, but you might. Know, I mean. She said she didn't want to ask you because it was a surprise. Was it a surprise?'

320

'A big one,' I said. 'Daddy was a lobsterman—'

'Bite your tongue, he was an *artist* – "a seacoast primitive." Ma still calls him that.' Siddy wasn't quite laughing.

'Shit, he sold lobster-pot coffee-tables and lawn-puffins to the tourists when he got too rheumatic to go out on the bay and haul traps.'

'*I* know that, but Ma's got her marriage edited like a movie for television.'

How true. Our own version of Blanche Du Bois. 'Dad was a lobsterman in Prout's Neck. He—'

Siddy interrupted, singing the first verse of "Pappa Was a Rollin' Stone" in a horrible offkey tenor.

'Come on, this is serious. He had his first boat from his father, right?'

'That's the story,' Sid agreed. 'Jack Noonan's *Lazy Betty*, original owner Paul Noonan. Also of Prout's. Boat took a hell of a pasting in Hurricane Donna, back in 1960. I think it was Donna'

Two years after I was born. 'And Daddy put it up for sale in '63.'

'Yep. I don't know whatever became of it, but it was Grampy Paul's to begin with, all right. Do you remember all the lobster stew we ate when we were kids, Mikey?'

'Seacoast meatloaf,' I said, hardly thinking about it. Like most kids raised on the coast of Maine, I can't imagine ordering lobster in a restaurant – that's for flatlanders. I was thinking about Grampy Paul, who had been born in the 1890s. Paul Noonan begat Jack Noonan, Jack Noonan begat Mike and Sid Noonan, and that was really all I knew, except the Noonans had all grown up a long way from where I now stood sweating my brains out.

They shit in the same pit.

Devore had gotten it wrong, that was all – when we Noonans weren't wearing polo shirts and being Memphis quality, we were Prout's Neckers. It was unlikely that Devore's great-grandfather and my own would have had anything to do with each other in any case; the old rip had been twice my age, and that meant the generations didn't match up.

But if he had been *totally* wrong, what had Jo been on about?

'Mike?' Sid asked. 'Are you there?'

'Yeah.'

'Are you okay? You don't sound so great, I have to tell you.'

'It's the heat,' I said. 'Not to mention your sense of impending doom. Thanks for calling, Siddy.'

'Thanks for being there, brother.'

'Kickin',' I said.

I went out to the kitchen to get a glass of cold water. As I was filling it, I heard the magnets on the fridge begin sliding around. I whirled, spilling some of the water on my bare feet and hardly noticing. I was as excited as a kid who thinks he may glimpse Santa Claus before he shoots back up the chimney.

I was barely in time to see nine plastic letters drawn into the circle from all points of the compass. CARLADEAN, they spelled . . . but only for a second. Some presence, tremendous but unseen, shot past me. Not a hair on my head stirred, but there was still a strong sense of being buffeted, the way you're buffeted by the air of a passing express train if you're standing near the platform yellow-line when the train bolts through. I cried out in surprise and groped my glass of water back on to the counter, spilling it. I no longer felt in need of cold water, because the temperature in the kitchen of Sara Laughs had dropped off the table.

I blew out my breath and saw vapor, as you do on a cold day in January. One puff, maybe two, and it was gone – but it had been there, all right, and for perhaps five seconds the film of sweat on my body turned to what felt like a slime of ice.

CARLADEAN exploded outward in all directions – it was like watching an atom being smashed in a cartoon. Magnetized letters, fruits, and vegetables flew off the front of the refrigerator and scattered across the kitchen. For a moment the fury which fueled that scattering was something I could almost taste, like gunpowder.

And something gave way before it, going with a sighing, rueful whisper I had heard before: 'Oh Mike. Oh Mike.' It was the voice I'd caught on the Memo-Scriber tape, and although I hadn't been sure then, I was now – it was Jo's voice.

But who was the other one? Why had it scattered the letters?

Carla Dean. Not Bill's wife; that was Yvette. His mother? His grandmother?

322

I walked slowly through the kitchen, collecting fridge-magnets like prizes in a scavenger hunt and sticking them back on the Kenmore by the handful. Nothing snatched them out of my hands; nothing froze the sweat on the back of my neck; Bunter's bell didn't ring. Still, I wasn't alone, and I knew it.

CARLADEAN: Jo had wanted me to know.

Something else hadn't. Something else had shot past me like the Wabash Cannonball, trying to scatter the letters before I could read them.

Jo was here; a boy who wept in the night was here, too.

And what else?

What else was sharing my house with me?

CHAPTER TWENTY

I didn't see them at first, which wasn't surprising; it seemed that half of Castle Rock was on the town common as that sultry Saturday afternoon edged on toward evening. The air was bright with hazy midsummer light, and in it kids swarmed over the playground equipment, a number of old men in bright red vests – some sort of club, I assumed – played chess, and a group of young people lay on the grass listening to a teenager in a headband playing the guitar and singing one I remembered from an old Ian and Sylvia record, a cheery tune that went

> *'Ella Speed was havin her lovin fun,*
> *John Martin shot Ella with a Colt forty-one . . .'*

I saw no joggers, and no dogs chasing Frisbees. It was just too goddam hot.

I was turning to look at the bandshell, where an eight-man combo called The Castle Rockers was setting up (I had an idea 'In the Mood' was about as close as they got to rock and roll), when a small person hit me from behind, grabbing me just above the knees and almost dumping me on the grass.

'Gotcha!' the small person cried gleefully.

'Kyra Devore!' Mattie called, sounding both amused and irritated. 'You'll knock him down!'

I turned, dropped the grease-spotted McDonald's bag I had been carrying, and lifted the kid up. It felt natural, and it felt wonderful. You don't realize the weight of a healthy child until you hold one,

324

nor do you fully comprehend the life that runs through them like a bright wire. I didn't get choked up ('Don't go all corny on me, Mike,' Siddy would sometimes whisper when we were kids at the movies and I got wet-eyed at a sad part), but I thought of Jo, yes. And the child she had been carrying when she fell down in that stupid parking lot, yes to that, too.

Ki was squealing and laughing, her arms outspread and her hair hanging down in two amusing clumps accented by Raggedy Ann and Andy barrettes.

'Don't tackle your own quarterback!' I yelled, grinning, and to my delight she yelled it right back at me: 'Don't taggle yer own quartermack! Don't taggle yer own quartermack!'

I set her on her feet, both of us laughing. Ki took a step backward, tripped herself, and sat down on the grass, laughing harder than ever. I had a mean thought, then, brief but oh so clear: If only the old lizard could see how much he was missed. How sad we were at his passing.

Mattie walked over, and tonight she looked as I'd half-imagined her when I first met her – like one of those lovely children of privilege you see at the country club, either goofing with their friends or sitting seriously at dinner with their parents. She was in a white sleeveless dress and low heels, her hair falling loose around her shoulders, a touch of lipstick on her mouth. Her eyes had a brilliance in them that hadn't been there before. When she hugged me I could smell her perfume and feel the press of her firm little breasts.

I kissed her cheek; she kissed me high up on the jaw, making a smack in my ear that I felt all the way down my back. 'Say things are going to be better now,' she whispered, still holding me.

'Lots better now,' I said, and she hugged me again, tight. Then she stepped away. 'You better have brought plenty food, big boy, because we plenty hungry womens. Right, Kyra?'

'I taggled my own quartermack,' Ki said, then leaned back on her elbows, giggling deliciously at the bright and hazy sky.

'Come on,' I said, and grabbed her by the middle. I toted her that way to a nearby picnic table, Ki kicking her legs and waving her arms and laughing. I set her down on the bench; she slid off it and beneath the table, boneless as an eel and still laughing.

'All right, Kyra Elizabeth,' Mattie said. 'Sit up and show the other side.'

'Good girl, good girl,' she said, clambering up beside me. 'That's the other side to me, Mike.'

'I'm sure,' I said. Inside the bag there were Big Macs and fries for Mattie and me. For Ki there was a colorful box upon which Ronald McDonald and his unindicted co-conspirators capered.

'Mattie, I got a Happy Meal! Mike got me a Happy Meal! They have toys!'

'Well see what yours is.'

Kyra opened the box, poked around, then smiled. It lit up her whole face. She brought out something that I at first thought was a big dustball. For one horrible second I was back in my dream, the one of Jo under the bed with the book over her face. *Give me that*, she had snarled. *It's my dust-catcher.* And something else, too – some other association, perhaps from some other dream. I couldn't get hold of it.

'Mike?' Mattie asked. Curiosity in her voice, and maybe borderline concern.

'It's a doggy!' Ki said. 'I won a doggy in my Happy Meal!'

Yes, of course. A dog. A little stuffed dog. And it was gray, not black . . . although why I'd care about the color either way I didn't know.

'That's a pretty good prize,' I said, taking it. It was soft, which was good, and it was gray, which was better. Being gray made it all right, somehow. Crazy but true. I handed it back to her and smiled.

'What's his name?' Ki asked, jumping the little dog back and forth across her Happy Meal box. 'What doggy's name, Mike?'

And, without thinking, I said, 'Strickland.'

I thought she'd look puzzled, but she didn't. She looked delighted. 'Stricken!' she said, bouncing the dog back and forth in ever-higher leaps over the box. 'Stricken! Stricken! My dog Stricken!'

'Who's this guy Strickland?' Mattie asked, smiling a little. She had begun to unwrap her hamburger.

'A character in a book I read once,' I said, watching Ki play with the little puffball dog. 'No one real.'

'My grampa died,' she said five minutes later.

326

We were still at the picnic table but the food was mostly gone. Strickland the stuffed puffball had been set to guard the remaining french fries. I had been scanning the ebb and flow of people, wondering who was here from the TR observing our tryst and simply burning to carry the news back home. I saw no one I knew, but that didn't mean a whole lot, considering how long I'd been away from this part of the world.

Mattie put down her burger and looked at Ki with some anxiety, but I thought the kid was okay – she had been giving news, not expressing grief.

'I know he did,' I said.

'Grampa was awful old.' Ki pinched a couple of french fries between her pudgy little fingers. They rose to her mouth, then gloop, all gone. 'He's with Lord Jesus now. We had all about Lord Jesus in VBS.'

Yes, Ki, I thought, *right now Grampy's probably teaching Lord Jesus how to use Pixel Easel and asking if there might be a whore handy.*

'Lord Jesus walked on water and also changed the wine into macaroni.'

'Yes, something like that,' I said. 'It's sad when people die, isn't it?'

'It would be sad if Mattie died, and it would be sad if you died, but Grampy *was* old.' She said it as though I hadn't quite grasped this concept the first time. 'In heaven he'll get all fixed up.'

'That's a good way to look at it, hon,' I said.

Mattie did maintenance on Ki's drooping barrettes, working carefully and with a kind of absent love. I thought she glowed in the summer light, her skin in smooth, tanned contrast to the white dress she had probably bought at one of the discount stores, and I understood that I loved her. Maybe that was all right.

'I miss the white nana, though,' Ki said, and this time she did look sad. She picked up the stuffed dog, tried to feed him a french fry, then put him down again. Her small, pretty face looked pensive now, and I could see a whisper of her grandfather in it. It was far back but it was there, perceptible, another ghost. 'Mom says white nana went back to California with Grampy's early remains.'

'*Earthly* remains, Ki-bird,' Mattie said. 'That means his body.'

'Will white nana come back and see me, Mike?'

'I don't know.'

'We had a game. It was all rhymes.' She looked more pensive than ever.

'Your mom told me about that game,' I said.

'She won't be back,' Ki said, answering her own question. One very large tear rolled down her right cheek. She picked up 'Stricken,' stood him on his back legs for a second, then put him back on guard-duty. Mattie slipped an arm around her, but Ki didn't seem to notice. 'White nana didn't really like me. She was just pretending to like me. That was her *job.*'

Mattie and I exchanged a glance.

'What makes you say that?' I asked.

'Don't know,' Ki said. Over by where the kid was playing the guitar, a juggler in whiteface had started up, working with half a dozen colored balls. Kyra brightened a little. 'Mommy-bommy, may I go watch that funny white man?'

'Are you done eating?'

'Yeah, I'm full.'

'Thank Mike.'

'Don't taggle yer own quartermack,' she said, then laughed kindly to show she was just pulling my leg. 'Thanks, Mike.'

'Not a problem,' I said, and then, because that sounded a little old-fashioned: 'Kickin.'

'You can go as far as that tree, but no farther,' Mattie said. 'And you know why.'

'So you can see me. I will.'

She grabbed Strickland and started to run off, then stopped and looked over her shoulder at me. 'I guess it was the fridgeafator people,' she said, then corrected herself very carefully and seriously. 'The *ree-fridge-a-rator* people.' My heart took a hard double beat in my chest.

'It was the refrigerator people what, Ki?' I asked.

'That said white nana didn't really like me.' Then she ran off toward the juggler, oblivious to the heat.

Mattie watched her go, then turned back to me. 'I haven't talked to anybody about Ki's fridgeafator people. Neither has she, until now. Not that there are any real people, but the letters seem to move around by themselves. It's like a Ouija board.'

'Do they spell things?'

For a long time she said nothing. Then she nodded. 'Not always, but sometimes.' Another pause. '*Most* times, actually. Ki calls it mail from the people in the refrigerator.' She smiled, but her eyes were a little scared. 'Are they special magnetic letters, do you think? Or have we got a poltergeist working the lakefront?'

'I don't know. I'm sorry I brought them, if they're a problem.'

'Don't be silly. You gave them to her, and you're a tremendously big deal to her right now. She talks about you all the time. She was much more interested in picking out something pretty to wear for you tonight than she was in her grandfather's death. I was supposed to wear something pretty, too, Kyra insisted. She's not that way about people, usually – she takes them when they're there and leaves them when they're gone. That's not such a bad way for a little girl to grow up, I sometimes think.'

'You both dressed pretty,' I said. 'That much I'm sure of.'

'Thanks.' She looked fondly at Ki, who stood by the tree watching the juggler. He had put his rubber balls aside and moved on to Indian clubs. Then she looked back at me. 'Are we done eating?'

I nodded, and Mattie began to pick up the trash and stuff it back into the take-out bag. I helped, and when our fingers touched, she gripped my hand and squeezed. 'Thank you,' she said. 'For everything you've done. Thank you so damn much.'

I squeezed back, then let go.

'You know,' she said, 'it's crossed my mind that Kyra's moving the letters around herself. Mentally.'

'Telekinesis?'

'I guess that's the technical term. Only Ki can't spell much more than "dog" and "cat."'

'What's showing up on the fridge?'

'Names, mostly. Once it was yours. Once it was your wife's.'

'Jo?'

'The whole thing – JOHANNA. And NANA. Rogette, I presume. JARED shows up sometimes, and BRIDGET. Once there was KITO.' She spelled it.

'Kito,' I said, and thought: *Kyra, Kia, Kito. What is this?* 'A boy's name, do you think?'

'I know it is. It's Swahili, and means precious child. I looked it

329

up in my baby-name book.' She glanced toward her own precious child as we walked across the grass to the nearest trash barrel.

'Any others that you can remember?'

She thought. 'REG has showed up a couple of times. And once there was CARLA. You understand that Ki can't even read these names as a rule, don't you? She has to ask me what they say.'

'Has it occurred to you that Kyra might be copying them out of a book or a magazine? That she's learning to write using the magnetic letters on the fridge instead of paper and pencil?'

'I suppose that's possible . . .' She didn't look as if she believed it, though. Not surprising. I didn't believe it myself.

'I mean, you've never actually seen the letters moving around by themselves on the front of the fridge, have you?' I hoped I sounded as unconcerned asking this question as I wanted to.

She laughed a bit nervously. 'God, no!'

'Anything else?'

'Sometimes the fridgeafator people leave messages like HI and BYE and GOOD GIRL. There was one yesterday that I wrote down to show you. Kyra asked me to. It's *really* weird.'

'What is it?'

'I'd rather show you, but I left it in the glove compartment of the Scout. Remind me when we go.'

Yes. I would.

'This is some spooky shit, *señor*,' she said. 'Like the writing in the flour that time.'

I thought about telling her I had my own fridgeafator people, then didn't. She had enough to worry about without that . . . or so I told myself.

We stood side by side on the grass, watching Ki watch the juggler. 'Did you call John?' I asked.

'You bet.'

'His reaction?'

She turned to me, laughing with her eyes. 'He actually sang a verse of "Ding Dong, the Witch Is Dead."'

'Wrong sex, right sentiment.'

She nodded, her eyes going back to Kyra. I thought again how beautiful she looked, her body slim in the white dress, her features clean and perfectly made.

330

'Was he pissed at me inviting myself to lunch?' I asked.

'Nope, he loved the idea of having a party.'

A party. He loved the idea. I began to feel rather small.

'He even suggested we invite your lawyer from last Friday. Mr Bissonette? Plus the private detective John hired on Mr Bissonette's recommendation. Is that okay with you?'

'Fine. How about you, Mattie? Doing okay?'

'Doing okay,' she agreed, turning to me. 'I *did* have several more calls than usual today. I'm suddenly quite popular.'

'Uh-oh.'

'Most were hangups, but one gentleman took time enough to call me a cunt, and there was a lady with a very strong Yankee accent who said, "Theah, you bitch, you've killed him. Aaa you satisfied?" She hung up before I could tell her yes, very satisfied, thanks.' But Mattie didn't look satisfied; she looked unhappy and guilty, as if she had literally wished him dead.

'I'm sorry.'

'It's okay. Really. Kyra and I have been alone for a long time, and I've been scared for most of it. Now I've made a couple of friends. If a few anonymous phone calls are the price I have to pay, I'll pay it.'

She was very close, looking up at me, and I couldn't stop myself. I put the blame on summer, her perfume, and four years without a woman. In that order. I slipped my arms around her waist, and remember perfectly the texture of her dress beneath my hands; the slight pucker at the back where the zipper hid in its sleeve. I remember the sensation of the cloth moving against the bare skin beneath. Then I was kissing her, very gently but very thoroughly – anything worth doing is worth doing right – and she was kissing me back in exactly the same spirit, her mouth curious but not afraid. Her lips were warm and smooth and held some faint sweet taste. Peaches, I think.

We stopped at the same time and pulled back a little from each other. Her hands were still on my shoulders. Mine were on the sides of her waist, just above her hips. Her face was composed enough, but her eyes were more brilliant than ever, and there were slants of color in her cheeks, rising along the cheekbones.

'Oh boy,' she said. 'I really wanted that. Ever since Ki tackled you and you picked her up I've wanted it.'

331

'John wouldn't think much of us kissing in public,' I said. My voice wasn't quite even, and my heart was racing. Seven seconds, one kiss, and every system in my body was red-lining. 'In fact, John wouldn't think much of us kissing at all. He fancies you, you know.'

'I know, but I fancy *you*.' She turned to check on Ki, who was still standing obediently by the tree, watching the juggler. Who might be watching *us*? Someone who had come over from the TR on a hot summer evening to get ice cream at Frank's Tas-T-Freeze and enjoy a little music and society on the common? Someone who traded for fresh vegetables and fresh gossip at the Lakeview General? A regular at the All-Purpose Garage? This was insanity, and it stayed insanity no matter how you cut it. I dropped my hands from her waist.

'Mattie, they could put our picture next to "indiscreet" in the dictionary.'

She took her hands off my shoulders and stepped back a pace, but her brilliant eyes never left mine. 'I know that. I'm young but not entirely stupid.'

'I didn't mean—'

She held up a hand to stop me. 'Ki goes to bed around nine – she can't seem to sleep until it's mostly dark. I stay up later. Come and visit me, if you want to. You can park around back.' She smiled a little. It was a sweet smile; it was also incredibly sexy. 'Once the moon's down, that's an area of discretion.'

'Mattie, you're young enough to be my daughter.'

'Maybe, but I'm not. And sometimes people can be too discreet for their own good.'

My body knew so emphatically what it wanted. If we had been in her trailer at that moment it would have been no contest. It was almost no contest anyway. Then something recurred to me, something I'd thought about Devore's ancestors and my own: the generations didn't match up. Wasn't the same thing true here? And I don't believe that people automatically have a right to what they want, no matter how badly they want it. Not every thirst should be slaked. Some things are just wrong – I guess that's what I'm trying to say. But I wasn't sure this was one of them, and I wanted her, all right. So much. I kept thinking about how her dress had slid when I put my arms around her

332

waist, the warm feel of her skin just beneath. And no, she wasn't my daughter.

'You said your thanks,' I told her in a dry voice. 'And that's enough. Really.'

'You think this is *gratitude*?' She voiced a low, tense laugh. 'You're forty, Mike, not eighty. You're not Harrison Ford, but you're a good-looking man. Talented and interesting, too. And I like you such an awful lot. I want you to be with me. Do you want me to say please? Fine. Please be with me.'

Yes, this was about more than gratitude – I suppose I'd known that even when I was using the word. I'd known she was wearing white shorts and a halter top when she called on the phone the day I went back to work. Had she also known what I was wearing? Had she dreamed she was in bed with me, the two of us screwing our brains out while the party lights shone and Sara Tidwell played her version of the white nana rhyming game, all that crazy Manderley-sanderley-canderley stuff? Had Mattie dreamed of telling me to do what she wanted?

And there were the fridgeafator people. They were another kind of sharing, an even spookier kind. I hadn't quite had nerve enough to tell Mattie about mine, but she might know anyway. Down low in her mind. Down below in her mind, where the blue-collar guys moved around in the zone. Her guys and my guys, all part of the same strange labor union. And maybe it wasn't an issue of morality *per se* at all. Something about it – about *us* – just felt dangerous.

And oh so attractive.

'I need time to think,' I said.

'This isn't about what you think. What do you *feel* for me?'

'So much it scares me.'

Before I could say anything else, my ears caught a familiar series of chord-changes. I turned toward the kid with the guitar. He had been working through a repertoire of early Dylan, but now he swung into something chuggy and up-tempo, something that made you want to grin and pat your hands together.

> *'Do you want to go fishin*
> *here in my fishin hole?*
> *Said do you want to fish some, honey,*

> *here in my fishin hole?*
> *You want to fish in my pond, baby,*
> *you better have a big long pole.'*

'Fishin Blues.' Written by Sara Tidwell, originally performed by Sara and the Red-Top Boys, covered by everyone from Ma Rainey to the Lovin' Spoonful. The raunchy ones had been her specialty, double-entendre so thin you could read a newspaper through it . . . although reading hadn't been Sara's main interest, judging by her lyrics.

Before the kid could go on to the next verse, something about how you got to wiggle when you wobble and get that big one way down deep, The Castle Rockers ran off a brass flourish that said 'Shut up, everybody, we're comin atcha.' The kid quit playing his guitar; the juggler began catching his Indian clubs and dropping them swiftly on to the grass in a line. The Rockers launched themselves into an extremely evil Sousa march, music to commit serial murders by, and Kyra came running back to us.

'The jugster's done. Will you tell me the story, Mike? Hansel and Panzel?'

'It's Hansel and *Gretel*,' I said, 'and I'll be happy to. But let's go where it's a little quieter, okay? The band is giving me a headache.'

'Music hurt your headie?'

'A little bit.'

'We'll go by Mattie's car, then.'

'Good thought.'

Kyra ran ahead to stake out a bench on the edge of the common. Mattie gave me a long warm look, then her hand. I took it. Our fingers folded together as if they had been doing it for years. I thought, *I'd like it to be slow, both of us hardly moving at all. At first, anyway. And would I bring my nicest, longest pole? I think you could count on that.* And then, afterward, we'd talk. Maybe until we could see the furniture in the first early light. When you're in bed with someone you love, particularly for the first time, five o'clock seems almost holy.

'You need a vacation from your own thoughts,' Mattie said. 'I bet most writers do from time to time.'

'That's probably true.'

'I wish we were home,' she said, and I couldn't tell if her fierceness was real or pretend. 'I'd kiss you until this whole conversation became irrelevant. And if there were second thoughts, at least you'd be having them in my bed.'

I turned my face into the red light of the westering sun. 'Here or there, at this hour Ki would still be up.'

'True,' she said, sounding uncharacteristically glum. 'True.'

Kyra reached a bench near the sign reading TOWN COMMON PARKING and climbed up on it, holding the little stuffed dog from Mickey D's in one hand. I tried to pull my hand away as we approached her and Mattie held it firm. 'It's all right, Mike. At VBS they hold hands with their friends everywhere they go. It's big people who make it into a big deal.'

She stopped, looked at me.

'I want you to know something. Maybe it won't matter to you, but it does to me. There wasn't anyone before Lance and no one after. If you come to me, you'll be my second. I'm not going to talk with you about this again, either. Saying please is all right, but I won't beg.'

'I don't—'

'There's a pot with tomato plants in it by the trailer steps. I'll leave a key under it. Don't think. Just come.'

'Not tonight, Mattie. I can't.'

'You can,' she replied.

'Hurry *up*, slowpokes!' Kyra cried, bouncing on the bench.

'*He's* the slow one!' Mattie called back, and poked me in the ribs. Then, in a much lower voice: 'You *are*, too.' She unwound her hand from mine and ran toward her daughter, her brown legs scissoring below the hem of the white dress.

In my version of 'Hansel and Gretel' the witch was named Depravia. Kyra stared at me with huge eyes when I got to the part where Depravia asks Hansel to poke out his finger so she can see how plump he's getting.

'Is it too scary?' I asked.

Ki shook her head emphatically. I glanced at Mattie to make sure. She nodded and waved a hand for me to go on, so I finished the story. Depravia went into the oven and Gretel found her secret

335

stash of winning lottery tickets. The kids bought a Jet Ski and lived happily ever after on the eastern side of Dark Score Lake. By then The Castle Rockers were slaughtering Gershwin and sunset was nigh. I carried Kyra to Scoutie and strapped her in. I remembered the first time I'd helped put the kid into her car-seat, and the inadvertent press of Mattie's breast.

'I hope there isn't a bad dream for you in that story,' I said. Until I heard it coming out of my own mouth, I hadn't realized how fundamentally awful that one is.

'I won't have bad dreams,' Kyra said matter-of-factly. 'The fridgeafator people will keep them away.' Then, carefully, reminding herself: '*Ree-fridge-a-rator*.' She turned to Mattie. 'Show him the crosspatch, Mommy-bommy.'

'Cross*word*. But thanks, I would've forgotten.' She thumbed open the glove compartment and took out a folded sheet of paper. 'It was on the fridge this morning. I copied it down because Ki said you'd know what it meant. She said you do crossword puzzles. Well, she said crosspatches, but I got the idea.'

Had I told Kyra that I did crosswords? Almost certainly not. Did it surprise me that she knew? Not at all. I took the sheet of paper, unfolded it, and looked at what was printed there:

d

go

w

ninety2

'Is it a crosspatch puzzle, Mike?' Kyra asked.

'I guess so – a very simple one. But if it means something, I don't know what it is. May I keep this?'

'Yes,' Mattie said.

I walked her around to the driver's side of the Scout, reaching for her hand again as we went. 'Just give me a little time. I know that's supposed to be the girl's line, but—'

'Take the time,' she said. 'Just don't take too much.'

I didn't want to take *any*, which was just the problem. The sex would be great, I knew that. But after?

There might *be* an after, though. I knew it and she did, too. With

Mattie, 'after' was a real possibility. The idea was a little scary, a little wonderful.

I kissed the corner of her mouth. She laughed and grabbed me by the earlobe. 'You can do better,' she said, then looked at Ki, who was sitting in her car-seat and gazing at us interestedly. 'But I'll let you off this time.'

'Kiss Ki!' Kyra called, holding out her arms, so I went around and kissed Ki. Driving home, wearing my dark glases to cut the glare of the setting sun, it occurred to me that maybe I could be Kyra Devore's father. That seemed almost as attractive to me as going to bed with her mother, which was a measure of how deep I was in. And going deeper, maybe.

Deeper still.

Sara Laughs seemed very empty after having Mattie in my arms – a sleeping head without dreams. I checked the letters on the fridge, saw nothing there but the normal scatter, and got a beer. I went out on the deck to drink it while I watched the last of the sunset. I tried to think about the refrigerator people and crosspatches that had appeared on both refrigerators: 'go down nineteen' on Lane Forty-two and 'go down ninety-two' on Wasp Hill Road. Different vectors from the land to the lake? Different spots on The Street? Shit, who knew?

I tried to think about John Storrow and how unhappy he was apt to be if he found out there was – to quote Sara Laughs, who got to the line long before John Mellencamp – another mule kicking in Mattie Devore's stall. But mostly what I thought about was holding her for the first time, kissing her for the first time. No human instinct is more powerful than the sex-drive when it is fully aroused, and its awakening images are emotional tattoos that never leave us. For me, it was feeling the soft bare skin of her waist just beneath her dress. The slippery feel of the fabric . . .

I turned abruptly and hurried through the house to the north wing, almost running and shedding clothes as I went. I turned the shower on to full cold and stood under it for five minutes, shivering. When I got out I felt a little more like an actual human being and a little less like a twitching bundle of nerve endings. And as I toweled dry, something else recurred to me. At some point I had thought of Jo's brother Frank, had thought that if anyone besides myself would

337

be able to feel Jo's presence in Sara Laughs, it would be him. I hadn't gotten around to inviting him down yet, and now wasn't sure I wanted to. I had come to feel oddly possessive, almost jealous, about what was happening here. And yet if Jo had been writing something on the quiet, Frank might know. Of course she hadn't confided in him about the pregnancy, but—

I looked at my watch. Quarter past nine. In the trailer near the intersection of Wasp Hill Road and Route 68, Kyra was probably already asleep . . . and her mother might already have put her extra key under the pot near the steps. I thought of her in the white dress, the swell of her hips just below my hands and the smell of her perfume, then pushed the images away. I couldn't spend the whole night taking cold showers. Quarter past nine was still early enough to call Frank Arlen.

He picked up on the second ring, sounding both happy to hear from me and as if he'd gotten three or four cans farther into the sixpack than I had so far done. We passed the usual pleasantries back and forth – most of my own almost entirely fictional, I was dismayed to find – and he mentioned that a famous neighbor of mine had kicked the bucket, according to the news. Had I met him? Yes, I said, remembering how Max Devore had run his wheelchair at me. Yes, I'd met him. Frank wanted to know what he was like. That was hard to say, I told him. Poor old guy was stuck in a wheelchair and suffering from emphysema.

'Pretty frail, huh?' Frank asked sympathetically.

'Yeah,' I said. 'Listen, Frank, I called about Jo. I was out in her studio looking around, and I found my typewriter. Since then I've kind of gotten the idea she was writing something. It might have started as a little piece about our house, then widened. The place is named after Sara Tidwell, you know. The blues singer.'

A long pause. Then Frank said, 'I know.' His voice sounded heavy, grave.

'What else do you know, Frank?'

'That she was scared. I think she found out something that scared her. I think that mostly because—'

That was when the light finally broke. I probably should have known from Mattie's description, *would* have known if I hadn't been so upset. 'You were down here with her, weren't you? In July of

338

1994. You went to the softball game, then you went back up The Street to the house.'

'How do you know that?' he almost barked.

'Someone saw you. A friend of mine.' I was trying not to sound mad and not succeeding. I *was* mad, but it was a relieved anger, the kind you feel when your kid comes dragging into the house with a shamefaced grin just as you're getting ready to call the cops.

'I almost told you a day or two before we buried her. We were in that pub, do you remember?'

Jack's Pub, right after Frank had beaten the funeral director down on the price of Jo's coffin. Sure I remembered. I even remembered the look in his eyes when I'd told him Jo had been pregnant when she died.

He must have felt the silence spinning out, because he came back sounding anxious. 'Mike, I hope you didn't get any—'

'What? Wrong ideas? I thought maybe she was having an affair, how's that for a wrong idea? You can call that ignoble if you want, but I had my reasons. There was a lot she wasn't telling me. What did she tell *you*?'

'Next to nothing.'

'Did you know she quit all her boards and committees? Quit and never said a word to me?'

'No.' I didn't think he was lying. Why would he, at this late date? 'Jesus, Mike, if I'd known that—'

'What happened the day you came down here? Tell me.'

'I was at the printshop in Sanford. Jo called me from . . . I don't remember, I think a rest area on the turnpike.'

'Between Derry and the TR?'

'Yeah. She was on her way to Sara Laughs and wanted me to meet her there. She told me to park in the driveway if I got there first, not to go in the house . . . which I could have; I know where you keep the spare key.'

Sure he did, in a Sucrets tin under the deck. I had shown him myself.

'Did she say why she didn't want you to go inside?'

'It'll sound crazy.'

'No it won't. Believe me.'

'She said the house was dangerous.'

339

For a moment the words just hung there. Then I asked, '*Did* you get here first?'

'Uh-huh.'

'And waited outside?'

'Yes.'

'Did you see or sense anything dangerous?'

There was a long pause. At last he said, 'There were lots of people out on the lake – speedboaters, water-skiers, you know how it is – but all the engine-noise and the laughter seemed to kind of . . . stop dead when it got near the house. Have you ever noticed that it seems quiet there even when it's not?'

Of course I had; Sara seemed to exist in its own zone of silence. 'Did it feel *dangerous*, though?'

'No,' he said, almost reluctantly. 'Not to me, anyway. But it didn't feel exactly empty, either. I felt . . . fuck, I felt *watched*. I sat on one of those railroad-tie steps and waited for my sis. Finally she came. She parked behind my car and hugged me . . . but she never took her eyes off the house. I asked her what she was up to and she said she couldn't tell me, and that I couldn't tell you we'd been there. She said something like, "If he finds out on his own, then it's meant to be. I'll have to tell him sooner or later, anyway. But I can't now, because I need his whole attention. I can't get that while he's working."'

I felt a flush crawl across my skin. 'She said that, huh?'

'Yeah. Then she said she had to go in the house and do something. She wanted me to wait outside. She said if she called, I should come on the run. Otherwise I should just stay where I was.'

'She wanted someone there in case she got in trouble.'

'Yeah, but it had to be someone who wouldn't ask a lot of questions she didn't want to answer. That was me. I guess that was always me.'

'And?'

'She went inside. I sat on the hood of my car, smoking cigarettes. I was still smoking then. And you know, I *did* start to feel something then that wasn't right. As if there might be someone in the house who'd been waiting for her, someone who didn't like her. Maybe someone who wanted to hurt her. Probably I just picked that up from Jo – the way her nerves seemed all strung up, the way she

340

kept looking over my shoulder at the house even while she was hugging me – but it seemed like something else. Like a . . . I don't know . . .'

'Like a vibe.'

'Yes!' he almost shouted. 'A vibration. But not a good vibration, like in the Beach Boys song. A *bad* vibration.'

'What happened?'

'I sat and waited. I only smoked two cigarettes so I don't guess it could have been longer than twenty minutes or half an hour, but it seemed longer. I kept noticing how the sounds from the lake seemed to make it most of the way up the hill and then just kind of . . . *quit*. And how there didn't seem to be any birds, except far off in the distance.

'Once, she came out. I heard the deck door bang, and then her footsteps on the stairs over on that side. I called to her, asked if she was okay, and she said fine. She said for me to stay where I was. She sounded a little short of breath, as if she was carrying something or had been doing some chore.'

'Did she go to her studio or down to the lake?'

'I don't know. She was gone another fifteen minutes or so – time enough for me to smoke another butt – and then she came back out the front door. She checked to make sure it was locked, and then she came up to me. She looked a lot better. Relieved. The way people look when they do some dirty job they've been putting off, finally get it behind them. She suggested we walk down that path she called The Street to the resort that's down there—'

'Warrington's.'

'Right, right. She said she'd buy me a beer and a sandwich. Which she did, out at the end of this long floating dock.'

The Sunset Bar, where I had first glimpsed Rogette.

'Then you went to have a look at the softball game.'

'That was Jo's idea. She had three beers to my one, and she insisted. Said someone was going to hit a longshot homer into the trees, she just knew it.'

Now I had a clear picture of the part Mattie had seen and told me about. Whatever Jo had done, it had left her almost giddy with relief. She had ventured into the house, for one thing. Had dared the spirits in order to do her business and survived. She'd had three

341

beers to celebrate and her discretion had slipped . . . not that she had behaved with any great stealth on her previous trips down to the TR. Frank remembered her saying if I found out on my own then it was meant to be – *que será, será*. It wasn't the attitude of someone hiding an affair, and I realized now that all her behavior suggested a woman keeping a short-term secret. She would have told me when I finished my stupid book, if she had lived. If.

'You watched the game for awhile, then went back to the house along The Street.'

'Yes,' he said.

'Did either of you go in?'

'No. By the time we got there, her buzz had worn off and I trusted her to drive. She was laughing while we were at the softball game, but she wasn't laughing by the time we got back to the house. She looked at it and said, "I'm done with her. I'll never go through that door again, Frank."'

My skin first chilled, then prickled.

'I asked her what was wrong, what she'd found out. I knew she was writing something, she'd told me that much—'

'She told everyone but me,' I said . . . but without much bitterness. I knew who the man in the brown sportcoat had been, and any bitterness or anger – anger at Jo, anger at myself – paled before the relief of that. I hadn't realized how much that fellow had been on my mind until now.

'She must have had her reasons,' Frank said. 'You know that, don't you?'

'But she didn't tell you what they were.'

'All I know is that it started – whatever it was – with her doing research for an article. It was a lark, Jo playing Nancy Drew. I'm pretty sure that at first not telling you was just to keep it a surprise. She read books but mostly she talked to people – listened to their stories of the old days and teased them into looking for old letters . . . diaries . . . she was good at that part of it, I think. Damned good. You don't know any of this?'

'No,' I said heavily. Jo hadn't been having an affair, but she *could* have had one, if she'd wanted. She could have had an affair with Tom Selleck and been written up in *Inside View* and I would have gone on tapping away at the keys of my PowerBook, blissfully unaware.

342

'Whatever she found out,' Frank said, 'I think she just stumbled over it.'

'And you never told me. Four years and you never told me any of it.'

'That was the last time I was with her,' Frank said, and now he didn't sound apologetic or embarrassed at all. 'And the last thing she asked of me was that I not tell you we'd been to the lake house. She said she'd tell you everything when she was ready, but then she died. After that I didn't think it mattered. Mike, she was my sister. She was my sister and I promised.'

'All right. I understand.' And I did – just not enough. What had Jo discovered? That Normal Auster had drowned his infant son under a handpump? That back around the turn of the century an animal trap had been left in a place where a young Negro boy would be apt to come along and step into it? That another boy, perhaps the incestuous child of Son and Sara Tidwell, had been drowned by his mother in the lake, she maybe laughing that smoke-broken, lunatic laugh as she held him down? You gotta wiggle when you wobble, honey, and hold that young 'un way down deep.

'If you need me to apologize, Mike, consider it done.'

'I don't. Frank, do you remember anything else she might have said that night? Anything at all?'

'She said she knew how you found the house.'

'She said *what*?'

'She said that when it wanted you, it called you.'

At first I couldn't reply, because Frank Arlen had completely demolished one of the assumptions I'd made about my married life – one of the biggies, one of those that seem so basic you don't even think about questioning them. Gravity holds you down. Light allows you to see. The compass needle points north. Stuff like that.

This assumption was that Jo was the one who had wanted to buy Sara Laughs back when we saw the first real money from my writing career, because Jo was the 'house person' in our marriage, just as I was the 'car person.' Jo was the one who had picked our apartments when apartments were all we could afford, Jo who hung a picture here and asked me to put up a shelf there. Jo was the one who had fallen in love with the Derry house and had finally worn down my resistance to the idea that it was

343

too big, too busy, and too broken to take on. Jo had been the nest-builder.

She said that when it wanted you, it called you.

And it was probably true. No, I could do better than that, if I was willing to set aside the lazy thinking and selective remembering. It was *certainly* true. I was the one who had first broached the idea of a place in western Maine. I was the one who collected stacks of real-estate brochures and hauled them home. I'd started buying regional magazines like *Down East* and always began at the back, where the real-estate ads were. It was I who had first seen a picture of Sara Laughs in a glossy handout called *Maine Retreats*, and it was I who had made the call first to the agent named in the ad, and then to Marie Hingerman after badgering Marie's name out of the realtor.

Johanna had also been charmed by Sara Laughs — I think anyone would have been charmed by it, seeing it for the first time in autumn sunshine with the trees blazing all around it and drifts of colored leaves blowing up The Street — but it was I who had actively sought the place out.

Except that was more lazy thinking and selective remembering. Wasn't it? Sara had sought *me* out.

Then how could I not have known it until now? And how was I led here in the first place, full of unknowing happy ignorance?

The answer to both questions was the same. It was also the answer to the question of how Jo could have discovered something distressing about the house, the lake, maybe the whole TR, and then gotten away with not telling me. I'd been gone, that's all. I'd been zoning, tranced out, writing one of my stupid little books. I'd been hypnotized by the fantasies going on in my head, and a hypnotized man is easy to lead.

'Mike? Are you still there?'

'I'm here, Frank. But I'll be goddamned if I know what could have scared her so.'

'She mentioned one other name I remember: Royce Merrill. She said he was the one who remembered the most, because he was so old. And she said, "I don't want Mike to talk to him. I'm afraid that old man might let the cat out of the bag and tell him more than he should know." Any idea what she meant?'

'Well . . . it's been suggested that a splinter from the old family

344

tree wound up here, but my mother's people are from Memphis. The Noonans are from Maine, but not from this part.' Yet I no longer entirely believed this.

'Mike, you sound almost sick.'

'I'm okay. Better than I was, actually.'

'And you understand why I didn't tell you any of this until now? I mean, if I'd known the ideas you were getting . . . if I'd had any *clue* . . .'

'I think I understand. The ideas didn't belong in my head to begin with, but once that shit starts to creep in . . .'

'When I got back to Sanford that night and it was over, I guess I thought it was just more of Jo's "Oh fuck, there's a shadow on the moon, nobody go out until tomorrow." She was always the superstitious one, you know – knocking on wood, tossing a pinch of salt over her shoulder if she spilled some, those four-leaf-clover earrings she used to have . . .'

'Or the way she wouldn't wear a pullover if she put it on backward by mistake,' I said. 'She claimed doing that would turn around your whole day.'

'Well? Doesn't it?' Frank asked, and I could hear a little smile in his voice.

All at once I remembered Jo completely, right down to the small gold flecks in her left eye, and wanted nobody else. Nobody else would do.

'She thought there was something bad about the house,' Frank said. 'That much I *do* know.'

I drew a piece of paper to me and jotted *Kia* on it. 'Yes. And by then she may have suspected she was pregnant. She might have been afraid of . . . influences.' There were influences here, all right. 'You think she got most of this from Royce Merrill?'

'No, that was just a name she mentioned. She probably talked to dozens of people. Do you know a guy named Kloster? Gloster? Something like that?'

'Auster,' I said. Below *Kia* my pencil was making a series of fat loops that might have been cursive letter *l*'s or hair ribbons. 'Kenny Auster. Was that it?'

'It sounds right. In any case, you know how she was once she really got going on a thing.'

345

Yes. Like a terrier after rats.

'Mike? Should I come up there?'

No. Now I was sure. Not Harold Oblowski, not Frank, either. There was a process going on in Sara, something as delicate and as organic as rising bread in a warm room. Frank might interrupt that process . . . or be hurt by it.

'No, I just wanted to get it cleared up. Besides, I'm writing. It's hard for me to have people around when I'm writing.'

'Will you call if I can help?'

'You bet,' I said.

I hung up the telephone, thumbed through the book, and found a listing for R. MERRILL on the Deep Bay Road. I called the number, listened to it ring a dozen times, then hung up. No newfangled answering machine for Royce. I wondered idly where he was. Ninety-five seemed a little too old to go dancing at the Country Barn in Harrison, especially on a close night like this one.

I looked at the paper with *Kia* written on it. Below the fat *l*-shapes I wrote *Kyra*, and remembered how, the first time I'd heard Ki say her name, I'd thought it was 'Kia' she was saying. Below *Kyra* I wrote *Kito*, hesitated, then wrote *Carla*. I put these names in a box. Beside them I jotted *Johanna*, *Bridget*, and *Jared*. The fridgeafator people. Folks who wanted me to go down nineteen and go down ninety-two.

'Go down, Moses, you bound for the Promised Land,' I told the empty house. I looked around. Just me and Bunter and the waggy clock . . . except it wasn't.

When it wanted you, it called you.

I got up to get another beer. The fruits and vegetables were in a circle again. In the middle, the letters now spelled:

lye stille

As on some old tombstones – *God grant she lye stille.* I looked at these letters for a long time. Then I remembered the IBM was still out on the deck. I brought it in, plonked it on the dining-room table, and began to work on my current stupid little book. Fifteen minutes and I was lost, only faintly aware of thunder someplace over the lake, only faintly aware of Bunter's bell shivering from time to

346

time. When I went back to the fridge an hour or so later for another beer and saw that the words in the circle now said

ony lye stille

I hardly noticed. At that moment I didn't care if they lay stille or danced the hucklebuck by the light of the silvery moon. John Shackleford had begun to remember his past, and the child whose only friend he, John, had been. Little neglected Ray Garraty.

I wrote until midnight came. By then the thunder had faded away but the heat held on, as oppressive as a blanket. I turned off the IBM and went to bed . . . thinking, so far as I can remember, nothing at all – not even about Mattie, lying in her own bed not so many miles away. The writing had burned off all thoughts of the real world, at least temporarily. I think that, in the end, that's what it's for. Good or bad, it passes the time.

CHAPTER TWENTY-ONE

I was walking north along The Street. Japanese lanterns lined it, but they were all dark because it was daylight – *bright* daylight. The muggy, smutchy look of mid-July was gone; the sky was that deep sapphire shade which is the sole property of October. The lake was deepest indigo beneath it, sparkling with sunpoints. The trees were just past the peak of their autumn colors, burning like torches. A wind out of the south blew the fallen leaves past me and between my legs in rattly, fragrant gusts. The Japanese lanterns nodded as if in approval of the season. Up ahead, faintly, I could hear music. Sara and the Red-Tops. Sara was belting it out, laughing her way through the lyric as she always had . . . only, how could laughter sound so much like a snarl?

'White boy, I'd never kill a child of mine. That you'd even think it!'

I whirled, expecting to see her right behind me, but there was no one there. Well . . .

The Green Lady was there, only she had changed her dress of leaves for autumn and become the Yellow Lady. The bare pine-branch behind her still pointed the way: go north, young man, go north. Not much farther down the path was another birch, the one I'd held on to when that terrible drowning sensation had come over me again.

I waited for it to come again now – for my mouth and throat to fill up with the iron taste of the lake – but it didn't happen. I looked back at the Yellow Lady, then beyond her to Sara Laughs. The house was there, but much reduced: no north wing, no south wing, no second story. No sign of Jo's studio off to the side, either. None of those things had been built yet. The ladybirch had travelled back with me from 1998; so had the one hanging over the lake. Otherwise—

'Where am I?' I asked the Yellow Lady and the nodding Japanese lanterns. Then a better question occurred to me. '*When* am I?' No answer. 'It's a dream, isn't it? I'm in bed and dreaming.'

Somewhere out in the brilliant, gold-sparkling net of the lake, a loon called. Twice. *Hoot once for yes, twice for no*, I thought. *Not a dream, Michael. I don't know exactly what it is – spiritual time-travel, maybe – but it's not a dream.*

'Is this really happening?' I asked the day, and from somewhere back in the trees, where a track which would eventually come to be known as Lane Forty-two ran toward a dirt road which would eventually come to be known as Route 68, a crow cawed. Just once.

I went to the birch hanging over the lake, slipped an arm around it (doing it lit a trace memory of slipping my hands around Mattie's waist, feeling her dress slide over her skin), and peered into the water, half-wanting to see the drowned boy, half-fearing to see him. There was no boy there, but something lay on the bottom where he had been, among the rocks and roots and waterweed. I squinted and just then the wind died a little, stilling the glints on the water. It was a cane, one with a gold head. A *Boston Post* cane. Wrapped around it in a rising spiral, their ends waving lazily, were what appeared to be a pair of ribbons – white ones with bright red edges. Seeing Royce's cane wrapped that way made me think of high-school graduations, and the baton the class marshal waves as he or she leads the gowned seniors to their seats. Now I understood why the old crock hadn't answered the phone. Royce Merrill's phone-answering days were all done. I knew that; I also knew I had come to a time before Royce had even been born. Sara Tidwell was here, I could watch her singing, and when Royce had been born in 1903, Sara had already been gone for two years, she and her whole Red-Top family.

'Go down, Moses,' I told the ribbon-wrapped cane in the water. 'You bound for the Promised Land.'

I walked on toward the sound of the music, invigorated by the cool air and rushing wind. Now I could hear voices as well, lots of them, talking and shouting and laughing. Rising above them and

349

pumping like a piston was the hoarse cry of a sideshow barker: 'Come on in, folks, *hurr*-ay, *hurr*-ay, *hurr*-ay! It's all on the inside but you've got to *hurr*-ay, next show starts in ten minutes! See Angelina the Snake-Woman, she shimmies, she shakes, she'll bewitch your eye and steal your heart, but don't get too close for her bite is *poy*-son! See Hando the Dog-Faced Boy, terror of the South Seas! See the Human Skeleton! See the Human Gila Monster, relic of a time God forgot! See the Bearded Lady and all the Killer Martians! It's on the inside, yessirree, so *hurr*-ay, *hurr*-ay, *hurr*-ay!'

I could hear the steam-driven calliope of a merry-go-round and the bang of the bell at the top of the post as some lumberjack won a stuffed toy for his sweetie. You could tell from the delighted feminine screams that he'd hit it almost hard enough to pop it off the post. There was the snap of .22s from the shooting gallery, the snoring moo of someone's prize cow . . . and now I began to smell the aromas I have associated with county fairs since I was a boy: sweet fried dough, grilled onions and peppers, cotton candy, manure, hay. I began to walk faster as the strum of guitars and thud of double basses grew louder. My heart kicked into a higher gear. I was going to see them perform, actually see Sara Laughs and the Red-Tops live and onstage. This was no crazy three-part fever-dream, either. This was happening right now, so hurr-ay, hurr-ay, hurr-ay.

The Washburn place (the one that would always be the Bricker place to Mrs M.) was gone. Beyond where it would eventually be, rising up the steep slope on the eastern side of The Street, was a flight of broad wooden stairs. They reminded me of the ones which lead down from the amusement park to the beach at Old Orchard. Here the Japanese lanterns were lit in spite of the brightness of the day, and the music was louder than ever. Sara was singing 'Jimmy Crack Corn.'

I climbed the stairs toward the laughter and shouts, the sounds of the Red-Tops and the calliope, the smells of fried food and farm animals. Above the stairhead was a wooden arch with

WELCOME TO FRYEBURG FAIR
WELCOME TO THE 20TH CENTURY

printed on it. As I watched, a little boy in short pants and a woman wearing a shirtwaist and an ankle-length linen skirt walked under the arch and toward me. They shimmered, grew gauzy. For a moment I could see their skeletons and the bone grins which lurked beneath their laughing faces. A moment later and they were gone.

Two farmers – one wearing a straw hat, the other gesturing expansively with a corncob pipe – appeared on the Fair side of the arch in exactly the same fashion. In this way I understood that there was a barrier between The Street and the Fair. Yet I did not think it was a barrier which would affect me. I was an exception.

'Is that right?' I asked. 'Can I go in?'

The bell at the top of the Test Your Strength pole banged loud and clear. Bong once for yes, twice for no. I continued on up the stairs.

Now I could see the Ferris wheel turning against the brilliant sky, the wheel that had been in the background of the band photo in Osteen's *Dark Score Days*. The framework was metal, but the brightly painted gondolas were made of wood. Leading up to it like an aisle leading up to an altar was a broad, sawdust-strewn midway. The sawdust was there for a purpose; almost every man I saw was chewing tobacco.

I paused for a few seconds at the top of the stairs, still on the lake side of the arch. I was afraid of what might happen to me if I passed under. Afraid of dying or disappearing, yes, but mostly of never being able to return the way I had come, of being condemned to spend eternity as a visitor to the turn-of-the-century Fryeburg Fair. That was also like a Ray Bradbury story, now that I thought of it.

In the end what drew me into that other world was Sara Tidwell. I had to see her with my own eyes. I had to hear her sing. *Had* to.

I felt a tingling as I stepped beneath the arch, and there was a sighing in my ears, as of a million voices, very far away. Sighing in relief? Dismay? I couldn't tell. All I knew for sure was that being on the other side was different – the difference between looking at a thing through a window and actually being there; the difference between observing and participating.

Colors jumped out like ambushers at the moment of attack. The smells which had been sweet and evocative and nostalgic on the lake side of the arch were now rough and sexy, prose instead of poetry. I could smell dense sausages and frying beef and the vast shadowy aroma of boiling chocolate. Two kids walked past me sharing a paper cone of cotton candy. Both of them were clutching knotted hankies with their little bits of change in them. 'Hey kids!' a barker in a dark blue shirt called to them. He was wearing sleeve-garters and his smile revealed one splendid gold tooth. 'Knock over the milk-bottles and win a prize! I en't had a loser all day!'

Up ahead, the Red-Tops swung into 'Fishin Blues.' I'd thought the kid on the common in Castle Rock was pretty good, but this version made the kid's sound old and slow and clueless. It wasn't cute, like an antique picture of ladies with their skirts held up to their knees, dancing a decorous version of the black bottom with the edges of their bloomers showing. It wasn't something Alan Lomax had collected with his other folk songs, just one more dusty American butterfly in a glass case full of them; this was smut with just enough shine on it to keep the whole struttin bunch of them out of jail. Sara Tidwell was singing about the dirty boogie, and I guessed that every overalled, straw-hatted, plug-chewing, callus-handed, clodhopper-wearing farmer standing in front of the stage was dreaming about doing it with her, getting right down to where the sweat forms in the crease and the heat gets hot and the pink comes glimmering through.

I started walking in that direction, aware of cows mooing and sheep blatting from the exhibition barns – the Fair's version of my childhood Hi-Ho Dairy-O. I walked past the shooting gallery and the ringtoss and the penny-pitch; I walked past a stage where The Handmaidens of Angelina were weaving in a slow, snakelike dance with their hands pressed together as a guy with a turban on his head and shoepolish on his face tooted a flute. The picture painted on stretched canvas suggested that Angelina – on view inside for just one tenth of a dollar, neighbor – would make these two look like old boots. I walked past the entrance to Freak Alley, the corn-roasting pit, the Ghost House, where more stretched canvas depicted spooks coming out of broken windows and crumbling chimneys. *Everything in there is death*, I thought . . . but from inside I could hear children who were very much alive laughing and squealing as they bumped into things in the dark. The older among them were likely stealing kisses. I passed the Test Your Strength pole, where the gradations leading to the brass bell at the top were marked BABY NEEDS HIS

BOTTLE, SISSY, TRY AGAIN, BIG BOY, HE-MAN, and, just below the bell itself, in red: HURCULES! Standing at the center of a little crowd a young man with red hair was removing his shirt, revealing a heavily muscled upper torso. A cigar-smoking carny held a hammer out to him. I passed the quilting booth, a tent where people were sitting on benches and playing Bingo, the baseball pitch. I passed them all and hardly noticed. I was in the zone, tranced out. 'You'll have to call him back,' Jo had sometimes told Harold when he phoned, 'Michael is currently in the Land of Big Make-Believe.' Only now nothing felt like pretend and the only thing that interested me was the stage at the base of the Ferris wheel. There were eight black folks up there on it, maybe ten. Standing at the front, wearing a guitar and whaling on it as she sang, was Sara Tidwell. She was alive. She was in her prime. She threw back her head and laughed at the October sky.

What brought me out of this daze was a cry from behind me: 'Wait up, Mike! Wait up!'

I turned and saw Kyra running toward me, dodging around the strollers and gamesters and midway gawkers with her pudgy knees pumping. She was wearing a little white sailor dress with red piping and a straw hat with a navy-blue ribbon on it. In one hand she clutched Strickland, and when she got to me she threw herself confidently forward, knowing I would catch her and swing her up. I did, and when her hat started to fall off I caught it and jammed it back on her head.

'I taggled my own quartermack,' she said, and laughed. 'Again.'

'That's right,' I said. 'You're a regular Mean Joe Green.' I was wearing overalls (the tail of a wash-faded blue bandanna stuck out of the bib pocket) and manure-stained workboots. I looked at Kyra's white socks and saw they were homemade. I would find no discreet little label reading Made in Mexico or Made in China if I took off her straw hat and looked inside either. This hat had been most likely Made in Motton, by some farmer's wife with red hands and achy joints.

'Ki, where's Mattie?'

'Home, I guess. She couldn't come.'

'How did you get here?'

'Up the stairs. It was a lot of stairs. You should have waited for me. You could have carrot me, like before. I want to hear the music.'

'Me too. Do you know who that is, Kyra?'

'Yes,' she said, 'Kito's mom. Hurry up, slowpoke!'

I walked toward the stage, thinking we'd have to stand at the back of the crowd, but they parted for us as we came forward, me carrying Kyra in my arms – the lovely sweet weight of her, a little Gibson Girl in her sailor dress and ribbon-accented straw hat. Her arm was curled around my neck and they parted for us like the Red Sea had parted for Moses.

They didn't turn to look at us, either. They were clapping and stomping and bellowing along with the music, totally involved. They stepped aside unconsciously, as if some kind of magnetism were at work here – ours positive, theirs negative. The few women in the crowd were blushing but clearly enjoying themselves, one of them laughing so hard tears were streaming down her face. She looked no more than twenty-two or -three. Kyra pointed to her and said matter-of-factly: 'You know Mattie's boss at the liberry? That's her nana.'

Lindy Briggs's grandmother, and fresh as a daisy, I thought. *Good Christ.*

The Red-Tops were spread across the stage and under swags of red, white, and blue bunting like some time-travelling rock band. I recognized all of them from the picture in Edward Osteen's book. The men wore white shirts, arm-garters, dark vests, dark pants. Son Tidwell, at the far end of the stage, was wearing the derby he'd had on in the photo. Sara, though . . .

'Why is the lady wearing Mattie's dress?' Kyra asked me, and she began to tremble.

'I don't know, honey. I can't say.' Nor could I argue – it was the white sleeveless dress Mattie had been wearing on the common, all right.

Onstage, the band was smoking through an instrumental break. Reginald 'Son' Tidwell strolled over to Sara, feet ambling, hands a brown blur on the strings and frets of his guitar, and she turned to face him. They put their foreheads together, she laughing and he solemn; they looked into each other's eyes and tried to play each other down, the crowd cheering and clapping, the rest of the Red-Tops laughing as they played. Seeing them together like that, I realized that I had been right: they were brother and sister. The resemblance was too strong to be missed or mistaken. But mostly what I looked at was

354

the way her hips and butt switched in that white dress. Kyra and I might be dressed in turn-of-the-century country clothes, but Sara was thoroughly modern Millie. No bloomers for her, no petticoats, no cotton stockings. No one seemed to notice that she was wearing a dress that stopped above her knees – that she was all but naked by the standards of this time. And under Mattie's dress she'd be wearing garments the like of which these people had never seen: a Lycra bra and hip-hugger nylon panties. If I put my hands on her waist, the dress would slip not against an unwelcoming corset but against soft bare skin. Brown skin, not white. *What do you want, sugar?*

Sara backed away from Son, shaking her ungirdled, unbustled fanny and laughing. He strolled back to his spot and she turned to the crowd as the band played the turnaround. She sang the next verse looking directly at me.

> *'Before you start in fishin*
> *you better check your line.*
> *Said before you start in fishin, honey,*
> *you better check on your line.*
> *I'll pull on yours, darlin,*
> *and you best tug on mine.'*

The crowd roared happily. In my arms, Kyra was shaking harder than ever. 'I'm scared, Mike,' she said. 'I don't like that lady. She's a scary lady. She stole Mattie's dress. I want to go home.'

It was as if Sara heard her, even over the rip and ram of the music. Her head cocked back on her neck, her lips peeled open, and she laughed at the sky. Her teeth were big and yellow. They looked like the teeth of a hungry animal, and I decided I agreed with Kyra: she was a scary lady.

'Okay, hon,' I murmured in Ki's ear. 'We're out of here.'

But before I could move, the sense of the woman – I don't know how else to say it – fell upon me and held me. Now I understood what had shot past me in the kitchen to knock away the CARLADEAN letters; the chill was the same. It was almost like identifying a person by the sound of their walk.

She led the band to the turnaround once more, then into another verse. Not one you'd find in any written version of the song, though:

'I ain't gonna hurt her, honey,
not for all the treasure in the worl'.
Said I wouldn't hurt your baby,
not for diamonds or for pearls.
Only one black-hearted bastard
dare to touch that little girl.'

The crowd roared as if it were the funniest thing they'd ever heard, but Kyra began to cry. Sara saw this and stuck out her breasts – much bigger breasts than Mattie's – and shook them at her, laughing her trademark laugh as she did. There was a parodic coldness about this gesture ... and an emptiness, too. A sadness. Yet I could feel no compassion for her. It was as if the heart had been burned out of her and the sadness which remained was just another ghost, the memory of love haunting the bones of hate.

And how her laughing teeth leered.

Sara raised her arms over her head and this time shook it all the way down, as if reading my thoughts and mocking them. Just like jelly on a plate, as some other old song of the time has it. Her shadow wavered on the canvas backdrop, which was a painting of Fryeburg, and as I looked at it I realized I had found the Shape from my Manderley dreams. It was Sara. Sara was the Shape and always had been.

No, Mike. That's close, but it's not right.

Right or wrong, I'd had enough. I turned, putting my hand on the back of Ki's head and urging her face down against my chest. Both her arms were around my neck now, clutching with panicky tightness.

I thought I'd have to bull my way back through the crowd – they had let me in easily enough, but they might be a lot less amenable to letting me back out. *Don't fuck with me, boys,* I thought. *You don't want to do that.*

And they didn't. Onstage Son Tidwell had taken the band from E to G, someone began to bang a tambourine, and Sara went from 'Fishin Blues' to 'Dog My Cats' without a single pause. Out here, in front of the stage and below it, the crowd once more drew back from me and my little girl without looking at us or missing a beat as they clapped their work-swollen hands together. One young man

356

with a port-wine stain swimming across the side of his face opened his mouth – at twenty he was already missing half his teeth – and hollered '*Yee-HAW!*' around a melting glob of tobacco. It was Buddy Jellison from the Village Cafe, I realized . . . Buddy Jellison magically rolled back in age from sixty-eight to eighteen. Then I realized the hair was the wrong shade – light brown instead of black (although he was pushing seventy and looking it in every other way, Bud hadn't a single white hair in his head). This was Buddy's grandfather, maybe even his great-grandfather. I didn't give a shit either way. I only wanted to get out of here.

'Excuse me,' I said, brushing by him.

'There's no town drunk here, you meddling son of a bitch,' he said, never looking at me and never missing a beat as he clapped. 'We all just take turns.'

It's a dream after all, I thought. *It's a dream and that proves it.*

But the smell of tobacco on his breath wasn't a dream, the smell of the crowd wasn't a dream, and the weight of the frightened child in my arms wasn't a dream, either. My shirt was hot and wet where her face was pressed. She was crying.

'Hey, Irish!' Sara called from the stage, and her voice was so like Jo's that I could have screamed. She wanted me to turn back – I could feel her will working on the sides of my face like fingers – but I wouldn't do it.

I dodged around three farmers who were passing a ceramic bottle from hand to hand and then I was free of the crowd. The midway lay ahead, wide as Fifth Avenue, and at the end of it was the arch, the steps, The Street, the lake. Home. If I could get to The Street we'd be safe. I was sure of it.

'Almost done, Irish!' Sara shrieked after me. She sounded angry, but not too angry to laugh. 'You gonna get what you want, sugar, all the comfort you need, but you want to let me finish my bi'ness. Do you hear me, boy? Just stand clear! Mind me, now!'

I began to hurry back the way I had come, stroking Ki's head, still holding her face against my shirt. Her straw hat fell off and when I grabbed for it, I got nothing but the ribbon, which pulled free of the brim. No matter. We had to get out of here.

On our left was the baseball pitch and some little boy shouting 'Willy hit it over the fence, Ma! Willy hit it over the fence!' with monotonous, brain-croggling regularity. We passed the Bingo, where some woman howled that she had won the turkey, by glory, every number was covered with a button and she had won the turkey. Overhead, the sun dove behind a cloud and the day went dull. Our shadows disappeared. The arch at the end of the midway drew closer with maddening slowness.

'Are we home yet?' Ki almost moaned. 'I want to go home, Mike, please take me home to my mommy.'

'I will,' I said. 'Everything's going to be all right.'

We were passing the Test Your Strength pole, where the young man with the red hair was putting his shirt back on. He looked at me with stolid dislike – the instinctive mistrust of a native for an interloper, perhaps – and I realized I knew him, too. He'd have a grandson named Dickie who would, toward the end of the century to which this fair had been dedicated, own the All-Purpose Garage on Route 68.

A woman coming out of the quilting booth stopped and pointed at me. At the same moment her upper lip lifted in a dog's snarl. I knew that face, too. From where? Somewhere around town. It didn't matter, and I didn't want to know even if it did.

'We never should have come here,' Ki moaned.

'I know how you feel,' I said. 'But I don't think we had any choice, hon. We—'

They came out of Freak Alley, perhaps twenty yards ahead. I saw them and stopped. There were seven in all, long-striding men dressed in cutters' clothes, but four didn't matter – those four looked faded and white and ghostly. They were sick fellows, maybe dead fellows, and no more dangerous than daguerreotypes. The other three, though, were real. As real as the rest of this place, anyway. The leader was an old man wearing a faded blue Union Army cap. He looked at me with eyes I knew. Eyes I had seen measuring me over the top of an oxygen mask.

'Mike? Why we stoppin?'

'It's all right, Ki. Just keep your head down. This is all a dream. You'll wake up tomorrow morning in your own bed.'

''Kay.'

The jacks spread across the midway hand to hand and boot to boot, blocking our way back to the arch and The Street. Old

Blue-Cap was in the middle. The ones on either side of him were much younger, some by maybe as much as half a century. Two of the pale ones, the almost-not-there ones, were standing side by side to the old man's right, and I wondered if I could burst through that part of their line. I thought they were no more flesh than the thing which had thumped the insulation of the cellar wall . . . but what if I was wrong?

'Give her over, son,' the old man said. His voice was reedy and implacable. He held out his hands. It was Max Devore, he had come back, even in death he was seeking custody. Yet it *wasn't* him. I knew it wasn't. The planes of this man's face were subtly different, the cheeks gaunter, the eyes a brighter blue.

'Where am *I*?' I called to him, accenting the last word heavily, and in front of Angelina's booth, the man in the turban (a Hindu who perhaps hailed from Sandusky, Ohio) put down his flute and simply watched. The snake-girls stopped dancing and watched, too, slipping their arms around each other and drawing together for comfort. 'Where am *I*, Devore? If our great-grandfathers shit in the same pit, then where am *I*?'

'Ain't here to answer your questions. Give her over.'

'I'll take her, Jared,' one of the younger men – one of those who were really *there* – said. He looked at Devore with a kind of fawning eagerness that sickened me, mostly because I knew who he was: Bill Dean's father. A man who had grown up to be one of the most respected elders in Castle County was all but licking Devore's boots.

Don't think too badly of him, Jo whispered. *Don't think too badly of any of them. They were very young.*

'You don't need to do nothing,' Devore said. His reedy voice was irritated; Fred Dean looked abashed. 'He's going to hand her over on his own. And if he don't, we'll take her together.'

I looked at the man on the far left, the third of those that seemed totally real, totally there. Was this me? It didn't look like me. There was something in the face that seemed familiar but—

'Hand her over, Irish,' Devore said. 'Last chance.'

'No.'

Devore nodded as if this was exactly what he had expected. 'Then we'll take her. This has got to end. Come on, boys.'

359

They started toward me and as they did I realized who the one on the end – the one in the caulked treewalker boots and flannel loggers' pants – reminded me of: Kenny Auster, whose wolfhound would eat cake 'til it busted. Kenny Auster, whose baby brother had been drowned under the pump by Kenny's father.

I looked behind me. The Red-Tops were still playing, Sara was still laughing, shaking her hips with her hands in the sky, and the crowd was still plugging the east end of the midway. That way was no good, anyway. If I went that way, I'd end up raising a little girl in the early years of the twentieth century, trying to make a living by writing penny dreadfuls and dime novels. That might not be so bad . . . but there was a lonely young woman miles and years from here who would miss her. Who might even miss us both.

I turned back and saw the jackboys were almost on me. Some of them more here than others, more vital, but all of them dead. All of them damned. I looked at the towhead whose descendants would include Kenny Auster and asked him, 'What did you do? What in Christ's name did you men do?'

He held out his hands. 'Give her over, Irish. That's all *you* have to do. You and the woman can have more. All the more you want. She's young, she'll pop em out like watermelon seeds.'

I was hypnotized, and they would have taken us if not for Kyra. 'What's happening?' she screamed against my shirt. 'Something smells! Something smells *so bad! Oh Mike, make it stop!*'

And I realized I could smell it, too. Spoiled meat and swampgas. Burst tissue and simmering guts. Devore was the most alive of all of them, generating the same crude but powerful magnetism I had felt around his great-grandson, but he was as dead as the rest of them, too: as he neared I could see the tiny bugs which were feeding in his nostrils and the pink corners of his eyes. *Everything down here is death,* I thought. *Didn't my own wife tell me so?*

They reached out their tenebrous hands, first to touch Ki and then to take her. I backed up a step, looked to my right, and saw more ghosts – some coming out of busted windows, some slipping from redbrick chimneys. Holding Kyra in my arms, I ran for the Ghost House.

'Get him!' Jared Devore yelled, startled. 'Get him, boys! Get that punk! Goddammit!'

360

I sprinted up the wooden steps, vaguely aware of something soft rubbing against my cheek – Ki's little stuffed dog, still clutched in one of her hands. I wanted to look back and see how close they were getting, but I didn't dare. If I stumbled—

'Hey!' the woman in the ticket booth cawed. She had clouds of gingery hair, makeup that appeared to have been applied with a garden-trowel, and mercifully resembled no one I knew. She was just a carny, just passing through this benighted place. Lucky her. 'Hey, mister, you gotta buy a ticket!'

No time, lady, no time.

'Stop him!' Devore shouted. 'He's a goddam punk thief! That ain't his young 'un he's got! Stop him!' But no one did and I rushed into the darkness of the Ghost House with Ki in my arms.

Beyond the entry was a passage so narrow I had to turn sideways to get down it. Phosphorescent eyes glared at us in the gloom. Up ahead was a growing wooden rumble, a loose sound with a clacking chain beneath it. Behind us came the clumsy thunder of caulk-equipped loggers' boots rushing up the stairs outside. The ginger-haired carny was hollering at them now, she was telling them that if they broke anything inside they'd have to give up the goods. 'You mind me, you damned rubes!' she shouted. 'That place is for kids, not th' likes of you!'

The rumble was directly ahead of us. Something was turning. At first I couldn't make out what it was.

'Put me down, Mike!' Kyra sounded excited. 'I want to go through by myself!'

I set her on her feet, then looked nervously back over my shoulder. The bright light at the entryway was blocked out as they tried to cram in.

'You asses!' Devore yelled. 'Not all at the same time! Sweet weeping Jesus!' There was a smack and someone cried out. I faced front just in time to see Kyra dart through the rolling barrel, holding her hands out for balance. Incredibly, she was laughing.

I followed, got halfway across, then went down with a thump.

'Ooops!' Kyra called from the far side, then giggled as I tried to get up, fell again, and was tumbled all the way over. The bandanna fell out of my bib pocket. A bag of horehound candy dropped from another pocket. I tried to look back, to see if they had got themselves sorted out and were coming. When I did, the barrel hurled me through another inadvertent somersault. Now I knew how clothes felt in a dryer.

I crawled to the end of the barrel, got up, took Ki's hand, and let her lead us deeper into the Ghost House. We got perhaps ten paces before white bloomed around her like a lily and she screamed. Some animal – something that sounded like a huge cat – hissed heavily. Adrenaline dumped into my bloodstream and I was about to jerk her backward into my arms again when the hiss came once more. I felt hot air on my ankles, and Ki's dress made that bell-shape around her legs again. This time she laughed instead of screaming.

'Go, Ki!' I whispered. 'Fast.'

We went on, leaving the steam-vent behind. There was a mirrored corridor where we were reflected first as squat dwarves and then as scrawny ectomorphs with long white vampire features. I had to urge Kyra on again; she wanted to make faces at herself. Behind us, I heard cursing lumberjacks trying to negotiate the barrel. I could hear Devore cursing, too, but he no longer seemed so . . . well, so *eminent*.

There was a sliding-pole that landed us on a big canvas pillow. This made a loud farting noise when we hit it, and Ki laughed until fresh tears spilled down her cheeks, rolling around and kicking her feet in glee. I got my hands under her arms and yanked her up.

'Don't taggle yer own quartermack,' she said, then laughed again. Her fear seemed to have entirely departed.

We went down another narrow corridor. It smelled of the fragrant pine from which it had been constructed. Behind one of these walls, two 'ghosts' were clanking chains as mechanically as men working on a shoe-factory assembly line, talking about where they were going to take their girls tonight and who was going to bring some 'red-eye engine,' whatever that was. I could no longer hear anyone behind us. Kyra led the way confidently, one of her little hands holding one of my big ones, pulling me along. When we came to a door painted with glowing flames and marked THIS WAY TO HADES, she pushed through it with no hesitation at all. Here red isinglass topped the passage like a tinted skylight, imparting a rosy glow I thought far too pleasant for Hades.

362

We went on for what felt like a very long time, and I realized I could no longer hear the calliope, the hearty *bong!* of the Test Your Strength bell, or Sara and the Red-Tops. Nor was that exactly surprising. We must have walked a quarter of a mile. How could any county fair Ghost House be so big?

We came to three doors then, one on the left, one on the right, and one set into the end of the corridor. On one a little red tricycle was painted. On the door facing it was my green IBM typewriter. The picture on the door at the end looked older, somehow — faded and dowdy. It showed a child's sled. *That's Scooter Larribee's*, I thought. *That's the one Devore stole.* A rash of gooseflesh broke out on my arms and back.

'Well,' Kyra said brightly, 'here are our toys.' She lifted Strickland, presumably so he could see the red trike.

'Yeah,' I said. 'I guess so.'

'Thank you for taking me away,' she said. 'Those were scary men but the spookyhouse was fun. Nighty-night. Stricken says nighty-night, too.' It still came out sounding exotic — *tiu* — like the Vietnamese word for sublime happiness.

Before I could say another word, she had pushed open the door with the trike on it and stepped through. It snapped shut behind her, and as it did I saw the ribbon from her hat. It was hanging out of the bib pocket of the overalls I was wearing. I looked at it a moment, then tried the knob of the door she had just gone through. It wouldn't turn, and when I slapped my hand against the wood it was like slapping some hard and fabulously dense metal. I stepped back, then cocked my head in the direction from which we'd come. There was nothing. Total silence.

This is the between-time, I thought. *When people talk about 'slipping through the cracks,' this is what they really mean. This is the place where they really go.*

You better get going yourself, Jo told me. *If you don't want to find yourself trapped here, maybe forever, you better get going yourself.*

I tried the knob of the door with the typewriter painted on it. It turned easily. Behind this door was another narrow corridor — more wooden walls and the sweet smell of pine. I didn't want to go in there, something about it made me think of a long coffin, but there was nothing else to do, nowhere else to go. I went, and the door slammed shut behind me.

Christ, I thought. *I'm in the dark, in a closed-in place . . . it's time for one of Michael Noonan's world-famous panic attacks.*

But no bands clamped themselves over my chest, and although my heart-rate was high and my muscles were still jacked on adrenaline, I was under control. Also, I realized, it wasn't entirely dark. I could only see a little, but enough to make out the walls and the plank floor. I wrapped the dark-blue ribbon from Ki's hat around my wrist, tucking one end underneath so it wouldn't come loose. Then I began to move forward.

I went on for a long time, the corridor turning this way and that, seemingly at random. I felt like a microbe slipping through an intestine. At last I came to a pair of wooden arched doorways. I stood before them, wondering which was the correct choice, and realized I could hear Bunter's bell faintly through the one to my left. I went that way and as I walked, the bell grew steadily louder. At some point the sound of the bell was joined by the mutter of thunder. The autumn cool had left the air and it was hot again – stifling. I looked down and saw that the biballs and clodhopper shoes were gone. I was wearing thermal underwear and itchy socks.

Twice more I came to choices, and each time I picked the opening through which I could hear Bunter's bell. As I stood before the second pair of doorways, I heard a voice somewhere in the dark say quite clearly: 'No, the President's wife wasn't hit. That's his blood on her stockings.'

I walked on, then stopped when I realized my feet and ankles no longer itched, that my thighs were no longer sweating into the longjohns. I was wearing the Jockey shorts I usually slept in. I looked up and saw I was in my own living room, threading my way carefully around the furniture as you do in the dark, trying like hell not to stub your stupid toe. I could see a little better; faint milky light was coming in through the windows. I reached the counter which separates the living room from the kitchen and looked over it at the waggy-cat clock. It was five past five.

I went to the sink and turned on the water. When I reached for a glass I saw I was still wearing the ribbon from Ki's straw hat on my wrist. I unwound it and put it on the counter between

364

the coffee-maker and the kitchen TV. Then I drew myself some cold water, drank it down, and made my way cautiously along the north-wing corridor by the pallid yellow glow of the bathroom nightlight. I peed (*you*-rinated, I could hear Ki saying), then went into the bedroom. The sheets were rumpled, but the bed didn't have the orgiastic look of the morning after my dream of Sara, Mattie, and Jo. Why would it? I'd gotten out of it and had myself a little sleepwalk. An extraordinarily vivid dream of the Fryeburg Fair.

Except that was bullshit, and not just because I had the blue silk ribbon from Ki's hat. None of it had the quality of dreams on waking, where what seemed plausible becomes immediately ridiculous and all the colors – both those bright and those ominous – fade at once. I raised my hands to my face, cupped them over my nose, and breathed deeply. Pine. When I looked, I even saw a little smear of sap on one pinky finger.

I sat on the bed, thought about dictating what I'd just experienced into the Memo-Scriber, then flopped back on the pillows instead. I was too tired. Thunder rumbled. I closed my eyes, began to drift away, and then a scream ripped through the house. It was as sharp as the neck of a broken bottle. I sat up with a yell, clutching at my chest.

It was Jo. I had never heard her scream like that in our life together, but I knew who it was, just the same. 'Stop hurting her!' I shouted into the darkness. 'Whoever you are, *stop hurting her!*'

She screamed again, as if something with a knife, clamp, or hot poker took a malicious delight in disobeying me. It seemed to come from a distance this time, and her third scream, while just as agonized as the first two, was farther away still. They were diminishing, as the little boy's sobbing had diminished.

A fourth scream floated out of the dark, then the house was silent. Breathless, the house breathed around me. Alive in the heat, aware in the faint sound of dawn thunder.

CHAPTER TWENTY-TWO

I was finally able to get into the zone, but couldn't do anything once I got there. I keep a steno pad handy for notes – character lists, page references, date chronologies – and I doodled in there a little bit, but the sheet of paper in the IBM remained blank. There was no thundering heartbeat, no throbbing eyes or difficulty breathing – no panic attack, in other words – but there was no story, either. Andy Drake, John Shackleford, Ray Garraty, the beautiful Regina Whiting . . . they stood with their backs turned, refusing to speak or move. The manuscript was sitting in its accustomed place on the left side of the typewriter, the pages held down with a pretty chunk of quartz I'd found on the lane, but nothing was happening. Zilch.

I recognized an irony here, perhaps even a moral. For years I had fled the problems of the real world, escaping into various Narnias of my imagination. Now the real world had filled up with bewildering thickets, there were things with teeth in some of them, and the wardrobe was locked against me.

Kyra, I had printed, putting her name inside a scalloped shape that was supposed to be a cabbage rose. Below it I had drawn a piece of bread with a beret tipped rakishly on the top crust. Noonan's conception of French toast. The letters L.B. surrounded with curlicues. A shirt with a rudimentary duck on it. Beside this I had printed QUACK QUACK. Below QUACK QUACK I had written *Ought to fly away 'Bon Voyage.'*

At another spot on the sheet I had written *Dean*, *Auster*, and *Devore*. They were the ones who had seemed the most there, the most dangerous. Because they had descendants? But surely all seven of those jacks must, mustn't they? In those days most families were whoppers. And where had *I* been? I had asked, but Devore hadn't wanted to say.

It didn't feel any more like a dream at nine-thirty on a sullenly hot Sunday morning. Which left exactly what? Visions? Time-travel? And if there was a purpose to such travel, what was it? What was the message, and who was trying to send it? I remembered clearly what I'd said just before passing from the dream in which I had sleepwalked out to Jo's studio and brought back my typewriter: *I don't believe these lies.* Nor would I now. Until I could see at least some of the truth, it might be safer to believe nothing at all.

At the top of the sheet upon which I was doodling, in heavily stroked letters, I printed the word **DANGER!**, then circled it. From the circle I drew an arrow to Kyra's name. From her name I drew an arrow to *Ought to fly away 'Bon Voyage'* and added *MATTIE*.

Below the bread wearing the beret I drew a little telephone. Above it I put a cartoon balloon with R-R-RINGGG! in it. As I finished this, the cordless phone rang. It was sitting on the deck rail. I circled *MATTIE* and picked up the phone.

'Mike?' She sounded excited. Happy. Relieved.

'Yeah,' I said. 'How are you?'

'Great!' she said, and I circled L.B. on my pad.

'Lindy Briggs called ten minutes ago – I just got off the phone with her. Mike, she's giving me my job back! Isn't that wonderful?'

Sure. And wonderful how it would keep her in town. I crossed out *Ought to fly away 'Bon Voyage,'* knowing that Mattie wouldn't go. Not now. And how could I ask her to? I thought again *If only I knew a little more . . .*

'Mike? Are you—'

'It's very wonderful,' I said. In my mind's eye I could see her standing in the kitchen, drawing the kinked telephone cord through her fingers, her legs long and coltish below her denim shorts. I could see the shirt she was wearing, a white tee with a yellow duck paddling across the front. 'I hope Lindy had the good grace to sound ashamed of herself.' I circled the tee-shirt I'd drawn.

'She did. And she was frank enough to kind of . . . well, disarm me. She said the Whitmore woman talked to her early last week.

367

Was very frank and to the point, Lindy said. I was to be let go immediately. If that happened, the money, computer equipment, and software Devore funnelled into the library would keep coming. If it didn't, the flow of goods and money would stop immediately. She said she had to balance the good of the community against what she knew was wrong . . . she said it was one of the toughest decisions she ever had to make . . .'

'Uh-huh.' On the pad my hand moved of its own volition like a planchette gliding over a Ouija board, printing the words PLEASE CAN'T I PLEASE. 'There's probably some truth in it, but Mattie . . . how much do you suppose *Lindy* makes?'

'I don't know.'

'I bet it's more than any three other small-town librarians in the state of Maine combined.'

In the background I heard Ki: 'Can I talk, Mattie? Can I talk to Mike? Please can't I please?'

'In a minute, hon.' Then, to me: 'Maybe. All I know is that I have my job back, and I'm willing to let bygones be bygones.'

On the page, I drew a book. Then I drew a series of interlocked circles between it and the duck tee-shirt.

'Ki wants to talk to you,' Mattie said, laughing. 'She says the two of you went to the Fryeburg Fair last night.'

'Whoa, you mean I had a date with a pretty girl and slept through it?'

'Seems that way. Are you ready for her?'

'Ready.'

'Okay, here comes the chatterbox.'

There was a rustling as the phone changed hands, then Ki was there. 'I taggled you at the Fair, Mike! I taggled my own quartermack!'

'Did you?' I asked. 'That was quite a dream, wasn't it, Ki?'

There was a long silence at the other end. I could imagine Mattie wondering what had happened to her telephone chatterbox. At last Ki said in a hesitating voice: 'You there too.' *Tiu.* 'We saw the snake-dance ladies . . . the pole with the bell on top . . . we went in the spookyhouse . . . you fell down in the barrel! It wasn't a dream . . . was it?'

I could have convinced her that it was, but all at once that seemed like a bad idea, one that was dangerous in its own way. I said: 'You had on a pretty hat and a pretty dress.'

'*Yeah!*' Ki sounded enormously relieved. 'And *you* had on—'

'Kyra, stop. Listen to me.'

She stopped at once.

'It's better if you don't talk about that dream too much, I think. To your mom or to anyone except me.'

'Except you.'

'Yes. And the same with the refrigerator people. Okay?'

'Okay. Mike, there was a lady in Mattie's clothes.'

'I know,' I said. It was all right for her to talk, I was sure of it, but I asked anyway: 'Where's Mattie now?'

'Waterin the flowers. We got lots of flowers, a billion at least. I have to clean up the table. It's a chore. I don't mind, though. I like chores. We had French toast. We always do on Sundays. It's yummy, 'specially with strawberry syrup.'

'I know,' I said, drawing an arrow to the piece of bread wearing the beret. 'French toast is great. Ki, did you tell your mom about the lady in her dress?'

'No. I thought it might scare her.' She dropped her voice. 'Here she comes!'

'That's all right . . . but we've got a secret, right?'

'Yes.'

'Now can I talk to Mattie again?'

'Okay.' Her voice moved off a little. 'Mommy-bommy, Mike wants to talk to you.' Then she came back. 'Will you bizzit us today? We could go on another picnic.'

'I can't today, Ki. I have to work.'

'Mattie never works on Sunday.'

'Well, when I'm writing a book, I write every day. I have to, or else I'll forget the story. Maybe we'll have a picnic on Tuesday, though. A barbecue picnic at your house.'

'Is it long 'til Tuesday?'

'Not too long. Day after tomorrow.'

'Is it long to write a book?'

'Medium-long.'

I could hear Mattie telling Ki to give her the phone.

'I will, just one more second. Mike?'

369

'I'm here, Ki.'

'I love you.'

I was both touched and terrified. For a moment I was sure my throat was going to lock up the way my chest used to when I tried to write. Then it cleared and I said, 'Love you, too, Ki.'

'Here's Mattie.'

Again there was the rustly sound of the telephone changing hands, then Mattie said: 'Did that refresh your recollection of your date with my daughter, sir?'

'Well,' I said, 'it certainly refreshed hers.' There was a link between Mattie and me, but it didn't extend to this — I was sure of it.

She was laughing. I loved the way she sounded this morning and I didn't want to bring her down . . . but I didn't want her mistaking the white line in the middle of the road for the crossmock, either.

'Mattie, you still need to be careful, okay? Just because Lindy Briggs offered you your old job back doesn't mean everyone in town is suddenly your friend.'

'I understand that,' she said. I thought again about asking if she'd consider taking Ki up to Derry for awhile — they could live in my house, stay for the duration of the summer if that was what it took for things to return to normal down here. Except she wouldn't do it. When it came to accepting my offer of high-priced New York legal talent, she'd had no choice. About this she did. Or thought she did, and how could I change her mind? I had no logic, no connected facts; all I had was a vague dark shape, like something lying beneath nine inches of snowblind ice.

'I want you to be careful of two men in particular,' I said. 'One is Bill Dean. The other is Kenny Auster. He's the one—'

'—with the big dog who wears the neckerchief. He—'

'That's Booberry!' Ki called from the middle distance. 'Booberry licked my facie!'

'Go out and play, hon,' Mattie said.

'I'm clearun the table.'

'You can finish later. Go on outside now.' There was a pause as she watched Ki go out the door, taking Strickland with her. Although the kid had left the trailer, Mattie still spoke in the lowered tone of

370

someone who doesn't want to be overheard. 'Are you trying to scare me?'

'No,' I said, drawing repeated circles around the word **DAN-GER**. 'But I want you to be careful. Bill and Kenny may have been on Devore's team, like Footman and Osgood. Don't ask me why I think that might be, because I have no satisfactory answer. It's only a feeling, but since I got back on the TR, my feelings are different.'

'What do you mean?'

'Are you wearing a tee-shirt with a duck on it?'

'How do you know that? Did Ki tell you?'

'Did she take the little stuffed dog from her Happy Meal out with her just now?'

A long pause. At last she said 'My God' in a voice so low I could hardly hear it. Then again: 'How—'

'I don't *know* how. I don't know if you're still in a . . . a bad situation, either, or why you might be, but I feel that you are. That you both are.' I could have said more, but I was afraid she'd think I'd gone entirely off the rails.

'He's *dead*!' she burst out. 'That old man is *dead*! Why can't he leave us alone?'

'Maybe he has. Maybe I'm wrong about all this. But there's no harm in being careful, is there?'

'No,' she said. 'Usually that's true.'

'Usually?'

'Why don't you come and see me, Mike? Maybe *we* could go to the Fair together.'

'Maybe this fall we will. All three of us.'

'I'd like that.'

'In the meantime, I'm thinking about the key.'

'Thinking is half your problem, Mike,' she said, and laughed again. Ruefully, I thought. And I saw what she meant. What she didn't seem to understand was that feeling was the other half. It's a sling, and in the end I think it rocks most of us to death.

I worked for a while, then carried the IBM back into the house and left the manuscript on top. I was done with it, at least for the time being. No more looking for the way back through the wardrobe; no more Andy Drake and John Shackleford until this was over. And, as

I dressed in long pants and a button-up shirt for the first time in what felt like weeks, it occurred to me that perhaps something – some force – had been trying to sedate me with the story I was telling. With the ability to work again. It made sense; work had always been my drug of choice, even better than booze or the Mellaril I still kept in the bathroom medicine cabinet. Or maybe work was only the delivery system, the hypo with all the dreamy dreams inside it. Maybe the real drug was the zone. Being in the zone. Feeling it, you sometimes hear the basketball players say. I was in the zone and I was really feeling it.

I grabbed the keys to the Chevrolet off the counter and looked at the fridge as I did. The magnets were circled again. In the middle was a message I'd seen before, one that was now instantly understandable, thanks to the extra Magnabet letters:

help her

'I'm doing my best,' I said, and went out.

Three miles north on Route 68 – by then you're on the part of it which used to be known as Castle Rock Road – there's a greenhouse with a shop in front of it. Slips 'n Greens, it's called, and Jo used to spend a fair amount of time there, buying gardening supplies or just noodling with the two women who ran the place. One of them was Helen Auster, Kenny's wife.

I pulled in there at around ten o'clock that Sunday morning (it was open, of course; during tourist season almost every Maine shopkeeper turns heathen) and parked next to a Beamer with New York plates. I paused long enough to hear the weather forecast on the radio – continued hot and humid for another forty-eight hours at least – and then got out. A woman wearing a bathing suit, a skort, and a giant yellow sunhat emerged from the shop with a bag of peat moss cradled in her arms. She gave me a little smile. I returned it with eighteen per cent interest. She was from New York, and that meant she wasn't a Martian.

The shop was even hotter and damper than the white morning outside. Lila Proulx, the co-owner, was on the phone. There was a little fan beside the cash register and she was standing directly in front of it, flapping the front of her sleeveless blouse. She saw me and twiddled her fingers in a wave. I twiddled mine back, feeling like someone else. Work or no work, I was still zoning. Still feeling it.

I walked around the shop, picking up a few things almost at random, watching Lila out of the corner of my eye and waiting for her to get off the phone so I could talk to her . . . and all the time my own private hyperdrive was humming softly away. At last she hung up and I came to the counter.

'Michael Noonan, what a sight for sore eyes you are!' she said, and began ringing up my purchases. 'I was awfully sorry to hear about Johanna. Got to get that right up front. Jo was a pet.'

'Thanks, Lila.'

'Welcome. Don't need to say any more about it, but with a thing like that it's best to put it right up front. I've always believed it, always will believe it. Right up front. Going to do a little gardening, are you?' *Gointer do a little ga'adnin, aaa you?*

'If it ever cools off.'

'Ayuh! Isn't it wicked?' She flapped the top of her blouse again to show me how wicked it was, then pointed at one of my purchases. 'Want this one in a special bag? Always safe, never sorry, that's my motto.'

I nodded, then looked at the little blackboard tilted against the counter. FRESH BLUEBERRYS, the chalked message read. THE CROP IS IN!

'I'll have a pint of berries, too,' I said. 'As long as they're not Friday's. I can do better than Friday.'

She nodded vigorously, as if to say she knew damned well I could. 'These were on the bush yest'y. That fresh enough for you?'

'Good as gold,' I said. 'Blueberry's the name of Kenny's dog, isn't it?'

'Ain't he a funny one? God, I love a big dog, if he's behaved.' She turned, got a pint of berries from her little fridge, and put them in another bag for me.

'Where's Helen?' I asked. 'Day off?'

'Not her,' Lila said. 'If she's in town, you can't get her out of this place 'less you beat her with a stick. She and Kenny and the kids went down Taxachusetts. Them and her brother's family club together and get a seaside cottage two weeks every summer. They all went. Old Blueberry, he'll chase seagulls until he drops.' She laughed – it was

373

a loud and hearty one. It made me think of Sara Tidwell. Or maybe it was the way Lila looked at me as she did it. There was no laughter in her eyes. They were small and considering, coldly curious.

Would you for Christ's sake quit it? I told myself. *They can't all be in on it together, Mike!*

Couldn't they, though? There *is* such a thing as town consciousness – anyone who doubts it has never been to a New England town meeting. Where there's a consciousness, is there not likely to be a subconscious? And if Kyra and I were doing the old mind-meld thing, could not other people in TR-90 also be doing it, perhaps without even knowing it? We all shared the same air and land; we shared the lake and the aquifer which lay below everything, buried water tasting of rock and minerals. We shared The Street as well, that place where good pups and vile dogs could walk side by side.

As I started out with my purchases in a cloth carry-handle bag, Lila said: 'What a shame about Royce Merrill. Did you hear?'

'No,' I said.

'Fell down his cellar stairs yest'y evening. What a man his age was doing going down such a steep flight of steps is beyond me, but I suppose once you get to his age, you have your own reasons for doing things.'

Is he dead? I started to ask, then rephrased. It wasn't the way the question was expressed on the TR. 'Did he pass?'

'Not yet. Motton Rescue took him to Castle County General. He's in a coma.' *Comber*, she said it. 'They don't think he'll ever wake up, poor fella. There's a piece of history that'll die with him.'

'I suppose that's true.' *Good riddance*, I thought. 'Does he have children?'

'No. There have been Merrills on the TR for two hundred years; one died at Cemetery Ridge. But all the old families are dying out now. You have a nice day, Mike.' She smiled. Her eyes remained flat and considering.

I got into my Chevy, put the bag with my purchases in it on the passenger seat, then simply sat for a moment, letting the air conditioner pour cool air on my face and neck. Kenny Auster was in Taxachusetts. That was good. A step in the right direction.

But there was still my caretaker.

*   *   *

374

'Bill's not here,' Yvette said. She stood in the door, blocking it as well as she could (you can only do so much in that regard when you're five-three and weigh roughly a hundred pounds), studying me with the gimlet gaze of a nightclub bouncer denying reentry to a drunk who's been tossed out on his ear once already.

I was on the porch of the neat-as-ever-you-saw Cape Cod which stands at the top of Peabody Hill and looks all the way across New Hampshire and into Vermont's back yard. Bill's equipment sheds were lined up to the left of the house, all of them painted the same shade of gray, each with its own sign: DEAN CARETAKING, No.1, No.2, and No.3. Parked in front of No.2 was Bill's Dodge Ram. I looked at it, then back at Yvette. Her lips tightened a little more. Another notch and I figured they'd be gone entirely.

'He went to North Conway with Butch Wiggins,' she said. 'They went in Butch's truck. To get—'

'No need lying for me, dear heart,' Bill said from behind her.

It was still over an hour shy of noon, and on the Lord's Day to boot, but I had never heard a man who sounded more tired. He clumped down the hall, and as he came out of its shadows and into the light – the sun was finally burning through the murk – I saw that Bill now looked his age. Every year of it, and maybe ten more to grow on. He was wearing his usual khaki shirt and pants – Bill Dean would be a Dickies man until the day he died – but his shoulders looked slumped, almost sprained, as if he'd spent a week lugging buckets that were too heavy for him. The falling-away of his face had finally begun, an indefinable something that makes the eyes look too big, the jaw too prominent, the mouth a bit loose. He looked old. There were no children to carry on the family line of work, either; all the old families were dying out, Lila Proulx had said. And maybe that was a good thing.

'Bill—' she began, but he raised one of his big hands to stop her. The callused fingertips shook a little.

'Go in the kitchen a dight,' he told her. 'I need to talk to my *compadre* here. 'Twon't take long.'

Yvette looked at him, and when she looked back at me, she had indeed reached zero lip-surface. There was just a black line where they had been, like a mark dashed off with a pencil. I saw with woeful clarity that she hated me.

'Don't you tire him out,' she said to me. 'He hasn't been sleepin. It's the heat.' She walked back down the hall, all stiff back and high shoulders, disappearing into shadows that were probably cool. It always seems to be cool in the houses of old people, have you noticed?

Bill came out on to the porch and put his big hands into the pockets of his pants without offering to shake with me. 'I ain't got nothin to say to you. You and me's quits.'

'Why, Bill? Why are we quits?'

He looked west, where the hills stepped into the burning summer haze, disappearing in it before they could become mountains, and said nothing.

'I'm trying to help that young woman.'

He gave me a look from the corners of his eyes that I could read well enough. 'Ayuh. Help y'self right into her pants. I see men come up from New York and New Jersey with their young girls. Summer weekends, ski weekends, it don't matter. Men who go with girls that age always look the same, got their tongues run out even when their mouths are shut. Now you look the same.'

I felt both angry and embarrassed, but I resisted the urge to chase him in that direction. That was what he wanted.

'What happened here?' I asked him. 'What did your fathers and grandfathers and great-grandfathers do to Sara Tidwell and her family? You didn't just move them on, did you?'

'Didn't have to,' Bill said, looking past me at the hills. His eyes were moist almost to the point of tears, but his jaw was set and hard. 'They moved on themselves. Never was a nigger who didn't have an itchy foot, my dad used to say.'

'Who set the trap that killed Son Tidwell's boy? Was it your father, Bill? Was it Fred?'

His eyes moved; his jaw never did. 'I dunno what you're talking about.'

'I hear him crying in my house. Do you know what it's like to hear a dead child crying in your house? *Some bastard trapped him like a weasel and I hear him crying in my fucking house!*'

'You're going to need a new caretaker,' Bill said. 'I can't do for you no more. Don't want to. What I want is for you to get off my porch.'

376

'What's happening? Help me, for Christ's sake.'

'I'll help you with the toe of my shoe if you don't get going on your own.'

I looked at him a moment longer, taking in the wet eyes and the set jaw, his divided nature written on his face.

'I lost my wife, you old bastard,' I said. 'A woman you claimed to love.'

Now his jaw moved at last. He looked at me with surprise and injury. 'That didn't happen *here*,' he said. 'That didn't have anything to do with *here*. She might've been off the TR because . . . well, she might've had her reasons to be off the TR . . . but she just had a stroke. Would have happened anywhere. *Anywhere.*'

'I don't believe that. I don't think you do, either. *Something followed her to Derry*, maybe because she was pregnant . . .'

Bill's eyes widened. I gave him a chance to say something, but he didn't take it.

'. . . or maybe just because she knew too much.'

'She had a stroke.' Bill's voice wasn't quite even. 'I read the obituary myself. She had a damn *stroke.*'

'What did she find out? Talk to me, Bill. Please.'

There was a long pause. Until it was over I allowed myself the luxury of thinking I might actually be getting through to him.

'I've only got one more thing to say to you, Mike – stand back. For the sake of your immortal soul, stand back and let things run their course. They will whether you do or don't. This river has almost come to the sea; it won't be dammed by the likes of you. Stand back. For the love of Christ.'

Do you care about your soul, Mr Noonan? God's butterfly caught in a cocoon of flesh that will soon stink like mine?

Bill turned and walked to his door, the heels of his workboots clodding on the painted boards.

'Stay away from Mattie and Ki,' I said. 'If you so much as go near that trailer—'

He turned back, and the hazy sunshine glinted on the tracks below his eyes. He took a bandanna from his back pocket and wiped his cheeks. 'I ain't stirrin from this house. I wish to God I'd never come back from my vacation in the first place, but I did – mostly on

377

your account, Mike. Those two down on Wasp Hill have nothing to fear from me. No, not from *me*.'

He went inside and closed the door. I stood there looking at it, feeling unreal – surely I could not have had such a deadly conversation with Bill Dean, could I? Bill who had reproached me for not letting folks down here share – and perhaps ease – my grief for Jo, Bill who had welcomed me back so warmly?

Then I heard a *clack* sound. He might not have locked his door while he was at home in his entire life, but he had locked it now. The *clack* was very clear in the breathless July air. It told me everything I had to know about my long friendship with Bill Dean. I turned and walked back to my car, my head down. Nor did I turn when I heard a window run up behind me.

'Don't you ever come back here, you town bastard!' Yvette Dean cried across the sweltering dooryard. 'You've broken his heart! Don't you ever come back! Don't you ever! Don't you *ever*!'

'Please,' Mrs M. said. 'Don't ask me any more questions, Mike. I can't afford to get in Bill Dean's bad books, any more'n my ma could afford to get into Normal Auster's or Fred Dean's.'

I shifted the phone to my other ear. 'All I want to know is—'

'In this part of the world caretakers pretty well run the whole show. If they say to a summer fella that he should hire this carpenter or that 'lectrician, why, that's who the summer fella hires. Or if a caretaker says this one should be fired because he ain't proving reliable, he is fired. Or *she*. Because what goes once for plumbers and landscapers and 'lectricians has always gone twice for housekeepers. If you want to be recommended – and *stay* recommended – you have to keep on the sunny side of people like Fred and Bill Dean, or Normal and Kenny Auster. Don't you see?' She was almost pleading. 'When Bill found out I told you about what Normal Auster did to Kerry, oooo he was so mad at me.'

'Kenny Auster's brother – the one Normal drowned under the pump – his name was Kerry?'

'Ayuh. I've known a lot of folks name their kids alike, think it's cute. Why, I went to school with a brother and sister named Roland and Rolanda Therriault, I think Roland's in Manchester now, and Rolanda married that boy from—'

'Brenda, just answer one question. I'll never tell. Please?'

I waited, my breath held, for the click that would come when she put her telephone back in its cradle. Instead, she spoke three words in a soft, almost regretful voice. 'What is it?'

'Who was Carla Dean?'

I waited through another long pause, my hand playing with the ribbon that had come off Ki's turn-of-the-century straw hat.

'You dassn't tell anyone I told you anything,' she said at last.

'I won't.'

'Carla was Bill's twin sister. She died sixty-five years ago, during the time of the fires.' The fires Bill claimed had been set by Ki's grandfather – his going-away present to the TR. 'I don't know just how it happened. Bill never talks about it. If you tell him I told you, I'll never make another bed in the TR. He'll see to it.' Then, in a hopeless voice, she said: 'He may know anyway.'

Based on my own experiences and surmises, I guessed she might be right about that. But even if she was, she'd have a check from me every month for the rest of her working life. I had no intention of telling her that over the telephone, though – it would scald her Yankee soul. Instead I thanked her, assured her again of my discretion, and hung up.

I sat at the table for a moment, staring blankly at Bunter, then said: 'Who's here?'

No answer.

'Come on,' I said. 'Don't be shy. Let's go nineteen or ninety-two down. Barring that, let's talk.'

Still no answer. Not so much as a shiver of the bell around the stuffed moose's neck. I spied the scribble of notes I'd made while talking to Jo's brother and drew them toward me. I had put *Kia*, *Kyra*, *Kito*, and *Carla* in a box. Now I scribbled out the bottom line of that box and added the name *Kerry* to the list. *I've known a lot of folks name their kids alike*, Mrs M. had said. *They think it's cute.*

I didn't think it was cute; I thought it was creepy.

It occurred to me that at least two of these soundalikes had drowned – Kerry Auster under a pump, Kia Noonan in her mother's dying body when she wasn't much bigger than a sunflower seed. And I had seen the ghost of a third drowned child in the lake.

Kito? Was that one Kito? Or was Kito the one who had died of blood-poisoning?

They name their kids alike, they think it's cute.

How many soundalike kids had there been to start with? How many were left? I thought the answer to the first question didn't matter, and that I knew the answer to the second one already. *This river has almost come to the sea*, Bill had said.

Carla, Kerry, Kito, Kia . . . all gone. Only Kyra Devore was left.

I got up so fast and hard that I knocked over my chair. The clatter in the silence made me cry out. I was leaving, and right now. No more telephone calls, no more playing Andy Drake, Private Detective, no more depositions or half-assed wooings of the lady fair. I should have followed my instincts and gotten the fuck out of Dodge that first night. Well, I'd go now, just get in the Chevy and haul ass for Der—

Bunter's bell jangled furiously. I turned and saw it bouncing around his neck as if batted to and fro by a hand I couldn't see. The sliding door giving on the deck began to fly open and clap shut like something hooked to a pulley. The book of *Tough Stuff* crossword puzzles on the end-table and the DSS program guide blew open, their pages riffling. There was a series of rattling thuds across the floor, as if something enormous were crawling rapidly toward me, pounding its fists as it came.

A draft – not cold but warm, like the rush of air produced by a subway train on a summer night – buffeted past me. In it I heard a strange voice which seemed to be saying *Bye-BY*, *bye-BY*, *bye-BY*, as if wishing me a good trip home. Then, as it dawned on me that the voice was actually saying *Ki-Ki*, *Ki-Ki*, *Ki-Ki*, something struck me and knocked me violently forward. It felt like a large soft fist. I buckled over the table, clawing at it to stay up, overturning the lazy susan with the salt and pepper shakers on it, the napkin holder, the little vase Mrs M. had filled with daisies. The vase rolled off the table and shattered. The kitchen TV blared on, some politician talking about how inflation was on the march again. The CD player started up, drowning out the politician; it was the Rolling Stones doing a cover of Sara Tidwell's 'I Regret You, Baby.' Upstairs, one smoke alarm went off, then another, then a third. They were joined a moment later by the warble-whoop of the Chevy's car alarm. The whole world was cacophony.

Something hot and pillowy seized my wrist. My hand shot forward like a piston and slammed down on the steno pad. I watched as it pawed clumsily to a blank page, then seized the pencil which lay nearby. I gripped it like a dagger and then something wrote with it, not guiding my hand but *raping* it. The hand moved slowly at first, almost blindly, then picked up speed until it was flying, almost tearing through the sheet:

help her don't go help her don't go help her help don't don't baby please don't go help her help her help her

I had almost reached the bottom of the page when the cold descended again, that outer cold that was like sleet in January, chilling my skin and crackling the snot in my nose and sending two shuddery puffs of white air from my mouth. My hand clenched and the pencil snapped in two. Behind me, Bunter's bell rang out one final furious convulsion before falling silent. Also from behind me came a peculiar double pop, like the sound of champagne corks being drawn. Then it was over. Whatever it had been or however many *they* had been, it was finished. I was alone again.

I turned off the CD player just as Mick and Keith moved on to a white-boy version of Howling Wolf, then ran upstairs and pushed the reset buttons on the smoke-detectors. I leaned out the window of the big guest bedroom while I was up there, aimed the fob of my keyring down at the Chevrolet, and pushed the button on it. The alarm quit.

With the worst of the noise gone I could hear the TV cackling away in the kitchen. I went down, killed it, then froze with my hand still on the OFF button, looking at Jo's annoying waggy-cat clock. Its tail had finally stopped switching, and its big plastic eyes lay on the floor. They had popped right out of its head.

I went down to the Village Cafe for supper, snagging the last Sunday *Telegram* from the rack (**COMPUTER MOGUL DEVORE DIES IN WESTERN MAINE TOWN WHERE HE GREW UP**, the headline read) before sitting down at the counter. The accompanying photo was a studio shot of Devore that looked about thirty years old. He was smiling. Most people do that quite naturally. On Devore's face it looked like a learned skill.

I ordered the beans that were left over from Buddy Jellison's Saturday-night beanhole supper. My father wasn't much for aphorisms – in my family dispensing nuggets of wisdom was Mom's job – but as Daddy warmed up the Saturday-night yelloweyes in the oven on Sunday afternoon, he would invariably say that beans and beef stew were better the second day. I guess it stuck. The only other piece of fatherly wisdom I can remember receiving was that you should always wash your hands after you took a shit in a bus station.

While I was reading the story on Devore, Audrey came over and told me that Royce Merrill had passed without recovering consciousness. The funeral would be Tuesday afternoon at Grace Baptist, she said. Most of the town would be there, many folks just to see Ila Meserve awarded the *Boston Post* cane. Did I think I'd get over? No, I said, probably not. I thought it prudent not to add that I'd likely be attending a victory-party at Mattie Devore's while Royce's funeral was going on down the road.

The usual late-Sunday-afternoon flow of customers came and went while I ate, people ordering burgers, people ordering beans, people ordering chicken salad sandwiches, people buying sixpacks. Some were from the TR, some from away. I didn't notice many of them, and no one spoke to me. I have no idea who left the napkin on my newspaper, but when I put down the A section and turned to find the sports, there it was. I picked it up, meaning only to put it aside, and saw what was written on the back in big dark letters: GET OFF THE TR.

I never found out who left it there. I guess it could have been any of them.

CHAPTER TWENTY-THREE

The murk came back and transformed that Sunday night's dusk into a thing of decadent beauty. The sun turned red as it slid down toward the hills and the haze picked up the glow, turning the western sky into a nosebleed. I sat out on the deck and watched it, trying to do a crossword puzzle and not getting very far. When the phone rang, I dropped *Tough Stuff* on top of my manuscript as I went to answer it. I was tired of looking at the title of my book every time I passed.

'Hello?'

'What's going on up there?' John Storrow demanded. He didn't even bother to say hi. He didn't sound angry, though; he sounded totally pumped. 'I'm missing the whole goddam soap opera!'

'I invited myself to lunch on Tuesday,' I said. 'Hope you don't mind.'

'No, that's good, the more the merrier.' He sounded as if he absolutely meant it. 'What a summer, huh? What a summer! Anything happen just lately? Earthquakes? Volcanoes? Mass suicides?'

'No mass suicides, but the old guy died,' I said.

'Shit, the whole *world* knows Max Devore kicked it,' he said. 'Surprise me, Mike! Stun me! Make me holler boy-howdy!'

'No, the *other* old guy. Royce Merrill.'

'I don't know who you – oh, wait. The one with the gold cane who looked like an exhibit from *Jurassic Park*?'

'That's him.'

'Bummer. Otherwise . . . ?'

'Otherwise everything's under control,' I said, then thought of

383

the popped-out eyes of the cat-clock and almost laughed. What stopped me was a kind of surety that Mr Good Humor Man was just an act – John had really called to ask what, if anything, was going on between me and Mattie. And what was I going to say? Nothing yet? One kiss, one instant blue-steel hard-on, the fundamental things apply as time goes by?

But John had other things on his mind. 'Listen, Michael, I called because I've got something to tell you. I think you'll be both amused and amazed.'

'A state we all crave,' I said. 'Lay it on me.'

'Rogette Whitmore called, and . . . you didn't happen to give her my parents' number, did you? I'm back in New York now, but she called me in Philly.'

'I didn't *have* your parents' number. You didn't leave it on either of your machines.'

'Oh, right.' No apology; he seemed too excited to think of such mundanities. I began to feel excited myself, and I didn't even know what the hell was going on. 'I gave it to Mattie. Do you think the Whitmore woman called Mattie to get it? Would Mattie give it to her?'

'I'm not sure that if Mattie came upon Rogette flaming in a thoroughfare, she'd piss on her to put her out.'

'Vulgar, Michael, *très vulgarino*.' But he was laughing. 'Maybe Whitmore got it the same way Devore got yours.'

'Probably so,' I said. 'I don't know what'll happen in the months ahead, but right now I'm sure she's still got access to Max Devore's personal control panel. And if anyone knows how to push the buttons on it, it's probably her. Did she call from Palm Springs?'

'Uh-huh. She said she'd just finished a preliminary meeting with Devore's attorneys concerning the old man's will. According to her, Grampa left Mattie Devore eighty million dollars.'

I was struck silent. I wasn't amused yet, but I was certainly amazed.

'Gets ya, don't it?' John said gleefully.

'You mean he left it to Kyra,' I said at last. 'Left it in trust to *Kyra*.'

'No, that's just what he did not do. I asked Whitmore three times, but by the third I was starting to understand. There was method in

384

his madness. Not much, but a little. You see, there's a condition. If he left the money to the minor child instead of to the mother, the condition would have no weight. It's funny when you consider that Mattie isn't long past minor status herself.'

'Funny,' I agreed, and thought of her dress sliding between my hands and her smooth bare waist. I also thought of Bill Dean saying that men who went with girls that age always looked the same, had their tongues run out even if their mouths were shut.

'What string did he put on the money?'

'That Mattie remain on the TR for one year following Devore's death – until 17 July 1999. She can leave on day-trips, but she has to be tucked up in her TR-90 bed every night by nine o'clock, or else the legacy is forfeit. Did you ever hear such a bullshit thing in your life? Outside of some old George Sanders movie, that is?'

'No,' I said, and recalled my visit to the Fryeburg Fair with Kyra. *Even in death he's seeking custody*, I had thought, and of course this was the same thing. He wanted them here. Even in death he wanted them on the TR.

'It won't fly?' I asked.

'Of *course* it won't fly. Fucking crackpot might as well have written he'd give her eighty million dollars if she used blue tampons for a year. But she'll get the eighty mil, all right. My heart is set on it. I've already talked to three of our estate guys, and . . . you don't think I should bring one of them up with me on Tuesday, do you? Will Stevenson'll be the point man in the estate phase, if Mattie agrees.' He was all but babbling. He hadn't had a thing to drink, I'd've bet the farm on it, but he was sky-high on all the possibilities. We'd gotten to the happily-ever-after part of the fairy-tale, as far as he was concerned; Cinderella comes home from the ball through a cash cloudburst.

'. . . course Will's a little bit old,' John was saying, 'about three hundred or so, which means he's not exactly a fun guy at a party, but . . .'

'Leave him home, why don't you?' I said. 'There'll be plenty of time to carve up Devore's will later on. And in the immediate future, I don't think Mattie's going to have any problem observing the bullshit condition. She just got her job back, remember?'

'Yeah, the white buffalo drops dead and the whole herd scatters!' John exulted. 'Look at em go! And the new multimillionaire goes back to filing books and mailing out overdue notices! Okay, Tuesday we'll just party.'

'Good.'

'Party 'til we puke.'

'Well . . . maybe us older folks will just party until we're mildly nauseated, would that be all right?'

'Sure. I've already called Romeo Bissonette, and he's going to bring George Kennedy, the private detective who got all that hilarious shit on Durgin. Bissonette says Kennedy's a scream when he gets a drink or two in him. I thought I'd bring some steaks from Peter Luger's, did I tell you that?'

'I don't believe you did.'

'Best steaks in the world. Michael, do you realize what's happened to that young woman? *Eighty million dollars!*'

'She'll be able to replace Scoutie.'

'Huh?'

'Nothing. Will you come in tomorrow night or on Tuesday?'

'Tuesday morning around ten, into Castle County Airport. New England Air. Mike, are you all right? You sound odd.'

'I'm all right. I'm where I'm supposed to be. I think.'

'What's that supposed to mean?'

I had wandered out on to the deck. In the distance thunder rumbled. It was hotter than hell, not a breath of breeze stirring. The sunset was fading to a baleful afterglow. The sky in the west looked like the white of a bloodshot eye.

'I don't know,' I said, 'but I have an idea the situation will clarify itself. I'll meet you at the airport.'

'Okay,' he said, and then, in a hushed, almost reverential voice: 'Eighty million motherfucking American dollars.'

'It's a whole lotta lettuce,' I agreed, and wished him a good night.

I drank black coffee and ate toast in the kitchen the next morning, watching the TV weatherman. Like so many of them these days, he had a slightly mad look, as if all those Doppler radar images had driven him to the brink of something. I think of it as the Millennial Video Game look.

'We've got another thirty-six hours of this soup to work through and then there's going to be a big change,' he was saying, and pointed to some dark gray scum lurking in the Midwest. Tiny animated lightning-bolts danced in it like defective sparkplugs. Beyond the scum and the lightning-bolts, America looked clear all the way out to the desert country, and the posted temperatures were fifteen degrees cooler. 'We'll see temps in the mid-nineties today and can't look for much relief tonight or tomorrow morning. But tomorrow afternoon these frontal storms will reach western Maine, and I think most of you are going to want to keep updated on weather conditions. Before we get back to cooler air and bright clear skies on Wednesday, we're probably going to see violent thunderstorms, heavy rain, hail in some locations. Tornados are rare in Maine, but some towns in western and central Maine could see them tomorrow. Back to you, Earl.'

Earl, the morning news guy, had the innocent beefy look of a recent retiree from the Chippendales and read off the TelePrompTer like one. 'Wow,' he said. 'That's quite a forecast, Vince. Tornados a possibility.'

'Wow,' I said. 'Say wow again, Earl. Do it 'til I'm satisfied.'

'Holy cow,' Earl said just to spite me, and the telephone rang. I went to answer it, giving the waggy clock a look as I went by. The night had been quiet – no sobbing, no screaming, no nocturnal adventures – but the clock was disquieting, just the same. It hung there on the wall eyeless and dead, like a message full of bad news.

'Hello?'

'Mr Noonan?'

I knew the voice, but for a moment couldn't place it. It was because she had called me Mr Noonan. To Brenda Meserve I'd been Mike for almost fifteen years.

'Mrs M.? Brenda? What—'

'I can't work for you anymore,' she said, all in a rush. 'I'm sorry I can't give you proper notice – I never stopped work for anyone without giving notice, not even that old drunk Mr Croyden – but I have to. Please understand.'

'Did Bill find out I called you? I swear to God, Brenda, I never said a word—'

'No. I haven't spoken to him, nor he to me. I just can't come back to Sara Laughs. I had a bad dream last night. A terrible dream. I dreamed that . . . something's mad at me. If I come back, I could

387

have an accident. It would *look* like an accident, at least, but . . . it wouldn't be.'

That's silly, Mrs M., I wanted to say. *You're surely past the age where you believe in campfire stories about ghoulies and ghosties and long-leggedy beasties.*

But of course I could say no such thing. What was going on in my house was no campfire story. I knew it, and she knew I did.

'Brenda, if I've caused you any trouble, I'm truly sorry.'

'Go away, Mr Noonan . . . Mike. Go back to Derry and stay for awhile. It's the best thing you could do.'

I heard the letters sliding on the fridge and turned. This time I actually saw the circle of fruits and vegetables form. It stayed open at the top long enough for four letters to slide inside. Then a little plastic lemon plugged the hole and completed the circle.

yats,

the letters said, then swapped themselves around, making

stay.

Then both the circle and the letters broke up.

'Mike, *please*.' Mrs M. was crying. 'Royce's funeral is tomorrow. Everyone in the TR who matters – the old-timers – will be there.'

Yes, of course they would. The old ones, the bags of bones who knew what they knew and kept it to themselves. Except some of them had talked to my wife. Royce himself had talked to her. Now he was dead. So was she.

'It would be best if you were gone. You could take that young woman with you, maybe. Her and her little girl.'

But could I? I somehow didn't think so. I thought the three of us were on the TR until this was over . . . and I was starting to have an idea of when that would be. A storm was coming. A summer storm. Maybe even a tornado.

'Brenda, thanks for calling me. And I'm not letting you go. Let's just call it a leave of absence, shall we?'

'Fine . . . whatever you want. Will you at least think about what I said?'

388

'Yes. In the meantime, I don't think I'd tell anyone you called me, all right?'

'No!' she said, sounding shocked. Then: 'But they'll know. Bill and Yvette . . . Dickie Brooks at the garage . . . old Anthony Weyland and Buddy Jellison and all the others . . . they'll know. Goodbye, Mr Noonan. I'm so sorry. For you and your wife. Your poor wife. I'm so sorry.' Then she was gone.

I held the phone in my hand for a long time. Then, like a man in a dream, I put it down, crossed the room, and took the eyeless clock off the wall. I threw it in the trash and went down to the lake for a swim, remembering that W. F. Harvey story 'August Heat,' the one that ends with the line 'The heat is enough to drive a man mad.'

I'm not a bad swimmer when people aren't pelting me with rocks, but my first shore-to-float-to-shore lap was tentative and unrhythmic – ugly – because I kept expecting something to reach up from the bottom and grab me. The drowned boy, maybe. The second lap was better, and by the third I was relishing the increased kick of my heart and the silky coolness of the water rushing past me. Halfway through the fourth lap I pulled myself up the float's ladder and collapsed on the boards, feeling better than I had since my encounter with Devore and Rogette Whitmore on Friday night. I was still in the zone, and on top of that I was experiencing a glorious endorphin rush. In that state, even the dismay I'd felt when Mrs M. told me she was resigning her position ebbed away. She would come back when this was over; of course she would. In the meantime, it was probably best she stay away.

Something's mad at me. I could have an accident.

Yes indeed. She might cut herself. She might fall down a flight of cellar stairs. She might even have a stroke running across a hot parking lot.

I sat up and looked at Sara on her hill, the deck jutting out over the drop, the railroad ties descending. I'd only been out of the water for a few minutes, but already the day's sticky heat was folding over me, stealing my rush. The water was still as a mirror. I could see the house reflected in it, and in the reflection Sara's windows became watchful eyes.

I thought that the focus of all the phenomena – the epicenter –

was very likely on The Street between the real Sara and its drowned image. *This is where it happened*, Devore had said. And the old-timers? Most of them probably knew what I knew: that Royce Merrill had been murdered. And wasn't it possible – wasn't it *likely* – that what had killed him might come among them as they sat in their pews or gathered afterward around his grave? That it might steal some of their force – their guilt, their memories, their *TR*-ness – to help it finish the job?

I was very glad that John was going to be at the trailer tomorrow, and Romeo Bissonette, and George Kennedy, who was so amusing when he got a drink or two in him. Glad it was going to be more than just me with Mattie and Ki when the old folks got together to give Royce Merrill his sendoff. I no longer cared very much about what had happened to Sara and the Red-Tops, or even about what was haunting my house. What I wanted was to get through tomorrow, and for Mattie and Ki to get through tomorrow. We'd eat before the rain started and then let the predicted thunderstorms come. I thought that, if we could ride them out, our lives and futures might clarify with the weather.

'Is that right?' I asked. I expected no answer – talking out loud was a habit I had picked up since returning here – but somewhere in the woods east of the house, an owl hooted. Just once, as if to say it *was* right, get through tomorrow and things will clarify. The hoot almost brought something else to mind, some association that was ultimately too gauzy to grasp. I tried once or twice, but the only thing I could come up with was the title of a wonderful old novel – *I Heard the Owl Call My Name*.

I rolled forward off the float and into the water, grasping my knees against my chest like a kid doing a cannonball. I stayed under as long as I could, until the air in my lungs started to feel like some hot bottled liquid, and then I broke the surface. I trod water about thirty yards out until I had my breath back, then set my sights on the Green Lady and stroked for shore.

I waded out, started up the railroad ties, then stopped and went back to The Street. I stood there for a moment, gathering my courage, then walked to where the birch curved her graceful belly out over the water. I grasped that white curve as I had on Friday evening and looked into the water. I was sure I'd see the child, his dead eyes looking up at me from his bloating brown face, and that my mouth and throat would once more fill with the taste of the lake: *help I'm drown, lemme up oh sweet Jesus lemme up*. But there was nothing. No dead boy, no ribbon-wrapped *Boston Post* cane, no taste of the lake in my mouth.

I turned and peered at the gray forehead of rock poking out of the mulch. I thought *There, right there*, but it was only a conscious and unspontaneous thought, the mind voicing a memory. The smell of decay and the certainty that something awful had happened right there was gone.

When I got back up to the house and went for a soda, I discovered the front of the refrigerator was bare and clean. Every magnetic letter, every fruit and vegetable, was gone. I never found them. I might have, probably would have, if there had been more time, but on that Monday morning time was almost up.

I dressed, then called Mattie. We talked about the upcoming party, about how excited Ki was, about how nervous Mattie was about going back to work on Friday – she was afraid that the locals would be mean to her, but in an odd, womanly way she was even more afraid that they would be *cold* to her, snub her. We talked about the money, and I quickly ascertained that she didn't believe in the reality of it. 'Lance used to say his father was the kind of man who'd show a piece of meat to a starving dog and then eat it himself,' she said. 'But as long as I have my job back, I won't starve and neither will Ki.'

'But if there really *are* big bucks . . . ?'

'Oh, gimme-gimme-gimme,' she said, laughing. 'What do you think I am, crazy?'

'Nah. By the way, what's going on with Ki's fridgeafator people? Are they writing any new stuff?'

'That is the weirdest thing,' she said. 'They're gone.'

'The fridgeafator people?'

'I don't know about them, but the magnetic letters you gave her sure are. When I asked Ki what she did with them, she started crying and said Allamagoosalum took them. She said he ate them in the middle of the night, while everyone was sleeping, for a snack.'

'Allama-*who*-salum?'

'Allamagoosalum,' Mattie said, sounding wearily amused. 'Another

391

little legacy from her grandfather. It's a corruption of the Micmac word for "boogeyman" or "demon" – I looked it up at the library. Kyra had a good many nightmares about demons and wendigos and the allamagoosalum late last winter and this spring.'

'What a sweet old grandpa he was,' I said sentimentally.

'Right, a real pip. She was miserable over losing the letters; I barely got her calmed down before her ride to VBS came. Ki wants to know if you'll come to Final Exercises on Friday afternoon, by the way. She and her friend Billy Turgeon are going to flannelboard the story of baby Moses.'

'I wouldn't miss it,' I said . . . but of course I did. We all did.

'Any idea where her letters might have gone, Mike?'

'No.'

'Yours are still okay?'

'Mine are fine, but of course mine don't spell anything,' I said, looking at the empty door of my own fridgeafator. There was sweat on my forehead. I could feel it creeping down into my eyebrows like oil. 'Did you . . . I don't know . . . sense anything?'

'You mean did I maybe hear the evil alpabet-thief as he slid through the window?'

'You know what I mean.'

'I suppose so.' A pause. 'I thought I heard something in the night, okay? About three this morning, actually. I got up and went into the hall. Nothing was there. But . . . you know how hot it's been lately?'

'Yes.'

'Well, not in my trailer, not last night. It was cold as ice. I swear I could almost see my breath.'

I believed her. After all, I *had* seen mine.

'Were the letters on the front of the fridge then?'

'I don't know. I didn't go up the hall far enough to see into the kitchen. I took one look around and then went back to bed. I almost *ran* back to bed. Sometimes bed feels safer, you know?' She laughed nervously. 'It's a kid thing. Covers are boogeyman kryptonite. Only at first, when I got in . . . I don't know . . . I thought someone was in there already. Like someone had been hiding on the floor underneath and then . . . when I went to check the hall . . . they got in. Not a nice someone, either.'

392

Give me my dust-catcher, I thought, and shuddered.

'What?' Mattie asked sharply. 'What did you say?'

'I asked who did you think it was? What was the first name that came into your mind?'

'Devore,' she said. '*Him*. But there was no one there.' A pause. 'I wish *you'd* been there.'

'I do, too.'

'I'm glad. Mike, do you have any ideas at all about this? Because it's very freaky.'

'I think maybe . . .' For a moment I was on the verge of telling her what had happened to my own letters. But if I started talking, where would it stop? And how much could she be expected to believe? '. . . maybe Ki took the letters herself. Went walking in her sleep and chucked them under the trailer or something. Do you think that could be?'

'I think I like the idea of Kyra strolling around in her sleep even less than the idea of ghosts with cold breath taking the letters off the fridge,' Mattie said.

'Take her to bed with you tonight,' I said, and felt her thought come back like an arrow: *I'd rather take you.*

What she said, after a brief pause, was: 'Will you come by today?'

'I don't think so,' I said. She was noshing on flavored yogurt as we talked, eating it in little nipping bites. 'You'll see me tomorrow, though. At the party.'

'I hope we get to eat before the thunderstorms. They're supposed to be bad.'

'I'm sure we will.'

'And are you still thinking? I only ask because I dreamed of you when I finally fell asleep again. I dreamed of you kissing me.'

'I'm still thinking,' I said. 'Thinking hard.'

But in fact I don't remember thinking about anything very hard that day. What I remember is drifting farther and farther into that zone I've explained so badly. Near dusk I went for a long walk in spite of the heat – all the way out to where Lane Forty-two joins the highway. Coming back I stopped on the edge of Tidwell's Meadow, watching the light fade out of the sky and listening to thunder rumble somewhere over New Hampshire. Once more there was that sense

393

of how thin reality was, not just here but everywhere; how it was stretched like skin over the blood and tissue of a body we can never know clearly in this life. I looked at trees and saw arms; I looked at bushes and saw faces. Ghosts, Mattie had said. Ghosts with cold breath.

Time was also thin, it seemed to me. Kyra and I had really been at the Fryeburg Fair – some version of it, anyway; we had really visited the year 1900. And at the foot of the meadow the Red-Tops were almost there now, as they once had been, in their neat little cabins. I could almost hear the sound of their guitars, the murmur of their voices and laughter; I could almost see the gleam of their lanterns and smell their beef and pork frying. '*Say baby, do you remember me?*' one of her songs went, '*Well I ain't your honey like I used to be.*'

Something rattled in the underbrush to my left. I turned that way, expecting to see Sara step out of the woods wearing Mattie's dress and Mattie's white sneakers. In this gloom, they would seem almost to float by themselves, until she got close to me . . .

There was no one there, of course, it had undoubtedly been nothing but Chuck the Woodchuck headed home after a hard day at the office, but I no longer wanted to be out here, watching as the light drained out of the day and the mist came up from the ground. I turned for home.

Instead of going into the house when I got back, I made my way along the path to Jo's studio, where I hadn't been since the night I had taken my IBM back in a dream. My way was lit by intermittent flashes of heat lightning.

The studio was hot but not stale. I could smell a peppery aroma that was actually pleasant, and wondered if it might be some of Jo's herbs. There was an air conditioner out here, and it worked – I turned it on and then just stood in front of it a little while. So much cold air on my overheated body was probably unhealthy, but it felt wonderful.

I didn't feel very wonderful otherwise, however. I looked around with a growing sense of something too heavy to be mere sadness; it felt like despair. I think it was caused by the contrast between how little of Jo was left in Sara Laughs and how much of her was still out here. I imagined our marriage as a kind of playhouse – and isn't that what marriage is, in large part? playing house? – where only half the stuff was held down. Held down by little magnets or hidden cables. Something had come along and picked up our playhouse by one corner – easiest thing in the world, and I supposed I should be grateful that the something hadn't decided to draw back its foot and kick the poor thing all the way over. It just picked up that one corner, you see. My stuff stayed put, but all of Jo's had slid . . .

Out of the house and down here.

'Jo?' I asked, and sat down in her chair. There was no answer. No thumps on the wall. No crows or owls calling from the woods. I put my hand on her desk, where the typewriter had been, and slipped my hand across it, picking up a film of dust.

'I miss you, honey,' I said, and began to cry.

When the tears were over – again – I wiped my face with the tail of my tee-shirt like a little kid, then just looked around. There was the picture of Sara Tidwell on her desk and a photo I didn't remember on the wall – this latter was old, sepia-tinted, and woodsy. Its focal point was a man-high birchwood cross in a little clearing on a slope above the lake. That clearing was gone from the geography now, most likely, long since filled in by trees.

I looked at her jars of herbs and mushroom sections, her filing cabinets, her sections of afghan. The green rag rug on the floor. The pot of pencils on the desk, pencils she had touched and used. I held one of them poised over a blank sheet of paper for a moment or two, but nothing happened. I had a sense of life in this room, and a sense of being watched . . . but not a sense of being *helped*.

'I know some of it but not enough,' I said. 'Of all the things I don't know, maybe the one that matters most is who wrote "help her" on the fridge. Was it you, Jo?'

No answer.

I sat awhile longer – hoping against hope, I suppose – then got up, turned off the air conditioning, turned off the lights, and went back to the house, walking in soft bright stutters of unfocused lightning. I sat on the deck for a little while, watching the night. At some point I realized I'd taken the length of blue silk ribbon out of my pocket and was winding it nervously back and forth between my fingers, making half-assed cat's cradles. Had it really come from the year 1900? The idea seemed perfectly crazy and perfectly sane at the same time. The night hung hot and hushed. I imagined old folks all over the TR – perhaps in Motton and Harlow, too – laying out their funeral clothes for tomorrow. In the doublewide trailer on Wasp Hill Road, Ki was sitting on the floor, watching a videotape of *The Jungle Book* – Baloo and Mowgli were singing 'The Bare Necessities.' Mattie was on the couch with her feet up, reading the new Mary Higgins Clark and singing along. Both were wearing shorty pajamas, Ki's pink, Mattie's white.

After a little while I lost my sense of them; it faded the way radio signals sometimes do late at night. I went into the north bedroom, undressed, and crawled on to the top sheet of my unmade bed. I fell asleep almost at once.

I woke in the middle of the night with someone running a hot finger up and down the middle of my back. I rolled over and when the lightning flashed, I saw there was a woman in bed with me. It was Sara Tidwell. She was grinning. There were no pupils in her eyes. 'Oh sugar, I'm almost back,' she whispered in the dark. I had a sense of her reaching out for me again, but when the next flash of lightning came, that side of the bed was empty.

CHAPTER TWENTY-FOUR

Inspiration isn't always a matter of ghosts moving magnets around on refrigerator doors, and on Tuesday morning I had a flash that was a beaut. It came while I was shaving and thinking about nothing more than remembering the beer for the party. And like the best inspirations, it came out of nowhere at all.

I hurried into the living room, not quite running, wiping the shaving cream off my face with a towel as I went. I glanced briefly at the *Tough Stuff* crossword collection lying on top of my manuscript. That had been where I'd gone first in an effort to decipher 'go down nineteen' and 'go down ninety-two.' Not an unreasonable starting-point, but what did *Tough Stuff* have to do with TR-90? I had purchased the book at Mr Paperback in Derry, and of the thirty or so puzzles I'd completed, I'd done all but half a dozen in Derry. TR ghosts could hardly be expected to show an interest in my Derry crossword collection. The telephone book, on the other hand—

I snatched it off the dining-room table. Although it covered the whole southern part of Castle County – Motton, Harlow, and Kashwakamak as well as the TR – it was pretty thin. The first thing I did was check the white pages to see if there *were* at least ninety-two. There were. The *Y*'s and *Z*'s finished up on page ninety-seven.

This was the answer. Had to be.

'I got it, didn't I?' I asked Bunter. 'This is it.'

Nothing. Not even a tinkle from the bell.

'Fuck you – what does a stuffed moosehead know about a telephone book?'

Go down nineteen. I turned to page nineteen of the telephone book, where the letter *F* was prominently showcased. I began to slip my finger down the first column and as it went, my excitement faded. The nineteenth name on page nineteen was Harold Failles. It meant nothing to me. There were also Feltons and Fenners, a Filkersham and several Finneys, half a dozen Flahertys and more Fosses than you could shake a stick at. The last name on page nineteen was Framingham. It also meant nothing to me, but—

Framingham, Kenneth P.

I stared at that for a moment. A realization began to dawn. It had nothing to do with the refrigerator messages.

You're not seeing what you think you're seeing, I thought. *This is like when you buy a blue Buick—*

'You see blue Buicks everywhere,' I said. 'Practically got to kick em out of your way. Yeah, that's it.' But my hands were shaking as I turned to page ninety-two.

Here were the *T*'s of southern Castle County, along with a few *U*'s like Alton Ubeck and Catherine Udell just to round things out. I didn't bother checking the ninety-second entry on the page; the phone book wasn't the key to the magnetic crosspatches after all. It did, however, suggest something enormous. I closed the book, just held it in my hands for a moment (happy folks with blueberry rakes on the front cover), then opened it at random, this time to the *M*'s. And once you knew what you were looking for, it jumped right out at you.

All those *K*'s.

Oh, there were Stevens and Johns and Marthas; there was Meserve, G., and Messier, V., and Jayhouse, T. And yet, again and again, I saw the initial *K* where people had exercised their right not to list their first name in the book. There were at least twenty *K*-initials on page fifty alone, and another dozen *C*-initials. As for the actual names themselves . . .

There were twelve Kenneths on this random page in the *M*-section, including three Kenneth Moores and two Kenneth Munters. There were four Catherines and two Katherines. There were a Casey, a Kiana, and a Kiefer.

'Holy Christ, it's like fallout,' I whispered.

I thumbed through the book, not able to believe what I was seeing and seeing it anyway. Kenneths, Katherines, and Keiths were everywhere. I also saw Kimberly, Kim, and Kym. There were Cammie, Kia (yes, and we had thought ourselves so original), Kiah, Kendra, Kaela, Keil, and Kyle. Kirby and Kirk. There was a woman named Kissy Bowden, and a man named Kito Rennie – Kito, the same name as one of Kyra's fridgeafator people. And everywhere, outnumbering such usually common initials as *S* and *T* and *E*, were those *K*'s. My eyes danced with them.

I turned to look at the clock – didn't want to stand John Storrow up at the airport, Christ no – and there was no clock there. Of course not. Old Krazy Kat had popped his peepers during a psychic event. I gave a loud, braying laugh that scared me a little – it wasn't particularly sane.

'Get hold of yourself, Mike,' I said. 'Take a deep breath, son.'

I took the breath. Held it. Let it out. Checked the digital readout on the microwave. Quarter past eight. Plenty of time for John. I turned back to the telephone book and began to riffle rapidly through it. I'd had a second inspiration – not a megawatt blast like the first one, but a lot more accurate, it turned out.

Western Maine is a relatively isolated area – it's a little like the hill country of the border South – but there has always been at least some inflow of folks from away ('flatlanders' is the term the locals use when they are feeling contemptuous), and in the last quarter of the century it has become a popular area for active seniors who want to fish and ski their way through retirement. The phone book goes a long way toward separating the newbies from the long-time residents. Babickis, Parettis, O'Quindlans, Donahues, Smolnacks, Dvoraks, Blindermeyers – all from away. All flatlanders. Jalberts, Meserves, Pillsburys, Spruces, Therriaults, Perraults, Stanchfields, Starbirds, Dubays – all from Castle County. You see what I'm saying, don't you? When you see a whole column of Bowies on page twelve, you know that those folks have been around long enough to relax and really spread those Bowie genes.

There were a few *K*-initials and *K*-names among the Parettis and the Smolnacks, but only a few. The heavy concentrations were all attached to families that had been here long enough to absorb the atmosphere. To breathe the fallout. Except it wasn't radiation, exactly, it—

I suddenly imagined a black headstone taller than the tallest tree on the lake, a monolith which cast its shadow over half of Castle County. This picture was so clear and so terrible that I covered my eyes, dropping the phonebook on the table. I backed away from it, shuddering. Hiding my eyes actually seemed to enhance the image further: a grave-marker so enormous it blotted out the sun; TR-90 lay at its foot like a funeral bouquet or a ceremonial slain dove. Sara Tidwell's son had drowned in Dark Score Lake . . . or *been* drowned in it. But she had marked his passing. Memorialized it. I wondered if anyone else in town had ever noticed what I just had. I didn't suppose it was all that likely; when you open a telephone book you're looking for a specific name in most cases, not reading whole pages line by line. I wondered if *Jo* had noticed – if she'd known that almost every longtime family in this part of the world had, in one way or another, named at least one child after Sara Tidwell's dead son.

Jo wasn't stupid. I thought she probably had.

I returned to the bathroom, relathered, started again from scratch. When I finished, I went back to the phone and picked it up. I poked in three numbers, then stopped, looking out at the lake. Mattie and Ki were up and in the kitchen, both of them wearing aprons, both of them in a fine froth of excitement. There was going to be a party! They would wear pretty new summer clothes, and there would be music from Mattie's boombox CD player! Ki was helping Mattie make biscuits for strewberry snortcake, and while the biscuits were baking they would make salads. If I called Mattie up and said *Pack a couple of bags, you and Ki are going to spend a week at Disney World*, Mattie would assume I was joking, then tell me to hurry up and finish getting dressed so I'd be at the airport when John's plane landed. If I pressed, she'd remind me that Lindy had offered her her old job back, but the offer would close in a hurry if Mattie didn't show up promptly at two P.M. on Friday. If I continued to press, she would just say no.

Because I wasn't the only one in the zone, was I? I wasn't the only one who was really feeling it.

I returned the phone to its recharging cradle, then went back into the north bedroom. By the time I'd finished dressing, my fresh shirt was already feeling wilted under the arms; it was as hot that morning as it had been for the last week, maybe even hotter. But

I'd be in plenty of time to meet the plane. I had never felt less like partying, but I'd be there. Mikey on the spot, that was me. Mikey on the goddam spot.

John hadn't given me his flight number, but at Castle County Airport, such niceties are hardly necessary. This bustling hub of transport consists of three hangars and a terminal which used to be a Flying A gas station – when the light's strong on the little building's rusty north side, you can still see the shape of that winged *A*. There's one runway. Security is provided by Lassie, Breck Pellerin's ancient collie, who spends her days crashed out on the linoleum floor, cocking an ear at the ceiling whenever a plane lands or takes off.

I popped my head into Pellerin's office and asked him if the ten from Boston was on time. He said it 'twas, although he hoped the paa'ty I was meetin planned to either fly back out before mid-afternoon or stay the night. Bad weather was comin in, good gorry, yes. What Breck Pellerin referred to as '*lectrical* weather. I knew exactly what he meant, because in my nervous system that electricity already seemed to have arrived.

I went out to the runway side of the terminal and sat on a bench advertising Cormier's Market (FLY INTO OUR DELI FOR THE BEST MEATS IN MAINE). The sun was a silver button stuck on the eastern slope of a hot white sky. Headache weather, my mother would have called it, but the weather was due to change. I would hold onto the hope of that change as best I could.

At ten past ten I heard a wasp-whine from the south. At quarter past, some sort of twin-engine plane dropped out of the murk, flopped on to the runway, and taxied toward the terminal. There were only four passengers, and John Storrow was the first one off. I grinned when I saw him. I had to grin. He was wearing a black tee-shirt with WE ARE THE CHAMPIONS printed across the front and a pair of khaki shorts which displayed a perfect set of city shins: white and bony. He was trying to manage both a Styrofoam cooler and a briefcase. I grabbed the cooler maybe four seconds before he dropped it, and tucked it under my arm.

'Mike!' he cried, lifting one hand palm out.

'John!' I returned in much the same spirit (*evoe* is the word that comes immediately to the crossword aficionado's mind), and slapped

401

him five. His homely-handsome face split in a grin, and I felt a little stab of guilt. Mattie had expressed no preference for John – quite the opposite, in fact – and he really hadn't solved any of her problems; Devore had done that by topping himself before John had so much as a chance to get started on her behalf. Yet still I felt that nasty little poke.

'Come on,' he said. 'Let's get out of this heat. You have air conditioning in your car, I presume?'

'Absolutely.'

'What about a cassette player? You got one of those? If you do, I'll play you something that'll make you chortle.'

'I don't think I've ever heard that word actually used in conversation, John.'

The grin shone out again, and I noticed what a lot of freckles he had. Sheriff Andy's boy Opie grows up to serve at the bar. 'I'm a lawyer. I use words in conversation that haven't even been invented yet. You have a tape-player?'

'Of course I do.' I hefted the cooler. 'Steaks?'

'You bet. Peter Luger's. They're—'

'—the best in the world. You told me.'

As we went into the terminal, someone said, 'Michael?'

It was Romeo Bissonette, the lawyer who had chaperoned me through my deposition. In one hand he had a box wrapped in blue paper and tied with a white ribbon. Beside him, just rising from one of the lumpy chairs, was a tall guy with a fringe of gray hair. He was wearing a brown suit, a blue shirt, and a string tie with a golf-club on the clasp. He looked more like a farmer on auction day than the sort of guy who'd be a scream when you got a drink or two into him, but I had no doubt this was the private detective. He stepped over the comatose collie and shook hands with me. 'George Kennedy, Mr Noonan. I'm pleased to meet you. My wife has read every single book you ever wrote.'

'Well thank her for me.'

'I will. I have one in the car – a hardcover . . .' He looked shy, as so many people do when they get right to the point of asking. 'I wonder if you'd sign it for her at some point.'

'I'd be delighted to,' I said. 'Right away's best, then I won't forget.' I turned to Romeo. 'Good to see you, Romeo.'

'Make it Rommie,' he said. 'Good to see you, too.' He held out the box. 'George and I clubbed together on this. We thought you deserved something nice for helping a damsel in distress.'

Kennedy now *did* look like a man who might be fun after a few drinks. The kind who might just take a notion to hop on to the nearest table, turn a tablecloth into a kilt, and dance. I looked at John, who gave the kind of shrug that means hey, don't ask *me*.

I pulled off the satin bow, slipped my finger under the Scotch tape holding the paper, then looked up. I caught Rommie Bissonette in the act of elbowing Kennedy. Now they were both grinning.

'There's nothing in here that's going to jump out at me and go booga-booga, is there, guys?' I asked.

'Absolutely not,' Rommie said, but his grin widened.

Well, I can be as good a sport as the next guy. I guess. I unwrapped the package, opened the plain white box inside, revealed a square pad of cotton, lifted it out. I had been smiling all through this, but now I felt the smile curl up and die on my mouth. Something went twisting up my spine as well, and I think I came very close to dropping the box.

It was the oxygen mask Devore had had on his lap when he met me on The Street, the one he'd snorted from occasionally as he and Rogette paced me, trying to keep me out deep enough to drown. Rommie Bissonette and George Kennedy had brought it to me like the scalp of a dead enemy and I was supposed to think it was *funny*—

'Mike?' Rommie asked anxiously. 'Mike, are you okay? It was just a joke—'

I blinked and saw it wasn't an oxygen mask at all – how in God's name could I have been so stupid? For one thing, it was bigger than Devore's mask; for another, it was made of opaque rather than clear plastic. It was—

I gave a tentative chuckle. Rommie Bissonette looked tremendously relieved. So did Kennedy. John only looked puzzled.

'Funny,' I said. 'Like a rubber crutch.' I pulled out the little mike from inside the mask and let it dangle. It swung back and forth on its wire, reminding me of the waggy clock's tail.

'What the hell is it?' John asked.

'Park Avenue lawyer,' Rommie said to George, broadening his

403

accent so it came out *Paa-aak Avenew lawyah.* 'Ain't nevah seen one of these, have ya, chummy? Nossir, coss not.' Then he reverted to normalspeak, which was sort of a relief. I've lived in Maine my whole life, and for me the amusement value of burlesque Yankee accents has worn pretty thin. 'It's a Stenomask. The stenog keeping the record at Mike's depo was wearing one. Mike kept looking at him—'

'It freaked me out,' I said. 'Old guy sitting in the corner and mumbling into the Mask of Zorro.'

'Gerry Bliss freaks a lot of people out,' Kennedy said. He spoke in a low rumble. 'He's the last one around here who wears em. He's got ten or eleven left in his mudroom. I know, because I bought that one from him.'

'I hope he stuck it to you,' I said.

'I thought it would make a nice memento,' Rommie said, 'but for a second there I thought I'd given you the box with the severed hand in it – I hate it when I mix up my gift-boxes like that. What's the deal?'

'It's been a long hot July,' I said. 'Put it down to that.' I hung the Stenomask's strap over one finger, dangling it that way.

'Mattie said to be there by eleven,' John told us. 'We're going to drink beer and throw the Frisbee around.'

'I can do both of those things quite well,' George Kennedy said.

Outside in the tiny parking lot George went to a dusty Altima, rummaged in the back, and came out with a battered copy of *The Red-Shirt Man*. 'Frieda made me bring this one. She has the newer ones, but this is her favorite. Sorry about how it looks – she's read it about six times.'

'It's my favorite, too,' I said, which was true. 'And I like to see a book with mileage.' That was also true. I opened the book, looked approvingly at a smear of long-dried chocolate on the flyleaf, and then wrote: *For Frieda Kennedy, whose husband was there to lend a hand. Thanks for sharing him, and thanks for reading, Mike Noonan.*

That was a long inscription for me – usually I just stick to *Best wishes* or *Good luck*, but I wanted to make up for the curdled expression they had seen on my face when I opened their innocent little gag present. While I was scribbling, George asked me if I was working on a new novel.

404

'No,' I said. 'Batteries currently on recharge.' I handed the book back.

'Frieda won't like that.'

'No. But there's always *Red-Shirt*.'

'We'll follow you,' Rommie said, and a rumble came from deep in the west. It was no louder than the thunder which had rumbled on and off for the last week, but this wasn't dry thunder. We all knew it, and we all looked in that direction.

'Think we'll get a chance to eat before it storms?' George asked me.

'Yeah. Just about barely.'

I drove to the gate of the parking lot and glanced right to check for traffic. When I did, I saw John looking at me thoughtfully.

'What?'

'Mattie said you *were* writing, that's all. Book go tits-up on you or something?'

My Childhood Friend was just as lively as ever, in fact . . . but it would never be finished. I knew that this morning as well as I knew there was rain on the way. The boys in the basement had for some reason decided to take it back. Asking why might not be such a good idea – the answers might be unpleasant.

'Something. I'm not sure just what.' I pulled out on to the highway, checked behind me, and saw Rommie and George following in George's little Altima. America has become a country full of big men in little cars. 'What do you want me to listen to? If it's home karaoke, I pass. The last thing on earth I want to hear is you singing "Bubba Shot the Jukebox Last Night."'

'Oh, it's better than that,' he said. 'Miles better.'

He opened his briefcase, rooted through it, and came out with a plastic cassette box. The tape inside was marked 7–20–98 – yesterday. 'I love this,' he said. He leaned forward, turned on the radio, then popped the cassette into the player.

I was hoping I'd already had my quota of nasty surprises for the morning, but I was wrong.

'Sorry, I just had to get rid of another call,' John said from my Chevy's speakers in his smoothest, most lawyerly voice. I'd have bet a million dollars that his bony shins hadn't been showing when this tape was made.

There was a laugh, both smoky and grating. My stomach seized up at the sound of it. I remembered seeing her for the first time standing outside The Sunset Bar, wearing black shorts over a black tank-style swimsuit. Standing there and looking like a refugee from crash-diet hell.

'You mean you had to turn on your tape-recorder,' she said, and now I remembered how the water had seemed to change color when she nailed me that really good one in the back of the head. From bright orange to dark scarlet it had gone. And then I'd started drinking the lake. 'That's okay. Tape anything you want.'

John reached out suddenly and ejected the cassette. 'You don't need to hear this,' he said. 'It's not substantive. I thought you'd get a kick out of her blather, but . . . man, you look terrible. Do you want me to drive? You're white as a fucking sheet.'

'I can drive,' I said. 'Go on, play it. Afterward I'll tell you about a little adventure I had Friday night . . . but you're going to keep it to yourself. They don't have to know' – I jerked my thumb over my shoulder at the Altima – 'and Mattie doesn't have to know. Especially Mattie.'

He reached for the tape, then hesitated. 'You're sure?'

'Yeah. It was just hearing her again out of the blue like that. The quality of her voice. Christ, the reproduction is good.'

'Nothing but the best for Avery, McLain, and Bernstein. We have very strict protocols about what we can tape, by the way. If you were wondering.'

'I wasn't. I imagine none of it's admissible in litigation anyway, is it?'

'In certain rare cases a judge might let a tape in, but that's not why we do it. A tape like this saved a man's life four years ago, right around the time I joined the firm. That guy is now in the Witness Protection Program.'

'Play it.'

He leaned forward and pushed the button.

John: 'How is the desert, Ms Whitmore?'
Whitmore: 'Hot.'

John: 'Arrangements progressing nicely? I know how difficult times like this can—'

Whitmore: 'You know very little, counsellor, take it from me. Can we cut the crap?'

John: 'Consider it cut.'

Whitmore: 'Have you conveyed the conditions of Mr Devore's will to his daughter-in-law?'

John: 'Yes ma'am.'

Whitmore: 'Her response?'

John: 'I have none to give you now. I may have after Mr Devore's will has been probated. But surely you know that such codicils are rarely if ever accepted by the courts.'

Whitmore: 'Well, if that little lady moves out of town, we'll see, won't we?'

John: 'I suppose we will.'

Whitmore: 'When is the victory party?'

John: 'Excuse me?'

Whitmore: 'Oh please. I have sixty different appointments today, plus a boss to bury tomorrow. You're going up there to celebrate with her and her daughter, aren't you? Did you know she's invited the writer? Her fuck-buddy?'

John turned to me gleefully. 'Do you hear how pissed she sounds? She's trying to hide it, but she can't. It's eating her up inside!'

I barely heard him. I was in the zone with what she was saying (*the writer her fuck-buddy*)

and what was *under* what she was saying. Some quality beneath the words. *We just want to see how long you can swim*, she had called out to me.

John: 'I hardly think what I or Mattie's friends do is any of your business, Ms Whitmore. May I respectfully suggest that you party with your friends and let Mattie Devore party with h—'

Whitmore: 'Give him a message.'

Me. She was talking about me. Then I realized it was even more personal than that – she was talking *to* me. Her body might be on the other side of the country, but her voice and spiteful spirit were right here in the car with us.

And Max Devore's will. Not the meaningless shit his lawyers had put down on paper but his *will*. The old bastard was as dead as Damocles, but yes, he was definitely still seeking custody.

John: 'Give who a message, Ms Whitmore?'
Whitmore: 'Tell him he never answered Mr Devore's question.'
John: 'What question is that?'

Does her cunt suck?

Whitmore: 'Ask him. He'll know.'
John: 'If you mean Mike Noonan, you can ask him yourself. You'll see him in Castle County Probate Court this fall.'
Whitmore: 'I hardly think so. Mr Devore's will was made and witnessed out here.'
John: 'Nevertheless, it will be probated in Maine, where he died. My heart is set on it. And when you leave Castle County the next time, Rogette, you will do so with your education in matters of the law considerably broadened.'

For the first time she sounded angry, her voice rising to a reedy caw.

Whitmore: 'If you think—'
John: 'I don't think. I know. Goodbye, Ms Whitmore.'
Whitmore: 'You might do well to stay away from—'

There was a click, the hum of an open line, then a robot voice saying 'Nine-forty A.M. . . . Eastern Daylight . . . July . . . twentieth.' John punched EJECT, collected his tape, and stored it back in his briefcase.

'I hung up on her.' He sounded like a man telling you about his first skydive. 'I actually did. She was mad, wasn't she? Wouldn't you say she was seriously pissed?'

'Yeah.' It was what he wanted to hear but not what I really believed. Pissed, yes. *Seriously* pissed? Maybe not. Because Mattie's

408

location and state of mind hadn't been her concern; Rogette had called to talk to me. To tell me she was thinking of me. To bring back memories of how it felt to tread water with the back of your head gushing blood. To freak me out. And she had succeeded.

'What was the question you didn't answer?' John asked me.

'I don't know what she meant by that,' I said, 'but I *can* tell you why hearing her turned me a little white in the gills. If you can be discreet, and if you want to hear.'

'We've got eighteen miles to cover; lay it on me.'

I told him about Friday night. I didn't clutter my version with visions or psychic phenomena; there was just Michael Noonan out for a sunset walk along The Street. I'd been standing by a birch tree which hung over the lake, watching the sun drop toward the mountains, when they came up behind me. From the point where Devore charged me with his wheelchair to the point where I finally got back on to solid ground, I stuck pretty much to the truth.

When I finished, John was at first utterly silent. It was a measure of how thrown for a loop he was; under normal circumstances he was every bit the chatterbox Ki was.

'Well?' I asked. 'Comments? Questions?'

'Lift your hair so I can see behind your ear.'

I did as he asked, revealing a big Band-Aid and a large area of swelling. John leaned forward to study it like a little kid observing his best friend's battle-scar during recess. 'Holy shit,' he said at last.

It was my turn to say nothing.

'Those two old fucks tried to drown you.'

I said nothing.

'They tried to drown you for helping Mattie.'

Now I *really* said nothing.

'And you never reported it?'

'I started to,' I said, 'then realized I'd make myself look like a whiny little asshole. And a liar, most likely.'

'How much do you think Osgood might know?'

'About them trying to drown me? Nothing. He's just a messenger boy.'

A little more of that unusual quiet from John. After a few seconds of it he reached out and touched the lump on the back of my head.

'Ow!'

'Sorry.' A pause. 'Jesus. Then he went back to Warrington's and pulled the pin. Jesus. Michael, I never would have played that tape if I'd known—'

'It's all right. But don't even think of telling Mattie. I'm wearing my hair over my ear like that for a reason.'

'Will you *ever* tell her, do you think?'

'I might. Some day when he's been dead long enough so we can laugh about me swimming with my clothes on.'

'That might be awhile,' he said.

'Yeah. It might.'

We drove in silence for a bit. I could sense John groping for a way to bring the day back to jubilation, and loved him for it. He leaned forward, turned on the radio, and found something loud and nasty by Guns 'n Roses – welcome to the jungle, baby, we got fun and games.

'Party 'til we puke,' he said. 'Right?'

I grinned. It wasn't easy with the sound of the old woman's voice still clinging to me like light slime, but I managed. 'If you insist,' I said.

'I do,' he said. 'Most certainly.'

'John, you're a good guy for a lawyer.'

'And you're a good one for a writer.'

This time the grin on my face felt more natural and stayed on longer. We passed the marker reading TR-90, and as we did, the sun burned through the haze and flooded the day with light. It seemed like an omen of better times ahead, until I looked into the west. There, black in the bright, I could see the thunderheads building up over the White Mountains.

CHAPTER TWENTY-FIVE

For men, I think, love is a thing formed of equal parts lust and astonishment. The astonishment part women understand. The lust part they only think they understand. Very few – perhaps one in twenty – have any concept of what it really is or how deep it runs. That's probably just as well for their sleep and peace of mind. And I'm not talking about the lust of satyrs and rapists and molesters; I'm talking about the lust of shoe-clerks and high-school principals.

Not to mention writers and lawyers.

We turned into Mattie's dooryard at ten to eleven, and as I parked my Chevy beside her rusted-out Jeep, the trailer door opened and Mattie came out on the top step. I sucked in my breath, and beside me I could hear John sucking in his.

She was very likely the most beautiful young woman I have ever seen in my life as she stood there in her rose-colored shorts and matching middy top. The shorts were not short enough to be cheap (my mother's word) but plenty short enough to be provocative. Her top tied in floppy string bows across the shoulders and showed just enough tan to dream on. Her hair hung to her shoulders. She was smiling and waving. I thought, *She's made it – take her into the country-club dining room now, dressed just as she is, and she shuts everyone else down.*

'Oh Lordy,' John said. There was a kind of dismayed longing in his voice. 'All that and a bag of chips.'

'Yeah,' I said. 'Put your eyes back in your head, big boy.'

He made cupping motions with his hands as if doing just that.

411

George, meanwhile, had pulled his Altima in next to us.

'Come on,' I said, opening my door. 'Time to party.'

'I can't touch her, Mike,' John said. 'I'll melt.'

'Come on, you goof.'

Mattie came down the steps and past the pot with the tomato plant in it. Ki was behind her, dressed in an outfit similar to her mother's, only in a shade of dark green. She had the shys again, I saw; she kept one steadying hand on Mattie's leg and one thumb in her mouth.

'The guys are here! The guys are here!' Mattie cried, laughing, and threw herself into my arms. She hugged me tight and kissed the corner of my mouth. I hugged her back and kissed her cheek. Then she moved on to John, read his shirt, patted her hands together in applause, and then hugged him. He hugged back pretty well for a guy who was afraid he might melt, I thought, picking her up off her feet and swinging her around in a circle while she hung on to his neck and laughed.

'Rich lady, rich lady, rich lady!' John chanted, then set her down on the cork soles of her white shoes.

'Free lady, free lady, free lady!' she chanted back. 'The hell with rich!' Before he could reply, she kissed him firmly on the mouth. His arms rose to slip around her, but she stepped back before they could catch hold. She turned to Rommie and George, who were standing side by side and looking like fellows who might want to explain all about the Mormon Church.

I took a step forward, meaning to do the introductions, but John was taking care of that, and one of his arms managed to accomplish its mission after all – it circled her waist as he led her forward toward the men.

Meanwhile a little hand slipped into mine. I looked down and saw Ki looking up at me. Her face was grave and pale and every bit as beautiful as her mother's. Her blonde hair, freshly washed and shining, was held back with a velvet scrunchy.

'Guess the fridgeafator people don't like me now,' she said. The laughter and insouciance were gone, at least for the moment. She looked on the verge of tears. 'My letters all went bye-bye.'

I picked her up and set her in the crook of my arm as I had on the day I'd met her walking down the middle of Route 68 in

412

her bathing suit. I kissed her forehead and then the tip of her nose. Her skin was perfect silk. 'I know they did,' I said. 'I'll buy you some more.'

'Promise?' Doubtful dark-blue eyes fixed on mine.

'Promise. And I'll teach you special words like "zygote" and "bibulous." I know lots of special words.'

'How many?'

'A hundred and eighty.'

Thunder rumbled in the west. It didn't seem louder, but it was more focused, somehow. Ki's eyes went in that direction, then came back to mine. 'I'm scared, Mike.'

'Scared? Of what?'

'Of I don't know. The lady in Mattie's dress. The men we saw.' Then she looked over my shoulder. 'Here comes Mommy.' I have heard actresses deliver the line *Not in front of the children* in that exact same tone of voice. Kyra wiggled in the circle of my arms. 'Land me.'

I landed her. Mattie, John, Rommie, and George came over to join us. Ki ran to Mattie, who picked her up and then eyed us like a general surveying her troops.

'Got the beer?' she asked me.

'Yessum. A case of Bud and a dozen mixed sodas, as well. Plus lemonade.'

'Great. Mr Kennedy—'

'George, ma'am.'

'George, then. And if you call me ma'am again, I'll punch you in the nose. I'm Mattie. Would you drive down to the Lakeview General' – she pointed to the store on Route 68, about half a mile from us – 'and get some ice?'

'You bet.'

'Mr Bissonette—'

'Rommie.'

'There's a little garden at the north end of the trailer, Rommie. Can you find a couple of good-looking lettuces?'

'I think I can handle that.'

'John, let's get the meat into the fridge. As for you, Michael . . .' She pointed to the barbecue. 'The briquets are the self-lighting kind – just drop a match and stand back. Do your duty.'

'Aye, good lady,' I said, and dropped to my knees in front of her. That finally got a giggle out of Ki.

Laughing, Mattie took my hand and pulled me back on to my feet. 'Come on, Sir Galahad,' she said. 'It's going to rain. I want to be safe inside and too stuffed to jump when it does.'

In the city, parties begin with greetings at the door, gathered-in coats, and those peculiar little air-kisses (when, exactly, did *that* social oddity begin?). In the country, they begin with chores. You fetch, you carry, you hunt for stuff like barbecue tongs and oven mitts. The hostess drafts a couple of men to move the picnic table, then decides it was actually better where it was and asks them to put it back. And at some point you discover that you're having fun.

I piled briquets until they looked approximately like the pyramid on the bag, then touched a match to them. They blazed up satisfyingly and I stood back, wiping my forearm across my forehead. Cool and clear might be coming, but it surely wasn't in hailing distance yet. The sun had burned through and the day had gone from dull to dazzling, yet in the west black-satin thunderheads continued to stack up. It was as if night had burst a blood-vessel in the sky over there.

'Mike?'

I looked around at Kyra. 'What, honey?'

'Will you take care of me?'

'Yes,' I said with no hesitation at all.

For a moment something about my response – perhaps only the quickness of it – seemed to trouble her. Then she smiled. 'Okay,' she said. 'Look, here comes the ice-man!'

George was back from the store. He parked and got out. I walked over with Kyra, she holding my hand and swinging it possessively back and forth. Rommie came with us, juggling three heads of lettuce – I didn't think he was much of a threat to the guy who had fascinated Ki on the common Saturday night.

George opened the Altima's back door and brought out two bags of ice. 'The store was closed,' he said. 'Sign said WILL RE-OPEN AT 5 P.M. That seemed a little too long to wait, so I took the ice and put the money through the mail-slot.'

They'd closed for Royce Merrill's funeral, of course. Had given up almost a full day's custom at the height of the tourist season to see

414

the old fellow into the ground. It was sort of touching. I thought it was also sort of creepy.

'Can I carry some ice?' Kyra asked.

'I guess, but don't frizzicate yourself,' George said, and carefully put a five-pound bag of ice into Ki's outstretched arms.

'Frizzicate,' Kyra said, giggling. She began walking toward the trailer, where Mattie was just coming out. John was behind her and regarding her with the eyes of a gutshot beagle. 'Mommy, look! I'm frizzicating!'

I took the other bag. 'I know the icebox is outside, but don't they keep a padlock on it?'

'I am friends with most padlocks,' George said.

'Oh. I see.'

'Mike! Catch!' John tossed a red Frisbee. It floated toward me, but high. I jumped for it, snagged it, and suddenly Devore was back in my head: *What's wrong with you, Rogette? You never used to throw like a girl. Get him!*

I looked down and saw Ki looking up. 'Don't think about sad stuff,' she said.

I smiled at her, then flipped her the Frisbee. 'Okay, no sad stuff. Go on, sweetheart. Toss it to your mom. Let's see if you can.'

She smiled back, turned, and made a quick, accurate flip to her mother – the toss was so hard that Mattie almost flubbed it. Whatever else Kyra Devore might have been, she was a Frisbee champion in the making.

Mattie tossed the Frisbee to George, who turned, the tail of his absurd brown suitcoat flaring, and caught it deftly behind his back. Mattie laughed and applauded, the hem of her top flirting with her navel.

'Showoff!' John called from the steps.

'Jealousy is such an ugly emotion,' George said to Rommie Bissonette, and flipped him the Frisbee. Rommie floated it back to John, but it went wide and bonked off the side of the trailer. As John hurried down the steps to get it, Mattie turned to me. 'My boombox is on the coffee-table in the living room, along with a stack of CDs. Most of them are pretty old, but at least it's music. Will you bring them out?'

'Sure.'

I went inside, where it was hot in spite of three strategically placed fans working overtime. I looked at the grim, mass-produced furniture, and at Mattie's rather noble effort to impart some character: the van Gogh print that should not have looked at home in a trailer kitchenette but did, Edward Hopper's *Nighthawks* over the sofa, the tie-dyed curtains that would have made Jo laugh. There was a bravery here that made me sad for her and furious at Max Devore all over again. Dead or not, I wanted to kick his ass.

I went into the living room and saw the new Mary Higgins Clark on the sofa end-table with a bookmark sticking out of it. Lying beside it in a heap were a couple of little-girl hair ribbons – something about them looked familiar to me, although I couldn't remember ever having seen Ki wearing them. I stood there a moment longer, frowning, then grabbed the boombox and CDs and went back outside. 'Hey, guys,' I said. 'Let's rock.'

I was okay until she danced. I don't know if it matters to you, but it does to me. I was okay until she danced. After that I was lost.

We took the Frisbee around to the rear of the house, partly so we wouldn't piss off any funeral-bound townies with our rowdiness and good cheer, mostly because Mattie's back yard was a good place to play – level ground and low grass. After a couple of missed catches, Mattie kicked off her party-shoes, dashed barefoot into the house, and came back in her sneakers. After that she was a lot better.

We threw the Frisbee, yelled insults at each other, drank beer, laughed a lot. Ki wasn't much on the catching part, but she had a phenomenal arm for a kid of three and played with gusto. Rommie had set the boombox up on the trailer's back step, and it spun out a haze of late-eighties and early-nineties music: U2, Tears for Fears, the Eurythmics, Crowded House, A Flock of Seagulls, Ah-Hah, the Bangles, Melissa Etheridge, Huey Lewis and the News. It seemed to me that I knew every song, every riff.

We sweated and sprinted in the noon light. We watched Mattie's long, tanned legs flash and listened to the bright runs of Kyra's laughter. At one point Rommie Bissonette went head over heels, all the change spilling out of his pockets, and John laughed until he had to sit down. Tears rolled from his eyes. Ki ran over and plopped on his defenseless lap. John stopped laughing in a hurry. 'Ooof!' he

416

cried, looking at me with shining, wounded eyes as his bruised balls no doubt tried to climb back inside his body.

'Kyra *Devore*!' Mattie cried, looking at John apprehensively.

'I taggled my own quartermack,' Ki said proudly.

John smiled feebly at her and staggered to his feet. 'Yes,' he said. 'You did. And the ref calls fifteen yards for squashing.'

'Are you okay, man?' George asked. He looked concerned, but his voice was grinning.

'I'm fine,' John said, and spun him the Frisbee. It wobbled feebly across the yard. 'Go on, throw. Let's see whatcha got.'

The thunder rumbled louder, but the black clouds were all still west of us; the sky overhead remained a harmless humid blue. Birds still sang and crickets hummed in the grass. There was a heat-shimmer over the barbecue, and it would soon be time to slap on John's New York steaks. The Frisbee still flew, red against the green of the grass and trees, the blue of the sky. I was still in lust, but everything was still all right – men are in lust all over the world and damned near all of the time, and the icecaps don't melt. But she danced, and everything changed.

It was an old Don Henley song, one driven by a really nasty guitar riff.

'Oh God, I love this one,' Mattie cried. The Frisbee came to her. She caught it, dropped it, stepped on it as if it were a hot red spot falling on a nightclub stage, and began to shake. She put her hands first behind her neck and then on her hips and then behind her back. She danced standing with the toes of her sneakers on the Frisbee. She danced without moving. She danced as they say in that song – like a wave on the ocean.

> '*The government bugged the men's room*
> *in the local disco lounge,*
> *And all she wants to do is dance, dance . . .*
> *To keep the boys from selling*
> *all the weapons they can scrounge,*
> *And all she wants to do, all she wants to do is dance.*'

Women are sexy when they dance – incredibly sexy – but that wasn't what I reacted to, or how I reacted. The lust I was coping with,

417

but this was more than lust, and not copeable. It was something that sucked the wind out of me and left me feeling utterly at her mercy. In that moment she was the most beautiful thing I had ever seen, not a pretty woman in shorts and a middy top dancing in place on a Frisbee, but Venus revealed. She was everything I had missed during the last four years, when I'd been so badly off I didn't know I was missing anything. She robbed me of any last defenses I might have had. The age difference didn't matter. If I looked to people like my tongue was hanging out even when my mouth was shut, then so be it. If I lost my dignity, my pride, my sense of self, then so be it. Four years on my own had taught me there are worse things to lose.

How long did she stand there, dancing? I don't know. Probably not long, not even a minute, and then she realized we were looking at her, rapt – because to some degree they all saw what I saw and felt what I felt. For that minute or however long it was, I don't think any of us used much oxygen.

She stepped off the Frisbee, laughing and blushing at the same time, confused but not really uncomfortable. 'I'm sorry,' she said. 'I just . . . I love that song.'

'All she wants to do is dance,' Rommie said.

'Yes, sometimes that's all she wants,' Mattie said, and blushed harder than ever. 'Excuse me, I have to use the facility.' She tossed me the Frisbee and then dashed for the trailer.

I took a deep breath, trying to steady myself back to reality, and saw John doing the same thing. George Kennedy was wearing a mildly stunned expression, as if someone had fed him a light sedative and it was finally taking effect.

Thunder rumbled. This time it *did* sound closer.

I skimmed the Frisbee to Rommie. 'What do you think?'

'I think I'm in love,' he said, and then seemed to give himself a small mental shake – it was a thing you could see in his eyes. 'I also think it's time we got going on those steaks if we're going to eat outside. Want to help me?'

'Sure.'

'I will, too,' John said.

We walked back to the trailer, leaving George and Kyra to play toss. Kyra was asking George if he had ever caught any crinimals. In the kitchen, Mattie was standing beside the open fridge and stacking

418

steaks on a platter. 'Thank God you guys came in. I was on the point of giving up and gobbling one of these just the way it is. They're the most beautiful things I ever saw.'

'You're the most beautiful thing *I* ever saw,' John said. He was being totally sincere, but the smile she gave him was distracted and a little bemused. I made a mental note to myself: never compliment a woman on her beauty when she has a couple of raw steaks in her hands. It just doesn't turn the windmill somehow.

'How are you at barbecuing meat?' she asked me. 'Tell the truth, because these are way too good to mess up.'

'I can hold my own.'

'Okay, you're hired. John, you're assisting. Rommie, help me do salads.'

'My pleasure.'

George and Ki had come around to the front of the trailer and were now sitting in lawn-chairs like a couple of old cronies at their London club. George was telling Ki how he had shot it out with Rolfe Neadau and the Real Bad Gang on Lisbon Street in 1993.

'George, what's happening to your *nose*?' John asked. 'It's getting so *long*.'

'Do you mind?' George asked. 'I'm having a conversation here.'

'Mr Kennedy has caught lots of crooked crinimals,' Kyra said. 'He caught the Real Bad Gang and put them in Supermax.'

'Yes,' I said. 'Mr Kennedy also won an Academy Award for acting in a movie called *Cool Hand Luke*.'

'That's absolutely correct,' George said. He raised his right hand and crossed the two fingers. 'Me and Paul Newman. Just like that.'

'We have his pusgetti sauce,' Ki said gravely, and that got John laughing again. It didn't hit me the same way, but laughter is catching; just watching John was enough to break me up after a few seconds. We were howling like a couple of fools as we slapped the steaks on the grill. It's a wonder we didn't burn our hands off.

'Why are they laughing?' Ki asked George.

'Because they're foolish men with little tiny brains,' George said. 'Now listen, Ki – I got them all except for the Human Headcase. He jumped into his car and I jumped into mine. The details of that chase are nothing for a little girl to hear—'

George regaled her with them anyway while John and I stood

419

grinning at each other across Mattie's barbecue. 'This is great, isn't it?' John said, and I nodded.

Mattie came out with corn wrapped in aluminum foil, followed by Rommie, who had a large salad bowl clasped in his arms and negotiated the steps carefully, trying to peer over the top of the bowl as he made his way down them.

We sat at the picnic table, George and Rommie on one side, John and I flanking Mattie on the other. Ki sat at the head, perched on a stack of old magazines in a lawn-chair. Mattie tied a dishtowel around her neck, an indignity Ki submitted to only because (a) she was wearing new clothes, and (b) a dishtowel wasn't a baby-bib, at least technically speaking.

We ate hugely – salad, steak (and John was right, it really was the best I'd ever had), roasted corn on the cob, 'strewberry snortcake' for dessert. By the time we'd gotten around to the snortcake, the thunderheads were noticeably closer and there was a hot, jerky breeze blowing around the yard.

'Mattie, if I never eat a meal as good as this one again, I won't be surprised,' Rommie said. 'Thanks ever so much for having me.'

'Thank *you*,' she said. There were tears standing in her eyes. She took my hand on one side and John's on the other. She squeezed both. 'Thank you all. If you knew what things were like for Ki and me before this last week . . .' She shook her head, gave John and me a final squeeze, and let go. 'But that's over.'

'Look at the baby,' George said, amused.

Ki had slumped back in her lawn-chair and was looking at us with glazing eyes. Most of her hair had come out of the scrunchy and lay in clumps against her cheeks. There was a dab of whipped cream on her nose and a single yellow kernel of corn sitting in the middle of her chin.

'I threw the Frisbee six fousan times,' Kyra said. She spoke in a distant, declamatory tone. 'I tired.'

Mattie started to get up. I put my hand on her arm. 'Let me?'

She nodded, smiling. 'If you want.'

I picked Kyra up and carried her around to the steps. Thunder rumbled again, a long, low roll that sounded like the snarl of a huge dog. I looked up at the encroaching clouds, and as I did, movement caught my eye. It was an old blue car heading west on Wasp Hill

Road toward the lake. The only reason I noticed it was that it was wearing one of those stupid bumper-stickers from the Village Cafe: HORN BROKEN — WATCH FOR FINGER.

I carried Ki up the steps and through the door, turning her so I wouldn't bump her head. 'Take care of me,' she said in her sleep. There was a sadness in her voice that chilled me. It was as if she knew she was asking the impossible. 'Take care of me, I'm little, Mama says I'm a little guy.'

'I'll take care of you,' I said, and kissed that silky place between her eyes again. 'Don't worry, Ki, go to sleep.'

I carried her to her room and put her on her bed. By then she was totally conked out. I wiped the cream off her nose and picked the corn-kernel off her chin. I glanced at my watch and saw it was ten 'til two. They would be gathering at Grace Baptist by now. Bill Dean was wearing a gray tie. Buddy Jellison had a hat on. He was standing behind the church with some other men who were smoking before going inside.

I turned. Mattie was in the doorway. 'Mike,' she said. 'Come here, please.'

I went to her. There was no cloth between her waist and my hands this time. Her skin was warm, and as silky as her daughter's. She looked up at me, her lips parted. Her hips pressed forward, and when she felt what was hard down there, she pressed harder against it.

'Mike,' she said again.

I closed my eyes. I felt like someone who has just come to the doorway of a brightly lit room full of people laughing and talking. And dancing. Because sometimes that *is* all we want to do.

I want to come in, I thought. *That's what I want to do, all I want to do. Let me do what I want. Let me—*

I realized I was saying it aloud, whispering it rapidly into her ear as I held her with my hands going up and down her back, my fingertips ridging her spine, touching her shoulderblades, then coming around in front to cup her small breasts.

'Yes,' she said. 'What we both want. Yes. That's fine.'

Slowly, she reached up with her thumbs and wiped the wet places from under my eyes. I drew back from her. 'The key—'

She smiled a little. 'You know where it is.'

'I'll come tonight.'

421

'Good.'

'I've been . . .' I had to clear my throat. I looked at Kyra, who was deeply asleep. 'I've been lonely. I don't think I knew it, but I have been.'

'Me too. And I knew it for both of us. Kiss, please.'

I kissed her. I think our tongues touched, but I'm not sure. What I remember most clearly is the *liveness* of her. She was like a dreidel lightly spinning in my arms.

'Hey!' John called from outside, and we sprang apart. 'You guys want to give us a little help? It's gonna rain!'

'Thanks for finally making up your mind,' she said to me in a low voice. She turned and hurried back up the doublewide's narrow corridor. The next time she spoke to me, I don't think she knew who she was talking to, or where she was. The next time she spoke to me, she was dying.

'Don't wake the baby,' I heard her tell John, and his response: 'Oh, sorry, sorry.'

I stood where I was a moment longer, getting my breath, then slipped into the bathroom and splashed cold water on my face. I remember seeing a blue plastic whale in the bathtub as I turned to take a towel off the rack. I remember thinking that it probably blew bubbles out of its spout-hole, and I even remember having a momentary glimmer of an idea – a children's story about a spouting whale. Would you call him Willie? Nah, too obvious. Wilhelm, now – *that* had a fine round ring to it, simultaneously grand and amusing. Wilhelm the Spouting Whale.

I remember the bang of thunder from overhead. I remember how happy I was, with the decision finally made and the night to look forward to. I remember the murmur of men's voices and the murmur of Mattie's response as she told them where to put the stuff. Then I heard all of them going back out again.

I looked down at myself and saw a certain lump was subsiding. I remember thinking there was nothing so absurd-looking as a sexually excited man and knew I'd had this same thought before, perhaps in a dream. I left the bathroom, checked on Kyra again – rolled over on her side, fast asleep – and then went down the hall. I had just reached the living room when gunfire erupted outside. I never confused the sound with thunder. There was a moment when my mind fumbled toward the idea of backfires – some kid's hotrod – and then I knew. Part of me had been expecting something to happen . . . but it had been expecting ghosts rather than gunfire. A fatal lapse.

It was the rapid *pah! pah! pah!* of an auto-fire weapon – a Glock nine-millimeter, as it turned out. Mattie screamed – a high, drilling scream that froze my blood. I heard John cry out in pain and George Kennedy bellow, 'Down, down! For the love of Christ, *get her down*!'

Something hit the trailer like a hard spatter of hail – a rattle of punching sounds running from west to east. Something split the air in front of my eyes – I heard it. There was an almost-musical *sproing* sound, like a snapping guitar string. On the kitchen table, the salad bowl one of them had just brought in shattered.

I ran for the door and nearly dived down the cement-block steps. I saw the barbecue overturned, with the glowing coals already setting patches of the scant front-yard grass on fire. I saw Rommie Bissonette sitting with his legs outstretched, looking stupidly down at his ankle, which was soaked with blood. Mattie was on her hands and knees by the barbecue with her hair hanging in her face – it was as if she meant to sweep up the hot coals before they could cause some real trouble. John staggered toward me, holding out a hand. The arm above it was soaked with blood.

And I saw the car I'd seen before – the nondescript sedan with the joke sticker on it. It had gone up the road – the men inside making that first pass to check us out – then turned around and come back. The shooter was still leaning out the front passenger window. I could see the stubby smoking weapon in his hands. It had a wire stock. His features were a blue blank broken only by huge gaping eyesockets – a ski-mask.

Overhead, thunder gave a long, awakening roar.

George Kennedy was walking toward the car, not hurrying, kicking hot spilled coals out of his way as he went, not bothering about the dark-red stain that was spreading on the right thigh of his pants, reaching behind himself, not hurrying even when the shooter pulled back in and shouted 'Go go go!' at the driver, who was also wearing a blue mask, George not hurrying, no, not hurrying a bit, and even before I saw the pistol in his hand, I knew why he had never taken off his absurd Pa Kettle suit jacket, why he had even played Frisbee in it.

The blue car (it turned out to be a 1987 Ford registered to Mrs Sonia Belliveau of Auburn and reported stolen the day before) had pulled over on to the shoulder and had never really stopped rolling. Now it accelerated, spewing dry brown dust out from under its rear tires, fishtailing, knocking Mattie's RFD box off its post and sending it flying into the road.

George still didn't hurry. He brought his hands together, holding his gun with his right and steadying with his left. He squeezed off five deliberate shots. The first two went into the trunk – I saw the holes appear. The third blew in the back window of the departing Ford, and I heard someone shout in pain. The fourth went I don't know where. The fifth blew the left rear tire. The Ford veered to that side. The driver almost brought it back, then lost it completely. The car ploughed into the ditch thirty yards below Mattie's trailer and rolled over on its side. There was a *whumpf!* and the rear end was engulfed in flames. One of George's shots must have hit the gas-tank. The shooter began struggling to get out through the passenger window.

'Ki . . . get Ki . . . away . . .' A hoarse, whispering voice.

Mattie was crawling toward me. One side of her head – the right side – still looked all right, but the left side was a ruin. One dazed blue eye peered out from between clumps of bloody hair. Skull-fragments littered her tanned shoulder like bits of broken crockery. How I would love to tell you I don't remember any of this, how I would love to have someone else tell you that Michael Noonan died before he *saw* that, but I cannot. *Alas* is the word for it in the crossword puzzles, a four-letter word meaning to express great sorrow.

'Ki . . . Mike, get Ki . . .'

I knelt and put my arms around her. She struggled against me. She was young and strong, and even with the gray matter of her brain bulging through the broken wall of her skull she struggled against me, crying for her daughter, wanting to reach her and protect her and get her to safety.

'Mattie, it's all right,' I said. Down at the Grace Baptist Church, at the far end of the zone I was in, they were singing 'Blessed Assurance,' . . . but most of their eyes were as blank as the eye now

424

peering at me through the tangle of bloody hair. 'Mattie, stop, rest, it's all right.'

'Ki . . . get Ki . . . don't let them . . .'

'They won't hurt her, Mattie, I promise.'

She slid against me, slippery as a fish, and screamed her daughter's name, holding out her bloody hands toward the trailer. The rose-colored shorts and top had gone bright red. Blood spattered the grass as she thrashed and pulled. From down the hill there was a guttural explosion as the Ford's gas-tank exploded. Black smoke rose toward a black sky. Thunder roared long and loud, as if the sky were saying *You want noise? Yeah? I'll give you noise.*

'Say Mattie's all right, Mike!' John cried in a wavering voice. 'Oh for God's sake say she's—'

He dropped to his knees beside me, his eyes rolling up until nothing showed but the whites. He reached for me, grabbed my shoulder, then tore damned near half my shirt off as he lost his battle to stay conscious and fell on his side next to Mattie. A curd of white goo bubbled from one corner of his mouth. Twelve feet away, near the overturned barbecue, Rommie was trying to get on his feet, his teeth clenched in pain. George was standing in the middle of Wasp Hill Road, reloading his gun from a pouch he'd apparently had in his coat pocket and watching as the shooter worked to get clear of the overturned car before it was engulfed. The entire right leg of George's pants was red now. *He may live but he'll never wear that suit again,* I thought.

I held Mattie. I put my face down to hers, put my mouth to the ear that was still there and said: 'Kyra's okay. She's sleeping. She's fine, I promise.'

Mattie seemed to understand. She stopped straining against me and collapsed to the grass, trembling all over. 'Ki . . . Ki . . .' This was the last of her talking on earth. One of her hands reached out blindly, groped at a tuft of grass, and yanked it out.

'Over here,' I heard George saying. 'Get over here, motherfuck, don't you even *think* about turning your back on me.'

'How bad is she?' Rommie asked, hobbling over. His face was as white as paper. And before I could reply: 'Oh Jesus. Holy Mary Mother of God, pray for us sinners now and at the hour of our death. Blessed be the fruit of thy womb Jesus. Oh Mary born without sin, pray for us who have recourse to Thee. Oh no, oh Mike, no.' He began again, this time lapsing into Lewiston street-French, what the old folks call La Parle.

'Quit it,' I said, and he did. It was as if he had only been waiting to be told. 'Go inside and check on Kyra. Can you?'

'Yes.' He started toward the trailer, holding his leg and lurching along. With each lurch he gave a high yip of pain, but somehow he kept going. I could smell burning tufts of grass. I could smell electric rain on a rising wind. And under my hands I could feel the light spin of the dreidel slowing down as she went.

I turned her over, held her in my arms, and rocked her back and forth. At Grace Baptist the minister was now reading Psalm 139 for Royce: If I say, Surely the darkness shall cover me, even the night shall be light. The minister was reading and the Martians were listening. I rocked her back and forth in my arms under the black thunderheads. I was supposed to come to her that night, use the key under the pot and come to her. She had danced with the toes of her white sneakers on the red Frisbee, had danced like a wave on the ocean, and now she was dying in my arms while the grass burned in little clumps and the man who had fancied her as much as I had lay unconscious beside her, his right arm painted red from the short sleeve of his WE ARE THE CHAMPIONS tee-shirt all the way down to his bony, freckled wrist.

'Mattie,' I said. 'Mattie, Mattie, Mattie.' I rocked her and smoothed my hand across her forehead, which on the right side was miraculously unsplattered by the blood that had drenched her. Her hair fell over the ruined left side of her face. 'Mattie,' I said. 'Mattie, Mattie, oh Mattie.'

Lightning flashed – the first stroke I had seen. It lit the western sky in a bright blue arc. Mattie trembled strongly in my arms – all the way from neck to toes she trembled. Her lips pressed together. Her brow furrowed, as if in concentration. Her hand came up and seemed to grab for the back of my neck, as a person falling from a cliff may grasp blindly at anything to hold on just a little longer. Then it fell away and lay limply on the grass, palm up. She trembled once more – the whole delicate weight of her trembled in my arms – and then she was still.

CHAPTER TWENTY-SIX

After that, I was mostly in the zone. I came out a few times – when that scratched-out scrap of genealogy fell from inside one of my old steno books, for instance – but those interludes were brief. In a way it was like my dream of Mattie, Jo, and Sara; in a way it was like the terrible fever I'd had as a child, when I'd almost died of the measles; mostly it was like nothing but itself. It was just the zone. I was feeling it. I wish to God I hadn't been.

George came over, herding the man in the blue mask ahead of him. George was limping now, and badly. I could smell hot oil and gasoline and burning tires. 'Is she dead?' George asked. 'Mattie?'

'Yes.'

'John?'

'Don't know,' I said, and then John twitched and groaned. He was alive, but there was a lot of blood.

'Mike, listen,' George began, but before he could say more, a terrible liquid screaming began from the burning car in the ditch. It was the driver. He was cooking in there. The shooter started to turn that way, and George raised his gun. 'Move and I'll kill you.'

'You can't let him die like that,' the shooter said from behind his mask. 'You couldn't let a dog die like that.'

'He's dead already,' George said. 'You couldn't get within ten feet of that car unless you were in an asbestos suit.' He reeled on his feet. His face was as white as the spot of whipped cream I'd wiped off the end of Ki's nose. The shooter made as if to go for him and George brought the gun up higher. 'The next time you move, don't stop,'

George said, 'because I won't. Guaranteed. Now take that mask off.'

'No.'

'I'm done fucking with you, Jesse. Say hello to God.' George pulled back the hammer of his revolver.

The shooter said, 'Jesus Christ,' and yanked off his mask. It was George Footman. Not much surprise there. From behind him, the driver gave one more shriek from within the Ford fireball and then was silent. Smoke rose in black billows. More thunder roared.

'Mike, go inside and find something to tie him with,' George Kennedy said. 'I can hold him another minute – two, if I have to – but I'm bleeding like a stuck pig. Look for strapping tape. That shit would hold Houdini.'

Footman stood where he was, looking from Kennedy to me and back to Kennedy again. Then he peered down at Highway 68, which was eerily deserted. Or perhaps it wasn't so eerie, at that – the coming storms had been well forecast. The tourists and summer folk would be under cover. As for the locals . . .

The locals were . . . sort of listening. That was at least close. The minister was speaking about Royce Merrill, a life which had been long and fruitful, a man who had served his country in peace and in war, but the old-timers weren't listening to him. They were listening to *us*, the way they had once gathered around the pickle barrel at the Lakeview General and listened to prizefights on the radio.

Bill Dean was holding Yvette's wrist so tightly his fingernails were white. He was hurting her . . . but she wasn't complaining. She *wanted* him to hold on to her. Why?

'Mike!' George's voice was perceptibly weaker. 'Please, man, help me. This guy is dangerous.'

'Let me go,' Footman said. 'You'd better, don't you think?'

'In your wettest dreams, motherfuck,' George said.

I got up, went past the pot with the key underneath, went up the cement-block steps. Lightning exploded across the sky, followed by a bellow of thunder.

Inside, Rommie was sitting in a chair at the kitchen table. His face was even whiter than George's. 'Kid's okay,' he said, forcing the words. 'But she looks like waking up . . . I can't walk anymore. My ankle's totally fucked.'

I moved for the telephone.

'Don't bother,' Rommie said. His voice was harsh and trembling. 'Tried it. Dead. Storm must already have hit some of the other towns. Killed some of the equipment. Christ, I never had anything hurt like this in my life.'

I went to the drawers in the kitchen and began yanking them open one by one, looking for strapping tape, looking for clothesline, looking for any damned thing. If Kennedy passed out from blood-loss while I was in here, the other George would take his gun, kill him, and then kill John as he lay unconscious on the smoldering grass. With them taken care of, he'd come in here and shoot Rommie and me. He'd finish with Kyra.

'No he won't,' I said. 'He'll leave her alive.'

And that might be even worse.

Silverware in the first drawer. Sandwich bags, garbage bags, and neatly banded stacks of grocery-store coupons in the second. Oven mitts and potholders in the third—

'Mike, where's my Mattie?'

I turned, as guilty as a man who has been caught mixing illegal drugs. Kyra stood at the living-room end of the hall with her hair falling around her sleep-flushed cheeks and her scrunchy hung over one wrist like a bracelet. Her eyes were wide and panicky. It wasn't the shots that had awakened her, probably not even her mother's scream. I had wakened her. My thoughts had wakened her.

In the instant I realized it I tried to shield them somehow, but I was too late. She had read me about Devore well enough to tell me not to think about sad stuff, and now she read what had happened to her mother before I could keep her out of my mind.

Her mouth dropped open. Her eyes widened. She shrieked as if her hand had been caught in a vise and ran for the door.

'No, Kyra, no!' I sprinted across the kitchen, almost tripping over Rommie (he looked at me with the dim incomprehension of someone who is no longer completely conscious), and grabbed her just in time. As I did, I saw Buddy Jellison leaving Grace Baptist by a side door. Two of the men he had been smoking with went with him. Now I understood why Bill was holding so tightly to Yvette, and loved him for it – loved both of them. Something wanted him to go with Buddy and the others . . . but Bill wasn't going.

Kyra struggled in my arms, making big convulsive thrusts at the door, gasping in breath and then screaming it out again. '*Let me go, want to see Mommy, let me go, want to see Mommy, let me go—*'

I called her name with the only voice I knew she would really hear, the one I could use only with her. She relaxed in my arms little by little, and turned to me. Her eyes were huge and confused and shining with tears. She looked at me a moment longer and then seemed to understand that she mustn't go out. I put her down. She just stood there a moment, then backed up until her bottom was against the dishwasher. She slid down its smooth white front to the floor. Then she began to wail – the most awful sounds of grief I have ever heard. She understood completely, you see. I had to show her enough to keep her inside, I had to . . . and because we were in the zone together, I could.

Buddy and his friends were in a pickup truck headed this way. BAMM CONSTRUCTION, it said on the side.

'Mike!' George cried. He sounded panicky. 'You got to hurry!'

'Hold on!' I called back. 'Hold on, George!'

Mattie and the others had started stacking picnic things beside the sink, but I'm almost positive that the stretch of Formica counter above the drawers had been clean and bare when I hurried after Kyra. Not now. The yellow sugar cannister had been overturned. Written in the spilled sugar was this:

go now

'No shit,' I muttered, and checked the remaining drawers. No tape, no rope. Not even a lousy set of handcuffs, and in most well-equipped kitchens you can count on finding three or four. Then I had an idea and looked in the cabinet under the sink. When I went back out, our George was swaying on his feet and Footman was looking at him with a kind of predatory concentration.

'Did you get some tape?' George Kennedy asked.

'No, something better,' I said. 'Tell me, Footman, who actually paid you? Devore or Whitmore? Or don't you know?'

'Fuck you,' he said.

I had my right hand behind my back. Now I pointed down the hill with my left one and endeavored to look surprised. 'What the hell's Osgood doing? Tell him to go away!'

Footman looked in that direction – it was instinctive – and I hit him in the back of the head with the Craftsman hammer I'd found in the toolbox under Mattie's sink. The sound was horrible, the spray of blood erupting from the flying hair was horrible, but worst of all was the feeling of the skull giving way – a spongy collapse that came right up the handle and into my fingers. He went down like a sandbag, and I dropped the hammer, gagging.

'Okay,' George said. 'A little ugly, but probably the best thing you could have done under . . . under the . . .'

He didn't go down like Footman – it was slower and more controlled, almost graceful – but he was just as out. I picked up the revolver, looked at it, then threw it into the woods across the road. A gun was nothing for me to have right now; it could only get me into more trouble.

A couple of other men had also left the church; a carful of ladies in black dresses and veils, as well. I had to hurry on even faster. I unbuckled George's pants and pulled them down. The bullet which had taken him in the leg had torn into his thigh, but the wound looked as if it was clotting. John's upper arm was a different story – it was still pumping out blood in frightening quantities. I yanked his belt free and cinched it around his arm as tightly as I could. Then I slapped him across the face. His eyes opened and stared at me with a bleary lack of recognition.

'Open your mouth, John!' He only stared at me. I leaned down until our noses were almost touching and screamed, '*OPEN YOUR MOUTH! DO IT NOW!*' He opened it like a kid when the nurse tells him just say aahh. I stuck the end of the belt between his teeth. 'Close!' He closed. 'Now hold it,' I said. 'Even if you pass out, hold it.'

I didn't have time to see if he was paying attention. I got to my feet and looked up as the whole world went glare-blue. For a second it was like being inside a neon sign. There was a black suspended river up there, roiling and coiling like a basket of snakes. I had never seen such a baleful sky.

I dashed up the cement-block steps and into the trailer again. Rommie had slumped forward on to the table with his face in his folded arms. He would have looked like a kindergartner taking a timeout if not for the broken salad bowl and the bits of lettuce in his hair. Kyra still sat with her back to the dishwasher, weeping hysterically.

I picked her up and realized that she had wet herself. 'We have to go now, Ki.'

'I want Mattie! I want Mommy! *I want my Mattie, make her stop being hurt! Make her stop being dead!*'

I hurried across the trailer. On the way to the door I passed the end-table with the Mary Higgins Clark novel on it. I noticed the tangle of hair ribbons again – ribbons perhaps tried on before the party and then discarded in favor of the scrunchy. They were white with bright red edges. Pretty. I picked them up without stopping, stuffed them into a pants pocket, then switched Ki to my other arm.

'I want Mattie! I want Mommy! *Make her come back!*' She swatted at me, trying to make me stop, then began to buck and kick in my arms again. She drummed her fists on the side of my head. 'Put me down! Land me! Land me!'

'No, Kyra.'

'*Put me down! Land me! Land me! PUT ME DOWN!*'

I was losing her. Then, as we came out on to the top step, she abruptly stopped struggling. 'Give me Stricken! I want Stricken!'

At first I had no idea what she was talking about, but when I looked where she was pointing I understood. Lying on the walk not far from the pot with the key underneath it was the stuffed toy from Ki's Happy Meal. Strickland had put in a fair amount of outside playtime from the look of him – the light-gray fur was now dark gray with dust – but if the toy would calm her, I wanted her to have it. This was no time to worry about dirt and germs.

'I'll give you Strickland if you promise to close your eyes and not open them until I tell you. Will you promise?'

'I promise,' she said. She was trembling in my arms, and great globular tears – the kind you expect to see in fairy-tale books, never in real life – rose in her eyes and went spilling down her cheeks. I could smell burning grass and charred beefsteak. For one terrible moment I thought I was going to vomit, and then I got it under control.

Ki closed her eyes. Two more tears fell from them and on to my arm. They were hot. She held out one hand, groping. I went down the steps, got the dog, then hesitated. First the ribbons, now the dog.

432

The ribbons were probably okay, but it seemed wrong to give her the dog and let her bring it along. It seemed wrong but . . .

It's gray, Irish, the UFO voice whispered. *You don't need to worry about it because it's gray. The stuffed toy in your dream was black.*

I didn't know exactly what the voice was talking about and had no time to care. I put the stuffed dog in Kyra's open hand. She held it up to her face and kissed the dusty fur, her eyes still closed.

'Maybe Stricken can make Mommy better, Mike. Stricken a magic dog.'

'Just keep your eyes closed. Don't open them until I say.'

She put her face against my neck. I carried her across the yard and to my car that way. I put her on the passenger side of the front seat. She lay down with her arms over her head and the dirty stuffed dog clutched in one pudgy hand. I told her to stay just like that, lying down on the seat. She made no outward sign that she heard me, but I knew that she did.

We had to hurry because the old-timers were coming. The old-timers wanted this business over, wanted this river to run into the sea. And there was only one place we could go, only one place where we might be safe, and that was Sara Laughs. But there was something I had to do first.

I kept a blanket in the trunk, old but clean. I took it out, walked across the yard, and shook it down over Mattie Devore. The hump it made as it settled around her was pitifully slight. I looked around and saw John staring at me. His eyes were glassy with shock, but I thought maybe he was coming back. The belt was still clamped in his teeth; he looked like a junkie preparing to shoot up.

'Iss ant eee,' he said – *This can't be*. I knew exactly how he felt.

'There'll be help here in just a few minutes. Hang in there. I have to go.'

'Go air?'

I didn't answer. There wasn't time. I stopped and took George Kennedy's pulse. Slow but strong. Beside him, Footman was deep in unconsciousness, but muttering thickly. Nowhere near dead. It takes a lot to kill a daddy. The jerky wind blew the smoke from the overturned car in my direction, and now I could smell cooking flesh as well as barbecued steak. My stomach clenched again.

I ran to the Chevy, dropped behind the wheel, and backed out of the driveway. I took one more look – at the blanket-covered body, at the three knocked-over men, at the trailer with the line of black bulletholes wavering down its side and its door standing open. John was up on his good elbow, the end of the belt still clamped in his teeth, looking at me with uncomprehending eyes. Lightning flashed so brilliantly I tried to shield my eyes from it, although by the time my hand was up, the flash had gone and the day was as dark as late dusk.

'Stay down, Ki,' I said. 'Just like you are.'

'I can't hear you,' she said in a voice so hoarse and choked with tears that I could barely make out the words. 'Ki's takin a nap wif Stricken.'

'Okay,' I said. 'Good.'

I drove past the burning Ford and down to the foot of the hill, where I stopped at the rusty bullet-pocked stop-sign. I looked right and saw the pickup truck parked on the shoulder. BAMM CONSTRUCTION on the side. Three men crowded together in the cab, watching me. The one by the passenger window was Buddy Jellison; I could tell him by his hat. Very slowly and deliberately, I raised my right hand and gàve them the finger. None of them responded and their stony faces didn't change, but the pickup began to roll slowly toward me.

I turned left on to 68, heading for Sara Laughs under a black sky.

Two miles from where Lane Forty-two branches off the highway and winds west to the lake, there stood an old abandoned barn upon which one could still make out faded letters reading DONCASTER DAIRY. As we approached it, the whole eastern side of the sky lit up in a purple-white blister. I cried out, and the Chevy's horn honked – by itself, I'm almost positive. A thorn of lightning grew from the bottom of that light-blister and struck the barn. For a moment it was still completely there, glowing like something radioactive, and then it spewed itself in all directions. I have never seen anything even remotely like it outside of a movie theater. The thunderclap which followed was like a bombshell. Kyra screamed and slid on to the floor on the passenger side of the car with her hands clapped to her ears. She still clutched the little stuffed dog in one of them.

A minute later I topped Sugar Ridge. Lane Forty-two splits left from the highway at the bottom of the ridge's north slope. From the top I could see a wide swath of TR-90 – woods and fields and barns and farms, even a darkling gleam from the lake. The sky was as black as coal dust, flashing almost constantly with internal lightnings. The air had a clear ochre glow. Every breath I took tasted like the shavings in a tinderbox. The topography beyond the ridge stood out with a surreal clarity I cannot forget. That sense of mystery swarmed my heart and mind, that sense of the world as thin skin over unknowable bones and gulfs.

I glanced into the rearview mirror and saw that the pickup truck had been joined by two other cars, one with a V-plate that means the vehicle is registered to a combat veteran of the armed services. When I slowed down, they slowed down. When I sped up, they sped up. I doubted they would follow us any farther once I turned on to Lane Forty-two, however.

'Ki? Are you okay?'

'Sleepun,' she said from the footwell.

'Okay,' I said, and started down the hill.

I could just see the red bicycle reflectors marking my turn on to Forty-two when it began to hail – great big chunks of white ice that fell out of the sky, drummed on the roof like heavy fingers, and bounced off the hood. They began to heap in the gutter where my windshield wipers hid.

'What's happening?' Kyra cried.

'It's just hail,' I said. 'It can't hurt us.' This was barely out of my mouth when a hailstone the size of a small lemon struck my side of the windshield and then bounced high into the air again, leaving a white mark from which a number of short cracks radiated. Were John and George Kennedy lying helpless out in this? I turned my mind in that direction, but could sense nothing.

When I made the left on to Lane Forty-two, it was hailing almost too hard to see. The wheelruts were heaped with ice. The white faded out under the trees, though. I headed for that cover, flipping on my headlights as I went. They cut bright cones through the pelting hail.

As we went into the trees, that purple-white blister glowed again, and my rearview mirror went too bright to look at. There

435

was a rending, crackling crash. Kyra screamed again. I looked around and saw a huge old spruce toppling slowly across the lane, its ragged stump on fire. It carried the electrical lines with it.

Blocked in, I thought. *This end, probably the other end, too. We're here. For better or for worse, we're here.*

The trees grew over Lane Forty-two in a canopy except for where the road passed beside Tidwell's Meadow. The sound of the hail in the woods was an immense splintery rattle. Trees *were* splintering, of course; it was the most damaging hail ever to fall in that part of the world, and although it spent itself in fifteen minutes, that was long enough to ruin a season's worth of crops.

Lightning flashed above us. I looked up and saw a large orange fireball being chased by a smaller one. They ran through the trees to our left, setting fire to some of the high branches. We came briefly into the clear at Tidwell's Meadow, and as we did the hail changed to torrential rain. I could not have continued driving if we hadn't run back into the woods almost immediately, and as it was, the canopy provided just enough cover so I could creep along, hunched over the wheel and peering into the silver curtain falling through the fan of my headlights. Thunder boomed constantly, and now the wind began to rise, rushing through the trees like a contentious voice. Ahead of me, a leaf-heavy branch dropped into the road. I ran over it and listened to it thunk and scrape and roll against the Chevy's undercarriage.

Please, nothing bigger, I thought . . . or maybe I was praying. *Please let me get to the house. Please let us get to the house.*

By the time I reached the driveway the wind was howling a hurricane. The writhing trees and pelting rain made the entire world seem on the verge of wavering into insubstantial gruel. The driveway's slope had turned into a river, but I nosed the Chevy down it with no hesitation – we couldn't stay out here; if a big tree fell on the car, we'd be crushed like bugs in a Dixie cup.

I knew better than to use the brakes – the car would have heeled sideways and perhaps have been swept right down the slope toward the lake, rolling over and over as it went. Instead I dropped the transmission into low range, toed two notches into the emergency brake, and let the engine pull us down with the rain sheeting against the windshield and turning the log bulk of the house into a phantom. Incredibly, some of the lights were still on, shining like bathysphere

436

portholes in nine feet of water. The generator was working, then . . . at least for the time being.

Lightning threw a lance across the lake, green-blue fire illuminating a black well of water with its surface lashed into surging whitecaps. One of the hundred-year-old pines which had stood to the left of the railroad-tie steps now lay with half its length in the water. Somewhere behind us another tree went over with a vast crash. Kyra covered her ears.

'It's all right, honey,' I said. 'We're here, we made it.'

I turned off the engine and killed the lights. Without them I could see little; almost all the day had gone out of the day. I tried to open my door and at first couldn't. I pushed harder and it not only opened, it was ripped right out of my hand. I got out and in a brilliant stroke of lightning saw Kyra crawling across the seat toward me, her face white with panic, her eyes huge and brimming with terror. My door swung back and hit me in the ass hard enough to hurt. I ignored it, gathered Ki into my arms, and turned with her. Cold rain drenched us both in an instant. Except it really wasn't like rain at all; it was like stepping under a waterfall.

'My doggy!' Ki shrieked. Shriek or not, I could hardly hear her. I could see her face, though, and her empty hands. 'Stricken! I drop Stricken!'

I looked around and yes, there he was, floating down the macadam of the driveway and past the stoop. A little farther on, the rushing water spilled off the paving and down the slope; if Strickland went with the flow, he'd probably end up in the woods somewhere. Or all the way down to the lake.

'Stricken!' Ki sobbed. 'My *DOGGY*!'

Suddenly nothing mattered to either of us but that stupid stuffed toy. I chased down the driveway after it with Ki in my arms, oblivious of the rain and wind and brilliant flashes of lightning. And yet it was going to beat me to the slope – the water in which it was caught was running too fast for me to catch up.

What snagged it at the edge of the paving was a trio of sunflowers waving wildly in the wind. They looked like God-transported worshippers at a revival meeting: *Yes, Jeesus! Thankya Lawd!* They also looked familiar. It was of course impossible that they should be the same three sunflowers which had been growing up through the boards of the stoop in my dream (and in the photograph Bill Dean had taken before I came back), and yet it was them; beyond doubt it *was* them. Three sunflowers like the three weird sisters in *Macbeth*, three sunflowers with faces like searchlights. I had come back to Sara Laughs; I was in the zone; I had returned to my dream and this time it had possessed me.

'Stricken!' Ki bending and thrashing in my arms, both of us too slippery for safety. 'Please, Mike, *please!*'

Thunder exploded overhead like a basket of nitro. We both screamed. I dropped to one knee and snatched up the little stuffed dog. Kyra clutched it, covered it with frantic kisses. I lurched to my feet as another thunderclap sounded, this one seeming to run through the air like some crazy liquid bullwhip. I looked at the sunflowers, and they seemed to look back at me – *Hello, Irish, it's been a long time, what do you say?* Then, resettling Ki in my arms as well as I could, I turned and slogged for the house. It wasn't easy; the water in the driveway was now ankle-deep and full of melting hailstones. A branch flew past us and landed pretty much where I'd knelt to pick up Strickland. There was a crash and a series of thuds as a bigger branch struck the roof and went rolling down it.

I ran on to the back stoop, half-expecting the Shape to come rushing out to greet us, raising its baggy not-arms in gruesome good fellowship, but there was no Shape. There was only the storm, and that was enough.

Ki was clutching the dog tightly, and I saw with no surprise at all that its wetting, combined with the dirt from all those hours of outside play, had turned Strickland black. It was what I had seen in my dream after all.

Too late now. There was nowhere else to go, no other shelter from the storm. I opened the door and brought Kyra Devore inside Sara Laughs.

The central portion of Sara – the heart of the house – had stood for almost a hundred years and had seen its share of storms. The one that fell on the lakes region that July afternoon might have been the worst of them, but I knew as soon as we were inside, both of us gasping like people who have narrowly escaped drowning, that it would almost certainly withstand this one as well. The log walls were so thick it

438

was almost like stepping into some sort of vault. The storm's crash and bash became a noisy drone punctuated by thunderclaps and the occasional loud thud of a branch falling on the roof. Somewhere – in the basement, I guess – a door had come loose and was clapping back and forth. It sounded like a starter's pistol. The kitchen window had been broken by the topple of a small tree. Its needly tip poked in over the stove, making shadows on the counter and the stove-burners as it swayed. I thought of breaking it off and decided not to. At least it was plugging the hole.

I carried Ki into the living room and we looked out at the lake, black water prinked up in surreal points under a black sky. Lightning flashed almost constantly, revealing a ring of woods that danced and swayed in a frenzy all around the lake. As solid as the house was, it was groaning deeply within itself as the wind pummelled it and tried to push it down the hill.

There was a soft, steady chiming. Kyra lifted her head from my shoulder and looked around.

'You have a moose,' she said.

'Yes, that's Bunter.'

'Does he bite?'

'No, honey, he can't bite. He's like a . . . like a doll, I suppose.'

'Why is his bell ringing?'

'He's glad we're here. He's glad we made it.'

I saw her want to be happy, and then I saw her realizing that Mattie wasn't here to be happy with. I saw the idea that Mattie would never be here to be happy with glimmer in her mind . . . and felt her push it away. Over our heads something huge crashed down on the roof, the lights flickered, and Ki began to weep again.

'No, honey,' I said, and began to walk with her. 'No, honey, no, Ki, don't. Don't, honey, don't.'

'I want my mommy! *I want my Mattie!*'

I walked her the way I think you're supposed to walk babies who have colic. She understood too much for a three-year-old, and her suffering was consequently more terrible than any three-year-old should have to bear. So I held her in my arms and walked her, her shorts damp with urine and rainwater under my hands, her arms fever-hot around my neck, her cheeks slathered with snot and tears, her hair a soaked clump from our brief dash through the downpour,

439

her breath acetone, her toy a strangulated black clump that sent dirty water trickling over her knuckles. I walked her. Back and forth we went through Sara's living room, back and forth through dim light thrown by the overhead and one lamp. Generator light is never quite steady, never quite still – it seems to breathe and sigh. Back and forth through the ceaseless low chiming of Bunter's bell, like music from that world we sometimes touch but never really see. Back and forth beneath the sound of the storm. I think I sang to her and I know I touched her with my mind and we went deeper and deeper into that zone together. Above us the clouds ran and the rain pelted, dousing the fires the lightning had started in the woods. The house groaned and the air eddied with gusts coming in through the broken kitchen window, but through it all there was a feeling of rueful safety. A feeling of coming home.

At last her tears began to taper off. She lay with her cheek and the weight of her heavy head on my shoulder, and when we passed the lakeside windows I could see her eyes looking out into the silver-dark storm, wide and unblinking. Carrying her was a tall man with thinning hair. I realized I could see the dining-room table right through us. *Our reflections are ghosts already*, I thought.

'Ki? Can you eat something?'

'Not hung'y.'

'Can you drink a glass of milk?'

'No, cocoa. I cold.'

'Yes, of course you are. And I have cocoa.'

I tried to put her down and she held on with panicky tightness, scrambling against me with her plump little thighs. I hoisted her back up again, this time settling her against my hip, and she subsided.

'Who's here?' she asked. She had begun to shiver. 'Who's here 'sides us?'

'I don't know.'

'There's a boy,' she said. 'I saw him there.' She pointed Strickland toward the sliding glass door which gave on the deck (all the chairs out there had been overturned and thrown into the corners; one of the set was missing, apparently blown right over the rail). 'He was black like on that funny show me and Mattie watch. There are other black people, too. A lady in a big hat. A man in blue pants. The rest are hard to see. But they watch. They watch us. Don't you see them?'

440

'They can't hurt us.'

'Are you sure? Are you, are you?'

I didn't answer.

I found a box of Swiss Miss hiding behind the flour cannister, tore open one of the packets, and dumped it into a cup. Thunder exploded overhead. Ki jumped in my arms and let out a long, miserable wail. I hugged her, kissed her cheek.

'Don't put me down, Mike, I scared.'

'I won't put you down. You're my good girl.'

'I scared of the boy and the blue-pants man and the lady. I think it's the lady who wore Mattie's dress. Are they ghosties?'

'Yes.'

'Are they bad, like the men who chased us at the fair? Are they?'

'I don't really know, Ki, and that's the truth.'

'But we'll find out.'

'Huh?'

'That's what you thought. "But we'll find out."'

'Yes,' I said. 'I guess that's what I was thinking. Something like that.'

I took her down to the master bedroom while the water heated in the kettle, thinking there had to be *something* left of Jo's I could pop her into, but all of the drawers in Jo's bureau were empty. So was her side of the closet. I stood Ki on the big double bed where I had not so much as taken a nap since coming back, took off her clothes, carried her into the bathroom, and wrapped her in a bath towel. She hugged it around herself, shaking and blue-lipped. I used another one to dry her hair as best I could. During all of this, she never let go of the stuffed dog, which was now beginning to bleed stuffing from its seams.

I opened the medicine cabinet, pawed through it, and found what I was looking for on the top shelf: the Benadryl Jo had kept around for her ragweed allergy. I thought of checking the expiration date on the bottom of the box, then almost laughed out loud. What difference did *that* make? I stood Ki on the closed toilet seat and let her hold on around my neck while I stripped the childproof backing from four of the little pink-and-white caplets.

441

Then I rinsed out the tooth-glass and filled it with cold water. While I was doing this I saw movement in the bathroom mirror, which reflected the doorway and the master bedroom beyond. I told myself that I was only seeing the shadows of windblown trees. I offered the caplets to Ki. She reached for them, then hesitated.

'Go on,' I said. 'It's medicine.'

'What kind?' she asked. Her small hand was still poised over the little cluster of caplets.

'Sadness medicine,' I said. 'Can you swallow pills, Ki?'

'Sure. I taught myself when I was two.'

She hesitated a moment longer – looking at me and looking *into* me, I think, ascertaining that I was telling her something I really believed. What she saw or felt must have satisfied her, because she took the caplets and put them in her mouth, one after another. She swallowed them with little birdie-sips from the glass, then said: 'I still feel sad, Mike.'

'It takes awhile for them to work.'

I rummaged in my shirt drawer and found an old Harley-Davidson tee that had shrunk. It was still miles too big for her, but when I tied a knot in one side it made a kind of sarong that kept slipping off one of her shoulders. It was almost cute.

I carry a comb in my back pocket. I took it out and combed her hair back from her forehead and her temples. She was starting to look put together again, but there was still something missing. Something that was connected in my mind with Royce Merrill. That was crazy, though . . . wasn't it?

'Mike? What cane? What cane are you thinking about?'

Then it came to me. 'A candy cane,' I said. 'The kind with stripes.' From my pocket I took the two white ribbons. Their red edges looked almost raw in the uncertain light. 'Like these.' I tied her hair back in two little ponytails. Now she had her ribbons; she had her black dog; the sunflowers had relocated a few feet north, but they were there. Everything was more or less the way it was supposed to be.

Thunder blasted, somewhere close a tree fell, and the lights went out. After five seconds of dark-gray shadows, they came on again. I carried Ki back to the kitchen, and when we passed the cellar door,

442

something laughed behind it. I heard it; Ki did, too. I could see it in her eyes.

'Take care of me,' she said. 'Take care of me cause I'm just a little guy. You promised.'

'I will.'

'I love you, Mike.'

'I love you, too, Ki.'

The kettle was huffing. I filled the cup to the halfway mark with hot water, then topped it up with milk, cooling it off and making it richer. I took Kyra over to the couch. As we passed the dining-room table I glanced at the IBM typewriter and at the manuscript with the crossword-puzzle book lying on top of it. Those things looked vaguely foolish and somehow sad, like gadgets that never worked very well and now do not work at all.

Lightning lit up the entire sky, scouring the room with purple light. In that glare the laboring trees looked like screaming fingers, and as the light raced across the sliding glass door to the deck I saw a woman standing behind us, by the woodstove. She was indeed wearing a straw hat, with a brim the size of a cartwheel.

'What do you mean, the river is almost in the sea?' Ki asked.

I sat down and handed her the cup. 'Drink that up.'

'Why did the men hurt my mommy? Didn't they want her to have a good time?'

'I guess not,' I said. I began to cry. I held her on my lap, wiping away the tears with the backs of my hands.

'You should have taken some sad-pills, too,' Ki said. She held out her cocoa. Her hair ribbons, which I had tied in big sloppy bows, bobbed. 'Here. Drink some.'

I drank some. From the north end of the house came another grinding, crackling crash. The low rumble of the generator stuttered and the house went gray again. Shadows raced across Ki's small face.

'Hold on,' I told her. 'Try not to be scared. Maybe the lights will come back.' A moment later they did, although now I could hear a hoarse, uneven note in the gennie's roar and the flicker of the lights was much more noticeable.

'Tell me a story,' she said. 'Tell me about Cinderbell.'

'Cinderella.'

'Yeah, her.'

'All right, but storyguys get paid.' I pursed my lips and made sipping sounds.

She held the cup out. The cocoa was sweet and good. The sensation of being watched was heavy and not sweet at all, but let them watch. Let them watch while they could.

'There was this pretty girl named Cinderella—'

'Once upon a time! That's how it starts! That's how they all start!'

'That's right, I forgot. Once upon a time there was this pretty girl named Cinderella, who had two mean stepsisters. Their names were . . . do you remember?'

'Tammy Faye and Vanna.'

'Yeah, the Queens of Hairspray. And they made Cinderella do all the really unpleasant chores, like sweeping out the fireplace and cleaning up the dogpoop in the back yard. Now it just so happened that the noted rock band Oasis was going to play a gig at the palace, and although all the girls had been invited . . .'

I got as far as the part about the fairy godmother catching the mice and turning them into a Mercedes limousine before the Benadryl took effect. It really was a medicine for sadness; when I looked down, Ki was fast asleep in the crook of my arm with her cocoa cup listing radically to port. I plucked it from her fingers and put it on the coffee-table, then brushed her drying hair off her forehead.

'Ki?'

Nothing. She'd gone to the land of Noddy-Blinky. It probably helped that her afternoon nap had ended almost before it got started.

I picked her up and carried her down to the north bedroom, her feet bouncing limply in the air and the hem of the Harley shirt flipping around her knees. I put her on the bed and pulled the duvet up to her chin. Thunder boomed like artillery fire, but she didn't even stir. Exhaustion, grief, Benadryl . . . they had taken her deep, taken her beyond ghosts and sorrow, and that was good.

I bent over and kissed her cheek, which had finally begun to cool. 'I'll take care of you,' I said. 'I promised, and I will.'

As if hearing me, Ki turned on her side, put the hand holding Strickland under her jaw, and made a soft sighing sound. Her lashes

444

were dark soot against her cheeks, in startling contrast to her light hair. Looking at her I felt myself swept by love, shaken by it the way one is shaken by a sickness.

Take care of me, I'm just a little guy.

'I will, Ki-bird,' I said.

I went into the bathroom and began filling the tub, as I had once filled it in my sleep. She would sleep through it all if I could get enough warm water before the generator quit entirely. I wished I had a bath-toy to give her in case she did wake up, something like Wilhelm the Spouting Whale, but she'd have her dog, and she probably wouldn't wake up, anyway. No freezing baptism under a handpump for Kyra. I was not cruel, and I was not crazy.

I had only disposable razors in the medicine cabinet, no good for the other job ahead of me. Not efficient enough. But one of the kitchen steak knives would do. If I filled the washbasin with water that was really hot, I wouldn't even feel it. A letter *T* on each arm, the top bar drawn across the wrists—

For a moment I came out of the zone. A voice – my own speaking as some combination of Jo and Mattie – screamed: *What are you thinking about? Oh Mike, what in God's name are you thinking about?*

Then the thunder boomed, the lights flickered, and the rain began to pour down again, driven by the wind. I went back into that place where everything was clear, my course indisputable. Let it all end – the sorrow, the hurt, the fear. I didn't want to think anymore about how Mattie had danced with her toes on the Frisbee as if it were a spotlight. I didn't want to be there when Kyra woke up, didn't want to see the misery fill her eyes. I didn't want to get through the night ahead, the day that was coming beyond it, or the day that was coming after that. They were all cars on the same old mystery train. Life was a sickness. I was going to give her a nice warm bath and cure her of it. I raised my arms. In the medicine cabinet mirror a murky figure – a Shape – raised its own in a kind of jocular greeting. It was me. It had been me all along, and that was all right. That was just fine.

I dropped to one knee and checked the water. It was coming in nice and warm. Good. Even if the generator quit now, it would be fine. The tub was an old one, a deep one. As I walked down to the kitchen to get the knife, I thought about climbing in with her after I had finished cutting my wrists in the hotter water of the basin. No, I decided. It might be misinterpreted by the people who would come here later on, people with nasty minds and nastier assumptions. The ones who'd come when the storm was over and the trees across the road cleared away. No, after her bath I would dry her and put her back in bed with Strickland in her hand. I'd sit across the room from her, in the rocking chair by the bedroom windows. I would spread some towels in my lap to keep as much of the blood off my pants as I could, and eventually I would go to sleep, too.

Bunter's bell was still ringing. Much louder now. It was getting on my nerves, and if it kept on that way it might even wake the baby. I decided to pull it down and silence it for good. I crossed the room, and as I did a strong gust of air blew past me. It wasn't a draft from the broken kitchen window; this was that warm subway-air again. It blew the *Tough Stuff* crossword book on to the floor, but the paperweight on the manuscript kept the loose pages from following. As I looked in that direction, Bunter's bell fell silent.

A voice sighed across the dim room. Words I couldn't make out. And what did they matter? What did one more manifestation – one more blast of hot air from the Great Beyond – matter?

Thunder rolled and the sigh came again. This time, as the generator died and the lights went out, plunging the room into gray shadow, I got one word in the clear:

Nineteen.

I turned on my heels, making a nearly complete circle. I finished up looking across the shadowy room at the manuscript of *My Childhood Friend*. Suddenly the light broke. Understanding arrived.

Not the crossword book. Not the phonebook, either.

My book. My manuscript.

I crossed to it, vaguely aware that the water had stopped running into the tub in the north-wing bathroom. When the generator died, the pump had quit. That was all right, it would be plenty deep enough already. And warm. I would give Kyra her bath, but first there was something I had to do. I had to go down nineteen, and after that I just might have to go down ninety-two. And I could. I had completed just over a hundred and twenty pages of manuscript, so I could. I grabbed the battery-powered lantern from the top of the cabinet where I still kept several hundred actual vinyl records, clicked it on, and set it on the table. It cast a white circle of radiance on the manuscript – in the gloom of that afternoon it was as bright as a spotlight.

On page nineteen of *My Childhood Friend*, Tiffi Taylor – the call-girl who had reinvented herself as Regina Whiting – was sitting in her studio with Andy Drake, reliving the day that John Sanborn (the alias under which John Shackleford had been getting by) saved her three-year-old daughter, Karen. This is the passage I read as the thunder boomed and the rain slashed against the sliding door giving on the deck:

```
FRIEND, by Noonan/Pg. 19

over that way, I was sure of it,' she said, 'but
when I couldn't see her anywhere, I went to
look in the hot tub.' She lit a cigarette. 'What I
saw made me feel like screaming, Andy - Karen was
underwater. All that was out was her hand . . . the
nails were turning purple. After that . . . I guess I
dived in, but I don't remember; I was zoned out.
Everything from then on is like a dream where stuff
runs together in your mind. The yard-guy - Sanborn -
shoved me aside and dived. His foot hit me in the
throat and I couldn't swallow for a week. He yanked
up on Karen's arm. I thought he'd pull it off her
damn shoulder, but he got her. He got her.'
    In the gloom, Drake saw she was weeping. 'God.
Oh God, I thought she was dead. I was sure she was.'
```

I knew at once, but laid my steno pad along the left margin of the manuscript so I could see it better. Reading down, as you'd read a vertical crossword-puzzle answer, the first letter of each line spelled the message which had been there almost since I began the book:

owls undEr stud O

Then, allowing for the indent two lines from the bottom:

Bill Dean, my caretaker, is sitting behind the wheel of his truck. He has accomplished his two purposes in coming here – welcoming me back to the TR and warning me off Mattie Devore. Now he's ready to go. He smiles at me, displaying those big false teeth, those Roebuckers. 'If you get a chance, you ought to look for the owls,' he tells me. I ask him what Jo would have wanted with a couple of plastic owls and he replies that they keep the crows from shitting up the woodwork. I accept that, I have other things to think about, but still . . . 'It was like she'd come down to do that errand special,' he says. It never crosses my mind – not then, at least – that in Indian folklore, owls have another purpose: they are said to keep evil spirits away. If Jo knew that plastic owls would scare the crows off, she would have known that. It was just the sort of information she picked up and tucked away. My inquisitive wife. My brilliant scatterbrain.

Thunder rolled. Lightning ate at the clouds like spills of bright acid. I stood by the dining-room table with the manuscript in my unsteady hands.

'Christ, Jo,' I whispered. 'What did you find out?'

And why didn't you tell me?

But I thought I knew the answer to that. She hadn't told me because I was somehow like Max Devore; his great-grandfather and my own had shit in the same pit. It didn't make any sense, but there it was. And she hadn't told her own brother, either. I took a weird kind of comfort from that.

I began to leaf through the manuscript, my skin crawling.

Andy Drake rarely frowned in Michael Noonan's *My Childhood Friend*. He scowled instead, because there's an owl in every scowl. Before coming to Florida, John Shackleford had been living in Studio City, California. Drake's first meeting with Regina Whiting occurred in her studio. Ray Garraty's last-known address was the Studio Apartments in Key Largo. Regina Whiting's best friend was Steffie Underwood. Steffie's husband was Towle Underwood – there was a good one, two for the price of one.

Owls under studio.

It was everywhere, on every page, just like the *K*-names in the telephone book. A kind of monument, this one built – I was sure of it

– not by Sara Tidwell but by Johanna Arlen Noonan. My wife passing messages behind the guard's back, praying with all her considerable heart that I would see and understand.

On page ninety-two Shackleford was talking to Drake in the prison visitors' room – sitting with his wrists between his knees, looking down at the chain running between his ankles, refusing to make eye-contact with Drake.

FRIEND, by Noonan/Pg. 92

```
only thing I got to say. Anything else, fuck,
what good would it do? Life's a game, and I
lost. You want me to tell you that I yanked
some little kid out of the water, pulled her
up, got her motor going again? I did, but
not because I'm a hero or a saint . . .'
```

There was more but no need to read it. The message, *owls under studio*, ran down the margin just as it had on page nineteen. As it probably did on any number of other pages as well. I remembered how deliriously happy I had been to discover that the block had been dissolved and I could write again. It had been dissolved all right, but not because I'd finally beaten it or found a way around it. *Jo* had dissolved it. *Jo* had beaten it, and my continued career as a writer of second-rate thrillers had been the least of her concerns when she did it. As I stood there in the flicker-flash of lightning, feeling my unseen guests swirl around me in the unsteady air, I remembered Mrs Moran, my first-grade teacher. When your efforts to replicate the smooth curves of the Palmer Method alphabet on the blackboard began to flag and waver, she would put her large competent hand over yours and help you.

So had Jo helped me.

I riffled through the manuscript and saw the key words everywhere, sometimes placed so you could actually read them stacked on different lines, one above the other. How hard she had tried to tell me this . . . and I had no intention of doing anything else until I found out why.

I dropped the manuscript back on the table, but before I could re-anchor it, a furious gust of freezing air blew past me, lifting the

449

pages and scattering them everywhere in a cyclone. If that force could have ripped them to shreds, I'm sure that it would have.

No! it cried as I grabbed the lantern's handle. *No, finish the job!*

Wind blew around my face in chill gusts – it was as if someone I couldn't quite see was standing right in front of me and breathing in my face, retreating as I moved forward, huffing and puffing like the big bad wolf outside the houses of the three little pigs.

I hung the lantern over my arm, held my hands out in front of me, and clapped them together sharply. The cold puffs in my face ceased. There was now only the random swirling air coming in through the partially plugged kitchen window. 'She's sleeping,' I said to what I knew was still there, silently watching. 'There's time.'

I went out the back door and the wind took me at once, making me stagger sideways, almost knocking me over. And in the wavering trees I saw green faces, the faces of the dead. Devore's was there, and Royce's, and Son Tidwell's. Most of all I saw Sara's.

Everywhere Sara.

No! Go back! You don't need no truck with no owls, sugar! Go back! Finish the job! Do what you came for!

'I don't *know* what I came for,' I said. 'And until I find out, I'm not doing *anything*.'

The wind screamed as if in offense, and a huge branch split off the pine standing to the right of the house. It fell on top of my Chevrolet in a spray of water, denting the roof before rolling off on my side.

Clapping my hands out here would be every bit as useful as King Canute commanding the tide to turn. This was her world, not mine . . . and only the edge of it, at that. Every step closer to The Street and the lake would bring me closer to that world's heart, where time was thin and spirits ruled. Oh dear God, what had happened to cause this?

The path to Jo's studio had turned into a creek. I got a dozen steps down it before a rock turned under my foot and I fell heavily on my side. Lightning zigged across the sky, there was the crack of another breaking branch, and then something was falling toward me. I put my hands up to shield my face and rolled to the right, off the path. The branch splashed to the ground just behind me, and I tumbled halfway down a slope that was slick with soaked needles. At last I was able to pull myself to my feet. The branch on the path was even

450

bigger than the one which had landed on the roof of the car. If it had struck me, it likely would have bashed in my skull.

Go back! A hissing, spiteful wind through the trees.

Finish it! The slobbering, guttural voice of the lake slamming into the rocks and the bank below The Street.

Mind your business! That was the very house itself, groaning on its foundations. *Mind your business and let me mind mine!*

But Kyra *was* my business. Kyra was my daughter.

I picked up the lantern. The housing was cracked but the bulb glowed bright and steady – that was one for the home team. Bent over against the howling wind, hand raised to ward off more falling branches, I slipped and stumbled my way down the hill to my dead wife's studio.

CHAPTER TWENTY-SEVEN

At first the door wouldn't open. The knob turned under my hand so I knew it wasn't locked, but the rain seemed to have swelled the wood . . . or had something been shoved up against it? I drew back, crouched a little, and hit the door with my shoulder. This time there was some slight give.

It was her. Sara. Standing on the other side of the door and trying to hold it shut against me. How could she do that? How, in God's name? She was a fucking ghost!

I thought of the BAMM CONSTRUCTION pickup . . . and as if thought were conjuration I could almost see it out there at the end of Lane Forty-two, parked by the highway. The old ladies' sedan was behind it, and three or four other cars were now behind them. All of them with their windshield wipers flopping back and forth, their headlights cutting feeble cones through the downpour. They were lined up on the shoulder like cars at a yard sale. There was no yard sale here, only the old-timers sitting silently in their cars. Old-timers who were in the zone just like I was. Old-timers sending in the vibe.

She was drawing on them. *Stealing* from them. She'd done the same with Devore – and me too, of course. Many of the manifestations I'd experienced since coming back had likely been created from my own psychic energy. It was amusing when you thought of it.

Or maybe 'terrifying' was the word I was actually looking for.

'Jo, help me,' I said in the pouring rain. Lightning flashed, turning the torrents a bright brief silver. 'If you ever loved me, help me now.'

I drew back and hit the door again. This time there was no resistance at all and I went hurtling in, catching my shin on the jamb and falling to my knees. I held on to the lantern, though.

There was a moment of silence. In it I felt forces and presences gathering themselves. In that moment nothing seemed to move, although behind me, in the woods Jo had loved to ramble – with me or without me – the rain continued to fall and the wind continued to howl, a merciless gardener pruning its way through the trees that were dead and almost dead, doing the work of ten gentler years in one turbulent hour. Then the door slammed shut and it began. I saw everything in the glow of the flashlight, which I had turned on without even realizing it, but at first I didn't know exactly what I was seeing, other than the destruction by poltergeist of my wife's beloved crafts and treasures.

The framed afghan square tore itself off the wall and flew from one side of the studio to the other, the black oak frame breaking apart. The heads popped off the dolls poking out of the baby collages like champagne corks at a party. The hanging light-globe shattered, showering me with fragments of glass. A wind began to blow – a cold one – and was quickly joined and whirled into a cyclone by one which was warmer, almost hot. They rolled past me as if in imitation of the larger storm outside.

The Sara Laughs head on the bookcase, the one which appeared to be constructed of toothpicks and lollipop sticks, exploded in a cloud of wood-splinters. The kayak paddle leaning against the wall rose into the air, rowed furiously at nothing, then launched itself at me like a spear. I threw myself flat on the green rag rug to avoid it, and felt bits of broken glass from the shattered light-globe cut into the palm of my hand as I came down. I felt something else, as well – a ridge of something beneath the rug. The paddle hit the far wall hard enough to split into two pieces.

Now the banjo my wife had never been able to master rose in the air, revolved twice, and played a bright rattle of notes that were out of tune but nonetheless unmistakable – wish I was in the land of cotton, old times there are not forgotten. The phrase ended with a vicious BLUNK! that broke all five strings. The banjo whirled itself a

453

third time, its bright steel fittings reflecting fishscale runs of light on the study walls, and then beat itself to death against the floor, the drum shattering and the tuning pegs snapping off like teeth.

The sound of moving air began to – how do I express this? – to *focus* somehow, until it wasn't the sound of air but the sound of voices – panting, unearthly voices full of fury. They would have screamed if they'd had vocal cords to scream with. Dusty air swirled up in the beam of my flashlight, making helix shapes that danced together, then reeled apart again. For just a moment I heard Sara's snarling, smoke-broken voice: '*Git out, bitch! You git on out! This ain't none of yours*—' And then a curious insubstantial thud, as if air had collided with air. This was followed by a rushing wind-tunnel shriek that I recognized: I'd heard it in the middle of the night. Jo was screaming. Sara was hurting her, Sara was punishing her for presuming to interfere, and Jo was screaming.

'No!' I shouted, getting to my feet. 'Leave her alone! Leave her be!' I advanced into the room, swinging the lantern in front of my face as if I could beat her away with it. Stoppered bottles stormed past me – some contained dried flowers, some carefully sectioned mushrooms, some woods-herbs. They shattered against the far wall with a brittle xylophone sound. None of them struck me; it was as if an unseen hand guided them away.

Then Jo's rolltop desk rose into the air. It must have weighed at least four hundred pounds with its drawers loaded as they were, but it floated like a feather, nodding first one way and then dipping the other in the opposing currents of air.

Jo screamed again, this time in anger rather than pain, and I staggered backward against the closed door with a feeling that I had been scooped hollow. Sara wasn't the only one who could steal the energy of the living, it appeared. White semeny stuff – ectoplasm, I guess – spilled from the desk's pigeonholes in a dozen little streams, and the desk suddenly launched itself across the room. It flew almost too fast to follow with the eye. Anyone standing in front of it would have been smashed flat. There was a head-splitting shriek of protest and agony – Sara this time, I knew it was – and then the desk struck the wall, breaking through it and letting in the rain and the wind. The rolltop snapped loose of its slot and hung like a jointed tongue. All the drawers shot out. Spools of thread, skeins of yarn, little flora/fauna

454

identification books and woods guides, thimbles, notebooks, knitting needles, dried-up Magic Markers – Jo's early remains, Ki might have called them. They flew everywhere like bones and bits of hair cruelly scattered from a disinterred coffin.

'Stop it,' I croaked. 'Stop it, both of you. That's enough.'

But there was no need to tell them. Except for the furious beat of the storm, I was alone in the ruins of my wife's studio. The battle was over. At least for the time being.

I knelt and doubled up the green rag rug, carefully folding into it as much of the shattered glass from the light as I could. Beneath it was a trapdoor giving on a triangular storage area created by the slope of the land as it dropped toward the lake. The ridge I'd felt was one of the trap's hinges. I had known about this area and had meant to check it for the owls. Then things began to happen and I'd forgotten.

There was a recessed ring in the trapdoor. I grabbed it, ready for more resistance, but it swung up easily. The smell that wafted up froze me in my tracks. Not damp decay, at least not at first, but Red – Jo's favorite perfume. It hung around me for a moment and then it was gone. What replaced it was the smell of rain, roots, and wet earth. Not pleasant, but I had smelled far worse down by the lake near that damned birch tree.

I shone my light down three steep steps. I could see a squat shape that turned out to be an old toilet – I could vaguely remember Bill and Kenny Auster putting it under here back in 1990 or '91. There were steel boxes – filing cabinet drawers, actually – wrapped in plastic and stacked up on pallets. Old records and papers. An eight-track tape player wrapped in a plastic bag. An old VCR next to it, in another one. And over in the corner—

I sat down, hung my legs over, and felt something touch the ankle I had turned in the lake. I shone my light between my knees and for one moment saw a black kid. Not the one drowned in the lake, though – this one was older and quite a lot bigger. Twelve, maybe fourteen. The drowned boy had been no more than eight.

This one bared his teeth at me and hissed like a cat. There were no pupils in his eyes; like those of the boy in the lake, his eyes were entirely white, like the eyes of a statue. And he was shaking his head. *Don't come down here, white man. Let the dead rest in peace.*

455

'But you're not at peace,' I said, and shone the light full on him. I had a momentary glimpse of a truly hideous thing. I could see through him, but I could also see *into* him: the rotting remains of his tongue in his mouth, his eyes in their sockets, his brain simmering like a spoiled egg in its case of skull. Then he was gone, and there was nothing but one of those swirling dust-helixes.

I went down, holding the lantern raised. Below it, nests of shadows rocked and seemed to reach upward.

The storage area (it was really no more than a glorified crawlspace) had been floored with wooden pallets, just to keep stuff off the ground. Now water ran beneath these in a steady river, and enough of the earth had eroded to make even crawling unsteady work. The smell of perfume was entirely gone. What had replaced it was a nasty riverbottom smell and – unlikely given the conditions, I know, but it was there – the faint, sullen smell of ash and fire.

I saw what I'd come for almost at once. Jo's mail-order owls, the ones she had taken delivery of herself in November of 1993, were in the northeast corner, where there were only about two feet between the sloped pallet flooring and the underside of the studio. *Gorry, but they looked real,* Bill had said, and Gorry if he wasn't right: in the bright glow of the lantern they looked like birds first swaddled, then suffocated in clear plastic. Their eyes were bright wedding rings circling wide black pupils. Their plastic feathers were painted the dark green of pine needles, their bellies a shade of dirty orange-white. I crawled toward them over the squelching, shifting pallets, the glow of the lantern bobbing back and forth between them, trying not to wonder if that boy was behind me, creeping in pursuit. When I got to the owls, I raised my head without thinking and thudded it against the insulation which ran beneath the studio floor. *Thump once for yes, twice for no, asshole,* I thought.

I hooked my fingers into the plastic which wrapped the owls and pulled them toward me. I wanted to be out of here. The sensation of water running just beneath me was strange and unpleasant. So was the smell of fire, which seemed stronger now in spite of the damp. Suppose the studio was burning? Suppose Sara had somehow set it alight? I'd roast down here even while the storm's muddy runoff was soaking my legs and belly.

456

One of the owls stood on a plastic base, I saw – the better to set him on your deck or stoop to scare the crows, my dear – but the base the other should have been attached to was missing. I backed toward the trapdoor, holding the lantern in one hand and dragging the plastic sack of owls in the other, wincing each time thunder cannonaded over my head. I'd gotten only a little way when the damp tape holding the plastic gave way. The owl missing its base tilted slowly toward me, its black-gold eyes staring raptly into my own.

A swirl of air. A faint, comforting whiff of Red perfume. I pulled the owl out by the hornlike tufts growing from its forehead and turned it upside down. Where it had once been attached to its plastic base there were now only two pegs with a hollow space between them. Inside the hole was a small tin box that I recognized even before I reached into the owl's belly and chivvied it out. I shone the lantern on its front, knowing what I'd see: JO'S NOTIONS, written in old-fashioned gilt script. She had found the box in an antiques barn somewhere.

I looked at it, my heart beating hard. Thunder boomed overhead. The trapdoor stood open, but I had forgotten about going up. I had forgotten about everything but the tin box I held in my hand, a box roughly the size of a cigar box but not quite as deep. I spread my hand over the cover and pulled it off.

There was a strew of folded papers lying on top of a pair of steno books, the wirebound ones I keep around for notes and character lists. These had been rubber-banded together. On top of everything else was a shiny black square. Until I picked it up and held it close to the side of the lantern, I didn't realize it was a photo negative.

Ghostly, reversed and faintly orange, I saw Jo in her gray two-piece bathing suit. She was standing on the swimming float with her hands behind her head.

'Jo,' I said, and then couldn't say anything else. My throat had closed up with tears. I held the negative for a moment, not wanting to lose contact with it, then put it back in the box with the papers and steno books. This stuff was why she had come to Sara in July of 1994; to gather it up and hide it as well as she could. She had taken the owls off the deck (Frank had heard the door out there bang) and had carried them out here. I could almost see her prying the base off one owl and stuffing the tin box up its plastic wazoo, wrapping both of them in plastic, then dragging them down here, all while her brother sat smoking Marlboros and feeling the vibrations. The bad vibrations. I doubted if I would ever know all the reasons why she'd done it, or what her frame of mind had been . . . but she had almost certainly believed I'd find my own way down here eventually. Why else had she left the negative?

The loose papers were mostly photocopied press clippings from the *Castle Rock Call* and from the *Weekly News*, the paper which had apparently preceded the *Call*. The dates were marked on each in my wife's neat, firm hand. The oldest clipping was from 1865, and was headed **ANOTHER HOME SAFE**. The returnee was one Jared Devore, age thirty-two. Suddenly I understood one of the things that had puzzled me: the generations which didn't seem to match up. A Sara Tidwell song came to mind as I crouched there on the pallets with my lantern shining down on that old-timey type. It was the ditty that went *The old folks do it and the young folks, too/And the old folks show the young folks just what to do* . . .

By the time Sara and the Red-Tops showed up in Castle County and settled on what became known as Tidwell's Meadow, Jared Devore would have been sixty-seven or -eight. Old but still hale. A veteran of the Civil War. The sort of older man younger men might look up to. And Sara's song was right – the old folks show the young folks just what to do.

What exactly had they done?

The clippings about Sara and the Red-Tops didn't tell. I only skimmed them, anyway, but the overall tone shook me, just the same. I'd describe it as unfailing genial contempt. The Red-Tops were 'our Southern blackbirds' and 'our rhythmic darkies.' They were 'full of dusky good-nature.' Sara herself was 'a marvellous figure of a Negro woman with broad nose, full lips, and noble brow' who 'fascinated men-folk and women-folk alike with her animal high spirits, flashing smile, and raucous laugh.'

They were, God keep us and save us, reviews. Good ones, if you didn't mind being called full of dusky good-nature.

I shuffled through them quickly, looking for anything about the circumstances under which 'our Southern blackbirds' had left. I found nothing. What I found instead was a clipping from the *Call* marked

458

19th July (*go down nineteen*, I thought) 1933. The headline read **VETERAN GUIDE, CARETAKER, CANNOT SAVE DAUGHTER**. According to the story, Fred Dean had been fighting the wildfires in the eastern part of the TR with two hundred other men when the wind had suddenly changed, menacing the north end of the lake, which had previously been considered safe. At that time a great many local people had kept fishing and hunting camps up there (this much I knew myself). The community had had a general store and an actual name, Halo Bay. Fred's wife, Hilda, was there with the Dean twins, William and Carla, age three, while her husband was off eating smoke. A good many other wives and kids were in Halo Bay, as well.

The fires had come fast when the wind changed, the paper said – 'like marching explosions.' They jumped the only firebreak the men had left in that direction and headed for the far end of the lake. At Halo Bay there were no men to take charge, and apparently no women able or willing to do so. They panicked instead, racing to load their cars with children and camp possessions, clogging the one road out with their vehicles. Eventually one of the old cars or trucks broke down and as the fires roared closer, running through woods that hadn't seen rain since late April, the women who'd waited found their way out blocked.

The volunteer firefighters came to the rescue in time, but when Fred Dean got to his wife, one of a party of women trying to push a balky stalled Ford coupe out of the road, he made a terrible discovery. Billy lay on the floor in the back of the car, fast asleep, but Carla was missing. Hilda had gotten them both in, all right – they had been on the back seat, holding hands just as they always did. But at some point, after her brother had crawled on to the floor and dozed off and while Hilda was stuffing a few last items into the trunk, Carla must have remembered a toy or a doll and returned to the cottage to get it. While she was doing that, her mother had gotten into their old DeSoto and driven away without rechecking the babies. Carla Dean was either still in the cottage at Halo Bay or making her way up the road on foot. Either way the fires would run her down.

The road was too narrow to get a vehicle turned around and too blocked to get one of those pointed in the right direction through the crush. So Fred Dean, hero that he was, set off on the run toward the smoke-blackened horizon, where bright ribbons of orange had already begun to shine through. The wind-driven fire had crowned and raced to meet him like a lover.

I knelt on the pallets, reading this by the glow of my lantern, and all at once the smell of fire and burning intensified. I coughed . . . and then the cough was choked off by the iron taste of water in my mouth and throat. Once again, this time kneeling in the storage area beneath my wife's studio, I felt as if I were drowning. Once again I leaned forward and retched up nothing but a little spit.

I turned and saw the lake. The loons were screaming on its hazy surface, making their way toward me in a line, beating their wings against the water as they came. The blue of the sky had been blotted out. The air smelled of charcoal and gunpowder. Ash had begun to sift down from the sky. The eastern verge of Dark Score was in flames, and I could hear occasional muffled reports as hollow trees exploded. They sounded like depth charges.

I looked down, wanting to break free of this vision, knowing that in another moment or two it wouldn't be anything so distant as a vision but as real as the trip Kyra and I had made to the Fryeburg Fair. Instead of a plastic owl with gold-ringed eyes, I was looking at a child with bright blue ones. She was sitting on a picnic table, holding out her chubby arms and crying. I saw her as clearly as I saw my own face in the mirror each morning when I shaved. I saw she was about

Kyra's age but much plumper, and her hair is black instead of blonde. Her hair is the shade her brother's will remain until it finally begins to go gray in the impossibly distant summer of 1998, a year she will never see unless someone gets her out of this hell. She wears a white dress and red stockings and she holds her arms out to me, calling Daddy, Daddy.

I start toward her and then there is a blast of organized heat that tears me apart for a moment – I am the ghost here, I realize, and Fred Dean has just run right through me. Daddy, *she cries, but to him, not me.* Daddy! *and she hugs him, unmindful of the soot smearing her white silk dress and her chubby face as he kisses her and more soot begins to fall and the loons beat their way in toward shore, seeming to weep in shrill lamentation.*

Daddy the fire is coming! *she cries as he scoops her into his arms.*

I know, be brave, *he says*. We're gonna be all right, sugarplum, but you have to be brave.

The fire isn't just coming; it has come. The entire east end of Halo Bay is in flames and now they're moving this way, eating one by one the little cabins where the men like to lay up drunk in hunting season and ice-fishing season. Behind Al LeRoux's, the washing Marguerite hung out that morning is in flames, pants and dresses and underwear burning on lines which are themselves strings of fire. Leaves and bark shower down; a burning ember touches Carla's neck and she shrieks with pain. Fred slaps it away as he carries her down the slope of land to the water.

Don't do it! *I scream. I know all this is beyond my power to change, but I scream at him anyway, try to change it anyway.* Fight it! For Christ's sake, fight it!

Daddy, who is that man? *Carla asks, and points at me as the green-shingled roof of the Dean place catches fire.*

Fred glances toward where she is pointing, and in his face I see a spasm of guilt. He knows what he's doing, that's the terrible thing — way down deep he knows exactly what he is doing here at Halo Bay where The Street ends. He knows and he's afraid that someone will witness his work. But he sees nothing.

Or does he? There is a momentary doubtful widening of the eyes as if he does spy something — a dancing helix of air, perhaps. Or does he feel me? Is that it? Does he feel a momentary cold draft in all this heat? One that feels like protesting hands, hands that would restrain if they only had substance? Then he looks away; then he is wading into the water beside the Deans' stub of a dock.

Fred! *I scream.* For God's sake, man, look at her! Do you think your wife put her in a white silk dress by accident? Is that anyone's idea of a play-dress?

Daddy, why are we going in the water? *she asks.*

To get away from the fire, sugarplum.

Daddy, I can't swim!

You won't have to, *he replies, and what a chill I feel at that! Because it's no lie — she won't have to swim, not now, not ever. And at least Fred's way will be more merciful than Normal Auster's when Normal's turn comes — more merciful than the squalling handpump, the gallons of freezing water.*

Her white dress floats around her like a lily. Her red stockings shimmer

461

in the water. She hugs his neck tightly and now they are among the fleeing loons; the loons spank the water with their powerful wings, churning up curds of foam and staring at the man and the girl with their distraught red eyes. The air is heavy with smoke and the sky is gone. I stagger after them, wading – I can feel the cold of the water, although I don't splash and leave no wake. The eastern and northern edges of the lake are both on fire now – there is a burning crescent around us as Fred Dean wades deeper with his daughter, carrying her as if to some baptismal rite. And still he tells himself he is trying to save her, only to save her, just as all her life Hilda will tell herself that the child just wandered back to the cottage to look for a toy, that she was not left behind on purpose, left in her white dress and red stockings to be found by her father, who once did something unspeakable. This is the past, this is the Land of Ago, and here the sins of the fathers are visited on the children, even unto the seventh generation, which is not yet.

He takes her deeper and she begins to scream. Her screams mingle with the screams of the loons until he stops the sound with a kiss upon her terrified mouth. 'Love you, Daddy loves his sugarplum,' he says, and then lowers her. It is to be a full-immersion baptism, then, except there is no shorebank choir singing 'Shall We Gather at the River' and no one shouting Hallelujah! *and he is not letting her come back up. She struggles furiously in the white bloom of her sacrificial dress, and after a moment he cannot bear to watch her; he looks across the lake instead, to the west where the fire hasn't yet touched (and never will), to the west where skies are still blue. Ash sifts around him like black rain and the tears pour out of his eyes and as she struggles furiously beneath his hands, trying to free herself from his drowning grip, he tells himself* It was an accident, just a terrible accident, I took her out in the lake because it was the only place I *could* take her, the only place left, and she panicked, she started to struggle, she was all wet and all slippery and I lost my good hold on her and then I lost *any* hold on her and then—

I forget I'm a ghost. I scream 'Kia! Hold on, Ki!' and dive. I reach her, I see her terrified face, her bulging blue eyes, her rosebud of a mouth which is trailing a silver line of bubbles toward the surface where Fred stands in water up to his neck, holding her down while he tells himself over and over that he was trying to save her, it was the only way, he was trying to save her, it was the only way. I reach for her, again and again I reach for her, my child, my daughter, my Kia (they are all Kia, the boys as well as the girls,

462

all my daughter), and each time my arms go through her. Worse — oh, far worse — is that now she is reaching for 'me,' her dappled arms floating out, begging for rescue. Her groping hands melt through mine. We cannot touch, because now I am the ghost. I am the ghost and as her struggles weaken I realize that I can't I can't oh I

couldn't breathe — I was drowning.

I doubled over, opened my mouth, and this time a great spew of lakewater came out, soaking the plastic owl which lay on the pallet by my knees. I hugged the JO'S NOTIONS box to my chest, not wanting the contents to get wet, and the movement triggered another retch. This time cold water poured from my nose as well as my mouth. I dragged in a deep breath, then coughed it out.

'This has got to end,' I said, but of course this *was* the end, one way or the other. Because Kyra was last.

I climbed up the steps to the studio and sat on the littered floor to get my breath. Outside, the thunder boomed and the rain fell, but I thought the storm had passed its peak of fury. Or maybe I only hoped.

I rested with my legs hanging down through the trap — there were no more ghosts here to touch my ankles, I don't know how I knew that but I did — and stripped off the rubber bands holding the steno notebooks together. I opened the first one, paged through it, and saw it was almost filled with Jo's handwriting and a number of folded typed sheets, (Courier type, of course), single-spaced: the fruit of all those clandestine trips down to the TR during 1993 and 1994. Fragmentary notes, for the most part, and transcriptions of tapes which might still be down below me in the storage space somewhere. Tucked away with the VCR or the eight-track player, perhaps. But I didn't need them. When the time came — *if* the time came — I was sure I'd find most of the story here. What had happened, who had done it, how it was covered up. Right now I didn't care. Right now I only wanted to make sure that Kyra was safe and stayed safe. There was only one way to do that.

Lye stille.

I attempted to slip the rubber bands around the steno books again, and the one I hadn't looked at slipped out of my wet hand and fell to the floor. A torn slip of green paper fell out. I picked it up and saw this:

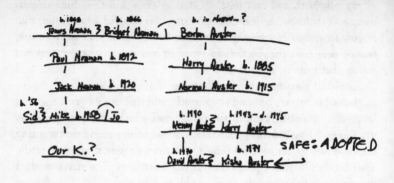

For a moment I came out of that strange and heightened awareness I'd been living in; the world fell back into its accustomed dimensions. But the colors were all too strong, somehow, objects too emphatically *present*. I felt like a battlefield soldier suddenly illuminated by a ghastly white flare, one that shows everything.

My father's people had come from The Neck, I had been right about that much; my great-grandfather according to this was James Noonan, and he had never shit in the same pit as Jared Devore. Max Devore had either been lying when he said that to Mattie . . . or misinformed . . . or simply confused, the way folks often get confused when they reach their eighties. Even a fellow like Devore, who had stayed mostly sharp, wouldn't have been exempt from the occasional nick in his edge. And he hadn't been that far off at that. Because, according to this little scratch of a chart, my great-grandfather had had an older sister, Bridget. And Bridget had married – Benton Auster.

My finger dropped down a line, to Harry Auster. Born of Benton and Bridget Noonan Auster in the year 1885.

'Christ Jesus,' I whispered. 'Kenny Auster's grandfather was the son of my great-grandfather's sister. And he was one of them. Whatever they did, Harry Auster was one of them. That's the connection.'

I thought of Kyra with sudden sharp terror. She had been up at the house by herself for nearly an hour. How could I have been so stupid? Anyone could have come in while I was under the studio. Sara could have used anyone to—

I realized that wasn't true. The murderers and the child victims had all been linked by blood, and now that blood had thinned, that river had almost reached the sea. There was Bill Dean, but he was staying well away from Sara Laughs. There was Kenny Auster, but Kenny had taken himself and his family off to Taxachusetts. And Ki's closest blood relations – mother, father, grandfather – were all dead.

Only I was left. Only I was blood. Only I could do it. Unless—

I bolted back up to the house as fast as I could, slipping and sliding my way along the soaked path, desperate to make sure she was all right. I didn't think Sara could hurt Kyra herself, no matter how much of that old-timer vibe she had to draw on . . . but what if I was wrong?

What if I was wrong?

465

CHAPTER TWENTY-EIGHT

Ki lay fast asleep just as I had left her, on her side with the filthy little stuffed dog clutched under her jaw. It had put a smudge on her neck but I hadn't the heart to take it away from her. Beyond her and to the left, through the open bathroom door, I could hear the steady *plink-plonk-plink* of water falling from the faucet and into the tub. Cool air blew around me in a silky twist, caressing my cheeks, sending a not unpleasurable shiver up my back. In the living room Bunter's bell gave a dim little shake.

Water's still warm, sugar, Sara whispered. *Be her friend, be her daddy. Go on, now. Do what I want. Do what we both want.*

And I *did* want to, which had to be why Jo at first tried to keep me away from the TR and from Sara Laughs. Why she'd made a secret of her possible pregnancy, as well. It was as if I had discovered a vampire inside me, a creature with no interest in what it thought of as talk-show conscience and op-ed page morality. A part that wanted only to take Ki into the bathroom and dunk her into that tub of warm water and hold her under, watching the red-edged white ribbons shimmer the way Carla Dean's white dress and red stockings had shimmered while the woods burned all around her and her father. A part of me would be more than glad to pay the last installment on that old bill.

'Dear God,' I muttered, and wiped my face with a shaking hand. 'She knows so many tricks. And she's so fucking *strong*.'

The bathroom door tried to swing shut against me before I could go through, but I pushed it open against hardly any resistance. The medicine-cabinet door banged back, and the glass shattered against

466

the wall. The stuff inside flew out at me, but it wasn't a very dangerous attack; this time most of the missiles consisted of toothpaste tubes, toothbrushes, plastic bottles, and a few old Vick's inhalers. Faint, very faint, I could hear her shouting in frustration as I yanked the plug at the bottom of the tub and let the water start gurgling out. There had been enough drowning on the TR for one century, by God. And yet, for a moment I felt an incredibly strong urge to put the plug back in while the water was still deep enough to do the job. Instead I tore it off its chain and threw it down the hall. The medicine-cabinet door clapped shut again and the rest of the glass fell out.

'How many have you had?' I asked her. 'How many besides Carla Dean and Kerry Auster and our Kia? Two? Three? Five? How many do you need before you can rest?'

All of them! the answer shot back. It wasn't just Sara's voice, either; it was my own, as well. She'd gotten into me, had snuck in by way of the basement like a burglar . . . and already I was thinking that even if the tub was empty and the water-pump temporarily dead, there was always the lake.

All of them! the voice cried again. *All of them, sugar!*

Of course – only all of them would do. Until then there would be no rest for Sara Laughs.

'I'll help you to rest,' I said. 'That I promise.'

The last of the water swirled away . . . but there was always the lake, always the lake if I changed my mind. I left the bathroom and looked in on Ki again. She hadn't moved, the sensation that Sara was in here with me had gone, Bunter's bell was quiet . . . and yet I felt uneasy, unwilling to leave her alone. I had to, though, if I was to finish my work, and I would do well not to linger. County and State cops would be along eventually, storm or no storm, downed trees or no downed trees.

Yes, but . . .

I stepped into the hall and looked uneasily around. Thunder boomed, but it was losing some of its urgency. So was the wind. What wasn't fading was the sense of something watching me, something that was not-Sara. I stood where I was a moment or two longer, trying to tell myself it was just the sizzle of my overcooked nerves, then walked down the hall to the entry.

I opened the door to the stoop . . . then looked around again sharply, as if expecting to see someone or something lurking behind the far end of the bookcase. A Shape, perhaps. Something that still wanted its dust-catcher. But I was the only Shape left, at least in this part of the world, and the only movement I saw was ripple-shadows thrown by the rain rolling down the windows.

It was still coming down hard enough to re-drench me as I crossed my stoop to the driveway, but I paid no attention. I had just been with a little girl when she drowned, had damned near drowned myself not so long ago, and the rain wasn't going to stop me from doing what I had to do. I picked up the fallen branch which had dented the roof of my car, tossed it aside, and opened the Chevy's rear door.

The things I'd bought at Slips 'n Greens were still sitting on the back seat, still tucked into the cloth carry-handle bag Lila Proulx had given me. The trowel and the pruning knife were visible, but the third item was in a plastic sack. *Want this one in a special bag?* Lila had asked me. *Always safe, never sorry.* And later, as I was leaving, she had spoken of Kenny's dog Blueberry chasing seagulls and had given out with a big, hearty laugh. Her eyes hadn't laughed, though. Maybe that's how you tell the Martians from the Earthlings – the Martians can never laugh with their eyes.

I saw Rommie and George's present lying on the front seat: the Stenomask I'd at first mistaken for Devore's oxygen mask. The boys in the basement spoke up then – murmured, at least – and I leaned over the seat to grab the mask by its elastic strap without the slightest idea of why I was doing so. I dropped it into the carry-bag, slammed the car door, then started down the railroad-tie steps to the lake. On the way I paused to duck under the deck, where we had always kept a few tools. There was no pick, but I grabbed a spade that looked up to a piece of gravedigging. Then, for what I thought would be the last time, I followed the course of my dream down to The Street. I didn't need Jo to show me the spot; the Green Lady had been pointing to it all along. Even had she not been, and even if Sara Tidwell did not still stink to the heavens, I think I would have known. I think I would have been led there by my own haunted heart.

There was a man standing between me and the place where the gray forehead of rock guarded the path, and as I paused on the

468

last railroad-tie, he hailed me in a rasping voice that I knew all too well.

'Say there, whoremaster, where's your whore?'

He stood on The Street in the pouring rain, but his cutters' outfit – green flannel pants, checked wool shirt – and his faded blue Union Army cap were dry, because the rain was falling through him rather than on him. He looked solid but he was no more real than Sara herself. I reminded myself of this as I stepped down on to the path to face him, but my heart continued to speed up, thudding in my chest like a padded hammer.

He was dressed in Jared Devore's clothes, but this wasn't Jared Devore. This was Jared's great-grandson Max, who had begun his career with an act of sled-theft and ended it in suicide . . . but not before arranging for the murder of his daughter-in-law, who'd had the temerity to refuse him what he had so dearly wanted.

I started toward him and he moved to the center of the path to block me. I could feel the cold baking off him. I am saying exactly what I mean, expressing what I remember as clearly as I can: I could feel the cold baking off him. And yes, it was Max Devore all right, but got up like a logger at a costume party and looking the way he must have around the time his son Lance was born. Old but hale. The sort of man younger men might well look up to. And now, as if the thought had called them, I could see the rest shimmer into faint being behind him, standing in a line across the path. These were the ones who had been with Jared at the Fryeburg Fair, and now I knew who some of them were. Fred Dean, of course, only nineteen years old in '01, the drowning of his daughter still over thirty years away. And the one who had reminded me of myself was Harry Auster, the firstborn of my great-grandfather's sister. He would have been sixteen, barely old enough to raise a fuzz but old enough to work in the woods with Jared. Old enough to shit in the same pit as Jared. To mistake Jared's poison for wisdom. One of the others twisted his head and squinted at the same time – I'd seen that tic before. Where? Then it came to me: in the Lakeview General. This young man was the late Royce Merrill's father. The others I didn't know. Nor did I care to.

'You ain't a-passing by us,' Devore said. He held up both hands. 'Don't even think about trying. Am I right, boys?'

They murmured growling agreement – the sort you could hear coming from any present-day gang of headbangers or taggers, I imagine – but their voices were distant; actually more sad than menacing. There was some substance to the man in Jared Devore's clothes, perhaps because in life he had been a man of enormous vitality, perhaps because he was so recently dead, but the others were little more than projected images.

I started forward, moving into that baking cold, moving into the smell of him – the same invalid odors which had surrounded him when I'd met him here before.

'Where do you think you're going?' he cried.

'For a constitutional,' I said. 'And no law against it. The Street's the place where good pups and vile dogs can walk side by side. You said so yourself.'

'You don't understand,' Max-Jared said. 'You never will. You're not of that world. That was our world.'

I stopped, looking at him curiously. Time was short, I wanted to be done with this . . . but I had to know, and I thought Devore was ready to tell me.

'*Make* me understand,' I said. 'Convince me that any world was your world.' I looked at him, then at the flickering, translucent figures behind him, gauze flesh heaped on shining bones. 'Tell me what you did.'

'It was all different then,' Devore said. 'When *you* come down here, Noonan, you might walk all three miles north to Halo Bay and see only a dozen people on The Street. After Labor Day you might not see anyone at all. This side of the lake you have to walk through the bushes that are growing up wild and around the fallen trees – there'll be even more of em after this storm – and even a deadfall or two because nowadays the townfolk don't club together to keep it neat the way they used to. But in our time—! The woods were bigger then, Noonan, distances were farther to go, and neighboring meant something. Life itself, often enough. Back then this really *was* a street. Can you see?'

I could. If I looked through the phantom shapes of Fred Dean and Harry Auster and the others, I could. They weren't just ghosts; they were shimmerglass windows on another age. I saw

a summer afternoon in the year of . . . 1898? Perhaps 1902? 1907?

470

Doesn't matter. This is a period when all time seems the same, as if time had stopped. This is a time the old-timers remember as a kind of golden age. It is the Land of Ago, the Kingdom of When-I-Was-a-Boy. The sun washes everything with the fine gold light of endless late July; the lake is as blue as a dream, netted with a billion sparks of reflected light. And The Street! It is as smoothly grassed as a lawn and as broad as a boulevard. It is a boulevard, I see, a place where the community fully realizes itself. It is the main conduit of communication, the chief cable in a township crisscrossed with them. I'd felt the existence of these cables all along – even when Jo was alive I felt them under the surface, and here is their point of origin. Folks promenade on The Street, all up and down the east side of Dark Score Lake they promenade in little groups, laughing and conversing under a cloud-stacked summer sky, and this is where the cables all begin. I look and realize how wrong I have been to think of them as Martians, as cruel and calculating aliens. East of their sunny promenade looms the darkness of the woods, glades and hollows where any miserable thing may await, from a foot lopped off in a logging accident to a birth gone wrong and a young mother dead before the doctor can arrive from Castle Rock in his buggy. These are people with no electricity, no phones, no County Rescue Unit, no one to rely upon but each other and a God some of them have already begun to mistrust. They live in the woods and the shadows of the woods, but on fine summer afternoons they come to the edge of the lake. They come to The Street and look in one another's faces and laugh together and then they are truly on the TR – in what I have come to think of as the zone. They are not Martians; they are little lives dwelling on the edge of the dark, that's all.

I see summer people from Warrington's, the men dressed in white flannels, two women in long tennis dresses still carrying their rackets. A fellow riding a tricycle with an enormous front wheel weaves shakily among them. The party of summer folk has stopped to talk with a group of young men from town; the fellows from away want to know if they can play in the townies' baseball game at Warrington's on Tuesday night. Ben Merrill, Royce's father-to-be, says Ayuh, but we won't go easy on ya just cause you're from N'Yawk. *The young men laugh; so do the tennis girls.*

A little farther on, two boys are playing catch with the sort of raw homemade baseball that is known as a horsey. Beyond them is a convention of young mothers, talking earnestly of their babies, all safely prammed and gathered in their own group. Men in overalls discuss weather and crops, politics and crops, taxes and crops. A teacher from the Consolidated High sits on the gray stone forehead I know so well, patiently tutoring a sullen boy who wants to be somewhere else and doing anything else. I think the boy will grow up to be Buddy Jellison's father. Horn broken – watch for finger, I think.

All along The Street folks are fishing, and they are catching plenty; the lake fairly teems with bass and trout and pickerel. An artist – another summer fellow, judging from his smock and nancy beret – has set up his easel and is painting the mountains while two ladies watch respectfully. A giggle of girls passes, whispering about boys and clothes and school. There is beauty here, and peace. Devore's right to say this is a world I never knew. It's

'Beautiful,' I said, pulling myself back with an effort. 'Yes, I see that. But what's your point?'

'My point?' Devore looked almost comically surprised. 'She thought she could walk there like everyone else, that's the fucking *point*! She thought she could walk there like a white gal! Her and her big teeth and her big tits and her snotty looks. She thought she was something special, but we taught her different. She tried to walk me down and when she couldn't do that she put her filthy hands on me and tumped me over. But that was all right; we taught her her manners. Didn't we, boys?'

They growled agreement, but I thought some of them – young Harry Auster, for one – looked sick.

'We taught her her place,' Devore said. 'We taught her she wasn't nothing but a

nigger. This is the word he uses over and over again when they are in the woods that summer, the summer of 1901, the summer that Sara and the Red-Tops become the musical act to see in this part of the world. She and her brother and their whole nigger family have been invited to Warrington's to play for the summer people; they have been fed on champagne and ersters . . . or so says Jared Devore to his little school of devoted followers as they eat their own plain lunches of bread and meat and salted cucumbers out of lard-buckets given to them by their mothers (none of the young men are married, although Oren Peebles is engaged).

Yet it isn't her growing renown that upsets Jared Devore. It isn't the fact that she has been to Warrington's; it don't cross his eyes none that she and that brother of hers have actually sat down and eaten with white folks, taken bread from the same bowl as them with their blacknigger fingers. The folks at Warrington's are flatlanders, after all, and Devore tells the silent, attentive young men that he's heard that in places like New York and Chicago white women sometimes even fuck blackniggers.

Naw! Harry Auster *says, looking around nervously, as if he expected a few white women to come tripping through the woods way out here on Bowie Ridge.* No white woman'd fuck a nigger! Shoot a pickle!

Devore only gives him a look, the kind that says When you're my age. *Besides, he doesn't care what goes on in New York and Chicago; he saw all the flatland he wanted to during the Civil War . . . and, he will tell you, he never fought that war to free the damned slaves. They can keep slaves down there in the land of cotton until the end of the eternity, as far as Jared Lancelot Devore is concerned. No, he fought in the war to teach those cracker sons of bitches south of Mason and Dixon that you don't pull out of the game just because you don't like some of the rules. He went down to scratch the scab off the end of old Johnny Reb's nose. Tried to leave the United States of America, they had! The Lord!*

No, he doesn't care about slaves and he doesn't care about the land of cotton and he doesn't care about blackniggers who sing dirty songs and then get treated to champagne and ersters (Jared always says oysters *in just that sarcastic way) in payment for their smut. He doesn't care about anything so long as they keep in their place and let him keep in his.*

But she won't do it. The uppity bitch will not do it. She has been warned to stay off The Street, but she will not listen. She goes anyway, walking along in her white dress just as if there was a white person inside it, sometimes with her son, who has a blacknigger African name and no daddy — his daddy probably just spent the one night with his mommy in a haystack somewhere down Alabama and now she walks around with the get of that just as bold as a brass monkey. She walks The Street as if she has a right to be there, even though not a soul will talk to her—

'But that's not true, is it?' I asked Devore. 'That's what really stuck in old great-granddaddy's craw, wasn't it? They *did* talk to her. She had a way about her — that laugh, maybe. Men talked to her about crops and the women showed off their babies. In fact they gave her their babies to hold and when she laughed down at them, they laughed back up at her. The girls asked her advice about boys. The boys . . . they just looked. But *how* they looked, huh? They filled up their eyes, and I expect most of them thought about her when they went out to the privy and filled up their palms.'

Devore glowered. He was aging in front of me, the lines drawing themselves deeper and deeper into his face; he was becoming the man who had knocked me into the lake because he couldn't bear to be crossed. And as he grew older he began to fade.

'That was what Jared hated most of all, wasn't it? That they didn't turn aside, didn't turn away. She walked on The Street and no one treated her like a nigger. They treated her like a neighbor.'

I was in the zone, deeper in than I'd ever been, down where the town's unconscious seemed to run like a buried river. I could drink from that river while I was in the zone, could fill my mouth and throat and belly with its cold minerally taste.

All that summer Devore had talked to them. They were more than his crew, they were his boys: Fred and Harry and Ben and Oren and George Armbruster and Draper Finney, who would break his neck and drown the next summer trying to dive into Eades Quarry while he was drunk. Only it was the sort of accident that's kind of on purpose. Draper Finney drank a lot between July of 1901 and August of 1902, because it was the only way he could sleep. The only way he could get the hand out of his mind, that hand sticking straight out of the water, clenching and unclenching until you wanted to scream *Won't it stop, won't it ever stop doing that.*

All summer long Jared Devore filled their ears with nigger bitch and uppity bitch. All summer long he told them about their responsibility as men, their duty to keep the community pure, and how they must see what others didn't and do what others wouldn't.

It was a Sunday afternoon in August, a time when traffic along The Street dropped steeply. Later on, by five or so, things would begin to pick up again, and from six to sunset the broad path along the lake would be thronged. But three in the afternoon was low tide. The Methodists were back in session over in Harlow for their afternoon Song Service; at Warrington's the assembled company of vacationing flatlanders was sitting down to a heavy mid-afternoon Sabbath meal of roast chicken or ham; all over the township families were addressing their own Sunday dinners. Those who had already finished were snoozing through the heat of the day – in a hammock, wherever possible. Sara liked this quiet time. Loved it, really. She had spent a great deal of her life on carny midways and in smoky gin-joints, shouting out her songs in order to be heard above the voices of redfaced, unruly drunks, and while part of her loved the excitement and unpredictability of that life, part of her loved the serenity of this one, too. The peace of these walks. She wasn't getting any younger, after all; she had a kid who had now left purt near all his babyhood behind him. On that particular Sunday she must have thought The Street almost *too* quiet. She walked a mile south from the meadow without seeing a soul – even Kito was gone by then, having stopped off to pick berries. It was as if the whole township were.

deserted. She knows there's an Eastern Star supper in Kashwakamak, of course, has even contributed a mushroom pie to it because she has made friends of some of the Eastern Star ladies. They'll all be down there getting ready. What she doesn't know is that today is also Dedication Day for the new Grace Baptist Church, the first real church ever to be built on the TR. A slug of locals have gone, heathen as well as Baptist. Faintly, from the other side of the lake, she can hear the Methodists singing. The sound is sweet and faint and beautiful; distance and echo has tuned every sour voice.

She isn't aware of the men – most of them very young men, the kind who under ordinary circumstances dare look at her only from the corners of their eyes – until the oldest one among them speaks. 'Wellnow, a black whore in a white dress and a red belt! Damn if that ain't just a little too much color for lakeside. What's wrong with you, whore? Can't you take a hint?'

She turns toward him, afraid but not showing it. She has lived thirty-six years on this earth, has known what a man has and where he wants to put it since she was eleven, and she understands that when men are together like this and full of redeye (she can smell it), they give up thinking for themselves and turn into a pack of dogs. If you show fear they will fall on you like dogs and likely tear you apart like dogs.

Also, they have been laying for her. There can be no other explanation for them turning up like this.

'What hint is that, sugar?' she asks, standing her ground. Where is everyone? Where can they all be? God damn! Across the lake, the Methodists have moved on to 'Trust and Obey,' a droner if there ever was one.

'That you ain't got no business walking where the white folks walk,' Harry Auster says. His adolescent voice breaks into a kind of mouse-squeak on the last word and she laughs. She knows how unwise that is, but she can't help it – she's never been able to help her laughter, any more than she's ever been able to help the way men like this look at her breasts and bottom. Blame it on God.

'Why, I walk where I do,' she says. 'I was told this was common ground,

475

ain't nobody got a right to keep me out. Ain't nobody has. You seen em doin it?'

'You see us now,' George Armbruster says, trying to sound tough.

Sara looks at him with a species of kindly contempt that makes George shrivel up inside. His cheeks glow hot red. 'Son,' she says, 'you only come out now because the decent folks is all somewhere else. Why do you want to let this old fella tell you what to do? Act decent and let a lady walk.'

I see it all. As Devore fades and fades, at last becoming nothing but eyes under a blue cap in the rainy afternoon (through him I can see the shattered remains of my swimming float washing against the embankment), I see it all. I see her as she

starts forward, walking straight at Devore. If she stands here jawing with them, something bad is going to happen. She feels it, and she never questions her feelings. And if she walks at any of the others, ole massa'll bore in on her from the side, pulling the rest after. Ole massa in the little ole blue cap is the wheeldog, the one she must face down. She can do it, too. He's strong, strong enough to make these boys one creature, his creature, at least for the time being, but he doesn't have her force, her determination, her energy. In a way she welcomes this confrontation. Reg has warned her to be careful, not to move too fast or try to make real friends until the rednecks (only Reggie calls them 'the bull gators') show themselves — how many and how crazy — but she goes her own course, trusts her own deep instincts. And here they are, only seven of em, and really just the one bull gator.

I'm stronger than you, ole massa, *she thinks, walking toward him. She fixes her eyes on his and will not let them drop; his are the ones that drop, his the mouth that quivers uncertainly at one corner, his the tongue that comes out as quick as a lizard's tongue to wet the lips, and all that's good . . . but even better is when he falls back a step. When he does that the rest of them cluster in two groups of three, and there it is, her way through. Faint and sweet are the Methodists, faithy music carrying across the lake's still surface. A droner of a hymn, yes, but sweet across the miles.*

> When we walk with the Lord
> in the light of His word,
> what a glory He sheds on our way . . .

I'm stronger than you, sugar, *she sends,* I'm meaner than you, you may be the bull gator but I'm the queen bee and if you don't want me stingin on you, you best clear me the rest of my path.

'*You bitch,*' *he says, but his voice is weak; he is already thinking this isn't the day, there's something about her he didn't quite see until he saw her right up close, some blacknigger hougan he didn't feel until now, better wait for another day, better—*

Then he trips over a root or a rock (perhaps it's the very rock behind which she will finally come to rest) and falls down. His cap falls off, showing the big old bald spot on top of his head. His pants split all the way up the seam. And Sara makes a crucial mistake. Perhaps she underestimates Jared Devore's own very considerable personal force, or perhaps she just cannot help herself – the sound of his britches ripping is like a loud fart. In any case she laughs – that raucous, smoke-broken laugh which is her trademark. And her laugh becomes her doom.

*Devore doesn't think. He simply gives her the leather from where he lies, big feet in pegged loggers' boots shooting out like pistons. He hits her where she is thinnest and most vulnerable, in the ankles. She hollers in shocked pain as the left one breaks; she goes down in a tumble, losing her furled parasol out of one hand. She draws in breath to scream again and Jared says from where he is lying, '*Don't let her! Dassn't let her holler!*'*

Ben Merrill falls on top of her full-length, all one hundred and ninety pounds of him. The breath she has drawn to scream with whooshes out in a gusty, almost silent sigh instead. Ben, who has never even danced with a woman, let alone lain on top of one like this, is instantly excited by the feel of her struggling beneath him. He wriggles against her, laughing, and when she rakes her nails down his cheek he barely feels it. The way it seems to him, he's all cock and a yard long. When she tries to roll over and get out from under that way, he rolls with her, lets her be on top, and he is totally surprised when she drives her forehead down on his. He sees stars, but he is eighteen years old, as strong as he will ever be, and he loses neither consciousness nor his erection.

*Oren Peebles tears away the back of her dress, laughing. '*Pig-pile!*' he cries in a breathy little whisper, and drops on top of her. Now he is dry-humping her topside and Ben is dry-humping just as enthusiastically from underneath, dry-humping like a billygoat even with the blood pouring down the sides of his head from the split in the center of his brow, and she knows that if she can't scream she is lost. If she can scream and if Kito hears, he'll run and get help, run and get Reg—*

But before she can try again, ole massa is squatting beside her and showing her a long-bladed knife. 'Make a sound and I'll cut your nose off,' he says, and that's when she gives up. They have brought her down after all, partly because she laughed at the wrong time, mostly out of pure buggardly bad luck. Now they will not be stopped, and best that Kito stay away — please God keep him back where he was, it was a good patch of berries, one that should keep him occupied an hour or more. He loves berry-picking, and it won't take these men an hour. Harry Auster yanks her hair back, tears her dress off one shoulder, and begins to sucker on her neck.

Ole massa the only one not at her. Old massa standing back, looking both ways along The Street, his eyes slitted and wary; old massa look like a mangy timberwolf done eaten a whole generation of chickenhouse chickens while managing to avoid every trap and snare. 'Hey Irish, quit on her a minute,' he tells Harry, then widens his wise gaze to the others. 'Get her in the puckies, you damn fools. Get her in there deep.'

They don't. They can't. They are too eager to have her. They arm-yank her behind the forehead of gray rock and call it good. She doesn't pray easily but she prays now. She prays for them to let her live. She prays for Kito to stay clear, to keep filling his bucket slow by eating every third handful. She prays that if he does take a notion to catch up with her, he will see what's happening and run the other way as fast as he can, run silent and get Reg.

'Stick this in your mouth,' George Armbruster pants. 'And don't you bite me, you bitch.'

They take her top and bottom, back and front, two and three at a time. They take her where anybody coming along can't help but see them, and ole massa stands off a little; first he looks at the panting young men grouped around her, kneeling with their trousers down and their thighs scratched from the bushes they are kneeling in, then he peers up and down the path with his wild and wary eyes. Incredibly, one of them — it is Fred Dean — says 'Sorry, ma'am' after he's shot his load feels like halfway up to east bejeezus. It's as if he accidentally kicked her in the shin while crossing his legs.

And it doesn't end. There's come down her throat, come running down the crack of her ass, the young one has bitten the blood right out of her left breast, and it doesn't end. They are young, and by the time the last one has finished, the first one, oh God, the first one is ready again. Across the river the Methodists are now singing 'Blessed Assurance, Jesus Is Mine' and as ole massa approaches her she thinks, It's almost over, woman, he the last, hold on hold steady and it be over. *He looks at the skinny redhead and the one who keeps squinching his eye up and tossing his head and tells them to watch the path, he's going to take his turn now that she's broke in.*

He unbuckles his belt, he unbuttons his flies, he pushes down his underwear — dirty black at the knees and dirty yellow at the crotch — and as he drops a knee on either side of her she sees that ole massa's little massa is just as floppy as a snake with its neck broke and before she can stop it, that raucous laugh bursts all unexpected from her again — even lying here covered with the hot jelly spend of her rapists, she can't help but see the funny side.

'Shut up!' Devore growls at her, and smashes the heel of one hard hand across her face, breaking her cheekbone and her nose. 'Shut up that howling!'

'Reckon it might get stiffer if it was one of your boys layin here with his rosy red ass stuck up in the air, sugar?' she asks, and then, for the last time, Sara laughs.

Devore draws his hand back to hit her again, his naked loins lying against her naked loins, his penis a flaccid worm between them. But before he can bring the hand down a child's voice cries, 'Ma! What they doin to you, Ma? Git off my mama, you bastards!'

She sits up in spite of Devore's weight, her laughter dying, her wide eyes searching Kito out and finding him, a slim young boy of eight standing on The Street, dressed in overalls and a straw hat and brandnew canvas shoes, carrying a tin bucket in one hand. His lips are blue with juice. His eyes are wide with confusion and fright.

'Run, Kito!' she screams. 'Run away h—'

Red fire explodes in her head; she swoons back into the bushes, hearing ole massa from a great distance: 'Get him. Dassn't let him ramble, now.'

Then she's going down a long dark slope, she's lost in a Ghost House corridor that leads only deeper and deeper into its own convoluted bowels; from that deep falling place she hears him, she hears, her darling one, he is screaming. I heard him screaming as I knelt by the gray rock with my carry-bag beside me and no idea how I'd gotten to where I was — I certainly had no memory of walking here. I was crying in shock and horror and pity. Was she crazy? Well, no wonder. No fucking wonder. The rain was steady but no longer apocalyptic. I stared at my fishy-white hands on the gray rock for a few seconds, then looked around. Devore and the others were gone.

The ripe and gassy stench of decay filled my nose — it was like a physical assault. I fumbled in the carry-bag, found the Stenomask Rommie and George had given me as a joke, and slipped it over my mouth and nose with fingers that felt numb and distant. I breathed shallowly and tentatively. Better. Not a lot, but enough to keep from fleeing, which was undoubtedly what she wanted.

'No!' she cried from somewhere behind me as I grabbed the spade and dug in. I tore a great mouth in the ground with the first swipe, and each subsequent one deepend and widened it. The earth was soft and yielding, woven through with mats of thin roots which parted easily under the blade.

'No! Don't you dare!'

I wouldn't look around, wouldn't give her a chance to push me away. She was stronger down here, perhaps because it had happened here. Was that possible? I didn't know and didn't care. All I cared about was getting this done. Where the roots were thicker, I hacked through them with the pruning knife.

'*Leave me be!*'

Now I *did* look around, risked one quick glance because of the unnatural crackling sounds which had accompanied her voice — which now seemed to *make* her voice. The Green Lady was gone. The birch had somehow become Sara Tidwell: it was Sara's face growing out of the crisscrossing branches and shiny leaves. That rain-slicked face swayed, dissolved, came together, melted away, came together again. For a moment all the mystery I had sensed down here was revealed. Her damp shifting eyes were utterly human. They stared at me with hate and supplication.

'I ain't done!' she cried in a cracked, breaking voice. 'He was the worst, don't you understand? He was the worst and it's his blood in her and I won't rest until I *have it out!*'

There was a gruesome ripping sound. She had inhabited the birch, made it into a physical body of some sort and intended to tear it free of the earth. She would come and get me with it if she could; kill me with it if she could. Strangle me in limber branches. Stuff me with leaves until I looked like a Christmas decoration.

'No matter how much of a monster he was, Kyra had nothing to do with what he did,' I said. 'And you won't have her.'

'Yes I *will!*' the Green Lady screamed. The ripping, rending sounds were louder now. They were joined by a hissing, shaky crackle. I didn't look around again. I didn't *dare* look around. I dug faster instead. 'Yes I *will* have her!' she cried, and now the voice was closer. She was coming for me but I refused to see; when it comes to walking trees and bushes, I'll stick to *Macbeth*, thanks. 'I *will* have her! He took mine and *I mean to take his*!'

'Go away,' a new voice said.

The spade loosened in my hands, almost fell. I turned and saw Jo standing below me and to my right. She was looking at Sara, who had materialized into a lunatic's hallucination – a monstrous greenish-black thing that slipped with every step it tried to walk along The Street. She had left the birch behind yet assumed its vitality somehow – the actual tree huddled behind her, black and shrivelled and dead. The creature born of it looked like the Bride of Frankenstein as sculpted by Picasso. In it, Sara's face came and went, came and went.

The Shape, I thought coldly. *It was always real . . . and if it was always me, it was always her, too.*

Jo was dressed in the white shirt and yellow slacks she'd had on the day she died. I couldn't see the lake through her as I had been able to see it through Devore and Devore's young friends; she had materialized herself completely. I felt a curious *draining* sensation at the back of my skull and thought I knew how.

'Git out, bitch!' the Sara-thing snarled. It raised its arms toward Jo as it had raised them to me in my worst nightmares.

'Not at all.' Jo's voice remained calm. She turned toward me. 'Hurry, Mike. You have to be quick. It's not really her anymore. She's let one of the Outsiders in, and they're very dangerous.'

'Jo, I love you.'

'I love you t—'

Sara shrieked and then began to spin. Leaves and branches blurred together and lost coherence; it was like watching something liquefy in a blender. The entity which had only looked a little like a woman to begin with now dropped its masquerade entirely. Something elemental and grotesquely inhuman began to form out of the maelstrom. It leaped at my wife. When it struck her, the color and solidity left Jo as if slapped away by a huge hand. She became a phantom struggling with the thing which raved and shrieked and clawed at her.

481

'*Hurry, Mike!*' she screamed. '*Hurry!*'

I bent to the job.

The spade struck something that wasn't dirt, wasn't stone, wasn't wood. I scraped along it, revealing a filthy mold-crusted swatch of canvas. Now I dug like a madman, wanting to clear as much of the buried object as I could, wanting to fatten my chances of success as much as I could. Behind me, the Shape screamed in fury and my wife screamed in pain. Sara had given up part of her discorporate self in order to gain her revenge, had let in something Jo called an Outsider. I had no idea what that might be and never *wanted* to know. Sara was its conduit, I knew that much. And if I could take care of her in time—

I reached into the dripping hole, slapping wet earth from the ancient canvas. Faint stencilled letters appeared when I did: J.M. McCURDIE SAWMILL. McCurdie's had burned in the fires of '33, I knew. I'd seen a picture of it in flames somewhere. As I seized the canvas, the tips of my fingers punching through and letting out a fresh billow of green and gassy stench, I could hear grunting. I could hear

Devore. He's lying on top of her and grunting like a pig. Sara is semiconscious, muttering unintelligibly through bruised lips which are shiny with blood. Devore is looking back over his shoulder at Draper Finney and Fred Dean. They have raced after the boy and brought him back, but he won't stop yelling, he's yelling to beat the band, yelling to wake the dead, and if they can hear the Methodists singing 'How I Love to Tell the Story' over here, then they may be able to hear the yowling nigger over there. Devore says 'Put him in the water, shut him up.' The minute he says it, as though the words are magic words, his cock begins to stiffen.

'*What do you mean?*' *Ben Merrill asks.*

'*You know goddam well,*' *Jared says. He pants the words out, jerking his hips as he speaks. His narrow ass gleams in the afternoon light. 'He seen us! You want to cut his throat, get his blood all over you? Fine by me. Here. Take my knife, be my guest!*'

'*N-No, Jared!*' *Ben cries in horror, actually seeming to cringe at the sight of the knife.*

He is finally ready. It takes him a little longer, that's all, he ain't a kid like these other ones. But now—! Never mind her smart mouth, never mind her insolent way of laughing, never mind the whole township. Let them all

show up and watch if they like. He slips it to her, what she's wanted all along, what all her kind want. He slips it in and sinks it deep. He continues giving orders even as he rapes her. Up and down his ass goes, tick-tock, just like a cat's tail. 'Somebody take care of him! Or do you want to spend forty years rotting in Shawshank because of a nigger boy's tattle?'

Ben seizes one of Kito Tidwell's arms, Oren Peebles the other, but by the time they have dragged him as far as the embankment they have lost their heart. Raping an uppity nigger woman with the gall to laugh at Jared when he fell down and split his britches is one thing. Drowning a scared kid like a kitten in a mudpuddle . . . that's another one altogether.

They loosen their grip, staring into each other's haunted eyes, and Kito pulls free.

'Run, honey!' Sara cries. 'Run away and get—' Jared clamps his hands around her throat and begins choking.

The boy trips over his own berry bucket and thumps gracelessly to the ground. Harry and Draper recapture him easily. 'What you going to do?' Draper asks in a kind of desperate whine, and Harry replies

'What I have to.' That's what he replied, and now I was going to do what I had to – in spite of the stench, in spite of Sara, in spite of my dead wife's shrieks. I hauled the roll of canvas out of the ground. The ropes which had tied it shut at either end held, but the roll itself split down the middle with a hideous burping sound.

'*Hurry!*' Jo cried. '*I can't hold it much longer!*'

It snarled; it bayed like a dog. There was a loud wooden crunch, like a door being slammed hard enough to splinter, and Jo wailed. I grabbed for the carry-bag with Slips 'n Greens printed on the front and tore it open as

Harry – the others call him Irish because of his carrot-colored hair – grabs the struggling kid in a clumsy kind of bearhug and jumps into the lake with him. The kid struggles harder than ever; his straw hat comes off and floats on the water. 'Get that!' Harry pants. Fred Dean kneels and fishes out the dripping hat. Fred's eyes are dazed, he's got the look of a fighter about one round from hitting the canvas. Behind them Sara Tidwell has begun to rattle deep in her chest and throat – like the sight of the boy's clenching hand, these sounds will haunt Draper Finney until his final dive into Eades Quarry. Jared sinks his fingers deeper, pumping and choking at the same time, the sweat pouring off him. No amount of washing will take the smell of that sweat out of these clothes, and when he begins to think of it as 'murder-sweat,' he burns the clothes to get shed of it.

Harry Auster wants to be shed of it all – to be shed of it and never see these men again, most of all Jared Devore, who he now thinks must be Lord Satan himself. Harry cannot go home and face his father unless this nightmare is over, buried. And his mother! How can he ever face his beloved mother, Bridget Auster with her round sweet Irish face and graying hair and comforting shelf of bosom, Bridget who has always had a kind word or a soothing hand for him, Bridget Auster who has been Saved, Washed in the Blood of the Lamb, Bridget Auster who is even now serving pies at the picnic they're having at the new church, Bridget Auster who is mamma; how can he ever look at her again – or she him – if he has to stand in court on a charge of raping and beating a woman, even a black woman?

So he yanks the clinging boy away – Kito scratches him once, just a nick on the side of the neck, and that night Harry will tell his mamma it was a bush-pricker that caught him unawares and he will let her put a kiss on it – and then he plunges the child into the lake. Kito looks up at him, his face shimmering, and Harry sees a little fish flick by. A perch, he thinks. For an instant he wonders what the boy must see, looking up through the silver shield of the surface at the face of the fellow who's holding him down, the fellow who's drowning him, and then Harry pushes that away. Just a nigger, *he reminds himself desperately.* That's all he is, just a nigger. No kin of yours.

Kito's arm comes out of the water – his dripping dark-brown arm. Harry pulls back, not wanting to be clawed, but the hand doesn't reach for him, only sticks straight up. The fingers curl into a fist. Open. Curl into a fist. Open. Curl into a fist. The boy's thrashing begins to ease, the kicking feet begin to slow down, the eyes looking up into Harry's eyes are taking on a curiously dreamy look, and still that brown arm sticks straight up, still the hand opens and closes, opens and closes. Draper Finney stands on the shore crying, sure that now someone will come along, now someone will see the terrible thing they have done – the terrible thing they are in fact still doing. Be sure your sin will find you out, *it says in the Good Book.* Be sure. *He opens his mouth to tell Harry to quit, maybe it's still not too late to take it back, let him up, let him live, but no sound comes out. Behind him Sara is choking her last. In front of him her drowning son's hand opens and closes, opens and closes, the reflection of it shimmering on the water, and Draper thinks* Won't it stop doing that, won't it ever stop doing that? *And*

484

as if it were a prayer that something is now answering, the boy's locked elbow begins to bend and his arm begins to sag; the fingers begin to close again into a fist and then stop. For a moment the hand wavers and then

I slammed the heel of my hand into the center of my forehead to clear these phantoms away. Behind me there was a frenzied snap and crackle of wet bushes as Jo and whatever she was holding back continued to struggle. I put my hands inside the split in the canvas like a doctor spreading a wound. I yanked. There was a low ripping sound as the roll tore the rest of the way up and down.

Inside was what remained of them – two yellowed skulls, forehead to forehead as if in intimate conversation, a woman's faded red leather belt, a moulder of clothes ... and a heap of bones. Two ribcages, one large and one small. Two sets of legs, one long and one short. The early remains of Sara and Kito Tidwell, buried here by the lake for almost a hundred years.

The larger of the two skulls turned. It glared at me with its empty eyesockets. Its teeth chattered as if it would bite me, and the bones below it began a tenebrous, jittery stirring. Some broke apart immediately; all were soft and pitted. The red belt stirred restlessly and the rusty buckle rose like the head of a snake.

'*Mike!*' Jo screamed. '*Quick, quick!*'

I pulled the sack out of the carry-bag and grabbed the plastic bottle which had been inside. Lye stille, the Magnabet letters had said; another little word-trick. Another message passed behind the unsuspecting guard's back. Sara Tidwell was a fearsome creature, but she had underestimated Jo ... and she had underestimated the telepathy of long association, as well. I had gone to Slips 'n Greens, I had bought a bottle of lye, and now I opened it and poured it, smoking, over the bones of Sara and her son.

There was a hissing sound like the one you hear when you open a beer or a bottled soft drink. The belt-buckle melted. The bones turned white and crumpled like things made out of sugar – I had a nightmare image of Mexican children eating candy corpses off long sticks on the Day of the Dead. The eyesockets of Sara's skull widened as the lye filled the dark hollow where her mind, her prodigious talent, and her laughing soul had once resided. It was an expression that looked at first like surprise and then like sorrow.

The jaw fell off; the nubs of the teeth sizzled away.

The top of the skull caved in.

Spread fingerbones jittered, then melted.

'*Ohhhhhh . . .*'

It whispered through the soaking trees like a rising wind . . . only the wind had died as the wet air caught its breath before the next onslaught. It was a sound of unspeakable grief and longing and surrender. I sensed no hate in it; her hate was gone, burned away in the corrosive I had bought in Helen Auster's shop. The sound of Sara's going was replaced by the plaintive, almost human cry of a bird, and it awakened me from the place where I had been, brought me finally and completely out of the zone. I got shakily to my feet, turned around, and looked at The Street.

Jo was still there, a dim form through which I could now see the lake and the dark clouds of the next thundersquall coming over the mountains. Something flickered beyond her – that bird venturing out of its safe covert for a peek at the rearranged environment, perhaps – but I barely registered that. It was Jo I wanted to see, Jo who had come God knew how far and suffered God knew how much to help me. She looked exhausted, hurt, in some fundamental way diminished. But the other thing – the Outsider – was gone. Jo, standing in a ring of birch leaves so dead they looked charred, turned to me and smiled.

'Jo! We did it!'

Her mouth moved. I heard the sound, but the words were too distant to make out. She was standing right there, but she might have been calling across a wide canyon. Still, I understood her. I read the words off her lips if you prefer the rational, right out of her mind if you prefer the romantical. I prefer the latter. Marriage is a zone, too, you know. Marriage is a zone.

—*So* that's *all right, isn't it?*

I glanced down into the gaping roll of canvas and saw nothing but stubs and splinters sticking out of a noxious, uneasy paste. I got a whiff, and even through the Stenomask it made me cough and back away. Not corruption; lye. When I looked back around at Jo, she was barely there.

'Jo! Wait!'

—*Can't help. Can't stay.*

Words from another star system, barely glimpsed on a fading

mouth. Now she was little more than eyes floating in the dark afternoon, eyes which seemed made of the lake behind them.

—Hurry . . .

She was gone. I slipped and stumbled to the place where she'd been, my feet crunching over dead birch leaves, and grabbed at nothing. What a fool I must have looked, soaked to the skin, wearing a Stenomask askew over the lower half of my face, trying to embrace the wet gray air.

I got the faintest whiff of Red perfume . . . and then only damp earth, lakewater, and the vile stink of lye running under everything. At least the smell of putrefaction was gone; that had been no more real than . . .

Than what? Than *what*? Either it was all real or none of it was real. If none of it was real, I was out of my mind and ready for the Blue Wing at Juniper Hill. I looked over toward the gray rock and saw the bag of bones I had pulled out of the wet ground like a festering tooth. Lazy tendrils of smoke were still rising from its ripped length. *That* much was real. So was the Green Lady, who was now a soot-colored Black Lady – as dead as the dead branch behind her, the one that seemed to point like an arm.

Can't help . . . can't stay . . . hurry.

Couldn't help with what? What more help did I need? It was done, wasn't it? Sara was gone: spirit follows bone, good night sweet ladies, God grant she lye stille.

And still a kind of stinking terror, not so different from the smell of putrescence which had come out of the ground, seemed to sweat out of the air; Kyra's name began to beat in my head, *Ki-Ki, Ki-Ki, Ki-Ki*, like the call of some exotic tropical bird. I started up the railroad-tie steps to the house, and although I was exhausted, by the time I was halfway up I had begun to run.

I climbed the stairs to the deck and went in that way. The house looked the same – save for the broken tree poking in through the kitchen window, Sara Laughs had stood up to the storm very well – but something was wrong. There was something I could almost smell . . . and perhaps I *did* smell it, bitter and low. Lunacy may have its own wild-vetch aroma. It's not the kind of thing I would ever care to research.

In the front hall I stopped, looking down at a heap of paperback

487

books, Elmore Leonards and Ed McBains, lying on the floor. As if they had been raked off the shelf by a passing hand. A flailing hand, maybe. I could also see my tracks there, both coming and going. They had already begun to dry. They should have been the only ones; I had been carrying Ki when we came in. They should have been, but they weren't. The others were smaller, but not so small that I mistook them for a child's.

I ran down the hall to the north bedroom crying her name, and I might as well have been crying *Mattie* or *Jo* or *Sara*. Coming out of my mouth, Kyra's name sounded like the name of a corpse. The duvet had been thrown back on to the floor. Except for the black stuffed dog, lying where it had in my dream, the bed was empty. And Ki was gone.

CHAPTER TWENTY-NINE

I reached for Ki with the part of my mind that had for the last few weeks known what she was wearing, what room of the trailer she was in, and what she was doing there. There was nothing, of course – that link was also dissolved.

I called for Jo – I think I did – but Jo was gone, too. I was on my own. God help me. God help us both. I could feel panic trying to descend and fought it off. I had to keep my mind clear. If I couldn't think, any chance Ki might still have would be lost. I walked rapidly back down the hall to the foyer, trying not to hear the sick voice in the back of my head, the one saying that Ki was lost already, dead already. I knew no such thing, couldn't know it now that the connection between us was broken.

I looked down at the heap of books, then up at the door. The new tracks had come in this way and gone out this way, too. Lightning stroked the sky and thunder cracked. The wind was rising again. I went to the door, reached for the knob, then paused. Something was caught in the crack between the door and the jamb, something as fine and floaty as a strand of spider's silk.

A single white hair.

I looked at it with a sick lack of surprise. I should have known, of course, and if not for the strain I'd been under and the successive shocks of this terrible day, I *would* have known. It was all on the tape John had played for me that morning . . . a time that already seemed part of another man's life.

For one thing, there was the time-check marking the point where John had hung up on her. *Nine-forty* A.M., *Eastern Daylight,* the robot voice had said, which meant that Rogette had been calling at six-forty in the morning . . . if, that was, she'd really been calling from Palm Springs. That was at least possible; had the oddity occurred to me while we were driving from the airport to Mattie's trailer, I would have told myself that there were no doubt insomniacs all over California who finished their East Coast business before the sun had hauled itself fully over the horizon, and good for them. But there was something else that couldn't be explained away so easily.

At one point John had ejected the tape. He did it because, he said, I'd gone as white as a sheet instead of looking amused. I had told him to go on and play the rest; it had just surprised me to hear her again. *The quality of her voice. Christ, the reproduction is good.* Except it was really the boys in the basement who had reacted to John's tape; my subconscious co-conspirators. And it hadn't been her *voice* that had scared them badly enough to turn my face white. The underhum had done that. The characteristic underhum you always got on TR calls, both those you made and those you received.

Rogette Whitmore had never left TR-90 at all. If my failing to realize that this morning cost Ki Devore her life this afternoon, I wouldn't be able to live with myself. I told God that over and over as I went plunging down the railroad-tie steps again, running into the face of a revitalized storm.

It's a blue-eyed wonder I didn't go flying right off the embankment. Half my swimming float had grounded there, and perhaps I could have impaled myself on its splintered boards and died like a vampire writhing on a stake. What a pleasant thought *that* was.

Running isn't good for people near panic; it's like scratching poison ivy. By the time I had thrown my arm around one of the pines at the foot of the steps to check my progress, I was on the edge of losing all coherent thought. Ki's name was beating in my head again, so loudly there wasn't room for much else.

Then a stroke of lightning leaped out of the sky to my right and knocked the last three feet of trunk out from beneath a huge old spruce which had probably been here when Sara and Kito were still alive. If I'd been looking directly at it I would have been blinded; even with my head turned three-quarters away, the stroke left a huge blue swatch like the aftermath of a gigantic camera flash floating in

490

front of my eyes. There was a grinding, juddering sound as two hundred feet of blue spruce toppled into the lake, sending up a long curtain of spray, which seemed to hang between the gray sky and gray water. The stump was on fire in the rain, burning like a witch's hat.

It had the effect of a slap, clearing my head and giving me one final chance to use my brain. I took a breath and forced myself to do just that. Why had I come down here in the first place? Why did I think Rogette had brought Kyra toward the lake, where I had just been, instead of carrying her away from me, up the driveway to Lane Forty-two?

Don't be stupid. She came down here because The Street's the way back to Warrington's, and Warrington's is where she's been, all by herself, ever since she sent the boss's body back to California in his private jet.

She had sneaked into the house while I was under Jo's studio, finding the tin box in the belly of the owl and studying that scrap of genealogy. She would have taken Ki then if I'd given her the chance, but I didn't. I came hurrying back, afraid something was wrong, afraid someone might be trying to get hold of the kid—

Had Rogette awakened her? Had Ki seen her and tried to warn me before drifting off again? Was that what had brought me in such a hurry? Maybe. I'd still been in the zone then, we'd still been linked then. Rogette had certainly been in the house when I came back. She might even have been in the north-bedroom closet and peering at me through the crack. Part of me had known it, too. Part of me had felt her, felt something that was not-Sara.

Then I'd left again. Grabbed the carry-bag from Slips 'n Greens and come down here. Turned right, turned north. Toward the birch, the rock, the bag of bones. I'd done what I had to do, and while I was doing it, Rogette carried Kyra down the railroad-tie steps behind me and turned left on The Street. Turned south toward Warrington's. With a sinking feeling deep in my belly, I realized I had probably heard Ki . . . might even have seen her. That bird peeking timidly out from cover during the lull had been no bird. Ki was awake by then, Ki had seen me – perhaps had seen Jo, as well – and tried to call out. She had managed just that one little peep before Rogette had covered her mouth.

How long ago had that been? It seemed like forever, but I had

491

an idea it hadn't been long at all – less than five minutes, maybe. But it doesn't take long to drown a child. The image of Kito's bare arm sticking straight out of the water tried to come back – the hand at the end of it opening and closing, opening and closing, as if it were trying to breathe for the lungs that couldn't – and I pushed it away. I also suppressed the urge to simply sprint in the direction of Warrington's. Panic would take me for sure if I did that.

In all the years since her death I had never longed for Jo with the bitter intensity I felt then. But she was gone; there wasn't even a whisper of her. With no one to depend on but myself, I started south along the tree-littered Street, skirting the blowdowns where I could, crawling under them if they blocked my way entirely, taking the noisy branch-breaking course over the top only as a last resort. As I went I issued what I imagine are all the standard prayers in such a situation, but none of them seemed to get past the image of Rogette Whitmore's face rising in my mind. Her screaming, merciless face.

I remember thinking *This is the outdoor version of the Ghost House.* Certainly the woods seemed haunted to me as I struggled along: trees only loosened in the first grand blow were falling by the score in this followup cap of wind and rain. The noise was like great crunching footfalls, and I didn't need to worry about the noise my own feet were making. When I passed the Batchelders' camp, a circular prefab construction sitting on an outcrop of rock like a hat on a footstool, I saw that the entire roof had been bashed flat by a hemlock.

Half a mile south of Sara I saw one of Ki's white hair ribbons lying in the path. I picked it up, thinking how much that red edging looked like blood. Then I stuffed it into my pocket and went on.

Five minutes later I came to an old moss-caked pine that had fallen across the path; it was still connected to its stump by a stretched and bent network of splinters, and squalled like a line of rusty hinges as the surging water lifted and dropped what had been its upper twenty or thirty feet, now floating in the lake. There was space to crawl under, and when I dropped to my knees I saw other knee-tracks, just beginning to fill with water. I saw something else: the second hair ribbon. I tucked it into my pocket with the first.

I was halfway under the pine when I heard another tree go over, this one much closer. The sound was followed by a scream – not

492

pain or fear but surprised anger. Then, even over the hiss of the rain and the wind, I could hear Rogette's voice: '*Come back! Don't go out there, it's dangerous!*'

I squirmed the rest of the way under the tree, barely feeling the stump of a branch which tore a groove in my lower back, got to my feet, and sprinted along the path. If the fallen trees I came to were small, I hurdled them without slowing down. If they were bigger, I scrabbled over with no thought to where they might claw or dig in. Thunder whacked. There was a brilliant stroke of lightning, and in its glare I saw gray barnboard through the trees. On the day I'd first seen Rogette I'd only been able to catch glimpses of Warrington's lodge, but now the forest had been torn open like an old garment – this area would be years recovering. The lodge's rear half had been pretty well demolished by a pair of huge trees that seemed to have fallen together. They had crossed like a knife and fork on a diner's plate and lay on the ruins in a shaggy X.

Ki's voice, rising over the storm only because it was shrill with terror: '*Go away! I don't want you, white nana! Go away!*' It was horrible to hear the terror in her voice, but wonderful to hear her voice at all.

About forty feet from where Rogette's shout had frozen me in place, one more tree lay across the path. Rogette herself stood on the far side of it, holding a hand out to Ki. The hand was dripping blood, but I hardly noticed. It was Kyra I noticed.

The dock running between The Street and The Sunset Bar was a long one – seventy feet at least, perhaps a hundred. Long enough so that on a pretty summer evening you could stroll it hand-in-hand with your date or your lover and make a memory. The storm hadn't torn it away – not yet – but the wind had twisted it like a ribbon. I remember newsreel footage at some childhood Saturday matinee, film of a suspension bridge dancing in a hurricane, and that was what the dock between Warrington's and The Sunset Bar looked like. It jounced up and down in the surging water, groaning in all its slatted joints like a wooden accordion. There had been a rail – presumably to guide those who'd made a heavy night of it safely back to shore – but it was gone now. Kyra was halfway out along this swaying, dipping length of wood. I could see at least three rectangles of blackness between the shore and where she stood, places where boards had snapped off. From beneath the dock came the disturbed *clung-clung-clung* of the empty steel drums that were holding it up. Several of these drums had come unanchored and were floating away. Ki had her arms stretched out for balance like a tightrope walker in the circus. The black Harley-Davidson tee-shirt flapped around her knees and sunburned shoulders.

'*Come back!*' Rogette cried. Her lank hair flew around her head; the shiny black raincoat she was wearing rippled. She was holding both hands out now, one bloody and one not. I had an idea Ki might have bitten her.

'*No, white nana!*' Ki shook her head in wild negation and I wanted to tell her don't do that, Ki-bird, don't shake your head like that, very bad idea. She tottered, one arm pointed up at the sky and one down at the water so she looked for a moment like an airplane in a steep bank. If the dock had picked that moment to take a hard buck beneath her, Ki would have spilled off the side. She regained some precarious balance instead, although I thought I saw her bare feet slide a little on the slick boards. '*Go away, white nana, I don't want you! Go . . . go take a nap, you look tired!*'

Ki didn't see me; all her attention was fixed on the white nana. The white nana didn't see me, either. I dropped to my belly and squirmed under the tree, pulling myself along with my clawed hands. Thunder rolled across the lake like a big mahogany ball, the sound echoing off the mountains. When I got to my knees again, I saw that Rogette was advancing slowly toward the shore end of the dock. For every step she took forward, Kyra took a shaky, dangerous step backward. Rogette was holding her good hand out, though for a moment I thought this one had begun to bleed as well. The stuff running through her bunchy fingers was too dark for blood, however, and when she began to talk, speaking in a hideous coaxing voice that made my skin crawl, I realized it was melting chocolate.

'Let's play the game, Ki-bird,' Rogette cooed. 'Do you want to start?' She took a step. Ki took a compensatory step backward, tottered, caught her balance. My heart stopped, then resumed racing. I closed the distance between myself and the woman as rapidly as I could, but I didn't run; I didn't want her to know a thing until she woke up. *If* she woke up. I didn't care if she did or not. Hell, if I could fracture the back of George Footman's skull with a hammer,

494

I could certainly put a hurt on this horror. As I walked, I laced my hands together into one large fist.

'No? Don't want to start? Too shy?' Rogette spoke in a sugary *Romper Room* voice that made me want to grind my teeth together. 'All right, *I'll* start. Happy! What rhymes with happy, Ki-bird? Pappy . . . and nappy . . . you were taking a nappy, weren't you, when I came and woke you up. And lappy . . . would you want to come and sit on my lappy, Ki-bird? We'll feed each other chocolate, just like we used to . . . I'll tell you a new knock-knock joke . . .'

Another step. She had come to the edge of the dock. If she'd thought of it, she could simply have thrown rocks at Kyra as she had at me, thrown until she connected with one and knocked Ki into the lake. But I don't think she got even close to such a notion. Once crazy goes past a certain point, you're on a turnpike with no exit ramps. Rogette had other plans for Kyra.

'Come on, Ki-Ki, play the game with white nana.' She held out the chocolate again, gooey Hershey's Kisses dripping through crumpled foil. Kyra's eyes shifted, and at last she saw me. I shook my head, trying to tell her to be quiet, but it was no good – an expression of joyous relief crossed her face. She cried out my name, and I saw Rogette's shoulders go up in surprise.

I ran the last dozen feet, raising my joined hands like a club, but I slipped a little on the wet ground at the crucial moment and Rogette made a kind of ducking cringe. Instead of striking her at the back of the neck as I'd meant to, my joined hands only glanced off her shoulder. She staggered, went to one knee, and was up again almost at once. Her eyes were like little blue arc-lamps, spitting rage instead of electricity. '*You!*' she said, hissing the word over the top of her tongue, turning it into the sound of some ancient curse: *Heeyuuuu!* Behind us Kyra screamed my name, stagger-dancing on the wet wood and waving her arms in an effort to keep from falling in the lake. Water slopped on to the deck and ran over her small bare feet.

'Hold on, Ki!' I called back. Rogette saw my attention shift and took her chance – she spun and ran out on to the dock. I sprang after her, grabbed her by the hair, and it came off in my hand. All of it. I stood there at the edge of the surging lake with her mat of white hair dangling from my fist like a scalp.

Rogette looked over her shoulder, snarling, an ancient bald gnome in the rain, and I thought *It's him, it's Devore, he never died at all, somehow he and the woman swapped identities,* she *was the one who committed suicide, it was* her *body that went back to California on the jet—*

Even as she turned the other way again and began to run toward Ki, I knew better. It was Rogette, all right, but she'd come by that hideous resemblance honestly. Whatever was wrong with her had done more than make her hair fall out; it had aged her as well. Seventy, I'd thought, but that had to be at least ten years beyond the actual mark.

I've known a lot of folks name their kids alike, Mrs M. had told me. *They think it's cute.* Max Devore must have thought so, too, because he had named a son Roger and his daughter Rogette. Perhaps she'd come by the Whitmore part honestly – she might have been married in her younger years – but once the wig was gone, her antecedents were beyond argument. The woman tottering along the wet dock to finish the job was Kyra's aunt.

Ki began to back up rapidly, making no effort to be careful and pick her footing. She was going into the drink; there was no way she could stay up. But before she could fall, a wave slapped the dock between them at a place where some of the barrels had come loose and the slatted walkway was already partly submerged. Foamy water flew up and began to twist into one of those helix shapes I had seen before. Rogette stopped ankle-deep in the water sloshing over the dock, and I stopped about twelve feet behind her.

The shape solidified, and even before I could make out the face I recognized the baggy shorts with their fading swirls of color and the smock top. Only Kmart sells smock tops of such perfect shapelessness; I think it may be a federal law.

It was Mattie. A grave gray Mattie, looking at Rogette with grave gray eyes. Rogette raised her hands, tottered, tried to turn. At that moment a wave surged under the dock, making it rise and then drop like an amusement-park ride. Rogette went over the side. Beyond her, beyond the water-shape in the rain, I could see Ki sprawling on the porch of The Sunset Bar. That last heave had flipped her to temporary safety like a human tiddlywink.

496

Mattie was looking at me, her lips moving, her eyes on mine. I had been able to tell what Jo was saying, but this time I had no idea. I tried with all my might, but I couldn't make it out.

'*Mommy! Mommy!*'

The figure didn't so much turn as revolve; it didn't actually seem to be there below the hem of the long shorts. It moved up the dock to the bar, where Ki was now standing with her arms held out.

Something grabbed at my foot.

I looked down and saw a drowning apparition in the surging water. Dark eyes stared up at me from beneath the bald skull. Rogette was coughing water from between lips that were as purple as plums. Her free hand waved weakly up at me. The fingers opened . . . and closed. Opened . . . and closed. I dropped to one knee and took it. It clamped over mine like a steel claw and she yanked, trying to pull me in with her. The purple lips peeled back from yellow toothpegs like those in Sara's skull. And yes – I thought that this time Rogette was the one laughing.

I rocked on my haunches and yanked her up. I didn't think about it; it was pure instinct. I had her by at least a hundred pounds, and three-quarters of her came out of the lake like a gigantic, freakish trout. She screamed, darted her head forward, and buried her teeth in my wrist. The pain was immediate and enormous. I jerked my arm up even higher and then brought it down, not thinking about hurting her, wanting only to rid myself of that weasel's mouth. Another wave hit the half-submerged dock. Its rising, splintered edge impaled Rogette's descending face. One eye popped; a dripping yellow splinter ran up her nose like a dagger; the scant skin of her forehead split, snapping away from the bone like two suddenly released windowshades. Then the lake pulled her away. I saw the torn topography of her face a moment longer, upturned into the torrential rain, wet and as pale as the light from a fluorescent bar. Then she rolled over, her black vinyl raincoat swirling around her like a shroud.

What I saw when I looked back toward The Sunset Bar was another glimpse under the skin of this world, but one far different from the face of Sara in the Green Lady or the snarling, half-glimpsed shape of the Outsider. Kyra stood on the wide wooden porch in front of the bar amid a litter of overturned wicker furniture. In front of her was a waterspout in which I could still see – very faintly – the fading shape of a woman. She was on her knees, holding her arms out.

They tried to embrace. Ki's arms went through Mattie and came out dripping. 'Mommy, I can't get you!'

The woman in the water was speaking – I could see her lips moving. Ki looked at her, rapt. Then, for just a moment Mattie turned to me. Our eyes met, and hers were made of the lake. They were Dark Score, which was here long before I came and will remain long after I am gone. I put my hands to my mouth, kissed my palms, and held them out to her. Shimmery hands went up, as if to catch those kisses.

'Mommy don't go!' Kyra screamed, and flung her arms around the figure. She was immediately drenched and backed away with her eyes squinched shut, coughing. There was no longer a woman with her; there was only water running across the boards and dripping through the cracks to rejoin the lake, which comes up from deep springs far below, from the fissures in the rock which underlies the TR and all this part of our world.

Moving carefully, doing my own balancing act, I made my way out along the wavering dock to The Sunset Bar. When I got there I took Kyra in my arms. She hugged me tight, shivering fiercely against me. I could hear the small dicecup rattle of her teeth and smell the lake in her hair.

'Mattie came,' she said.

'I know. I saw her.'

'Mattie made the white nana go away.'

'I saw that, too. Be very still now, Ki. We're going back to solid ground, but you can't move around a lot. If you do, we'll end up swimming.'

She was good as gold. When we were on The Street again and I tried to put her down, she clung to my neck fiercely. That was okay with me. I thought of taking her into Warrington's, but didn't. There would be towels in there, probably dry clothes as well, but I had an idea there might also be a bathtub full of warm water waiting in there. Besides, the rain was slackening again and this time the sky looked lighter in the west.

'What did Mattie tell you, hon?' I asked as we walked north along The Street. Ki would let me put her down so we could crawl under

498

the downed trees we came to, but raised her arms to be picked up again on the far side of each.

'To be a good girl and not be sad. But I am sad. I'm *very* sad.' She began to cry, and I stroked her wet hair.

By the time we got to the railroad-tie steps she had cried herself out . . . and over the mountains in the west, I could see one small but very brilliant wedge of blue.

'All the woods fell down,' Ki said, looking around. Her eyes were very wide.

'Well . . . not all, but a lot of them, I guess.'

Halfway up the steps I paused, puffing and seriously winded. I didn't ask Ki if I could put her down, though. I didn't *want* to put her down. I just wanted to catch my breath.

'Mike?'

'What, doll?'

'Mattie told me something else.'

'What?'

'Can I whisper?'

'If you want to, sure.'

Ki leaned close, put her lips to my ear, and whispered.

I listened. When she was done I nodded, kissed her cheek, shifted her to the other hip, and carried her the rest of the way up to the house.

'Twasn't the stawm of the century, chummy, and don't you go thinkin that it was. Nossir.

So said the old-timers who sat in front of the big Army medic's tent that served as the Lakeview General that late summer and fall. A huge elm had toppled across Route 68 and bashed the store in like a Saltines box. Adding injury to insult, the elm had carried a bunch of spitting live lines with it. They ignited propane from a ruptured tank, and the whole thing went kaboom. The tent was a pretty good warm-weather substitute, though, and folks on the TR took to saying they was goin down to the MASH for bread and beer – this because you could still see a faded red cross on both sides of the tent's roof.

The old-timers sat along one canvas wall in folding chairs, waving to other old-timers when they went pooting by in their rusty old-timer cars (all certified old-timers own either Fords or Chevys, so I'm well on my way in that regard), swapping their undershirts for flannels as the days began to cool toward cider season and spud-digging, watching the township start to rebuild itself around them. And as they watched they talked about the ice storm of the past winter, the one that knocked out lights and splintered a million trees between Kittery and Fort Kent; they talked about the cyclones that touched down in August of 1985; they talked about the sleet hurricane of 1927. Now *there* was some stawms, they said. *There* was some stawms, by Gorry.

I'm sure they've got a point, and I don't argue with them – you rarely win an argument with a genuine Yankee old-timer, never if it's about the weather – but for me the storm of 21 July, 1998 will always be *the* storm. And I know a little girl who feels the same. She may live until 2100, given all the benefits of modern medicine, but I think that for Kyra Elizabeth Devore that will always be *the* storm. The one where her dead mother came to her dressed in the lake.

The first vehicle to come down my driveway didn't arrive until almost six o'clock. It turned out to be not a Castle County police car but a yellow bucket-loader with flashing yellow lights on top of the cab and a guy in a Central Maine Power Company slicker working the controls. The guy in the other seat was a cop, though – was in fact Norris Ridgewick, the County Sheriff himself. And he came to my door with his gun drawn.

The change in the weather the TV guy had promised had already arrived, clouds and storm-cells driven east by a chilly wind running just under gale force. Trees had continued to fall in the dripping woods for at least an hour after the rain stopped. Around five o'clock I made us toasted-cheese sandwiches and tomato soup . . . comfort food, Jo would have called it. Kyra ate listlessly, but she did eat, and she drank a lot of milk. I had wrapped her in another of my tee-shirts and she tied her own hair back. I offered her the white ribbons, but she shook her head decisively and opted for a rubber band instead. 'I don't like those ribbons anymore,' she said. I decided I didn't, either, and threw them away. Ki watched me do it and offered no objection. Then I crossed the living room to the woodstove.

500

'What are you doing?' She finished her second glass of milk, wriggled off her chair, and came over to me.

'Making a fire. Maybe all those hot days thinned my blood. That's what my mom would have said, anyway.'

She watched silently as I pulled sheet after sheet from the pile of paper I'd taken off the table and stacked on top of the woodstove, balled each one up, and slipped it in through the door. When I felt I'd loaded enough, I began to lay bits of kindling on top.

'What's written on those papers?' Ki asked.

'Nothing important.'

'Is it a story?'

'Not really. It was more like . . . oh, I don't know. A crossword puzzle. Or a letter.'

'Pretty long letter,' she said, and then laid her head against my leg as if she were tired.

'Yeah,' I said. 'Love letters usually are, but keeping them around is a bad idea.'

'Why?'

'Because they . . .' *Can come back to haunt you* was what rose to mind, but I wouldn't say it. 'Because they can embarrass you in later life.'

'Oh.'

'Besides,' I said. 'These papers are like your ribbons, in a way.'

'You don't like them anymore.'

'Right.'

She saw the box then – the tin box with JO'S NOTIONS written on the front. It was on the counter between the living room and the sink, not far from where old Krazy Kat had hung on the wall. I didn't remember bringing the box up from the studio with me, but I suppose I might not have; I was pretty freaked. I also think it could have come up . . . kind of by itself. I *do* believe such things now; I have reason to.

Kyra's eyes lit up in a way they hadn't since she had wakened from her short nap to find out her mother was dead. She stood on tiptoe to take hold of the box, then ran her small fingers across the gilt letters. I thought about how important it was for a kid to own a tin box. You had to have one for your secret stuff – the best toy, the prettiest bit of lace, the first piece of jewelry. Or a picture of your mother, perhaps.

'This is so . . . *pretty*,' she said in a soft, awed voice.

'You can have it if you don't mind it saying JO'S NOTIONS instead of KI'S NOTIONS. There are some papers in it I want to read, but I could put them somewhere else.'

She looked at me to make sure I wasn't kidding, saw I wasn't.

'I'd love it,' she said in the same soft, awed voice.

I took the box from her, scooped out the steno books, notes, and clippings, then handed it back to Ki. She practiced taking the lid off and then putting it back on.

'Guess what I'll put in here,' she said.

'Secret treasures?'

'Yes!' she said, and actually smiled for a moment. 'Who was Jo, Mike? Do I know her? I do, don't I? She was one of the fridgeafator people.'

'She—' A thought occurred. I shuffled through the yellowed clippings. Nothing. I thought I'd lost it somewhere along the way, then saw a corner of what I was looking for peeking from the middle of one of the steno notebooks. I slid it out and handed it to Ki.

'What is it?'

'A backwards photo. Hold it up to the light.'

She did, and looked for a long time, rapt. Faint as a dream I could see my wife in her hand, my wife standing on the swimming float in her two-piece suit.

'That's Jo,' I said.

'She's pretty. I'm glad to have her box for my things.'

'I am too, Ki.' I kissed the top of her head.

When Sheriff Ridgewick hammered on the door, I thought it wise to answer with my hands up. He looked wired. What seemed to ease the situation was a simple, uncalculated question.

'Where's Alan Pangborn these days, Sheriff?'

'Over New Hampshire,' Ridgewick said, lowering his pistol a little (a minute or two later he holstered it without even seeming to be aware he had done so). 'He and Polly are doing real well. Except for her arthritis. That's nasty, I guess, but she still has her good days. A person can go along quite awhile if they get a good day every once and again, that's what I think. Mr Noonan, I have a lot of questions for you. You know that, don't you?'

502

'Yes.'

'First off and most important, do you have the child? Kyra Devore?'

'Yes.'

'Where is she?'

'I'll be happy to show you.'

We walked down the north-wing corridor and stood just outside the bedroom doorway, looking in. The duvet was pulled up to her chin and she was sleeping deeply. The stuffed dog was curled in one hand – we could just see its muddy tail poking out of her fist at one end and its nose poking out at the other. We stood there for a long time, neither of us saying anything, watching her sleep in the light of a summer evening. In the woods the trees had stopped falling, but the wind still blew. Around the eaves of Sara Laughs it made a sound like ancient music.

EPILOGUE

It snowed for Christmas – a polite six inches of powder that made the carollers working the streets of Sanford look like they belonged in *It's a Wonderful Life*. By the time I came back from checking Kyra for the third time, it was quarter past one on the morning of the twenty-sixth, and the snow had stopped. A late moon, plump but pale, was peeking through the unravelling fluff of clouds.

I was Christmasing with Frank again, and we were the last two up. The kids, Ki included, were dead to the world, sleeping off the annual bacchanal of food and presents. Frank was on his third Scotch – it had been a three-Scotch story if there ever was one, I guess – but I'd barely drunk the top off my first one. I think I might have gotten into the bottle quite heavily if not for Ki. On the days when I have her I usually don't drink so much as a glass of beer. And to have her three days in a row . . . but shit, *kemo sabe*, if you can't spend Christmas with your kid, what the hell is Christmas for?

'Are you all right?' Frank asked when I sat down again and took another little token sip from my glass.

I grinned at that. Not is *she* all right but are *you* all right. Well, nobody ever said Frank was stupid.

'You should've seen me when the Department of Human Services let me have her for a weekend in October. I must have checked on her a dozen times before I went to bed . . . and then I *kept* checking. Getting up and peeking in on her, listening to her breathe. I didn't sleep a wink Friday night, caught maybe three hours on Saturday. So this is a big improvement. But if you ever blab any of what I've told you, Frank – if they ever hear about me filling up that bathtub before the storm knocked the gennie out – I can kiss my chances of adopting her goodbye. I'll probably have to fill out a form in triplicate before they even let me attend her high-school graduation.'

I hadn't meant to tell Frank the bathtub part, but once I started talking, almost everything spilled out. I suppose it had to spill to someone if I was ever to get on with my life. I'd assumed that John Storrow would be the one on the other side of the confessional when the time came, but John didn't want to talk about any of those events except as they bore on our ongoing legal business, which nowadays is all about Kyra Elizabeth Devore.

'I'll keep my mouth shut, don't worry. How goes the adoption battle?'

'Slow. I've come to loathe the State of Maine court system, and DHS as well. You take the people who work in those bureaucracies one by one and they're mostly fine, but when you put them together . . .'

'Bad, huh?'

'I sometimes feel like a character in *Bleak House*. That's the one where Dickens says that in court nobody wins but the lawyers. John tells me to be patient and count my blessings, that we're making amazing progress considering that I'm that most untrustworthy of creatures, an unmarried white male of middle age, but Ki's been in two foster-home situations since Mattie died, and—'

'Doesn't she have kin in one of those neighboring towns?'

'Mattie's aunt. She didn't want anything to do with Ki when Mattie was alive and has even less interest now. Especially since—'

'—since Ki's not going to be rich.'

'Yeah.'

'The Whitmore woman was lying about Devore's will.'

'Absolutely. He left everything to a foundation that's supposed to foster global computer literacy. With due respect to the number-crunchers of the world, I can't imagine a colder charity.'

'How is John?'

'Pretty well mended, but he's never going to get the use of his right arm back entirely. He damned near died of blood-loss.'

Frank had led me away from the entwined subjects of Ki and custody quite well for a man deep into his third Scotch, and I was willing enough to go. I could hardly bear to think of her long days and longer nights in those homes where the Department of Human Services stores away children like knickknacks nobody wants. Ki didn't live in those places but only existed in them, pale and listless, like a well-fed rabbit kept in a cage. Each time she saw my car turning in or pulling up she came alive, waving her arms and dancing like Snoopy on his doghouse. Our weekend in October had been wonderful (despite my obsessive need to check her every half hour or so after she was asleep), and the Christmas holiday had been even better. Her emphatic desire to be with me was helping in court more than anything else . . . yet the wheels still turned slowly.

Maybe in the spring, Mike, John told me. He was a new John these days, pale and serious. The slightly arrogant eager beaver who had wanted nothing more than to go head to head with Mr Maxwell 'Big Bucks' Devore was no longer in evidence. John had learned something about mortality on the twenty-first of July, and something about the world's idiot cruelty, as well. The man who had taught himself to shake with his left hand instead of his right was no longer interested in partying 'til he puked. He was seeing a girl in Philly, the daughter of one of his mother's friends. I had no idea if it was serious or not, Ki's 'Unca John' is closemouthed about that part of his life, but when a young man is of his own accord seeing the daughter of one of his mother's friends, it usually is.

Maybe in the spring: it was his mantra that late fall and early winter. *What am I doing wrong?* I asked him once – this was just after Thanksgiving and another setback.

Nothing, he replied. *Single-parent adoptions are always slow, and when the putative adopter is a man, it's worse.* At that point in the conversation John made an ugly little gesture, poking the index finger of his left hand in and out of his loosely cupped right fist.

That's blatant sex discrimination, John.

Yeah, but usually it's justified. Blame it on every twisted asshole who ever decided he had a right to take off some little kid's pants, if you want; blame it on the bureaucracy, if you want; hell, blame it on cosmic rays if you want. It's a slow process, but you're going to win in the end. You've got a clean record, you've got Kyra saying 'I want to be with Mike' to every judge and DHS worker she sees, you've got enough money to keep after them no matter how much they squirm and no matter how many forms they throw at you . . . and most of all, buddy, you've got me.

I had something else, too – what Ki had whispered in my ear as I paused to catch my breath on the steps. I'd never told John about that, and it was one of the few things I didn't tell Frank, either.

Mattie says I'm your little guy now, she had whispered. *Mattie says you'll take care of me.*

I was trying to – as much as the fucking slowpokes at Human Services would let me – but the waiting was hard.

Frank picked up the Scotch and tilted it in my direction. I shook my head. Ki had her heart set on snowman-making, and I wanted to be able to face the glare of early sun on fresh snow without a headache.

'Frank, how much of this do you actually believe?'

He poured for himself, then just sat for a time, looking down at the table and thinking. When he raised his head again there was a smile on his face. It was so much like Jo's that it broke my heart. And when he spoke, he juiced his ordinarily faint Boston brogue.

'Sure and I'm a half-drunk Irishman who just finished listenin to the granddaddy of all ghost stories on Christmas night,' he said. 'I believe all of it, you silly git.'

I laughed and so did he. We did it mostly through the nose, as men are apt to do when up late, maybe in their cups a little, and don't want to wake the house.

'Come on – how much really?'

'All of it,' he repeated, dropping the brogue. 'Because Jo believed it. And because of her.' He nodded his head in the direction of the stairs so I'd know which her he meant. 'She's like no other little girl I've ever seen. She's sweet enough, but there's something in her eyes. At first I thought it was losing her mother the way she did, but that's not it. There's more, isn't there?'

'Yes,' I said.

'It's in you, too. It's touched you both.'

I thought of the baying thing which Jo had managed to hold back while I poured the lye into that rotted roll of canvas. An Outsider, she had called it. I hadn't gotten a clear look at it, and probably that was good. Probably that was very good.

'Mike?' Frank looked concerned. 'You're shivering.'

508

'I'm okay,' I said. 'Really.'

'What's it like in the house now?' he asked. I was still living in Sara Laughs. I procrastinated until early November, then put the Derry house up for sale.

'Quiet.'

'Totally quiet?'

I nodded, but that wasn't completely true. On a couple of occasions I had awakened with a sensation Mattie had once mentioned – that there was someone in bed with me. But not a dangerous presence. On a couple of occasions I have smelled (or thought I have) Red perfume. And sometimes, even when the air is perfectly still, Bunter's bell will shiver out a few notes. It's as if something lonely wants to say hello.

Frank glanced at the clock, then back at me, almost apologetically. 'I've got a few more questions – okay?'

'If you can't stay up until the wee hours on Boxing Day morning,' I said, 'I guess you never can. Fire away.'

'What did you tell the police?'

'I didn't have to tell them much of anything. Footman talked enough to suit them – too much to suit Norris Ridgewick. Footman said that he and Osgood – it was Osgood driving the car, Devore's pet broker – did the drive-by because Devore had made threats about what would happen to them if they didn't. The State cops also found a copy of a wire-transfer among Devore's effects at Warrington's. Two million dollars to an account in the Grand Caymans. The name scribbled on the copy is Randolph Footman. Randolph is George's middle name. Mr Footman is now residing in Shawshank State Prison.'

'What about Rogette?'

'Well, Whitmore was her mother's maiden name, but I think it's safe to say that Rogette's heart belonged to Daddy. She had leukemia, was diagnosed in 1996. In people her age – she was only fifty-seven when she died, by the way – it's fatal in two cases out of every three, but she was doing the chemo. Hence the wig.'

'Why did she try to kill Kyra? I don't understand that. If you broke Sara Tidwell's hold on this earthly plane of ours when you dissolved her bones, the curse should have . . . why are you looking at me that way?'

'You'd understand if you'd ever met Devore,' I said. 'This is the man who lit the whole fucking TR on fire as a way of saying goodbye when he headed west to sunny California. I thought of him the second I pulled the wig off, thought they'd swapped identities somehow. Then I thought *Oh no, it's her all right, it's Rogette, she's just lost her hair somehow.*'

'And you were right. The chemo.'

'I was also wrong. I know more about ghosts than I did, Frank. Maybe the most important thing is that what you see first, what you think first . . . that's what's usually true. It was him that day. Devore. He came back at the end. I'm sure of it. At the end it wasn't about Sara, not for him. At the end it wasn't even about Kyra. At the end it was about Scooter Larribee's sled.'

Silence between us. For a few moments it was so deep that I could actually hear the house breathing. You can hear that, you know. If you really listen. That's something else I know now.

'Christ,' he said at last.

'I don't think Devore came east from California to kill her,' I said. 'That wasn't the original plan.'

'Then what was? Get to know his granddaughter? Mend his fences?'

'God, no. You still don't understand what he was.'

'Tell me, then.'

'A human monster. He came back to *buy* her, but Mattie wouldn't sell. Then, when Sara got hold of him, he began to plan Ki's death. I suspect that Sara never found a more willing tool.'

'How many did she kill in all?' Frank asked.

'I don't know for sure. I don't think I want to. Based on Jo's notes and clippings, I'd say that there were perhaps four other . . . directed murders, shall we call them? . . . in the years between 1901 and 1998. All children, all *K*-names, all closely related to the men who killed her.'

'My God.'

'I don't think God had much to do with it . . . but she made them pay, all right.'

'You're sorry for her, aren't you?'

'Yes. I would have torn her apart before I let her put so much as a finger on Ki, but of course I am. She was raped and murdered.

510

Her child was drowned while she herself lay dying. My God, aren't *you* sorry for her?'

'I suppose I am. Mike, do you know who the other boy was? The crying boy? Was he the one who died of blood-poisoning?'

'Most of Jo's notes concerned that part of it – it's where she got started. Royce Merrill knew the story well. The crying boy was Reg Tidwell, Junior. You have to understand that by September of 1901, when the Red-Tops played their last show in Castle County, almost everyone on the TR knew that Sara and her boy had been murdered, and almost everyone had a good idea of who'd done it.

'Reg Tidwell spent a lot of that August hounding the County Sheriff, Nehemiah Bannerman. At first it was to find them alive – Tidwell wanted a search mounted – and then it was to find their bodies, and then it was to find their killers . . . because once he accepted that they were dead, he never doubted that they'd been murdered.

'Bannerman was sympathetic at first. *Everyone* seemed sympathetic at first. The Red-Top crowd had been treated wonderfully during their time on the TR – that was what infuriated Jared the most – and I think you can forgive Son Tidwell for making a crucial mistake.'

'What mistake was that?'

Why, he got the idea that Mars was heaven, I thought. *The TR must have seemed like heaven to them, right up until Sara and Kito went for a stroll, the boy carrying his berry-bucket, and never came back. It must have seemed that they'd finally found a place where they could be black people and still be allowed to breathe.*

'Thinking they'd be treated like regular folks when things went wrong, just because they'd been treated that way when things were right. Instead, the TR clubbed together against them. No one who had an idea of what Jared and his protégés had done condoned it, exactly, but when the chips were down . . .'

'You protect your own, you wash your dirty laundry with the door closed,' Frank murmured, and finished his drink.

'Yeah. By the time the Red-Tops played the Castle County Fair, their little community down by the lake had begun to break up – this is all according to Jo's notes, you understand; there's not a whisper of it in any of the town histories.

'By Labor Day the active harassment had started – so Royce told Jo. It got a little uglier every day – a little scarier – but Son Tidwell flat didn't want to go, not until he found out what had happened to his sister and nephew. He apparently kept the blood family there in the meadow even after the others had taken off for friendlier locations.

'Then someone laid the trap. There was a clearing in the woods about a mile east of what's now called Tidwell's Meadow; it had a big birch cross in the middle of it. Jo had a picture of it in her studio. That was where the black community had their services after the doors of the local churches were closed to them. The boy – Junior – used to go up there a lot to pray or just to sit and meditate. There were plenty of folks in the township who knew his routine. Someone put a leghold trap on the little path through the woods that the boy used. Covered it with leaves and needles.'

'Jesus,' Frank said. He sounded ill.

'Probably it wasn't Jared Devore or his logger-boys who set it, either – they didn't want any more to do with Sara and Son's people after the murders, they kept right clear of them. It might not even have been a friend of those boys. By then they didn't *have* that many friends. But that didn't change the fact that those folks down by the lake were getting out of their place, scratching at things better left alone, refusing to take no for an answer. So someone set the trap. I don't think there was any intent to actually kill the boy, but to maim him? Maybe see him with his foot off, condemned to a lifetime crutch? I think they may have gotten that far in their imagining.

'In any case it worked. The boy stepped in the trap . . . and for quite awhile they didn't find him. The pain must have been excruciating. Then the blood-poisoning. He died. Son gave up. He had other kids to think about, not to mention the people who'd stuck with him. They packed up their clothes and their guitars and left. Jo traced some of them to North Carolina, where many of the descendants still live. And during the fires of 1933, the ones young Max Devore set, the cabins burned flat.'

'I don't understand why the bodies of Sara and her son weren't found,' Frank said. 'I understand that what you smelled – the putrescence – wasn't there in any physical sense. But surely at the time . . . if this path you call The Street was so popular . . .'

'Devore and the others *didn't* bury them where I found them, not to begin with. They would have started by dragging the bodies deeper into the woods – maybe up to where the north wing of Sara Laughs stands now. They covered them with brush and came back that night. Must have been that night; to leave them any longer would have drawn every carnivore in the woods. They took them someplace else and buried them in that roll of canvas. Jo didn't know where, but my guess is Bowie Ridge, where they'd spent most of the summer cutting. Hell, Bowie Ridge is still pretty isolated. They put the bodies somewhere; we might as well say there.'

'Then how . . . why . . .'

'Draper Finney wasn't the only one haunted by what they did, Frank – they all were. Literally *haunted*. With the possible exception of Jared Devore, I suppose. He lived another ten years and apparently never missed a meal. But the boys had bad dreams, they drank too much, they fought too much, they argued . . . bristled if anyone so much as mentioned the Red-Tops . . .'

'Might as well have gone around wearing signs reading KICK US, WE'RE GUILTY,' Frank commented.

'Yes. It probably didn't help that most of the TR was giving them the silent treatment. Then Finney died in the quarry – committed suicide in the quarry, I think – and Jared's logger-boys got an idea. Came down with it like a cold. Only it was more like a compulsion. Their idea was that if they dug up the bodies and reburied them where it happened, things'd go back to normal for them.'

'Did Jared go along with the idea?'

'According to Jo's notes, by then they never went near him. They reburied the bag of bones – without Jared Devore's help – where I eventually dug it up. In the late fall or early winter of 1902, I think.'

'She *wanted* to be back, didn't she? Sara. Back where she could really work on them.'

'And on the whole township. Yes. Jo thought so, too. Enough so she didn't want to go back to Sara Laughs once she found some of this stuff out. Especially when she guessed she was pregnant. When we started trying to have a baby and I suggested the name Kia, how that must have scared her! And I never saw.'

'Sara thought she could use you to kill Kyra if Devore played out before he could get the job done – he was old and in bad health, after all. Jo gambled that you'd save her instead. That's what you think, isn't it?'

'Yes.'

'And she was right.'

'I couldn't have done it alone. From the night I dreamed about Sara singing, Jo was with me every step of the way. Sara couldn't make her quit.'

'No, she wasn't a quitter,' Frank agreed, and wiped at one eye. 'What do you know about your twice-great-aunt? The one that married Auster?'

'Bridget Noonan Auster,' I said. 'Bridey, to her friends. I asked my mother and she swears up and down she knows nothing, that Jo never asked her about Bridey, but I think she might be lying. The young woman was definitely the black sheep of the family − I can tell just by the sound of Mom's voice when the name comes up. I have no idea how she met Benton Auster. Let's say he was down in the Prout's Neck part of the world visiting friends and started flirting with her at a clambake. That's as likely as anything else. This was in 1884. She was eighteen, he was twenty-three. They got married, one of those hurry-up jobs. Harry, the one who actually drowned Kito Tidwell, came along six months later.'

'So he was barely seventeen when it happened,' Frank said. 'Great God.'

'And by then his mother had gotten religion. His terror over what she'd think if she ever found out was part of the reason he did what he did. Any other questions, Frank? Because I'm really starting to fade.'

For several moments he said nothing − I had begun to think he was done when he said, 'Two others. Do you mind?'

'I guess it's too late to back out now. What are they?'

'The Shape you spoke of. The Outsider. That troubles me.'

I said nothing. It troubled me, too.

'Do you think there's a chance it might come back?'

'It always does,' I said. 'At the risk of sounding pompous, the Outsider eventually comes back for all of us, doesn't it? Because we're all bags of bones. And the Outsider . . . Frank, the Outsider wants what's in the bag.'

He mulled this over, then swallowed the rest of his Scotch at a gulp.

'You had one other question?'

'Yes,' he said. 'Have you started writing again?'

I went upstairs a few minutes later, checked Ki, brushed my teeth, checked Ki again, then climbed into bed. From where I lay I was able to look out the window at the pale moon shining on the snow.

Have you started writing again?

No. Other than a rather lengthy essay on how I spent my summer vacation which I may show to Kyra in some later year, there's been nothing. I know that Harold is nervous, and sooner or later I suppose I'll have to call him and tell him what he already guesses: the machine which ran so sweet for so long has stopped. It isn't broken – this memoir came out with nary a gasp or missed heartbeat – but the machine has stopped, just the same. There's gas in the tank, the sparkplugs spark and the battery bats, but the wordygurdy stands there quiet in the middle of my head. I've put a tarp over it. It's served me well, you see, and I don't like to think of it getting dusty.

Some of it has to do with the way Mattie died. It occurred to me at some point this fall that I had written similar deaths in at least two of my books, and popular fiction is heaped with other examples of the same thing. Have you set up a moral dilemma you don't know how to solve? Is the protagonist sexually attracted to a woman who is much too young for him, shall we say? Need a quick fix? Easiest thing in the world. 'When the story starts going sour, bring on the man with the gun.' Raymond Chandler said that, or something like it – close enough for government work, *kemo sabe*.

Murder is the worst kind of pornography, murder is let me do what I want taken to its final extreme. I believe that even make-believe murders should be taken seriously; maybe that's another idea I got last summer. Perhaps I got it while Mattie was struggling in my arms, gushing blood from her smashed head and dying blind, still crying out for her daughter as she left this earth. To think I might have written such a hellishly convenient death in a book, *ever*, sickens me.

Or maybe I just wish there'd been a little more time.

I remember telling Ki it's best not to leave love letters around; what I thought but didn't say was that they can come back to haunt you. I am haunted anyway . . . but I will not willingly haunt myself,

515

and when I closed my book of dreams I did so of my own free will. I think I could have poured lye over those dreams as well, but from that I stayed my hand.

I've seen things I never expected to see and felt things I never expected to feel – not the least of them what I felt and still feel for the child sleeping down the hall from me. She's my little guy now, I'm her big guy, and that's the important thing. Nothing else seems to matter half so much.

Thomas Hardy, who supposedly said that the most brilliantly drawn character in a novel is but a bag of bones, stopped writing novels himself after finishing *Jude the Obscure* and while he was at the height of his narrative genius. He went on writing poetry for another twenty years, and when someone asked him why he'd quit fiction he said he couldn't understand why he had trucked with it so long in the first place. In retrospect it seemed silly to him, he said. Pointless. I know exactly what he meant. In the time between now and whenever the Outsider remembers me and decides to come back, there must be other things to do, things that mean more than those shadows. I think I could go back to clanking chains behind the Ghost House wall, but I have no interest in doing so. I've lost my taste for spooks. I like to imagine Mattie would think of Bartleby in Melville's story.

I've put down my scrivener's pen. These days I prefer not to.

Center Lovell, Maine: 25 May, 1997 – 6 February, 1998